AMALTHEAN QUESTS TWO

JERI DION

STOCKWELL
PUBLISHERS SINCE 1898

First published in 2018
This edition published in 2022 by
A.H. Stockwell Ltd.
West Wing Studios, Unit 166
The Mall, Luton
ahstockwell.co.uk

Copyright © 2018, 2022 Jeri Dion

The right of Jeri Dion to be identified as the author of this work has been asserted in accordance with the Copyright, Designs and Patents Act 1988.

All rights reserved. No part of this publication may be reproduced, stored in a retrieval system, or transmitted, in any form or by any means without the prior written permission of the publisher, nor be otherwise circulated in any form of binding or cover other than that in which it is published and without a similar condition being imposed on the subsequent purchaser. Any person who does so may be liable to criminal prosecution and civil claims for damages.

British Library Cataloguing-in-Publication Data: A catalogue record for this book is available from the British Library.
ISBN 9780722352205

All characters appearing in this work are fictitious. Any resemblance to real persons, living or dead, is purely coincidental.

For my late dad, who loved science fiction.

For Dick Hall, a man of many writing talents, thank you for your guidance.

Also my laptop, 'A-mal', who processed the words.

Contents

Dedication iii
Names in this Book v
Amalthea Two Layout vi
Team Members of Amalthea Two ix
Amalthean Quests Update 1

1. New Voyage 3
2. A Charan Prince .24
3. Questa Rescue 45
4. Headquarters Base Two 65
5. Cripion Arrest and the Test 87
6. The Space Triangle 110
7. Trauns Reunited 134
8. Tremanexan Bore-radds 157
9. Distress Call at Entronet 180
10. The Sexton Berenices 203
11. A Traun Elected 225
12. Virus and Apprehension 247
13. Deluca 273
14. The Aemiliyana Threat 296
15. Influential Forces on Maldigri 317
16. Lance 346
17. Final Confrontation 374
18. Thealysis HB 2 399
19. The Boglayons' Final Return 424
20. Last Duties 444

The Amalthean Quests Continue... 469
For My Readers 470

Names in this Book

Amal   Pronounced A-mal, short for Amalthea
Romid   Robotic original mobile intelligent drone
Stavern   Champagne
Level Steps Steps between the decks/levels of the cruiser
Vardox   Vodka
MLC   Medical Life Centre
DC   Discuss Centre

Amalthea Two Layout

FRONT AND REAR DECKS

LEVEL 1: *Main Organisation Deck*

Organisation Centre
DC (Discuss Centre, formally known as the Meeting Centre)
Resources and Study Centre
Slazer Emergency Store and Charge Point
Emergency Hatch for escaping Amalthea Two, which incorporates passage to Life Escape Pods (which are stored at the rear of the cruiser)
Total Shutdown Centre for the whole cruiser.

LEVEL 2: *Life Deck*

Medical Life Centre (MLC)
Emergency Treatment Room
Slazer Burns Centre (for the treatment of burns from weapon fire)
Dr Tysonne's Officette
Medical Supplies Store.
Body Scanner Room (for injuries)
Transpot Centre
Docking Bay With Boarding Tube
Leisure and Refreshments Centre
Male Sanitary Room (for cleansing after a Quest)
Female Sanitary Room (for cleansing after a Quest)
Pios Sanctuary Centre
Medical Experimental Lab A (especially for diagnosing diseases)

LEVEL 3: Quarters Deck

Main Crew Quarters (situated at the front of the cruiser)
    Tayce Traun, 1A
    Marc Dayatso, 2B
    Dairan Loring, 3C
    Donaldo and Treketa Tysonne, 4D

Second-Rank Officers' Quarters
    Kelly Travern, 5E
    Lance Largon, 6F
    Craig Bream, 7G
    Mac Danford, 8H (note: halfway through the voyage these quarters become Nick Berenger's)
    Sallen Vargon, 9I
    Aldonica Darstayne, 10J
    Jaul Naven, 11K

Guest Quarters
    Deluca Marrack (team member)

Flight Hanger Bay Entrance

Flight Maintenance Unit

Quest Suiting-Up Room

LEVEL 4: Science And Botany Deck

Garden Dome (rear of the cruiser)
Plant Specimen Growing and Prep Room
Botany Study Centre
Astrono Centre
Dairan Loring's Officette
Sallen Vargon's Officette
Medical Experimental Lab B (Larger facility than lab A)
Botany Equipment and Seed Stores.

LEVEL 5: Combat And Tech Level Deck

Combat Training and Practice Centre
Robot and Technical Service Section
Weaponry Design Centre (Aldonica's domain).
Gym and Sauna Rooms
Shower Rooms for Gym
Recreational Room (for sports)
Weaponry Testing Room
Engine Room
Electronics Centre (serving the whole cruiser)
Engine Access Shaft (for maintenance)
Access Room (for the main weaponry cannons for the cruiser)

LEVEL 5 (REAR): Freight Hold And Interrogation Deck

Interrogation Centre
Confinement Cells 1–9
Slazer Energy Force-Field Doors to Cells' Control Room
Cruiser Electronic Defence Operational Room
Invis Shield Control Room
Service Area (for shuttles/fighters and other spacecraft)

Team Members of Amalthea Two

Tayce Traun
Captain

Marc Dayatso
Commander

Dairan Loring
Lieutenant Commander / Astronomer
(New Member)

Lance Largon
Quests Research Information Officer

Kelly Travern
Navigationalist
(From Greymaren; New Member)

Mac Danford
COMMUNICATIONS OFFICER
(New member)

Craig Bream
Computer Analysing Technical Officer
(New Member)

Nick Berenger
Replacement Communications Chief
(New Member)

Deluca Marrack
Quests Assistant
(From The Planet Marrack; New Member)

Donaldo Tysonne
Doctor / Laser Surgeon

Treketa Tysonne
Medic / Nurse
(Née Stavard, Tom's Sister From *Amalthea One*)

Aldonica Darstayne
Weaponry Specialist
(New Member)

Sallen Vargon
Science Tech
(Sallen is the evil daughter of the Countess, but she has undergone a memory-reprogramming procedure and has been given a new identity with no recollection of her old past; new member)

Jaul Naven
Science, Medical And Botany Officer
(New member)

Twedor
Escort And Romid To Tayce Traun
(Formally Midge, the guidance and operations computer on *Amalthea One*; Romid = robotic original mobile intelligent drone; new member)

Amal
Female Guidance And Main Operations Computer
(Link-up to Twedor; new member; Amal, pronounced A-mal, is short for *Amalthea*)

AMALTHEAN QUESTS TWO

Amalthean Quests Update

At the end of the first voyage, when Tayce didn't know if she could go on without Tom, her husband, the team and cruiser were called back to Questa unexpectedly. The future looked unsure for all the members for the vastly recognised Amalthean Quests team, even though they had been classed as Legends of the Universe. In 2418 the team were disbanded by new council ruling, by a man everyone despised, namely Layforn Barkin, who was at this time in charge of the new man-made sister colony to Questa, Enlopedia. Barkin, as many addressed him, because of the disrespect they had for the man, had the Amalthean Quests team disbanded on to new assignments without further word. Hence the Amalthean Quests team fell apart. He claimed that the Amalthean Quests voyage was taking up too much funding to be kept operational, and as he had to make cutbacks it was wiped of the face of the universal map. The Amalthean cruiser was placed in an area known as 'out of service' and shut down at Enlopedia, pending a final decision on what to do with it. Councillor Lydia Traun was furious—she had managed to gain all but one vote to keep her daughter's Amalthean Quests crime-orientated voyage continuing.

In 2420 Layforn Barkin after his unpopular conduct with the people of both Questa and Enlopedia made a fatal error of duty in his cutbacks, assigning 200 newly trained cadets in their late teens on a dangerous and life-threatening assignment, where safety was not what it should have been. All 200 young people were sent to their deaths, horrifically. This finally was the turning point for Lydia Traun, when the other members began to see Layforn Barkin for what he was. A power-happy and dangerous councillor with no regard for life or duty. He was sentenced for his misconduct and sent to live out the rest of his dayons on a remote penal colony

Layforn Barkin was replaced by Waynard Bayden, Jonathan Largon's friend and someone that knew a lot more about running a colony such as Enlopedia. Soon he put the harmony back where it belonged, in the every-dayon existence of what both colonies stood for and what the late Jonathan Largon had built up over the yearons' peace and justice. One of the things he reinstated was the Amalthean Quests voyages. Everyone was pleased at both the colonies that life was returning to what it should be, and many congratulated Waynard when they saw him in the city square, as he checked personally on buildings and duties that went into restoring what life should be. That had been closed down or cut back. As for Amalthea One, he gave orders for it to be taken out of where it had been placed, stripped back to its bare frame and redesigned, but still keeping its sleek 'A' shape. Craig Bream, a young expert in the field of computer design and technology, was placed in charge of removing all of Midge's computer circuitry, character memory and voice and placing them into a brand-new design of a free walking-talking escort-type robot, that was classed as a just over three-foot high Romid with a new name, Twedor. Twedor was given the same friendly characteristics that he had when he was guidance and main operations computer aboard Amalthea One, so he could become Tayce Traun's new companion. He would also protect Tayce in any dangerous situation. Top construction designers in the fields of engineering, weaponry, interior electronics and quarters design worked around the clock to restore the sleek design with an up-to-date feel that was to become Amalthea Two. As the cruiser was Tayce's to begin with, many of the chiefs in the relevant teams working aboard the cruiser welcomed her input. Craig Bream worked with her also, as there was to be a high-frequency link-up between Twedor and new female guidance and main operations computer named Amal, pronounced A-mal, short for Amalthea.

For Tayce life had been hard after the death of Tom Stavard, but she had had a good friend on Questa in Jan Barnford, now chief of the Security Patrol Division. He and Tayce had become firm friends and she had helped him on many an assignment until she felt that she could return to a life of independence once more. Jan had escorted Tayce to many social functions and put the laughter back in her life.

At the end of 2419 Amalthea Two was complete, except for the final check by Maintenance Chief Jamie Balthansar. New team members making the team bigger were interviewed by Lydia Traun, Waynard Bayden and Tayce. Some of the old team, upon hearing that they could drop their forced assignments and head back to being team members, dropped what they were doing and headed home.

Amalthean Quests was getting ready to be reborn once more, with a second voyage...

1. New Voyage

It was roughly forty-eight hourons to the commencement of the new voyage. It was hard to think that it was almost two and a half yearons since the Amalthean Quests team had been disbanded to assignments that were not of their choosing. Tayce cringed with anger every time she thought back to that dayon, when her team had so callously been sent off in different directions and there was nothing she or her mother could do to stop it. She felt Layforn Barkin got everything he deserved. She was near completion of yet another assignment for Chief Jan Barnford, on Naninda. A new planetary retreat for the latest and notorious pirates in the present time. The Nanindan pirates. They were just as ruthless as any other pirates to date, only their motto was take prisoners home as hostages and feed them to their so-called flesh-eating herds of animals. Tayce with the new Romid Twedor (Midge) in his blue metallic metlon capacity of escort by her side, on full scan alert, made her way to the point that Twedor's scanner had identified as the point of rescue and assignment. They carefully wandered through the cavernous corridors, on total lookout for any of the Nanindan pirates that might have been roaming below surface and had picked up that she had landed not far from their domain. The air was filled with the strong smell of the vardox kind. Twedor felt his circuits were giving him bad vibes. Tayce glanced at him, noticing that for a Romid he was shaking. This could only mean one thing—his sensors were giving him the equivalent of extreme nervousness, something that was new to him.

"Twedor, I'm not happy you being here. Go back to the rescue cruiser and prepare the onboard medical facility in case we need it," ordered Tayce.

"Just as long as you think you can go on alone?" he asked.

"I can handle it from here, now go!"

Twedor turned and wandered off back the way he had come, on alert. His Slazer primed ready to use if he had to. Tayce continued on, so that she could see through a gap in the cave wall large enough to crawl through if she had to escape quickly. As she looked, so she could see men dressed in scruffy-looking attire, mining for rare crystals, which as far as she could make out were white in colour, in various shapes and sizes. These, she thought, would probably be sold on the black market, and would no doubt go towards some dubious use. In making weapons and space equipment, which would be sold on the same kind of market. She'd seen these kinds of crystals once before many yearons ago and they were classed as molybdenum-orientated. Which only confirmed one thing. These Nanindan pirates had their retreat somewhere they could make more profit below surface.

Just as she thought it was safe to continue on in the final yardons to her designated point of assignment, she was grabbed roughly from behind. She realised it wasn't good when she was blasted by a mixture of strong odour of sweat and vardox. This meant only one thing: she had been detected by a Nanindan pirate. He moved his leatherex gloved right hand across her mouth and nose, whilst restraining her tightly against his sweaty bulk of a body with the left. Tayce struggled—she was finding it near impossible to breathe.

He hauled her away, still in a restraining hold, off through the poorly lit winding cavernous tunnel. They headed toward a blue fluorescent force-field-type door. Upon approach, with his right hand—taking it from Tayce's mouth and nose, much to her relief—he deactivated the entrance and threw her into the dimly lit cell, where the walls were solid rock, laughing callously as he did so.

Tayce sailed straight across the interior and right into the back of a humanoid male. She looked up. Light, such as it was, played to her advantage. Before her was the young dark-haired Questonian she had been sent to rescue—she recognised him from the image earlier.

Without warning she passed out. The young Questonian turned quickly, catching her in mid fall, wondering who she was. Supporting her, he guided her to the only stonex-type seat in the cell, sitting her down. Sitting beside her he began to pat her cheeks lightly to bring her back to consciousness. He looked at her with warm brown concerned eyes. Had these pirates tortured her? he wondered. Dairan Loring was his name. It stated this on his uniform identification badge.

Tayce opened her eyes, slowly looking about her surroundings. Her focus was fuzzy. She looked up, and as her focus cleared she found herself looking into the most warm good-looking features she'd seen in a long time. For a moment she found herself lost just looking into his brown eyes.

"Are you all right? The name's Dairan Loring, astro-explorer for Questa," he said, introducing himself.

"Tayce Traun. Hello!" replied Tayce, still caught by his handsome features.

Dairan quickly realised he was staring at none other than the legendary Tayce Traun, of the Amalthean Quests team. He began wondering if the Amalthean Cruiser was in orbit just outside. He was about to ask her when suddenly the grid-type force-field doors were turned off and the grids vanished. In walked a large paunchy scruffily dressed Nanindan pirate, who Tayce could read was the leader. He reached out roughly, grabbing her by the upper arm, pulling her sharply in front of him. She winced at the smell of his strong breath hitting her in the face. In behind him came another more-ugly-looking male, his eyes showing great interest in Tayce. He paused, leaning on the wall by the doorway. The first Nanindan put his left hand to Tayce's face and jaw, forcing her to look at him. He congratulated his accomplice in a gruff slurred tone on capturing such a legend—she would fetch a pretty sum on the next trade trip. With this, he threw Tayce back at Dairan and walked from the cell, laughing evilly as he went. His accomplice fell in behind and the force-field grid type doors activated behind him once more.

Tayce rubbed her jaw, trying to bring it back.

"Not the best of hosts, are they?" said Dairan, trying to cheer her up.

"Believe me, he's no more than what I've come up against in the past. We've got to get out of here. I would contact my Romid, but that idiot that grabbed me the first time around must have made me hit my wrist against the wall, because it's broken my Wristlink," she replied, furious at the fact.

"Take it off. I'll have a look—I know a great deal about electronics, and they didn't take everything off me on throwing me in here," he said, reaching into his brown jacket pocket and retrieving what looked like a small pencil-shaped object, in silver.

Tayce removed her Wristlink. The glassene display was smashed. She handed it to Dairan without much hope of seeing it work again. He leant back against the wall in the better glow of the light that was illuminating their surroundings, beginning to work on restoring communications. Tayce slowly began to pace back and forth, agitated. She paused, turning in thought.

Then she began. "Dairan—can I call you Dairan?" she asked.

"Yeah!" he replied, giving her half his attention.

"I want to tell you something, though you might find it slightly unnerving," she began apprehensively.

"Go on," he prompted, still trying to fix the Wristlink.

"I'm telepathic with added abilities; and if you can't fix my Wristlink, I could try and send a message to Twedor at the rescue cruiser. He's my Romid, so he can pinpoint our location and blow the forcefield doors via a high-frequency sound wave. I can do this by thought transference," she explained

Dairan gave her a blank surprised look, trying to take in what she had just said. He then went back to trying to fix the Wristlink in hand, saying nothing. She had a feeling she had just insulted him, when he figured he was doing his best to repair her Wristlink. Dairan continued to point the pencil-shaped object at different points on the Wristlink display. A fine beam of orange light hit the display, sometimes for short bursts, sometimes for long.

Tayce sauntered back to the force-field grid-type entrance and looked out through into the winding tunnel-like distance. She wanted to be back on Questa. Time was moving on in her destined beginning of the new voyage. Dairan, after a few moments of trying various ideas he had to restore the Wristlink, crossed and handed it back to her. Tayce looked up and he shook his head in a no-go way. He explained that the main relay chip for transmitting and receiving was totally destroyed—it had obviously happened when she hit her wrist. He could try further to see if he could bypass some circuits that were working, rig up something temporary to get them out of their present surroundings if she wanted him to. As he continued, on her nod for him to do so, she watched his look of great concentration. Tayce found her agitation of wanting to get out of their present surroundings nagging at her strongly. Dairan glanced at her. Then it hit him—he always carried spare digit bombs in his other pocket. Fudging inside, he found one. The digit delay bomb was the latest explosive device to come into circulation at Enlopedia and it was used on missions of exploration and danger. It was no bigger than a large marble, but the blast effect was the size of a megaton bomb. Tayce looked at the small device, then met his look. What next was he going to pull out of his jacket pocket? she wondered.

"Those Nanindan pirates might be good at making money on the unlawful trade market; but when it comes to searching enemies, I think they need to go back to the manual, if you know what I mean," said Dairan.

"What are you going to do? I've never seen one of those before," said Tayce, studying the small marble-shaped object in his hand.

"Get us out of here. Stand back and look away while I set this," he ordered.

Crossing near to the entrance, he set the digit bomb and set it down quickly, crossing to shield Tayce. A few minons elapsed and the bomb blew a disruptive break in the form of a large gaping hole in the force-field grid for them to make an escape. Dairan hurried over to the doorway, quickly joined by Tayce. He stepped out on to the sandy-type soil of the tunnel.

Much to Tayce and his surprise, they'd been under watch by two guards, who now lay dead, caught in the blast. Dairan turned, outstretching his hand back through the gap in the energy force-field. Tayce grasped it, exiting the cell carefully so as not to get hurt. Dairan suggested they take the guards' weapons—they could come in handy, especially if the pirates had heard the explosion above. Tayce agreed.

They both set off. Tayce explained that her rescue cruiser was about half a milon from their present surroundings. Both ran at full pelt with the Nanindan guns set on 'disintegrate'. Halfway along the last part of the corridor to the surface Dairan noticed Tayce had fallen behind. He glanced back to see she had paused for something shiny and sparkly on the sandy soil.

"Tayce! What are you doing? Do you want to be recaptured? Leave it!" he said sharply to her.

As she showed no sign of taking any notice until she got what she wanted, he hurried back and grabbed her by the arm, pulling her on, ordering her to move. Tayce grabbed the shiny crystal and followed on, almost tripping as she tried to keep up with Dairan. He paused for a brief cencron himself, to get his breath back. Both ran on, on the last yardons until they reached outside. But as they broke the surface, shots rang out around and above them. Tayce, dodging the weapon fire, led the rest of the way to the Quest rescue cruiser. The open entrance hatch was a welcome sight.

Tayce climbed up and ran into the pilot area and slid into the seat, quickly starting the engines. Dairan glanced at Twedor, impressed by the little Romid, then hurried to get into the co-pilot's seat next to Tayce as the entrance hatch closed and the rescue cruiser took to the Nanindan sky under the immense power of the nucleus engines. Once airborne, it headed off into the increasingly darkened sky of the planet, into the Universe, off towards Questa Headquarters Base, home.

"The Nanindan pirates are still firing on us, and their orbital vessels are in pursuit, Tayce," said Twedor.

Tayce, on this, activated the defence shields just as a precaution. At the speed they were travelling they'd soon be entering 'D' space (defended space) of Questa and Enlopedia and would be protected. She glanced at Dairan, who was showing signs of concern regarding the fact that even though they'd escaped Naninda they could still be blown to hell by the pursuing Nanindan pirates in their fighter-type vessels.

"It's OK, Dairan, I'm a good pilot. A couple of minons and we'll be in 'D' space. If they follow us in there they will wish they hadn't," assured Tayce.

"Thanks for saving me back on Naninda. Another dayon on that place and I would have been animal feed. Thank you," he said sincerely.

"You're welcome. Chief Barnford was the one to send me; you were nearly never rescued, as there wasn't anyone to fly out and take on the rescue. Then Chief Traun offered it to me. I had one more rescue mission to run, so I agreed. In the end, you could say we rescued each other," she replied casually.

Dairan agreed. On approach to Questa with the Nanindan pirates nowhere in sight, Tayce asked for her usual clearance to go in to land. It was immediately granted. She looked up at the top-ranking space Construction Port, where the completed result of a shining new Amalthea Two hung suspended in stabilising gravity. Her thoughts were on Marc Dayatso, wondering if her mother had managed to find him for the beginning of the new Amalthean Quests voyage tomorron.

Dairan could see, as he glanced at her, she was in deep thought about something, and enquired if he could help. Tayce decided he was only being friendly and asked if he had heard of a well-known member of her first team, Marc Dayatso. Dairan nodded, asking what had happened to him—he was well known for being a computer genius—the best, in fact?

"At the end of the last and first voyage on the Amalthean Quests, Marc was having none of Barkin's laws about putting him on other assignments. He just took off and found his own work commanding a friend's cruiser. He's been down there ever since. The last report I had from him, he was off on a dangerous mission. I hope Chief Traun has managed to find him—he's wanted for the start of the new voyage,"explained Tayce.

"Tell me to forget it if you want; but if you need any replacement team members, I would be more than glad to help out—join your team, I mean," said Dairan, being pushy.

"You get straight to the point, don't you? Won't your section chief want you to return to your current position and duty?" asked Tayce, finding Dairan's cheek quite amusing.

"He's likely to kick me out of my section. I was supposed to return in three dayons with the report on the Nanindan mining survey; now I'm returning without that and the fighter I flew down there in, it's going to be goodbye, Loring, and don't come back," he replied.

"Well, if you have nothing else to go on to, be at Chief Traun's Officette this evening between the times of 19:40 and 20:30 hourons. I'm still looking for an astronomer lieutenant-commander grade, to join the team—someone who has both knowledge in the Universe and is able to be part of the crime-fighting-orientated team that Amalthean Quests is," put Tayce.

The moment the rescue cruiser had landed and they'd exited out into the Docking Port, Lydia Traun was waiting to see Tayce with good news. She knew that it was the kind she'd want to hear. Tayce smiled at her mother and crossed the moment she left the cruiser. Lydia began. She had good news: there was someone waiting to see her up on Amalthea Two.

"Will you see Jan gets this? It's the rescue report. Come on, Twedor, let's go and see who's waiting," said Tayce, turning and heading away from her mother, heading on across the port.

Lydia briskly went after her daughter, saying she had forgotten to say that Treketa had telelinked to say she and Donaldo had left the Medical Colony Assignment Division and couldn't wait to start the new voyage.

Tayce smiled upon her mother's words. It felt good to know her old team were coming together once more. She continued across the marblex floor towards the Vacuum Lift with Twedor in tow, to take her all the way to the Construction Port. Pausing, waiting for the lift to ascend, she began thinking—she would have to visit the Memorial Park to visit Tom's memorial before she departed. The Vacuum Lift arrived. Several people stepped out, heading away to their destination. Tayce boarded, requesting the construction port. Upon the glassene and steelex doors closing, the lift began to ascend above Q City. The people below began to look like space migins (ants) milling around. She leant on the rail that ran round the lift. Twedor was silent beside her. He hated lifts—especially clear-vision ones. It made his sight circuits act up with the motion he considered was not natural; it was like having a vertigo attack.

A while later, as Tayce and Twedor walked aboard the new Amalthea Two, Tayce found there was still the strong smell of newness in the air as she and Twedor began on the walk towards the new central-operations centre of the cruiser. It was once known as the Organisation Deck and was now known as the Organisation Centre. She wondered who the on board person was, waiting to see her.

They soon arrived at the entrance to the Organisation Centre, a centre that was large and gave the feeling of being a comfortable and spacious working environment. Tayce could see that out of all the duty positions around the centre there was one black and chrome chair that was in a certain position at navigations, as if someone was seated there.

"You'd better be a friend; if you're a reporter wanting a scoop for the news channel, I do not have the time," she said, not knowing who it was.

After a few cencrons the chair slowly turned to face her, and none other than Marc Dayatso looked at her with a warm, handsome smile. He stood up and walked over. She gave him a warm overwhelmed smile that said it all. She was glad he was back. He opened his arms to her upon approach and closed them around her as she walked into them, giving her a strong hug that conveyed he'd missed her. Upon releasing her, he held her so that he could study her for a few minons.

"You certainly look better than when I last saw you," he began, pleased.

"Are you ready to start the new voyage as commander?" she asked, wondering if he had come back for good, or had just visited the base to say hello before heading back out to his friend's cruiser.

"Yes, I'm here for good. Tom and your father would never forgive me if I left you alone to take on the many vagabonds of this Universe. I'm here for as long as you need me as part of your new team," he replied, full of enthusiasm.

Marc looked past Tayce and saw the new form of Midge in Twedor. He was impressed beyond words. Twedor walked forth, welcoming Marc back to the team in his original voice, telling him he was no longer immobile, as he could see; he was now free to roam and protect Tayce as her escort. He now had a small plasmatronic ultra-thought brain, which was like a human's and could process a number of things all at the same time. He could smell, touch with the right amount of pressure and act in a split cencron if required. He had a small built-in operating system that enabled him to link up with Amal via high-frequency link-up. Marc gave a look of total amazement that this just above three-foot-high Romid was once Midge and was now under the title of Twedor. Tayce crossed and pushed a small white key on the main operations panel for the cruiser, below a circular wall screen. Marc watched, interested as to what was going to happen next to amaze him. Amal, the new female guidance and main operations computer introduced herself in eloquent soft-spoken English.

"Welcome aboard Amalthea Two, Commander. I'm Amal. I have logged your presence into my memory system and your quarters are allocated to you, with everything fully operational when you are ready," she stated, much to Marc's surprise.

"This cruiser has just got even better; and as for the amazing new major change to Midge, being this amazing little robot, it astounds me. I'm speechless," began Marc, impressed, but he was cut off by Twedor.

"I'm a Romid. A robot is an insignificant form of the lowest grade compared with me," said Twedor.

"Apologies. I'd like to shake the hand of the person responsible for achieving the redesign of both Twedor and Amal here. What they've done is truly exceptional," said Marc, truly speechless.

Tayce began back to the new wider entrance, exclaiming that he could meet that man tomorrow. In the meantime Lydia was expecting her in an houron for refreshment, so she had to cleanse and change into a clean uniform.

"Do you mind if I tag along?" he put to her, glancing around the new Organisation Centre, impressed by what he was seeing.

"Not at all. It will give you a chance to see some of the changes we've made around here—that's me and the design team. Come on, Twedor, let's go," commanded Tayce.

Marc followed on behind Twedor, still not believing the impressive change in the once guidance and main operations computer, in him becoming a highly sophisticated robot, classed as a Romid.

One thing that Marc noticed as he went was that Amalthea Two was a lot larger in size than Amalthea One. He put it to Tayce and she confirmed that in fact the cruiser was wider by a milon and longer by half a milon; this was to incorporate the new improved changes. They both discussed the many changes that had taken effect and why on the way to Level 3.

* * *

The Enlopedian Cruiser and Redesign Team at the Enlopedian Dome had stripped Amalthea One back to its bare frame. It had taken five monthons to undertake the task. Tayce then attended meetings, being in on each stage of the redesign and construction with many of the heads of each stage, including the new improved computerised functions and capabilities to bring the cruiser up to date. Her input was welcomed and she was considered like one of the team from start to finish. Now, finally, after fifteen monthons of hard overtime duty for the workers concerned to get Amalthea Two ready for the new voyage, she was ready. The final signal for completion was signalled with an elaborate appreciation party thrown by Tayce for all the hard work the men and women had put in and finished just prior to twenty-five hourons into the galactic new yearon of 2420. Amalthea Two had had many extras incorporated into her larger design. The original Transpot had been up dated to Transpot 2, which was quicker and more risk-free than its original. Enabling travel from one spot to another within a fifty milon radius. A fail-safe return was incorporated, making sure everyone returned safely. More weaponry had been incorporated with Slazer cannons, giving an immediate setting of 'disintegration' if required in battle. A new improvement for Amalthean Two, was the new Invis Shield. A shield that made the cruiser totally invisible to the eye and undetected on any vessel, colony or base.

The Organisation Centre was the new immediate working and operations hub of the cruiser. Tayce's Officette was now incorporated in the new Meeting Centre, which was named the Discuss Centre, or DC for short. In the new DC was a new meeting-centre table in chrome and tinted glassene, which seated the whole team plus any guests that were visiting the cruiser. There was a mouldable cream leather soffette that had been placed against one wall for a more relaxed atmosphere. Tayce's desk was situated in front of the almost floor-to-ceiling sight port. The colour scheme in the DC was cream and beige. Amalthea was bigger and better than before.

* * *

Tayce, down in her new quarters, was soon cleansed and changed and was checking her final appearance in the imager. She looked the true successful leader of the Amalthean Quests team that she was! Marc, who had dropped his bags off at his new quarters to unpack later, admired her, thinking she was still as gorgeous as ever, despite what she had gone through, as he leant on the soffette waiting for her. She did one final turn, this way and that. Upon seeing she was pleased with the end result, she headed for the entrance, asking was he waiting for something?

Once off Amalthea Two Tayce exclaimed whilst they walked that when they'd got down in Q City she'd leave him to go on to her mother's and meet him there. There was something she had to do before leaving next dayon.

Marc nodded understandingly as they began across to the Vacuum Lift. Once aboard, they soon travelled back down to the main city level—Q City Square. Marc glanced around through the clear glassene walls as they descended slowly and smoothly.

"So what's with these new changes? I go away and there is one headquarters base; come back, there's a new second one. Enlopedia?" he asked, curious.

"When the team split in 2418 Lydia decided to divide the council chamber, as so many heads of Questa sections were being formed. Questa wasn't coping with the increasing changes, so Enlopedia was designed and constructed. Even our population was growing, because people and aliens from other words came to live and work here. With just the one base, it was impossible to cater for everyone," explained Tayce.

"Really? I noticed there was more security around—why?" asked Marc.

"It's been a different attitude since Barkin was put in charge. Morale throughout the base began to wane; people no longer tolerated something just because it was classed as right. Peace was falling apart and unrest was on the increase. The way people were being treated in their duty was like—and still is in places—they are easily replaced. Loyalty was coming to mean nothing. This mornet I returned with a young male astro-explorer for Questa, and because he's failed to return without his fighter and mission report he'll be out of job by the end of the dayon. Dairan Loring is his name. I offered him a place on the team—you'll probably meet him later."

"Still helping out strays, then?" he teased with a cheeky grin.

"You know me," she replied, laughing.

"I got the evil eye when I landed, by security that I hadn't seen before," said Marc, recalling the fact.

"Mother had a threat made on her life. They've now moved her to a new Officette area under the city, where it's guarded by personal security all the time. Things have changed around here, Marc—not for the better," said Tayce.

"So the changes are related to this Layforn Barkin, then. Why did they choose him for being on the council? Surely they must have checked his background?" asked Marc.

"Someone had it in for Mother, they said. She got the duty she was given too easily. They wanted to unseat her, but try as hard as they could no one could find out who was sending the threats. But they ceased mysteriously when Barkin was escorted from the base," explained Tayce.

Marc raised his eyes in surprise. The Vacuum Lift softly stopped on city level and, as the doors drew apart to reveal people and aliens waiting to board, Tayce, with Marc and Twedor, walked forth. Tayce with Twedor walked as far as the offshoot corridor that would take Marc down to her mothers new Officette, then she informed him she'd see him later with her mother. He nodded and continued on, wondering what had happened to the rest of the old team.

Tayce began on the walk across to the Memorial Park, where Tom's memorial was. She soon entered the park and began on the walk along the rusty-coloured marblex path to come to stand before Tom's plaque in a secluded area of greenery.

She began.

"Well, this is it. Tomorron I'm heading out—second voyage, would you believe, Tom? If someone had said to me at the end of the last voyage I would be starting again without you, I wouldn't have believed them. Marc's back and taking on the role of Commander. Well, I won't be seeing you for a while. I'll come again soon. Bye, my love!"

Twedor noticed as Tayce turned she had tears in her eyes. He could see she would never really forget what unfolded before her eyes that fateful dayon. He slipped his metlon hand in hers and squeezed it lightly. She looked down and smiled. Even in this new Romid form, he knew how she felt. She heard someone familiar talking not far away. Turning, she saw Lance Largon visiting his father's memorial too. She decided to let him have his moment and walked on out of the Memorial Park, off to see her mother.

When she exited the park she was surprised to find Marc waiting for her.

"What's wrong? I thought you were heading to Mother's Officette?" she asked, concerned.

"I got lost, would you believe? After a scrutinising look from security, I came back to find you," he explained.

"Come on, I'll take you there," she said, amused.

"So what happened to the rest of our team from the last voyage?" he asked, curious.

"Lance has been teaching combat to cadets, would you believe? He hated it so much that when I asked him to become part of the new team for this voyage he jumped at it. He's in the Memorial Park at the moment, paying his respects to Jonathan. The rest of the team were scattered here and there, throughout the Universe on different bases. I've found Treketa and Donaldo—they were on the Intergalactic Medical Colony, but are on their way back.

"You've worked hard to bring us all back together. I'm proud of you, considering what you've been through to get us here," he said praisingly

After crossing through the busy atmosphere of city life, in the city square, they walked down along the glassene offshoot partitioned corridor, turning into a large walkway.

"You can see the need for the second base. I noticed, coming across the city square back there, that it was very busy!" Marc exclaimed.

"Quite!" replied Tayce.

Marc wondered if anything happened to Questa, would Lydia Traun take care of its sister colony Enlopedia.

They neared a large white doorway, guarded by two light-blue-platex-shielded guards. They saluted to Tayce with a quick, efficient hand-to-forehead gesture, then went back on guard. They respected her gaining such a high rank at such a young age, as captain. But Marc was not so fortunate as to be allowed to just enter what was classed as a restricted area. They asked him for his identification, prepared to arrest or shoot him if he didn't comply with the new precautionary rules. Marc, feeling he didn't want to rub the guards up the wrong way, took out his ID wallet and handed it to the fair-haired more-officious-looking guard of the two. He studied Marc in great cold security-orientated interest, then handed the ID back with a much kinder expression and nod.

Both Tayce and Marc continued on in through the floor-to-almost ceiling heavy doors, followed by Twedor. Lydia came forth, her arms held out to greet Marc, whom she considered almost like a son. She was dressed in a white silkene high-necked suit and matching high-heeled boots, in cream.

"You found your onboard guest, then?" she asked Tayce with a warm smile.

"Yes she did, and she's been filling me in on what's been happening around here," said Marc with a hint of displeasure in the tone of his voice.

Both Lydia and Marc hugged affectionately, then released, as Lydia explained she had had an update from Treketa and Donaldo in that they'd be arriving in about an houron, via the next Medical Launch.

"There's something that will surprise you as far as Treketa and Donaldo are concerned. Three monthons ago they became legally joined. Treketa is now known as Medic/Nurse Tysonne. I was unfortunately too busy with the redesigning of Amalthea Two to attend," said Tayce, wishing Lydia would close the file she was working on, on screen, and put her screen to standby mode.

"Well, before any more of the new team arrive for the forthcoming voyage, I suggest a bit of refreshment—so let's go, shall we?" suggested Lydia, coming from behind her desk.

Both Tayce and Marc didn't get the chance to protest as Lydia led the way and Twedor followed on first. Marc draped a friendly arm around Tayce's shoulders, like a big brother, as they walked on out together. Lydia glanced over her shoulder to see her daughter and Marc laughing and talking like old buddies. He hadn't changed a bit, thought Lydia. He might have been a couple of yearons older and he had been in the position of command on his friend's cruiser, but he was still the Marc they had come to know and love and consider one of the family, the 'warm, friendly and ready for anything' attitude was still present.

All three walked from the Officette deeper into the corridors to Lydia's new apart-house (named apart-house, because one part of the dwelling was like an apartment and the other was like a two-storey house), where refreshment had been prepared by the Questa Catering Dome techs. Once refreshment was through, Lydia, Tayce and Marc sat around discussing many of the things in general that had gone on in the past yearons. Both on Questa and in Marc's life.

Suddenly Lydia's private cordless Telelinkphone buzzed. Tayce reached across and picked it up. Adam Carford's voice came through, informing her that Treketa and Donaldo had arrived. Tayce thanked him.

Upon replacing the handset, she rose to her feet and began moving over towards the entrance, telling Lydia she was going to meet Donaldo and Treketa and she'd see them later. With this, she walked from the Living Area as the main doors opened automatically before her, and began on the walk down to the Docking, Departure and Arrival Dome. She soon crossed Q City Square and entered briskly into the Arrival and Waiting Centre. Pausing, she looked about in all directions, even over the heads of arriving passengers. She glanced up at the digital display arrival-and-departure board, reading down until she found the Medical Launch. It was in. She pushed on through the arriving crowd, coming from the same flight. Without warning there came a cry out from Treketa to get her attention. Treketa broke into a sprint, leaving Donaldo behind with the luggage.

"Welcome home. It's good to see you both," said Tayce as Treketa paused and gave her once sister by law a long-awaited missed-you hug, excited to see her again after the long absence.

"Hello, Tayce. Long time no see," said Donaldo, giving Tayce a hug upon reaching her, leaving the luggage carrier in Treketa's care for a moment.

"I hear congratulations is in order—so sorry I missed your dayon. It's been hectic around here, getting the cruiser completed."

"No need for apologies. We were amazed to hear Waynard had done what he had, considering what Barkin had done. You've done well to bring us all back together," said Donaldo praisingly, studying her as he spoke like a friend, yet doctor.

"That's just what Marc said. Anyway, Mrs Tysonne—it has a nice sound to it…" began Tayce.

"Nurse/Medic Tysonne, if you don't mind," she said, laughing.

"She doesn't change," cut in Donaldo, putting a loving arm around Treketa, pulling her to him affectionately.

"Shall we go? We'll head for Mother's Officette, though it's not where it used to be," said Tayce.

They all began walking on across the Arrival and Waiting Centre. Treketa, as she went, noticed the different-uniformed guards that she hadn't noticed the last time she was on the base, just on two yearons ago. They seemed dressed in uniforms other than those at Questas previously, as she remembered. Tayce saw the look on her face and explained there had been quite a few changes since they'd all been together. The three of them soon exited the Docking, Departure and Arrival Dome, entering into Q City Square. As they went they talked about many things that had changed. Treketa commented on how well Tayce looked, considering what had happened for them both in losing Tom last voyage. She'd done well to come through it. Tayce didn't want to say anything, but deep down she still found there were times when she missed Tom. Donaldo understood and could see she was doing a good job in hiding the fact.

* * *

Later that same dayon on Questa in Lydia Traun's Officette Chambers, a pre-voyage party was in full swing to celebrate the coming-together of the old team and the joining of some of the new members. New members present, and nervous of meeting the old familiar ones, were as follows. Jaul Naven, a science medical and botany officer from Canardan 5, was a pleasant young man with sandy-coloured hair. Aldonica Darstayne, a young female genius in the field of weaponry, was around 1.70 metres tall and was joining the team as weaponry specialist. She was Questonian/human, fresh from training, and had passed her grade with flying colours. She was top of her field. Next was Craig Bream, a young, blonde, curly-haired, well-built Questonian/human male, responsible for the redesign and update of both Twedor and the Amalthea's new guidance and main operations computer, Amal, pronounced A-mal. He was to be Amalthea's new computer-analysing tech officer and would be responsible for Amal and the upkeep of Twedor. Making sure they were kept in working order. Craig was a pleasant bit-of-a-jack-the-lad type, but good at his job. He took great pride in what he did. Tayce had offered him the position on the team when they'd got on so well in working to get both Twedor and Amal up and running. She knew that he would fit in with the others, as he got on well with everyone around him whilst working with teams in Amalthea Two's construction. He was chatting with Kelly Travern, the team's third new recruit. Straight from Greymaren, she was to be Amalthea's new navigationalist. Kelly was rescued on the last voyage and had decided to join the team upon Tayce's invitation to do so, in looking for a good all-round navigationalist. The familiar regulars of the team returning were Lance Largon, who was reprising his position as Quests research and information officer, though his title had now been shortened to Quests research officer. Donaldo Tysonne was back to be the cruiser's doctor. He had returned with Treketa as his assistant in the new role of medic/nurse and his new intimate joined partner. Marc Dayatso was back in the rank of commander, bringing with him the experience of commanding a cruiser. Everyone stood around with a fluted glassene filled with celebratory liquid of some kind, talking, getting to know one another.

"If I could have everyone's attention for a minon, the reason I've called this get-together is so firstly you can all get to know each other, and to introduce you to one more new member—someone who has spent the last two yearons after special medical treatment putting her new life together, with no recollection of her old one whatsoever. Some of you might remember her because of what she has done in her old life, but due to mind reprogramming she is no longer the person she used to be and has a completely new life and identity. If asked who was her mother, you would get the simple reply she is an orphan who was adopted and put through science academy," explained Tayce.

"Before you ask your final member in, Tayce, I have authority to hand you a surprise you weren't expecting. From tonight, care of Waynard, you are hereby given the new rank of captain, officially," said Lydia proudly.

"What!" said Tayce, both surprised and overjoyed.

Congratulations and applause in the honour of the joyous news erupted into the air. Whilst Tayce took in the moment, pleased such a thing had been bestowed on her, Lydia turned, ordering one of the aides to show in Amalthea's last recruit. The doors to the room soon opened and in walked someone that the old regulars of the Amalthean Quests team didn't expect to see ever again. Treketa gave a wide-eyed look of shock and surprise. What was Tayce thinking?

she wondered. How could she invite this person to be part of the team? Marc gave a look to say had she lost her mind? They were forgetting what Tayce had said—that this person present had no recollection of what she used to be.

Feeling nervous, and not understanding why some of the team were looking at her coldly, she felt she wasn't wanted and wanted to turn tail and run. Pausing in the middle of the room, this last new team member was none other than the once evil daughter of Countess Vargon—Sallen. She was a far cry from the old dayons, when she dressed like an evil vixen. Instead she was dressed in an Amalthean Quests science uniform, in the rank of science tech, looking like she was ready for duty. Tayce glanced at Treketa and slowly shook her head. Sallen felt awkward. She didn't know what to do or say, having no recollection of her old past.

Kelly, after a few minons broke the ice by walking forth and welcoming Sallen to the team with a gentle hug. She was prepared to adjust to the fact that Sallen was not what she once was. After Kelly broke the tense moment, slowly everyone else came forth and did as she had done and wiped the slate clean, welcoming Sallen to the team. Tayce sighed a gentle sigh of relief, glad the uneasy moment was over. She knew it wasn't going to be easy for Sallen. She mingled with the others, answering questions that they had, then suggested that as they were leaving tomorrow she would see them in the mornet and she expected the team to be ready for duty then—in other words, not to remain too long. Sleep was what they needed, to be ready to leave at first light.

Everyone agreed, saying goodnight to her.

Tayce turned and walked from the chambers, meeting Adam Carford in the doorway, who handed her her new silver metallic attaché case for the new voyage, wishing her luck. Tayce nodded, then walked on with Twedor in tow. Everyone had loved Twedor as the new addition to the team in his new form and had spent most of the evening congratulating Craig for his excellent work.

Tayce had no sooner entered the outer anteroom when Dairan Loring entered.

"Dairan! Are you here to be part of my new team tomorrow?" she asked, finding her heart jumping with excitement at the warmth of his mysterious brown eyes as he looked at her.

"You're leaving—am I too late?" he said, hoping not.

"No, go right on in. I'll see you tomorrow—a little more punctual, I hope," she replied.

"What do I say?" he asked, walking to her and about to walk past her.

Tayce felt their closeness was all too much to bear, and she began to blush. The feelings she was feeling were less than professional. Was he doing this on purpose, winding her up? He could see he was unnerving her and slightly smiled—a bright smile that broke the moment.

"Tell Chief Traun I sent you and you're the new astronomer, lieutenant-commander grade—that's if you still want to be?" she said, trying to concentrate.

"Sure I do, Commander," he replied, not knowing her new rank.

"Actually, it's now Captain, but when we're on the cruiser you can call me Tayce," she replied, liking what she was picking up from this Dairan Loring.

"Sorry! Congratulations, by the way. See you first light," he said softly and continued on in to meet with the others.

Tayce thought to herself she had to get a grip on this feeling she was feeling whenever she was around Dairan Loring. She was going to be his team leader and duty was duty. She would have to stop feeling like a love-struck teenager meeting her idol and treat him like a friend.

After Dairan had walked on in to join with the others, she continued on towards the construction port Vacuum Lift to take her back to the cruiser.

"He liked you, you know, I read his vital signs. His adrenaline level was a little elevated," said Twedor at her side as they walked.

"Twedor! Dairan Loring is just another member of the new part of the team, nothing more," she replied sharply at him.

"Um!" said Twedor. His readings were telling him otherwise.

*　*　*

Sometime later in the Vacuum Lift, when the doors had sealed shut, Tayce felt she could breathe a sigh of great relief as the lift rose above Q City Square, on the way back to Amalthea Two, which once again was to be known as just Amalthea. She began thinking that all the hard work was done. She could feel proud of herself. Tomorron was finally arriving, when she could leave Questa for the new voyage.

Upon leaving the lift with Twedor, she walked over to the Docking-Bay doors. Suddenly she heard the familiar voice of none other than Empress Tricara behind her. Tayce had confided to Twedor the fact that she would forgive Tricara for what had happened on Trinot with Tom and had put it down to fate playing a cruel blow. The two of them had come back to being friends again. Tricara asked if it was possible to talk with her, as after tomorron they wouldn't be seeing each other until she was in port again. It would be a good time to go over what she had been taught about focusing her abilities, making sure she fully understood. In the last yearons Tricara had been appointed Tayce's guide in adjusting her to her new powers. Both women walked aboard as the Docking-Bay doors drew apart on the original Level 2, and began on the walk to the Organisation Centre, talking as they went. As soon as Tayce entered Organisation, Amal came on standby and illuminated the overhead lights. She continued on through to the DC. Entering, she placed the attaché case down by the side of her new desk. As Tricara sat down relaxingly on the cream mouldable soffette, Tayce crossed the floor to fix them two drinks from the small wall dispenser.

"Here, I thought we could toast to new beginnings all round and let the past remain where it is," said Tayce, walking to Tricara with a glass filled with stavern.

"I totally agree," she said softly, smiling, glad Tayce had said what she had.

"Is there anything I should expect during this voyage, as far as my abilities go?" said Tayce, turning and looking out through the floor-to-ceiling sight port back at Questa.

"Honitonia!" she simply announced.

"What or who is Honitonia?" asked Tayce, glancing back at her questioningly.

"He's emperor of the Realm of Honitonia and someone you will be turning to over the yearons ahead, as your superior being in your gifts, as they mature, he will come to mean a great deal to you. But you must be careful—he will reprimand you should he feel the need to. He is an extremely powerful being," explained Tricara as gently as she could.

"Why should he pick this voyage?" asked Tayce, curious.

"He has consulted with me and feels during this voyage he will set you a test, to test your true loyalty to the Empire of Honitonia with your powers, whether you can be trusted to carry the blue power crystal. Before you say anything, I know you're true to the Realm of Honitonia, but he doesn't," said Tricara, seeing Tayce was about to protest.

On the words Tricara had just spoken, Tayce felt strangely uneasy and wished she hadn't asked. Tricara could see she was worried, but there was nothing she could do. Tayce had to face the final test of her powers to be granted studentship of the Realm of Honitonia, so she could hold on to the Telepathian blue crystal. She thought for a moment. Then it struck her that there was one thing she could do and that was to give her the Tristarcan blue crystal that she'd already handed back to her during the last voyage and had held safely for fear of it falling into the wrong hands and its powers being used for evilness. She informed Tayce she would hand the crystal back to her again next dayon.

Both she and Tayce talked on well into the early hourons of the dayon of launch of the new voyage. When Tayce finally headed back to her quarters to get what sleep she could, she ordered Twedor to make sure she woke in time for her to cleanse herself and be ready for the new voyage at first light.

* * *

08:00 hourons QMT (Quests Mean Time). It was the first dayon of the new voyage. It had finally arrived. All the monthons of planning, meetings and preparations had been done. The new team members and old regular members were waiting down in Q City dressed in their new Amalthean uniforms. The Vacuum Lift descended to meet them. Inside was Tayce, dressed like the true captain and team leader she was; beside her was Twedor. As the Vacuum Lift gently stopped, the doors drew apart. The team waiting turned and smiled, glad to see Tayce. Lydia was also present. Tayce walked forth, admiring her well-turned-out and smart team in their blue-and-white striped uniforms. Lydia for a moment wondered what Tayce's father would say if he saw her todayon, considering what she'd gone through since that fateful night when she'd left Traun. She guessed he would be proud of what she had accomplished to date. Tricara approached Tayce, carrying the item she had promised her the night hourons before. She was dressed in her all-in-one elegant uniform for the school for gifted children, of a crimson colour. Tricara had fulfilled her ambition, and that was to be head of a school for gifted students and children, in helping them adjust to a life of abilities like Tayce. Tayce had spent some off-duty time having private lessons on how to handle her own new abilities, and she was grateful for them. The team looked on as Tricara handed Tayce the familiar purple velveteen box containing the crystal.

"This is something that we talked about last night. Keep it safe. It will protect you, and should you achieve what is expected of you, which I have no doubt you will, it will remain yours forever," said Tricara, taking Tayce's hands and placing the box gently in her hold.

Tricara stepped back beside Lydia, and on Tayce's command the team began into the awaiting Vacuum Lift, waiting for Tayce and Twedor to join them.

"Be safe and stay in touch," said Lydia, giving Tayce a warm motherly loving hug.

"I will. After all, I have a good team and Twedor here to make sure of that," assured Tayce.

With this she turned and walked on into the Vacuum Lift to join the team. The doors soon drew closed and the lift began to ascend back to Amalthea's Docking-Bay doors. Marc, catching Tayce's apprehensive look, gave her a warm reassuring wink to make her feel a bit more relaxed. He knew going back out into space on Amalthea was not going to be easy. But he would be there for her. Once the Vacuum Lift stopped, the doors drew open and the team walked out along and in through the already open Docking-Bay doors, loaded with their garment carriers and holdalls, holding personal belongings for making their quarters home.

"Marc, before we depart, I want a meeting in the DC and I want to talk to you alone," she asked as the others began moving away."

"Sure! I'll just drop these bags off. I shouldn't be long," he promised, heading away.

As Marc followed the others off down the corridor, Twedor looked at Tayce and they began on the walk up to the Organisation Centre. On arriving a while later, Tayce immediately ordered Amal to go to full operational mode, ready for departure.

Amal came back: "Commencing operational command now, Captain. Preparing procedures for final departure, commencing in roughly forty-five minons and counting. All team present and confirmed. Docking-Bay doors sealed," announced Amal in her crisp, clear voice.

Tayce looked out of the new wide-expanse sight port that almost filled the front hull of the cruiser and watched as they began to draw out of the place she had called home for the best part of two yearons.

* * *

The vast-sized graceful-looking exploration cruiser slowly moved from its construction hold out into the Universe. It was an awesome sight. There was a lot of spectators watching them from both Questa and Enlopedia. Three of those people were the man who had made it all happen for Tayce, Waynard Bayden, and, on Questa, Lydia Traun and Tricara. The white new exterior with the familiar line of red trim travelling from bow to stern was clearly seen. The outer hull reflected the powerful lights of both the Construction Port and Questa. Lights shone from on board the new cruiser as sections and rooms became fully operational, as it slowly withdrew from the port. Many workers that had been responsible for making the Amalthea Two what she was all stood watching, pleased with their work. Leaving what they were working on to watch with pride. Some waved the cruiser off as she had been the focal point of their every-dayon point of interest and duty. Amalthea Two was now officially on its second voyage. What lay ahead no one knew for sure. Tayce was standing looking out of the DC sight port, waving back at some of the waving workers as the cruiser manoeuvred further and further away from Questa Headquarters Base. She felt glad she'd won the battle for a second voyage, and she would do it all again if she had to. It felt good to be back in the Universe crime fighting and seeing justice would be served where it needed to be served.

Marc Dayatso entered the DC. Tayce turned and sat down at her chrome-and-smoked-glassene desk. He waited a few minons, then opened his right lapel jacket pocket, withdrawing a small blue box. The size that would generally hold a ring. He crossed and placed it down on the desktop before her. He then ordered the DC doors closed. Amal picked up his orders and the two doors began to slowly slide together.

"What's this?" asked Tayce, wondering.

"Open it! I guarantee you'll get a surprise—it was a surprise to me when someone handed it to me during a routine search-and-rescue mission. They handed it to me because they couldn't trace you." Tayce cautiously did as Marc suggested, opened the box carefully. The first sight she got of the slightly worn exquisite man's ring was a stone that was called the Traunian Emerald. This she had seen numerous times before and recognised to be her father's ring. She looked up at Marc, speechless.

"It's Father's ring, but how?" she asked in outright astonishment.

Did this mean her father was still alive somewhere, somehow.

"The Chief said it was discovered on an assignment to a small solar world called Planus. He said it was discovered in the remains of a burnt-out Life Pod on the surface. One of his men found fragments of the pod with our old Traunian emblem on, but no there was no body—only this with the initials 'D. T.' for Darius Traun engraved on the inside," explained Marc.

She took the ring from the blue small box and turned her chair so that she could look out of the DC sight port in thought, without taking her attention from studying the ring and looking out into the Universe.

"Do you honestly think Father could be alive somewhere, or is there no hope of ever finding him again and I have to resign myself to the fact I'll never see him again?" she asked, hoping not.

"I have no idea, but the team that were on Planus did a planet-wide sweep for any life signs and found nothing, only the animals and insects that roamed there," he explained.

"Maybe someone picked up his life-pod signal and rescued him before he crashed," she said suddenly.

"If he's out here, then whoever rescued him may just help in tracing you and Lydia," he assured.

Marc could see she felt upset and walked around the back of the chair, pulling her up into his strong arms, giving her a warm hug. Tayce didn't want to think of the worst, but what if her father had been picked up by no do-gooders? Marc held her so he could look down at her.

"If Darius is alive, believe me, he probably wants to know if you're alive too, Lydia also, so he's going to do his damnedest to find you both if he can."

"What if he has amnesia and doesn't even know we're alive?" asked Tayce, thinking.

"If you're meant to come face-to-face with him, then it will happen," he replied assuringly.

No more was said on the matter, but Tayce was now wondering. She placed the ring back in the box. It was not the box it was originally kept in. Maybe her father had left it at the scene as a kind of clue. That if anyone found it and his body was not present, then it would tell her he was alive—she would rather think along those lines. Marc held her slightly away from him, studying her for a few minons. Tayce broke away from him and began saying that during the current voyage she would be called to the Telepathian Empire on Honitonia to undertake a test to secure her right to use her abilities and meet a man that was going to play a big part in her future. Marc remembered hearing Tricara mention something earlier about the blue crystal and assured her that, whatever happened, he would fall in and take command when it occurred, that he would be there when she needed him.

"Do you want me to tell the others of this?" he asked.

"No, I'll tell them," she assured.

Marc ordered Amal to open the DC doors. Within minons the doors drew apart, revealing the Organisation Centre. The team were waiting to walk in and seat themselves around the Meeting-Centre table for the first meeting of the voyage.

Tayce stood and waited until all the team were seated.

The second voyage, on Amalthea Two, had just begun.

2. A Charan Prince

Life on board the new Amalthean cruiser was settling down for the team. Since leaving Questa Headquarters Base Construction Port, any new problems that had arisen with Amalthea Two being fresh out of port had been taken care of quickly by Craig Bream, returning the cruiser to smooth full running operation once more. The Universe was not the place to have an under-functioning cruiser. It would be considered a sitting target for anyone who fancied their chances to use Amalthea as target practice. The team members old and new were getting used to each other, and the frosty atmosphere that had been present where Sallen Vargon was concerned was slowly easing. Treketa and Sallen were slowly becoming friends.

* * *

It was the first dayon of the second monthon. Whilst on his first duty watch Craig Bream discovered without warning two milons away from Amalthea and drifting was a strange-looking vessel that looked somewhat royal in appearance. It was small in size and looked void of all life. There were no lights shining from on board to signify otherwise. He quickly called Tayce from the DC. After a few minons Tayce hurried out and across to see what he was worried about. Coming to a pause by his side, she looked out to where he was pointing through the main sight port. Upon seeing the vessel in distress, she turned to new team member Kelly Travern at navigations.

"Kelly, run a scan for hostile intent. It could be a elaborate trap," said Tayce.
"Running scan now," replied Kelly, her fingers flying over the touchpad keys.
"Amal, have Aldonica and Dairan come to Organisation," ordered Marc.
"Requesting now," replied Amal.
Marc crossed and paused just beside Kelly's chair. She looked up at him, explaining that the mystery vessel appeared just as it looked, drifting and void of all life. It had two engines, but only one was operational at present. Dairan and Aldonica ran into Organisation, one behind the other, coming to a gentle

pause. As Aldonica crossed to Kelly, she looked out to see the vessel. She was a slim pretty girl with doll-like beautiful features, blue eyes and long thick straight blonde hair. Upon pausing just beside Marc, she enquired what weaponry did the vessel have, if any? Kelly explained, she was unable to detect any through normal scan, as all the readings that had come back through were 'nil'.

"Amal, give me a scan freeze of the whole vessel. Bring it up so we can see what the name and origination of it is," said Dairan beside Tayce.

"Operating scan freeze now. Would you like me to run the sweep facility?" asked Amal.

"Yes," replied Dairan, waiting.

Lance, at his research console, began getting the scan-freeze information appearing on screen before him. He began reading back what he was receiving as it came in.

"Humanoid male life form on board. Heat scan just confirmed he's in some kind of suspended hibernation state. Weaponry: there isn't any. The emblem that appears on the side of the vessel is one even our database can't identify," he explained.

Aldonica gave a puzzled look. She was unsure what to make of the vessel. Tayce came to the conclusion whoever was aboard had to be from a peaceful civilisation, with no weaponry of any sort; either that or they had to be downright stupid not to have any, in the current times. Marc glanced to Tayce, who was in deep thought of what to do for the best.

"Amal, can we bring the vessel into the bay?" asked Tayce.

"Calculating now," replied Amal.

"What are you thinking of doing?" asked Marc, crossing, interested.

"Calculations complete. It's possible to bring the vessel through decontamination procedure aboard. Would you like me to undertake this, Captain?" asked Amal.

Tayce gave the go-ahead, then stood watching through the main sight port as the tractor beam latched on to the small vessel and brought it aboard. She studied the size in general and could see it was large enough to carry one person, no more. But she too had to admit she never remembered seeing a vessel before such as this one, in her past travels, ever!

"Marc, you're in charge. Dairan, Craig, Aldonica, come with me. We're going down to see what the reason is for that vessel drifting into our spacial path—that's if we can revive whoever is on board successfully," announced Tayce, heading across Organisation to the entrance, in a true walk of command.

The three members followed on behind. They headed on out of Organisation. Twedor exited the DC, where he had been on standby, and decided to take a closer look at the vessel coming into the Flight Hangar Bay. He came to a pause beside Marc and stood silently watching the nearing of the vessel.

Tayce and the others briskly walked along discussing the arriving vessel, trying to piece together some ideas on who was aboard. Aldonica and Craig found themselves having a certain understanding when it came to technology. Craig noticed how pretty she was—her innocent features and small round face with clear complexion. He could see in time they were going to be good close friends. It was hard to imagine she was a genius in her field, by appearance. She looked like she would be at home on some modelling catwalk somewhere, not designing weaponry and other gizmos to destroy or protect. But, studying her as they talked, he bet if the moment came when she would need to protect herself, then she looked like she could more than handle any action that was thrown at her.

Aldonica was thinking to herself as they went, she had seen the emblem on the vessel before, but would it come to her? No! Then, just like a blinding flash, it suddenly did. It was three yearons ago on a weaponry assignment during her training. The vessel was from the Charan Empire in the future—400,000 yearons to be exact—through a strange phenomenon known as the Time-Shift Tunnel. She immediately informed Tayce, explaining where the vessel was from. Both Dairan and Craig looked at her in sheer amazement at what she was divulging—how the planet the vessel was from was from 400,000 yearons in the future, down the Time-Shift Tunnel, and it was near impossible to find just by star chart. The people of the Charan Empire were the only people who knew how to call up the entrance.

"But what's this vessel doing so far from home, especially in this time and space?" asked Tayce, curious something had forced whoever was on board to escape his own time for some reason.

"Maybe it was some unknown force that pushed him into our path, off course from his," said Aldonica.

"The information I found earlier upon keying our mysterious vessel into the research database system was the Time-Shift Tunnel is roughly fifty milons from our current orbit. It's puzzling to know what it's doing here," said Dairan, much to the surprised looks of the others around him as they didn't think there was any information to be had.

"How come you managed to find it? It's generally not easily found—like I said earlier, only by Charan Empire inhabitants." Aldonica was astounded Dairan had found the information she couldn't so easily.

"Anything else we should know that you can recall, Aldonica?" asked Tayce, stepping in.

"There is one other thing. I heard the Charan Empire people aren't hostile, like some races. I guess, when you come to think about it, that's why the vessel doesn't have any weaponry," she replied.

"Is that it?" asked Craig, teasing her.

"Only I heard from an old friend of mine they are as good as you in computers. You'll find it near impossible to try and fix their engines—they are way ahead of this Universe for technology."

"Nothing is too sophisticated for me. I class it as a resourceful exciting challenge. Remember Twedor and Amal—way ahead of their time, but I designed and built them," replied Craig.

"Enough teasing, you two. Now let's see what we've got in here with our mystery guest from the Charan Empire, shall we?" said Tayce, entering the Flight Hangar Bay and looking about then across the vast-sized area for the first sign of the mystery vessel.

The Charan travel-pod-type vessel was undergoing the last cencrons of the decontamination process. It was bathed in a bright-red sweeping light. It ceased. Next it was manoeuvred by tractor-beam crane to be placed in the Service Area. All four Amaltheans waited patiently. On touchdown, the electronic sensory energy crane ceased and retracted back to its resting place back up in the ceiling, where it belonged, and shut down with a hum and a click.

"Dairan, Wristlink Donaldo. Tell him I want him and Treketa down here. Tell him it's a code orange and to bring his new Emergency Medical Kit," ordered Tayce in true commanding tone.

Dairan quickly contacted Donaldo via Wristlink, informing him of Tayce's request. No sooner had he ceased communications than both Donaldo and Treketa were hurrying into the Flight Hangar Bay, bringing with them the Hover Trolley and Emergency Medical Kit—a kit that had been improved since the first voyage to carry a lot more items to treat extreme emergencies, hence the light name change. Donaldo looked towards the now stationary vessel with interest as he came to a stop beside Tayce. He glanced at her questioningly for a moment, then looked back at the silver-and-green-bullet shaped vessel. He had changed in his attitude in handling emergency situations. He was a lot calmer and for the moment in hand—in fact he had become a first-class understanding medical man who knew how to handle situations quickly and confidently.

"Is this the emergency?" he asked casually.

"Yes! There's a humanoid male inside, in some kind of hibernation state. The vessel was picked up a while ago. It was drifting way off course, operating on one engine with no weaponry. I would like you present in case we need your help in reviving him," confided Tayce.

"Decontamination complete. The vessel is now cleansed for entry," said Amal overhead.

"May I, Captain?" asked Aldonica. "I'm familiar with Charan technology, to get us inside the vessel."

Without further word she began walking forward to the entrance hatch. She turned, glancing at Tayce questioningly. Tayce nodded for her to continue. She figured as Aldonica obviously knew a great deal about the Charan Empire and its technology she should be the one to gain entry to the vessel. Donaldo stood waiting to act at a minon's notice if he had to. Everyone watched as Aldonica tried various entry codes into the small circular inset keypad by the entrance, which was made up of symbols. After a few minons, success was achieved. The half-moon-shaped entrance hatch clicked and began to slide back with a gentle easiness.

Tayce began forward and walked up the two inset steps, boarding the darkened interior. Donaldo followed on. Dairan placed his hand on his handgun, out in the Flight Hangar Bay, ready to use at a minon's notice if he had to do so. He was ready to protect Tayce if he had to. There was no telling what was on board, in the vessel's interior. Without warning the vessel's interior changed to a red glow as Tayce entered. Donaldo pulled Tayce back, concerned they'd triggered something off like an intruder system. He suggested she remain at a safe distance whilst he ran the Examscan over the hibernation container first. Tayce wasn't going to argue, and her hand moved to her gun in case she needed to protect the both of them. Donaldo guided the small handheld device all over the long illuminated hibernation chamber. Standing back, he waited for a reading. A few cencrons elapsed and the reading came back as all clear of contamination. Treketa entered the interior. She noticed the inside of the small vessel was high quality. Computers lined one side whilst the hibernation container almost filled the other. Donaldo nodded to Tayce, signifying everything was fine, there wasn't any danger. Both leant over the smoked-glassene domed cover with the Charan Empire emblem on, looking inside. A young boy around the age of twelve, lay in deep sleep.

"He's very young to be out here alone," said Donaldo.

"You're right. Is he alive?" asked Tayce, somewhat surprised.

"It looks like whoever he is he's someone high-up. Judging by the emblem on his uniform, maybe he's royalty of some kind," said Treketa, studying the young lad, noticing he was someone of high standing.

He looked like he had been well bred—a kind of designer child.

Aldonica managed to get into the interior, wondering what was happening. She enquired was there anything she could do to help?

Tayce gestured for her to take a look in the hibernation chamber. "Perhaps you can throw some light on who we have here?" she asked.

Aldonica squeezed past Treketa and Donaldo so she could get a clear look into the top of the hibernation chamber. She gave a look of total astonishment at whom she was looking at. Tayce and Donaldo glanced at each other, then back at Aldonica questioningly.

"Who do we have here? Is he some kind of threat to us and the cruiser? If so, we'll put him back where he belongs," said Tayce, not prepared to put everyone in danger.

"This is Prince Tieman. He's the son of the king of the royal house of Charan," expressed Aldonica to the shocked faces of Tayce, Donaldo and Treketa.

"According to the latest reading, his vital signs are wavering," said Donaldo, checking the Examscan.

"In that case, do what you have to and what you consider necessary to revive him safely and restore him to a healthy consciousness, then call me," ordered Tayce.

"I'll help," volunteered Aldonica eagerly.

As Tayce began on out of the vessel, she couldn't believe the first real rescue of the second voyage was one that was going to be remembered for some yearons to come. A royal prince aboard Amalthea. She was wondering what to do to help the young prince return to his home, as she exited the vessel. Dairan picked up on her thoughtful expression and crossed. Donaldo came out behind her briefly, to get the Hover Trolley, whilst Aldonica stayed and helped with gaining entry into the hibernation chamber so the Prince could gain the help he needed to come back to reality. Eventually the chamber was unsealed and both Treketa and Donaldo worked fast to get the Prince on to a portable life support and on to the awaiting Hover Trolley. Donaldo then took hold of the small handheld control pad, pushing a white key to operate the trolley. It slowly moved off forward just in front of him. He followed on with Treketa by his side, carrying the Emergency Medical Kit, heading away towards the Medical Life Centre, which was termed the MLC for short. Tayce watched him leave, hoping they'd be able to revive the Prince successfully. Aldonica climbed from the small vessel, suggesting she follow Donaldo and find out what she could about their onboard guest. Tayce nodded. With this she hurried on out to try and catch Donaldo and Treketa up. Craig stood summoning up the engine department—two powerful-looking engines were situated on the outside under the wing. This was not going to be easy, he thought.

"This vessel, if I'm not mistaken, has been in a fast flight to escape some kind of enemy. The engines, as far I can see, have been pushed for maximum power for a long duration," he explained to Tayce on approach.

"So it could have been in some kind of battle?" asked Tayce, approaching.

"I don't know, but whoever fired upon His Highness wanted him to be left to be picked off by criminals of the worst kind," replied Craig.

"Can you see what damage is done? After all, you said you like a challenge," said Tayce light-heartedly.

"I'll give it go," he said cheerfully in his Australton tone.

Tayce walked briskly on out of the Flight Hangar Bay, joined by Dairan, leaving Craig to see what damage was done. He stood scratching his head, remembering what Aldonica told him about finding it impossible to repair the Charan engines—their technology was so far advanced.

'A challenge is a challenge,' he thought as he continued on with what he had to do in hand.

Craig was around 1.85 metres tall. His eyes were a dark blue, almost grey. He was an easy-going kind of person, as well as having his Jack-the-Lad traits. He was fast with the wit and quick off the mark for a good joke. In a situation he could turn from sad or awkward to a light-hearted moment to cheer everyone up. Even though he was of strong muscular build, it could be seen he possessed good stamina and would move very quickly from one situation to another, no matter how tough it became, in the line of needed action.

* * *

Tayce and Dairan, as they neared the Deck Travel, began discussing their royal guest. Dairan suggested he try and find out something about Prince Tieman. Tayce agreed eagerly. They both boarded the Deck Travel as it arrived and the doors opened. No sooner had the doors closed then the Deck Travel under Dairan's request headed for Level 5, to drop him off, before taking Tayce to Level 1, so he could head off and start the astro-research into the planet Charan. Upon the Deck Travel stopping on Level 5 and Dairan exiting, he turned before heading away and informed Tayce he'd see her later with what he could come up with. She agreed with a nod. She noticed for the first time, when she looked at him, there was a different kind of feeling. She felt there was more of a genuine friendship forming, instead of the thoughts she shouldn't have been having the first time she looked at him. As the doors closed and Tayce began on the ascent to Level 1 she stood in thought over the way Dairan and herself were becoming good teammates. She was glad she had taken him on the team. He was going to be a worthwhile member of the new team and, in time, a real good friend.

The Deck Travel stopped on Level 1. As soon as the doors opened Tayce walked out, beginning along the corridor to enter back into the Organisation Centre. Noticing the team at work, she passed through, going on into the DC. Marc, upon seeing her pass, left Craig Bream's empty duty position, informing Kelly to continue on with the information they were checking. He sauntered on into the DC to find out how things had gone down in the Flight Hangar Bay. He paused, leaning on the wall just inside the doorway, as Tayce seated herself on her swivel high-backed chair.

"How did things go in the Flight Hangar Bay? Who's our first rescue of the new voyage? he asked casually.

"We have a prince on board, would you believe? He's the son of the king of the Charan Empire. Do you know anything about the Charan Empire, by any chance?" asked Tayce, wondering if he might have come across the name in his travels aboard his last cruiser, in the last yearons.

"I've heard about them, but only they're based in a future time so many yearons beyond ours. Why?" replied Marc, thinking about it.

"It puzzles me what the Prince is doing here in this particular sector of the Universe," said Tayce, thinking.

"So what are your plans, or don't you know yet?" enquired Marc, wondering.

"As soon as he regains consciousness, find out just what he is doing so far from his home world. Aldonica's with him at present, to see what she can find out, if anything, the moment he is revived."

"Is anything being done to contact his father, to let him know what's happened?" asked Marc seriously.

"No not yet, though I'd better talk to him, as Captain of this cruiser. Dairan's finding everything he can about the Charan Empire. It will be intriguing, to say the least."

"I guess you have it in hand. I'll carry on in Organisation—leave you to contact the King. Oh, if he appears on screen, don't forget to curtsey!" said Marc cheekily as he turned in the doorway, walking back down into Organisation.

"Very funny, Marc," replied Tayce after him, giving a look that said it all.

As Marc continued on with his duty in Organisation, Tayce picked up the Telelinkphone on her desk and depressed the key code sequence to connect her with Dairan down in the Astrono Centre. He answered. She asked how could she go about contacting the King of the Charan Empire? Dairan thought about it for a few minons, then suggested as soon as he found out perhaps she would allow him to do it. He was currently sifting through reams of information that were somewhat complex on the said empire. Tayce thought about it for a minon. She thought she really should be the one to contact the King herself, but then agreed, telling him the moment he made contact he was to remember he was representing Amalthea and to address the King as His Highness. Dairan agreed, exclaiming he would see her later with the results. He quickly cut communications. Tayce placed the handset back on its triangular slim base and turned to look out of the DC sight port at the passing Universe in thought.

* * *

Dairan an houron later entered the DC carrying charts and printed information relating to the Charan Empire. Marc walked back in and stood at ease, waiting to find out what he had managed to discover.

"How did it go, contacting the King?" he asked Tayce, interested.

"Actually, I know I should have done it, but Dairan offered," she replied, looking at Dairan in a questioning way.

"Did you bow when he appeared on screen?" teased Marc as Dairan set up the information he had.

"What! No—did I have to?" replied Dairan, not getting the fact Marc was winding him up.

Marc smiled. Exhaling, he shook his head.

Dairan needed to lighten up. Dairan handed Tayce the information he'd printed. She took it, studying it. Dairan informed her their onboard guest, as she knew, was Prince Tieman, and his father, the King of the Charan Empire, was thankful they'd rescued his only son and heir. He explained his son had been separated from a protective party on the way to a meeting in another sector. It was near impossible to track him because of a storm that had crossed their path in the remainder of the journey with the escort team. He also expressed great gratitude and explained he had been deeply concerned about his son's whereabouts, thinking the worst. He thought he was never to see his son again, through being picked off by criminals of the worst kind. They'd been invited to visit the Charan Empire to return the Prince as soon as possible.

Marc, upon this, smiled and shook his head, thinking to himself, 'What next?' He nudged Dairan, suggesting it was time to get out his VIP uniform.

Tayce smiled to herself. She had to admit their latest Quest was something out of the ordinary. It had been the first time ever they'd rescued royalty. Though her family on Traun had been treated like the equivalent of royalty by the people of her world. Dairan turned as Lance entered the DC with a message.

"Hope you've brought your VIP uniform. We're off to visit royalty," Marc told Lance.

"Why, what's happening?" asked Lance, curious, handing Tayce the message.

"We've been asked by the King of the Charan Empire to personally return our onboard guest, Prince Tieman," explained Tayce.

"There is one thing I would like to say here: I know Amalthea is a lot more stable and better and tougher in design, but do you think she can handle the interior of the Time-Shift Tunnel?" asked Marc, concerned.

"Yes, I certainly do. Twedor here will back me up. We were there, remember, at the design and construction stages of this cruiser. The designers specifically worked in the toughened flexibility for tremendous turbulence into the main frame," pointed out Tayce in a no-nonsense tone.

Her desktop Telelinkphone suddenly sounded three short soothing sounds at the side of her. She turned her swivel chair so she could press a small blue key on the base. She picked up the slim handset and placed it to her right ear. Aldonica's voice came through. She informed Tayce their onboard guest was conscious and demanding to speak to the person in charge. Tayce informed her to tell the Prince she was on her way down and she could return to her section. Aldonica acknowledged, then ceased communication. Tayce placed the handset back and rose to her feet.

"Come on, Twedor—we're going to meet a prince," ordered Tayce, walking out from behind her desk.

"Do you want me along?" asked Marc.

"Yes! And seriously, no more joking. This guest is important," replied Tayce as she and Twedor headed over to the entrance.

Marc agreed. He knew when to call a halt to a moment of light-heartedness. He followed on, seriously thinking about the situation in hand and the fact this rescue had to beat all rescues. No wonder they were being classed as new legends on the space waves. He followed Tayce and Twedor through Organisation. Dairan hurried on behind. He was going back to the Astrono Centre, to see if he would find anything further on the Time-Shift Tunnel.

Down in the MLC Treketa was busy running constant checks on the young prince, to keep him constantly monitored until he returned to normal health. The results she was receiving were somewhat amazing. She kept her thoughts to herself and just took the results to Donaldo. He was watching from the other side of the centre. The Prince's health and rate of recovery amazed him as a highly qualified physician. He was intrigued as to why the Prince showed no concern over what he'd gone through. Then he guessed the Prince was in a suspended animated state when they boarded the vessel back in the Flight Hangar Bay and knew nothing of what had happened. Something else also bugged him: what he'd discovered about the Prince's general health and normal well-being. On the outside he had the normal appearance of any royal child of roughly twelve yearons old, but on the inside he had the most amazing strong bone structure he'd ever seen; but the most surprising thing about it was Amal had given him an estimated age of 140 for the Prince's true age. It didn't add up. He shook his head at the puzzling discovery. Treketa handed him her findings, then returned to watch over their guest.

Donaldo's thoughts for a moment left what he was studying and his eyes fell on Treketa. He studied her. She worked with more confidence and efficiency on this new voyage, he thought, because of her spell at the Intergalactic Medical Colony. It had done her good. As he studied the findings, he also continued to study her in general, thinking she'd come a long way from losing Tom, her brother, to the present dayon. She was still a pretty feminine blonde, which had attracted him to her. He liked the way her hair fell into a bob style just under her chin. Her slim figure that still showed the small shapely curves in all the right places. He smiled to himself. She was still the slim attractive girl she was when she had joined the team back in the last voyage, just a little older. She was now twenty-eight. Treketa's uniform had changed since the first voyage. It now consisted of a miniskirt in flared design with matching close-fitting bolero jacket, which was all in white with a pencil-thin line running from her shoulder to her wrist on each sleeve of her jacket and from the waist to the hem of her skirt in a grey stripe. Her new uniform was topped off with white matching tights and ankle boots with two-inch heels. Again in white. All the team now had name-and-rank badges on the right-hand side of their uniform jackets, or long-sleeved vests. Treketa caught the Prince trying to make out the name on her badge. She smiled.

"I'm Medic/Nurse Stavard, Your Highness," she announced politely.

Donaldo crossed with another injection to steady the Prince's blood level, as it was again for some strange reason decreasing into an unhealthy reading. As a doctor, Donaldo was greatly concerned. He had to steady the level or there was no telling what might occur, considering the Prince was from the future and his body chemistry was different to a normal humanoid of his age. Treketa watched him like she'd done numerous times before. She could see the concern in his features. Donaldo's uniform was the same patten as Treketa's—white with a pencil-thin grey line that ran from shoulder to wrist of his medical top and from the waist to the ankle of his trousers. His boots were flat, in white.

Suddenly the entrance doors drew open with the soft sound of compressed air. Tayce entered, elegantly crossing to the Prince's bunk, closely followed by Marc and Twedor.

"At last someone to save me from this mad doctor! Who are you?" the young dark-haired prince demanded.

"I'm Captain Traun, Your Highness—the person in charge of this cruiser, who rescued you from the path of danger," announced Tayce in an authoritative tone.

"Why does this being keep on sticking sharp-pointed objects in me?" he demanded in the true tone of a royal child and prince.

"Dr Tysonne, I can assure you Your Highness, is not doing you any harm. He is my main medical man. Let me introduce you. He's trying to give you the best medical treatment there is, to make you well enough to face your father. We want you well enough to return to Charan. Your father is pleased to hear you're safe," assured Tayce.

"You told my father where I am? Oh, fantastic!" said the Prince, throwing his hands in the air in outrage at the thought that his father now probably considered him an idiot for getting separated from his travelling party.

"Yes, your father was informed, Your Highness," replied Tayce to the point, but politely.

"Is there a problem with it?" asked Marc. He didn't like the way the Prince thought he could be rude to Tayce and get away with it.

"No, no problem. Couldn't you have just left me alone out in the Universe?" continued the prince angrily.

"You fancy yourself as galactic pirate bait, do you; because if Captain Traun here had left where you were, that's what you would have become," pointed out Marc behind Tayce. He was finding it impossible to keep his temper at the continued disrespect this young prince was showing her.

"Captain, a private word in my Officette, please?" asked Donaldo, gesturing towards his Officette doorway.

"Of course," agreed Tayce, following him briskly over to enter into his Officette.

Once inside Donaldo crossed to his desktop computer and keypad. He keyed in a sequence to bring up the Prince's file information and body scans. As they began materialising on-screen, he began to explain. He turned the screen so she could see what he'd discovered. He expressed that it intrigued him greatly, the strange and fascinating readings that had arisen. He paused for a minon to close the door, to give them some privacy. Tayce sat down on the edge of the desk. Donaldo reached over and handed her a medical print-out, asking her if she thought it was the scan she'd expect from a normal twelve-yearon child, royal or otherwise? Tayce studied the scan for a few minons. She'd taken medical exams back on her home world, so she had some idea of what she was studying. She gave a look of surprise. She was baffled, to say the least.

"This scan shows amazing bone structure for a child his age. Looking at this, I would put him at the rough age of around 140 internally, but at some time these bones seem to have been damaged yet healed in such a way like nothing I can think of. There's still a fine line in several places where it's healed—it's like the bones are somehow constructed to withstand anything thrown at them and easily heal themselves. I'm baffled over the fact that on the outside he is a lot younger than he is on the inside," said Tayce, not believing what she was seeing.

"I agree—old on the inside and young on the outside. I'd love to know how this happens?" confided Donaldo calmly and quietly.

"Absolutely! If you look, however, at some of the bones more closely, you can just make out where they have taken a severe blow and healed to near perfection, only showing a slight indentation," said Tayce, tracing an area on-screen on the right leg.

"It's hard to believe the Prince is who he is—a twelve-yearon boy—and on the inside he has the inner bone growth of a man of much older yearons," agreed Donaldo, shaking his head in utter disbelief at what he was seeing and treating.

"There is one theory—maybe the Charan Empire has some kind of process where a person reaches a certain age and rejuvenates back to any age they choose to be, by some process unknown to the likes of you and me," said Tayce, thinking.

"I wouldn't mind it. It's got to be something like that—I'd certainly be interested to find out more, if it was possible?" said Donaldo in utterly baffled thought.

"Me too," replied Tayce. She was finding the whole make-up of Prince Tieman intriguing.

Donaldo opened the Officette doors. Tayce began back out to Marc and Twedor. Donaldo followed on, asking, as the King of the Charan Empire had asked her to take the Prince home, could he be part of the visiting Quest team? Tayce thought about it for a minon. She didn't see any harm in him going along and agreed to his request. He thanked her. He couldn't wait to find out if the King would allow him to know how the process regarding age and unusual bone structure worked.

Tayce paused mid floor and discreetly asked him how it felt to be back as part of the new team.

He began by saying it was good to be back on board and back where he belonged, travelling the stars as part of the Amalthean Quests team.

They continued on to the Prince's bunk-side. Tayce was surprised to see Twedor was keeping the Prince in intelligent conversation. Marc had calmed down to hear the many interesting situations the Prince had been through. He'd told Marc about life in the Charan Empire—some of the things Marc found quite unbelievable, yet fascinating.

"I think we need to leave you to rest, Your Highness," said Tayce coming to a pause.

"I am feeling a bit fatigued. Nice meeting you, Twedor; you too, Commander Dayatso," announced the Prince in a much better polite tone than earlier.

Marc nodded in acknowledgement, then turned with Tayce to head on out, Twedor following on in his own little walking way. Upon approach, the doors drew apart in front of them, the overhead sensor picking up their presence. Tayce called back over her shoulder to Donaldo before leaving, saying she would see him later. With this, she, Marc and Twedor continued on out on their return to the Organisation Centre, known sometimes just as Organisation.

* * *

By 16:00 hourons QMT, the Amalthea was on course to rendezvous with the Time-Shift Tunnel entrance to head into the future time and orbit of the Charan Empire. All the team were watching the journey unfold in Organisation. The visiting Quest members going to Charan had been picked. They were all dressed in ceremonial attire. The ceremonial dress was the same as the normal Amalthean Quest uniform, but in white with gold. The pencil-thin stripe of gold ran from shoulder to cuff of the top and there were smart close-fitting trousers for both female and male members of the team. The Prince was well enough to be escorted to Organisation.

As he entered so Tayce turned, welcoming him. "Welcome to what we term the Organisation Centre, Your Highness. This is our main operations centre of the whole cruiser," began Tayce politely. She went on to introduce the present team members.

Marc had warned the team about the Prince's appearance and that he was not all he appeared to be. As the team individually met him, they tried not to show their surprise. Tayce introduced Craig Bream as he entered Organisation, explaining he was responsible for repairs to his royal vessel, which had been badly damaged.

"Would you show me the repairs you've done, if your Captain here doesn't mind releasing you from your current duties?" asked the Prince, glancing at Tayce questioningly.

"I don't see why not," replied Tayce.

Both the Prince and Craig began away. The team returned to their current duties. Amalthea soon came to the last moments before entering the Time-Shift Tunnel entrance. The team present in Organisation watched as a flash of red light burst open before the cruiser, through the main sight port. It engulfed the entire centre, bathing it in the brilliance of red reflection. Outside it surrounded the whole of the cruiser, bathing the hull in the same brilliance. Tayce secretly hoped she'd been right when she'd said the outside hull had been constructed to withstand tremendous force. Amal controlled the entire journey, both navigationally and operatively, constantly adjusting for compensation of the cruiser travelling against forces of the interior of the tunnel. Lance, at his position, pressed a small inset key on his console as Amal transferred her findings of the interior journey to his duty position. He tore off a printout and studied it. Marc watched the journey unfold and figured that if the cruiser was as good as Tayce claimed he didn't see why they couldn't change speed to hyper-thrust turbo and suggested so. Tayce quickly stopped the request, stating there was too much of a strong gravitational pull.

"Commander, I can confirm Captain Traun's words of concern. Even though this cruiser is strong in design and able to withstand more turbulence than it used to, it would be unwise to attempt it. The turbulence would be too great," said Amal, backing Tayce up.

"Point taken," said Marc, seeing sense in the fact.

Prince Tieman, a while later, walked back into Organisation with Craig just as Amal gave an update on the current journey—that everything was running smoothly. All compensations for turbulence were well in hand.

"Your Highness," greeted Tayce, turning.

"You're concerned for your cruiser during this journey, Captain, I understand, though I can assure you both you and your cruiser are quite safe," assured the prince.

"Commander Dayatso suggested the use of hyper-thrust turbo—is this possible? I thought it would be too much for this cruiser and flatly refused?" Tayce asked quietly.

"It will be absolutely fine to use hyper-thrust turbo. The interior of our Time-Shift Tunnel may concern you, but it is merely a precaution for criminals trying to use this means to travel to our Universe. If there were any kind of detection during the journey that whoever had entered this tunnel had done so unlawfully they'd be destroyed. The tunnel has a built-in sensory system that can penetrate the hull and read the intentions of the person making the passage. As you are bringing me back to my people, it has been put in place, even though the journey is somewhat uneasy, shall we say? You're safe and it will also be safe when you return to your Universe when you leave my empire," explained the Prince.

"Commence hyper-thrust turbo, Kelly," ordered Tayce, to Marc's utter surprise.

"Activating hyper-thrust turbo now," announced Kelly.

Marc shook his head, but said nothing. Through the main sight port it could be seen that Amalthea was going straight into hyper-thrust turbo speed, heading off like a shot out of a gun, at great speed into the future realm of the Charan Empire Universe. But Amalthea looked graceful as she made the transition from slow speed to hyper-thrust turbo, heading inside. The tunnel interior colours changed as the cruiser travelled deeper into the journey. Within 200 milons, the cruiser had travelled 400,000 yearons into the future. Kelly, upon Tayce's orders, keyed in the sequence to slow the cruiser for final approach to the future. Amalthea slowed to warp 5 with the assistance of Amal. The Prince looked out through the main sight port at the front of Organisation to the pear-shaped world, with shining gold and silver spires, that reached high up into the outer orbit of the planet. There was a honeycomb shape two storeys high.

'This,' thought Tayce, 'must be the building for their Flight Control for arriving vessels, etc., coming from space.'

It seemed like it. The building was constructed of steelex and glassene. Charan looked the true idea of a kingdom, sparkling like a mystical wonder to be explored with interest. It was truly a breathtaking sight.

"That's my home, the Charan Empire—all three miltons of it," announced the Prince proudly, forgetting for a moment he had broken away from the travelling party and he would have to answer to his father, the King, for his actions.

"It's truly a breathtaking sight, Your Highness," said Tayce, impressed.

"If I may, Captain, Commander, please cease all engines and deactivate any protection shields you may have operational at present. We are about to enter through the scanner gates, to dock with my world. If you do not, then this lovely cruiser and your team captain will cease to exist," said the Prince in an advising tone.

"Amal, shut down all engine power and deactivate all shields. Prepare to dock," commanded Marc.

"All engine power at standstill, Commander," confirmed Amal in her soft tone.

Donaldo walked into Organisation ready to go over to the Charan Empire as part of the visiting team. Tayce acknowledged he was present with a slight friendly smile. Treketa was remaining on the cruiser to carry on sorting the medical supplies that had been loaded at Questa a monthon before, and they hadn't been placed where they needed to go. She also didn't feel the need for them to both go on the Quest. Amalthea, once inside the scanner gates, was suddenly latched on to by a strong guiding white tractor beam from the landing area of Charan below them and pulled in for docking at the large futuristic white stonex port. As the cruiser neared, so a boarding tube extended out to lock on to the Docking-Bay doors on Level 2. There came a slight bump in motion as the boarding tube locked in place. Amalthea had now successfully completed docking with Charan.

Dairan walked into Organisation looking very handsome in his ceremonial dress uniform. He looked at Tayce and she smiled softly. Twedor could tell there was a growing spark becoming a deep friendship between the two, but he was keeping it to himself.

The prince turned. "If you're ready, Captain, I would like it if you would escort me back to my father and meet him," he said calmly and politely.

Tayce nodded.

Placing Marc in overall command, ordering him to have the Prince's vessel transferred to the Charan Empire, she turned, ready to walk out of Organisation. Her ceremonial dress uniform was a cream wrap-over calf-length gown, with matching belt and cream high-heeled boots. There was a decorative slit up to the knee of the gown. Her hair was swept up in a cream clasp, keeping it looking elegant back behind her head. Dairan studied her. God she was beautiful. He wished she was his. He considered her fit to be a princess in her present attire. Tayce glanced towards him—she'd been reading his thoughts. He quickly changed his train of thought, but it was too late. Tayce gave a discreet amused smile. She knew how he felt about her now. Marc watched the little exchange between the two of them and smiled, thinking it was nice to see her getting to know someone special since Tom's demise. Tayce, Dairan, Donaldo, Twedor and Prince Tieman walked on out through the Organisation entrance. Marc continued on in command, putting forth the orders to transfer the Prince's vessel. Then he returned to check everything was all right and as it should be with Kelly at navigations.

The Quest visiting team escorted Prince Tieman in the direction of the Docking-Bay doors on Level 2. A while later, Prince Tieman was the first to exit the cruiser and set foot back on his home world, via the boarding tube. Tayce followed on with Dairan, whilst Twedor walked beside Donaldo.

The King soon came into view. He was plumpish and was dressed in a tight-fitting smart dark-red suit with a royal emblem in gold on the right lapel. But his most striking feature was the strangest colour of baldness on his head that could be imagined. It was decorated with pin-sized spots of purple, all over. His eyes were brown completely—there was no white or dark pupil like a normal human eye. He was around 1.75 metres in height. He didn't look a dayon over forty. Donaldo wondered what his real age was.

The King eagerly and pleasantly asked everyone to accompany him, which they did. Tayce walked with the King and Prince Tieman, whilst Dairan had fallen back to talk to Donaldo with Twedor. Donaldo leant close to Dairan and discreetly discussed the King's appearance with the purple spots and how it could have something to do with the ageing-effect process. Dairan nodded.

A young, beautiful, tall, slender woman came into view. She had clear tanned skin, not like the King's. Her attire was made up of colour chiffons and satinex.

Her make-up was truly exquisite and her long dark-brown hair cascaded about her shoulders in a thick mane of tight curls. Everyone paused upon coming to meet her.

"Captain Traun, allow me to introduce you to the Prince's mother and my joined partner, Queen Shayner," he said proudly.

"Your Highness, it's an honour to meet you. You have such a beautiful world here—it's truly exquisite," began Tayce. She didn't curtsey as she feared she would insult the queen—it might not be what they did on Charan, and it could be classed as offensive.

"Thank you for returning my son, Captain. We had feared the worst when he broke away from the travel party," said Queen Shayner, giving the Prince a reprimanding look, then reached out to shake Tayce's hand.

"You're welcome. This is my team—Lieutenant Commander Loring and Dr Donaldo Tysonne. Dr Tysonne was responsible for looking after your son," announced Tayce proudly, shaking the Queen's hand.

"Who is this?" asked the Queen, smiling at seeing Twedor standing like an obedient servant.

"I am Twedor, escort and protector to the Captain here," announced Twedor informatively.

"Oh, he's wonderful, Captain," said the Queen, impressed, with a delighted smile.

"Captain, you must forgive me, I have not formally introduced myself. I'm King Raynard of the Charan Empire. Maybe we should start again," he said, laughing lightly.

He shook hands with the various members of the Amalthean team and even grasped Twedor's hand to shake, much to his impressed delight. Tayce thought to herself King Raynard wasn't what she expected for royalty. He outstretched his hand in gesture, explaining all that the team could see for as far as the eye could see was the whole of the Charan Empire. The surface was miltons of beautiful glistening scenery that stretched way into the distance.

"Captain, I would also personally like to thank you for returning my son safely to us. Who knows what would have happened to him if you hadn't come to his rescue!" said the King in sheer appreciation, also throwing his son an unimpressed look, at his actions that could have so easily ended his life.

"You're welcome. We have what's termed in our Universe the worst kind of criminal, called pirates, and they are rampant throughout the sector. Because of who your son is, they would have held him for a high ransom or done worse," said Tayce knowingly.

"Shall we proceed? I have in your honour, had refreshments served." The King gestured for the Amaltheans to proceed along an ivory-coloured path

Tayce and Dairan walked with King Raynard, whilst Queen Shayner walked with Donaldo, Twedor and Prince Tieman. As everyone went, so the Amaltheans found themselves in between, talking with the King and Queen, looking around at the futuristic buildings, realising the empire was truly into the future and beyond with their designs and technology. Buildings tall and short, yet not any two in the same design or colour. The King's main palace was in cream marblex material—the only one of its design.

Everyone stopped after walking for a while, pausing at what looked to be a small Hover-Rail terminal. Two glassene and metlex railcars were waiting, with royal couriers. The King stepped into the first with his wife, Dairan and Tayce, whilst in the second one Donaldo and Twedor travelled with the Prince. A glassene canopy came down, sealing the passengers inside. The step they'd boarded by retracted neatly back into the car's lower body and the door slid shut with a slow humming sound until it had locked home. The King gave a spoken command and the first car of the two started away, slightly lifting just above the rails so it was sitting on a cushion of air, then took off at great speed (almost 90 mph) along the suspended track. The second car did the same, keeping up with the first. Dairan glanced around as they went, finding the magnificent futuristic splendour and architectural designs of the many buildings unbelievable and so clean. There were techs attending the many streets, keeping them tidy.

After travelling around bends and down long stretches of rail, the two railcars came to a declining gentle stop outside the King's palace. The glassene canopies opened, rising so everyone could exit. The retractable step extended back out. King Raynard stepped out, taking his wife's slender hand, helping her out to stand beside him. Dairan did the same for Tayce.

The Amalthean team members followed the Prince and his parents into the grand-looking palace. The palace was not a mystical kind, as they had first thought from a distance. The three-storey palace was in cream marblex on each level. The three levels were stacked on top of the each other, facing in different directions, one level just balanced on the one below it, until ground level. The overall design was something along the lines of a digital 'S' shape. The team found themselves walking down a long shiny-floored corridor in the same cream marblex as the rest of the palace was constructed in. The royal guards were stationed here and there. They were dressed in mustard-and-gold-coloured smart close-fitting uniforms, with gold-coloured head shields and black knee-length leatherex boots. As the King passed they stood to attention with their Slazer lances upright close to them, in respect of him passing. Everyone soon entered the equivalent of a lift, with transparent doors. They closed on a command from King Raynard once everyone was safely inside. The lift swiftly but almost silently took the small Amalthean Quests team, the King, Twedor, Prince Tieman and his mother, the Queen, to the second level of the building. The lift soon stopped. King Raynard, as the doors drew apart, walked out and across the cream corridor and through an alcove, in through large floor-to-almost-ceiling doors that opened on his approach. The Quests team followed on into the grand vast-looking chamber.

The King commanded his servants to serve the Amalthean Quests team—they were honoured guests.

Everyone walked to a large white ornately carved table, where refreshments were served. Tayce seated herself upon the King's gesture for her to do so. Twedor stood beside Tayce, almost at the corner of the table, and went into standby temporary-hibernation mode. The others of the Amalthean Quests team sat around on high-backed white woodenex chairs. Dairan seated himself next to Tayce, the Queen sat at the other end of the table and Prince Tieman sat next to Donaldo.

"From what you have seen of our world, Captain, what do you think?" asked the King, interested to hear her views.

"It's a beautiful place. I can feel a sense of harmony here," said Tayce in thought.

"Charan is peaceful place. We don't stand on parade here. The Queen and myself are not your typical royals—we like to work with our people and treat them fairly. We take time to know our people and share in their every-dayon existence. If they have a grievance, we want to know about it and we work to sort it out. Our people, to us, are like family, as unconventional as it sounds," explained the King.

"I think that's wonderful. My home world used to be the same," replied Tayce, recalling the fact.

"Really! What was the name of your world? asked the King, interested.

"Traun, though sadly it was destroyed, but it still has a place in my heart as being special," replied Tayce.

The gathered group talked on, back and forth over the specially prepared meal of the Charan authentic meats and fresh fruit, in the strangest of shapes, sizes and colours. Queen Shayner and Donaldo talked about what life was like in 2420 in general. Tayce discussed what her team were about, which the King and Prince found fascinating and a good idea.

After a while the King announced he would like to award the team with a small gift as a token of thanks for returning the Prince safely to Charan. He clapped his hands in a summoning gesture and a guard approached, carrying a gold tray of red velveteen gift boxes. He paused beside the King as he removed them one by one, handing them around to the Amaltheans. Tayce not only received a velveteen box, but also a multicoloured Perspexon one. Upon opening the lid and looking inside, she saw the most exquisite scaled-down replica of the Charan Empire with its tall spires. She overwhelmingly thanked the King and Queen. Dairan and Donaldo nodded in thanks also. Queen Shayner turned to Donaldo putting forth the idea that as he had earlier showed an interest in the ageing process perhaps she could get one of her aides to take him and show him how the process was achieved. The King looked at the Queen, somewhat surprised at her suggestion, but then figured it would help should Donaldo come face-to-face with the Charan race again. He agreed, with a discreet nod.

The Queen called her personal aide, ordering him to take Donaldo to the Empire Lab of Ageing. As Donaldo rose to his feet, Tayce quickly ordered him not to be late back—they had a schedule to keep. He agreed, informing her he would meet her back at Amalthea in time for departure. Prince Tieman suggested he go with Donaldo, as he would make sure he would make it back in time.

Tayce nodded thankfully. She knew what Donaldo was like when he became engrossed in research—he lost all track of time. He'd been like it right back from when she'd first met him. He'd always liked to get really into studying when faced with an interesting situation, such as the current age situation with the Prince.

"You've a dedicated team, Captain," said the Queen, impressed.

"I like to think so. Donaldo has been with me since he joined me in the first voyage," replied Tayce casually.

"I assume this is your second voyage, then?" asked the King, interested.

"Yes," replied Tayce, her Wristlink suddenly sounding, breaking the conversation.

Twedor came on operational mode, informing her Amal had sent him a message, Marc was trying to reach her in case she could not be reached. Tayce excused her presence for a moment, leaving Dairan to talk to the King and Queen whilst she took the call. She walked away to a discreet alcove, where there was also a pane to look out on the Charan view. She paused, raising the Wristlink, activating it.

Marc's voice came through—Tayce noticed there was a certain urgency to it.

"I received an urgent call—we're needed back in our own Universe, like yesteron. Questa needs us and it sounds urgent," said Marc, greatly anxious at the news he'd received.

"All right, I'm on my way," replied Tayce, ceasing communications.

As she did so she felt the strongest feeling that something was badly wrong back in their own time, but she tried to hide it. She deactivated the Wristlink, returning to the table where they'd had the meal.

Dairan looked up, seeing something was wrong by the look on her face.

"King Raynard, that was my cruiser. I apologise for cutting this visit short with you and the Queen here, but myself and my team are wanted urgently in our own Universe. Thank you for making us truly welcome, but I have to return to my cruiser for departure immediately," said Tayce in a true apologetic tone.

"You do what you have to. I hope your urgent call does not mean too much trouble on your return. My wife will inform Prince Tieman of the change in circumstances. He'll join you in a short while with Dr Tysonne. Maybe we'll cross paths one dayon again," he said understandingly.

The Queen rose to her feet and hurried away in her pastel body-hugging chiffon outfit, the wind slightly blowing the chiffon trails to her top as she went. Twedor fell in beside Tayce and walked with Dairan and an aide back out of the palace. The King walked to a balcony, from where he could see the Amaltheans leave the palace and head back to the arrival and departure area safely.

* * *

Once everyone had regrouped by the Hover-Rail car point, and the Prince had made sure they got back to the walkway adjoining Amalthea, they said their goodbyes, then parted for the walk back to the cruiser Docking-Bay doors. The Prince smiled and waved until the team that had saved him was gone from sight, then he too turned and headed back to the palace, his aide walking beside him.

Amalthea soon began to withdraw from docking at Charan and turned to head back down the Time-Shift Tunnel, home. The new Amalthean Quest team had successfully done their first Quest of the new voyage, and it would be one they would be talking about for quite a while.

3. Questa Rescue

As Amalthea headed back down the Time-Shift Tunnel, back to 2420, Tayce ran into Organisation followed by Dairan and Twedor. Upon entering, she ordered the team to make sure they were ready to handle whatever was waiting for them upon arrival in their own time. Crossing, she requested Amal to send a message to Questa ahead of them, that they were on their way, then relay the message around the cruiser that had come in, in all sections occupied, including their surroundings. Quite suddenly the main Sight Screen flashed into life. A live message from her mother, Lydia Traun, dressed in her council attire appeared. Tayce noticed she looked troubled, as if she was about to be in some kind of extreme danger that was going to unfold at any minon. The Organisation team and others around the cruiser shared her concern, wondering if they were about to hear bad news.

"The final threat has been issued towards me and this base. It's a serious one—it states there would be lives lost and this base would be destroyed. As yet there is no reason for this act to be carried out, other than for all the wrong reasons. Someone has already slipped through our Arrival and Departure Dome, avoiding our tight security, almost gaining entry to this Officette, brandishing a Pollomoss, would you believe? Just get here as soon as you can, Tayce," said Lydia with an extremely worried tone.

Tayce was furious, but tried not to show it. She sighed impatiently. Lydia, on screen, glanced away, worried, then her look changed to one of relief upon Adam coming into view.

Glancing back at the screen, Lydia added, "Adam has an update on the approaching attack fleet."

Tayce waited, interested to hear further as Adam handed her mother the update printout. She had to admit she didn't like the sound of what was unfolding. Lydia exclaimed that the Questa fighter squadron was standing by, ready for the attack to defend Questa. Tayce thought for a moment. This was like her old home world all those yearons ago, preparing for the full-on attack from

Vargon and her army. No wonder her mother was feeling uneasy. Lydia finally requested she wanted emergency assistance from the team. With this, the screen went blank. Tayce was even more determined to take on the task ahead—she was damned if she was going to lose her mother all over again. Marc put his hand on her shoulder, reassuringly exclaiming he knew how she felt, but this time they'd do their damnedest to save not only Lydia, but the Questonians as well if they had to. Tayce thought about how men, women and children were going to be in exactly the same situation as she had been in all those yearons ago, on that fateful night. She just hoped they stood more of a chance than her people did.

"Amal, did you send the message that we're on our way to Questa to assist?" asked Tayce.

"Yes, Captain, and I can confirm the message has been received," replied Amal.

Kelly turned on her chrome and black chair, informing Tayce they'd be at Questa just ahead of the attack fleet at their current speed. Tayce nodded, then informed her to keep her up to date—she would be in the DC if anything else came in in the meantime. Kelly agreed. Tayce continued up the two steps into the DC, ordering the moment they broke back into 2420 she wanted a Satlelink to Questa. Craig agreed as Kelly was currently busy. He immediately went about gaining the Satlelink link-up, ready to put into action as soon as they were back in home space. The year 2420 appeared as the cruiser broke back free from the Time-Shift Tunnel. Questa was just ahead, surrounded by both Enlopedia and a Questa fighter squadron, ready in a stationary orbit, waiting to commence protection of the base from the advancing attack force. Craig informed Tayce through the open doorway of the DC that she had her connection with Questa. Tayce quickly seated herself at her desk. Twedor watched her, knowing this was going to be like a case of déjà vu all over again for her. He still had his memories of the night he'd had to take matters into his command and got her safely away from Traun as her guidance and operations computer. Tayce placed the slim handset to her right ear, pressing the connect transfer button to transfer the call to the desktop slim screen. After a few minons, Lydia appeared on-screen, relieved to see her daughter.

"How's it going, Mother?" she asked—like any true caring daughter, concerned for her mother's safety.

"It's panic everywhere down here. We're trying to shift the majority of non-essential personnel and families to Enlopedia until this is all over," replied Lydia.

"We're back in 2420 and we're on our way to assist in any way we can," assured Tayce, sounding like the true leader and captain she was.

"We need all the assistance we can get. The attack fleet are still not letting us know their reason for attack, or who they are, but they are about ten milons from here and closing. We picked up on long range. They're a massive force. We'll be lucky if we keep Questa—they mean business," replied Lydia.

"Are they a pirate force?" asked Tayce. She was thinking of one man, though she didn't know why, who could have possibly regrouped with a new force and he was a being that made her sensually shudder at the mere thought of him—Dion!

"No idea. We're just going to be prepared to fight for this base when they arrive," said Lydia.

"Don't worry, they haven't anticipated the likes of this cruiser and Amal's quick-fire response to oncoming enemy firepower," said Tayce with a smile.

"I now know why you had that incorporated in the design. I've a feeling you'll be using it for the first time with what's about to unfold," replied Lydia.

Tayce looked up as Marc entered the DC, then back at the screen, advising Lydia to stay calm—she knew it would be difficult, but to try. They'd be landing at Questa soon. A slight smile crossed Lydia's features and she simply announced she loved Tayce, before signing off. This sent an uneasy shiver through Tayce. It was just like she would never see her again.

She pressed the button on the Telelinkphone, deactivating the connection with Questa. Sitting back in thought, her mind took her back to the past, to the fateful night on Traun when her mother said the same thing before her departure.

Kelly brought her back to the present by calling her out into Organisation.

"Are you OK? She'll be all right this time—it will be different," said Marc, as if he had been reading her thoughts.

"I'll be fine once I know Mother will be safe. I want a fighter team put together," she replied.

"All right—but hold on a minon, are you thinking of going in alone, because I strongly advise against it! We don't know what we could find down there. Tell me you're not." He looked at her questioningly, hoping she wasn't.

"I've a fighter team to get together. In answer to your question, I'm not going to act irrationally if that's what you're worried about," she replied over her shoulder, walking from the DC.

"I'll pick the team if you like," he said, glad she was not going to be foolish and try going in alone.

"I need members of this team that are good at manoeuvres and have excellent weaponry skills," she said as he caught her up out in Organisation.

"Count me in for a start. I'll take Lance, Dairan, Craig and Aldonica," suggested Marc.

"All right, sort it out then head on out. I'll meet you on Questa. We have to get Mother off that base alive. She's very anxious—it's becoming a danger zone."

"Don't worry, we will," he assured her.

"Kelly, I want you to monitor the situation as it unfolds. You and Amal will be main link to us; so if we need to be pulled out at a minon's notice, then we can call on you," said Tayce, seeing Kelly was wondering what she was required to do.

"You can count on me," she assured.

"See you in the impossible zone," joked Marc.

"Yes! Be careful," she replied.

Marc winked at her affectionately. He was trying to make her feel a little more at ease, instead of worrying about Lydia. He lightly summoned both Lance and Craig to accompany him, exclaiming they'd a job to do. As he walked from Organisation he explained they were in for some flying action. Pausing briefly, Marc ordered Kelly over his shoulder to have Aldonica bring appropriate ground weaponry and to prepare for combat, also to have Dairan report to the Flight Hangar Bay—he was needed for combat. Kelly acknowledged and got straight on with the request. Tayce, who had returned to her desk in the DC, walked back to Kelly, waiting until she had finished the request, then informed her that she wanted to know the moment the team left the Flight Hangar Bay. Also she wanted their every move tracked and seen through the sight port. She wanted to be kept up to date on the enemy's advancing attack fleet, heading to Questa. Kelly agreed. Sallen Vargon entered Organisation. Pausing, she enquired was there anything she could do to help? Tayce glanced about, suggesting that if she could do it she might take Lance's position and keep her up to date. Sallen nodded. Without a further word she headed straight to the position in question. Kelly looked at her for a brief moment in thought, thinking it was hard to imagine what Sallen had been and what she had become. It was amazing how medical science could take someone like Sallen and turn her from being Vargon's evil daughter and sidekick to being a nice normal person, like she was. As time passed Amal and Kelly guided Amalthea successfully under shields into an orbit of Questa's uncertain future. Tayce stood watching for the first signs of the Quest 3 shuttles/fighters heading into space. Treketa and Donaldo sauntered into the Organisation Centre, wanting to know what was happening as far as their duty requirements went on Questa. Both paused beside Tayce, looking out through the main sight port, which was now showing the Amalthean Quests fighter team heading across to join the protection fleets. Tayce turned, concerned for her team and uneasy for her mother's safety. This was not going to be easy, she thought.

"We've heard from Marc what's happening. We passed him earlier on Level 2, coming back from break," said Donaldo, glancing out into the Universe, then back at Tayce's worried face.

"You must be worried for your mother. She looked worried on the on-screen message. I wouldn't want to be in her position," said Treketa, understanding Tayce's uneasiness.

"I'm fine. I'd just like to get my hands on that attack force who are doing this just because they want Questa for some reason," replied Tayce in anger.

"Do you want us to assist in the medical emergencies that are arising over on Questa, when you go over to help shortly?" enquired Donaldo.

"Yes, I may need you when we go in to rescue Mother," replied Tayce, thinking for a moment.

"When you're ready, we'll be ready—just ask," promised Donaldo sincerely.

"We'll be arriving at Questa in roughly an houron, Tayce," said Kelly, turning to her.

"OK, keep me informed. You two had better go and get Emergency Medical Kits. We could be up against the worst in attack fleets—we just don't know. You'll also need your hand Slazers," suggested Tayce.

Donaldo nodded in total understanding. He and Treketa walked on out, to go and do what they had to do in order to be prepared for the impossible ahead. Kelly, at communications, exclaimed Councillor and Chief Waynard was on Satlelink to speak with her. Tayce, upon hearing this, left, watching the action unfolding through the main sight port, ordering Kelly to put the call through to the DC. Without a further word, Kelly went about keying in the sequence to transfer the call through to the DC. Tayce hurried back to her desk, pressing the connect button on her approach. Twedor came on alert—he wanted to hear what was unfolding as he was quite sure Tayce would want him to go with her.

"Captain Traun here, Chief. Go ahead," said Tayce.

Being supreme chief and councillor of sister base to Questa, until a new member could be found with sound knowledge to run Enlopedia, Waynard requested her, if it had not been done, to send her fighter team to assist in the onslaught attack for the protection of Questa immediately! Tayce quickly assured him that five of their fighters were en route, heading straight for Questa with one thing in mind. Protecting the base in any way they could. She herself was preparing to board Questa and help in the rescue of her mother. A thankful smile crossed Waynard's kind mellowed features. Nodding, he thanked her, exclaiming he was then leaving for Enlopedia to see about moving the sister colony to a safe orbital distance from Questa. Tayce nodded and he signed off.

Moving Enlopedia was a major manoeuvre in itself, but it had been built into its construction should it need to be moved to a new orbit in an extreme emergency, then all twenty-one of the powerful engines would kick in all in succession and slowly but effortlessly move the base to a safe distance. So the inhabitants would be safe and unharmed during the onslaught of attack.

The call suddenly gave a usual static signalling sound, signalling all communications had been severed between herself and Waynard. Tayce sat back in thought. There were going to be a lot of changes owing to this unprovoked attack. She also thought about the people of Questa leaving what they'd figured would be their home for the foreseeable future, leaving behind memories. She felt their pain having to do such a thing, as she herself had lived through it many yearons ago. She was glad Waynard was in charge and not the original leader, Barkin. He would have been hopeless in such a situation—probably would have denied anything was actually happening until it was to late to rescue anyone, let alone her mother. He deserved to rot his life away on that desolate colony made for criminals, which is what he'd become. Kelly entered the DC, bringing Tayce back to the present.

"Marc and the others are rendezvousing with the Questa and Enlopedia fighter squadrons," she announced softly.

"Good! I think it's time I went over to Questa. Come on, Twedor, you're with me in rescuing Mother. Thank you, Kelly keep up the good work," said Tayce.

Both women and Twedor walked from the DC. Kelly knew what she and Sallen had to do in Tayce's absence, and that was monitor the situation as it played out and assist where necessary. Twedor was glad to be going. He liked to be part of the action these dayons, considering when he was the original guidance computer he was always fixed on board the cruiser and never ventured anywhere. Tayce headed across Organisation in a determined way, going on out through the entrance as she reached it, with Twedor in hot pursuit. As she went, so she realised this second voyage was going to be a bit more action-packed than her first. Her thoughts went to Marc and the others out flying, protecting Questa and putting their lives in danger in doing so. Her mother too crossed her thoughts. Waynard also, hoping when all that was currently going on was through they'd all be where they should be—Questa, assuming that it would only be slightly damaged instead of obliterated. She soon was leaving the Deck Travel on Level 3 and heading along to her quarters to change attire for the Quest ahead, even though it was an unscheduled one. Twedor managed to keep up with her. As soon as the quarters doors opened, she passed through, taking off her duty high-heeled boots, ready to change into her combat attire. Twedor stood waiting like an obedient servant as his mistress headed to change clothes. The doors closed behind him with the gentle sound of compressed air.

* * *

Amalthea Two slowed to an orbit within safe distance of Questa Headquarters Base. Even though it was vastly becoming somewhat of a battleground, by the arrival of the enemy attack fighters and following main vessel, which was firing off round after round of immense weapon fire as they came at the QSEC (Questa Space Exploration Colony) protection fleet. The Quest team from Amalthea and Enlopedia destroyed many of their enemy targets, which they did on several direct strikes. Enlopedia could be seen nearing its safe orbit fifteen milons in the distance from its original orbital bearing of five milons from Questa. The engine rocket thrusters could be seen illuminated faintly from underneath the colony, but in short bursts as it neared the end of its journey from its original orbit. Explosions erupted on both sides—the enemy and Questa—as men lost their lives and fighters blew up. The head vessel of the attack fleet had been identified in the last houron by Amal, in searching the main vessel's computer system for their enemy's identity, as the Cripions. She had, though, just managed to gain the information she required, before they pinpointed the source of their infiltration, namely, Amal. But she had covered her tracks well, keeping the information she'd gained beside the identity, in case her mistress required it.

***

Tayce down in her quarters, walked out into the Living Area, telling Twedor it was time to go. He came on alert, walking over from the sight port, where he had been waiting for her. Following on, they exited from the quarters, heading along to the Deck Travel, letting the quarters doors close behind them. Upon reaching the Deck Travel, they quickly headed through the opening doors. Tayce requested Level 2 as the doors closed. The Deck Travel began on its ascent to Level 2. As the doors opened and Tayce walked forth, so Donaldo and Treketa were leaving the MLC, to begin on the walk to the Transpot 2 Centre. Both were dressed in their all-in-one white Rescue Quest medical suits. Both were carrying Emergency Medical Kits. Tayce, with Twedor by her side, walked to meet them, suggesting they get going. All three plus Twedor continued in the direction of the Transpot 2 Centre doors. Once inside, Treketa crossed to the Transpot 2 control podium and stepped up on the one-step podium platform to operate the controls.

"There's a change in plans. I want you two to remain here until we get back, or I'll call you via Amal to come down for assistance. There's no telling what I alone will run into down on Questa. I don't want you two running into any more danger, than me and Twedor, it's too dangerous, I don't want to lose you both," said Tayce, not wanting to put either Donaldo or Treketa in a life-threatening situation intentionally.

"Fine! No problem, just call us. We'll be ready to leave the moment you want us," replied Donaldo, seeing her point.

Tayce crossed to the Transpot 2 floor area, waiting for Twedor to take up his special triangular spot on the floor that had been specially designed so when Transpot 2, just known as Transpot, went into operation he wouldn't explode in the process of transference from cruiser to destination.

"We'll be waiting," assured Treketa as she keyed in the sequence for Transpot operation.

Transpot generally held twelve members of the team plus Twedor. Each segment was marked out on the floor in a triangular shape; and as Transpot took on, it travelled in a swirling motion, starting out underneath the soles of the boots of the person, or Twedor, stood on the triangular spot and travelled up the body heading into the Dematerialisation Chamber above their heads. Before Tayce gave Treketa the nod to continue, she took out her Pollomoss, checking it was fully loaded, then set it to 'kill/disintegrate', holding it ready to open fire the moment they set foot on Questa. Tayce, as she gave the nod to Treketa to commence Transpot, wondered if this was where, of all places, she would be summoned for the test Empress Tricara had told her about at the beginning of the voyage. Being summoned by the Telepathian Empire and Emperor Honitonia. She certainly hoped not—otherwise she'd lose the chance to save her mother and would be back exactly where she was at the beginning of the first voyage, without her. The Transpot's soft green vaporising energy swirled up from underfoot into the ceiling until Tayce and Twedor had dematerialised from the centre.

"I hope she arrives safely, considering what's going on down there," confided Treketa.

"According to this reading, both are down safely," said Donaldo checking the destination reading to conclude successful arrival.

"Good! You could see she was really concerned about Lydia and has every right to be. She keeps her worry inside, it concerns me, she can be quite vulnerable at times without even realising it," said Treketa having known Tayce a long time.

"Quite! Is the MLC ready if we receive any sudden emergencies?" Donaldo asked.

"Yes! Let's hope we don't need it and everyone gets to Enlopedia safely, before Questa is destroyed," replied Treketa, thinking on Questas possible outcome.

More than anything, she hoped Tayce and the others would come back safely, as they were heading into an extremely difficult and perhaps impossible situation. Both crossed and sat down on the seat by the far wall of the centre to wait and watch the battle rage on outside the Transport 2 Centre sight port, as the Cripions were advancing on Questa, using every available means to destroy whatever got in their path. They both watched in sheer amazement at the fierceness of bombardment of weapon fire, on both sides, that was almost blinding at times. Donaldo pulled Treketa close, hoping they themselves would be all right and it wouldn't be long before they were needed.

* * *

Far from the peace and smooth running of Amalthea on Questa, the situation was becoming way out of hand fires raged in the once beautiful Q City square. Rescue crews were losing the battle to put out fires, caused by incoming direct hits of weapon fire. Buildings were falling to the ground without warning having been struck with bombs from the Cripions. People trying to escape the turmoil who had wanted to remain to try and save their businesses were being killed as they tried to run for it. Explosions filled the air. Bodies were beginning to litter the area. Some were badly scorched with missing limbs, having been caught in an explosion not running fast enough. The whole base was turning into a sheer crumbling wreck. Marc Dayatso, who was somewhat of an expert in landing in near-impossible situations, miraculously brought his Quest in to land in what was left of the first-class arrival and departure area, narrowly missing a collision with the second-floor balcony crashing near to where he went to set down. As it was, when he did set down he wondered if he was going to get out? There were bricks and debris cascading all around from high up on the second level. As he climbed out and slid to the floor he narrowly missed being killed himself by falling masonry. He was smothered in a cloud of dust as another explosion across the area blew out in his direction. He cursed to himself. This was damned near impossible and downright life-threatening he thought. His vision was impaired by the vast growing smokescreens that were also making him cough. He managed to check his Pollomoss. He didn't want to be picked off by a gun-wielding Cripion. He had agreed to help Tayce—if he could find her in all the commotion going on around him. He sighed, then made a run for it, heading across the landing area, ducking and diving, sidestepping near misses, to take his life, from one source or another—explosion or weapon fire deployed by the Cripions, looking to take out anything crossing their sights and aim. Firepower sailed above and all around him. He eventually returned fire, just to stay ahead and alive. As he glanced back, he was glad to see he'd taken out a few of the enemy. A pleased smile crossed his handsome features as he ran on. He could see Tayce waiting in an alcove with Twedor, using his weaponry finger to assist her in returning fire.

"This whole rescue is totally crazy," said Marc as he finally came to her side, still returning fire to cover the both of them.

"I know, but we've no choice. If this is anything like where Mother is, she could be in danger. We can't leave her," shouted Tayce above the commotion.

Marc further informed her that if it wasn't for the fact they were there to rescue Lydia, he would have aborted the idea of coming into land, called everyone off the Quest and returned to Amalthea, as the situation was turning out to be a no-win situation. Twedor, Tayce and Marc suddenly found they were being surrounded by mean-looking gun-shooting Cripions, who had detected they were in the area. Another building crashed under the strain of damaged support, just behind them, and all three were showered in debris and dust. Marc glanced up and could see the latest descending huge piece of masonry was descending fast in Tayce's direction. He pushed her out of the way with split-cencron timing, leaving Twedor to follow her.

"That was too close. Let's get the hell out of here before we join the many dead lying around," suggested Marc, looking far from the handsome man he was.

"Oh, I agree. Come on, Twedor let's go. Keep alert," ordered Tayce.

"All this dust is going to get stuck in my parts for weekons," said Twedor, following on.

He was quite happy to fall in with Tayce's suggestion. He was glad he was no longer stuck in the corner of Organisation as guidance and main operations computer, when it came to being in on the action like he was now—the retaliation of firepower. It was, however, his first time in a dangerous situation such as they were in, but he was loving every minon of it. It didn't bother him. Debris was descending past him and all around him, but he was made of extreme attack-proof steelex, made for battle situations like this currently was. Marc suggested they head for Lydia's Officette, as they rounded what was the first calm corner in quite a while. As luck would have it, it was the corridor that would take them down to Lydia's Officette. But just when it was thought to be all calm and clear, it was too good to be true. Marc was blown of his feet by an undercover Cripion. Twedor, without thought, quickly pinpointed the shooter and took him out with a direct precision shot, sending the Cripion into oblivion. Tayce hurried to Marc's side, horrified to think he'd been killed. Much to her relief, he was struggling back on to his feet, clutching his upper left arm in agony. Now Marc had been wounded, she was extremely concerned for all their safety. It was getting much too dangerous to remain in the city square—it was time to leave.

"Marc, lean on me for support. Twedor, protect us while we make our way down to Mother's Officette," ordered Tayce.

Tayce, realising Marc was struggling, helped him into a nearby alcove so he could get some rest. She didn't like the idea of staying where they were too long, because trouble wasn't too far away in the form of more Cripions discovering Twedor had just killed one of their own. If they fancied returning the same weapon fire that had been used earlier, they'd both wind up dead. There would be no one to rescue her mother and Adam if they were killed. All four of them would probably perish, and Twedor would either be taken to sell on as material parts or blown up. Marc glanced at her, seeing her concern.

"Let's go—I'll be fine. Look, on second thoughts I'll slow you down—go on ahead, I'll catch you up.

Twedor, take Tayce and get out of here," ordered Marc.

He was growing concerned himself. It was bad enough he was beginning to feel weak from the injury; he didn't want them all sitting targets for the Cripions to pick off.

"I'm not leaving you here—it's too dangerous. You'll never make it alone. I could use my powers and heal you," offered Tayce.

"No chance—there's no time. We'll make it—come on, Twedor. You keep on alert and if any of those Cripions appear, let them have it," ordered Marc, grimacing from the pain.

"You've got it," replied Twedor, moving to the rear to watch for any sign of trouble as they advanced. Tayce put her arm around Marc, steadying him as they proceeded. Twedor kept watch from the rear and backed up close to Tayce and Marc as they headed in the direction of Lydia's Officette, firing as he went at any oncoming weapon fire. Marc switched his Slazer to his right hand and tried to forget the near-unbearable searing pain that was burning in his upper left arm and shoulder, helping Twedor in firing back. All three were glad to make it to below what was left of Q City.

The doors opened to Lydia's outer anteroom. Adam Carford stood facing them, injured, with a primed Pollomoss in his good hand, aimed straight at them, ready to shoot if it had been the enemy. He lowered the weapon immediately, glad to see who it was, apologising and crossing to help Marc. Lydia rushed out of her wreck of an Officette to her daughter, glad to see her, but paused mid floor on seeing a wounded Marc. He glanced at her, trying to conceal the pain he was suffering, not sure of how much longer he was going to remain on his feet. Tayce raised her Wristlink, contacting Donaldo back on Amalthea, giving him the fixed bearings of where they currently were. Donaldo could be heard informing her that he was on his way down and to stand by.

Within a short time Donaldo was present via Transpot, with Emergency Medical Kit in hand. Treketa followed on, bringing with her the extra Transpot wristbands for Adam and Lydia. She handed them to Tayce to distribute. Donaldo opened his Emergency Medical Kit, taking out a pain-easing injection, pressing it to Marc's shoulder, near to the region of the injury, telling him it would hold off the pain until they got back to the MLC.

"I don't think we should hang around here too long," he said, hearing the growing chaos that was nearing outside.

"I agree. I think Questa is coming under the destructive hold of the Cripions," replied Tayce, thinking.

After a few minons she decided to contact Kelly back on Amalthea, giving her the order to immediately Transpot everyone back aboard apart from herself and Twedor. Kelly agreed. Everyone present looked at Tayce in alarm, wondering what she was thinking of doing. Suddenly she began—much to their horror, she was heading back to get the shuttle/fighter Marc had arrived in, with Twedor. Lydia immediately and angrily forbade her to attempt such a stupid unwise thing, adding it was totally out of the question. Tayce ignored her mother's words and raised her Wristlink, ordering immediate Transpot without a further word. Before anyone had time to stop her, Lydia, Adam, Marc, Treketa and Donaldo disappeared from their current surroundings back to the cruiser. Tayce checked her Pollomoss Slazer, making sure it still had enough firepower to take on what she might have to do in order to fight back to get to the shuttle/fighter.

"Ready, Twedor? This is going to be treacherous, but we can do it. Come on," she ordered, heading back out into the thick smoky atmosphere.

Twedor stuck to her like glue, with his Slazer finger ready to fire. Chaos still rained in the sound of crashing masonry, exploding glassene and debris being thrown out ahead. Fires still raged out of control, even though men had tried to bring them under control. The men had given up and left the base. As they came back into what was left of Q City Square, it almost made Tayce want to cry at the saddened burnt state it had become. The number of dead bodies had increased. Some were Cripions; some were Questa personnel. The atmosphere was nauseating; the stench was horrendous. Checking that the way to the arrival and departure area was almost clear, apart from debris that littered the floor, Tayce called Twedor and they ran on together. But, unfortunately for her, she couldn't quite make out the direction she was running in through the thick smoke and ran straight into the path of a gun-wielding Cripion, looking like thunder about to erupt. Twedor wondered what Tayce was going to do, as both she and the Cripion had come to a standstill facing each other. A few split cencrons sealed the Cripion's fate. As he went for his dark-grey powerful-looking weapon, Twedor didn't think twice in protecting his mistress and took him out with one single shot.

"Thanks, Twedor. For a cencron he took me totally by surprise. I guess he caught me off guard, because I was unsure of what to do next," confided Tayce.

"I guessed so, but at least we have a clear way ahead now," replied Twedor.

"Let's get out of here before any more of the enemy show up. Next time we might not be so lucky."

Both ran as fast as they could, dodging bodies, fallen bits and pieces and hanging cables—the usual wreckage that would be left behind after a massive bombardment. Finally they entered through a half-constructed entrance that was once the arrival and departure area. Fires were still raging out of control and walls caved in owing to the unsecured support, crashing to the floor, starting more fires and explosions that sent sparks flying. Again, bodies were everywhere of people who had obviously tried to leave Questa, but failed. The Quest 3, much to her relief, was still in one piece. It was sitting in the middle of a crater of fallen debris. Covered in dust, it still looked like it could lift off. Twedor ran over with Tayce, upon her word. She took the de-locking key out of her pocket, rubbing off the dust. She aimed it at the Quest, praying it would work, pressing the de-locking key as she neared. The entrance hatch opened, much to her relief upon final approach. Tayce lifted Twedor up and almost threw him on board. He righted himself and together they went straight through to the pilot section. No sooner had Tayce seated herself than she strapped herself in and started the powerful rocket engines. Out behind the shuttle/fighter blue and yellow rockets fired, blowing the rubble across the area that had built up behind it.

"That killed a few Cripions," said Twedor.

"Take one last look at this place, Twedor. It will be the last time we'll know it as Questa Headquarters Base."

Tayce looked up and could see the roof of the dome had gone above them, but it was still going to be tricky to manoeuvre up through. Twedor strapped in next to her. He knew it was going to be precarious, but she'd been in tighter spots and he had every faith in her to do it. Slowly the Quest rose off the floor and up into the air, keeping a steady gentle pace, with the defence shields activated so the moment they entered space they 'd have some protection against the main Cripion vessel. Going through the broken and jagged domed roof was like squeezing through a tight, spiky gap that wouldn't hesitate to rip the Quest to shreds if they made any move in the wrong direction. Finally they emerged from Questa and it was a sorry sight to see. As they left it behind and glanced back, fires raged high into space and explosions continued. The time of total annihilation of the once first base of the QE fleet was fast approaching. Tayce shook her head. Questa would always hold a special place in her heart. It was where it had all begun for her. She headed across space, informing Kelly via Aircom she was on the way back. Dairan Loring had waited for her in orbit of Questa on guard and flew alongside, asking if she was all right. Tayce nodded in acknowledgement. The Cripion vessel slowly began to retreat, and what fighters were left headed back in underneath the vessel to go aboard. The deed had been accomplished. Within a split cencron the armed-to-the-teeth, ferocious-looking Cripion vessel vanished in the blink of an eye.

* * *

Dairan was the first to bring his Quest in to land in the Flight Hangar Bay, back aboard Amalthea, followed closely by Tayce. Both landed slowly and expertly down on the bay floor side by side. Tayce was glad to be back in the safe environment of the cruiser. Dairan, no sooner had he landed, was out of his Quest and heading around to help Tayce and Twedor. He'd watched her manoeuvre out of the tight remains of Questa and felt she was one special woman, with guts. He immediately lifted Twedor down, standing him on the bay floor. He then took Tayce's right hand, helping her down, looking dusty from her ordeal, but still attractive.

"That was one hell of a tricky manoeuvre you've just pulled, getting off Questa the way you did, if you don't mind me saying," said Dairan in a congratulating way, impressed.

"Thanks, though I did wonder if I could do it especially as it was a bit tight," she replied, thinking how lucky she'd been.

"I could see it," replied Dairan.

As he set her down on the bay floor, Tayce looked up and found she was looking into his gorgeous brown eyes again. What was it she was feeling every time she did? Whatever it was, it was growing enticingly deep between them. He smiled, breaking the moment.

"I want to check on Marc, Adam and Mother. Donaldo brought them back, whilst I went to get the Quest. Will you get us under way? I'll be up in Organisation as soon as I can," said Tayce.

"Sure! I'll just get changed and head on up there. I hope they're OK," he said, watching her walk away.

Tayce paused at the entrance to the Flight Hangar Bay. She turned, warning him her mother would probably be in Organisation and he was to make her feel welcome at all costs, be polite to her. Dairan nodded in an understanding way. She continued on out along to the Deck Travel, whilst Dairan exited the Flight Hangar Bay and headed for the Level Steps to take him down to his quarters. On Level 2, Tayce exited the Deck Travel with Twedor silent by her side. She figured the little Romid had been through a lot on this Quest and he was processing some of what he'd witnessed, sharing it with Amal for a future report if one was needed.

Walking along the spacious corridor, she soon entered into the MLC. Donaldo looked up, glad to see she'd made it in one piece. He gave her a warm smile of relief. Adam Carford was sitting propped up on one of the medical bunks enjoying every minon of Treketa's care as she attended to the wound over his left eye he'd sustained trying to dodge fallen masonry in Lydia's Officette. It was his first time aboard Amalthea Two and he was impressed by what he saw.

"This is truly impressive. Amalthea Two is everything you designed her to be," he said praisingly.

"We like to think so. I would give you a guided tour, but judging by your wound you need to rest. Maybe later?" suggested Tayce.

"Yes, good idea—I'd like that," Adam replied, feeling dizzy, relaxing back on the pillet.

Donaldo moved away with her from Adam, exclaiming he had sustained a bad cut and concussion, but would be fine. Tayce nodded as he moved on to Marc. Marc gave her a look that was far from pleased at what she'd done regarding the Quest shuttle/fighter. Donaldo moved to check the upper wound and how it was healing under the Healentex.

"You managed to survive, then?" he said, plainly far from impressed.

"Twedor and I ran into the most friendly Cripion on the way out, if you know what I mean, but Twedor put him out of his misery in a hurry. It wasn't the most easy of manoeuvres I've had to date—a bit tight. Part of the dome-shaped ceiling of the arrival and departure area had collapsed. There wasn't much room to squeeze through, but I did it and the Quest is in the hangar bay, safe and sound," said Tayce in a way that showed she was quite pleased with herself—she'd managed the manoeuvre to escape danger.

"You should have seen it—best manoeuvre I've seen in a long time," said Twedor, backing up Tayce.

"You concerned me when you had the notion to head back for my Quest, knowing how bad it was to get to your mother," said Marc casually.

"I knew I could do it, and in the last yearons before this voyage started I came into contact with some pretty awkward situations and got out of a lot tighter spots than leaving Questa. You needn't have worried," replied Tayce to Marc.

"But I did, and as your long-standing friend I wouldn't have done anything else," he replied.

"I need Marc to remain here for a couple of dayons. The injury he sustained is quite deep and I want him to rest and make sure it heals like it should," said Donaldo.

"It's fine. Dairan's in temporary command. He can do Marc's duty until he's able to return," said Tayce, fully understanding where Donaldo was coming from.

Tayce could see her mother in discussion with Treketa and figured she would try and keep out of her way. She had hoped she'd gone to Organisation. She figured she would come in for a heavy lecture about her craziness to head off after the Quest on Questa, and right at that moment in time she wasn't in the mood to have the discussion over it. Upon satisfying herself everyone was all right, she headed back to the entrance of the MLC, telling Donaldo she'd leave him to it.

Continuing on out as the doors parted before her, she headed on up the corridor, hoping her mother wouldn't follow. It didn't work. Halfway along she could hear her mother coming up behind softly. Lydia, upon reaching her daughter, reached out and gently halted her by the upper arm.

"Feel better for your foolish behaviour? Quests can be replaced; your life can't," began Lydia softly, but to the point, showing she was far from impressed at her daughter's irresponsible behaviour.

"Shuttles/fighters are expensive. I can't afford to replace them at present. I stretched myself as it was financing this voyage—you know how the expenditure came up when there was a shortfall in the council funding. I knew I could get out of Questa. I wouldn't have done it if I didn't think I could," replied Tayce, recalling the fact.

She knew as usual she was probably overreacting to her mother's genuine concern. But she couldn't help it. Lydia said no more, changing the subject, talking over what she might be doing when she reached Enlopedia, which would be the new main headquarters base.

Later during the same duty hourons, back in Organisation, Lance informed Tayce that the Cripion vessel they'd all thought had left orbit was in fact only twenty milons from their present reference. Tayce gave a look that was far from pleased and ordered for the Cripion vessel to be put up on the main Sight Screen. The Cripion vessel came back into clear view in all her evil battle-filled glory, stationary. Lydia, next to Dairan, gave a look of sheer anger. She knew what she'd like to do to the vessel, considering what it had done to Questa.

"What's left of home is about to explode," said Lance suddenly.

Without warning the unstable shell that was once home to Lance and the starting of the Amalthean Quests exploded, sending a colourful array of debris and sparks for milons, or as far as the eye could see, just like a universal spectacular firework display. Once it was all over, there was nothing but a starscape. Like Questa had never been. It filled the team with a sudden sadness. Kelly Travern put her hands to her face and began to weep. Memories of the late Jonathan Largon and her father in happier times flashed into her immediate thoughts that were now no longer to be relived every time she would set foot on the base, for it was no more. Her memories would remain in the past forever. Lance rose to his feet and crossed to comfort her as he understood where she was coming from. Questa held a special place in his heart too—it was his birthplace and home for a lot of yearons. He too had memories, some good, some bad, but he had them. Tayce left Dairan in command and walked on into the DC. She wanted to be alone with her memories for a few minons. They involved her father and Jonathan laughing on many matters. Once inside the DC, she crossed to her desk, walking round. She sat relaxingly down on her high-backed chair, in thought of what had just happened. Questa was gone forever. Dairan, after a few minons, sauntered in, not quite knowing how to approach her. He'd heard about her father and guessed right at that moment she was thinking about him amongst other things relating to Questa and the past.

"It's not easy, is it? If you want to talk, I'm here," he said calmly.

"Thanks! It's just memories of Father and Jonathan. When I was at Questa on a visit, I suddenly saw them laughing and talking in what was Jonathan's Officette; also, there's the time Tom and I first visited Questa, where this voyage first began, when Jonathan believed in my concept for a crime-fighting team," she replied softly.

"You'll never lose those moments—they will always be with you," assured Dairan.

"You OK?" asked Marc as he suddenly walked in.

"You're suppose to be in the MLC for a couple of dayons," said Tayce, surprised, wondering if he'd slipped out when Donaldo wasn't looking.

"I've got a portable Healentex fixed to the wound, though I'm not allowed to put any weight on it. I forgot to thank you for pulling me to safety back on Questa. I was prepared to meet my Maker, you could say," he said softly.

"You would have done the same if it was me. Dairan, put the procedures to get this cruiser to Enlopedia in operation, please," she ordered softly.

"Sure!" he replied, turning and heading on back out into Organisation.

Marc stayed behind. He walked over and around to Tayce, who was fighting back the tears she so wanted to unleash. She looked up at his warm handsome features and dark-brown curly hair she'd seen so many times before. As he came to a pause before her, he held out his good hand. She gently took hold of it, standing. He pulled her in for a gentle warm hug, telling her he understood her feelings. They stayed together for a few minons as Tayce finally let go of the pent-up tears. Marc knew Questa held a special place in her heart. It had not only been where they'd all come together on occasions, it was also full of past memories of her father and was the place where Tom had had his memorial.

"We all feel the same—believe me. We all have links to the past where Questa is concerned. They will build a new Memorial Park and Tom will have a new memorial somewhere some dayon, but I know he wouldn't worry about it. You've got to look forward now with this voyage and make new memories, also to a new future—we'll make fresh moments to look back on, you'll see," he said soothingly as Lydia walked into the DC and caught Marc with Tayce in a gentle hold.

She smiled softly, seeing them both together. She had always thought even though they were just friends they looked the ideal couple.

"Dairan's entered the coordinates for the journey to Enlopedia!" she exclaimed, breaking their moment.

"Mother! What happened to Empress Tricara?" asked Tayce, breaking away from Marc, suddenly concerned by what had happened to her Telepathian friend. Had she perished in the ambush on Questa?

"It's all right—she's perfectly safe on Enlopedia. I made her leave with Councillor Waynard, with her special-abilities group before the Cripions arrived," assured Lydia.

"Panic over," said Marc, looking down at Tayce softly.

"I know you came to thank me for saving your life. Well, Marc Dayatso, you've done so. Now I want you off duty, resting. Mother, will you take him out of here and don't let him back until Donaldo lets him?" ordered Tayce, giving Marc a look.

She'd rumbled the fact he'd so neatly sneaked back on duty.

"I'm going—you win," he said in soft protest, laughing.

He continued over to the entrance to the DC. Pausing, he looked back, softly asking was she going to be all right regarding Questa now they'd had their talk? Tayce nodded. With this he walked on out with Lydia. He would escort her to temporary quarters so she could unwind before facing the utter chaos awaiting her at the sister colony, Enlopedia, the only remaining headquarters base in existence for the time being. He wondered what lay ahead for Lydia. She was obviously going to be in charge of Enlopedia, just like she was at Questa. There would be people now needing new proper accommodation, new homes and new duty positions. He decided to talk it over with her, like he did when they were back on Traun.

Dairan, having got the cruiser under way for Enlopedia, sauntered back into the DC. Once inside, he let the doors close behind him. Tayce, glanced up from reading the latest on the attack from Enlopedia, on Questa. He began across. She met his caring concerned look as he came to a pause before her and felt a certain softness she had only felt once before in her life, and that was when she and Tom had fallen in love. She quickly reminded herself silently she was his captain and brushed it aside. This was duty time anyway, not pleasure time. She was sure he loved playing with her feelings just for the fun of it and she didn't like having her feelings played with—she wished he wouldn't. It was beginning to make her feel feelings she shouldn't whilst on duty. Was he wanting to be serious about them, or not? She would have to clear the air between them once and for all, soon, before either one of them got hurt, and she didn't want that.

"As Marc has gone off duty for a couple of dayons, if he shows up in Organisation you have my permission to tell him he should be resting. You're going to be the only one in assisting command until he returns," she announced casually.

Dairan smiled and nodded. Turning, he suggested he get on with it then. Knowing once more he had unnerved her in the intimate stakes, it made him smile at the thought on the way out, amused. One dayon she would succumb to his playing with her emotions. She wouldn't always be able to hide behind the title of captain. He could see there was a softer, vulnerable side to her and he wanted to get to know it more seriously. He could wait. The doors opened back into Organisation and he walked on through.

Tayce gave a look and shook her head, thinking, 'Men!'

Twedor shook his head, wishing the pair of them would stop all the playing around and get down to something serious in being an item. The readings he was receiving when the two of them were near were quite compatible, to say the least.

* * *

Amalthea Two cruised at a steady warp on the fifteen-milon journey to rendezvous with the new headquarters base, Enlopedia, where Lydia Traun would resume leadership over the whole colony and Waynard would step aside and let her do what she had done so well on Questa: be chief over the whole base. Waynard had only taken the command temporarily until a new leader could be found, and after what had happened with Questa Lydia was that person. Her career had taken a move no one could have foreseen.

* * *

On board Amalthea on Level 3, the Quarters Deck, Marc opened Lydia's temporary-quarters doors, letting her go on in and following on behind as the ceiling lights activated to a soft mode. Activated by Amal, picking up Lydia's presence. The guest quarters were roomy and comfortable with a lighting system that could give a natural light. There were just enough furnishings not to make it look crowded. Lydia walked over to the nearest dark-blue mouldable soffette and sat down relaxingly, sighing, glad she could take a break at long last.

"Would you like some liquid refreshment?" he began.

"Please! I haven't had a thing since the refreshments stopped early this mornet, when everyone was shipped to Enlopedia," she replied.

Marc quickly keyed a sequence in and retrieved a nourishing meal and beverage from Amal's serving system for refreshments in the quarters wall. He picked it up with his good hand, sauntering over to her, suggesting she enjoy. Lydia sat in thought for a moment. It had suddenly hit her: Questa was no more. Her life had now changed in a matter of hourons. She had gone from being in charge of Questa, trying to make sure everyone that had to leave Questa for Enlopedia did, trying to make their move as smooth as possible, to now being leader of a new base, which would be a new way of life for her. It took some taking in. Marc could see she was shocked. He understood how she was feeling, but he also knew she would make a first-class leader. She had done a grand job in taking over from Jonathan Largon, even though there were a few ruffled feathers because of the fact she had just been handed the position easily. But in time people had turned to her, like they had Jonathan, because she was a woman who showed good leadership and was fair-minded and kind.

"It takes a bit of getting used to knowing I'll be in charge of Enlopedia," she announced in between eating.

"You've done a grand job so far. Jonathan would have been proud of you. He probably wouldn't have done any more than you've done. As I see it, you've done your best and no one should expect more," replied Marc praisingly.

"Tayce has certainly settled into this second voyage. Do you think there's something growing between her and Dairan Loring?" confided Lydia wondering.

"Oh, there's something, but after what happened at the end of voyage one with Tom, I think she's a little cautious, considering what she's lost," replied Marc.

Both continued on, catching up on what had been happening to date, how on the last Quest they'd rescued a prince and taken him home to a future time. They talked on well into the late hourons about Questa and Enlopedia, amongst other universal topics of interest. Both had a lot to catch up on.

* * *

Up in Organisation, Dairan, was taking to the duty of relief commander with great ease. The team didn't mind he'd been temporarily placed in charge, as they found he was more like a buddy than someone who was giving orders. Tayce stood in the DC doorway, just taking in the way he handled his responsibilities, realising not only was he good at what he was qualified to do, astronomy, he was good at taking charge of a cruiser too, at short notice. This she would keep in mind for future reference. She decided to let him continue taking care of the journey to Enlopedia and headed off duty to go and see her mother as she wouldn't get much of a chance once they arrived at Enlopedia.

Dairan looked up from Kelly's side as she walked out of the DC with Twedor by her side. Pausing, Tayce informed him she'd be in her mother's guest quarters. Should an emergency arise, he could contact her there. Dairan nodded. She and Twedor continued on out. Dairan moved over to Lance to check he was OK. He'd been concerned he hadn't said much since Questa's demise and he wanted to be there should he want to talk his thoughts through on the demise, as a buddy.

* * *

Tayce as she walked along the corridor with Twedor towards the Deck Travel, found herself thinking about what Layforn Barkin would think about her mother taking over Enlopedia. One thing was for sure, she would love to see the look on his evil, smug face at finding out. The Deck Travel soon arrived on Level 1. She and Twedor entered as the doors drew open, requesting Level 3. The doors drew closed and the Deck Travel descended to the desired level. On Level 3 the doors drew open and they walked forth along to the guest quarters. Upon approach she could hear the familiar laughter of her mother and Marc enjoying something amusing in conversation.

"Are they having a party and not invited us?" asked Twedor, hearing the laughter from within.

"No, I think it's what's called reminiscing," replied Tayce as the doors opened to her mother and Marc, who looked over to her and Twedor about to enter.

Marc wondered what was wrong. Had she come to find him for some reason? But he quickly realised it wasn't anything particular and she was just dropping in to check on them.

"I can hear you two halfway down the corridor. Twedor thought you were having a party," said Tayce.

"No, just recalling old funny memories, that's all," replied Marc casually.

"How long until we arrive at Enlopedia?" asked Lydia, interested.

"Not long. Why, Mother, you're not getting nervous surely! You did a wonderful job at Questa till now," said Tayce, proud of what her mother had achieved to date.

"No! I just want to look my best for taking over that's all," she replied positively

"Don't worry, I'll let you know as soon as possible so you have plenty of time to prepare. I just came to tell you Donaldo has called on Wristlink. He said Adam is doing fine. I won't stay—carry on catching up on old times. I'll see you later," she announced and turned back to the doors.

"You should take a break," said Lydia, noticing how tired Tayce looked.

"No, I'm fine. This cruiser needs two people in command, as you know. Catch you later," she replied, heading out through the doors with Twedor in tow.

Once outside, Twedor put to her that she really didn't want to stay, and the thing about two people needing to run the cruiser was just an excuse, wasn't it? Tayce agreed, explaining that reminiscing about the old dayons of Traun was really something she preferred to leave in the past now. They continued to talk about Questa on the return walk back to Level 1. Twedor figured it would help Tayce to adjust to life without the base.

* * *

Lydia, back in the guest quarters, realised the injection Marc had been given had finally induced a peaceful sleep. He'd rested his head on the back of the seat and was in deep sleep. She smiled, thinking he was a good man and someone she was glad had survived the Traun destruction for Tayce's sake. She rose to her feet, sauntering over to the full-length sight port, looking out into the stars in thought. She was wondering what life would be like on what was to be her new home, Enlopedia. Questa would live on for many yearons to come in everyone's memories. It certainly would be remembered for it was where it had all begun for all of them, in some kind of way.

4. Headquarters Base Two

With the destruction of Questa behind the team, Dairan Loring's concerns over the way in which Lance had been affected over the whole ordeal had come true. Tayce walked back into Organisation to find Lance missing from his duty position. She glanced at Dairan questioningly. He crossed, asking her for a brief word, looking apprehensive, not quite knowing how to tell her what he had to. She agreed, then ordered Kelly to let her know when final approach was under way for Enlopedia. Kelly nodded in agreement, glancing at Dairan, then back at her screen in front of her. Craig was busy running computer checks and offered to keep an eye on Lance's position until he returned. Tayce agreed. Both Dairan and herself headed on into the DC. He paused mid floor, his eyes showing a darker, angrier shade of brown than normal.

"Why do I have a feeling this is about Lance, considering he's missing from his duty position?" demanded Tayce.

"We've got a problem—one I was concerned about the moment we left Questa's orbit," he put to her.

"Go on," said Tayce, preparing to listen.

"Lance just stopped his duty, stood up, said he couldn't take any more and walked out without a further word. I tried to ask him what was wrong, but he just threw me a plain look, mumbled something along the lines he wanted to be left alone, then continued on out. Believe me, I wanted to stop this from happening. I had a feeling something like this was going to surface somehow—I've seen it before. He seemed quiet with his own thoughts when Kelly was upset at the demise of Questa, but he didn't show his feelings," explained Dairan.

"OK, leave it with me. Next time something like this happens, call me on Wristlink," she ordered.

"Sure! Sorry—I figured I could handle it," he replied apologetically.

"It's all right. Lance can be unpredictable when it comes to being hurt," replied Tayce. She could see he felt bad about letting her down, considering she'd left him in charge.

She thought to herself, she too had a feeling something was going to happen. Lance had been too quiet, like something was bothering him since the demise of his birthplace. Dairan had been right. She put a friendly hand on Dairan's arm, assuring him he was doing a good job. Lance would have done the same thing if Marc or herself was on duty—what had happened would have occurred anyway. Dairan gave a look of relaxed relief with a warm smile. In his estimation Tayce was one fair leader. Anyone else would have probably called him an idiot for not sorting it before it had happened. She suggested he head on back to duty—she could take care of the situation. He nodded, following her out. He returned to duty, whilst Tayce headed to the Organisation entrance. Twedor pushed past Dairan in a hurry to catch Tayce up, as he'd been on standby mode. Some dayons, thought Twedor, he wished Tayce would remember he was suppose to be with her, as her personal escort. Especially when she walked off without him. Dairan and the others present laughed at the little Romid running to catch Tayce up.

* * *

Amalthea was travelling at a smooth warp 4 in the direction of the only headquarters base in existence, Enlopedia. Since the redesign of the cruiser at the end of the first voyage, everything had been made a lot smoother in operation and a lot quicker in reaction. When the operation called for it to happen, it was there. Amalthea Two, being the second cruiser in the line of the name Amalthea, was the best so far. She ripped through space like a blade through paper as she travelled the last steps towards Enlopedia.

Upon Twedor finally catching Tayce up, they both stepped into the Deck Travel together. Tayce requested Level 5. Twedor had undertaken a cruiser-wide sweep scan and pinpointed Lance down in the Combat and Training Practice Centre. He further added that it looked like Lance was letting off pent-up frustrated emotion, as the readings he was receiving were way off what they should be for a normal person in combat practice. Tayce said nothing, but she was far from pleased with the fact he had just stood up and walked off duty without a word to Dairan, only a mumble. But she also knew he always let off his pent-up emotions the way he was currently doing. He'd done it in the past. She just wished he had come clean to Dairan and told him he needed time off duty. The Deck Travel stopped on Level 5. As the doors opened, Tayce walked out, Twedor trying to keep up with her as she walked determinedly along. She could hear the sounds of Slazer fire in the distance, growing nearer. The newness smell still hung in the naturally lit corridor as she went, and she wished it would fade. As she stood before the doors to the Combat and Training Practice Centre, her powerful ability was sensing Lance was going beyond the true natural force of human endurance. He was likely to collapse from his pent-up anger and frustration at any moment. She had to act fast. The doors slid back to reveal the action screen simulation and an almost darkened interior. She and Twedor walked inside. Lance, to Tayce's surprise, spun round to face her, sweat pouring off him. His eyes as wild as fire, with the gun aimed at her. Tayce side-stepped a shot Lance fired off. It hit the wall just behind her. She gasped in heart-stopping shock. Twedor activated his Slazer finger on 'stun' setting, figuring Lance had truly lost it and was going to hurt his mistress. Tayce reached for the cut-off of the simulation, which appropriately was on on-coming Cripions, and hit it hard, stopping all action.

"Lower your weapon, Lance—that's an order, now!" commanded Tayce angrily, shaken up by the fact he'd nearly killed her without a thought of what he was doing.

Lance lowered his Slazer, standing with sweat running down his face from the pent-up strain and energy he'd used in the fierceness of the actions towards the Cripions in the simulation. He'd let it get out of control. His features were blank as he looked at Tayce. It was as if he was frozen in time. His breathing was the equivalent of someone who had done a vigorous workout, which in some ways he had. His normally Spanish-brown eyes were darker than normal and conveyed a certain piercing sharpness. Tayce realised she had to do something—he was lost in the onslaught of the emotion of pent-up fury. But suddenly, as if someone had snapped their fingers, Lance came back to normal. Tayce breathed a silent sigh of relief. He realised he still held the gun in his grasp and quickly let it drop to the floor. It all came flooding back, what he'd done.

"God, Tayce, I am so sorry! Honest, you know I would never hurt you," he said, feeling disgusted with himself for doing such a thing, for letting the action get the better of him.

"Questa's destruction is behind this, isn't it? Believe me, you're not the only one that's feeling angry over what's happened; we all are. I have personal reasons to be silently furious. Tom had a memorial there—now I have to wait until they erect one on Enlopedia," pointed out Tayce, slowly calming down from nearly joining Tom in the next realm.

"What can I say? I'm sorry, really I am, believe me. I guess I let my emotions get way out of control. It isn't so much the fact Questa has gone; it's how it went, at the damn hands of those Cripions, and there wasn't anything I could do to stop it," he explained, taking the wipe towel and wiping the sweat from his face and neck.

"You want to hear something, between you and me? I think this attack by the Cripions has been in the background for ages. If it hadn't been the Cripions, I think it would have been someone else; and if it could be proven, I think it goes right back to when Layforn Barkin was in charge," she announced.

"You could be right. I guess Dairan's mad at me for walking off duty like I did. I just couldn't handle holding in the hurt any more. You know me—when I blow I just have to get out of where I am and let off what's inside," he said, smiling kindly at her, hoping she would forgive him.

"Believe me, when it comes to feeling angry I know what that feels like—especially losing your home. I felt the same anger you're feeling right now the night that bitch Vargon destroyed my home world, and like you there wasn't anything I could do to fight back; so the way you're feeling right now is how I was feeling then. I was left alone with only Twedor here, in his old form, as someone to share the hurt with. The memories will always be with you, like they are in my mind," confided Tayce.

"It's strange really, Sallen is now part of this team—Vargon's daughter, even though she doesn't know it," said Lance, deactivating and wiping the programme with a few key command strokes on the computer-simulation console.

"Yes, but I know which version I'd rather have. Do you know, what makes my dayon is knowing one dayon should Vargon come sniffing round for her daughter and expect to find her, Sallen would probably have her arrested, because she has no recollection of who she is."

Lance smiled, seeing Tayce's point. Both hugged. Tayce forgot about his outburst. They'd been friends too long for her to take him wrongly. But if he had lost his mind, then he would have either been shot by Twedor or stunned and dropped from the team and brought before her mother for an act of violence against his captain.

"You all right now?" she put to him in a caring tone.

"Yeah, thanks. I guess I just have to look to the future," he replied, trying to sound optimistic.

"When they ask about the memorial for Tom, I'll have one placed for your father too; then we'll both have somewhere to still pay our respects. Now get cleansed and changed and report back to Organisation. We'll be arriving at Enlopedia soon—and above all else, apologise to Dairan," suggested Tayce.

"Of course," he replied.

"Come on, Twedor," said Tayce, walking back over to the entrance doors of the Combat and Training Practice Centre.

As the doors drew apart in front of her, she passed through with Twedor behind her. Lance watched her go, thinking even though she had undergone many things, confronting life changes in the past three yearons, she'd always been a good leader and been there for all of them at different times when she was needed. She was the best friend and captain anyone could have. He had been on another assignment in the last yearons and he figured he wouldn't want to be on any other team than where he was. Even if someone offered him a million partecs. He wiped the remaining sweat from his neck with the towel. Picking up his Wristlink, he depressed the keypad to log the simulation score into the memory to recheck at a later date. He then walked off in the direction of the Cleanse Unit to cleanse and change attire for duty. As he went, so he realised he felt a lot more at ease in himself for letting go of his pent-up feelings, despite what happened. Tayce had helped him see the future a lot easier.

* * *

The spectacular sight that was about two milons from Amalthea was the sister colony, and now the only one in existence, Enlopedia, which was to be the new home to thousands of Questonians that had been driven out of Questa Headquarters Base by the onslaught of attack. The colony was situated in what was termed the 7th North Sector. It was constructed by over 1750 construction workers and designers, electronics technicians and numerous other personnel, plus robots that went into positions suited and unsuited workers couldn't go. The shape resembled a jellyfish with spires reaching into orbit, and covered roughly eight milons in diameter. Incorporated in the vast constructed base was a Medical Hospital Dome, known as just Medical Dome to most, and the Flight Arrival and Departure Dome. In the many buildings that had been built there was also a Planetary and Personnel Research/Search and Rescue Centre, a new Security, Crime and Patrol Division building and an Assignment Centre, where chief councillors' chambers were incorporated. This would be where Lydia Traun would take up her new post, in overall control of the base. Enlopedia's living area, where personnel lived when not on duty, was known as the apart-house area. One part of the dwelling was built like an apartment, and the other like a house. Built up behind it, joining as one unit where families, couples and single people could dwell, there was a Construction and Service Port, which was an added bonus for the new colony, as it was where new Quest shuttles/fighters were constructed and serviced when called for. As Questa never had a big enough area, Enlopedia incorporated a lot more different advanced areas than Questa, but Questa had been in operation for quite a long time. The colony would serve space for many yearons to come, unless the unforeseen happened, as it had for Questa.

* * *

Amalthea was less than an houron from the orbital distance to Transpot to Enlopedia. The first sight that greeted the team was the vast expanse of steelex and glassene which the base was constructed of. The glassene domed roof of the colony reflected the lights shining from within. It looked something along the lines of a sparkling round glassene ornament, catching the light at certain angles. Enlopedia was a first-class sight of a fresh new colony, worth visiting.

Lance walked back on duty into Organisation. Dairan glanced at him. He crossed over and came to a pause before him.

"I guess I owe you an apology for just walking off duty, but I—" began Lance, but he was cut of by Dairan.

"It's all right. I understand. I wish you'd talked it through with me first, though. I would have listened you know that," said Dairan in an understanding tone.

Lance walked to his position, glancing back to the view of Enlopedia through the main sight port.

Lydia and Marc walked into Organisation. They came to a pause to watch the nearing of Enlopedia. Tayce and Twedor came from the DC to join them.

"Marc, has Donaldo given you permission to be up here?" demanded Tayce.

"Yes. I figured you'll need someone to take command when you're over on Enlopedia, so I'm volunteering to do it, considering I've been grounded, so to speak, for a couple of dayons and it can still be classed as light duties," he announced, knowing she wouldn't argue as he was right regarding the light duties.

Tayce looked at her mother. She shook her head. Marc had crept back to duty in a certain degree and got his own way to be in Organisation, even if it was on light duties. Lydia smiled at the situation and suggested discreetly that she should let Marc do what he wanted, as Amal wouldn't let him do any more than he was meant to if Tayce informed Amal of the situation and asked her, to keep an eye on him. Tayce nodded in agreement.

"All right, you've got the duty, but I'm ordering Amal to keep an eye on you, so you won't do what you're not suppose to—it's too early," said Tayce firmly.

"Fine! I won't, I assure you," Marc replied, feeling peeved that he was going to be watched by Amal.

Tayce said no more on the matter and turned her attention to Lydia, inquiring whether she'd like to talk in the DC before docking at Enlopedia. They had a little time. Lydia agreed—she knew there wouldn't be much time for a mother-and-daughter talk when they set foot upon Enlopedia. Both turned with Twedor and went back into the DC. Tayce paused in the doorway, letting her mother pass.

"Kelly, check with Enlopedia Medical Emergency Team and find out what preparations we need to have Adam Carford transferred, then relay the information to Donaldo for arrival," ordered Tayce.

"I'll get right on to it," replied Kelly, her fingers beginning to key away, to gain the contact code.

Tayce continued on into the DC to be with her mother. Lydia was sitting on the soffette in deep thought. Tayce studied her—she could see she was worried about what she might face when she stepped on to the base that was to be her new home.

"You're worried about what awaits you, aren't you?" said Tayce in a soft, understanding tone.

"Sometimes I wonder if I'm as adaptable and as good as Jonathan or your father," she replied quietly.

Lydia stood and sauntered over to the DC floor-to-almost-ceiling sight port and paused, staring out into the eluding Universe. Tayce didn't like to see her mother the way she was, but she guessed she'd felt the same when she came back aboard Amalthea after two yearons absence from being head of the team. Even though some of the members were familiar to her.

"You gathered this team together and helped me in getting this cruiser back to what is. I believe Jonathan and Father would be proud to see what you've achieved. Jonathan once said to me that you had leadership skills and would make a fine leader, and I and members of this team believe you do too," said Tayce, trying to cheer Lydia up.

"You really think so?" replied Lydia softly, turning to face her daughter with a slight smile.

"Yes!"

"I second that. Without you, Chief, I would still be in the corner of the Organisation, not what I am," spoke up Twedor.

"Thank you, both of you. I want to make a good job of running Enlopedia, just as I did Questa, if not better," replied Lydia, smiling.

Lydia walked back from the sight port, back to the soffette. She paused, turning, waiting for Tayce to say anything she wanted to share with her. She studied Tayce, thinking how proud Darius, her husband and Tayce's father, would have been if he could see how their daughter had grown into an independent young woman. It was hard to imagine she was once a naïve privileged daughter of a commodore and somewhat of a tomboy back on Traun. Tayce smiled at her mother, reading her thoughts with her ability. She realised it must be strange to think she had come such a long way, as she herself never thought she would be the leader of a crime-fighting team and captain.

Suddenly Tayce's desktop Communcom sounded. She turned her attention to it, pressing a small square grey connect button. Lance's voice came through.

"Sorry to disturb—just letting you know we'll be within Transpot distance in twenty minons," he informed.

"Has Kelly found out what we have to do where Adam is concerned, for Donaldo?" asked Tayce.

"Yes, everything is finalised—it's all in hand," assured Lance.

"Good work—thanks," said Tayce, praising him. She knew even the smallest praise at the moment for Lance would boost his morale.

He signed off and the small screen above the Communcom deactivated, going back to showing the 'QE'-entwined emblem. Lydia suggested they'd better go. Tayce agreed, waiting for her mother to head for the DC entrance first. As the doors opened before her, Lydia continued on out briskly back into Organisation. Twedor followed on. Upon exiting the DC, the sight through the main sight port of Enlopedia greeted them. Dairan crossed to Tayce, informing her there was a slight change in arrival plans. She gave him her full listening attention. He began by saying they were going to dock at the base instead of Transpot over. Enlopedia had problems in the fact many of the Questonians had heard their chief had made it off Questa and were gathering to ask questions and look for advice. It was a scene of chaos and they figured Chief Traun would want to settle into her position before being bombarded with problems. Tayce nodded, totally understanding where the powers that be were coming from. Without warning there was a slight bump. Amalthea had successfully docked home at the High-Ranked Docking Port. Tayce, Dairan, Lance, Twedor and Lydia all began on out of Organisation. Marc called out to have a good time and immediately took command under the watchful eyes of the team present and Amal, as Tayce had ordered her to watch Marc, in that he wasn't to use his injured arm for anything duty-wise. She had the notion that because he was out of her sight he would no doubt try and do something when she wasn't around.

* * *

Both Dairan and Lance, with Twedor, walked behind Lydia and Tayce in discussion about Enlopedia. How they were glad the base was going to be under Lydia's rules and not Layforn Barkin's. Dairan assured Lance that with the chief of Questa being in overall charge, things were going to be a lot more easier than last time both of them were on the base, for different reasons. Lydia smiled to herself, pleased Dairan and Lance were already feeling glad she was going to be in overall charge. Lance continued, saying he had had a home to return to at Questa, in duty breaks from the cruiser; but now that was gone, there was no telling what would happen or where he would reside when off the cruiser. Dairan shook his head. He realised Lance had lost everything except his duty on Amalthea and his quarters, with its belongings. It had been tough—he wouldn't have wanted to go through losing so many memories and personal mementoes in one go.

After a while the team members exited Amalthea via the Docking-Bay doors. They all walked down the long boarding tube and out into the high-ranked area. Lydia looked across the vast wide-open expanse and spotted Chief Waynard walking to meet her. He was to be her new deputy, and was prepared to stand down from running Enlopedia for her. She had insisted he remain as he was a valuable member of her team and she wanted him to stay, so offered him a much higher salary to remain, which he accepted. As he saw her and the Amalthean Quests team, he gave a wave of acknowledgement and a welcoming smile. As he approached, so Lydia wondered if he would feel awkward handing over his total command of Enlopedia to her. She would try and make it an easy transition, as he was considered a dear and long-standing friend.

"Welcome, all of you, to Enlopedia—especially you, Lydia. It's good to know the rescue was a success," he said, joyous to see she had made it safely.

"We have Tayce here and the team to thank for my safe arrival, though Commander Dayatso was injured, and Adam Carford," said Lydia.

"Hello, young lady. I hope Commander Dayatso will be all right. One of my aides informed me you did some fancy manoeuvres to get out of what was left of Questa. Is this true?" asked Waynard, giving her his full attention.

"Let's just say I wouldn't want to do it again in a hurry. It was pretty tight," assured Tayce.

"Here here! But it was good," spoke up Twedor.

Two young male aides walked forth. They came to a pause in an official manner beside Waynard, on each side of him. Upon seeing Lydia, they immediately came to attention and saluted—precise, straight, sideways, hand to right temple just the once.

"At ease, gentlemen. Chief Traun, you can see it's still a bit hectic around here, so I will leave you in the hands of these two young aides.

"When will we meet to discuss our new situation?" asked Lydia eargerly. "I'm eager to get things back to normal for the people of Questa, who are now Enlopedian citizens, as soon as possible?"

"Later. Don't concern yourself. You get settled in—remember you appointed me as deputy. We'll talk soon," he assured her with a gentle smile, then walked away to take care of the continuing business to get the people from Questa sorted out with their many wants.

Tayce watched Waynard leave. She could see it had been a strain with the converging of the two bases into one and she thought he looked tired. She turned to her mother and informed her of as much. Lydia assured her that the moment she was in full command and things were settling he would be allowed time off for a break. This Tayce was glad to hear. Waynard had always treated her with fairness, and she didn't want to think something would happen to him because he worked too hard.

"Excuse me, Chief Traun, I'm Dayboard, your personal aide until you are settled. Let me personally welcome you to your new home, Enlopedia Headquarters Base. It's an honour to be serving you for the temporary period Mr Carford is unable to serve you," announced one of the aides politely, who was tall and slim with chestnut-coloured hair and pleasant looks.

"Have you been briefed on what is required of you, duty-wise?" asked Lydia in the true tone of chief.

"Yes, ma'am, by our temporary galactic assignments officer. What is your first requirement?" he asked in an obliging tone with a warm smile.

"You can start by showing me to my new chambers," ordered Lydia.

Dayboard gestured without a further word for Lydia and the team, plus Twedor, to follow him. Lydia went first, followed by Tayce, who had grabbed Twedor's metlon hand—she didn't want him being caught up in any crowds that might be waiting outside in E City. Dairan and Lance took in the surrounding area as they followed on. Dayboard led the way out into the city and across the shiny marblex beige floor, watching for signs Lydia would be under siege by people of all ages, wanting answers to questions. People came and went, discussing business. Dairan and Lance glanced up to see repairs going on that needed to be carried out by the design and construction team after the slight damage caused during the attack by the Cripions' misfired shots that had missed Questa and hit Enlopedia. Lydia looked up, noticing the damage also. She asked Dayboard if the base had sustained any real structural damage. Dayboard immediately put Lydia's mind at ease, explaining it was merely cosmetic. Though some electronics that had gone off line were in the process of being repaired and would be up and running by duty end. They soon approached the clear-vision Vacuum Lift. As the doors parted, everyone entered. The doors glided shut and the Vacuum Lift began to rise slowly above E City Square. Twedor pointed back to the city square below, to the medical team taking Adam Carford to the new Medical Dome for further treatment and aftercare. Tayce looked to where Twedor was pointing, watching the many beings milling around below.

Her mind went back to the first dayon she'd arrived on Questa. It was the same all over again, only it was her mother in charge instead of Jonathan Largon, and this was Enlopedia rather than Questa, and she was without Tom. It was hard to imagine how time had changed certain things. Like Tom and herself being married and now she was alone. Her mother was now chief of Enlopedia. This was her second voyage.

Lance, unbeknown to Tayce, was also casting his mind back over past memories. He was thinking back to his dayons on Questa and his father. Moments of heated differences between them. The good times they'd shared.

Once they were at the required level, the lift doors opened. Dayboard walked out and stood holding back the doors, allowing Lydia to walk forth, followed by Twedor and the Amalthean team members. As Dairan stepped forth, he glanced about, noticing the whole of the top floor was devoted to the running of the base and Lydia as the chief of Enlopedia. As they walked, so he looked in rooms that were staffed by personnel, both male and female, busy at work. He noticed there was a Meeting Centre and the corridors were light and airy with plant foliage in decorative containers, making the area welcome to visitors. The walls and floors were light beige in a shiny tough-wearing marblex. As they went, so the sound of their boots echoed in the air. Twedor walked along at Tayce's side. He was taking in the surroundings and relaying them back to Marc and the others aboard the cruiser so they could see what the new base was like. Everyone came to two floor-to-almost-ceiling white decorative engraved doors. Dayboard reached out and placed his right palm on the yellow lit panel beside the entrance. The panel sensor read his palm print and the doors clicked and began to open. From within a warm breeze rushed out to meet them. Dayboard entered the outer anteroom of what was to be Lydia's immediate working area and chambers, with a Meeting Centre off to one side. He turned, gesturing for Lydia to enter. Tayce accompanied her. As she did, she knew how it felt to walk into somewhere new for the first time. Once inside, she found herself liking the roomy interior, impressed by the high-quality ornate and plush furnishings, the brown mahoganex meeting table with beige leatherex swivel chairs and beige plain walls and almost-floor-to-ceiling inset sight panes, with tinted glassene. It was truly a chief's domain of great sophisticated modern splendour. Tayce glanced around her mother's new surroundings, also surprised by the good quality of the layout. She too had to admit she was impressed. She glanced towards Dairan, who was, as it happened, glancing at her. As he met her look, he raised his eyes in surprise. Tayce nodded in agreement, thinking to herself that Chief Waynard had obviously known her mother's high expectations in furnishings and design for a working and meeting environment, for greeting and impressing people and alien races with impressiveness.

"Chief Traun, I trust you find everything to your liking. Chief Waynard took into consideration your choice for design and a comfortable working environment. I will leave you to settle in and will return later. It has been an honour to meet you all," he said politely.

"Yes, it's perfect. Relay to Deputy Waynard that he's done an excellent job. I'll be very happy here. Would you also make sure Mr Carford has the best medical treatment? Make sure he's not in need of anything," ordered Lydia, realising she'd given her first new order of being in charge.

"Of course, ma'am," he replied obligingly, turning and heading on out through the open doorway.

Tayce studied Dayboard as he met her briefly as he turned to leave. She found even though he was her mother's temporary aide, he reminded her of one of her old male friends back home. Nice eyes, reasonably handsome features and someone she felt her mother would come to trust and rely on. He smiled at her kindly, then looked ahead, going on out. He was just right to replace Adam temporarily, she thought. Dairan glanced at Tayce, noticing her interest in Dayboard, wondering was it common interest or was she seeing something in him that made her enticingly interested? The moment Tayce glanced his way, Dairan smiled a warm, gentle smile then looked away. Tayce read Dairan's thoughts and was surprised to read that it was jealousy. It made her amused. Lydia crossed and sat down behind her new desk, asking everyone present, except Twedor, to take a seat.

"Lance, would you help in the operation of the Vidfilm of Questa's attack?" asked Lydia carefully.

"Sure!" he replied, unaware he would have to witness the whole destruction of his once home all over again.

He soon activated the screen and returned to his seat. Dairan and Tayce exchanged unsure glances. Was it a good idea that Lance was doing what he was, considering what had happened when he had left duty earlier because he couldn't face what had happened to his home. The Vidfilm flashed up on the large circular wall screen. First to appear was the date and time the film had been shot. Then the title: '**DESTRUCTION OF QUESTA HEADQUARTERS BASE ONE**'. As the film commenced, Tayce watched Lance. She could see he was becoming more uneasy as time went on. She could also see he was determined to try and stay with it, but his stomach began to churn at the sheer bloody violence that was being exchanged between the Cripions and the innocent Questonians, many of them people he knew. It was making it gut-wrenchingly difficult. Lydia hadn't noticed him finding it near impossible to live through. Lance left his seat and ran from the chambers. Tayce shook her head—why had he tried to do something he knew he couldn't?

"Shall I go and check he's all right?" asked Dairan, concerned.

"No, leave him. He'll want to be alone. He shouldn't have put himself through the torture," replied Tayce, feeling angry. Lance had been foolish to try such a thing when the destruction was still fresh.

"Is it wise to let him go off like this? I feel bad. I should have known he would have reacted like he did—Questa was everything to him," said Lydia apologetically.

"Forget it, Mother. Lance should have had more sense. He'll be fine. If there is one thing I have learned about him of late, it is to leave him to adjust to situations like this one in his own way," assured Tayce.

"I am sorry," continued Lydia, thinking about her actions.

"He's all right. I'm keeping track of him," said Twedor.

He'd been scanning where Lance was heading and was tracking his every move. He would alert Tayce should Lance get into any trouble.

"Thank you, Twedor. Let's get off the subject of Questa's destruction for a minon, shall we? Whilst at Questa I was putting into action a plan for you to have a communications officer on Amalthea, only you said before the voyage began you could do with one. Are you still interested?" put Lydia.

"Yes, it would free up some of Kelly Travern's time," replied Tayce eagerly.

"I'll go ahead and notify him that the plans are still going ahead," suggested Lydia.

"Do we have a name for this communications officer?" asked Tayce, interested.

"Mac Danford. He's the best in his field of communications on his colony. He can converse in seventeen space dialects, which I figure will be helpful if you visit planets, vessels or come across races that need his skills. He was recommended by his chief. He's here on Enlopedia already. He arrived ready to join you before all the turmoil of Questa. I'll have him meet you at the boarding tube. Now back to the Quest I'm about to hand you—you probably know what it is," put Lydia.

"Tracking down the Cripions, to bring them to justice?" asked Tayce.

"Try, don't you mean? You see what they did to Questa—what chances do we have?" cut in Dairan, finding the whole idea stupid. Considering what the Cripions did to Questa, Amalthea was small fry.

"Dairan, that's enough," said Tayce, not liking his sudden outburst.

"No, Tayce, Dairan has a good point. I understand your concern. That's why I want you to work with Jan Barnford on this Quest. It's too dangerous to attempt alone—don't think of doing it either," said Lydia sternly. She didn't want to think because of Tayce's stupidity she'd die at the hands of the Cripions—too many had died already unnecessarily.

"You have my promise on this one—I don't want to lose mine or any of the team's lives," assured Tayce.

"Good. I know what a risk-taker you are, but you'll work with Jan Barnford?" asked Lydia, making sure Tayce was seeing sense like she claimed.

"Sure! Love to," confirmed Tayce.

Lydia wondered whether she was doing the right thing, handing Tayce the Quest and one that was extremely dangerous, but she also knew the Amalthean Quest team was the right team for the job; plus joined with the forces of Chief Commander Jan Barnford, it would be a Quest that could have excellent results.

"Well, Mother, we'd better find Lance and get back to Amalthea for the first official Quest for Enlopedia. By the way, it suits you behind that desk!" she announced with a smile.

"I guess I'm already settling in," Lydia replied light-heartedly.

Tayce began back to the entrance followed by Dairan and Twedor. Lydia watched her go. She had a feeling Dairan Loring was going to be good for her daughter, in the respect that he'd try and make her see sense when she felt like taking bold risks. Tayce glanced back at her mother as the doors parted before her, then continued on out with Dairan and Twedor. Outside the three of them walked back along the shiny-floored wide corridor towards the Vacuum Lift. Twedor could see his reflection in the floor and was finding it somewhat amusing. He was walking on himself in the reflection. Both Tayce and Dairan laughed at him, not realising it was something new to the little Romid.

Dairan thought to himself as they continued on that the forthcoming Quest was going to be dangerous in the extreme. His concern was for Tayce. He knew how to handle himself against anything thrown at him, but Tayce—he would have to watch her for safety's sake. He also wondered what it would be like working with Chief Commander Barnford. He'd heard he was a stickler for the rules and didn't suffer fools gladly when it came to being in the line of extreme danger.

They soon paused at the clear-vision Vacuum Lift. As they waited for it to arrive, Twedor undertook a scan for Lance's whereabouts. The lift soon arrived and the doors parted. Tayce entered first, followed by Dairan and Twedor. The doors closed and the lift descended, gliding back to E City Square below. As the doors drew apart Tayce walked out on to the busy bustling city square.

"Lance is in the refreshment bar, better known as the Twone Bar, announced Twedor, looking up at Tayce.

"If you don't mind me saying, that place is rowdy at the best of times and it's no place for a lady like you. I'll go and fetch him," volunteered Dairan, beginning away.

"When are you going to stop ordering me around, Dairan Loring? Don't you think I'm capable of going into a rowdy atmosphere?" asked Tayce, making Dairan stop in his tracks, surprised at Tayce's words.

"This time, no," he replied, going on, not listening any further.

Tayce gave a look that conveyed she was angry at Dairan. Who did he think she was! She wasn't hopeless in a rowdy atmosphere and could hold her own against anything that made a move towards her she didn't want. Then she heard the kind of rowdiness atmosphere of the refreshment bar. She didn't care to enter any time soon. She ordered Twedor to accompany him—there might be trouble and he was to protect Dairan at all costs, even if he did like taking matters into his own hands. God knows what was in the bar as far as travellers went, considering the loud noise. After letting Twedor go, she wondered if she'd done the right thing. She hoped Dairan would look after him. Falling into the wrong hands was the last thing she wanted. She walked on over to the high-ranked arrival and departure area, but was halted halfway by a male voice calling out to her. She paused, glancing around. He appeared from behind a crowd of people. It was no one she recognised. Was this the new communications officer? He was nothing to write home about. Of slim build, around 1.75 metres tall. In appearance he was far from what she would term communications-officer material. He wasn't like any she'd seen in the past. His hair was mousy and rough-looking, but short. His features were rugged, but conveyed he was a take-it-or-leave-it kind of man. His eyes were the darkest brown she'd ever seen. She thought as he met her on approach that he was not ready for duty—in fact he looked like he'd just stepped off of an expedition vessel back from an archaeology trip. She guessed he had to be in his thirties—her mother hadn't told her how old he was. He gave her a nervous but mischievous smile to try and make the moment light.

"Mac Danford. I guess you're Captain Traun. I figured if I didn't yell above the noise, I would have missed you. Call me Mac—everyone does," he said politely, in a friendly tone that was rather along the lines of an old earth American light Mid West drawl.

"Mac! Welcome. Yes, I'm Captain Traun—everyone on the team calls me Tayce. When we're on board, only call me captain when we have to attend a special situation. I'm heading back to the cruiser—are you ready to come along?" asked Tayce, studying Mac, wondering how he would fit into the team.

"Sure! Of course, after you," he said eagerly, gesturing for her to go first.

Mac flung his holdall over his shoulder and followed Tayce on to Amalthea. That was to be his new duty position and his new home for the foreseeable future. Nearing the boarding tube, Jan Barnford approached, dressed in his security-mission attire. Mac stayed silent and looked about the immediate vicinity whilst Tayce paused to talk with Jan.

"Your mother said your first assignment is going after the Cripions with me and my team. Is this true?" he demanded casually, in his usual abrupt gruff tone.

"Yes!" replied Tayce.

"Not being rude here and taking over—I know you'd hate that—but don't you think you ought to leave this one to me and my men?" he asked seriously.

"No! Mother has issued this Quest to me and the team as our first official Quest for Enlopedia and I'm looking forward to the both of us working together. We haven't done it for a while and I definitely think we can pull it off," replied Tayce.

"All right, fair enough; but knowing more about the Cripions than you on this one, please work with me. No bold independent heroic moves when we catch up with these idiots! This assignment is going to be extremely dangerous. You know my old saying, I don't want to have to come back here and tell Chief Traun you're dead," he said.

"You have my word, I don't intend to put myself or the team in the deliberate path of death, defying danger without some kind of backup from you and your team. I'll see you later out in space."

"Right," he replied, beginning away, still wondering if she'd try anything bold.

"Oh, Jan, would you do me a favour? Check in the Twone Bar and see how Dairan Loring's doing on helping Lance back to the cruiser. Lance took it badly what happened to Questa, so you can guess what's he up to right now—drowning his sorrows. I want him, Twedor and Dairan back on board asap," asked Tayce, knowing Jan would help as they were good friends.

"Leave it with me. I'll get him back to you," he assured, continuing on.

Mac didn't pry who Jan was as they both walked on together. He simply said he thought he seemed like a good man. Tayce explained that he was and his bark was worse than his bite, as the saying went. Once at the Docking-Bay doors they drew apart on their approach and they both walked aboard. Mac paused once on the cruiser, asking what would she like him to undertake first? She suggested he go and get unpacked, then, once changed for duty, to report to Organisation. Mac nodded in understanding, heading away whilst Tayce headed on up to Organisation. She began thinking that in a way she was glad Jan Barnford was along for the first official Quest for Enlopedia. There was no telling what the Cripions would do, knowing they were in the throes of being brought to justice, especially after what they'd done to Questa.

* * *

Back down in E City Square in the Twone Bar Dairan and Twedor were in amongst the smoky atmosphere of bright-colour laser cell lights, rowdy travellers worse for wear, strange sophisticated music that was like some rock song gone horribly wrong and dancers dancing in scanty outfits. There was the odd sudden eruption of uncouth laughter from darkened tables, from groups, followed by cheers. Twedor felt uneasy. He didn't like some of these misfits and the way they seemed to be eyeing him with interest. Dairan was nearing the end of his patience, trying to get Lance to see sense. It was damned near impossible, as Lance had been drinking. He was pointing out to him that what he was doing wouldn't solve anything. It was falling on deaf ears. Lance was too far gone to care, or listen. Without warning, Twedor had an unfriendly and noisy drunk put a callous hand on his blue metlon shoulder. He didn't like being handled in the way he was. He activated his heat protection shield, which was his way of defending himself. His outer casing became hot to the touch, even though his internal parts were safe from overheating. Much to Twedor's delight the drunk traveller found his hand was beginning to sting, with an increasing burning sensation. The traveller quickly pulled his hand away, gripping it, swearing in some alien garbled language and was about to knock Twedor off his feet.

"Yes, I'm hot property. Keep your hands off me, you miscreant," retorted Twedor defensively.

"I wouldn't if you don't want to find yourself looking at the wall of a security holding cell. Go about your drinking before I impound you," said Jan, quickly taking the situation in hand.

The overweight scruffy moody-looking drinker threw a vile threatening look at Jan for a few minons. He wasn't scared one bit. He in fact fancied pushing his luck, until Jan brought out his ID card, thrusting it under the traveller's nose. He gave a displeased grunt, then sauntered away, heading back to his drinking, saying something incoherent under his breath.

Jan looked across to Lance, who was seated at the round moon-shaped bar, and Dairan trying unsuccessfully to get him to see reason. He shook his head. Lance was not doing himself any favours downing vardox after vardox. This situation was growing more uneasy by the cencron. The growing interest in Twedor was telling him it was time he stepped in.

"Dairan, I think it would be wise if you thought about leaving, taking Lance and Twedor with you. He's had enough," said Jan in a gruff tone, finding Lance's drunk state somewhat amusing.

"Believe me, Chief, no one more than me wants to get him out of here, but he won't budge," replied Dairan.

"Let me give you a hand before I have to call for backup support for all of us, especially for Twedor and the growing interest he's getting. His parts could fetch a pretty sum on the unauthorised market," explained Jan.

"Right! Ready when you are," said Dairan, only too happy to get out of the current surroundings.

The traveller who had been interested in Twedor watched at a distance for a few minons, hovering around, wondering if there would be a possibility he could get another chance at Twedor. Jan, seeing him, threw a warning look in his direction. He gave a snarl back and sauntered off out of sight. Jan grabbed Lance away from drowning his sorrows and, with Dairan, guided him in a very difficult motion of sorts towards the bar entrance, back out into the city square. Once outside, Jan beckoned to one of his patrol guards, ordering him upon approach to help Dairan take Officer Largon back to Amalthea. The stockily-built ginger-haired guard grabbed Lance supportingly with Dairan and they began away with Twedor close by and Lance mumbling something incoherent off in the direction of the cruiser. Jan shook his head in amusement at the sight, thinking Tayce was sure to give Lance hell when he arrived back, being a member of her team. He couldn't understand Lance acting the way he did. He was always a strong, level-headed person and coped exceedingly well with past disappointments. Why the destruction of Questa had let him turn into someone getting drunk for the shear fun of it he couldn't understand. He knew Jonathan Largon would have hit the roof if he'd been around still. He turned when the three were out of sight and began back to his Officette in the Security and Patrol Complex off the domed area.

Marc, on Amalthea, had been notified by Tayce upon her return to Organisation about Lance's misconduct. He was far from amused and was awaiting his return at the Docking-Bay doors. Dairan and the security patrol guard came into view with a very unsteady-on-his-feet and happy intoxicated Lance. Dairan looked up at Marc as he and the guard walked up the walkway boarding tube, noticing he was like thunder about to erupt.

"Escort him down to his quarters and leave him there," ordered Marc angrily. He would have liked to put him in confinement, but because of the circumstances surrounding what had happened he figured sending him to his quarters was the next best thing.

Dairan began away, supporting Lance, whilst the security patrol guard, upon Marc thanking him, turned and went off back to duty in E City. Marc, as Twedor walked around to his side and they began on the way to Level 1, ordered Amal to close the Docking-Bay doors and get them under way, via Wristlink.

* * *

As the cruiser began drawing away from Enlopedia, Tayce in Organisation watched it get further and further away into the distance through the main sight port. Kelly at her console looked up at Tayce questioningly, waiting for her next orders. Craig was heading on out. He had some technical checks to make—something in the system was fluctuating, making the process of information slow one minon, fast the next. Tayce let him get on with what he had to. If there was one thing about Craig, he worked under his own schedule during duty time, keeping the cruiser running smoothly, mingling in the background unless called upon by herself to join a Quest as part of the team. She crossed to Kelly, ordering her to download the information sent from Enlopedia on the Cripion battlecruiser, to be stored for retrieval later, and to key the orbital bearings into the navigational computer and set course. Amal heard Tayce's request and began assisting Kelly in sorting the information into relevant files. A sequence of small coloured lights flashed in front of Kelly, confirming course to rendezvous with the Cripions was in place. Amalthea turned in the direction of the programmed set course and headed off at warp 8—1,488,000 milons a cencron.

Dairan returned from escorting Lance to his quarters. He entered Organisation along with Marc and Twedor, whom he'd caught up on the Level Steps. Both paused in the middle of Organisation. Tayce turned, deciding the present time was the best time to introduce Mac Danford to the team, as he'd just taken up his seat at communications.

"I know we have a difficult Quest ahead, but I'd like your attention for a moment. I'd like you all to meet our new communications officer, Mac Danford. He's now part of this team," introduced Tayce.

Everyone present welcomed Mac in a friendly way to the team. Kelly informed him she was glad he was there—it would take a lot off her shoulders, duty-wise, as it had been part of her duty to handle all incoming and outgoing communications. Mac assured her that she was welcome.

"Lance was out cold when I left him on the soffette in his quarters," said Dairan discreetly.

"He's lucky I'm prepared to overlook the circumstances behind this act; otherwise I could have had you escort him to confinement," said Tayce, far from pleased Lance had behaved in such a way, being a member of the Amalthean Quests team.

"I hope he has the mother of all headaches when he sobers up," spoke up Marc, just as displeased as Tayce.

She turned, walking away up into the DC with Twedor going on ahead of her. Upon entering the DC she sauntered over to her desk and around to sit on her high-backed swivel chair. Relaxing, she began thinking about Lance's behaviour, even though she'd understood his loss of a place associated with his past memories, his home. She wished he had considered for just a moment that he was part of the team and everyone felt the same over Questa. There was a certain decorum to uphold, considering they were upholding the law. She sighed. What had been done had been done, but when they got the chance she would have it out with him. She expected him to act like a law-abiding member of her team, not some low-grade officer. Marc and Dairan sauntered in and Tayce told them of her decision over Lance. They wholeheartedly agreed. Tayce noticed Marc's arm was back to normal—something she hadn't expected to see.

"Donaldo said it's fine—I'm cleared, honestly!" he announced.

"You're not telling me lies, Marc Dayatso, just to get back to duty?" asked Tayce, studying him. She knew he was eager to do so.

"No, Donaldo said it had healed a lot more quickly and easily than he thought it would," assured Marc.

Dairan felt peeved in one way. He would be taking a step back from full command in Marc's place. He had enjoyed his time in full command and it was a shame it had come to an end. Tayce noticed the look of deflation in the fact he had to give up his time and return to normal duty. But one dayon she could see him making a first-class full duty commander—whether it would be for her or someone else time would tell. Dairan turned without a further word, going back to duty. Marc followed on, exclaiming to Tayce that he would take care of the business with Lance. Even though she would rather have handled it herself, she found herself agreeing. As Marc and Dairan exited the DC, so the doors drew closed. Tayce turned in her swivel chair to look out of the floor-to-almost-ceiling sight port. Twedor walked to stand before her desk. He could see she was drifting into deep thought about something. She was thinking about the past dayons. Questa had played a big part in all their lives, and even though Lance had acted the way he had she could understand his reason for his actions. She hoped Marc would think things over when handling the situation and think back to Traun.

Her desktop Telelinkphone suddenly sounded. She turned and lifted the cordless handset. Mac's voice came through, informing her that Chief Commander Barnford was on the line from his Patrol Officette on Enlopedia. Tayce was surprised to hear this. She thought he would be under way to rendezvous with her later. The Satlelink relay-link screen flashed into life on her desktop. Jan appeared. Even though his title was Chief Commander Barnford, he preferred to be called just Chief Barnford, or Jan to his immediate friends.

"I want you to hold the orbit you're currently in," he ordered sternly.

"Why, what's the problem?" asked Tayce, concerned.

"As you know, the Cripions are a dangerous bunch. You wait for me—remember we're suppose to be going into this together. I don't want you going in alone. They'll think you're small fry, if you know what I mean," he said seriously.

"All right, we'll wait for you within a five-milon orbit," replied Tayce, sounding the true leader she was.

"I'm bringing a SSWAT team. We'll be there in roughly two hourons. Nothing is to start until I get there—understood?" he asked, hoping she would see the seriousness of the task ahead.

"You have my word. I don't want to put this team in any more danger than is necessary," assured Tayce.

Jan signed off and the screen went blank. Tayce knew they'd have to slow things down at their current speed. She pressed the Communcom key to connect her to Kelly out in Organisation. To Tayce's surprise Kelly announced she was getting sightings of the Cripion battlecruiser already ahead. Tayce rose to her feet urgently, almost shouting at Kelly to stop the course. She headed briskly on out, hitting the door mechanism panel upon reaching the DC entrance. As the doors parted she ran out into Organisation and crossed, pausing by Marc, who was watching the sight through the main sight port. It was the most repulsive, evil-looking shape that could ever be imagined. Twedor had followed Tayce out of the DC and he came to a pause beside her, forming his own opinion on the silver-and-black Starshant design from the Cripion Empire.

The battlecruiser was approximately one and a half milons in overall diameter and loaded with every available weapon for space battle and destruction. It had dents in its hull and it showed the battlecruiser was never far from a battle. As menacing as the Cripion battlecruiser looked, it was along the lines of an old earth one—a prehistoric dinosaur without legs. It had a bullet-shaped head section that would have obviously been the command part of the powerful cruiser. Powerful-looking guns protruded from what would have been the left and right nostril of the nose shape. Behind was a long neck, which was connected to the main body of the cruiser. This was probably the living and working main quarters. Bulbous in shape, the main part looked overbearing and more than a powerful match for Amalthea Two. All the team in Organisation looked at the sight, wondering just what they were up against.

Dairan spoke up from behind Tayce. "It's in a class considered the most deadly of all galactic war machines in the entire Universe," he announced.

"Capture a scan shot in scan mode. I want to know if there are any weak spots, Amal," ordered Tayce.

"Hold on—what are you thinking of doing? You know Chief Barnford ordered us to do nothing until he has joined us," said Marc beginning to get alarmed that Tayce was thinking of ignoring the Chief's words and putting the Quest into action to finish off the attack vessel once and for all.

Tayce ignored Marc's sudden panic, standing ready to hear what Amal had found in the scan results on the battlecruiser. Marc was looking at Tayce, waiting to hear she was not going to be irrational, but he had a feeling he was not going to hear it.

"Scan reveals no weaknesses, Captain," informed Amal.

"Not making it easy for us, are they? We'll have to find a weakness," replied Tayce.

"I'm reading from the scan there's little movement on board," said Kelly, reading the information in front of her.

"Perhaps they're on sleep time," replied Mac.

"Criminals of this nature never sleep. They make you think they are," replied Marc, knowing the fact.

"He's right—having been through a lot of this type of encounter back on Traun, working for my Father." said Tayce in a prompting tone.

"Yes, there were quite a few encounters in which the enemy played dead back in those dayons," replied Marc, thinking back to the past and his old life.

Marc glanced out through the main sight port in thought, wondering if this menacing battlecruiser before them would be another one to add to his list of encounters where he had discovered all was not what it should be and had to fight his way out. Tayce hoped Jan's arrival was not going to be too far off. She felt like they were sitting targets in their current orbit. Kelly turned, announcing much to Tayce's relief, that Chief Barnford's Patrol Cruiser was coming up behind on scanner, gaining speed to manoeuvre into position to come alongside. Tayce turned, ordering Mac to inform Chief Barnford that she would meet him in the Transpot Centre in about an houron. Mac nodded, turning back to his console to carry out the order.

Tayce began on out of Organisation. She paused in the entrance, informing Marc that she was off to change, ready for the Quest ahead. He nodded. Twedor walked on behind her as she continued on out, off to her quarters. Kelly looked in the direction of the entrance to Organisation, thinking and hoping everything would be all right on this dangerous Quest, and that the team picked to go would all come back safely. She looked up at Marc. He caught her concerned look, seeing her looking towards the entrance after Tayce had gone. He assured her that whatever the boarding team encountered, they'd take care of it. There was nothing to worry about. Kelly hoped he was right, as she remembered a similar race back from her growing-up dayons on Greymaren. She lost friends like Tayce in conflicts such as they were about to enter into. An houron elapsed. The Quest team had been picked to go on the Quest. Lance Largon had sobered up and had been warned by Marc that the next time he thought about being irresponsible Tayce might not be quite so lenient.

The Quest team began to gather in the Transpot Centre, dressed ready to go. Chief Barnford materialised in the centre and waited for Tayce to arrive. She soon walked in, dressed in a navy-blue all-in-one lightly padded combat suit. She came to a pause upon seeing Jan. He crossed and gently took hold of her by the upper arm, guiding her to one side. The rest of the Quest members stood around waiting when they arrived. Aldonica and Sallen walked in and crossed to Lance. They noticed he looked somewhat sheepish for his earlier behaviour on Enlopedia. Aldonica had brought her PolloAld bombs, named PolloAld because they'd been a designed and created on her last place of duty, by herself. Hence there was a capital A in the name. 'Pollo' was the high-energy explosive and 'Ald' was from the front part of her name. She showed Craig, Lance and Dairan, explaining about the impact they gave, much to their amazement. They all stood discussing the benefits they could bring to the forthcoming Quests. Once everyone was present and ready, they waited. Jan turned and in a friendly tone informed everyone he would see them over on the Cripion battlecruiser. With this, he stepped into the Transpot and transpoted back to the Patrol Cruiser to brief his men ready to transport over to the cargo hold of the Cripion battlecruiser. Tayce warned the team of the severity of the Quest ahead in that no one was to take any chances. Herself, Twedor and the team going stepped into the Transpot and stood ready to transpot over on Jan's word via her Wristlink. As soon as word was given, the Transpot activated, sending the Quest team members from Amalthea over to uncertain danger aboard the Cripion battlecruiser's cargo hold.

5. Cripion Arrest and the Test

Upon materialising on the Cripion battlecruiser, Jan Barnford and his team of tough, efficient officers were already waiting. Tayce noticed straight away Jan's men were wearing their blue platex armour. Was there more than she was being told about on the dangerous side of this Quest? Sure enough, she knew what the Cripions were capable of, but should she have brought Twedor?

"Chief Barnford, a word, please, now!" demanded Tayce in an annoyed discreet tone.

"What's the problem?" he asked, glancing around, knowing they were in danger staying in their current surroundings for long.

"Your men are wearing protective armour—why? I understand they need protection, but what about us? You didn't say anything about us needing any?" demanded Tayce in furious discreet tone.

"They are wearing it to protect your team. We're working together, right? My men are going to protect your team as well as do their job—that's what they're trained in," he replied, with a look that said stop panicking.

"Fine! Just as long as I know," replied Tayce, wishing he'd been up front about that aspect.

"Shall we get started?" he replied, giving her a slight smile.

Without a further word Jan turned, ordering his blue platex-armoured men to fall in line with the Amalthean Quest team. All thirty-five highly skilled SSWAT members did as requested by their chief. Everyone, including Twedor with his Slazer finger primed, began cautiously off on alert into the darkly lit corridor to the centre of the proposed action, with a hoped-for successful outcome. The teams expected trouble waiting around every corner they ventured. Tayce and Dairan were up front with Twedor and Jan. The two teams followed close behind in search of the first signs of the Cripion leader, working their way to the centre of operations, where the Cripion leader no doubt unleashed his or her orders for the destruction of Questa. What were they going to find? Dairan looked at Tayce as they proceeded. He had to admit what he'd been studying in the last hourons before leaving the cruiser—he was concerned for her safety and felt in his mind as he glanced to one of Jan's officers in his blue armour, that as Tayce was leader of the Amalthean Quests team, maybe this was one Quest she should have sat out on for her own safety. But this was just his opinion and he didn't dare tell her. Instead he gave her a reassuring smile. Noises suddenly filled the air, signifying there was life on board. It grew louder as they progressed towards the front of the battlecruiser. The interior had seen better dayons. Lance announced that the interior's smell reminded him of the old dayons in the changing rooms during training on Questa. Sallen, next to him, agreed, exclaiming that the strong stench was certainly not of the sweet kind! Jan was finding the conversation amusing between the two Amaltheans. A broad smile crossed his rugged features. Craig Bream shone the infrared heat-seeking device in different directions, checking to see how many crew were ahead and which way they seemed to be heading. Tayce glanced at the readings as they came up.

"You know the Cripion leader is a woman?" said Jan discreetly to Tayce, much to her surprise.

"What's that supposed to mean?" asked Tayce, wondering if Jan was implying all female leaders were trouble.

"All I'm saying is remember Vargon—we could be looking at the same, only worse," he replied.

"Do we have a name for this woman leader?" enquired Dairan.

"Hydran Corvous," replied Jan, to the point.

Craig suddenly stopped and everyone nearly piled into the back of him. He exclaimed that Hydran Corvous's men were situated in the main Operations Centre up ahead. This, thought Tayce, would be where the Quest would end, alive or—the worst—dead! Craig continued. The readings he was continuously getting signified Corvous's men appeared to be spread out all over the cruiser and there were quite a few of them. Jan, upon hearing this, turned, briefing his men, ordering them to remain on alert. As they continued on, both the Quest members and Jan's patrol officers waited for the sudden appearance of Corvous's men, primed with weapons to open fire as they came. Craig continued to update both Tayce and Jan as they went. Both teams checked their Slazers were set to 'disintegrate'. Nearing the entrance, finding not a sign of what they were expecting, Jan began positioning his men ready for the possible onslaught. There was going to be no mercy shown to this murderous female and her bunch of killers. Jan's officers were used to this kind of criminal, but some of the officers were like Lance—they'd personal reasons for wanting to see this murderess, Hydran Corvous, brought to justice. They were Questonians that had friends, lovers and relatives perish at this murdering female's command, to destroy Questa.

"Chief, Kelly Travern on our team said her father had had dealings with this race a long time ago. She said they didn't show any mercy the last time on attacking Greymaren. Kelly also said her father considered this Hydran Corvous to be ruthless and cunning, and she would work a situation to her advantage just to get what she wanted," informed Sallen.

"Information appreciated," replied Jan abruptly, finding it difficult talking to Sallen. He still couldn't get the past thoughts out of his mind—what she stood for—as hard as he tried, but he hid the fact very professionally.

"You're welcome, sir!" replied Sallen, glad she had been able to help, not knowing what Jan was feeling.

"Tayce, you OK, only you look a bit uneasy?" enquired Dairan in a caring tone, noticing she seemed as if she was fighting something from within.

"I'm fine! Why shouldn't I be? Honestly, I'm all right," she assured him with a smile, trying to dismiss the strong feeling of overpowering dizziness and unable to understand why.

"Prepare your men, Maitland. We're closing in when I give the word, Captain?" said Jan, checking Tayce was ready as he walked by to his men.

"Yes, ready," replied Tayce, still fighting internal powerful feelings that had only come on since nearing the main Operations Centre, though she couldn't understand why.

"Check Slazers are set to 'disintegrate'. Let's go," commanded Jan, authoritatively striding off in the direction of the main Operations Centre ahead.

Both teams went forth. Jan Barnford's men were the first to burst through the automatically opening doors with their Pollomoss weapons primed ready to shoot the first member of the Cripion crew that didn't cooperate. Coming to a stop, they aimed their weapons at the shocked workers that had immediately stopped what they were doing. Thirty-five tough-looking SSWAT men in platex armour were ready to do whatever their chief so wished them to do to bring the crew and its leader to justice for Questa. Tayce couldn't believe how quickly the securing of the Operations Centre had occurred. The men now all looked like statues in their actionable stance. Weapons were aimed at the operatives in front of them. The leader came from a side room and was surprised to see her team had been taken under gun watch by total strangers. She paused mid floor, her eyes wide with anger. She was a slim woman, roughly in her mid forties with sandy-coloured hair that was wiry and swept back behind her head, clasped in a decorative comb in a brilliant red. She was dressed in a velveteen grey gown that seemed to hug her tightly. Tayce thought she looked the perfect female criminal leader in every way. This, thought Tayce, had to be Hydran Corvous. She might have thought she was beautiful, but her make-up made her look like a painted doll. There was something else that unnerved Tayce and she found herself reading into this leader of the Cripions, discovering she held powers of her own and was an equal match for herself. Tayce stepped out, walking clear of Jan and the others.

"Hydran Corvous, I presume. I'm Captain Traun, representing the earth/space headquarters base Enlopedia and the base you annihilated, Questa. You're under arrest for the total destruction of Questa. I strongly advise against you making any sudden moves to escape. These men you see before you are highly trained marksmen. Each has a personal reason for wanting to see you taken down and nothing would give them greater pleasure than to see you get what you deserve, so no power tricks," pointed out Tayce in a cold tone, much to Jan's surprise.

"Young woman, you think you can threaten me. I am the great Hydran Corvous of twenty-three empires—you can think again," retorted Corvous in a grating tone, giving Tayce an unimpressed look.

Tayce stood her ground as Hydran Corvous pushed the guns aside that were primed on her and walked toward her. The men whose weapons were primed on Corvous followed her, ready to shoot if they had to protect Tayce. Dairan didn't like this woman. She reminded him of a galactic sorceress of the worst kind. Twedor stayed out of sight. He feared what she might do to him. Jan studied Corvous. She was one cunning female all right! He could see if he and his men didn't play this right, they could end up being the next victims instead of Corvous. He glanced to Tayce. He could see she was thinking along the same lines, like himself, and it was best to play it cool and give Corvous the idea that she would evade being taken under arrest, then they could take the upper hand just as Corvous made the wrong move and everything could be brought to a quick conclusion. The whole battlecruiser would be theirs to impound or destroy, whatever was best.

"The Captain's right, Corvous—you're under arrest. You can count your dayons of murder and destruction well and truly over. Make it easy on yourself and my men will go easy on you. The outcome will still be the same for you, of course," said Jan, sounding convincing, coming between Corvous and Tayce, giving Corvous a cold look as he knew what he'd like to do to her for what she'd done to Questa and the innocent lives that were lost.

"You are?" she said right back at Jan in her grating voice, giving him an evil displeased look to match.

"Chief Commander Barnford of Enlopedia Security Patrol," he replied, motionless.

"Very well, you win. Maybe I'm tired of destroying things' maybe a change of scenery will do me good, and once I take a look at this Enlopedia I might make it a new target next time around," she said in a careless attitude, surrendering easily.

Tayce upon this was rather glad, but wondered why the whole thing seemed too easy, especially as Corvous had powers. She was suspicious. She ordered Aldonica and Sallen to force-field handcuff Corvous. Both did as requested, but they too wondered why it seemed just too easy and were wondering what plan this Hydran Corvous had in mind once she'd managed to fool them. Jan's men continued to keep her in their current watch status. Aldonica activated the force-field handcuffs around Hydran's skinny wrists.

"You all think you've seen and heard the last of me. Well, my race will come looking for me and when they do they will bring a lot more than one battlecruiser. They will wipe your Enlopedia off the face of the Universe and you along with it. What I've done to Questa will be small compared to what will happen," she retorted.

Tayce and Jan exchanged alarmed glances of wonder. Lance, Craig and Dairan with Twedor decided to join the SSWAT officers, in aiming their Slazers at the Cripion workers at their consoles. They quietly agreed between themselves that the Cripion workers and outside warriors were just biding their time before they turned on their action against the arrest of their leader. They knew Jan's men would no doubt take out the workers present—it was the warriors outside they had to worry about. Sallen, along with Aldonica, pushed Hydran over to the entrance to the Operations Centre. Dairan took out the PolloAld bombs Aldonica had given him earlier, before carrying out Tayce's orders to handcuff Hydran Corvous, getting ready to set it. Jan ordered his men to move back, but stay on alert. He then pulled Tayce out of the centre by the upper arm. Twedor hurried to keep up. Both Dairan and Lance, who had the PolloAld bombs, activated them, twisting the small dial and pushing a small blue button. They continued to the entrance and both threw them together in a rolling motion to send them across the deck floor towards the operatives, then took to their heels, running out through the entrance. The doors closed when everyone was clear. From outside the explosions could be heard going off.

In a matter of minons, all hell broke loose as the Cripion warriors found out Hydran Corvous had been apprehended and were converging on the Amaltheans, the SSWAT members and Jan. They emerged with guns firing. Jan gave the order to take them out and work with the Amaltheans. Twedor activated his Slazer finger and shots rang past him as he joined in the action. Dairan made sure Tayce was beside him in the exchange of orange and blue Slazer fire, out of harm's way. She tried to fire back, but found for some strange reason her dizziness was making her lose her concentration and focus every five minons. She was fighting an inner fight of her own, as well as trying to return fire. It was as if something or someone was pulling her from inside her very existence into total nothingness. She fought back against passing out, the feeling was so strong. Her Telepathian ability was giving her strangest of feelings, as if she was losing total control of her entire body. She could feel something was trying to consume her, take her away to somewhere else. Was this the test? she wondered. She couldn't leave at the present time—it was impossible. She had to think and think fast. She would have to leave the team and Quest in Dairan's command. She looked up at him as he shielded her from the Slazer onslaught, seeing something wasn't right with her.

In the weapon-fire exchange and noise that was going off around them, she made him hear the following words: "You're in command," said Tayce, fighting her immense takeover to wherever.

Before Dairan had a chance to ask again, to make sure he'd heard right, there was a blinding flash and Tayce vanished right before his eyes. The light was so strong it gave the Amalthean team and Jan's team an advantage over the onslaught of advancing warriors, because it lit up the whole corridor and section. Dairan knew it was down to him to lead the team and Quest to a successful conclusion. Where had Tayce gone? he wondered. Was this the test she'd said about at the beginning of the voyage? he wondered.

Quite suddenly, as if Tayce had been still beside him, he heard her voice say to him, "Dairan, I'm putting my trust in you. Get everyone back to the cruiser safely."

Dairan shook his head, thinking this Telepathian test, whoever was behind it certainly had lousy timing. His thoughts quickly returned to the confrontation before him. Lance glanced across to him, asking was he all right? He'd noticed he looked troubled about something. Dairan nodded, immediately continuing without Tayce, knowing she was relying on him to pull off this dangerous situation without anyone getting killed. Jan ordered for Corvous to be taken back to the Patrol Cruiser. He figured that with her out of the way it would make the situation a lot easier. Silence unexpectedly filled the air. Dairan called out around the team, making sure everyone was alive. Cries from each member, giving the OK, came back, much to his relief. He quickly realised it wasn't a bright thing to do, when another wave of Cripion warriors came out of nowhere and another onslaught of firepower erupted. Aldonica came running back down the corridor, dodging weapon fire, having laid more PolloAld bombs under the watchful eye of a couple of Jan's men.

The area was a mass of explosive power on both sides. Even Twedor, beside Dairan, was getting in on the act, giving as good as what was flying through the air towards him and past him. Eventually the SSWAT officers and the Amaltheans won through. The Cripion warriors, much to Jan and the other's relief, were sprawled about the corridor floor in different positions, scorched. For some strange reason they hadn't disintegrated, like they should have. No one could understand this, as everyone's weapon had been set to 'disintegrate', which should have made them vanish on being shot.

"Where's Tayce?" demanded Jan, thinking the worst.

"She had a date with something to do with her power ability—when the powers that be call, you go. You don't argue with them, apparently."

"Just as long as she's all right. I guess you're in charge, then?" asked Jan casually, giving Dairan an uneasy look.

"Yeah, I was kind of thrown in the deep end, you could say," replied Dairan.

Jan turned, ordering his armour-clad officers to prepare to head back to the cruiser. They'd a criminal to return for trial at Enlopedia. Everyone on both teams shook hands. Jan began to say that the battlecruiser might be destroyed in a matter of minons, but they could bet they hadn't seen the last of the Cripion race. Dairan nodded, then wristlinked to Marc back on Amalthea, requesting Transpot. Jan walked to his officers as the Amaltheans dematerialised off the battlecruiser back to Amalthea. He heard the first explosion of Aldonica's PolloAld bombs and ordered immediate Transpot. He made it off the cruiser with split cencron timing, as the corridors in succession began exploding one by one, up as far as where they'd all been fighting.

* * *

Tayce found herself in the equivalent of a dark, misty nowhere. Mist bellowed all around her feet. She could only see a few yards in any one direction. Why was she here? she wondered. There was absolutely nothing in any direction. One thing was for sure: the ground was solid—otherwise she would be falling to God knows where, she thought. Why was she here in this place? she wondered again. There was a certain mysterious creepy feeling that could be felt. What was she expected to do? She decided to walk forward—she certainly couldn't remain where she was. She would be stood there on the same spot forever. Out of the mist, to her utter startled amazement, came new team member Mac Danford, looking uneasy as to why he was present like she was. What was he doing there? she wondered. He seemed unarmed and began walking towards her. Much to her relief, he began assuring her no harm would come to her—she was perfectly safe—even though the current environment was making her feel otherwise. How did he know she was going to be safe? she wondered.

"Where is this place? Why am I here? Come to think about it, what are you doing here? I want some answers and I want them now?" demanded Tayce. She began feeling she'd been dragged into a trap of some kind and Mac was somehow connected with it. She was far from amused.

"Firstly, you're in the Telepathian Realm of Honitonia. Secondly, the reason you've been brought here will be explained to you soon. That's all I've been told," assured Mac. He could see she was very uneasy.

She didn't feel like dropping her guard, even though Mac was present. How did she know this was the real Mac? How did she know this was not someone this so called Empire of Honitonia had conjured up? It bothered her. If this was the real Mac Danford, how come there was nothing in his personal record to specify he originated from their current surroundings? Through the swirling mist walked a tall, thin being of human appearance, roughly in his late forties, in white heavy, long robes with a stand-up collar that shielded half the back of his bald head. His features were chiselled, with the look of pure marblex about them, they were so smooth. He stared at her, giving her a whimsical smile, trying to make her feel a little less under threat. His eyes were the most striking thing about his features. They were the most amazing, darkest blue Tayce had ever seen. They powerfully sparkled. She studied him, trying not to be probing or rude. But at the same time she wondered who he was and whether his age in appearance was his true age. Something was telling her he was a lot older than he appeared. But what she didn't realise was that he was reading her every thought with his amazing powers, as she did. She could see he was a man of very high standing—there was a kind of great supremacy about him, as if he commanded a great source, higher than any normal sense of life. But she could also see he was a being that would not tolerate being pushed beyond his tolerance. He came to a pause just a small way away from her, to make her not feel intimidated by his supreme presence. He might have been powerful, but he could read she was afraid of him deep down. Tayce stepped back. He was like something out of a ghostly dream, she thought.

"Do not be afraid of who I am, Tayce Amanda. I, from this moment forward in your life, will come to play a great role in your future and the future of your abilities. As you grow, so will your gift. I will be there watching from afar to assist where I feel it will help and guide you, for full benefit of your powers," he began pleasantly.

"Why am I here now? What's Mac doing, involved in all this? You tell me you're going to be a part of my future, but not who you are?" demanded Tayce. She wasn't prepared to be totally trusting just yet—she wanted more.

"I am Emperor Honitonia, head of this vast realm you see before you. It's known as the Empire of Honitonia. Your crew person here was picked because you haven't any strong ties with him, unlike other members of your team. They'd allow their personal feelings to discourage you from the tests I will set before you. I asked Mr Danford to bring an item you will need for your tasks ahead. The blue power crystal, Mr Danford, if you please?" asked the Emperor in true command, holding out his slim hand to Mac, to accept the crystal.

"I'm far from pleased. When you abducted me for this so-called test I was in the middle of a dangerous Quest. I had to leave my team to hopefully return to the cruiser alive. I also object to you using Mac here."

"Tayce Amanda, there is something you need to know about Mr Danford here. His mother owed the empire a debt many yearons ago, when we stepped in to help in a matter of life or death with her husband. In return she gave us the privilege to use Mac in circumstances such as yours for the rest of his natural life. We arranged for your communications officer to be Mr Danford, so he would be in a position to help us with what we had in store for you," explained Honitonia, much to Tayce's shock.

Tayce glanced at Mac. She could see he was just as mad as herself at being used. It came to Tayce that the only way out of the debt for Mac was to bargain with the Emperor.

"You want me to undertake this test. All right. If I succeed and gain what is required of me, in the stage of my abilities, then Mac can be allowed to go free and the debt that was owed will have been paid in full; he would have done his duty in bringing me—and God knows how he found it!—the blue power crystal before you. If I fail, then I still take Mac here back to Amalthea, you keep the blue power crystal and I will surrender my abilities. One way or another I won't return without Mac," said Tayce straightforwardly.

The Emperor shook his head. This Tayce Amanda Traun was just like others of her bloodline who had visited the empire before her. Very spirited. He considered her proposal for a minon silently, his features remaining motionless. It looked like he was consulting with others somewhere else. Tayce glanced at Mac—he silently thanked her. After a few minons the Emperor walked forth to come to stand before her. She suddenly felt small against him, because of his powerfulness. What was he going to do? she wondered.

"You have your wish—Mr Danford will go free," said the Emperor.

He reached out and took hold of her right hand, placing the blue power crystal in the centre of her palm. He then discreetly advised her to relax. He could read her nervous feelings of being afraid getting out of hand. He placed a cloaked arm around her shoulders and guided her towards a dark entrance ahead. Mac stood watching her being led away in the Emperor's company, hoping all would go well and she would succeed in her test. Not only so the debt that was owed to the empire could be paid, but because he liked her, and he hoped she walked away with her powers still intact too. He stood in thought. He had no idea she was even gifted until they both arrived at their current surroundings and he had been summoned to help her.

"Your test awaits you in the next grade of your abilities. Let your power and the power of the crystal be your guide. Trust in what you know to be true," said the Emperor calmly.

Even though Tayce wanted to feel brave inside, she was scared for probably the first time in her galactic life. The dark entrance loomed ahead of her and she was soon walking in through the swirling mist. As she entered, the atmosphere grew extremely eerie. The surface beneath her was a dark earthen kind of soil. Not something she expected. Tayce found herself both unsure and unaware of what dangers would strike and when. What would she be expected to overcome first? She kept herself alert, waiting for the first sign of something to present itself. Turning right as the corridor rounded at the end, she was presented with a kind of doorway into a room. Here she was struck with a dilemma—what to do? Making the decision to venture forth, she quickly realised it had been a mistake, as the ground beneath her suddenly vanished and she dropped like a stone. She screamed as she fell. It was like falling down a long dark chute to nowhere. Tayce tried with all her might to grab something—anything—but there was nothing. The drop seemed to go on forever. Dirty soil fell around her as she hurtled at great speed out of control downwards. Was this it? Was she going to die? She'd failed. Suddenly there came the sound of whispering and it seemed to surround her. The voices, both male and female, were very persuasive. They told her to give up the power crystal, give up her powers, over and over again. As she continued descending to God knows where her inner strength rose within her.

"Come on, think of the team. Think of Dairan, but don't listen to the voices," she sternly told herself.

She felt the power of the crystal grow stronger in her grasp and her inner ability grew stronger as well. Without warning the blue power crystal began to literally melt into the palm of her slim, delicate hand. Her Amalthean Quests uniform began to change into a cream wrap-over calf-length gown with wide cream leatherex belt. An aura of bright blue illumination began forming around her head and travelled down her whole form to her feet in a swirling motion. When the transformation was complete, she looked stunning and powerful. Finally she landed on solid ground. Falling to the floor, on landing on her rear she was glad to discover the surface was solid after what she'd been through. She gathered herself together for a minon, summoning up her surroundings. Before her there was a kind of round tunnel heading off into the distance, and a wind was blowing up from somewhere ahead. What did it mean? Where was it coming from?

Climbing back on to her feet, she brushed herself off, then looked both ways. She hadn't realised it before, but the tunnels ran in both directions on either side of her. Back behind her and forwards. Both directions seemed to head into darkness. She looked forward and out of the darkness. At the end of the forward tunnel a diamond-shaped entrance took form. She was unsure of what to do. A male voice spoke, and it was one that made her jump. It had been two yearons since she'd heard Tom's voice, but how could it be him if he was dead? As if by magic he appeared, as real as life itself. This was one sick joke the empire was having with her, bringing a dead man back to life for their so-called test. This was hurtful. Her heart sank as she thought back to the end of the last voyage and how he was stolen from her with a single gunshot. She still missed him. But was this the real Tom, or was this some elaborate trick being conjured up by the Emperor for her test? Perhaps he was part of the next task ahead, she thought. Was this to test her loyalty to the empire? Tom was dressed in the same attire as the dayon he'd disintegrated at the hands of the killer on Trinot. She felt overwhelmed as he reached out to touch her face. He was real all right, but how? He pulled her in towards him in a convincing pleasurable way.

"I'm here for you. I'm here to help you through this. You'll succeed if you give them what they want—you know what that is," he said softly, close to her right ear.

"What! My ability? No! Get away from me! You're not Tom; you're a trick!" said Tayce, pushing the empire form of Tom away from her with force. She knew the real Tom would never ask her to give up her powers.

The Emperor's plan so far was working, in testing if she would give up her powers and the crystal to a copy of something she once loved and trusted. So far the Emperor's estimation of Tayce was proving true—she was turning out to be quite a good student. How could she have been so foolish as to think Tom had come back? Tears formed in her eyes and began to fall. This was hard, she thought, but she had to focus; otherwise she would lose her gift. Tom, before her, smiled and confirmed she had passed her second phase. She found it near impossible, for some strange reason, to not be enticed by this Tom before her. Even though she had pushed him away, she found it impossible to resist the pull of his allure. As he lowered his head to kiss her, she let him. But quickly realised she'd been fooled again when his hand slid around her delicate neck and he tightened his grip. She fought to get him to stop—why had she been so stupid as to lose all sense of the moment and drop her guard?

"Stop! Please, no! You're hurting me. Why?" she begged, as she was losing the struggle to break free.

He didn't answer and the look in his eyes changed from a softness to pure powerful coldness, darkness. His features turned from handsome to an evilness. Deep down inside, Tayce suddenly knew that to survive this she had to fight back using her powers. Slowly she began and the strength grew from within her. Her powerful ability rose inside and she pushed Tom off with force. He vanished into thin air. Tayce, for a moment, tried to gain her composure as her body was shaking and her breathing had all but been throttled out of her. But she'd won. Walking on down the tunnel, wiping the tears from her face through the emotional hurt, with the sleeve of her gown, she felt cheated to think the empire could have done such a thing towards her when she hadn't done any vile act towards them. This test was evil and unfair.

* * *

Back on board Amalthea Dairan entered Organisation with Lance and Twedor not far behind. Marc stood in the middle of the centre, looking angry, waiting to hear why Tayce was not with them. Dairan saw the look of thunder on Marc's face, wondering what was wrong.

"Where's Tayce?" he demanded, giving a look to say he was waiting to hear.

"We need to talk in the DC for a moment," suggested Dairan.

Marc nodded, then turned to head on inside with Dairan following on behind. The doors closed, sealing them off from the Organisation team so they wouldn't hear what was being discussed. Marc walked around the back of Tayce's desk and dropped into her swivel chair. He looked at Dairan in a questioning way.

Dairan leant on the wall nearest the desk, looking at the floor then up again, not knowing how to begin what he had to say.

"It all started when we were finishing the apprehension of the Cripion leader. She looked at me as if she was trying to tell me something was about to happen, then without warning she just disappeared in a blinding flash, which blinded all of us for a few cencrons. I heard her order me to make sure the others got back safely. If you want my opinion here, I think the test she told us about has begun and she's where she needs to be to achieve it," explained Dairan casually and calmly.

"Sorry—I thought the worst had happened, considering what she's like for being irrational. I guess all we can do is wait for her return. Let's hope it all goes well for her. Good work in getting everyone back safely," praised Marc, relaxing, knowing Tayce was safe and not dead.

He thought for a minon about Tayce, hoping she wasn't going through too bad a time. He asked what Hydran Corvous was like. Dairan began by saying she had sandy-coloured hair, which was swept back off her face, and eyes that were somewhat cunning, to say the least. The average run-of-the-mill female criminal. She had quite a curvy figure, which to some would be appealing. Definitely not his type! Marc laughed, then asked if he'd seen Mac on his travels up from below, as he'd gone for his break about an houron ago and somehow vanished and no one had managed to find him. Dairan shook his head, exclaiming he hadn't seen him since before he'd left for the Quest to the Cripion battlecruiser.

"Where is he and what the hell's he playing at?" asked Marc, far from amused at Mac's sudden vanishing act.

The desktop screen activated and Kelly confirmed she had done a cruiser scan sweep and Mac was not in his quarters and was nowhere to be found on board.

"Thanks, Kelly," said Marc.

"I know this is a long shot, but do you think by some bizarre coincidence he could have disappeared where Tayce has gone and somehow he's connected with the test where she is?" put Dairan, thinking about it.

"You might have something, but why didn't it mention about his link to wherever Tayce is in his personnel record when he joined?" replied Marc, thinking of the possibility the two were linked—Tayce vanishing to wherever and Mac disappearing not long after.

"Maybe I'm being an idiot here—I don't know," replied Dairan, wondering if it was a silly thought.

"No! It does seem feasible. We don't really know much about Mac other than that Lydia put him up for the communications position. I guess we'll just have to wait until the test is over and see who comes back. Anyway, you're in charge," ordered Marc, rising to his feet, walking out from behind the desk.

"Where will you be if I need to contact you?" enquired Dairan as Marc began on the way to the entrance.

"I'm going to wait in Tayce's quarters. She's going to need a familiar face when she returns. I've got some work I can do via Amal until she does," replied Marc, thinking about Tayce and what she'd said about her fear of failing the Telepathian test.

As the doors parted, the warm air rushed in from Organisation. Marc walked on out, off to Tayce's quarters, whilst Dairan resumed his command, being in charge of the Organisation team. Something he hadn't thought he would be doing so soon after Marc returned to his duty, after his accident. He figured both Marc and Tayce must have realised they liked what they saw in him taking command the last time at such short notice.

* * *

In the Realm of Honitonia Tayce was progressing in her test. The empire was in the universal realms of Mid Zone. Some people had been known to call it Nothing Space because if you weren't careful travelling through it, you could drift endlessly forever, or until you no longer existed. But if it was the Realm of Honitonia you sought, then you would find it if you were gifted. Mac felt lost as he sat on the stonex slab seat. He was praying silently to himself, that Tayce would make it through the test and come back safely. He also wondered how in space sake he was going to explain to Commander Dayatso how he'd disappeared upon going for his duty break nearly two hourons ago, and where he'd been during that time. He glanced across the vast open space at the Emperor, watching Tayce endure her many feats put forth before her, on a podium screen. A smile crossed his calm features when he felt the whole test was looking very much in his favour of gaining the power crystal and Tayce's powers to keep at the empire forever. But he was also realising that Tayce Amanda Traun was somewhat different to other young Traunian candidates in the past. She showed spirit, determination and courage. Maybe she deserved to hold on to her gift, as she certainly was worthy of it. But it wasn't just his decision to allow her to do so. It was a decision for the empire's higher minds. He watched as Tayce had to endure the fourth of her tasks, and that was the test of illusion, of good and evil.

* * *

Tayce found herself walking into a chamber filled with a bright-purple misty telepathic energy force. She looked down at her right hand, and once again the white aura of the power crystal was swirling fast in the centre of her palm. Out from nowhere came a pure ball of light. Tayce sensed it was evil by the way in which it glowed. It hung for a few minons in mid-air in front of her, then without warning it came straight for her. As it neared, so it enlarged until as it reached her it engulfed her. She was trapped inside like being inside a non-penetrable bubble of clear platex. The evil force within the aura had trapped her and was trying to make her give up her powers for good. The evil force planted untrue situations in her mind, of close friends trying to entice her to let go of her ability. Incidents that seemed real, that would never generally happen, played out in her mind. Tayce knew she had to keep her wits about her, keep in mind the fact that all that was happening was down to the test. The more the power between good and bad prevailed, the more the white and pink forces fought back and forth. Occasions flashed into Tayce's mind seemed so real. She fought back the onslaught of tears and emotional pain in trying to handle what was untrue. In the moments of struggle that passed, the white aura of protection and the pink evil force were mingling so fast it was near impossible for Tayce to comprehend. Abruptly everything stopped. Tayce stumbled, giving a great sigh of relief. These tasks weren't getting any easier, she thought. She felt drained and staggered weakly against the chamber's stonex wall, resting there for a few cencrons.

"How many more of these do I have to endure?" she called out into the empty surroundings.

No reply came, and the Emperor conjured up another illusion, this time of someone Tayce didn't want to come face-to-face with ever again and knew wouldn't be present—Countess Vargon. Also an old version of someone Tayce knew not to be the real thing—Sallen! All around Tayce her surroundings changed. She was placed in a situation where Vargon had recaptured her daughter from the present dayon. Vargon's intention was to put back the evil past that had been wiped from her mind. Strangely enough, this Sallen was remarkably like the current Sallen, on Amalthea. She had no recollection of her evil past and called out for Tayce to help her. This illusion, thought Tayce, was even more lifelike than the last.

"You can free her if you give me the crystal, Traun," said the lifelike countess, promptly holding out her hand to accept the crystal, with an evil cold look.

"I would give her the crystal, Tayce Amanda. You want Sallen back, don't you?" said the Emperor inside her mind, testing her loyalty to the empire once again.

"No! This whole illusion is total lies. Her being present is just another of your powerful tricks to make me give up my powers. I refuse to believe this. I won't be fooled any longer," said Tayce, fed up.

In her mind and without warning came the voice of Empress Tricara. She advised Tayce to be extremely careful—the Emperor was a powerful being—but at the same time she should take the action that was right for her in her final judgement on this task. But if she didn't complete it, it would be considered as a total fail for the whole test set before her and she would return to Amalthea powerless. Luckily for Tayce, the Emperor was unaware Tricara was helping her. Because in her power ability she was an equal match for Emperor Honitonia. She had shut him out, picking up the fact she was there to help in mind transference from Enlopedia. But it was wondered whether he did have some notion that something was not as it should be, that there was someone else interfering.

Because Tayce found she suddenly became brave in tackling her last task and wanted to show him she could complete the test. She walked forward towards the conjured-up illusion of the Countess and threw a ball of pure energy at her. Upon impact, the Countess screamed in ear-piercing agony and turned to pure pink evil energy in the silhouette of her true form, then blew apart in a thousand sparks. Sallen vanished too. Tayce smirked. Did this Emperor think she was that naïve? It had been too easy to get rid of the Countess for her to have been the real thing, and she was still locked up as far as she knew. She would have retaliated anyway in some way. She knew her to be a treacherous bitch.

Abruptly the task stopped, signifying the test was complete. Everything around Tayce returned to normal. But she wondered if this was the calm before another dangerous task took form. The mist returned, blowing all about her. She was back where she entered the test earlier. The Emperor walked forth with Mac by his side, delighted she'd accomplished everything set before her. Mac noticed she looked drained.

He silently mouthed, "Thank you."

"You have done well, Tayce Amanda. I'm pleased to tell you you retain your abilities. You have achieved all that has been set before you. I hereby keep my word regarding what you asked earlier. Mac Danford is to go free—the debt has been paid. You're a good student of the empire, young woman, even if a bit spirited. You will represent the empire well. We are pleased to have you as a student, to serve us," announced the Emperor with a whimsical smile.

"Let me say this before I go—it's Tayce, not Tayce Amanda. Also, the powers that be here need to brush up on what Countess Vargon is about. Your version gave in too easily. As for Tom, he never would have done what he did to me," pointed out Tayce.

"The people in your test were mere test subjects, but your comments have been noted. Well, Tayce, use your abilities only for the greater good. I will be watching you and might even visit on occasions. I will let Mac tell you more of why he was used by the empire in his own time," replied the Emperor.

The Emperor looked at Tayce. He noticed she'd gone pale. Mac glanced at her also noticing as much.

"Captain, are you all right, only you look pale?" asked Mac, truly concerned.

Upon his words, what little strength Tayce had drained and she fainted. Mac quickly caught her in his arms. Honitonia suggested he take her back to Amalthea where she could rest. With this, he used his powers and returned both Tayce, who was totally exhausted, and Mac back to Amalthea. He raised his hands and a strong and powerful wind blew up out of nowhere, accompanied by a blue aura. It enlarged and engulfed both Tayce and Mac.

"By the power of the Empire of Honitonia, return these two mortals to their rightful place of existence," he commanded.

Both Tayce and Mac vanished from the Realm of Honitonia. Tayce would be returned to her quarters and placed on her bunk, by Mac, for a much needed rest. It would be here Mac would tell Tayce the whole story behind his being used by the empire, how his father, a member of the empire, was near to death when his mother offered up his life as payment for bringing her husband back. Mac appeared in Tayce's quarters with a blinding blue flash. He scooped her up and gently placed her on her bunk. Marc, who had been waiting for Tayce, had to shield his eyes from the blinding brilliance of the flash for a few minons. Once over, he was surprised to see Mac standing by the bunk. Tayce began to come round from her faint and sat up, resting on her elbows, focusing on the familiar surroundings, glad to be back. Marc crossed to her, glancing at Mac, wondering what was going on. He sat on the bunk beside her. She looked at him, tired.

"Don't be angry with Mac—he's innocent in all that's gone on. Mac, everything is fine now. We'll talk later if you want," she assured him.

Mac left Tayce in Marc's care and walked on out, heading off to his quarters, feeling in a way happy knowing he no longer had to help the empire. But how was he going to explain his absence for such a long time away from duty? He had only one option: to tell the truth. The quarters doors opened on approach, and he walked on out. Tayce in the meantime fell into the warm and secure arms of Marc and he assured her it was all over. Tayce relaxed against his warm chest, glad to be back.

"Thanks for waiting here for me," she said softly and tiredly.

"Where else would I be? You mean the Universe to me. You're kind of like a little sister," he said softly to her.

After a few minons of warm comfort, Tayce broke away and looked up at Marc. He looked down with a gentle, warm smile, noticing she had been crying by her wet tear-stained face. He suggested Donaldo check her over, just to make sure she was all right and only tired from her ordeal. Tayce agreed. She swung her feet round to slide down to a standing position on the Repose Centre floor. She slightly toppled. Marc quickly steadied her, understanding how she was feeling. She quickly assured him she'd be fine in a while. Both began on out of the Repose Centre, across the Living Area of the quarters to the entrance. Upon approach, the doors to the outside corridor opened and they continued on out. Heading on down the corridor, Tayce began to explain why Mac Danford had been with her. Marc listened, giving her his full attention, and found what she was telling him hard to believe, even though it was true. On the way to the MLC she explained about the power test, but was finding it hard as her concentration was coming and going, owing to her tiredness.

Upon reaching the MLC, they entered as the doors opened before them. Donaldo turned, concerned by her tiredness. Treketa began over as Tayce stumbled yet again. With Marc's help, they lifted Tayce on to a medical bunk and gently lowered her down so she could rest. Donaldo crossed with the Examscan.

He looked down at Tayce as he approached, concerned. Treketa stood by, patiently waiting for orders of what Donaldo needed.

"I'm guessing this has something to do with what you told me about the test?" asked Donaldo softly.

"Yes, and I managed to keep my abilities. How did the Quest finish? Has Corvous been brought to justice?" asked Tayce, glancing at Marc questioningly.

"Yes! She's safely on her way back to headquarters for a much deserved trial, though Jan did ask where you had suddenly vanished. Dairan explained what happened," replied Marc, watching Donaldo.

"That's something I wish I could have seen," replied Tayce, thinking amused of Dairan doing his best to try and explain her mysterious sudden departure. Jan probably thought he had lost the plot.

Tayce found herself drifting off into a deep slumber. Donaldo glanced at the overhead monitor, making sure all her vital signs were what they should be, in that she hadn't relapsed into some kind of power-drained unconscious state. But it was fine. He ordered Treketa to fetch an injection that would aid in Tayce regaining her full strength and health. Whilst he waited, he asked if there was any sign of the missing Mac Danford. Marc explained he'd arrived back at the same time as Tayce did, strangely enough. But he would let Tayce explain more when she was feeling up to it. As Treketa walked back, Tayce began to wake up. She looked up into Donaldo's brown warm, caring eyes.

"Enjoy the sleep?" he asked calmly, taking the injection from Treketa and administering it to her neck.

"Sorry—did I drift off?" she asked in a tired way.

"It's fine. You probably needed it after all you've just gone through" he assured.

As the injection Donaldo had administered hit home, Tayce found herself feeling a little more restored from her ordeal. It was obviously fast-acting and she could feel her inner self beginning to come back to normal.

"Feeling a little better?" asked Donaldo, interested.

He glanced at her vital signs on the monitor once more and noticed they were levelling nicely to what they should be.

"Am I going to live?" asked Tayce, noticing him studying the readings, waiting.

"Apart from a bit of exhaustion from your ordeal, you'll live. That injection I've given you will restore your health back to normal, but I want you to take it easy for a couple of hourons. Is that understood?" he said, looking at her in a more stern way.

Whether she would take his advice was another thing. She slowly sat up and Marc helped her back down off the bunk. She thanked Donaldo for making sure she was OK, then began on out in the company of Marc. As she reached the entrance doors, they parted and she and Marc walked through. Treketa went back to clearing up behind Donaldo, putting the equipment away, he'd used.

* * *

Tayce sighed as they began on up the corridor. Marc paused and reached out pulling her back gently in front of him. As she came face-to-face with him, he put his hands on her slim shoulders and looked softly into her blue eyes, studying her for a minon. After a few minons he firmly advised her to for once take Donaldo's advice—take it easy for a while. He could take command until she felt up to returning to duty. He did not want a repeat of her astral exhaustion, like she suffered back in 2417. Upon his stern but caring words, she smiled.

"All right, you win. I'm not going to argue this time," she announced, much to his relief.

He removed his hands, suggesting he go and relieve Dairan from temporary full command. Tayce headed away towards the Deck Travel. She wanted to see how Mac was doing after their visit to the Realm of Honitonia. She realised Marc was beginning to trust Dairan being in command, and she was glad see it.

She soon reached Mac Danford's quarters on Level 3. Depressing the door intercom system, she waited. After a few minons, the doors slid open to reveal Mac waiting on the other side. He gave her a thankful warm, friendly smile, glad she was all right. Tayce read his thoughts and found he seemed a lot more relaxed and was glad to be free of the debt to the realm.

"I was really worried when I left you in your quarters earlier," he began.

"I'm fine—just a bit tired, that's all," she replied, walking into his quarters.

"I feel you were really brave—what you went through. Would you like a drink to celebrate the fact you got to keep your abilities and I'm a free man?" he asked, heading over to the drinks dispenser.

"Great idea, but no thanks. Donaldo just gave me something to restore my health, after what I went through. I really came to see if you were OK, I can see you're fine," she said, glancing around, impressed at how quickly he'd made his quarters like home.

"Before you go, I just want to apologise for the fact I didn't tell you who I was when we met on Enlopedia—my connection with the Empire of Honitonia. I'll tell you the full story one dayon."

"Forget it. We now know you were sent here firstly because of your connection to the empire. Let's start afresh. I suggest you start by heading back to your duty post and we'll take it from there," said Tayce calmly with a slight smile.

Mac nodded in reply. Tayce turned and began back to the entrance doors. They opened and as she walked through she called back to him to say she'd see him up on duty. As she began up the corridor she began thinking she was nearly back to her normal self. With this in mind, she decided to head on up to Organisation to see what was happening instead of what Marc had suggested earlier.

* * *

Amalthea was gliding at cruise warp 4 through the current calm sector of space. Everything on board had returned to normal since the apprehension of Hydran Corvous. Marc was in full command once more, watching over the duties of the team in Organisation. Tayce sauntered in a while later. He glanced up, surprised to see she was even present, considering what Donaldo had suggested earlier. He left looking at what Lance was showing him and walked to join her mid floor. Just as he paused, Mac Danford hurried in and headed to his duty position, much to everyone's surprised looks, wondering where he'd been.

"What are you doing up here? I thought Donaldo wanted you to take it easy, and that's just what I suggested too," he discreetly reminded her.

"Don't start, Marc! I'm fine," she replied insistingly.

He said no more. He knew better than to push his concern too far where Tayce was concerned. She headed away and went to walk past Lance in the direction of the DC, but he reached out and grabbed her gently by the wrist. She halted and looked back as he squeezed her wrist gently. He silently asked was everything all right? Was it all over?—meaning the test. Tayce nodded, informing him everything was fine. With this he let her go on. He watched her go, realising for the first time they'd come a long way since the dayons they were childhood buddies. In the last few yearons, they'd become really close true friends. He could confide in her as she could him on any matter. He thought for a moment and figured that if both their fathers were watching over them at that moment, they would probably be proud to know the fact.

Upon entering the DC, Tayce crossed to her desk. Upon reaching it, she turned to look out into the Universe for a few minons, noticing how calm it was. Then she turned back and sat down relaxingly on her chair. Dairan entered the DC carrying two cups of liquid refreshment. He hit the door-closing panel as he passed, with his elbow. Crossing, he set Tayce's drink down on the desktop and began informing her that they were back on voyage course to continue exploring. He studied her as she looked up at him.

"How did it go—you breaking the news to Chief Barnford about my sudden disappearance?"

"After you disappeared and left me to explain to the Chief where you'd gone, I think he thought I'd lost the plot, so to speak. He gave me a real uneasy look when I told him you were gone for a test of powers," replied Dairan, sipping his Coffeen, amused about it.

"Don't worry, I guess I put you on the spot," she replied with a gentle smile.

"Forget it. You couldn't help it. Before I go off duty, one thing puzzles me—Mac. Where does he fit into this?" asked Dairan, interested. "Marc said he arrived back with you?"

"It's a long story. I'll tell it to you when we have a quiet moment. You go and take your duty break—you've earned it," suggested Tayce, not wanting to talk about it at that moment.

Suddenly the Telelinkphone on her desktop made a buzzing sound. Twedor, who had been on standby mode, came on full operation mode and picked it up, ready to hand it to her. Tayce was reaching out to take it when the DC doors opened and Marc rushed in. He was far from his normal calm self. His friendly features were alert and he looked gravely concerned about something. Tayce let Twedor find out who was on the other end and prepared to listen to what was bothering him. Dairan hung around, giving Marc his full attention. Twedor put the call on hold and turned his attention to Marc. It appeared it had something to do with the cruiser he had served on—the Astrona Star—before the current voyage. As soon as Tayce could see Marc's problem was urgent, she ordered Dairan, before he went off duty, to have Mac find out what the caller wanted on the Telelinkphone, telling him she would come back to them later. On this, Twedor suddenly announced it was Empress Tricara.

"Dairan, tell Mac I'll get back to her," ordered Tayce.

He nodded in agreement, heading on out, as he could see Tayce was preoccupied by Marc's problem involving the Astrona Star. As he went, so he shrugged off the thought of relaxing for a couple of hourons, forcing the tiredness to the back of his mind. Tayce rose to her feet, crossing to Amal's wall drinks dispenser to get a refill for her Coffeen, which she'd finished. Marc didn't know how to break the news he had to put to her. She'd only just got back from her ordeal in the Realm of Honitonia.

"I really don't want to lay this on you so soon after what you've just been through: they need me on the Astrona Star, like yesteron, apparently," he said thoughtfully.

"But I thought your friend returned to full command of the Astrona Star when you returned to us for this new voyage. How long will you be needed for?" asked Tayce, startled by the news.

"A monthon at the most. I'm sorry, really I am, but I did promise, if they ever needed me, to just call. I had no idea it would be so soon," he replied. He could see she was far from pleased.

"What's it for anyway? Will you be in command again?" she asked, curious.

"Probably. Timec Bayston was good to me when I was on the Astrona Star. He had a lot of faith in me. He was the only one to give me a chance when I was cast out at the end of the first Amalthean voyage. I owe him. He has to attend to an emergency on his home world and he couldn't think of anyone he could put his trust in to command the cruiser in his absence. Really, the cruiser is half mine anyway. I brought a share of it when I joined his crew. I'll be back as soon as possible, I promise."

Tayce paced in thought. Really his duty was to Amalthea and she was far from pleased. Poor Dairan would be expected to step back as her second in command; but if it had to be done, then it had to be. Twedor watched as she continued to think for a cencron, pacing back and forth. Marc studied her, hoping she would let him go. Twedor looked from his mistress to Marc and back again, waiting for something to be decided.

"I can't say I'm pleased at the untimely request; but if you have to do this, then you have to. You can take my Quest 3 shuttle/fighter. It will get you there in no time. I want to hear everything you've been doing when you return," she said sternly.

"You've got it," he replied wholeheartedly and walked over to her.

He brought her into a thank-you hug, thanking her for being so understanding, then kissed her gently on the cheek. He let her go and hurried away to get packed to leave. Twedor watched him go, hoping he would be safe whilst he was gone. Tayce realised it had been the first time Marc had kissed her on the cheek goodbye. She shivered and her senses gave her an uneasy feeling he wouldn't return.

"It's certainly going to be quiet around here whilst he's gone," spoke up Twedor in his usual childlike male voice.

"He's only going for a monthon—besides, Dairan will be filling his place and he can more than make up for Marc at times in volume," replied Tayce, not that she was implying Dairan was rowdy in any way.

Without further word, she walked on over to the doorway of the DC and out through the open doors into Organisation, looking around at the busy team. Lance caught her eye. He was finishing some late research work.

"Looking for anyone in particular?" he enquired.

"Dairan. I have to tell him he's taking over from Marc once again," she replied casually.

"Just after informing Mac about the call you had come in and put on hold, he headed off duty," he replied.

"Thanks, Amal. You're in command—that goes for Marc's departure also. I'm turning in. See you in the mornet. Don't work too late," said Tayce to Lance in a soft ordering tone.

She walked out of Organisation and off down the corridor. Twedor followed on, looking about as he walked beside her. He was making sure the functions on board with Amal were operating as they should, as she had informed him via high-frequency link that the cruiser had gone into 'night-hourons mode'. He began running the scan checks on the many onboard operating functions, ready to report to her via the same high-frequency link if a particular operating function wasn't working as it should be. It would be noted and Craig would check into it at first light, when he came on duty. As Tayce and Twedor were about to walk down the Level Steps, Lance called out to her, asking her to wait. She naturally waited. As he reached her, so he suggested they head on down to Level 3 together. She agreed. As they went on, Lance began to say he hadn't had the chance to congratulate her for bringing everyone back together for the current voyage. This Tayce was pleased to hear, as she had wondered how the team felt. He continued, saying that he for one was glad to be back travelling in the perilous Universe and among friends he thought he would never see again. Tayce figured on these words that this current voyage was going to hopefully be as successful as the first. On the Quarters Level, Level 3, both went their separate ways. Lance went on to his quarters and Tayce and Twedor walked in the opposite direction to Dairan's quarters. She came to a pause outside. She pushed the intercom/announcement button, waiting. After a few minons the doors drew back to a sight Tayce wasn't expecting to see, and it slightly made her feel flushed. Dairan stood inside in a state of half-undress. She tried to hide her somewhat shock at his appearance. Sure enough she'd, seen Tom in a similar state many times, but they were joined. She found herself studying his well-formed and maintained upper tanned torso, with interest. Twedor did what was termed a wolf whistle, just for the sheer cheek of the moment. Dairan caught on to what Tayce was thinking and smiled a relaxed warm smile to make light of the awkward moment. He could see what she was thinking and found it quite amusing. He'd just stepped from the solar massage shower with a towelling wrap around his waist to his knees, his short dark-brown hair glistening in the ceiling lights. How much more could she take? she wondered. Was he doing this on purpose? She noticed the way he was looking at her.

"Would you like to come in? Sorry for my appearance," he said, breaking the silence of the moment.

"I won't take up much of your time. You're probably busy," she began, and found herself sounding like she'd never seen a half-naked man before. She was nervous which was stupid.

"What's the problem?" he asked casually, ignoring her feeling awkward.

"I need you to take back your duty of full command with me. Marc has had to leave the cruiser for urgent business, so tomorron I need you back as my deputy, so to speak," she announced, finding it near impossible to keep her mind on what she had to ask him, in his current state of undress.

"Sure—of course. Actually I caught Marc before he left. He gave me strict instructions to take care of you in his absence," he replied, not the least bit uneasy about his appearance.

Tayce, without warning, went into a fit of the giggles, much to Dairan and Twedor's surprise. She was thinking if she needed protecting at that moment, or if he had to rescue her, he'd look far from what he was—a member of a crime-fighting team, dressed in his towelling wrap. Dairan gave a look as much to say do you want to share the joke? Tayce did and they both ended up laughing. He suggested that if she'd like to stay he would slip into something more comfortable. How about a double bunk, with her? she thought. Then she quickly tried to bring her feelings back to normal, which wasn't easy having seen what she'd just seen. Dairan hurried away, leaving Tayce to make herself comfortable. He soon returned and crossed to the drinks dispenser, asking would she like a drink?

She agreed. Twedor stood to one side, going into standby mode to conserve his energy. Tayce and Dairan soon began to relax in each other's company. They talked well on into the early hourons of the next dayon, when a new Quest dayon would begin.

6. The Space Triangle

It had been three weekons since the Cripions had been destroyed and their leader, Hydran Corvous, taken for trial at Enlopedia. The trial had taken place where Hydran Corvous had answered for her unmerciful act of destroying Questa and had been sentenced to immediate termination of life. In her case, considering she had powers, the person in charge of carrying out the befitting end would make sure she died an agonising and justifiedly slow death. The Amalthean Quests team had accomplished the bringing to justice of yet another galactic criminal at large. But it was wondered whether her race would surface in the future and carry out what she threatened on the ambush of her battlecruiser. Marc Dayatso, who had left Amalthea, had contacted Mac Danford, informing him he had safely arrived for his temporary command of the Astrona Star. Amalthea was en route to the next point of investigation, whatever it might be. Nothing had come out of Enlopedia to take care of in urgency.

In the onboard Lab Garden Dome, Science Tech Sallen Vargon was planting out new specimens she had grown from seedlings in the Botanical Lab Centre, which was the equivalent of a huge greenhouse. Besides being a science tech, Sallen was in charge of the Lab Garden Dome general maintenance. She had jumped at the chance when Tayce offered her the extra duties, to take care of the plants and make the dome somewhere to go and sit to unwind. She was busy at work when Lance sauntered in, carrying what appeared to be the resemblance of a once healthy plant in a decorative pot. Though it looked, in its current state, as though it was more fit for the recycling bin! He stood waiting patiently until Sallen backed out from between two bushes. He congratulated her on the colourful array of blooms and how the dome was beginning to look truly spectacular in the weekons since she'd taken over its maintenance. Upon standing, Sallen looked at the poor excuse for a plant, then looked at Lance questioningly.

"Can you do anything for this?" he asked sheepishly. "Father gave it to me, to remind me of home."

"Give it the kiss of life maybe!" came Sallen's humorous reply.

Lance guessed he deserved her reply. He then went on to explain that the plant had sentimental value. It was considered a good-luck symbol. Sallen studied the plant, thinking his luck must have run out, because in its current state it didn't look like it could give anyone any luck. It was brown and straggly. She took the plant and walked away to the Gynaebotany Centre, which was generally where Jaul Naven resided, but he was out around the cruiser somewhere. It was adjacent to the dome. She told him she'd try, but she wasn't promising any miracles. She removed a brown leaf from the plant as she entered the centre, crossing to the analysis computer. Upon pausing, she placed the deteriorated leaf into the diagnostic scanner, then pressed a sequence of coloured keys. They both stood waiting and watching as the scan took place. Lance hoped his plant could be saved.

Without warning, the cruiser began shaking violently. Sallen fought to stay on her feet and grabbed Lance for support. The both of them looked around as their surroundings suddenly seemed to be raining chaos. Specimen tubes and numerous storage containers fell from the shelves, some smashing on impact with the centre floor. Equipment shook and rattled on the centre work surfaces. Everything that could slide off somewhere, or fall, did.

Abruptly the shaking stopped; silence filled the air.

"Are you all right?" Lance asked Sallen. "I wonder what that was all about."

"Yes!" replied Sallen with a frightened look on her face, wondering what was going to happen next.

Just as Lance figured they were going to be all right, the onboard alarms sounded. It was emergency red alert. It followed an overhead announcement from Tayce, recalling all Organisation team members back to duty positions immediately! Lance made sure Sallen was all right to continue sorting out the caused mess. Then he left her holding his dying plant, taking to his heels in urgency. Pausing by the door, he apologised for running out on her. Sallen just gestured for him to go on. The doors parted before him. He continued on out, heading on up to the emergency ahead.

All around the cruiser, various team members in off-duty pursuits were leaving what they were doing, heading back to the Organisation Centre for the emergency that had arisen. Treketa and Donaldo left what they were doing, heading back to the MLC in case they were needed for a medical emergency.

* * *

In the Organisation Centre, Dairan, who was acting as commander, crossed to Lance, who had run in and taken up his console. He stood studying the present information arriving on the VDU from Amal, doing a scan of the immediate

Universe. Lance keyed in a sequence. Information began appearing on the screen under the heading 'phenomenon'. The scene that appeared showed a red-and-black swirling giant triangle, big enough to swallow Amalthea. Dairan keyed in a further command to see where the phenomenon sat in the orbit of the cruiser. To his surprise, it was right in their current flight path. It looked as if it could pull Amalthea into uncertainty and a perilous journey in a matter of minons. It would be one that would be treacherous and no doubt life-threatening. Tayce walked from the DC and came to the middle of Organisation, pausing. She crossed her arms as she stood looking out into the Universe through the main sight port. Her immediate point of interest was the swirling sight right in their current flight path. Mac turned at his position, informing her she had a Satlelink relay link call from Chief Traun on Enlopedia. Tayce sighed. She could do without a mother-and-daughter chat at the present time. She turned, ordering Mac to put it through to the DC. As she headed back in, she wondered if her mother's call had anything to do with the fact she'd failed to return Empress Tricara's call earlier. Even so, this communication wasn't needed right there and then, considering what they were facing. The rest of the Organisation team began arriving for their emergency duty, walking in and heading straight for their positions and sitting down. They each took on their specified task and began sorting the information that was currently pouring in on the phenomenon. Twedor was working alongside Kelly at navigations, calculating a possible and safe journey through the triangular phenomenon and out the other side, even if it might be a journey to uncertainty. Dairan crossed the Organisation floor to retrieve a printout of information from the printer that served all the consoles in Organisation. He glanced down, studying it, raising his eyes in surprise at the content, which told him what they were about to enter into. He began briskly across the centre and headed on into the DC, knowing Tayce would want to see the latest. He paused as he saw she was on the Telelinkphone and in conversation with Chief Traun. Upon seeing he was waiting to see her, Tayce quickly informed her mother he had just brought in what looked like the latest information on the current situation ahead of them. He sauntered over and handed her the information, then stood back patiently waiting for her orders on what she wanted to do next. She decided to read the contents to Lydia, saying that the phenomenon was known as the Space Triangle, then continued to read the report on what they were up against. When she finished, Dairan gestured that he could explain further if her mother wanted to know more. Tayce agreed, handing over the handset. He stepped forward and waited until she'd walked out from behind her desk; then he walked around beginning to explain more fully what they were heading into in case there was some unforeseen complications and they didn't return from the journey.

"Hang up when you're finished. I'll head on out into Organisation to see what's happening so far," said Tayce, leaving Dairan to continue in conversation with her mother.

He began by saying that what they were being drawn into was what was termed extreme danger as far as Quests went, but this one was unavoidable. This time it might mean there would be no means of return to the current Universe. Tayce had just reached the entrance and heard Dairan's last words. It hit her quite suddenly that she might never see her mother ever again. She was almost rooted to the spot at the thought. She'd lost her for three yearons last time; now it looked like, due to this Space Triangle, she might lose touch with her mother for good. It didn't bear thinking about. Then there was Marc—he'd never find her or the team if they couldn't return. Dairan looked up and saw her looking suddenly sad. Had he said something wrong? he wondered. He had no idea she'd just heard what he'd said about being unable to come back. He rose to his feet and announced that the Chief wanted a further word. She crossed back to her desk, realising it might be the last time she would talk to Lydia. Sadness rose inside her as she accepted the handset from Dairan. He gave her a gentle smile, taking the information back out into Organisation. Tayce realised she wouldn't be the only one shocked at the fact they might not come back. The team each had families somewhere in this current Universe and not seeing them ever again would be quite a wrench. She heard Dairan order Mac to have everyone on board attend an emergency meeting in the DC. This was not going to be easy, she thought, telling everyone they might not come back from this unplanned journey.

* * *

In the Organisation Centre Mac carried out Dairan's request, already himself feeling pangs of uneasiness that he might not return to their current time. Kelly turned, announcing that the gravitational pull from the interior of the swirling mass known as the Space Triangle was steadily increasing every half-houron. Twedor agreed with her.

"As the power increases from the gravitational pull, we should decrease the cruiser engines to compensate for the force from the interior; otherwise, if we continue at the current speed, Amalthea will tear apart under the immense strain we'll be under," said Twedor.

Dairan nodded. He could see Twedor's point. He glanced at Tayce, who was now standing at the top of the steps down from the entrance to the DC. She gave the go-ahead for the decrease to take place. She did not want to lose the cruiser for the sake of not taking some advice. Twedor knew what he was talking about because of his experience of similar situations in the past, where the cruiser's speed was concerned. Just as Tayce had given the order, all the onboard lighting and electronics failed. After a few minons, emergency power cut in. Craig Bream stood up and moved his swivel chair out from his console. Getting down under the console, he removed the main electronics panel, beginning to examine the internal workings. But as he brushed his hand near to one of the circuit panels, so an electrical blue surge spat at him, making him withdraw quickly to avoid being burnt. Tayce, seeing what happened, crossed, activating her light pencil torch, handing it down to him on pausing beside him.

"Try this. It will be a lot easier. Get power back as soon as possible," she ordered, feeling like they were all suddenly vulnerable, not having the cruiser at full operating power.

"Don't worry, I'll have it up and operable in no time," he replied assuringly.

"No more accidents! We don't want you injured, especially with what we're facing," said Tayce, concerned.

"I'll be fine, I promise!" he said, starting to find the root of the problem.

"We've lost all communications with sudden power loss. If there were any communications coming in from Enlopedia, they have crashed in the system transit wave," announced Mac.

"Last navigational bearings I managed to get before power failure were that we were within half a milon of the Space Triangle's immense gravitational pull. Sorry to say this, but we've no chance of breaking free once it hits," expressed Kelly, not wanting to deliver bad news.

Upon these words, Tayce knew it was too late to turn back and it was time to hold the meeting. They were on a dangerous journey to God knows where. It was time to put preparations into place to get them safely through. She turned, asking for everyone's attention and for Donaldo, Aldonica and Sallen to be told via the onboard emergency channel the following.

"We are obviously in the full pulling force of this phenomenon known as the Space Triangle, so we now need to secure anything on board against being damaged, in case we encounter strong turbulence," announced Tayce.

As the cruiser began entering the Space Triangle entrance, so the gravitational pull increased rapidly minon by minon until it became the highest degree it could possibly climb to. On board, even though everyone had done their best in such a short time to secure any loose objects, equipment shook and rattled in corridors and rooms all over the cruiser. Where there was equipment and personal belongings that had not been secured properly, everything fell and broke, or was damaged on impact with the surface they fell on. From Sallen in the Lab Garden Dome, through to Tayce and the team in Organisation, except Twedor, they were suddenly finding it impossible to breathe because of the immense force. One by one, all the team members at their duty positions found themselves drifting into an unconscious state, falling to the ground or slumping over their consoles. Twedor glanced around at all his teammates becoming unconscious before his sight circuits. He wasn't let off the effects either. His circuits began to tingle and make him shake. He was, however, glad that before Craig dropped he had managed to restore full power and Amal was back online.

"It's up to you and me, Amal. With my experience and your new technology, we should be able to guide the team and get us through safely, right?" he began, sounding like he was in charge.

"You're correct, Twedor. The team's safety and the transition of this cruiser in one piece through this turbulent journey is our top priority. We'll work together," agreed Amal.

Twedor glanced around at the team in a state of induced deep sleep in their different positions. He hoped this situation was not going to become permanent. Everyone looked peaceful, he thought. There was Mac—he'd slid off his chair. Craig had dropped on to his side and gone into deep sleep where he had been working. Kelly upon standing to leave her duty position had collapsed and was lying on the floor near to the DC entrance. He noticed how her curly brown hair was down across her face and out of its usual neat style. She looked so calm. On looking around, his sight fell on his mistress. He did a soft whistle on seeing her. She was lying in a crumpled heap with Dairan not far from her, as if he'd gone to catch her in mid fall as she passed out. He shook his metlon head in awe at the strange sight. He wished the gravity would ease. It was making his little metlon blue leg sensors strain with fighting to stay in a standing position. He decided to anchor on to Amal's console, with one metlon hand applying a locking pressure, to give his strained sensors some rest. Amalthea travelled on in a gravitational-pulling way into the interior of the swirling red-and-black mass known as the Space Triangle. There was no means of escape. As it travelled into uncertainty, the cruiser's interior was slowly becoming stable, as Twedor and Amal worked together. Twedor began wondering how much more his sensor functions and circuitry were going to take. If his legs didn't feel like they were being pulled from underneath him, then his circuits kept tingling from the sudden power-force energy fluctuations. He hoped this whole galactic trip of involuntary terror wouldn't last long and they would soon be back in normal space on the other side.

Time elapsed—three hourons to be exact—Amalthea was emerging on the other side of the tunnel. Twedor ran navigational checks, having gained full control of his functions when the force began to decrease whilst Amal did a section-by-section, level-by-level check to make sure the cruiser was as good as when it entered into the triangle. It was another Universe, but a calm one. Twedor wondered what yearon it was, as obviously they weren't in 2420 any more. They'd made it, he and Amal, even though for a female she could be downright bossy sometimes. For a guidance computer, she'd done a good job in getting them through, though he wished she'd realise he once held her position on the old Amalthea and had done a great job and would have easily done what she'd done with her technology.

"All onboard functions are fully operational. The cruiser, despite the journey, is unscathed. As you would put it, Twedor, we made it," confirmed Amal.

"I guess we did," he replied, quite chuffed.

"You're correct," replied Amal, to the point.

Throughout the cruiser, it looked like the equivalent of a whirlwind attack. Debris littered many of the rooms, centres and corridors, from bow to stern. The cruiser would need a mass clean-up. Everything was almost silent. The only sounds that could be heard were the quick-reaction engines and interior general operating sounds, confirming all was well and back to normal.

* * *

Back in the DC Dairan was the first person to regain consciousness. He slowly opened his eyes, focusing on his immediate surroundings. A few cencrons elapsed and his vision cleared. He sat up to find Twedor standing beside him with a drink to refresh him. He took the drink and glanced around, noticing everything was as it should be.

"Did we make it?" asked Dairan. "Obviously I'm not dead."

"We're through, but as yet I can't make out what yearon we're in. We're travelling at warp 1. Command is in Amal's guidance," assured Twedor, leaving Dairan to wake Tayce.

Dairan sprang to his feet and crossed to Tayce. He crouched down and sat her up in a supporting hold, with his arm around her shoulders. He lightly patted her cheeks to rouse her from the sleep she'd been induced into by the immense force.

"Come on, wake up. We're through the triangle on the other side," he said softly, looking down at her.

After a while of waiting, Tayce gently opened her eyes, focusing on the shady figure above her. Once her vision cleared, she found herself looking up into Dairan's warm, concerned features and meeting his enticing, warm brown eyes, unable to break free. Dairan also found he was unable to break away from looking down at her. It was like the off-duty time all over again, when they'd really got to know each other, when she'd come to tell him he was taking Marc's place. There was an attraction growing between the both of them and it was growing stronger by the dayon, which was proving tricky. She was his captain—they couldn't mix duty with pleasure, it wouldn't be right.

Twedor came running back into the DC, announcing Kelly had woken and gone straight into sudden convulsions. Upon these words, Tayce slid out from Dairan's supporting hold, breaking the moment between them. She climbed to her feet and hurried on out into Organisation. Duty came first, thought Dairan. He'd been right not to act on impulse and kiss her—she probably would have reprimanded him. He quickly followed on. Even though Tayce was not truly back to herself after the induced state, she had to muster all the concentration she could, making Kelly top priority.

"Get Donaldo up here and fast if he's awake—this is serious," ordered Tayce, kneeling down beside Kelly.

Dairan quickly took care of the request, hoping Donaldo had regained consciousness. Tayce took hold of Kelly, trying to calm her, assuring her she would be all right. Kelly drifted in and out of a sleepy state as her slim body jerked with the convulsions she was suffering. Tears rolled down her doll-like features. She was scared beyond all reason of what was happening to her. Donaldo's voice could be heard answering Dairan's emergency request, much to Tayce's relief. He confirmed he would be on his way just as soon as he could find his Emergency Medical Kit. Dairan turned, informing Tayce, watching Kelly in Tayce's caring hold. Donaldo was on his way. Craig Bream and Mac watched too. Having come back to consciousness, they sat for a moment getting their bearings. Craig felt his head, wondering why it hurt. Then it came back to him: he'd hit it on the way down, on the console ledge. He cursed under his breath, rubbing it. When he brought his hand down, he was glad there was only a slight trace of blood—the kind that signified a slight scratch. He'd live, he thought, and quickly pushed the thought he might have done worse to the back of his mind, proceeding to put the circuitry panel back in its place. Once done, he then helped Mac in getting Organisation back up and running. Twedor assisted where he could. After a while life was slowly beginning to return to some kind of normality. Donaldo and Treketa hurried into Organisation, bringing a Hover Trolley and Emergency Medical Kit. They quickly took over from Tayce. She gently let Treketa take hold of Kelly in a supporting hold, explaining to Donaldo as he began to treat Kelly, what had happened. She had already administered a muscle relaxant from the centre's Emergency Medical Kit to try and calm her. He nodded, knowing she had certain medical knowledge.

"All right, let's get her back to the MLC, where I can make a full diagnosis and run some tests," he began.

Dairan stepped forth, and between himself and Donaldo they carefully lifted Kelly on to the Hover Trolley. Treketa stepped in and covered her with a heat-sealant blanket, up to her chin. As Donaldo began away with the Hover Trolley, he suggested to Treketa that she should check the team around for injuries and treat them, then go below to check the rest of the team. He would get started on treating Kelly. Treketa agreed and took the Emergency Medical Kit to begin checking around the team. The Hover Trolley slowly moved forward down the corridor ahead of Donaldo as he operated it via a handheld slim pad. Tayce watched it go, hoping whatever Kelly had caught was treatable. Treketa moved from one team member to the next, checking their injuries and symptoms of the sudden impact of falling into a deep sleep, during the gravitational pull. Craig was back making sure all the replacements he'd done were fully operational and the cruiser was back to full running capacity. He called Twedor, and with Tayce's permission, took the little Romid to check that the rest of the cruiser was back up to full power.

Without warning, as Tayce turned to ask Dairan to step into the DC, she mysteriously saw her father's face appear in her mind and he was talking to a man. The flash happened so quickly it made her stop in her tracks for a few minons.

"Father!" she said softly to herself.

"Did you say something?" asked Dairan, not catching what she said.

"Would you join me in the DC?" she casually asked, ignoring what had just happened.

"Sure!" he replied, following on behind her.

He wondered if this was duty or pleasure, considering their recent encounter. Upon entering, Tayce crossed to her desk. Walking round, she sat relaxingly down on her swivel chair, relaxing back. Dairan could see it was duty, by the look on her face. He put any notion this was otherwise to the back of his mind till they were off duty.

"Twedor and Amal did a great job getting us through safely. I began to wonder if we would make it at the beginning. But where are we?" asked Tayce. "That's the point?"

"Leave it with me—I'll find out. At least wherever we are it looks calm space out there," he said, looking past her out through the sight port.

"Yes! By the way, thanks for what you did out in Organisation, acting so quickly to make sure we were all all right. Marc would have done the same. Good work!" praised Tayce, pleased.

"Thanks! But it's not needed—I enjoy working with you, you know that," he said casually.

"Well, so far you're proving to be a good relief commander," replied Tayce light-heartedly.

"I'll go and see what I can find out about our current new Universe," he said with a warm smile.

"Let me know the moment you find anything," called Tayce as he headed on out.

Tayce didn't want to say anything about her father's face in her mind for those split cencrons. She wanted to keep it to herself, but she felt a certain familiar feeling—like the both of them were going to meet. Maybe Marc had been right at the beginning of the voyage when he handed her her father's ring. Her father could still be alive somewhere. Maybe somehow this was where he was. She turned to look out into the Universe for a moment, in thought of her father.

"Father, if you're alive and here somewhere in this new Universe, I'm here," she said to herself.

She sat in thought, wondering what he would look like if he was alive and what he would make of what she had become. Then she heard this little voice of caution: was she getting her hopes up too much?

Dairan, out in Organisation, crossed to work with Lance at the research console. Treketa, having finished checking the team, picked up her Emergency Medical Kit and headed on into the DC to check over Tayce, to make sure she hadn't done any damage during the ride of turbulence. She guided the Examscan about Tayce as she sat in her chair. Twedor, to Tayce's surprise, soon returned to her side in the DC.

"That was quick!" said Tayce surprised.

"Craig doesn't need me any longer. Everything seems to be checking out just fine," he replied.

"That's good," replied Tayce, glad everything was as it should be.

"You're fine, Tayce—there's nothing strained," assured Treketa, deactivating the Examscan.

"Thanks! What's the matter, Twedor?" asked Tayce. She could see he was fidgeting, and this generally meant he was troubled by something.

"Nothing! Just musing," he replied, not wanting to say.

"Treketa, tell Donaldo I want a report on Kelly's condition as soon as possible," ordered Tayce.

"Right! I'll ask him as soon as I get back to the MLC," she replied, closing the Emergency Medical Kit and heading on back across the DC to the entrance to leave.

Tayce glanced back at Twedor. She figured the trip through the Space Triangle might have affected him and he needed time for his plasmatronic brain to sort itself out. She sat back in her chair and turned to look back through the sight port into the Universe again. Twedor could see she had something on her mind—and she always shared her concerns with him he wanted to know what was wrong.

"Something bothering you you want to share?" he asked.

"I saw Father's face in my mind a while ago. I wondered if it meant something—that somehow he might be alive after all and out here in this area of space somehow," confided Tayce.

"I hate to disillusion you, but the kind of powerful vortex we just came through gave off some real strange forces. My mind is still in a spin, maybe seeing your father was one of those mind illusionary forces that got left behind while you were in the sleeping state and triggered suddenly, like a leftover strand, when we had passed through. Remember we've been through similar journeys in our time together before, like this, when your mind played tricks," explained Twedor, understanding her need for what she saw to be a reality—Darius Traun, her father, alive somewhere after all.

Tayce smiled. He was right—they'd been through similar occurrences when it was just the two of them. But, somehow, this time around it felt different. She rose to her feet and patted Twedor on the head in friendly way. He was more like a buddy than a Romid sometimes. He was always there when she needed him. Just like the good old dayons when he cheered her up. She headed over to the entrance, wanting to find out if Lance and Dairan had managed to find anything on their current new universal surroundings, other than that they were on the other side of the Space Triangle. Twedor followed her like an obedient child. Once out in Organisation, Tayce paused, glad to see things were back to normal, that the team were back at their duty positions working away.

"Amal, take over navigational guidance until Kelly Travern returns," ordered Tayce.

"Yes, Captain. Taking control now," replied Amal efficiently.

Sallen entered Organisation. She'd managed to escape being hurt in the turmoil and wanted to know if there was anything she could do to help. Tayce thought for a moment, then it came to her: if she was familiar with navigations, she could take over from Amal. She put it to her. Sallen nodded, exclaiming that she could do it. She'd done training in navigational guidance at her training complex on Questa. Tayce gestured for her to take over.

"Amal, release guidance controls to Sallen," she announced.

"Releasing control now," replied Amal.

Sallen looked over the keys for a moment to familiarise herself, then began running checks on their current speed and direction. Her fingers flew over the command keys with ease and speed. Within a few minons she'd picked up something on the navigational scanner. It was large and stationary. Tayce went to her side as everyone around paid attention.

"How far away is it from us?" asked Tayce, coming to a pause just behind her.

"According to this, about a milon. I can't detect if there is any life aboard, though. Whoever they are, they're in total darkness. All engine power and operational functions seem to be in a terminated state," explained Sallen.

"Anything, Lance, to say what it is?" asked Tayce.

"Information coming in states… I don't believe what I'm reading… it's the missing space exploration port, the Quentron, apparently. And I know this for a fact: it first set out in 2416 and, according to this, it's been here in this Universe for the best part of four yearons. It's obviously a victim, like us. As I recall, Father closed the voyage file knowing there was no way of ever finding the port or crew again. Searchers were sent out, but found nothing," explained Lance, astounded the port was right before them.

He wished his father were alive to see the sight he was seeing—that the Quentron was still in one piece. He wondered if Paul Trukanne was still alive. He had been the captain of the space port. It was the first port to be able to move about the Universe, using specially designed engine power. It had been considered the first of its kind and a marvel in the Questa history logs, designed by a genius in the field of ports.

"Amal, run a penetrating power scan over the entire port just to make sure that all power is drained as first thought," ordered Tayce. She was making sure they were receiving what they should be in information.

Amal did as requested and the information materialised on Sallen's screen in front of her. Tayce glanced back at Sallen's screen, studying the information filtering in. Feedback confirmed there were in fact two humanoids on board and that there was low power output. It stated the function for communications was severely damaged. Upon reading the fact, Tayce knew there was no way the Quentron could possibly contact them, or receive anything she sent. She thought for a moment. They were going over to the Quentron. The moment she thought about the port, her father's face flashed back into her mind yet again, followed by the feeling that somehow—she didn't know how—she was going to see him soon. She quickly considered that whoever was left on the port might need medical attention urgently. She began announcing the visiting team to accompany her. Craig of course would go. He could see if he could repair the communications system. Dairan, because he was acting commander. Lance, because he had met Captain Trukanne many yearons ago and would be able to identify him upon possibly meeting him. Finally Donaldo, for the medical treatment that may be required by whoever was on board. Twedor would go, as he was considered protection for herself.

"Mac, you're in charge," ordered Tayce casually.

"You give the word when you reach Transpot. I'll transpot you to the Quentron," suggested Sallen.

Tayce nodded, then began on out of Organisation followed by the visiting team members. Once out in the corridor she began to say as they began walking that she would meet them all in the Transpot Centre. She wanted to change attire for the Quest ahead. Dairan nodded understandingly, suggesting he see her in a while. Tayce ran on ahead, off to get changed into her cream all-in-one Quests suit, leaving Twedor to walk on with the others. Lance and Dairan began discussing the Quentron as Dairan didn't know much about the port. Lance shared some of his memories of the time the port was launched into operation.

* * *

About an houron later Amalthea came into the stationary orbit of the Quentron space port. It manoeuvred to within a milon of the Docking Port. The port was in total darkness. It was a hexagonal shape, roughly four decks in depth and constructed of steelex and glassene. The overall size was a diameter of four square milons. At the head of the hexagonal shape was another. This was obviously the main operations module. The usual Questaline colours ran round the middle of the port—a white, red and green stripe. The top half of the port was white, the bottom black. At the top at the front was the title of the port, 'QSHC QUENTRON SPACE PORT'. QSHC stood for Questa Space Headquarters Colony. Quite suddenly, there seemed dimmed light coming from somewhere aboard. It could be seen through the rhombus-shaped sight ports in one particular area. Hopefully Paul Trukanne was one of the life forms they had detected on board.

Lance Largon, having experienced the construction, and being connected to the launch of the Quentron with his father, stood waiting patiently in the Transpot Centre in deep thought, wondering if Captain Trukanne would remember him as Jonathan Largon's son, if he was alive. It had been a lot of yearons. He glanced around the Transpot Centre, looking at the others, thinking that the Captain would be surprised at where he was todayon. Considering he was something of a tearaway in bygone dayons, when he was with his father. When he thought about it, he wondered if the Captain even knew his father was no longer alive. Tayce walked into the centre as the doors parted, dressed for the Quest ahead. Dairan turned, giving her an impressed smile, noticing her somewhat sexy yet professional appearance. Donaldo followed her, carrying his Emergency Medical Kit.

"This is a déjà-vu trip for me," spoke up Lance as Tayce came towards him.

"Yes, it must be. I can't remember the Quentron quite like you probably can. What intrigues me is who the second life form could be. I keep seeing my father's face appear in my mind suddenly," she confided.

"And your premonitions are never wrong. Lets hope this one proves right for you," he replied.

All five stepped into the Transpot area. Tayce gave Sallen the word when Twedor was ready to commence Transpot, via her Wristlink. She, as the team around her began to dematerialise, stepped outside the area and used her powers to travel to the Quentron. A blue aura surrounded her and she dematerialised, using mind transference to take her from cruiser to port. Hoping the remaining fragments of the force from inside the Space Triangle wouldn't catapult her into God knows where.

* * *

On board the Quentron space port, in a deserted white corridor, the Amalthean Quests small investigative team materialised via the Transpot aura in separate shafts of swirling light. Tayce successfully arrived, much relieved she hadn't failed because of the presence of after-power strands from the Space Triangle. Once everyone had fully materialised, they all glanced around the clean and tidy environment. The port was just like it had left Questa—all shiny and new. It was hard to imagine it was four yearons old and there had been a crew on board. The air was filled with an eerie silence. It was as if at any moment they'd be met by a sudden unwelcome being or whatever. Tayce glanced at Dairan questioningly. He met her questioning look and shrugged his shoulders in jest, not having any idea of what they could expect. They knew who they should be expecting, but would it be who they thought? Craig took out his handheld scanner and began scanning for the two life forms supposed to be aboard.

"They have to be here somewhere," said Tayce beside Craig.

Tayce saw her father again in her mind in a blinding flash. The feeling was a lot stronger than the last time, she thought. She felt it wasn't the Space Triangle playing tricks; it felt incredibly real for some strange reason, as if he was present—nearby even. But where?

"It is known that if the Quentron was abandoned after four monthons, her electronics would automatically shut down," spoke up Lance.

"Well, she can't be abandoned—there are two life forms here on this port, so let's find them," snapped Tayce as the feelings she was feeling over her father's possible presence were pulling at her too strongly to withstand. If he was present, she wanted to know.

"Take it easy. I know you think your father may be here—I heard you talking with Lance earlier—but it's been a long time and perhaps they're nervous about meeting us, as we are them," pointed out Dairan discreetly.

"Let's just go, shall we? Craig, keep trying to find out where those life forms' readings are coming from. Dairan, keep your Slazer ready—you too, Twedor. There's no telling what we're going to be classed as. If this is other than who we think it could be, this port could be on wide alert and consider us intruders, if it's not Captain Trukanne. We don't know yet what or who we're dealing with," said Tayce, heading off towards the entrance doors ahead in eager determination to find out, but on her guard.

"Don't worry, I'll protect you," replied Twedor, activating his Slazer finger ready.

"Lance, you know this port better than anyone—where's the main operations point?" asked Tayce.

"Follow me," replied Lance, heading off and remembering the layout as if it had been yesteron he had been on board with his father.

Tayce walked beside Lance. She apologised for snapping. Dairan was concerned that Tayce was going to be disappointed if they found Darius Traun and he didn't recognise her for some reason, considering how many yearons it was since he had last seen his daughter and how long he had been in space. He could have even lost his memory. He noticed as they went that Tayce was heading on further and further up ahead, out of his and Twedor's protection. He broke into a gentle sprint, Twedor joining him to catch her up. There was no way of telling what was through the entrance doors at the end of the long corridor. It crossed his mind that who they thought was Captain Paul Trukanne and possibly Darius Traun could be in fact be vagabonds that had found the port for stealing, for a pricey haul, back to their home world to be sold.

Just as he reached her and they paused before the doors, they drew back and from what appeared to be the equivalent of the Deck Travel out stepped a humanoid male in his mid thirties. He was tall, of medium build and reasonably handsome. His eyes were hazel; his features were the kind any woman would take a liking to. This was topped off with ash-blonde short neatly styled hair that was swept away from his face. It could be seen, as he came towards Tayce, that he was a man who was friendly yet held great authority. As he saw the team behind Tayce, so he pleasantly introduced himself.

"Please don't be concerned. I'm Captain Paul Trukanne. You have nothing to fear," he began in an Australton Outback twang—Outback Australian Earth-1 tone.

"Captain Tayce Traun," introduced Tayce apprehensively.

"I must apologise for not meeting you on your arrival. I was held up with repairs. Welcome to the Quentron Space Port. It's been a long time since I've welcomed any visitors," he said in true friendly manner, glancing past Tayce at Dairan, who had placed his hand on his Slazer in his side holster, ready to use it if he had to.

"Paul, is it really you after all these yearons? It's me, Lance Largon, Jonathan's son?" said Lance, overjoyed to see his father's old friend after all the lost yearons.

"Lance! Yes, I remember you. You were somewhat of a tearaway in the old dayons. How's your father? This young man, Captain, showed great interest in travelling the stars yearons ago," said Paul, thinking back.

"My father is sadly no longer with us. He died about two yearons ago. It was his heart—they couldn't repair it," said Lance, swallowing hard at the thought.

"I'm sorry to hear that, Lance. Your father was a good man. A female captain? Don't get me wrong, I admire you, having encountered some of the criminals I've encountered along my journey. And who is this little chap?" asked Paul, looking down at Twedor, impressed.

"I am Twedor, escort to Captain Traun," announced Twedor.

"This is Dairan Loring. He's my relief commander. Craig Bream is our computer-analysing technical officer and, finally, Dr Donaldo Tysonne—he takes care of our onboard medical needs. This is just part of my team; there are others aboard my cruiser that make up the Amalthean Quests team," introduced Tayce.

"Come, we'll talk about what has brought you to the other side of the Space Triangle up in my main Action Centre." He gestured for everyone to follow.

As they all began away, Tayce felt she was eager to find out who this second of the life forms that were suppose to be on board was. She noticed Paul hadn't mentioned his or her name yet. She began to feel a bit saddened—it might not be who she thought it was. Upon hearing her surname, she figured Paul would have said he had another person on board that shared the same surname as herself. They all entered the Deck Travel-type lift and the doors closed. They were soon on a fast and smooth journey to the main point of the port. When the Deck Travel-type lift stopped on the requested level, the doors opened. Tayce and the team followed Paul out into the corridor and along to the main Action Centre. Tayce felt confused. Why was it she was still feeling she was going to be coming face-to-face with her father as she neared. She was finding it near impossible to fight the strong continuing feeling that someone she knew was nearby. She forced herself to think about something else, just to keep herself from going insane.

They all turned into a wide open archway that led into a white-and-burgundy-coloured elaborate centre of action where a team would normally be seated around the various consoles working, which were currently vacant. The centre was a standard size. It held twenty working consoles, ten down each side. There was a large lectern-cum-star-chart podium in the centre. At the head of the Action Centre was the Private Meeting Centre belonging to Paul.

"Captain, we were unable to communicate with you as your communications link didn't seem to be working. What's the problem?" asked Tayce, sounding helpful.

"It happened during the transit through the Space Triangle. The force took out the main transmit-and-receive system. It's beyond my capabilities to repair it," replied Paul.

"I could take a look if you'd like me to. Nothing is beyond repair when I'm around," volunteered Craig.

"Help yourself. You will find tools that might help in the store over there," replied Paul, glad someone could help at long last with repairs.

Craig immediately set about checking out the communications console and underneath circuitry, finding it was standard Questonian along the lines of Amaltheas own communications circuitry layout. He knew, by assessing the situation, he could repair it. Tayce looked towards the doors that led into the Private Meeting Centre, wondering why the doors were closed, as on Amalthea her DC doors were always open, except for private moments. Was this where the second life form was hiding?

Twedor looked around at the many computerised facilities. Seeing the main Quentron computer was a standard Questonian type, he decided to try his high-frequency link-up to do a little scan probing of his own and withdraw what he wanted to know. As half the port was down on power, he knew he'd get what he wanted without the system rebuffing him with an electronic shock. As he silently worked away, he glanced at Paul Trukanne, looking like he was listening as he discussed the Space Triangle and its force with Tayce and the others.

"Captain Traun, how would you like to meet the only other member of this crew? I picked him up almost four yearons ago, before I entered the Space Triangle," said Paul.

"Yes, of course, if he wants to meet us," replied Tayce in eager anticipation that it would be who her mind and heart kept telling her it was.

Paul raised his equivalent of a Wristlink and contacted the person, or being, on the other side of the Private Meeting Centre doors, asking him to come out as they had guests. After a few minons the doors drew back and the other life form walked forth. He paused at the top of the two steps. Tayce couldn't believe who she was seeing and gasped. She felt fixed to the spot at the sight of someone she had believed was dead for the past yearons since Traun's destruction. Lance shared her stunned surprise at who was present. He was just as Tayce remembered him—broad-shouldered and tall in stature, with short platinum-grey hair, neatly styled. He had the same handsome features, with a look of great authority about them, the same bluey-grey eyes. He was just a little older and more tired-looking. He still retained the high-ranked dignity of a commodore though, with the fair-minded approach to life, but the warmth she knew as her loving father wasn't there and she could sense great sadness. He began down the steps slowly—not like he would have walked on Traun, with a certain determined authority. Tayce couldn't take her eyes off him. She found it hard to take in the fact that she was looking at her father again after all the lost yearons. She felt like her heart would erupt with joy that he was present and not dead after all.

Dairan was growing concerned. As he had no idea who this man was, he kept his hand on his gun ready.

"My God, Tayce, is it you? You're alive! It's been a long time—let me look at you," said Darius upon reaching her, taking hold of her gently by the upper arms then pulling her into a warm strong loving hug.

Lance quickly halted Dairan in his suspicious concerned action to protect Tayce, mouthing silently that it was OK—it was her father. Dairan sighed, relaxing, studying him. He saw there was a resemblance between father and daughter to convey as much.

"I have so much to ask you," he began in a tired tone, releasing Tayce slightly so he could look at her.

"Don't worry, Father, I'm not going anywhere. We have all the time in the Universe now. You remember Lance, and this is my crew—or part of it. This is Dairan Loring. He's relief commander. That over there is Craig Bream. He's computer-analysing tech officer. And this is Dr Donaldo Tysonne," introduced Tayce.

"It's wonderful to meet you all. A crew!" replied Darius with an impressed nod, looking back at Tayce.

He gave Tayce another warm affectionate hug. Tayce felt secure again, back in her father's loving hold. It brought a slight tear to her eyes. How she'd missed him! She felt the family was back together again. Darius released her gently, taking a more studying look at her, thinking it was hard to imagine that the last time he saw her she was a naïve young girl just starting out in a dangerous Universe. He could see what she had become was a true leader, and a beautiful one at that, obviously doing well with a crew and vessel. Tayce thought to herself it was strange to think of all the yearons that had passed from that fateful night, never knowing her father was alive, and here he was. She wished she'd known he would come back into her life. If she'd known, it would not have been so bad.

"Father, there is just one more person—or should I say Romid?—and member of my team I would like you to meet: Twedor!" said Tayce, introducing him.

Twedor stopped searching the Quentron computer and storing the information. He looked up at Darius and did a quick scan to make sure he was seeing who he was—Darius Traun. His scan confirmed this was Tayce's father all right, even though he was in need of medical attention and rest.

"Hello, Twedor!" said Darius, smiling, impressed by the little Romid.

"Commodore, it's good to see you again, sir!" replied Twedor politely, holding up his hand for Darius to shake.

"Would you believe this is the original Midge from Amalthea One? Craig redesigned him in this new form.

"Really! I'm impressed, young man," said Darius to Craig. Darius nodded, impressed.

Paul could see this was a family reunion of sorts and talked with Lance and Dairan about how he had come to find the Commodore. How he had been surveying a planet called Planus and found a burnt-out Life Pod. Upon looking for a sign of the body, luckily for the Commodore he had been found a milon away, uninjured though unconscious. He was brought back to the Quentron and the then doctor of the Quentron crew, before he vanished during the journey through the Triangle, managed to bring him back to full health. Tayce continued to study her father. It felt good to know he was back.

"I thought I'd lost you forever that night. I thought you were dead when Marc dragged me away, because you were suddenly cut off from my sight in the falling masonry of our home. Marc's alive, Father. He's part of my team. He's just away on a personal assignment at the moment. He was the one at the beginning of this second voyage to hand me your emerald ring. He said it had been found in the burnt-out remains of a Life Pod on a solar world called Planus," said Tayce softly.

"It's a long story, but I put your mother in a Life Pod that night. There were only two left after Marc had successfully got you under way. He came back and helped me escape, the same way your mother did. Tell me, Tayce, is she alive? Did she make it?" he asked, hoping so.

"Yes! She's fine—in fact, she's holding down a leadership position these dayons. She's the chief of Enlopedia Headquarters Base. There have been so many changes, Father. You were telling me how you came to be here?" continued Tayce, listening.

"To cut a long story short, I knew I was going to crash on this planet, then everything went dark. Next thing, I woke up here in their medical facility," said Darius sincerely.

"Thank you, Captain, for rescuing my father. We wondered whether he was alive or not. Many search parties were sent out from Questa, but nothing was found and after a while they gave up," said Tayce, recalling the fact with sadness. Then she smiled, now knowing Darius was safe.

"You don't have to thank me, Captain. Your father here was lucky we found him when we did, but, believe me, he has helped in a lot of onboard repairs, which I'm grateful for," replied Paul with a warm smile.

"Excuse me, Captain—all repairs are complete. It was just minor, but tricky if you didn't know where to find it. It's as good as new—all communications are back online," confirmed Craig, packing the tools away he'd used to fix the fault.

"Much appreciated, Craig. I won't feel quite so cut off now—you've saved me from being isolated," praised Paul.

Darius and Tayce continued to talk about what she'd been doing since she'd left Traun. Darius found some of the things amazing, some not so surprising—namely, Countess Vargon. He liked the concept of the Amalthean Quests team. He was saddened to learn, though, of the demise of Jonathan Largon and conveyed this to Lance.

"Lance, I'm sorry to hear about your father. He was a good man. We used to call him the backbone of the planetary council. He will be missed," said Darius, thinking about the fact his dear friend had gone.

"Thank you. I miss him too," replied Lance, suddenly feeling sad.

Paul shook his head in awe at Jonathan's demise. He shared Darius's feelings—Jonathan had been a good man and a good leader. Tayce let Donaldo take a look at her father whilst she discussed the proposal of offering Amal's services to calculate a safe return journey back through the Space Triangle. That would hopefully return everything back to normal, involving both port and cruiser. Twedor, standing beside Tayce, suddenly cut in, exclaiming that he'd already been recalculating the return journey to 2420. He'd already fed in the Quentron's journey into Amal, via high-frequency link, as they'd been talking. If successful, it would return both port and cruiser back to the original Universe. Paul agreed wholeheartedly with the idea, thinking about the possible return of his 456 crew that had been locked in limbo for the past four yearons. It began to give him hope that he and his crew would be back to normal in 2420.

"Just give the word, Captain. I'll be ready to attempt anything if it means getting this port and crew back," said Paul eagerly.

"When I've done the final calculations I'll transmit the necessary information directly to your main guidance computer!" exclaimed Twedor.

Paul nodded understandingly, amazed at Twedor's capabilities. Tayce turned back to her father, who was sitting down in one of the cream and chrome swivel console chairs, with Donaldo talking to him. She could see Donaldo was trying to assess his condition and fitness, so when they got back to the cruiser he would know what medical treatment he could safely administer to return him to full health, as it had been some time since he had been checked by a medical professional.

"Well, Father, ready to join me and the team here and come aboard Amalthea?" enquired Tayce, hoping he would want to go with her.

"Are you going to be all right here, Paul?" asked Darius concerned. "I could remain until we've reached the original Universe if you want me to."

"It's fine. You go with your daughter. I'll be fine here," assured Paul.

"Did you say Amalthea?" asked Darius, wondering if he'd heard right.

"Yes, but it's not the original cruiser I left Traun in. This one is a lot better than its predecessor. It's called Amalthea Two, though we just call it Amalthea," replied Tayce to her father's amazed look.

"Thank you, Paul, for all you've done. Thank your medical staff also when they hopefully return," expressed Darius.

"You're welcome. I speak for the med team here when I say we were only too glad to bring you back to near-normal health. I'm also glad to see you and your charming daughter have been reunited. Good luck," said Paul, happy for him and Tayce.

Tayce removed her Wristlink/Transpot bracelet, handing it to her father. He, for a moment, tried to figure out how to fasten it, until she took it in hand and did it for him. She would use her gift to travel back to the cruiser.

"Won't you need this? How will you get back if you give me this?" he asked, concerned.

"No, I'll be fine. I'll use my ability. I'm gifted like Empress Tricara, Father. I only have to see in my mind where I want to be and I can be there just like Transpot," she said softly.

"You mean the gift of the Realm of Honitonia of telepathy has come out in you. Well, use it wisely and only for the greater good—never evil," he said, studying her, pleased for her.

Dairan, on Tayce's nod, contacted Sallen back on Amalthea via his Wristlink and requested her to commence Transpot. Tayce closed her eyes and concentrated, using her telepathic power of body transference. She, along with the others, dematerialised from the Quentron, leaving Paul alone to face the return journey ahead. But being alone wouldn't last long if the plan worked. Whatever took the crew of the Quentron would restore them on the journey through the triangle. Paul realised he was totally alone. It felt weird considering he'd had Darius Traun to talk with for the last three to four yearons. He continued on with the repairs in the main Action Centre, as all he could do was wait for the transfer of information to get him under way for the return journey.

* * *

The team and Darius materialised on board Amalthea in the Transpot Centre. Once fully present, Darius looked around impressed by the redesign and spaciousness of the new cruiser in the Amalthean series. It had certainly changed since the last time he'd seen the original design more than four yearons ago. He was glad Tayce hadn't changed the name. The name had originated from a small planet belonging to Jupiter named Amalthea. Tayce brought him back to the present by asking Lance to escort him down to the clothing store to get a clean uniform, then on to Donaldo for a full check-up. Lance agreed, only to happy to do so. As Darius was about to leave he turned back. As the others left he took hold of Tayce again for another fatherly hug, telling her it was good to know she was alive, and he was proud of her. He released her, telling her he'd see her later. He continued on in the company of Lance. Tayce watched him walk away, thinking he hadn't really lost that certain leadership way. Twedor informed her he had work to do if they were going to leave their current unpleasant surroundings. With this, he hurried on out at a brisk pace, leaving Tayce to walk on behind in thought about her father with Dairan, who was waiting for her outside. They walked along back to Level 1, discussing her father in general.

* * *

Three hourons later, Darius Traun entered Organisation feeling a lot more refreshed. He'd had a Vitboost injection, an anti-space-disease jab, plus a health-rejuvenating injection to restore his health to the full in a matter of hourons. Lance left him in the middle of the centre and returned to his duty.

"Welcome to the Organisation Centre. How are you feeling?" asked Dairan politely.

"Amazed! You could say this is quite a cruiser—a vast improvement on the first one. Where's Tayce?" he asked, looking about.

"I'm in here, Father," called Tayce from the DC.

Darius discreetly suggested to Dairan to keep up the good work, then walked on into the DC to see Tayce seated at her desk. As he entered, a great feeling of extreme pleasure and satisfaction came over him, seeing her in the position she was in—the leader of a good team, seated at what he would term her desk of command. She had proved him and Lydia wrong when she was that naïve privileged daughter all those yearons ago. She was now a beautiful grown-up mature woman and an excellent leader and daughter to be proud of. As he crossed the airy modern DC, so the Telelinkphone buzzed. Tayce transferred the call to her desktop screen. Donaldo appeared and began by telling her there was still no change in Kelly's condition. Her help would be appreciated. Tayce agreed. She deactivated the screen and rose to her feet in urgency. She hurried across the DC and out into Organisation, leaving her father smiling to himself, thinking she reminded him of himself back in the dayons on Traun—never a moment to keep still. Tayce, realising she was rushing out on her father, stepped back, apologising for running out on him. But she told him to feel free to explore the cruiser and do whatever he wished—she would catch him later. Darius realised this was one busy environment. Twedor shot past him to catch Tayce up, being her escort. He was doing the final calculations en route for the return journey. Darius walked back out to talk with Dairan, who was more than happy to discuss things. Both laughed at the speed Twedor hurried on out through the entrance, mumbling to himself occasionally as he replied to Amal en route, as they worked on many of the factors that needed to be taken into account for the journey.

* * *

Down in the MLC, Kelly Travern lay on a medical bunk. Attached to her forehead and temple region were cordless discs, relaying her vital signs to the overhead monitor, allowing Donaldo to keep constant checks, as did Treketa. Kelly had remained in a suspended state ever since they'd come out of the Space Triangle and it concerned Donaldo. She lay silent, not twitching or moving like anyone else in a sleeping state—nothing. He shook his head. It was totally baffling and he was unable to put a finger on why she wasn't improving. They'd tried all necessary tests and administered the right drugs to bring her out of her current state—but nothing. It was beyond all the experience he'd gained over the last yearons. He'd never known anything like it. Kelly's symptoms were the weirdest he'd ever heard of or seen. One minon she would be in a total convulsive state, then sudden calm, with extremely high temperature.

The centre doors drew apart and Tayce briskly walked in with Twedor not far behind. Donaldo glanced in her direction, finishing the final checks, then crossed as soon as he'd finished, explaining that he'd just had to sedate Kelly to keep her calm. Tayce walked up to Kelly's bunk-side and studied her, concerned. Without warning, Kelly broke the sedated state, opened her eyes and looked directly at Tayce with a glazed wild expression. It was as if she was about to lash out. Tayce silently used her powers to probe into Kelly's mind. She could see Donaldo needed her help.

"I'd like to try something if you'll permit me?" asked Tayce.

"If you have a solution I'd welcome anything; but if it comes to you being hurt using your abilities, I don't want you injured," he replied, worried she would suffer.

"Don't worry—if there's a chance I'm going to get hurt, I'll pull out," replied Tayce assuringly.

Donaldo watched as she placed her hands on Kelly's forehead and closed her eyes to concentrate, entering into the young navigationalist's mind. Tayce slowly formed a glow and placed her hands, palm down, over Kelly's forehead, just a small distance above, letting the power glow grow. The glow began to pulsate and began forming into a small vortex of swirling energy, with the point going down into Kelly's mind. Treketa watched, amazed Tayce showed no strain. She remained totally calm. Donaldo ordered her to stand by with a sedative just in case he needed it. Tayce, once she'd entered into Kelly's mind, found the power force of the Space Triangle. It was black and swirling and locked into controlling her thought and senses regions. Tayce knew she had to try and sever the connection and save Kelly, as it seemed to be slowly consuming the young woman's sanity. As Tayce increased her powers, the space-triangle force struck back. A pencil-thin brilliant white beam fired from Kelly's eyes straight into Tayce's shut eyes. It threw Tayce across the room with force. She landed near the far wall, feeling dazed, with her eyes hurting. The doors opened at that precise moment and Darius entered, alarmed to see her where she was. He rushed to help her back on to her feet. He quickly lifted her up gently. Twedor helped on the other side of her.

"What were you doing to cause this?" he asked, concerned making sure she was OK.

"I tried to help Kelly. The Space Triangle has her totally in its grip. She's totally possessed. She won't change until we get out of our current Universe. I've seen what's affecting her," said Tayce, calming back to normal, blinking her eyes to regain her focus.

"Can I ask what you saw?" asked Donaldo carefully.

"It's like a smaller version of the swirling journey we took to end up here, only with a much darker and more sinister feel to it. It's beyond my gift to tackle," said Tayce, thinking about it.

Donaldo knew she'd done all she could—her best. They were back to square one. Darius put a fatherly warm arm around Tayce's shoulders, asking her gently was she sure she was all right? Tayce nodded. She wasn't concerned about herself; she was more concerned about Kelly's state of mind. Donaldo began to explain to Darius what had been happening with Kelly, in that she would suddenly go into convulsions the moment she regained consciousness as if she was being possessed. Darius could see where he was coming from in his account of the symptoms Kelly was suffering. He explained that on the Quentron when the crew disappeared they all had gone into the same violent state before being consumed by a dark shadow, disappearing to God knows where. It was hard to understand why certain people were affected and some were not. Both himself and Paul Trukanne had tried to work on many theories, but nothing had come back with any answers. Behind them Kelly began reacting violently once more. She was jerking and lashing out uncontrollably. Darius and Donaldo hurried to her side and, whilst they took hold of her firmly, Treketa administered a further muscle relaxant. Within a few cencrons, Kelly stopped. It was like a switch being thrown.

"Thanks, Commodore. I don't know how much more I'm going to be able to administer before this relaxant causes permanent damage to her," said Donaldo, concerned.

"Do what you have to—even use force-field restraints," ordered Tayce.

"We're reversing the journey through the Space Triangle and, no doubt, as soon as we break back into 2420 she will return to normal."

"All right, we'll do what we can to keep her safe and well," agreed Donaldo.

"Final calculations have been achieved and a set has been sent to the Quentron," spoke up Twedor.

Tayce thought for a minon, then decided maybe the science medical and botany officer, Jaul Naven, could come up with something that would make Kelly get through the journey, using something more natural as a relaxant until the return journey was through. Donaldo agreed. He could see where Tayce was coming from. He said he'd call Jaul immediately. Tayce turned and walked back to the entrance. Upon reaching the opening doors she turned, telling Donaldo everything would work out fine—he was doing all he could in such difficult circumstances. With this she continued on out of the centre in the company of her father and Twedor. As they began down the corridor, heading back to Level 1, she hoped everything would soon return to normal for all their sakes and they were back in 2420.

7. Trauns Reunited

Tayce was silent on the walk back up to Organisation. Darius could see she was concerned over Kelly's well-being. He slipped a fatherly supportive arm around her slim shoulders and informed her he knew what she was going through. But sometimes some things were beyond help, and in the case of Kelly all she could do was wait and see. He hugged her to him, telling her to cheer up. She glanced at him, managing a small smile, glad he was back in her life again after such a long absence. Twedor, down beside her, suggested he head on. Tayce agreed, letting him. She continued on to the Deck Travel in the company of her father, talking on different matters, namely the demise of Questa and the new base Enlopedia. Upon reaching the Deck Travel, it arrived after a few cencrons and they boarded. It quickly took them to Level 1. Upon stepping from the Deck Travel on Level 1, Tayce's Wristlink bleeped. She raised it, pressing for contact. After a few minons Dairan's voice came through, informing her Amal was all set to go ahead with the return journey, just as soon as she could get back to the Organisation Centre.

"I'm on Level 1 now, heading on in," she informed him, deactivating her Wristlink.

Lowering her Wristlink, father and daughter hugged at the idea they'd soon be saying goodbye to the phenomenon known as the Space Triangle. Soon everything would be all right again—the Quentron could return to headquarters for an overhaul and, with luck, the crew could materialise back on board and return to see their loved ones, upon their return to Enlopedia, who'd thought they'd gone forever. Kelly Travern would hopefully return to her normal healthy self. As they went on, so Tayce explained more about Lydia. Darius listened, greatly interested in what his only love and legal intimate joining partner had been up to to date. They soon entered back into Organisation, to meet Lance looking up from his duty position announcing the return journey was almost about to begin, and it looked like it was going to be far from smooth! Tayce looked down at his screen, seeing the information to confirm as much. Darius noticed the apprehensive look on her face. He discreetly assured her it would be all right in the end. Dairan shared Darius's reassurance and gave Tayce a warm, gentle smile as she glanced at him. But it still didn't stop her wondering if they'd survive a return journey going against the gravitational pull, in reverse. Dairan glanced around the immediate team members, seeing the same look Tayce had of apprehensive uncertainty about whether they'd live to see 2420 again. It wasn't going to be easy for any of them, he thought.

"Lance, have a scan placed on the Quentron during our return journey. I want to know the moment the crew hopefully return," ordered Tayce over his shoulder.

"Scanner activated and ready to take the reading when it occurs," replied Lance.

Without warning the return journey commenced. Amalthea Two, under the guidance monitoring of Twedor and Amal, began its journey back to 2420. After a few minons, the cruiser began to rock slowly from side to side at first, in the reverse pull. It then began to feel like the whole cruiser was fighting against the most immense reverse pulling power that could be imagined. So much so, it began to jolt—and it wasn't a slight jolt, it was so forceful that Tayce lost her footing and fell in front of her father. But, before he could help her on to her feet, one by one the team began falling back into the unconscious state they'd succumbed to the first time around upon entering into the phenomenon. Some were even thrown against their consoles; some were just dropping to the floor. Darius never got the chance to see Tayce had struck her head in falling on the corner of the console by the entrance to the DC, as he dropped, like Dairan, to the floor and lay in an induced state of deep sleep. Soon the whole team were once again under the influence of the mysterious effects of the force from the Space Triangle. Twedor glanced around at the now silent team and Darius in different sleeping positions and whistled in disbelief at how quickly he and Amal were alone once more, to make sure the cruiser and Quentron made it through.

* * *

Out in the turbulent Universe, in the interior of the Space Triangle, behind Amalthea Two came the Quentron space port under tractor beam. As the return journey progressed, so the whole crew of the port began returning to their last duty positions, where they'd disappeared from almost four yearons ago. Like the Amalthean Quests team and Darius, they too were unconscious upon return. Paul Trukanne was awake to see them beginning to materialise before he became unconscious also. Both the Amalthea and the Quentron space port passed through the swirling reverse-gravitational tunnel, pulling with a jolting motion as both fought against the immense resisting forces to head back to 2420. An aura of protecting energy, created by Twedor and Amal, protected both port and cruiser from any lasting damage that might have occured as the journey progressed. On board Amalthea, Twedor was playing a vital role in guiding Tayce and the unconscious team through the triangle's interior. The whole journey was one not anyone would want to endure ever again in a hurry. The Quentron was under immense strain as the tractor beam was being almost severed at times as the interior force danced off the beam joining port and cruiser together. The whole death-defying journey took just on three hourons, until both the port and cruiser broke out into normal calm space once more.

* * *

Ten milons from the Space Triangle they reached calm space—2420 to be exact. They'd made it. Both the Amalthea and the Quentron space port were now in a stationary orbit, both having survived the treacherous journey under the guidance of Twedor and Amal. On board the cruiser, the team were still in an unconscious state. Darius Traun lay face down, not moving. Dairan Loring was the first to regain consciousness. He sat up, looking around at his immediate teammates still out cold. Like before, Twedor crossed to him with a cup of plicetar (water).

"We're through, both of us—the Quentron and us. I can confirm we are back in the yearon 2420," informed Twedor glad.

"Nice work, mate!" congratulated Dairan.

At least they'd made it through safely, he thought as he glanced around at his unconscious teammates. Twedor prodded Dairan and drew his attention to Tayce, lying under the far console at the foot of the steps to the DC. He immediately noticed she'd been injured—he could see the bloodied gash from where he was sitting.

"Get the Emergency Medical Kit, Twedor—hurry!" ordered Dairan, crawling over to Tayce's side.

He carefully lifted her up into a sitting position, wondering what had happened to cause the wound on her temple. She began to come round, moaning about her head hurting. Dairan soothingly informed her she was going to be all right, but told her to remain still for a few minons. Twedor quickly returned with the kit, handing it to him. He opened it, taking out the Examscan. Upon activating it, he guided the small handheld device over the wound. Checking the reading, he was glad to see she hadn't done any serious damage. He took out the Healentex, which healed wounds, from the kit and proceeded to treat her.

"This may hurt. Try and bear with it," he said, treating the area.

Twedor, to take her mind off what Dairan, was doing informed her they'd made it through and now were back in calm space in 2420. Tayce cringed as she felt a cold feeling from the Healentex as it healed her skin like new, as if there had never been a wound in the first place. She looked at Dairan as he held the handheld device over the wound.

"You OK? Nearly through. You'll need to take it easy for a while after this," he said softly.

"Thanks. I knew I'd hit my head when I fell, but had no idea I'd made it bleed," she replied casually as she began to sit up.

Twedor looked across as the others began coming round—Darius, in particular, was still sprawled face down where he had fallen unconscious, not making any signs of recovering. Twedor prodded Tayce with his metlon hand and pointed to her father. She forgot all about recovering from her own injury and hurried to her father's side, thinking the worst. The triangle was not prepared to give up a victim if it could claim one. Surely she wasn't going to lose him again so soon after they had come together as father and daughter. Dairan glanced at her. He could see she was quickly trying to work out what to do. Twedor stood by like an obedient servant, waiting for any orders that would come his way. Tayce checked her father's pulse, then looked over at Dairan.

"It's weak. Get Donaldo up here—tell me if he hasn't regained consciousness yet. I'll have to revive Father myself," she ordered, meaning she'd have to use her power ability.

She gently turned her father over on to his back and glanced towards Dairan, waiting to find out whether Donaldo was answering Dairan's request for emergency assistance. Dairan shook his head. He left Tayce to use her powers to revive her father and walked away to check on the rest of the Organisation team. Upon checking with the others, he was satisfied they were getting back to normal. He glanced back at Tayce, busy reviving her father, and it amazed him how skilfully and calmly she used her powerful force. Her hands were over her father's heart with a powerful glow underneath, pulsating, until Darius Traun began to breathe normally and come back to them. Tayce opened her eyes, waiting for her father to open his. Dairan brought her a drink to hand to him when he did rouse. Both stood watching as Darius slowly opened his eyes and sat up.

"Did we make it—did the Quentron and Paul make it?" he asked, greatly interested.

"Yes! Twedor just told me we're back in 2420 and our original Universe. Here, drink this," suggested Tayce, handing him the drink.

Darius began getting back to his feet, drinking the much needed plicetar. Tayce suggested he sit for a moment in the DC before thinking of doing anything else. Both walked in, talking about what they'd all just gone through. He sat relaxingly on Tayce's swivel chair, finishing his drink as Tayce stood by studying him in a concerned way. He began to feel a bit stronger as the moments went on. He smiled at her, then reached out to take her hand and squeeze it to reassure her that he was going to be all right. Tayce smiled a loving smile, glad he was OK in return. Twedor entered the DC, looking at a revived Darius, glad his mistress had managed to save him from the clutches of the phenomenon.

"Are you feeling stronger now, sir?" enquired Twedor in his usual friendly childlike voice.

"Yes! Getting stronger by the minon. Tell me, did the crew return to the Quentron all right?" asked Darius.

"Yes! All crew materialised just after we broke back into 2420. Captain Trukanne was overjoyed to get his crew back and wishes you luck for the future," replied Twedor.

"Twedor, you and Amal have done an excellent job guiding us safely through that treacherous journey whilst we were unconscious," praised Darius.

"I agree," spoke up Tayce, agreeing with her father.

She patted Twedor praisingly on his metlon head, telling him he was one special Romid to be proud of considering he'd saved all of them. Darius studied Twedor. He was something special all right, and he was certainly right to assist his daughter in protecting her. It was nice to know Craig Bream had managed to move Midge's entire character into such a small form, from having been a guidance computer.

"Twedor, you can stay with Father here and tell him more about the Amalthean Quests to date, Questa and Enlopedia," suggested Tayce.

"Yes, you only gave me a brief outline of what's been happening to date," replied Darius, looking at Tayce.

"Sorry, Father, but Twedor will give you the rest," said Tayce lightly.

Tayce, with this, turned and went back out into Organisation to see how the team were coming along in getting back to normal duty. As soon as she stepped back out into the centre she could see everything was back to normal. Dairan was in the middle of receiving a damage report on the cruiser. Craig was checking onboard operations, making sure nothing had been strained during the transit through the triangle's interior. Sallen was trying to establish some kind of current navigational bearing. It was a busy scene. For a moment she stood taking in all that was unfolding around her and felt pleased that she and the team had made it back to 2420. From what she was hearing, there hadn't been any real structural damage, only scorching to the outside hull. Three of the letters in the name of the cruiser had been scorched off, so the name now read A AL HEA T O. She crossed over to Mac at communications.

"Mac, now we're back in our own Universe, contact Jamie Balthansar at Construction and Maintenance on Enlopedia. Tell him what's happened and say we'll meet him on arrival," ordered Tayce.

"Sure—of course," said Mac obligingly, getting on with the request.

Tayce walked back across to Sallen to see how she was doing at Kelly's position. She enquired how things were coming along. Sallen began by saying she'd found the journey somewhat frightening at first, but everything on the navigation front was returning to normal and she was happy to report that they were back in calm space.

"You're doing a good job. Well done," praised Tayce—something she thought she would never do.

She continued over to Dairan. He walked towards her, meeting her mid floor. She discreetly confided that she was glad the whole triangle ordeal was over. He nodded, smiling gently as she looked at him, glad they'd both made it. Dairan placed Lance in charge, suggesting they take a break. Both glanced into the DC, wondering if her father would want to join them, but they had the feeling that Twedor had him engrossed in a game of space checkers on the three-tier crystal board. They were gaining levels against each other and enjoying it. Maybe it was best to leave them to it. It was nice to know, thought Tayce, that someone else besides herself was enjoying the relaxing game she kept in the DC for quieter moments. She smiled at the sight of her father and Twedor doing moves to outsmart each other. Dairan suggested discreetly over her shoulder that they should leave the two of them to enjoy what they were doing. Tayce nodded. Together they turned to walk from Organisation, discussing the journey they'd been through as they went—also how she was going to break the news to her mother that her father was alive, as it would come as a shock to her to know he was back. They soon boarded the Deck Travel and it was descending smoothly to Level 2. Upon stepping on to level 2, Donaldo was exiting the MLC. He was glad to see them as they'd saved him a journey up to Organisation. Both waited.

"Good news—Kelly is all right and returning to her normal self," said Donaldo, happy about the fact.

"Oh, thank goodness! That's great news," said Tayce, glad.

"She'll be ready to return to duty just as soon as she has rested for a while," said Donaldo casually.

"Tell her I'm glad she's all right. I look forward to seeing her back on duty," replied Tayce.

Donaldo nodded, turned and headed back into the MLC whilst she and Dairan continued on to their break. It had been one hell of an ordeal in the clutches of the Space Triangle for all of them. But life aboard Amalthea was slowly returning to normal, and, apart from the slight cosmetic damage, the cruiser had successfully stood up to its most challenging journey of the second voyage so far.

* * *

Three hourons later Amalthea brought the Quentron space port to Enlopedia. It wasn't its original home, but a better port. Here she would be given the utmost, latest refit and overhaul before heading back into space. When near the headquarters base, within a seven-milon radius, Amalthea severed all tractor-beam ties, allowing the rescue teams to move in and help the Quentron and its crew. Once Amalthea was free, the cruiser headed on to dock at the base.

* * *

On board Amalthea Mac Danford informed Tayce as she entered Organisation that they were currently going through final docking procedures and Waynard Bayden was waiting to meet her on arrival. Tayce nodded understandingly, then went on through to the DC, leaving Dairan to take care of telling the team everyone would be remaining on board to get the cruiser ready for heading back out into space.

"You're in charge when we go over to Enlopedia," said Dairan as he came to a pause behind Lance.

"Sure!" replied Lance in acknowledgement.

Tayce, as she reached the entrance to the DC, saw her father and Twedor coming to the end of their current game and talking about Enlopedia. She found it somewhat amusing to see her father putting up a good fight in trying to win the game against Twedor. By the look on his face, he was somewhat determined to try and outsmart the little Romid. It was hard to imagine that her father was once commodore of Traun, giving orders in the every-dayon running of their planetary world, as he played such a challenging checkers game against Twedor.

"Twedor, you're not cheating, are you? It's not me you're playing against. Watch him, Father—he's prone to cheat and play a mean game whilst he's doing it," said Tayce in a commanding tone, finding the situation amusing.

"No! He's fine. It's very interesting. Are we at Enlopedia yet?" asked Darius.

"We're in the process of docking now," replied Tayce.

"It feels strange knowing that after all these yearons we will be a family again, even if you are travelling around the Universe most of the time, hunting for criminals. You could say it's Trauns reunited," replied Darius a smile of happiness at the thought they were all going to be together once more crossing his features.

"Excuse me, we've docked, Tayce. Are you ready, Commodore? Enlopedia is a wonderful place," assured Dairan, stepping just into the doorway of the DC.

"Yes, I'm ready. Tayce is right, Twedor—you play a mean game of space checkers. We'll have to have a rematch someday," said Darius, rising to his feet.

Tayce let Dairan and Twedor walk on ahead, then followed on with her father. Once out in Organisation, Darius walked around each of the team, shaking hands with individual members, saying how glad he was to have met them, saying a few words more to some members than others. He came to Sallen and paused for a few minons, studying her. He remembered her when she was a small child and member of the Vargon family. 'Vargon's daughter!' he thought. He smiled, then turned to walk on out, saying nothing as he couldn't think of anything to say. The hurt of what the Countess did to Traun, even though it wasn't Sallen's fault, was still fresh in his mind. Darius turned and followed Tayce over to the Organisation Centre entrance.

"Until we all meet again, take care," said Darius with a nod to the team watching him leave.

"Goodbye, sir!" came the reply from the various members.

He continued on out in the company of Dairan and Tayce, leaving the team behind to discuss how pleasant he was for a commodore. Lance cut in, announcing he'd always been a fair man since as far back as he could remember, but he could be as authoritative as any other leader if he had to be. Sallen felt awkward. She had no idea why the Commodore had made her feel uncomfortable in his presence, considering she'd never met him before. Lance glanced over and immediately assured her it was nothing personal, even though he knew otherwise—he knew her real past, of which she had no recollection. She decided to take her duty break and informed Lance of such. Craig decided he would go with her. He could see she needed cheering up, and he had done all he needed to do on restoring the systems back to normal, for the time being. He'd do the rest when they'd left port and headed back into space. They both walked off together, and Lance and Mac were the only members left in Organisation.

* * *

Darius asked Tayce how long Sallen had been a member of the team. He did it in such a way that he seemed to be asking how could she recruit the daughter of the woman that had destroyed their home world?

"Father, let me explain. The Sallen you saw back there is not the same girl. There's a new mind-reprogramming technique and it's used on criminals. Sallen was running with the Countess, taking part in her many unlawful actions, until she and the Countess were apprehended. Sallen was sent for memory reprogramming, where they wiped all her past and replaced it with a new life of a science tech. Gone are any memories of what she was going to become. She's someone now that's a far cry from the original Sallen. She'll do anything for anyone and has become a real team player. The team found it awkward at first, knowing what she used to be, but they soon realised this Sallen is a very different one from the bad one we all knew," explained Tayce.

"Is there any chance she could remember her old life—say if her mother escapes where she is and comes back to find her?" asked Darius, curious.

"No, the memory reprogramme has a 100 per cent success rate. No one so far has found a way to put back what was taken out, as what is removed is destroyed once and for all."

Darius nodded understandingly as the three of them exited the Deck Travel they'd boarded on Level 1, on Level 2. Dairan and Twedor walked along behind, listening, as both father and daughter talked about the new technique and Sallen. As they went, Darius found himself becoming nervous of meeting Lydia, rather like a young man going on his first date. It had been a long time of absence since he'd seen the woman that had meant and still did mean the Universe to him. He wondered how she would react. Had she fallen out of love with him? Had things changed so much in her world that she wouldn't want him back in it? Would she feel, seeing him walking back into her life, that as a former member of the original planetary council he would automatically be handed her leadership of Enlopedia? He hoped not. Tayce looked at him, noticing his apprehension, and read his thoughts. It made her smile.

"Everything will be all right, Father. You'll love Enlopedia," she assured him.

"I've heard there are people there that know of you and are waiting to welcome you back, sir," said Dairan over Darius's shoulder.

As they walked out to the Construction-Area walkway, Chief Jamie Balthansar walked over to meet them. He studied Darius, seeing he was like Tayce in appearance.

"Hello, Jamie. This is Commodore Traun, my father," introduced Tayce proudly.

"Welcome to Enlopedia, Commodore. It's good to know you're back with us. What's the damage, Tayce?" asked Jamie, glancing at her.

"Lance will give you a report. He's in Organisation waiting. Jamie does all the maintenance and keeps us in space, Father," said Tayce.

"Looks like you and your team do a good job," praised Darius, shaking hands with Jamie.

"Thank you, sir. Don't worry, Tayce, Amalthea will be ready to leave in first-class condition as always," he said pleasantly.

"That's great! She's all yours," replied Tayce.

Darius smiled, thinking Jamie was a good man. He was a man that certainly knew his job, judging by the way in which he presented himself. Both he and Tayce walked over to the Vacuum Lift to join Dairan and Twedor, who were standing waiting. They boarded and waited for the doors to close. Darius turned to see for the first time the far-reaching architecturally orientated panoramic view that was Enlopedia. The tall white buildings that almost touched the roof of the base, the grey two- and three-storey different designs. As the lift began to descend, so Tayce and Dairan explained many of the buildings around. Darius found himself impressed by what he was seeing. It was rather like their old home world, but under cover. He watched groups of young and middle-aged men, women and students, come and go smartly dressed, some in uniforms of different colours carrying equipment, meeting in the centre of E City, talking—in fact the whole busy every-dayon life unfolding before his eyes. As the lift came to ground level, he saw her, even though he was expecting Waynard. Tayce had asked Lydia to come to meet her, and she was waiting in the city square instead of Waynard, looking every inch the beautiful leader she was. Lydia had glanced away for a few minons to acknowledge a member of the base that had walked past and she hadn't seen Darius. She looked back in front and was transfixed by the face from her past and of someone she thought she would never see again. She couldn't believe her eyes. Strong overwhelming emotional feelings of utter joy grabbed at her heart with a vengeance. Tears began to fill her vision. Darius felt the same and smiled a loving smile at her. She was just as breathtakingly beautiful as he remembered and just as elegant too. Lydia smiled a warm smile and at the same time tears of utter overwhelming joy brimmed in her sapphire-blue eyes and began to slide down her cheeks. It was like it was just the two of them in the whole base for a moment and time had halted everything around them. The fears each had in never seeing each other again faded, to be replaced by the true strong pull of love.

The doors to the lift drew back and Darius walked out, coming to a pause for a few minons before his one true love. Lydia couldn't control her longing any longer to hold him at bay and ran straight towards his open arms with tears of utter joy streaming down her delicate cheeks. Dairan and Tayce stood back to allow the two to come together as one for a moment. Darius closed his arms around Lydia, feeling the warmth of her body against his, taking in her softness, the smell of the perfume she loved wearing. Savouring the moment he thought he would never see again. She announced tearfully that she loved him so much. Passing people saw the situation and wondered what was happening. Security were becoming twitchy, wondering if they should intervene, concerned that this person might try to abduct Lydia. Dairan managed to stave off the notion something was awry by waving that everything was fine, there was no problem. Darius, after a few minons, held Lydia so he could study her for a while. God, she was still his beautiful Lydia, even if she was a little older with the yearons. Lydia wondered if she was in one of the dreams she'd had of this moment so many times before and would wake up to the cold reality that he wasn't there.

He hugged her to him again, telling her, "You're still as lovely as the dayon I met you. It's good to be back," he said softly.

Lydia felt the warmth of his tender closeness. It was real, all right, and long-awaited. Tears were flowing again of joy as she looked over Darius's shoulder at Tayce and silently thanked her daughter with a warm smile. Twedor gave a soft whistle of awe at the two reunited. He glanced at his mistress, noticing she was sharing the joy of her parents coming together. Dairan put his arm around her shoulders. He looked down at her, noticing she had tears in her eyes of pure pleasure, seeing her parents united once more.

"Here! Before you dampen your uniform, take it easy. Come on," he said, handing her a disposable wipe for her tears, hugging her to him like the true friend he'd become.

"Thanks! It's just I'm so happy to see them like this. I thought it would never happen," replied Tayce, wiping her tears away with the dry disposable wipe Dairan had given her.

He turned her to face him and pulled her into a friendly warm hug as the tears of joy rolled down her face at a sight she thought she would never see again. She realised she liked being in his warm, gentle hold. He pulled away, looking down at her with a warm smile.

"All this water—I'll rust in a minon," spoke up Twedor.

Passers-by looked at the happy reunion and smiled. Some, though, wondered what all the fuss was about. Darius and Lydia held each other's hands face-to-face, studying each other with such strong emotions of deep love in their eyes, neither one wanting to break from the other for fear they might disappear.

"I just can't believe you're actually here. I thought I would never see you again," said Lydia softly.

"The last I saw of you was when I set off into space, from what was left of our home world, when I was rescued by Paul Trukanne of the Quentron. He sent out a search deep-space probe, hoping somehow we would find you. When nothing came back I figured I was alone and I prayed to God that, wherever you were, you had found peace," replied Darius.

"I escaped all right. I was thrown into deep space by an explosion on our world. Then I was rescued by a young pilot on Micacer. He took me back to Micacer and got me well," explained Lydia.

"Well, we're all here now back together. What Vargon attempted, she failed in. We're a family once again, and that's all that matters even if our daughter is flying around the Universe crime-busting," said Darius with a teasing smile on his face, looking at Tayce.

"Father! We have Twedor here to thank for what's happened. He and Amal have to take most of the credit for bringing us back together. They worked out a safe way to bring us and the Quentron space port out of the Space Triangle," expressed Tayce.

"He's quite something, aren't you, Twedor? And he plays a mean game of space checkers too," praised Darius, laughing and patting Twedor on the head.

"Shall we head to my chambers?" suggested Lydia.

"After you," said Darius, gesturing with his hand behind her back gently.

Tayce explained as they all began off across the city square, towards the Vacuum Lift on the other side, how the team and herself had found her father on being sucked into the Space Triangle. As Tayce talked with her mother, her father fell a little behind to talk with Dairan in general about Enlopedia. He could see the many areas that had scope to be improved on, as Dairan explained the bad current state after the rule of Layforn Barkin. Darius listened and nodded understandingly. They soon reached the level in Lydia's building that her chambers were in. They entered through double doors into the outer anteroom. Adam Carford, recovered from his ordeal at the destruction of Questa, stood up from behind his desk and walked round.

"Adam, this is Commodore Traun, my husband. Darius, this is Adam, my assistant," introduced Lydia softly.

"It's an honour to meet you, sir. Welcome home," said Adam, stretching out his hand in a friendly gesture.

"Thank you, Adam. It's good to be home," said Darius, pleased.

He studied Adam and could see he was a polite and obliging young man. He had done a wonderful job in taking care of Lydia, assisting her as best he could. He had a feeling that if they got to work together in the future, they would work well. Lydia turned, ordering Adam to postpone all her council meetings and deal with all her calls, no matter how important they might seem. Adam nodded in total understanding. Lydia further requested that techs should bring refreshment to the new inner chambers and Empress Tricara should be paged. Adam nodded, then walked away to carry out her requests. Lydia continued on into the new inner chambers, which were roomy and had been lavishly furnished in light relaxing colours—a cream suite and pastel peach walls. The carpetron tiles underfoot were a soft fawn colour, giving the chambers a relaxing atmosphere to be in during off-duty times. Darius walked across towards the large sight pane that looked down on E City Square, to look out impressed. Lydia entered the chambers as Dairan and Tayce sat down together on the nearest of the two facing soffettes. Lydia crossed to the drinks dispenser, keying in the request she wanted—four glassenes of stavern for celebratory purposes. Four tall-stemmed glassenes materialised on the delivery tray, filled with stavern. Taking them, she handed one each to Dairan, Tayce and Darius, proposing a toast.

"To the safe return of my husband, and Tayce's father, Darius!" announced Lydia, raising her glassene.

Everyone present raised a glassene in toast, then drank down the stavern, which was equivalent to Earth-1 champagne. Tayce stood and sauntered over to the sight pane, looking down on the busy E City below. People were briskly coming and going in their every-dayon work-related existence. Some were standing, chatting and pointing to something in particular in discussion. Tayce glanced at her father watching the ongoing life in the city. He glanced at her with a warm smile and put a fatherly arm around her shoulders. As they stood watching life unfold for the many Enlopedian inhabitants, Tayce found she was glad to feel her father by her side once again. Until he was found, there had always seemed there was a part of her missing.

They both stood talking about Enlopedia and its similarities with Traun, their old home world, when quite suddenly Marc's face flashed into Tayce's mind with force and he seemed to be in immense pain. It made her gasp. She realised he was in danger somewhere but where? Silently, by her father's side, she concentrated on trying to reach where he was, only to discover, quite surprisingly, he was being brought into Enlopedia's Medical Dome as an emergency. Tayce pulled away quickly from her father's gentle hold. Turning to her mother, she asked if there had been any word from Marc, as she hadn't heard anything lately on how he was getting on on the Astrona Star.

"Are you worried about him?" asked Darius, turning, interested.

"Yes, though at the moment I can't put my finger on what it is," explained Tayce, trying to make sense of what she was seeing in her mind.

Just at that moment, and as if by coincidence, the Telelinkphone sounded on the first of the occasional tables that were at each end of the soffette's. Lydia set down her half-filled glassene, picking up the handset, wondering why Adam hadn't dealt with this call. As she had said, she didn't want to be disturbed. She spoke into it and to the point.

"Chief Traun," she announced, waiting for whoever to speak on the other end.

Darius was recalling with Dairan the first dayon Marc had started duty and how he didn't much like the idea he had to watch Tayce, as she was prone to get away with anything she cared to get past his nose. But in time they'd become good friends, rather like a brother and a close sister. Dairan listened with interest as Darius explained. The inner-chamber doors opened as Lydia continued to talk to whoever was on the other end of Telelinkphone. Empress Tricara walked in, in her usual graceful gliding way. Darius broke the conversation. Apologising, he walked towards Tricara in a true friendly way.

"Welcome back, Darius. I couldn't believe it when Adam said you were alive and back with us," said Tricara, overjoyed to see her long-time friend.

"It's good to be back and to know all the people I once knew and loved are still here," said Darius, hugging Tricara in a strong way for a few minons.

"Darius, is Tayce all right, only I sense something is troubling her?" asked Tricara discreetly. "She looked a little worried when I walked in."

Lydia at this moment placed the Telelinkphone handset back down with a look on her face that said she didn't quite know how to deliver the news she'd just been given. Tricara stopped talking with Darius about the new Enlopedian Council, as she could see something was wrong. She studied her friend's worried face.

"Lydia, whatever has happened?" she asked in a true soft caring tone.

"Tayce, you were right to be concerned about Marc. He's just been brought into the Medical Dome as an extreme emergency.

"What! I had a feeling something was suddenly wrong. I've got to be there for him—come on, Dairan, let's go," commanded Tayce, heading briskly towards the entrance to the inner chamber.

Behind her the small gathering of Lydia, Darius and Tricara looked on, wondering what could have possibly gone wrong for Marc. Twedor hurried on, breaking into a small sprint to catch his mistress and Dairan up as they hurried out through the opening doors. Tayce was soon out of sight. She was running with such urgency that Dairan soon lost her. Twedor pointed ahead, having scanned further in their current direction. Dairan finally caught sight of Tayce, noting she hadn't stopped for the Vacuum Lift but had headed on for the descending walkway that would take her to the steps down to the Medical Dome. He slowed and decided Tayce was going to get to where she was heading quicker than him and Twedor. Tayce ran as fast as she could. Her thoughts were on Marc and what condition she'd find him in. She was also wondering what had gone wrong on the

Astrona Star. Dairan at last was gaining on her, as both he and Twedor decided to break into a further sprint in order to gain a bit of distance.

"I wish she wouldn't run so fast. It's near impossible to keep up," protested Twedor.

"You're doing your best, buddy, you can do no more," assured Dairan in a true encouraging tone.

As Twedor came to a pause, Dairan lifted him up and ran on with the little Romid, so they could finally come alongside Tayce. As Dairan did weight training every mornet before duty, carrying Twedor was relatively easy. They finally caught her up at the concretex steps that would take them down to the side entrance of the Medical Dome. Dairan put Twedor down and they went on down, two at a time. Twedor was muttering under his breath about Tayce and her actions. It was hard for him to keep up. Dairan waited for him at the foot of the steps, whilst Tayce walked on in urgency. He then followed on.

Tayce approached the side-entrance glassene and steelex doors. They opened with the sound of compressed air. Once inside she looked for the main reception desk through the crowds. Seeing it was ahead on the far side of the waiting area, she began across, letting Dairan and Twedor follow on behind. Dairan dodged a wounded Enlopedian, passing on the way to get treatment, on a Hover Trolley. As he passed, he glanced back to make sure it wasn't Marc. Upon seeing it wasn't, he wondered where Marc was. As Tayce reached the main reception desk, Dairan and Twedor came to a pause just behind her. Glancing around at the many situations occurring that would go on in a medical environment, he figured it was like being in the middle of a rush-houron zone, with medical staff coming and going in urgency, and names being called out for attendance. He also noticed the usual smell of hospital-type antiseptic hanging in the warm air. A pretty female nurse walked up and passed him, giving him an enticing, interested look, conveying she liked what she saw in him, on passing. She glanced back, giving him a playful come-on look. Then she looked where she was going. This amused Dairan. He smiled, shaking his head at the sudden interesting situation. Twedor shook his head. Tayce turned, whilst waiting for someone to come to the desk, just in time to see the situation going on between the young impressed nurse and Dairan. She gave the nurse a look of total displeasure, then pointed out to Dairan that she needn't remind him he was on duty. He found the whole situation funny. He had a young nurse interested in him and he had Tayce being slightly jealous over someone else liking him. Twedor slightly prodded Dairan in the thigh as a warning that it was time to behave.

The reception administrator came towards Tayce, apologising for keeping her waiting. She was a buxom woman in her mid forties, with dark curly hair that cascaded down her back, and features that conveyed she could put anyone in their place, in her profession. Her eyes were blue, but held no warmth. It could be seen she was a total career woman. Tayce silently thought to herself that she wished she'd come to the desk at the same time as the young nurse was flirting with Dairan—she would have been severely reprimanded. Tayce glanced at her name—Officer Carlan Morting.

"Can I help you?" she plainly demanded, without a smile.

"I'm Captain Traun of Amalthea Two. I believe you have an injured survivor from the Astrona Star. His name is Commander Marc Dayatso. I'm here to see him," explained Tayce in her true tone of leader and captain.

"Dayatso? One moment, Captain—I'll call Dr Sellecson. I believe he's expecting you. Chief Traun has informed us you were coming here," replied the officer.

Officer Morting headed off to find Dr Sellecson. Tayce, even though she was there to see Marc, didn't like dealing with Sellecson. He always studied her to make sure she was taking care of herself. She hated it. It made her feel like she was under a microscope. She hated waiting.

Dairan sighed. He hated medical facilities at the best of times. Tayce looked at him. She could see his uneasiness at being where they were, so put a gentle reassuring hand on his right shoulder, informing him quietly that it wouldn't be long. Twedor too offered his support by slipping his metlon hand in Dairan's, applying the right pressure to gently grasp it, to let him know there was nothing to be concerned about.

Officer Morting soon returned, informing Tayce that Dr Sellecson was on his way down and would be there shortly. Tayce nodded. She wished it wasn't him, but some other doctor on the base.

"Maybe we should go and wait in the Botanical Waiting Area?" put Dairan casually.

"That's a good idea. Could you inform Dr Sellecson, when he arrives, where we'll be?" asked Tayce to Officer Morting.

"Yes, Captain," she replied, politely this time.

Tayce walked away with Twedor and Dairan in the direction of the Botanical Waiting Area. It was an area of plants with beautiful blooms, waterfalls and ponds. A really nice place to relax. Dairan was impressed as he entered, stepping from the sterile medical environment into a true garden of beauty.

"How are you bearing up?" asked Dairan casually as they crossed to a white platex bench-type seat. "It must be quite a shock to find Marc is here?"

"Yes! Quite! But I'm all right," she replied, thinking what a state Marc might be in.

She figured all she wanted to do was see him and find out if he was going to recover to full health and come back to the team. She sighed impatiently. Dairan for the first time reached over and took hold of her hand, gently squeezing it reassuringly. She looked at him, realising he was being a true friend, and that was just what she needed right then. He knew what Marc meant to her—they went back a long way together. He quietly assured her that Marc was tough and said he wouldn't be surprised if Marc made a full recovery in no time. Tayce smiled at him in an appreciative way. She could see he understood her feelings. Glancing through the glassene partition, she could see Dr Sellecson exiting the Intensive Care Unit, walking on his way to meet them. She noticed he looked pensive. Could this mean bad news? she wondered. Dr Sellecson was dressed in an Enlopedian surgeon's attire of navy-blue tunic with white doctor's protective thigh-length coat over the top and grey casual shoes. He smiled, seeing Tayce was watching him approach. He recalled the time when she'd given him the wrath of her tongue on voyage one when he ordered her to rest because she was exhausted. It amused him still. He soon rounded the corner, entering into the Botanical Waiting Area.

"Tayce, good to see you're looking well," said Paclan.

"This is Dairan Loring, my relief commander. We came as soon as Chief Traun told me. How bad is it?" asked Tayce, waiting for the worst.

"Dairan! Marc should be regaining consciousness soon. It's touch and go. I can't lie to you—he's been hurt bad. In fact he's lucky to be alive. Come with me—I'll explain en route."

Twedor walked with Dairan, taking in all Dr Sellecson was explaining about how Marc had been the fortunate one of the Astrona Star crew. But he nearly wasn't saved. In fact, the Astrona Star was nothing but debris and Marc was found in the nick of time by a passing Research Patrol Cruiser. The remains of one member of the crew were brought back. Whatever attacked the vessel was pretty gruesome—it was as if some kind of horrific space beast had attacked savagely. They soon crossed from the Botanical Waiting Area and went on into Intensive Care. As they walked to where Marc's room was, Dr Sellecson talked more about what the rescue team had discovered. Dairan, having listened, was putting two and two together on who he thought might have carried out the attack, and when he heard Dr Sellecson say the other victims of the attack had their eyes sucked out of their sockets it came to him.

"This to me sounds like the callous work of a bunch you wouldn't want to run into. They're known as the Tremanexan Bore-radds—a race that steals the sight of their victims and then savagely destroys their bodies, making them unrecognisable. It happened to a close friend of mine. He became one of their victims on a training mission," said Dairan, recalling the hurtful memory of his brother, but not saying as much.

"I've heard of this race. Dairan's right—you wouldn't want to meet them if they were the last form of help in the Universe," expressed Paclan.

"Who was this friend?" asked Tayce, glancing at Dairan in a questioning way.

"Well, he wasn't a friend, actually. He was my brother Ben. All they found were his remains. It happened just on five yearons ago," replied Dairan like it had happened yesteron.

"I'm sorry—you never told me you had a brother," replied Tayce, feeling stupid for asking him, as she could see the memory still hurt.

"It's all right—it's a memory I and my family would rather forget," replied Dairan casually.

All three paused outside a private Intensive-Care room—the kind that was specially available for high-ranked injured personnel. Medical personnel passed as they stood in the corridor waiting to receive the command to enter. The medical teams that had passed carried life-saving equipment and entered a room further up, in urgency. Tayce braced herself for what she might find as the doors to Marc's room opened. Dr Sellecson walked ahead into the dimly lit but cool room. Dairan stepped back, allowing Tayce to enter with Twedor, then followed on. Once inside, there was the usual medical bunk and overhead monitor relaying Marc's current vital signs in various illuminated colours. Tayce walked more fully into the room so she could get a better look at Marc. When she did, she almost gasped at his injured state. It was something she wasn't expecting to see—not quite so severe injuries anyway. Both his arms were encased in special bone-repairing platex white supports. There were deep and not so deep cuts to his normally handsome features, with bruising in places. His eyes were protected by dark eye-protection shields. Tayce could see he had put up a good fight, with bruising here and there all over his upper body. She sighed, wondering just what had happened out in space aboard the Astrona Star.

"What are the eye-protection shields for? He will see again, won't he?" asked Tayce, turning to Paclan.

"Yes! Don't worry—Marc's eyes have just sustained some swelling and bruising, plus scratching to his cornea. The protection shields are protecting his sight from the brilliant light as they are sore. He'll be able to discard them once his eyes are back to normal," assured Paclan. He could see Tayce was worried.

Tayce walked around to come to the side of Marc's bunk, along with Twedor and Dairan. Paclan meantime began checking the latest readings concerning Marc's repair and healing, hoping Marc would soon be coming back to them.

Dairan stood looking down at his injured team buddy and shook his head. 'No one deserves to end up like this,' he thought.

"Marc, it's Tayce. I'm here. Don't worry—you're safe. Dairan and Twedor are here too," said Tayce softly as she sat on the white and chrome stool by him.

"He's coming to. He must have heard you," spoke up Paclan quietly, looking down at Marc, watching Marc in a true doctor's studying way.

Tayce gently put her hand on his right hand, so as not to disturb the healing process. She studied it, thinking it was an experienced hand—one that had flown many fighter craft and held a gun to fire a marksman's shot with precision, to take out many an enemy. It had also pulled her to safety the night Traun was destroyed, and designed Twedor as Midge in Amalthea One using the computer design board. She didn't like seeing him so wounded and it brought a tear to her eyes.

He began to speak in a groggy tone. "Thank God you're here," he said slowly, trying to squeeze Tayce's hand.

"You're safe. You're on Enlopedia in the Medical Dome, under Dr Sellecson. You're going to be fine. You just need to put yourself in the medical team's hands and forget about anything else right now," said Tayce softly.

Dairan couldn't stand seeing Marc the way he was any more. He was a true friend and it reminded him of his older brother Ben. He left Tayce by Marc's side and sauntered over to the tinted sight pane, fighting back his own tears of hurt in recalling the past. The memories were flooding back—of his mother, sitting like Tayce was beside his brother's bunk, in tears, knowing that Ben was not going to make it.

"Excuse me, Doc, I've got to take a walk," he announced, trying to hide his feelings.

Dr Sellecson understood. He, like any doctor would be, was concerned for Dairan. He could see he wasn't handling the situation well. He left Tayce to talk with Marc, going in search of Dairan, making sure he was going to be all right.

As Marc could see through the eye-protection shields, he wondered why his buddy was walking out on him.

"What's with him?" asked Marc lightly.

"His brother was a victim of the same lot that attacked you," replied Tayce, leaning close to the bunk.

"You'd better go and find him—see if he's OK," suggested Marc with difficulty.

Just as Tayce was about to rise to her feet, Paclan walked back into the room. He beckoned her over, asking as she neared for a brief word. Halfway she glanced back at Marc and gave him a direct order. He was to rest until he was better and until he was released—no leaving beforehand just because he felt well enough to do so. She continued on out with Twedor in tow, following Dr Sellecson, the door soon closing behind them. After discussing Marc in the corridor, and the fact Tayce wanted him to have the best possible care, Paclan assured her he would see to it; as Commodore Traun had already called down and ordered the same, saying he would take care of any medical bills that accrued in order to get Marc back on his feet. Paclan enquired was Dairan going to be all right, only he looked somewhat pale when he caught up with him earlier? Tayce nodded. Suddenly Paclan's Wristlink sounded three short beeps.

"Better go—you take care. Don't worry—Marc is in safe hands," he assured her with a gentle reassuring smile.

"You've always sorted my problems out," she replied, feeling a little easier in his presence for the first time.

Both went their separate ways. Tayce went down the corridor with Twedor by her side, in search of Dairan. She ordered Twedor to try scanning for him, as otherwise they might end up walking around the Medical Dome for hourons. Twedor did as requested, and after a few minons he announced that Dairan was on the Stargazers balcony area, an area in the Medical Dome, on their level, that was for patients and visitors to be alone for a moment in thought and reflection. Tayce gestured for him to lead the way. She followed on and soon they were turning a corner on to a wide open expanse that had a panoramic sight pane and clear domed roof, looking into space. Dairan was standing studying the Universe in thought with his back to her. Twedor stood back patiently, watching as Tayce walked up to him. She came to a gentle stop beside him.

"It's Ben, isn't it? I understand, honestly I do. Marc was concerned because you had left; but when I told him why, he fully understood," said Tayce, leaning on the marblex sill, looking at him.

"Sorry—it's just that all the memories came flooding back. It was like it was yesteron," he said in an apologetic tone, meeting her concerned look.

Dairan turned to face her, then reached out, bringing her gently towards him. She let him and he hugged her, thanking her for being so understanding. She assured him that being there for each other was what made a good team spirit. As his friend and captain, she would always be ready to listen any time. She broke away from his warm hold, suggesting that, if he was ready, they would head off to see Chief Barnford. The Tremanexan Bore-radds were not going to get away with any more of their criminal savage acts on unsuspecting targets. They could consider themselves brought to justice just as soon as she could arrange it, unless their evil lives were terminated first as a result of their latest actions. Dairan assured her that she could count on him if she thought about taking the matter on herself with the Chief's assistance.

Both he and Tayce with Twedor left Marc in the care of the medical staff of the dome and continued on out of the area, down the corridor and back out to the entrance into E City Square, off to see Chief Barnford in the Security Crime and Patrol Division building. Just as they were about to leave, Darius Traun was about to enter. Both paused, as did Twedor.

"Father, what brings you over here? You're all right, aren't you?" asked Tayce, studying him, concerned.

"I'm fine—couldn't feel better. I've come to see Marc. How is he doing?" asked Darius, greatly interested. Marc had been a good officer on Traun and Darius had always considered him like one of the family.

"Not too good at the moment. He'll pull through, though. Dr Sellecson said he'll make a full recovery and will be back on duty in no time. He's conscious and talking, but you'll see he's had a bad attack," explained Tayce.

"Where are you two heading now—back to the cruiser?" asked Darius, curious.

"I have decided the Tremanexan Bore-radds' callous acts need to be stopped. We're on our way to discuss the fact with Chief Barnford and suggest a possible Quest," replied Tayce.

"From what I've heard about that race from Adam Carford, are you sure you think it's wise to attempt such a Quest? Don't you think the Chief and his team should handle it completely?" he asked, greatly concerned.

"Don't worry, Father—I'm hoping to get Jan to join us and bring his SSWAT team along. Then we can take care of the Tremanexan Bore-radds once and for all. I've worked with his team of specialist officers in the apprehension of Countess Vargon and that was quite a battle," assured Tayce.

"If the chief agrees to your idea, will you call in and see your mother before you depart?" asked Darius.

"No! If Chief Barnford gives the go-ahead, we'll be leaving straight away," replied Tayce in a tone of true authority.

"I'll say goodbye to your mother for you. Dairan, take care of my daughter out there on this one," Darius asked Dairan.

"You have my word, sir," assured Dairan sincerely.

Tayce hoped that now her father had returned he wasn't going back to the protective way he used to treat her. She was a grown-up girl now and certainly didn't need his protection any more. Darius realised, as Tayce walked away in the company of Dairan, it was a part of his daughter's life, taking on dangerous Quests. He hadn't visualised her rarely being at the headquarters base he was to call home, but it had to be. He had to realise she wasn't his little girl any more. He continued on into the Medical Dome to go and see Marc Dayatso. Tayce had a feeling, as she walked along with Dairan and Twedor, that her father wasn't pleased she was thinking of risking her life on such a life-threatening Quest. But in time he would adjust and see what she had become and be proud of all she had achieved. They crossed the city square towards the Security, Crime and Patrol Division building. The city square was busy, as it always was at mid dayon. They walked in through the main entrance doors to the destined building as security guards and officers came and went. Some were escorting criminals that were being brought in worse for wear from the city bar. Dairan watched Tayce protectively as they made their way through the loud noise of verbal abuse from criminals, and officers speaking loud commands to other officers and criminals, trying to bring them under control. Smoke hung in the air from smokers who had refused to give up the age-old habit, which killed well over 85 billion people until it was banned in public places three centuries ago. Some still refused and did it behind closed doors. Twedor stuck as close to Dairan as he could get as they pushed through the scene of utter chaos. He didn't like the look of some of the misfits. Tayce had been to Jan's Officette many times and was, against all odds, determined to head there.

"Excuse me, ma'am—you can't go in there," shouted a stout-looking desk clerk with very little hair and law-inforcing features.

"I'm Captain Traun. It's all right—Chief Barnford knows me. It's urgent," replied Tayce, realising this had to be a new desk clerk; otherwise he would have recognised her from previous times.

"Captain Traun, my apologies, ma'am. We've poor lighting until it's fixed. You go right on in," he said in an apologetic tone with a smile.

He felt a total idiot not recognising Tayce, but it had been one of those dayons and there was bad lighting in the building because of the base taking a hit during the ambush on Questa and the main lighting throughout the base had been knocked out. It was hard to see at the best of times. The division building was one of the buildings still waiting to be repaired. It was tough-going making out anyone properly. Tayce continued on to Jan's Officette, Twedor now with his metlon hand firmly in hers, for safety reasons. As a vagabond had taken a studying interest in him for all the wrong reasons, Dairan kept glancing back discreetly to the scene of chaos, glad he didn't work in these current surroundings.

Upon reaching the floor-to-almost-ceiling double brown doors to Jan's Officette, Tayce placed her hand on the doors' sensory panel. After a few minons the doors drew back, revealing Jan sitting at his glassene-and-chrome desk, busy behind a computer. Upon him seeing it was Tayce, he rose to his feet with a welcome smile. He gestured for her and Dairan to take a seat. Tayce sauntered to the nearest oversized brown leatherex chair and sat down relaxingly, followed by Dairan, whilst Twedor stood by Tayce. Jan was about to enquire what was the nature of her visit? Then his desktop intercom sounded. He pushed a button, telling whoever it was abruptly he did not want to be disturbed. Tayce smiled at his tone. She recalled what he was like the first time she'd met him, back in voyage one—just as abrupt.

"To what do I owe the pleasure of this unscheduled visit?" he asked, giving her his full attention.

"I have a Quest which I would be glad of your assistance on, and your SSWAT team," began Tayce.

"Commander! I guess this has something to do with the Tremanexan Bore-radds. I've heard they ambushed the Astrona Star," he replied, acknowledging Dairan.

"Quite! Marc's injuries are horrific. I want to stop these killers and bring them to trial, or destroy them once and for all before they mutilate any more unnecessary victims," said Tayce plainly.

"You know what you're proposing won't be easy, even with the best of my men, the Tremanexan Bore-radds are a race that take their victims in a split cencron, then mutilate them, stealing their eyes right out of their sockets, cutting any attaching blood vessels and skin, leaving their victims dead—and not a pretty sight either. My men might not want any part of this—they've seen what happens when victims have been torn to shreds by the knife-sharp claws of those bastards."

"I understand what you're saying, but they have to be stopped. Think of what we'll both get out of this. There will be the reward for you, knowing you've brought to justice a race no one in this Universe wants to encounter, and I'll get justice for Marc," replied Tayce.

"I would like to see them get their just deserts, also for personal reasons," backed up Dairan.

"All right, you've got my assistance. Give me time to get my men together, though they're not going to be keen on this one. I'll see you out in space."

"Thanks! You won't regret this, and justice will be served," said Tayce, rising to her feet.

Dairan stood also, and together they left Jan to sort out the procedures to get his expert team together, to join her out in space. Tayce and Dairan with Twedor walked from the Officette. The doors opened on their approach. With Twedor in her tight grip, Tayce pushed back through the jostling crowds, which hadn't thinned out. They headed back to the entrance. Halfway back across E City, Dairan turned to Tayce and apologised for his behaviour earlier when they were both in with Marc, in running out on her. Tayce assured him that it was understandable, and told him not to think anything of it. Her mind was on the Quest ahead, hoping that what they were proposing to pull off Quest-wise would not go wrong. If it did, it would spell the end of the legendary Amalthean Quests team, as they were now known.

* * *

A while later, on board Amalthea, as Tayce stepped aboard she raised her Wristlink, ordering Amal to gather everyone together for an emergency meeting. As she walked along the corridor, she could hear the familiar voice of Jamie Balthansar talking with Lance somewhere up ahead. As she rounded the corner of the Level Steps Lance and Jamie came down towards them. Jamie paused, letting Lance and Dairan carry on back up to Level 1 whilst he and Tayce discussed the cruiser, walking back along to the Docking-Bay doors. Upon stepping back outside the cruiser, Jamie paused, leaning on the chrome rail. He was a tall, strongly-built man in his late thirties to early forties, with short-cropped brown hair. His features were pleasant. His eyes were brown, yet held a lot of knowledge, and you could tell he was giving you his full attention when discussing something. In past yearons on earth it could be said he resembled a rugby player in build. He smiled relaxingly, glancing around across the wide-open expanse that was the Service Port.

"Amalthea is quite a cruiser. She's back to her usual working order. There were a couple of things that needed replacing, but the good news is that everything is back running fine, considering what you've just been through. The Space Triangle sounds pretty hair-raising," said Jamie.

"It's not something I want to travel through again any time soon. Thanks for checking Amalthea over so quickly," replied Tayce, thankful.

"You're welcome. She's a pleasure to work on and keep running. I hear you're going after the most dangerous race in the Targonic Universe—an area known as a no-go land. Anyone that ventures in generally never comes back," said Jamie.

"Yes, but we'll pull it off. We've never been defeated before," replied Tayce, taking in what Jamie said about the area of space they were about to take on during the next Quest.

"I hope it all goes well for you. I've heard some pretty awful reports about what they do to their victims. Let's hope you all stay in one piece. Good luck. Better go—duty calls," he said, beginning away.

"Bye, Jamie," called Tayce as he went.

"See you next time, and take care of my favourite cruiser. She's one of a kind," he called back jokingly.

Tayce glanced around the area, then walked back aboard Amalthea. The Docking-Bay doors closed behind her. Twedor was waiting for her, to walk back to Level 1 together.

* * *

Amalthea Two after a while began to withdraw from the Docking-Bay Port area. At the same time, at the Crime Port area Jan Barnford's men were loading supplies to take along for the most dangerous and life-threatening mission to date. Jan glanced up to see Amalthea under way and ordered his men to get moving. They needed to leave—Amalthea Two was already heading back out into space.

* * *

Darius Traun, as it happened, looked up through the glassene domed roof of E City Square to see Amalthea leave, upon leaving the Medical Dome.

"May God go with you, Tayce—you're going to need it," he said in a near whisper.

8. Tremanexan Bore-radds

Tayce and the various members of the team were seated around the meeting-centre table in deep discussion on the next dangerous Quest—namely, the bringing to justice of the Tremanexan Bore-radds. Jan Barnford was space-borne and heading out to rendezvous with Amalthea for the forthcoming mission. Not any of his men were particularly keen to undertake it, considering what had happened to the Astrona Star crew. Jan himself wasn't too happy about putting his men in the line of probable death, but he knew they were the kind never to let him down. If they had to die in the line of duty, then it was meant to be.

* * *

The wall Sight Screen flashed into life in the Meeting Centre. Tayce began by saying that what they were about to be shown was recorded by the Astrona Star Intruder Image Recorders, on board, during the attack, and some of the scenes were somewhat graphically horrific. Twedor turned and walked from the centre, not needing to watch the replay of what occurred. He headed on back out into Organisation to assist Amal in guiding the cruiser to their most vicious of Quests yet. Tayce continued to explain that no matter how gruesome the scenes might be, they all had to take note of how the Tremanexan Bore-radds attacked, so when it came to it they could avoid it at any cost. Many of the members present glanced at one another, uneasy about what they could face. Tayce nodded to Dairan, who commenced the image recording via a few key strokes. The first scene began, showing what happened to Marc, how the onslaught of attack began on the unsuspecting crew the moment the Tremanexan Bore-radds boarded the Astrona Star. Some of the crew didn't have time to react to being attacked. Screams and voices pleading not to be killed rang out in the utter chaos of the scenes that unfolded. Some of the crew were in sleep time and were brutally murdered and their eyes removed before they'd even left reality. Tayce, even though she found the scenes just as gory as everyone else did, noticed that when the Bore-radds stole the eyes from their victims they did it with a very powerful force emitting from their own eyes and in split cencrons. She almost jumped when Marc became the last victim, but watched, pleased he put up a hell of a fight to keep his life and sight, using his last ounce of strength in pulling his Pollomoss handgun from its holster, pushing it into the face of the pitiless big bulk of a dark and merciless Bore-radd, and firing one single shot before falling unconscious because of his horrific injuries. The recording suddenly ceased. Silence filled the Meeting Centre for a few minons. Tayce nodded to Dairan to deactivate the wall Sight Screen. Jaul Naven, the science medical and botany officer, whistled in utter amazement at what he'd just witnessed and gave a stunned look to match. His brown eyes widened in disbelief.

"Marc was certainly brave. I think I would have caved after the first severe beating," said Jaul in his true Canardan accent, not believing what he'd just witnessed, shaking his head.

"Me too. They have to be the most evil beings I've ever seen!" backed up Lance in agreed disbelief.

"He probably figured someone had to survive to give the report of the attack, to get someone to stop the Bore-radds in their gruesome game," said Mac.

"I know none of us wants this Quest, but we know now what we're up against. We have to keep our guard up, keep alert. If they come, we must kill them without a further thought. Is that understood?" asked Tayce glancing around the table at her various team members.

"Are we working alone on this one?" asked Craig, wondering.

"No! Chief Barnford and his SSWAT team are assisting. We'd be the same as the Astrona Star crew if we tried this one alone. I don't think any of us want that," said Tayce.

"You can count on us—we won't let you down, and I speak for everyone around this table. This is for Marc, right?" asked Lance, glancing around at his teammates.

Everyone nodded in total agreement. They all realised the seriousness of the looming Quest and the fact they had to give their all in honour of Marc. Plus the Tremanexan Bore-radds had to be terminated in the Universe from carrying out any more gruesome strikes on unsuspecting victims.

Craig spoke up, asking why had they been picked for the Quest? Surely it was a job solely for Chief Barnford's SSWAT team. Lance was quick to say Marc was their teammate and commander, so it was only right they should put an end to this group.

"Let me ask you a question here. If someone you knew close to you was taken out by these so-called Bore-radds, wouldn't you want revenge for what they did?" asked Dairan seriously.

"Sure I would," replied Craig, thinking about it for a moment.

Tayce glanced at Dairan, wondering if he was thinking about revenge for Ben, his brother, on this Quest. She wasn't happy about the fact he was becoming slightly heated when the team were being difficult in their reluctance to take on what had to be done. She would have to watch he didn't let his feelings cloud his judgement and get himself killed.

"So it's unanimously agreed that ourselves and Chief Barnford will bring the Tremanexan Bore-radds to justice?" asked Tayce, glancing around the table once again at the team individually before she closed the meeting.

Everyone nodded, agreeing wholeheartedly.

Dairan gave a verbal and strong "Yes."

This just fuelled Tayce's concern that Ben was his reason for going after the Bore-radds. Should she take him along? she wondered. Could she rely on him when it came to the crucial moment in taking out the Bore-radds? He was relief commander. She would just have to be on her guard in case he let her down and forgot he was part of the Amalthean Quests team, there to do a job as part of a team, not on a personal revenge trip. She declared the meeting closed and suggested everyone get back to duty. There was a lot to do before the Quest commenced. Everyone rose to their feet and headed back to duty.

"Lance, I want you to find out everything you can on who we're going up against. Look for any weaknesses that might prove useful," ordered Tayce.

"Sure! I saw the way in which Dairan gave a triumphant "yes" in reply to your last words before you closed the meeting. He's thinking of handling the Bore-radds on his own, in a kind of revenge trip, isn't he, because of what happened to his brother?" asked Lance, ready to listen.

"To be honest, it worries me that he may put the safety of this team and Quest in jeopardy because of his personal feelings about what happened to Ben," confided Tayce.

"Don't worry—I'll keep an eye on him. If he does do what you suspect, I'll step in and remind him he's part of this team first and foremost," he assured.

He put a friendly arm around her shoulders, pulling her towards him, giving her a reassuring hug. He assured her that if the worst came to the worst he would step in and watch the team's backs. This made Tayce a lot happier, knowing she could rely on him if Dairan turned his back on the team for personal reasons. Lance released her, then walked on out back to his duty. Tayce watched him go, thinking their friendship had continued to go from strength to strength since his father's untimely death. In off-duty sport pursuits she played against him and they'd done their weaponry practice sessions together, trying just for the fun of it to outsmart each other. She looked out into Organisation, seeing the many thoughtful faces of the team. She sensed it had something to do with the Quest ahead and wondered if she had done right in taking on this latest one. It wasn't going to be easy for any of them, but the Tremanexan Bore-radds had to be brought to justice—and they did have Jan Barnford along, so they weren't alone without back-up protection. She crossed to her desk and sat down. There wasn't much to do herself until they reached their destination, so she would catch up on some Porto Compute work she'd been putting off. Twedor stood beside her in standby mode, as there was nothing for him to do at present either. Everything was at a standstill until they were at the destined port of call.

After a few minons, and finding she couldn't concentrate, she deactivated the Porto Compute and stood to walk out into Organisation. As she crossed the DC, Twedor came back into full operational mode and followed on. He could see his mistress was agitated because of the fact there was nothing more she could do until they reached their destination. He'd seen it many times before. Tayce came to a pause at the top of the steps leading down into Organisation. Twedor paused beside her, looking up, seeing she was looking for someone among the team and wondered who.

"Lance, where's Dairan?" she asked, noticing he wasn't present.

"He said he was off to get some combat practice in for the Quest ahead," replied Lance.

"You're in command. I'll be around the cruiser—you can contact me on Wristlink should you need me," she informed, far from pleased that Dairan had walked off duty, without permission to do so.

Without a further word she continued on out of Organisation with Twedor walking beside her. He could see she was far from pleased. They headed straight for the Deck Travel. Tayce found her thoughts were drifting to Marc, wondering how he was coming along back at Enlopedia. She wished he was all right and on board; but then, they wouldn't be going after the Tremanexan Bore-radds. Twedor silently scanned her thoughts and found a high tense reading that showed she was under great stress. One thought he read said her greatest fear in their upcoming Quest was that they should all share the same cruel fate as the Astona Star crew did. He put to her, as they reached the open doors of the Deck Travel, that if she felt like she did, why didn't she hand over the Quest to Chief Barnford and leave their current orbit? Tayce was quick to point out, as they entered and the doors closed, that it was her idea to go after the Tremanexan Bore-radds. Leaving Chief Barnford to take on the Quest alone wouldn't be right. The more people there were to take on the eye-stealing race, the quicker they could be put a stop to. Twedor saw her point, but he still didn't like seeing her so anxious.

The Deck Travel descended with the gentle sound of compressed air, to Level 5. Once on the destined level, Tayce could hear just what she expected to hear: the sound of combat weapon fire in the distance, in the direction of the Combat and Training Practice Centre. As she and Twedor walked out of the Deck Travel, she shook her head at what was coming from the said direction. This could only mean one thing. Dairan was letting his pent-up emotions go, and she bet the targets in the simulation he was using were their destination. Why was he getting his skills primed for facing the Tremanexan Bore-radds when he was good at combat in the first place? she wondered. Why had he walked off duty without some word of what he was intending to do?

* * *

Further down the corridor on the same Level, Dairan, in the Combat and Training Practice Centre, loaded another recharged cartridge into his handgun, then selected a higher degree of action to match his angered emotions. All four holographic walls surrounding him suddenly activated on his command. He went straight into action against the oncoming Bore-radds, which were twice his size and twice as fast as they came. He had to shoot round after round in quick succession, sometimes ducking and diving to avoid the attack swipes. He was doing what a couple of monthons ago he had advised Lance never to do again, when Questa was destroyed. His movements were quick and precise. As the programme played out, he began to feel more at ease with himself. He soon became one with the action surrounding him. He was beginning to feel as if the whole situation was real. He was so engrossed in the action that he didn't hear Tayce enter with Twedor behind him. She stood for a few minons, arms folded, displeased at his decision to leave his duty, watching with a studying eye the way in which he handled himself against their next foes.

"Twedor, deactivate the simulation. I think we've seen enough, but take note of his scores," she ordered discreetly.

Twedor, through high frequency link, stopped the simulation. It abruptly ceased and Dairan spun round, his eyes sharp and dark from being fuelled by the action he'd been lost in, sweat running down his handsome features. Upon seeing it was Tayce, he didn't register at first, until he calmed down.

"Quite impressive, but who were you fighting for—this team or your brother?" asked Tayce plainly.

"I could have taken it all the way to the end. I only had another thirty minons left," he protested.

"Another thirty minons and you would have been in the MLC, suffering from illness caused by what I would term going beyond your endurance. You haven't answered my question, Dairan," replied Tayce sternly, refusing to budge on what she'd asked him.

"You know I would serve this team to the best of my ability. I'm honing my skills both to take care of this team and in memory of Ben," he replied without thought. He didn't like what she was implying.

"I'm having doubts about taking you on this forthcoming Quest. I can't be sure that at the last moment you won't forget this team you claim you would protect and act vengefully for Ben, putting us in jeopardy, despite what you claim. You promised my father you would take care of me during this dangerous Quest ahead, but it seems you're prepared to forget that for something that happened in your past," she said getting angry.

"Sorry! Right now I'm going through very mixed emotions. I'm trying to work them out," he replied, sounding apologetic.

"It's simple. Every round of weapon fire you use against the Bore-radds for real, make it count as a strike for the honour of your brother. And when it comes to the final take-down, you put yourself first and foremost on the side of this team, making the final shot of confrontation for Ben. I'm ordering you to get cleaned up and get back to duty, but first you can accompany me to see what Aldonica has come up with for the Quest ahead," said Tayce in an ordering tone, turning towards the entrance, far from pleased.

"So I take it I'm going, then?" he asked over her shoulder.

"You're going, but if I find any sign you're going to let us down, I'll have Amal bring you back to the cruiser in an instant. Is that understood?" replied Tayce, walking on across to the entrance with Twedor.

Dairan threw a fresh towelling wrap around his neck in a roll and followed on. They walked out as the doors drew apart, back into the corridor. As the doors closed behind them, all three began on up the corridor towards the Weaponry Design Centre. After a few minons Dairan realised he'd been wrong regarding his thoughts during the simulated attack, and what Tayce advised seemed like the right way to look at what he was feeling. Ben was gone and he was part of the best team he could be in. He had a good meaningful friendship with her; and if he stepped out of line, she might look at him differently. She could even de-rank him. Also he didn't want Marc coming back and finding out he'd put himself above the team when he was in the temporary position of commander. It wouldn't look good.

On approach to the Weaponry Design Centre, or, as some of the team had come to term it, Aldonica's domain, as she spent many of her duty hourons in the centre, the doors opened to reveal her working. She looked up, acknowledging Tayce and Dairan, then continued to dismantle a small electronic object with a laser split torch, wearing eye-protection shields to protect her from the dangerous glare. Craig crossed the shiny grey speckled floor to meet both Tayce and Dairan. Craig spent some of his time working with Aldonica, especially when they were working on a creation to be used on the next Quest.

"How is it coming along? Is it something we can use this time around?" asked Tayce.

"We've come up with an idea—it looks like it's going to be a good one. Well, we think so," said Craig, pleased at what was materialising.

"The idea is that one of our PolloAld bombs could be a lot more powerful if we use a more powerful explosive circuit from the Pollomoss 2 range, which should make a very good impact on destroying what has to be destroyed. If I can get it ready in time, and it tests all right in the Test Chamber, we could use it on Tollatex like you want to," expressed Aldonica, stopping her work and explaining.

"Tollatex? Where's that?" asked Tayce, not knowing this was the home of the Bore-radds.

"Home of the Tremanexan Bore-radds," replied Dairan without a further word.

"Oh, OK. Good luck with the test. Let's hope it all works out and it's ready in time," said Tayce, pleased at what was unfolding.

"Yeah," backed up Dairan, looking forward to seeing the end results.

"Just as long as we don't get blown up with it when you come to test it," spoke up Twedor.

"He doesn't have much faith in me, does he, Tayce?" said Aldonica, looking at Twedor and laughing.

She removed her eye-protection shields and pulled the clasp from her long blonde hair, which had kept it up in a ponytail whilst working. She let her hair fall back around her shoulders, shaking her head to put the style back into position.

"He's just being concerned, aren't you, Twedor? How long do you think it will be to test the first one?" asked Tayce, interested.

"About two hourons. I'll give you the results when it's done," assured Aldonica in her soft Australton accent.

"That's if we're still here in two hourons," said Twedor, continuing to wind Aldonica up.

"That's enough, Twedor," reprimanded Tayce. She could see he was enjoying being mischievous.

She knew if Aldonica's design was a success, then Enlopedia would want to see it and consider it for one of their forthcoming ideas, to be put into production, as she had done something similar before with the PolloAld bomb, and that had become a great success all over the Universe.

"I'll let you continue. I can't wait to see the finished result," said Tayce.

"Thanks! I'm hoping it's going to give the impact I'm looking for," replied Aldonica, chuffed Tayce was pleased with what she was trying to accomplish.

Dairan and Twedor followed Tayce back to the entrance and back out into the corridor. Twedor was thinking as they walked on out through the parting doors that if the new improved bombs worked they'd be a godsend on the Quest. He followed Tayce up the corridor as the doors closed behind them, listening to his mistress and Dairan discussing Aldonica and Craig—how well they worked together as a good inventive small team. Dairan decided to confide in Tayce as it seemed she had forgiven him for his behaviour earlier. He figured she had been right to be angry at him, and when he'd thought it through he realised he was putting his feelings before the team and he wanted to apologise. Tayce listened and suggested he forget the whole thing. Changing the subject, she informed him that apart from his behaviour earlier she was generally pleased with the way in which he was handling his responsibility as relief commander; it was quite a shock when Marc decided to join the Astrona Star crew at short notice. He nodded, agreeing, smiling at her. As she looked at him, he was glad he'd come near to Marc's standards in his duties. Tayce read his thoughts and it made her smile that he was glad to hear he was as good as Marc, even though Marc had been doing his job for yearons. He continued, saying that one good thing had come out of his new responsibilities. That was stepping back into the combat simulator and achieving a simulation level of 35, which he had been trying to reach since he did combat training in his early dayons. Despite what he did earlier, she was pleased for him. She could see he was glad of his achievement. As they went, so they continued to discuss Marc and Ben. Tayce figured that if she could find out more about him, it would help her understand his pain and anger and the reason he wanted revenge. She was not just his captain; she was fast becoming more than just a friend. At the Deck Travel on Level 5 at the doors drew open. Dairan suggested he catch her later on duty; meanwhile he'd head off to get cleansed and changed. Tayce nodded, stepping into the Deck Travel with Twedor, whilst he sprinted on to his quarters on Level 3.

* * *

On Level 1, the Deck Travel doors opened. Both Tayce and Twedor exited and walked along to Organisation in a brisk manner to see what was progressing on the journey to Tollatex, home of the Tremanexan Bore-radds. Lance looked up as she entered and headed on through to the DC. He jumped up with the latest information and followed on. Tayce walked across the DC to her desk. She paused once by her swivel chair, looking out into the calm Universe. Lance entered the DC and approached her desk. She turned, sitting down relaxingly, looking at him questioningly as he came to a pause. Twedor stood ready to listen beside her to what Lance had to deliver, so he could store any vital information.

"Dairan's still not back yet. Did you manage to find him?" asked Lance, interested.

"Yes, thanks. Between you and me, it was a good thing I did. He was in the combat simulator on a simulation for fighting the Bore-radds—at level 35, would you believe?"

"That's high. Did he achieve it?" asked Lance, surprised.

"Yes! He said it was something he's been trying to do for yearons, but I feel his anger towards the Bore-radds had something to do with achieving it; otherwise he wouldn't have," confided Tayce.

"Well, this is the latest information I could retrieve—quite interesting too, you'll find. Ready?" he asked, getting ready to read it to her.

Tayce relaxed, ready to listen, leaning back in her chair. Lance began by saying the final analysis was that the planetary temperature was below 51°C. The atmosphere was a cold, snowy one, but breathable. The surface of Tollatex, besides being snowy and rocky, had mountains, where they'd have to be careful. If the Bore-radds were aware they were landing, they might try and pick them off from hidden positions. Precautions for the Quest would be that they should all dress in warm thermal attire to withstand the low temperatures and they should take weaponry good enough to fight the likes of the Bore-radds with. It was known that when the Bore-radds attacked they did it with split-cencron timing and so fast that if anyone was in the line of attack, who wasn't ready or on alert, they'd become the next unforeseen victim. Lance continued saying he'd checked storage and they'd specially designed hyper-acting thermally insulated suits, fit for the climate. They had four layers of thermal insulation and reflected body heat, sealing the warmth close to the body, shutting out the extreme cold. The suits would protect them. As Tayce wanted Twedor along, she ordered Lance to check there was one fit for Twedor. He nodded. She suggested he go ahead and inform the others that they'd need to change into their special suits well in advance of arrival. Twedor was storing the points Lance had brought up in his little memory system, as he was going on the Quest. He might need to access the information should the need arise, especially if he and Tayce got separated from the team. Lance placed the information sheet on the desk, then said that if there was anything else she wanted to know she should just let him know. Tayce agreed, letting him walk back out to his duty position with her request about the team and the suits. Kelly turned out in Organisation and was next into the DC, informing Tayce that the Tremanexan Bore-radds' base on the surface of Tollatex was about three milons into their distant future and closing. She might like to take a look at it. Upon this Tayce rose to her feet and followed Kelly back on out into Organisation. Lance, at research, was surprised Kelly could give Tayce a close-up view on screen so soon, as he hadn't been able to get one less than ten minons previously.

"Are you sure it's Tollatex, Kelly?" asked Lance somewhat surprised. "I checked about ten minons ago and it was only just becoming detectable. It seemed a lot nearer than what you're saying."

"Check for yourself. My coordinates give me a visual clear enough to see it on magnifyied scan," replied Kelly.

"To be doubly sure—not that I'm doubting either one of you—check both your readings. We don't want any slip-ups at this stage," ordered Tayce, wanting to make sure one set of readings was correct.

"According to this, Tollatex is 1.5 milons off its original course," replied Kelly in surprise, after checking her readings.

"She's right!" spoke up Twedor before Lance had a chance to confirm the fact.

"Lance, are you sure the information you've given me is all there is, considering this latest orbital shift of the planet?" asked Tayce, becoming seriously concerned that maybe the information was out of date.

"Of course I'm sure," he replied, surprised she had doubted him. He'd always been spot-on before.

"Take a break. You've earned it and, as I recall, you were on duty before anyone else this mornet," ordered Tayce. She realised he could be getting duty fatigue, if

Kelly could pick up the orbital shift and he hadn't noticed it. As Quests research and information officer, it was his duty to pick up the finest point.

She left him to go on his duty break and stood watching what Kelly wanted her to see, through the main sight port: the drawing-near of the first sight of Tollatex as a whitish-looking globe. She wondered what lay ahead. The nearer it drew, the clearer the sight of the Tremanexan Bore-radds' base became. It was, as Lance said, covered with snow and ice.

Just as Tayce stood in thought, her desktop Telelinkphone sounded in the DC. Mac informed her, at communications, that it was Chief Barnford. He'd just transferred it to the DC for privacy. Tayce quickly headed into the DC and across to answer the call. Soon herself and Jan were in conversation. He suggested she should transfer the call to the desktop screen. That way they could talk to each other face-to-face. Tayce did as requested and sat down in her chair. Jan soon appeared on the screen with a rugged smile. She prompted him to go ahead. He began asking had their navigational computer gone wrong, only his was making Tollatex about 1.5 milons from where it should be? What was going on? Twedor, near Tayce, was finding Jan's accusation annoying—to claim Amal was going wrong! He stood tapping his little metlon foot in agitation. Tayce tried not to laugh at his actions, explaining quickly that the original bearings were correct; there had been what was termed an orbital shift. There was nothing to be concerned about.

"Computer gone wrong! I'll have him know Amal is a very sophisticated computer," said Twedor, heading away across the DC, mumbling further in disgust at Jan's words.

Tayce watched him go, amused by the way he was behaving, especially his disgust at Jan's comment. But Jan heard it all, exclaiming that he guessed he was in trouble. Tayce simply replied that Twedor didn't like Amal being insulted, believe it or not. Twedor had been designed with a feelings pick-up system and Jan had just stepped on them. Jan saw the funny side. He had come a long way since Tayce had met him on voyage one—he had learnt to relax a bit and see the funny side in amusing situations. He laughed, then apologised, shaking his head in utter disbelief.

"Are you aware it's going to be minus 50°C down on Tollatex? I take it you have adequate warm suits over there?" he enquired seriously.

"Yes, all the team get given them when they join the team. It's part of the Quest attire. We're all ready over here—what about you?" asked Tayce casually.

"We're also ready, but my men still aren't keen. They know it's all in the line of duty, but it doesn't take away the fact they could still be killed on this one. To be honest, Tayce, I'm not happy your team are going in," said Jan, still not liking the idea.

"We'll be fine. I'm bringing Twedor and, yes, he does have a specially padded suit."

"I'd like to see those Bore-radds try and get their hands on his eyes. They probably won't have encountered anyone like him before," said Jan, laughing.

Tayce tried not to laugh, but she could see where he was coming from in the fact that the Bore-radds were roughly seven feet tall and hugely built with the ability to move like lightning in their actions to get what they wanted. She could clearly see Twedor raising his Slazer finger as a Bore-radd loomed large over him, opening fire. Jan suggested she contact him when she was ready to head down to the surface and do justice or hopefully terminate the Tremanexan Bore-radds forever. With this, he ceased communications. The desktop screen deactivated just as Dairan entered the DC looking a lot more refreshed from his cleanse and change of uniform.

"I've just met Lance. He told me you're worried about me on the Quest ahead. Why?" he asked casually.

"I was, but you've assured me the team comes first on Tollatex," replied Tayce, to the point.

"You know there's something I want to tell you in the light of this most dangerous of Quests to date," he began, not quite knowing how to tell her what he wanted.

"You're not suited to this team after all, and when this is over you want out. I fully understand that filling Marc's shoes on a temporary basis isn't easy. I can understand you're struggling…" began Tayce in reply, ignoring the fact Dairan was waiting to say what he had on his mind.

"You'll probably think I need to be cautioned for what I'm about to say, but in the last seven monthons my feelings for you have grown and grown. Now we're working really closely. I…" he began apprehensively

"Yes, go on," prompted Tayce, sensing that he was wondering if he should continue.

Without warning, Dairan just went for it. He reached out and pulled her up out of her seat and in close to him with gentle swift force. He lowered his head to kiss her full on the lips, letting all the feelings he felt for her rush forth. As Tayce had found herself taken totally by surprise, she was shocked at first and resisted as his lips met hers, then slowly melted in his strong hold, relaxing totally, succumbing to the same feelings. She draped her arms around his lightly tanned neck, feeling the sudden unexpected shudder of excitement rush through her. This had been a long time coming. He'd toyed with her affections from the moment they'd met and she had felt there was a certain chemistry that had grown between them. This had now erupted. All the feelings behind her rank of captain and leader came forth. She responded to his strong kisses and caressing, picking up on his longing to become more than just friends. In the moments that elapsed, both herself and Dairan moved a step closer to an intimate situation that could be classed as forbidden between captain and relief commander. He scooped her up in his arms and ordered Amal to close and lock the entrance doors. He carried her over to the mouldable soffette, placing her gently down, lowering her back into a lying position. Tayce looked at him, but not in a way that forbade him to continue; quite the reverse. Dairan came down on her gently and they became totally lost in the moment. They became engrossed in what each other wanted to feel and needed in the heat of a passion that had caught them totally by surprise and seemed to drive them on to total fulfilment. Sealing their feelings, which had been bottled up for some time, which had exploded and come to the surface for each other.

One houron later, the intercom sounded on Tayce's desk. She was now back to normal and at her desk, acting as if nothing had happened—which was very hard to do, considering what she and Dairan had shared. Dairan, as the entrance doors opened, winked affectionately upon seeing her looking at him. She pressed the intercom, trying to bring herself back to her duty as leader, instead of the lover she'd been in the last houron.

"Tollatex is now coming into orbital position for us to go into a stationary orbit. What would you like me to do?" asked Kelly casually.

"Go ahead and bring us into a stationary orbit. Then tell everyone it's time to change for the Quest," ordered Tayce.

"Very well," replied Kelly, signing off.

Tayce looked at Dairan. Things had changed between the two of them. Gone was the rank difference; there was now a deep meaningful understanding that had come out of their somewhat untimely intimate encounter. She had discovered the love she had lost with Tom, in Dairan, and more. Now they were looking more like becoming a loving couple, because both had realised there was a deep meaningful love that had formed between the two of them. That, if they were lucky, would last well into their future and beyond. He winked at her affectionately once more, then turned to head on out of the DC, saying he'd better go and get changed into his thermal suit. Tayce announced that what they'd no doubt become would have to be kept to off-duty hourons. He totally agreed. Twedor passed him in the doorway, then continued on in, over to his mistress. Dairan thought to himself that the somewhat heated and passionate moment between himself and Tayce would linger for a while in his mind. She was one exceptionally gifted woman. Tayce read his thoughts. This was real all right between them, she thought. She had no idea he had felt something so strong towards her and she guessed she felt the same. She rose to her feet. She too had to go and change. Twedor scanned his mistress discreetly and found her levels in her system were elevated slightly, just as they were in Dairan when he scanned him earlier as he passed him in the doorway. The kind of levels that signified extreme pleasure had occurred within just under two hourons. He put two and two together, but kept what he'd discovered to himself. He was pleased for his mistress, if she had become more seriously involved with Dairan. She had been a long time without someone in her life to love her seriously, since Tom. They both stepped out into Organisation just as Mac Danford turned to inform Tayce that Craig was about to test-launch the new PolloAld 2 bomb. She paused and in the few cencrons that followed there was a blinding flash of light that made both herself and Mac shield their eyes. This signified that the test had taken place, then was confirmed by the cruiser slightly shaking. Mac gave a whistle of amazement, exclaiming that it looked like Aldonica had done it again, created yet another masterpiece in weaponry. Tayce agreed, suggesting he inform Craig that the weapon should be ready to use on Tollatex and tell him to bring at least enough to use for a possible onslaught of attack. Mac nodded, going on with the request. With this, Tayce turned and called Twedor to go with her, heading on out of Organisation to go and change into her Quest suit and put Twedor in his.

* * *

An houron later, Tayce walked back into Organisation wearing her Quest thermal-protection attire, which consisted of a suit and low-heeled cream boots. The type that would be suitable for walking in freezing landscapes. Lance turned, also kitted out in his Quest suit, complimenting her on her appearance.

"You look like a snow princess," he said, impressed.

"I might look like one, but I don't feel like one, with what we're about to take on," replied Tayce seriously.

Twedor began complaining that he felt like a delicate piece of glassene, not the tough Romid he was. The suit was restricting his movements—why did he have to wear it? He did have thermal controls he could adjust to compensate for the conditions of the planet surface. Tayce firmly informed him that if he didn't wear the suit he would seize up from the frozen conditions. If he didn't want to explode from frozen seizure of his internal parts, then he should wear the suit. Twedor fell silent. He didn't say any more. The thought of his internal parts seizing up, then exploding, made him tolerate his undignified state. Dairan entered the centre looking truly like an Arctic explorer. He acknowledged Lance, then paused as Tayce was suggesting to Mac he contact Chief Barnford and let him know they were ready to go when he was. Mac nodded.

"Lance, head on down and meet Craig and Aldonica in the Transpot Centre. We'll be along soon."

"Right!" he replied, heading on out of Organisation.

"Chief Barnford is informing me he's preparing his men now. He'll be setting down on Tollatex in around twenty-five minons," said Mac, listening to Jan and relaying to Tayce.

"Right, let's go. To give you time, Mac, to head down and get changed, we'll meet you down in the Transpot Centre," suggested Tayce.

"Thanks! Just transferring controls to Amal, then I'll go," he assured, keying in the command for Amal to take overall control of communications.

"Kelly, you're best off here in the warm, but I promise the next Quest is yours," assured Tayce, seeing that the young navigationalist was feeling a bit left out.

"I'm fine. I'll be waiting for your orders," she replied, not bothered she wasn't going, as she didn't want to come face-to-face with the so-called Bore-radds.

"Let us know if anything transpires to threaten our actions down on the surface," asked Tayce.

"Will do. Stay safe," said Kelly, smiling softly.

Tayce followed Dairan with Twedor on out of the Organisation Centre, leaving Kelly in overall command with Amal. In a way Tayce didn't like leaving Kelly on her own, but it wasn't the kind of Quest she would want to send her on, for she was the kind of girl who would probably freeze if she came face-to-face with the Bore-radds. Both she and Dairan soon entered the Deck Travel with Twedor and were heading for Level 2. Tayce took the opportunity to remind him that when the crunch came to the crunch he was not to try anything stupid he couldn't get out of, in revenge for Ben. Dairan nodded. Even though he'd heard it all before, he assured her he wouldn't. The Deck Travel descended and stopped on Level 2 and the doors parted. Tayce was first out, followed by Dairan and Twedor, who looked more like a padded toy than a sophisticated Romid. They briskly walked in the direction of the Transpot Centre, thinking about the Quest ahead. Dairan took out his Pollomoss, checking it was loaded in case he needed to start shooting the moment they set down on the surface.

In the Transpot Centre, everyone was present and waiting, dressed in their white thermal suits. Lance stood next to Aldonica, who was carrying the new PolloAld 2 bombs in a small clear case. The bombs were silver in colour. The size of a small Earth-1 golf ball. Donaldo held his Emergency Medical Kit. Mac came running into the centre, out of breath, pausing. Craig handed him a portable scanner to detect the onslaught of Bore-radds, so none of them got caught out. Jaul Naven was present for the Quest. He was going along as combat back-up. He checked his Pollomoss, in his side holster, making sure it was fully charged and on the right setting to take out any waiting Bore-radds that were aware of their landing on the surface. Tayce, Twedor and Dairan entered the centre. Twedor glanced around at everyone present, as did Tayce, making sure the whole Quest team was present.

"Can I have everyone's attention? As you all know, this is probably the most dangerous of Quests to date. It has two aims. First, with Chief Barnford and his men of the Space Special Weapons and Tactics team, is to find the murdering lawbreakers the Tremanexan Bore-radds—that's if they haven't already detected us and are waiting down on the surface for us. We will bring them to justice. Our second aim is to destroy their base. That's where you come in, Aldonica. We'll be using your latest success. Don't take chances down on Tollatex, any of you. I want this team to come back in one piece—is that understood?" said Tayce, glancing at Dairan and around the team.

Everyone nodded in total understanding around the centre. They knew if they made any slip-ups it would be goodbye life in the most horrific of ways.

"We all saw the Vidfilm on Marc being attacked. Is this definitely the kind of force we're up against and about to face?" enquired Jaul, wanting to know.

"I'm afraid so, Jaul, but Chief Barnford's men are there to assist. If it's any consolation, they aren't feeling any easier than we are, but this is a task that has to be undertaken to stop what happened to Marc happening again to someone else, whoever it may be. Let's go," ordered Tayce.

Everyone began taking up their marks on the Transpot floored area. Tayce made sure Twedor was right where he needed to stand. The team took out their handguns ready, and stood poised in case they needed to start shooting the moment they landed. Tayce raised her Wristlink, ordering Kelly in Organisation to commence Transpot. The soft green swirling aura of Transpot took form underfoot, rising around the bodies of each individual team member. Tayce used her transference gift of power to take her from the cruiser to the surface, linking her thoughts with the computer bearings of Amal. Upon closing her eyes, Tayce along with the others began to dematerialise off the cruiser on the way to Tollatex. Treketa and Sallen watched them leave. Treketa hoped to God that Donaldo would be OK. She turned and walked back out up the corridor to see Kelly, to track the Quest with her in Organisation. Though she would be ready to head down to the surface at a moment's notice if needed.

* * *

Tollatex, a cold and white hostile world. A world belonging to the murderous eye-stealing race known as the Tremanexan Bore-radds. There was snow and mountains for as far as the eye could see. It greeted the Quest team upon their arrival. To make the conditions of the surface worse, there were howling winds blowing the snow about. Jan Barnford arrived with his men and they were just as padded out in their attire for the task ahead they had to undertake as was the Amalthean Quests team. They quickly sheltered behind some rocks, dug out in the rock face of one of the snow covered mountains, and went about scanning for any forces that could emerge from nowhere—namely, the Bore-radds. The Quest team quickly hurried to join them. All wore snow protection, including anti-glare eye shields, to protect their eyes. Jan looked Tayce up and down, impressed, trying not to make it obvious he was doing it, thinking how breathtaking she looked considering the task they had ahead. Both team leaders were soon in discussion about the best course of action to take first. After a while, Jan pointed in the decided direction they'd all head off in.

"Listen up. Our object, as some of you may know, is to get into that large building about a milon from here. It is believed (and a scan confirms it) to be the main domain of the Bore-radds. I need not remind you, don't let your defences down for one cencron when we're inside. Is that understood? I don't want to return to Enlopedia and have to fill out a death report because someone here failed in their concentration. I don't think the Captain here wants to do the same for anyone in the Amalthea team either, so no heroics—is that understood? We work in unison with each other on both teams," said Jan, pacing back and forth, glancing at his own men and the members of the Amalthean Quests team as both teams listened.

"I hope you all listened in my team because, like Chief Barnford said, I don't want to have to compile death reports either," said Tayce straightforwardly.

Everyone nodded in total understanding, then began moving off as Jan gave the word to move out. Both teams set off across the snowy treacherous terrain in the direction of the Bore-radds' central building. Twedor looked up at Tayce as they walked along on the snow-covered ground. She kept him close to her as they walked through the howling winds that seemed to push against them as they ventured forth into the open. Jan's men kept a lookout for any sudden sign of advancing Bore-radds, but nothing materialised.

Craig glanced at Aldonica, exclaiming, "Not only do they get a killer Quest; they get the killer temperatures that go with it!"

Aldonica couldn't help but laugh.

Tayce heard the conversation between the two of them and a smile crossed her face. Even on serious Quests, such as they were on, Craig's humour always came through, she thought, to keep everyone's spirits up.

After walking for what seemed an eternity—the best part of a full milon—Craig checked his portable scanner and found it difficult to push the inset keys for a clear reading, because of the snow being whipped up by the winds that in the last houron had seemed to grow stronger. After Aldonica grabbed him, sheltering what he was trying to do, he scanned and found what appeared to be a large object covering the best part of five square milons in area ahead. He drew Tayce's attention to the large heat source ahead, covered in snow, and the smaller heat sources moving within. Jan listened, stopping his men. His bearings had been confirmed by Craig. It was Bore-radd Central. On Tayce's word, he gathered his men around and ordered them to be ready—they were going in. The two teams realised this was it. Time to face the Bore-radds. As they continued on the last steps to the base, there were almost sixty people in the combined team heading through the snow, including Twedor. Everyone had their hands on their Slazers, primed ready for the first Bore-radd to appear—but there was nothing. Craig couldn't understand why they hadn't been detected yet, unless the Bore-radds' scanning equipment had frozen solid. As they came to what looked like large wide doors, the snow underfoot became deep and hard to walk in. It was equivalent to a solid ice-skating platform underfoot. Both teams found it treacherous. Members steadied one another when they slipped. Aldonica took one of the PolloAld 2 bombs and set it ready to go off in silent mode. Both teams ran behind a mound of rock and snow, near to the entrance, as Aldonica threw the bomb in a rolling motion towards the entrance doors, then ran to be with the others in hiding.

The entrance doors shook, signifying the lock mechanism had blown. It was time to go in. Both teams held their weapons primed ready to open fire once inside, because they didn't have time to think about drawing and shooting, because of the fast way in which the Bore-radds attacked. Once inside, there was a wide open expanse, rather like a large foyer. The smell of fresh raw flesh hung in the air in a strong stench. It was so strong it nearly made the female members of the Quest team want to throw up. The deeper the teams walked, the worse the smell became. But the entrance area soon turned into wide cavernous corridors, formed out of the rocks the building had been carved from. Water, or some other kind of liquid, dripped from above. Out of the corner of his eye, Dairan spotted a Bore-radd. It was the ugliest thing he'd ever seen, covered in dark scales, with a thin body and long limbs with pointed fingers that were almost like needles. Its eyes were purple with a small slit for its pupil, with a crazy look about them and set at the top of its head, rather like the eyes of a fly. Dairan wondered if they were a set stolen from an unsuspecting victim of another race. It made him feel sick to his stomach just thinking about it. The Bore-radd's features were narrow and pointed. What would have been its chin was coated with smaller dark scales. The whole creature looked like it had originated from a sea creature of the twenty-first century. Without alerting anyone, Dairan decided to take off and get a better look at the creature, even though he had promised Tayce he wouldn't. Lance followed suit, upon the nod from Tayce to do so. Jan immediately called two of his officers to assist. They took to their heels with their guns primed, and went off in pursuit of Lance and Dairan. Jan gave a look of total annoyance that said it all. Words failed Tayce over Dairan's actions. She was furious at him. After a few minons, Jan discreetly assured her that no harm would come to him or Lance, despite his rash actions. His men would see to that. He suggested they head in the same direction as Craig's scanner readings confirmed the Bore-radds' main gathering point was, dead ahead, in the same cavernous corridor.

Just as they were about to follow on, out of nowhere leapt a Bore-radd, right into the path of Tayce. It leered down on her, studying her for a moment with its piercing eyes almost weighing her up for the disastrous strike, to take her life and her sight. But before it had a chance to take her, Tayce used her powers, instead of her weapon, and drove it to an untimely death just by using her thoughts. It writhed in agony as it fell to the ground and cried out before death. Jan and his officers backed her up, firing at the creature also. Jan quickly rushed forth to check she was all right. She felt shaken, but pleased. For the first time she'd used her powers to save herself, which the Empress had taught her at Questa after the end of the first voyage. Jan had a look of alarm in his eyes. Tayce gave him a look that said she was shaken, but OK.

They continued on for about a milon, deeper into the darkly lit cavernous corridor. Suddenly there came the sound of Amalthean Pollomoss Slazer fire and SSWAT weapon fire. Aldonica, on Tayce's word, began setting the PolloAld 2 bombs and placing them with enough time to get them into the heart of Bore-radd Central. But there was a surprise waiting for both teams in the form of the Tremanexan Bore-radd leader, which neither team was expecting. When everyone came together—Jan, Tayce, Aldonica and Mac, plus some of Jan's officers—they began attacking the onslaught of Bore-radds. It was like they'd ventured into a nest. They were everywhere in their onslaught to take out the members of both teams, falling from cavernous hideouts and leaping from spaces in rock faces.

"Next time you feel like making a bold move, count me out. These things are hideous," said Lance, firing on the advancing Bore-radds with highly skilled shots, taking them out one by one.

"I've got a feeling this isn't all of them. There's an entrance of some sorts over there," replied Dairan, pointing as he continued to fire round after round, wishing he hadn't acted on his stupid impulse to take out the one Bore-radd he saw.

Craig checked the scanner reading out of sight to see where the entrance led, firing occasionally. He confirmed it was an entrance all right and there was possibly an inner chamber further in, or what looked to be one. When the present wave of Bore-radds had vaporised and Jan's men had checked the loading of their weapons, Jan ordered them to spread out around the entrance across from their current point, ready to shoot any Bore-radds advancing in their direction the moment the door opened. They slowly advanced forth, coming to a pause around the entrance. He pointed out to his men that Tremanexor, the Bore-radd leader, was their main priority, if he could be found. Tayce, Dairan, Jan, Lance and Mac began over to the entrance under the watchful protection of Jan's men. They paused, studying how they were going to get in. It was a heavy steelecreate-type door. There was only one thing and that was to blow the door from its hold. Aldonica came forth with a PolloAld bomb, setting it with just enough force to blow the mechanism. Twedor sheltered with Tayce as Aldonica stepped back after placement. There was a mild explosion and the door, to their amazement, separated in the middle and each side slid back into the wall on either side. No more Bore-radds rushed forth, much to the relief of both teams. They cautiously ventured inside, into the near darkness of the room that had been revealed.

"You three, come with me; you others, remain here on guard. Alert me if any trouble arrives," ordered Jan, to the point.

"Yes, sir!" came the reply from the men, in acknowledgement.

Without warning, the moment Tayce stepped inside, lighting activated, illuminating their entire surroundings. No one was prepared for the sight that greeted them. It was totally beyond belief. The team were totally speechless at what they were seeing all around them. In row upon row, from floor to ceiling, encased in glassene casings, were sets of human and alien eyes in every shape and colour. Set on supports, all looking like they were staring back at those who had just entered the room. Aldonica, with her strong constitution as weaponry specialist, who had seen some pretty horrendous sights during her training, was finding the sight unbelievable and creepy. Twedor whistled in disbelief. Dairan looked up and found he was staring right into the familiar brown eyes of his brother. Tears of sheer gut-wrenching hurt tore at him in every way. The torture Ben had gone through, he thought, before his untimely death, didn't bear thinking about. Tayce turned. Even though she was angry at him deep down for what he'd done earlier, she understood what he was thinking. She placed an understanding hand on his arm, after reading his thoughts. Dairan glanced at her with an expression of true hurt. He looked away and his sight caught a further door at the end of the room.

"You mentioned an inner chamber, Craig. What's in there?" enquired Dairan, trying to gain his composure, which wasn't easy after what he'd just seen.

Craig checked his scanner and announced one life form occupied the next chamber, and the readings seemed to be human and alive. Jan summoned the rest of his men from out on enemy watch, back where they'd just left. The officers soon entered the room. Glancing around, they were both horrified and taken aback by the sight of the encased sets of eyes around the walls from floor to ceiling. Some shook their heads at the gut-wrenching sight. Jan quickly brought them back to attention with a few words of command to pay attention. Upon their chief's words, they immediately returned to being upstanding elite officers, ready to obey their chief's orders. Jan ordered his men to aim their weapons at the far door of the room and fire. The door blew from its hold, shattering several sets of the encased eyes before it. The eyes fell to the floor and rolled. One landed near Twedor. He squirmed and stepped back behind Tayce. It made Tayce cringe to think someone's eye had just rolled in their direction and was looking up at her. The Amalthean Quests members set their weapons to 'disintegrate' in case there was more than one being in the next room and some kind of force was shielding him or it, even though Craig had only detected one. Dairan was the only one who didn't set his gun to the same setting as the others. Instead, he set it on a long burst of energy fire, so the being in the next room, if it was found to be the leader, would feel the wrath of justice on behalf of his brother. He wanted the creep to suffer the same agonising pain his brother felt in the eye-stealing clutches of his Bore-radds. Twedor could see the setting he'd set and nudged Tayce with his little metlon hand. Upon her turning, Twedor whisperingly announced what Dairan had done. Tayce glanced over at the Pollomoss setting to see he was right. She concentrated on switching the setting back to 'stun'. She didn't want Jan arresting Dairan for interfering in the apprehension of the leader of the Bore-radds, if he was the being in the next room. Everyone went forth, weapons primed. As Lance passed the side of the entrance, to enter in, he caught sight of a small red flashing light. He drew Jan's attention to it. It meant only one thing. They'd been detected and their immediate vicinity would be crawling with Bore-radds at any cencron. Jan didn't like the situation at all, as it stood. He turned to Aldonica, suggesting she start setting and laying the PolloAld 2 bombs, allowing enough time for them to get what they hoped was inside and leave. She nodded understandingly.

As they entered the room more fully, she discreetly went here and there, setting and placing the PolloAld 2 bombs neatly out of sight. Jan, as he saw the being in the middle of the room on a dark stonex throne, was surprised by his appearance. For the being was human up to its neck, and at the neck he had the same head and features as the Bore-radds. What was he? Jan wondered. Human or Bore-radd? Had this been someone the Bore-radds had captured and tortured to be a leader, giving him these features by some kind of mistreatment surgery so he would look like them? As Jan neared on alert, the half-human half-Bore-radd turned his head. His eyes were dark purple with black circular pupils, smaller than a human eye. This wasn't right, thought Jan in total surprise and awe. The room was in almost total darkness, so it was difficult to see. There was just enough light to make out someone or something. Lance glanced around. This, he thought, had to be the main command room, the centre of all of the Tremanexan Bore-radd operations. There were plenty of gadgets to put forth orders to attack vessels, such as the Astrona Star, and do what they wished.

After a few minons of studied silence, the leader of the Tremanexan Bore-radds introduced himself, amazingly in spoken English. As he did so, on either side of the vast room, from every corner entrance, came grey-clad beings that were human in body form, with heads like the Bore-radds, carrying some kind of black spear-like weapons. Dairan was finding his temper hard to control. The Amaltheans and Jan's men readied themselves, taking aim with their weapons. Dairan studied the weapons the Bore-radd obvious guards were carrying, wondering if this was the kind of weapon they used on his brother. The obvious leader stood and came down from the throne as his men encircled the outer edge of the room. He gestured for his guards to lower their weapons. Tayce studied him, trying to read his evil mind. The leader picked up on what she was doing and glared back at her with a cold, threatening stare.

"My guards are primed—death is certain for you all if you don't say your reasons for being here, considering you've strayed on to this world without permission," demanded Tremanexor in an icy-cold tone.

His half-human, half-Bore-radd guards all around the room watched on, primed ready to commence obeying their leader's orders. Both teams present felt extremely uneasy, ready to spring into action at a moment's notice to protect themselves against the threatening Bore-radd guards.

"The name's Barnford. I'm chief of security at Enlopedia Headquarters Base. We're here to place you under arrest for the destruction of one of our vessels—

the Astrona Star, to be exact. Before you give the order to your goons all around, I would think carefully. Your men, or whatever you want to term them, may be fast, but my men will take yours out before they even move a muscle—and they never miss," said Jan with meaning.

Upon Jan's words, Tremanexor grunted something to his men and just what Jan suspected would happen did. All hell broke loose on both sides, whilst Tremanexor retreated swiftly to make a quick exit. The spear-type weapons the guards were holding quickly began firing round after round at the Quest team and SSWAT team. Many of the shots hit home on the blue armour of the SSWAT officers. Slazer bolts of immense firepower flew from the Amaltheans and Twedor. It was a mass crossfire, of sheer weapon fire, on both sides.

Tayce, amongst the onslaught of weapon fire, realised Dairan was nowhere to be seen. Glancing around in the near darkness, shooting back in retaliation, her sight was caught by Dairan at the end of a death-defying arrival of none other than a Bore-radd that had him on the floor and was about to tear him to shreds. She knew, even though he had disobeyed orders not to stray earlier, she could not let him die. She quickly retreated behind the others and used her powers to do what she had done earlier to the last Bore-radd they'd encountered—she drove it to its death. This time, though, she emitted a blue powerful force from her eyes and sent it straight into the heart of the Bore-radd. After a few minons the Bore-radd turned its evil head in her direction, screamed and dropped to the floor. Dairan glanced at Tayce, trying to get his composure back to normal.

The action stopped abruptly. All the guards were gone—vaporised. The room was empty. Jan glanced around his men, glad to see they were still present apart from two who he knew had taken off after Tremanexor earlier. He gave a look of concern towards the entrance. Tayce walked over to Dairan.

"You disobeyed my orders, but I wasn't going to let you die," she stated, holding out her hand to help him up on to his feet.

He took hold of her hand and, as she hauled him back to a standing position, he thanked her. Two of Jan's officers that had seen Tremanexor try and make a run for it had apprehended him at the entrance and were hauling him back into the room, much to Jan's relief. Dairan almost flew across the room and was going to lunge at Tremanexor. Tayce quickly acted to stop Dairan getting in his way.

"No, Dairan, leave it. He's not worth it. He'll pay for what he's done—and, believe me, it's going to be a death far worse than what he did to your brother and Marc. Forget it—that's an order!" ordered Tayce sharply.

Dairan's eyes were dark and wide with anger. He backed down on Tayce's command, even though he wanted to deal with the murderous jerk himself. He had already disobeyed one too many orders. Donaldo put away his weapon and began to attend to the injured on both teams. Jaul Naven had sustained a cut above his left eye, but nothing serious. Aldonica checked on the settings on the PolloAld 2 bombs. She quickly spoke up and suggested they left—there was little time left on the timers, before things would start coming apart as the explosives went off. Jan immediately ordered his two officers who had Tremanexor to secure him in a force field and take him back to the cruiser.

Dairan, as the former leader of the Bore-radd race walked past in the company of two of Jan's men, gave him a look of pure hatred. Lance put a friendly advising hand on his shoulder, advising him to do what Tayce suggested: forget it. Tayce crossed to Jan, enquiring what was going to happen to Tremanexor? He turned and began to explain that he'd be taken back to trial by the Enlopedian Criminal Council where Dairan would no doubt be required to make a report on what he could recall of Ben's demise. Dairan heard what was being said.

"You have my total support. Just call," assured Dairan, helpfully, to the point.

"We'd better get out of here before this planet blows and we go up with it," announced Jan.

"I agree," replied Tayce gladly.

"Chief, before you leave, thanks for seeing justice done—not only for Marc, but for my brother," announced Dairan, pleased.

"Think nothing of it. When you've seen and dealt with situations like I have over the past yearons, you're glad justice can be done to criminals like Tremanexor. I class it as all in a dayon's duty," replied Jan, glad to have achieved what he had come to do.

"Yes, thanks for taking this one on with us," backed up Tayce casually.

"Like I said to Dairan—all in a dayon's duty," he replied with a rugged smile.

"Keep me informed of what the outcome is," said Tayce, joining the others for Transpot with Twedor.

Jan did as Tayce had done and joined his men to transport back to the Patrol Cruiser. He raised his Wristlink, ordering his Patrol Cruiser captain to transport him and the team immediately. Within the next few cencrons Jan and his officers were gone in the Transpot aura back to the Patrol Cruiser. Tayce glanced around her team, glad they'd succeeded in yet another Quest in the cause of justice and lived to tell about it.

"Are we ready to go?" she asked.

"Let's just get out of here," said Aldonica in urgency.

Tayce glanced at Twedor, glad he had come through unscathed and had fought well as a little Romid. Then she saw he hadn't escaped entirely. He had some damage, but nothing Craig couldn't put right. She raised her Wristlink, contacting Kelly on Amalthea, ordering immediate Transpot. In the next moments, like Jan and his team, the Amalthean Quests team and Twedor disappeared in the swirling green aura back to Amalthea.

* * *

Outside, as the explosions began blowing rock and snow sky-high, the rest of the remaining Bore-radds that were converging on where the teams had been were instantly being blown apart. The Tremanexan Bore-radds and Tollatex were rapidly becoming a thing of the past, never to operate again. In space, as the final explosion occurred, there was a spectacular array of planetary debris erupting into space and Tollatex was no more. Justice had been served again. The Universe was safe from the murderous eye-stealing race.

9. Distress Call at Entronet

Night hourons aboard Amalthea, after the successful apprehension that dayon of Tremanexor. The cruiser had resumed its normal voyage course. Tayce was the only one on duty after the Organisation team had handed over the controls to Amal for the night hourons and gone off duty. Twedor was keeping her company, as she sat at her desk talking with Jan Barnford on the Telelinkphone in the DC at Enlopedia. Much to her surprise Dairan came through the doorway. She had expected him to head off to his off-duty pursuits. He could see she was in conversation and decided to hang around, perching on the edge of the soffette arm until she'd finished. Whilst waiting, he glanced in the direction of Organisation, thinking how strange it was it was team-less. Tayce, after a few minons, finished the call. Placing the handset down, she explained what Jan had just told her, that Tremanexor was to be put on trial at first light in the new Council Chamber, and her father would be present to read both his and Marc's report on what happened to both his brother and Marc. The reading would be taken into consideration as part of the evidence before a final decision was made on what would become of Tremanexor. Dairan nodded understandingly. She continued, saying Jan had expressed the opinion that it was most likely to be classed as 'termination of life', which meant Tremanexor would be taken from the trial and his life terminated with one shot of a marksman's weapon in the Termination Chamber. This pleased Dairan—Tremanexor's death couldn't come soon enough for the type of crimes he had committed. Tayce rose to her feet and walked round to the front of the desk, perching on the edge.

"This might not be as cut and dry as we'd like to think. There was a murder similar to what Tremanexor did and it happened just on two yearons ago. Everyone thought it was a foregone conclusion. There was enough evidence set against the guilty party, but out of the blue someone paid a large sum of currency for his release and, believe it or not, he walked free."

"So even after all the evidence that's stacked against Tremanexor, if someone comes up with the same, or springs him in some way, he could walk free?" asked Dairan in utter disbelief.

"We'll just have to wait and see. Father will do all he can, but the outcome will be out of his hands," pointed out Tayce softly. She could see how furious he felt, by the look on his face.

"So it's a case of thanks for nothing. Great! See you in the mornet," he said, forgetting what he had come to see her about, heading back to the entrance, not looking back.

"Hold on—Coffeen before you turn in for the night?" she called after him, but it fell on deaf ears.

She understood how he felt about Tremanexor. He was right—he did deserve to have his life terminated—but there was nothing she could do, except be there for him should the decision go against what he wanted. Nobody ever could assume a case would go in their favour. It was a kind of sod's law—when you want something badly, fate sometimes steps in and the decision ten to one wanted is never achieved. She could see Dairan was in that position. He wanted the decision to be given in his favour, against Tremanexor.

"Yeah, why not?" he replied, walking back in from the outside corridor, much to her surprise.

Tayce crossed to the programmable drinks-and-refreshment dispenser unit, keying in a sequence of numbers on the slim keypad at the side as she reached it. After a few minons, two cups of fresh Coffeen materialised on her desk, as she could key in wherever she wanted them set down. She crossed back and was about to pick up the cups, which were of half heat-resistant glassene set in a metlon base. Dairan, much to her surprise, had walked up behind her. He slipped his hands slowly around her waist, to the front, and pulled her back against him. slowly lowering his head to kiss her on the neck softly. She caved as his lips touched her skin, falling back against him, enjoying his close presence. He took this as the signal to continue, and moved his head to kiss her more softly and slowly, in such a way that she felt an uncontrollable soft shudder rush through her, spreading throughout her existence. Twedor was watching silently, realising his mistress and Dairan were truly made for each other. He could see it. He just hoped the same unforeseen fate that met Tom Stavard, Tayce's first husband, didn't happen again, to Dairan. Tayce pulled away softly and turned to face him, looking up into his brown eyes for a few minons. She felt sensually lost. She could read what he wanted and she felt the same. Love had become strong for them. He pulled her in close, swiftly and gently. They were looking into each other's eyes, letting everything melt away around them. Twedor wanted to whistle as Dairan looked at her in a sexual questioning way, asking if she wanted to go further, like they'd done before. Tayce, for some strange reason—and it hadn't happened before—was suddenly afraid, feeling the amazing tenderness she was feeling and more. Even though it had been some time since the death of Tom, it was like she was scared to commit her feelings fully for Dairan in case something happened to him, like it did to Tom. It was as if Dairan had been able to read what she was thinking.

"Relax! Nothing bad is going to happen. I'm not going anywhere, I promise," he said softly, then slowly brought his lips down on hers, beginning to kiss her.

He kissed her lightly at first, then, as Tayce let go of what she feared in going forward, he kissed her with stronger meaning. He wanted her just like he had before. Tayce draped her arms around his uniformed neck, giving in to the pure passion that was materialising between them, letting go of the past. Tayce was finding that a power she never knew existed in her abilities was suddenly growing within her, and it was one that was extremely sensual and soft. They both found each other responding to each other's wants and needs to fulfil their desire for each other. Tayce's power was growing by the cencron and it seemed to drive Dairan on. Empress Tricara had told her of such a power and said it could be triggered in a moment of intimate bliss. It was known as the Telepathian Sensuality of Ultimate Pleasure. As it grew to a higher pitch, the power rushed forth and encased both her and Dairan's bodies, making them as one. An orange aura bathed them in a warm, soft, pleasurable glow as they stood in the middle of the DC. Dairan swept her up in his strong arms and carried her towards the DC doorway, kissing her with soft tentative kisses, and suggested they continue what they were feeling in his quarters.

"Yes," came the soft reply from Tayce, captivated by the feeling of wanting him.

She couldn't resist the feelings she was feeling, and what Dairan was doing to her was making her sensually lost. The attraction this night hourons was strong to the extreme. It was as if this whole situation was just waiting to surface between the two of them. But this time, unlike the first time, there was some unexplainable force that was driving them deeper. A kind of strong bond was forming in their relationship for each other that would luckily last forever. Twedor watched them go, and in his own little way he figured this night was going to be the beginning of a meaningful relationship for his mistress and Dairan. She had found happiness again. It made him feel good to see Tayce happy again. It had been a long time coming. He went to standby mode, putting his systems into self-recharge for the night hourons. The lights in the DC went to semi-darkness and all that could be heard was the familiar sound of the cruiser in operational mode.

***

It was 02:30 hourons. Amal was receiving what was termed a distress call from a paradise world named Entronet. Upon receiving it and considering whether there were any nearer vessels that could assist, it was decided it was for Tayce's attention. Even though Amal did not want to disturb her mistress, she contacted

Tayce's quarters, sounding her intercom in the Living Area. She found there was no answer. She had been told by Tayce that she did not want to be disturbed unless it was extremely urgent. Amal ran a scan of Level 3, finding her mistress was, in fact, in Dairan's quarters. To be discrete and respectful to her, she contacted Tayce's Wristlink, making it light up intermittently.

* * *

Down in Dairan Loring's quarters in the Repose Centre, on the bunk-side top, sat Tayce's slim silver Wristlink. In the grey silkene sheets of the double bunk adjacent was Tayce, lying in the strong, slightly tanned arms of Dairan. She was peaceful, with her bare left arm draped over Dairan's bare upper torso. He was also in a silent peaceful sleep. The alarm sounded on Tayce's Wristlink as Amal could wait no longer. She slowly opened her eyes, wondering if she'd heard right. She looked up at Dairan, smiling, remembering the onslaught of their soft, pleasurable time, which had unfolded and had gone on for the best part of two hourons. It would be a night that would always stand out for her. This night he'd treated her with the utmost respect and softness in his experienced moves to please her. Her Wristlink sounded again, pulling her back to reality. She put what had happened between her and Dairan to the back of her mind, sitting up and taking the Wristlink from the bunk-side top. She tried not to wake Dairan, but he'd felt her sit up beside him. He too sat up, concerned something was wrong. He lightly touched her on the bare arm in a questioning way. She turned to smile at him for a few minons, then climbed from the bunk, reaching for her uniform. Dairan reached out for his 'D' gown and threw it on, doing it up as he slid from the bunk. Tayce quickly but reluctantly put her uniform back on. She would have liked to cleanse herself before the arising emergency. Dairan, upon reaching her, reached out and gently gave her a kiss on her cheek, whispering close to her that she was very special, especially with the perfect powerful gift of intimacy he'd remember forever. Tayce broke away, quickly answering the sounding Wristlink, wondering what was wrong.

"Captain, we have an emergency. I need you in Organisation immediately," said Amal.

"I'm on my way, Amal," replied Tayce, ceasing communications.

She left Dairan standing and hurried towards the outer quarters entrance doors. As they drew apart she ran out and on her way to Organisation in urgency. What she and Dairan had done in the last hourons was purely off duty and had to be left there. Now it was time to turn her attention to the present emergency. A while later, halfway up the Level Steps, Craig and Lance caught up with her in their night attire, saying Amal was recalling them to Organisation for an emergency.

"What's happening, Amal?" demanded Tayce as she ran into the Organisation Centre on Level 1.

"I'm receiving a distress call from a planet in our near orbital distance. It's the planet Entronet, I've been picking up the message from the surface. I've scanned and pinpointed the origin of the signal. It's coming from a group of buildings there," explained Amal.

"What are the buildings used for—any information?" asked Tayce, interested, standing looking at the yellowish planet through the sight port.

"It's research and space exploration. It drifted away from its mother planet about nine yearons ago. It holds a living, thriving colony of humanoid-type inhabitants—around 4,500 of oriental origin," replied Amal.

"Can they communicate with us, other than sending a distress signal?" asked Tayce.

"They seem only to be able to deliver a distress message at this time," replied Amal.

"What do you reckon?" asked Lance, close to her, then glancing out.

"I'll try and let them know somehow we've picked up their distress signal," said Mac, having entered the centre in his night attire to hear what was unfolding.

He briskly went to his duty position and began finding a way to send some kind of message, saying who they were, that the Amalthea had picked up their distress call and they were on their way to help.

"What's going on?" asked Dairan, walking in, cleansed and in a uniform.

"We've received a distress call from that planet out there. It's name is Entronet. We're in the process of letting them know we've received it and we're on our way to help," she replied casually.

Mac soon turned at communications, explaining that, whatever had happened to communications on the surface of Entronet, they only had one way to communicate and that was through sending a distress message. On Mac's words, Tayce went into thought for a moment, then ordered Amal to run a plague scan over the entire planet. Everyone present looked at Tayce, wondering why. Dairan glanced at her too, wondering, then looked out through the sight port at Entronet, realising she was just being cautious. Amal soon returned with a scan report, which had come back with an all-clear reading.

"Right, that's it. We're going down to the surface. Amal check on the Entronet temperature and pick a team for going," ordered Tayce in the true tone of captain.

"Planetary temperatures are in the nineties. It's the same as the Earth-1 season known as summer, in the month known as July. Clothing for the Quest should be light and comfortable, though there does seem to be the threat of what is termed a shower of plicetar," explained Amal informatively.

"Plicetar—drinking water. That will be handy!" said Craig, seeing the funny side.

"She means water, not drinking water. Lance, I want you to remain on board in command. Check if there is a dayon/night-hourons rota," replied Tayce, though she did find what Craig said amusing.

"Sure you want this now?" he asked, gesturing to the fact he was hardly dressed for duty.

"Yes, now!" replied Tayce, ignoring his night attire of just silkene pj bottoms.

Lance said no more. In no time at all he had seated himself at his console and had called up the information on Entronet. He scrolled down through until he came to the information he wanted, then turned to Tayce.

"Information states there's a dayon/night-houron cycle. At the present time they are in their dayon time and have six hourons left before nightfall sets in."

"Fine! Then I suggest whoever has been picked to go on the Quest with me head off and get cleansed and changed. Please announce to all concerned, Amal," said Tayce.

Going on the emergency Quest was Dairan, Craig, Kelly, Twedor, Tayce, Sallen, Jaul, Donaldo and Treketa. Tayce ordered Amal to inform Donaldo and Treketa that they were requested to go and to bring the Emergency Medical Kit. Amal confirmed the request as Tayce headed on out of Organisation to go and get cleansed and changed for the Quest ahead. The members in Organisation picked to go followed on. Amal took back control of some of the operations for night duty, telling Lance that if he wanted to cleanse and change for duty she would take control until he returned. Lance agreed and headed on out quickly, telling Amal he wouldn't be long.

* * *

Craig, roughly half an houron later, cleansed and changed for the Quest ahead, hurried down to the Robot and Technical Service Section, where he'd left Twedor earlier that night after collecting him from Organisation, after Tayce had left him in the DC. He'd repaired the slight damage from their Quest to Tollatex and was just letting Twedor remain in the section until first light. He soon entered the section, crossing to Twedor, who was suspended on a secure harness three feet above the ground, attached by slim cables from the Diagnostic and Energy Replenishing Bench.

"Come on, mate, activate to normal mode. It's time to go—you're wanted on an emergency," said Craig, taking the small slim connectors off Twedor's outer casing, pushing a button on the diagnostic energy crane to lower him to the floor. Upon Twedor setting down he clicked and hummed as every circuit came back to full operational power and his plasmatronic brain began returning to full operational function. Twedor was like a humanoid child in build, around the age of five, waking up from a deep sleep, moving all his metlon joints one by one. Craig smiled and waited, thinking back to the first time he'd activated him, when he'd completed him after five yearons of perfecting the perfect companion and being recruited to design a companion and escort for Tayce.

"You ready to go?" Craig asked Twedor.

"Yes, right with you," replied Twedor walking to catch Craig up.

They both walked across the Robot and Technical Service Section, on up to Level 3, to rendezvous with the others on the Quest team. Twedor was finding his limbs were stiff as he'd been in the suspended position off the floor for the best part of four hourons as Amal helped Craig put him right. Craig made sure they walked up the Level Steps to get his little legs moving again, so he would be all right for the Quest ahead.

The Flight Hangar Bay—05:00 hourons. The Quest team walked in ready for the Quest ahead. They were dressed in a lightweight uniform of navy trousers and navy T-shirt with a white thin stripe running across the chest with a 'QE' emblem in gold on the right-hand side, just above the stripe. Footwear was shoes in a leisure-type design, in white, but with enough protection to protect the sole of the foot from dangerous objects protruding from the surface. Sallen and Jaul walked in carrying specimen kits and a diagnostic pack, just in case they found anything interesting plant-wise to safely bring back to the cruiser. Craig and Twedor walked in. Craig carried his tech kit in case it was needed to repair the damage to the communications system where they were going. Donaldo and Treketa were next to walk in, carrying their Emergency Medical Kits. Last was Dairan. He had a hunch he'd be the last to arrive. Tayce caught him looking at her as he entered briskly and came to a pause. She could see their time together, a couple of hourons ago, had shattered him slightly, but he'd been the one to turn on the enticement, not her.

Everyone soon loaded their emergency equipment into the small luggage hold of the Quest shuttle/fighter, then climbed aboard. They each strapped themselves into the safety restraints. Dairan slid into the pilot seat—the one Marc would normally occupy. Craig took the co-pilot seat once he'd made sure everyone was present and secure. Tayce sat just behind Dairan once she'd made sure Twedor was safely seated. She pulled the safety restraints over her shoulders and secured them. Soon the Quest 3 lifted off the Flight Hangar Bay floor, heading towards the opening hangar doors to leave the cruiser. Tayce relaxed back. She looked out of one of the five side ports as they broke into space, leaving the cruiser behind. She couldn't help it, but she began thinking about herself and Dairan and what had unfolded between them suddenly in the last hourons. She was wondering where they'd take what had happened next. Was there a chance it could become something more on a permanent footing for them, in becoming a couple, or would they become so engrossed in duty first that it would fade away? Only time would tell. Treketa looked at Tayce. She could see she was thoughtful about something.

"Are you all right? You look troubled. Anything you want to share?" asked Treketa softly.

"No, I'm fine. I'm just thinking about this unscheduled Quest, that's all," replied Tayce, giving her a warm smile to convey nothing was wrong.

"Are you sure you're feeling all right? You're looking a little pale," said Donaldo, studying her, concerned.

"Stop it, both of you. I'm fine. I just didn't get to sleep earlier, that's all," replied Tayce, glancing discreetly at Dairan.

Dairan, up in the pilot seat, announced that Entronet was dead ahead. With that, he brought the shuttle/fighter smoothly but sharply round and began to find a clearing where he could set down. Finally he set the Quest down a short distance from the base. As the Quest descended, so the team aboard could make out groups of one- and two-storey square grey buildings on the surface. Dairan looked out as he brought the engines to a standstill. So far the area seemed safe, he thought. He turned, asking Craig what he thought about their immediate surroundings. Craig agreed that everything looked reasonably calm at present. Dairan suggested it would be wise to keep their wits about them, though, just in case it was an elaborate trap of some sort. Craig agreed wholeheartedly. Tayce stood Twedor on his feet, from his seat, and glanced at Dairan, thinking that since he had taken over Marc's position temporarily he'd adapted well to being in assisting charge and had learnt not to overrule her, when it came to her making decisions regarding the team. It could be said that his attitude to life had become more grown-up and he was taking his duty more seriously.

"What do you reckon?" Dairan asked her. "Everything looks calm enough—no onslaught of weapon fire."

"Quite, but you can never be sure it's not an elaborate trap, or know what's lurking in the vicinity," replied Tayce as Craig pressed the entrance mechanism panel.

All agreed with her.

Tayce further suggested they be on their guard when outside, just in case. Entronet might be like a paradise world, but there could be dangers that caused the distress call waiting. The entrance hatch slid back, revealing a warm, sunny, breathable atmosphere, rather like an earth summer day on. But was everything as peaceful and tranquil as it seemed? Tayce stepped out, down the retractable steps on to the sandy-type soil, and was followed by the rest of the team, all glancing around as they did so. Dairan helped Twedor down. Craig Bream immediately began to scan the area, using his hand-held scanner, activating the heat-seeking device. Dairan locked the Quest by lifting the de-locking silver-toned flap by the entrance and entering a four-digit security code. Craig, as Tayce turned her full attention to what he was doing, announced that there seemed to be a heat source in the far single-storey building, which was the largest of several in the area.

Dairan suddenly drew Tayce's attention to a young, beautiful slim oriental female making her way towards them. She seemed to stumble, then gain her composure and continue on towards them, crying out for help. Quite suddenly she dropped into long pale-yellow grass and didn't get up again. Donaldo, with Tayce, immediately ran towards where the young woman had fallen. Donaldo, upon reaching her, crouched down at her side as she was lying with her eyes closed. He immediately placed his Emergency Medical Kit down, beginning to retrieve his Examscan. He activated it and began guiding it over the young woman. Tayce noticed her uniform was scorched and ripped. What had been going on? she wondered. Tayce noticed the female looked like she'd been the victim of sheer mistreatment and wondered if she'd been the one to send the distress call. Donaldo soon finished reading the diagnosis from the Examscan and reached into his kit for a silver inject pen, which contained a drug that would revive the young woman

"Are you sure that's wise? What if she reacts against our medicine?" asked Tayce, unsure.

"It's fine. The Examscan works out the compatibility and what dosage to give her so that it won't clash with her system. It's a universal reviving drug," assured Donaldo, with a calm reassuring smile.

He gently injected the drug into the young woman's tanned neck. Treketa, who had reached them, began opening a sealed pack from her medical kit and shook out a heat-sealant blanket, ready to put around the young woman. After a few minons she began to come round. She sat bolt upright in alert fright. Tayce quickly assured her that she had nothing to fear—she was quite safe—everyone present was there because of the distress call that was received. Treketa draped the heat sealant blanket around her as she was going into shock.

"I'm Captain Traun of Amalthea Two. We represent Enlopedia Headquarters Base. We're known as the Amalthean Quests team. My cruiser's computer picked up your distress call. What's happened here?" asked Tayce carefully in an enquiring tone.

The young woman with round exquisite-looking oriental features looked at Tayce with dark eyes—eyes that were also red and sore from crying during the torturing ordeal she'd endured at the hands of whoever had invaded the present surroundings.

"I am Cinva, once governor of all of Entronet. It is nothing now, ruined by the attackers that bombarded our world. Please help us, Captain," asked Cinva in a pleading gentle tone.

"Are there any more of your people left here, or are you the only one?" enquired Dairan, glancing around then back at Cinva.

She rose to her feet, with help from Treketa and Donaldo, and pointed to where the rest of what was left of her people resided, which was the large building Craig had found the heat source emitting from earlier, explaining they were hiding for fear of another attack.

"If you would permit me, I would advise you let me and my team take over," put Tayce.

"Please! Captain, we are now the remaining few of what we used to be here," replied Cinva in agreement.

With this, Tayce turned, ordering Kelly to return to the shuttle/fighter with Cinva and to remain there until they returned with the other inhabitants. Kelly nodded obligingly and began to escort the Governor away back to the Quest shuttle/fighter. The Governor paused. Turning, she advised Tayce to be careful and be aware of the security precautions she had put in place. What were termed Entrodroids patrolled the base, and if Tayce and her team weren't careful, the Entrodroids might take them for enemy attackers who had come back. Twedor's hearing circuits came on alert at the mention of Entrodroids and security precautions. He listened as the Governor explained that the Entrodroids were in place to protect what was left of her people. Furthermore, there was one Entrodroid malfunctioning. It had turned defective when it was attacked by the raiders to her world. It would shoot to kill in a split cencron. Kelly thought back to the first voyage, when the team had come to rescue her on Greymaren, remembering what the Securidroids did to make things difficult for the team back then. Craig looked at Tayce on these words. He had a feeling she was going to ask him to try and stop the uncontrollable machine. Tayce raised her eyes in reply, then assured Cinva they could handle the situation—not to worry.

Donaldo closed his case. Picking it up, he followed on as the team went on their way towards the largest of the grey buildings, in a group, that were home to the people of Entronet. They soon stepped on to a pathway which would take them down to the half-ruined building ahead. After a while they came to double glassene-and-steelex patterned doors. Craig and Dairan took out their Pollomoss handguns, setting them to 'stun'. Twedor activated his Slazer finger, ready to join in the action and protect his mistress if he had to. He had no intention of ending up as Entrodroid bait!

The doors drew apart as they stepped into the pickup area. Inside was a long corridor with a hard, shiny floor in a shade of white and pillared walls with archways inset in grey mottled stonex. Upon finding the area was calm and empty, the team walked forward, entering inside. No sooner had they done so than Twedor announced he could sense an Entrodroid coming in their direction and his inbuilt scanning system was picking up some weird signals to confirm the fact.

"This place is certainly impressive," said Treketa in a whisper, looking about and up at the high arched and patterned oriental ceiling of many colours and designs.

"Whatever happened here happened fast. The big question is was it provoked or unprovoked?" asked Donaldo, looking about the wrecked area.

"What does your scanner tell us, Craig? Any sign of Twedor's Entrodroid?" asked Tayce, keeping a look out now with her gun primed.

"There's a reading dead ahead, but the heat source doesn't tell me whether it's Entronian or Entrodroid," he replied, tapping the side of the scanner as he was at the same time picking up interference from somewhere else.

"I think we need to show extreme caution. Whoever did this damage could be still on this base, in hiding, lying in wait for someone to answer the distress call—namely us," said Tayce, glancing around at the various amounts of damage done—the broken glassene and charred pieces of oriental furniture scattered here and there.

The team cautiously continued and turned into what must have been a work area for the inhabitants, which was littered with wreckage everywhere once again. Broken furniture, computer consoles and workstations had been smashed to smithereens. They continued on through and entered into yet a further room, which again hadn't escaped the onslaught of attack. Bits of ceiling and cable wire hung freely, swinging back and forth. Smoke was rising from different places within the room, where fires had been put out. Donaldo, who had walked on with Sallen, paused to look through an open double doorway. He leant inside and came to the conclusion it had to be the Control Room for the whole base. Donaldo could suddenly hear the sound of a small child crying. He ventured in and continued on into a side room and his sight was immediately drawn to the far corner, where a child was sheltering with a young frightened couple. Upon seeing Donaldo they panicked.

"It's all right, you've nothing to fear. I've come in peace. I'm not here to harm you. My name is Dr Tysonne. I'm part of the Amalthean Quests team. We're here in response to your distress call," assured Donaldo sincerely and gently.

Tayce soon appeared in the doorway, wondering who Donaldo was trying to assure. Upon seeing who it was, she could see they had been victims of the onslaught of the attackers, judging by their cowering state; the young child was clinging to the young woman, petrified.

"It's all right, we're here to help. Like Dr Tysonne said, you can trust us, I promise. We have already rescued your governor. She is perfectly safe. I'm Captain Traun. You've met Dr Tysonne here. He wants to check your wounds. I assure you, he won't hurt you," explained Tayce, trying her utmost to get the freaked-out threesome to trust her and Donaldo.

Just as Tayce finished her calm words and figured she'd gained the trust of the threesome, a roaring sound seemed to begin in the distance and grow closer minon by minon. Craig joined Tayce and immediately did a scanner reading on what could be approaching.

In the small group, the male child cried out, "They're coming back!" with a look of sheer fright in his young brown oriental eyes.

"Who's coming back—the race who attacked this planet? Tell me—I need to know to help you," demanded Tayce in a tone of urgency as the sound grew louder as it came towards them.

From the group the male adult, who was roughly in his forties, with short, dark, spiky hair, decided to trust Tayce and spoke up. He further allowed Donaldo to attend to the wound in his shoulder. He began by saying that a warrior woman had been the being who led the attack on their peaceful surroundings. Everyone had been going about their daily living when the woman led an army to wipe out most of their people. It sounded like she was returning to finish what she started as they had not handed over what she wanted.

"Did she say who she was and why she should attack?" asked Tayce, finding it near impossible to put a finger on who the attack force might be. There was one woman—but she didn't want to think it could be her—and that was Vargon, but she was sent to a confinement colony for her evil acts in the last voyage.

"She told us and our governor she wanted our world because it was in this particular sector of the Universe—no other reason. And as she came with such force, and so quickly, we were helpless to act against her," stated the male Entronian.

Donaldo was soon joined by Treketa and they exchanged curious glances, wondering who it could be. Craig looked up as he gained the final readings from the heat scan in the direction of the approaching sound. He had a look of great concern on his normally calm and easy-going features. He began by saying he'd picked up heat-seeking explosive devices and they were inward bound to their present surroundings. At the current speed, they'd be with them in roughly twenty-five minons. On this, everyone, including the three Entronians, ran from the current area and out of the building as fast as they could go. Twedor ran as fast as his little metlon legs would take him. As they went Tayce contacted Kelly back at the shuttle/fighter, ordering her to put Invis Shield into operation, close the entrance hatch, get airborne and head back to Amalthea. Kelly could be heard asking how were they going to get back. Tayce quickly informed her she'd contact Aldonica and have her Transpot them back. Kelly said no more, other than that they'd see her back on Amalthea.

"Captain Traun, we are sorry for involving you in all this," said the male Entronian in an apologetic way.

"It's a bit late now," said Dairan under his breath, looking away.

"We picked up your distress call and we're here to help. If it wasn't us, it would have been someone else. You haven't told me who you are?" asked Tayce, ignoring Dairan's outspokenness.

"Paracrose, I am Governor Cinva's personal aide. I was separated from her, caught with my people when the warrior woman and her army struck. It was impossible to reach the governor, to help her," he said in clear English, with a hint of an oriental accent in his voice.

"You did what you could in such a short time. I think you did well; and as for involving me, this is what we do as a team. We're known as the Amalthean Quests team, and rescuing you and your friends here is part of our duty in the Universe.

As Tayce and Paracrose spoke in the safe area they figured they'd found, from outside there came the sound of heavy boots marching up the walkway towards them. The Amalthean Quests team took out their Slazers and activated them, taking aim, as did Twedor, activating his Slazer finger. Tayce ordered everyone to take cover, dividing the team, ordering Donaldo and Treketa to look after the Entronian group. Craig informed Tayce, glancing at the scanner as a missile exploded nearby in the background, that there was a female walking briskly ahead of the army, approaching like she meant business.

"Paracrose, we're right behind you, but I want you to play along with her," ordered Tayce. She had a feeling about this woman and wanted her in full clear view, where she could see her.

"But, Captain, she could kill me," he protested. He didn't want to die.

"She won't get the chance—I'll see to that," assured Tayce, her senses telling her she knew who it was.

On Tayce's promise, Paracrose agreed reluctantly. He knew what this warrior woman was capable of. On her last visit she had killed almost all of his people coldly. Tayce read in his ashen face that he was scared, but he had to do it. Just as everything looked like it was going as planned, more Entronians came into the area. Paracrose forgot all about meeting the warrior woman and guided them into safety. Tayce realised her plan had fallen apart and decided to head further on to a safer area, with Craig, Dairan and the others. They ran behind some tall white pillars set back into a deep recess that led to a room. Twedor was the last to be squeezed in out of sight.

As soon as Paracrose saw the warrior woman walk into view, he gave Tayce a nod, then walked out, trying not to feel apprehensive though he was facing death in the form of this dark-haired witch-type warrior woman. She was just who Tayce thought she was, but how she'd come to escape from where she'd been sent was another thing. She shook her head, not surprised at who she was seeing. She had entered the area and had come into full view in her usual certain cold-prowess kind of way. Dressed in a black all-in-one close-fitting suit and shiny black boots, and looking as spitefully evil as ever, she came to a stop, arms folded, with a look that said she was waiting for the handing over of Entronet. Tayce sighed impatiently and in exasperation. She knew this bitch would surface again. Jan Barnford had been right about her popping up when she least expected her to again. In spite of Dairan's protest for her not to, Tayce walked out elegantly into view.

Vargon looked at Tayce plainly, but continued.

"Well, man, are your people going to hand over Entronet to me, or do I take it from you?" she demanded in her usual spiteful, ruthless way.

"Not on this dayon, Vargon. It's all right, Paracrose, I can take it from here. Join your people," said Tayce.

Paracrose did not know what it was between Captain Traun and this warrior woman, but he knew there was something bad. He hurried to be with his people, leaving Tayce to take over.

"Tayce Traun, I lay claim to this world and it's not for negotiating," said Vargon coldly.

"I thought Mother sending you to that confinement colony was too easy for you. Now you're up to your old tricks again, stealing worlds from people who just want to live in peace. Why this world in particular? Haven't you claimed enough paradise worlds—mine included?" replied Tayce with a tone of sheer cold hatred in her demand to know.

Much to Tayce's dismay, Sallen came into view with the rest of the Amalthean Quests team in front of the Entronians. Vargon looked at her once daughter, studying her, then gave her a look of total disgust, seeing her in an Amalthean Quest uniform. Tayce read Vargon's thoughts, for the first time breaking through the block she tried to put up the moment she knew what Tayce was doing. Tayce felt pleased Vargon was feeling the way she was about Sallen wearing one of her uniforms.

"This is nice—you've brought Sallen along. I must say she looks well, but she'll always be mine. It doesn't matter what uniform you put her in, or what you've tried to do to her, because one dayon I will claim her back and she will serve again at my side," retorted Vargon, seething.

"She'll never know you for who you truly are. You'll be wasting your time," said Tayce calmly, prepared to protect Sallen if she had to.

"Putting this matter of Entronet aside for a moment, come here girl," demanded Vargon of Sallen.

As Sallen began forth, not knowing that this evil dark-clad woman was once her mother, she looked at Tayce, afraid of what this woman would do to her. Tayce took hold of Sallen's arm and gently restrained her, by her side, not letting Vargon get too close as she was scaring Sallen.

"Leave her alone. Let's get back to the real reason you attacked these innocent people. You still haven't told me why you want this world in particular?" asked Tayce plainly.

"Yes! Leave her alone," backed up Donaldo, coming up behind Sallen, making Sallen a little less scared.

"With looks like yours, Doctor, I could never understand why you never became a pirate. Women would have thrown themselves at you. I could have done with someone like you in my quarters. Medical knowledge and a handsome pirate—quite a catch and quite intriguing to say the least!" she said, thinking on it, ignoring Tayce's demand.

"Because, unlike you, Countess, I prefer to be on the good side of the law. That's something you'll never see and somewhere you'll never be," said Donaldo in a straightforward unemotional tone.

Tayce had been wondering, as the words were being exchanged between Countess Vargon and Donaldo, why she should want Entronet in particular. Then it came to her.

"I know why you're here with a new army. It's coming to me now—you're in a sector of space I don't believe is covered by Enlopedian intergalactic criminal ruling. This means you can never be arrested again after your escape. That's it, isn't it? God, you don't change! I heard rumours you were set free from where you were sent for good behaviour, when we both know otherwise, don't we? You've probably been plotting to take Entronet as a safe haven since just after your escape. That's right, isn't it?" demanded Tayce, glancing around at the others, then back at Vargon, not surprised she was still playing the same old sly game she always played to get what she wanted.

"Do we have to continue this hostility towards each other? Can't we let what happened with your world remain in the past? It was yearons ago, girl," said Vargon, changing the subject because she knew Tayce was right.

"As long as you're in this Universe, never. I will never forgive you for destroying my world, and as long as you continue to attack people like my people, namely these Entronians, I will continue to fight for justice against you. You see, you and I are on opposite sides of the law and that's the way it will always be, so if you think for one minon I wouldn't deter you from taking this base, rendering these people homeless, think again," said Tayce coldly.

"Nice speech," said Dairan discreetly behind her.

"So tell me, Tayce, what will you do to stop me?" asked Vargon, her hands on her hips, her head tilted to one side, waiting.

"Besides what I did to you the last time you tried to take me on, I'll report you to these people's headquarters base. No doubt they won't hesitate to track you down and arrest you for what you've done, and here is where they will start looking first," replied Tayce spitefully.

Vargon looked at Sallen, ignoring what Tayce just said, studying her once daughter again, wondering what the Enlopedians had done to turn her away from her evil side to what she'd become, so she no longer recognised her as her mother. Sallen looked back at her, afraid of this powerful woman, not knowing who she truly was. She didn't like her. Twedor glanced from woman to woman, thinking he never did like Vargon, even back when he was guidance computer on Amalthea One. She gave him the creeps, to say the least. He wondered why she couldn't just die when she was defeated time after time. He stepped behind Tayce to Sallen, ready to protect her if Vargon made any moves to take her.

"Seen enough of what was once yours? I give you an houron to get yourself, your new army and your no doubt new battlecruiser out of this planet's orbit, or I'll contact Amalthea and have one of my team activate our Slazer cannons and turn them on your vessel. Nothing would give me greater pleasure than to rid this Universe of the likes of you once and for all," said Tayce in a warning tone.

"Before I leave, I'll strike a bargain with you. You let me take Sallen and I'll leave these pathetic planetary people in peace, or I'll kill her right where she stands," announced Vargon, looking dark with evilness.

Twedor activated his Slazer finger, ready to block Vargon's attempt. Both Dairan and Craig put their hands on their Pollomoss handguns, ready to do the same. Tayce cut Vargon's idea dead by announcing she didn't make deals with criminals such as she was. Dairan, Twedor and Craig, on Tayce's discreet words, slowly got ready to act to protect Sallen. Tayce gave Vargon a look that made her think again in her proposed actions, as she recalled the last time she'd challenged Tayce and lost badly, power-wise, when Tayce had taken her on and left her licking her wounds, so to speak.

"One dayon you will have to fight on the same side as me—you'll see," retorted Vargon.

"Never!" said Tayce under her breath with meaning.

The Countess withdrew her handgun, deciding to go ahead with what she had in mind. Dairan and Craig withdrew theirs and stood ready, Twedor also, giving a look as though he wanted her to carry out the action. Vargon knew she had been beaten for the first time. She called her army to withdraw in a displeased sharp command, then began on the way out of their surroundings. She paused midway down the pathway, turning back to face Tayce, watching her leave.

"One dayon, Traun, you and I will meet alone and you won't have your teammates to protect you," she said angrily, then went on.

"I'll look forward to that dayon. Then you can repay the debt you owe my people—with your life!" replied Tayce without a further word.

"That woman gives me the creeps. Who was she?" asked Sallen softly at Tayce's side.

"You have nothing to fear from her while you're with us. She has a bad case of mistaken identity," said Tayce, trying to reassure Sallen she was all right.

Treketa put a friendly reassuring arm around Sallen and assured her also, no one liked the evil woman. She was a bit loopy and bad with it! Even though she herself knew of Sallen's background, but she had been prepared to bury what had been in their past because of what had happened to her, in a way Treketa felt sorry for the new Sallen as she had no idea of the true reason Vargon wanted her. Paracrose walked over to Tayce with the rest of the Entronians.

"Captain, how can we thank you enough? You handled her well—almost like you've had dealings with her before," he said sincerely and thankfully.

"You're right, Paracrose, I have. That woman destroyed my world and killed my people many yearons ago, like the way she was trying to take Entronet. She was apprehended for her murderous acts in my last voyage and sentenced to a confinement colony for the rest of her natural life, though, by the looks of it, during her sentence she probably escaped. But there's been rumours she was found to be behaving herself, so they released her on the understanding she didn't cause any further trouble. Little did they know she would go right back into it, coming after your planet," explained Tayce.

"Excuse me—may I suggest we take these people back to the MLC for proper medical treatment?" asked Donaldo, cutting in politely.

"Yes, of course. Carry on. Contact Lance and tell him we need a group Transpot and that we're returning with casualties," commanded Tayce.

"Right!" he replied, turning away to contact Lance via Wristlink.

"Paracrose, I understand from the fact you couldn't acknowledge our reply to your distress call you have some trouble with your communications system. Am I not right? If you think it's worth me doing so, I would be pleased to take a look and see if I can repair it for you," offered Craig helpfully.

"Please! We're in the dark at the present time. We need our communications above all else, otherwise we're cut off from the Universe and our outlying bases," said Paracrose.

"Show me where it is and I'll get straight on to it," said Craig eagerly.

"Follow me. It's in this building over here," suggested Paracrose, leading the way across and into a small building big enough to hold a communications main-operations facility.

"Come on, Twedor, you can assist," said Craig, walking on behind.

Tayce watched Twedor follow Craig away, then turned, ordering Dairan to return to the cruiser with the rest of the injured inhabitants for the medical attention needed. She was putting them under his watchful care. Dairan nodded understandingly. Donaldo had made sure everyone had a Transpot band and turned to inform Tayce they were ready to go up to the cruiser. Dairan crossed, joining the Entronians and Donaldo, giving the word on his Wristlink to transpot. A cencron passed—the Entronians and Dairan vanished off Entronet in the Transpot, back to the cruiser, with Donaldo and Treketa.

* * *

Once everyone who had left Entronet had arrived back on Amalthea, Donaldo and Treketa with Dairan escorted them straight to the MLC. Once at the entrance, Donaldo assured Dairan he could take over and told him to go and do what he had to until it was time to escort the Entronians back to the surface. With this, he headed straight on up to Organisation. Lance met him halfway, on the Level Steps, going down to meet him. They both turned and walked back to the Organisation Centre together. Upon entering the centre, Dairan ordered him to find the nearest headquarters base for the Entronians. Lance agreed, getting straight on to it. After a while of keying in different sets of information requests, Lance had a name appear on screen—'Osmarea' and the following information appeared underneath. It was the main base for the Entronians to be answerable to should anything go wrong in the every-dayon smooth running of Entronet. Lance continued to read about the race in general and found they were a peaceful race. After Dairan filled him in on who was leading the attack on Entronet, he realised the head of the headquarters base was going to look upon her unprovoked attack as a serious threat—and a criminal one at that. No doubt they would track her down and put her on trial and the outcome would be an execution on their terms.

He turned as Dairan approached to see how the request was coming along, and Lance explained that he'd found the headquarters base and Dairan should take a look at what he'd just read about it. Dairan leant forward so he could read the contents on the screen. Studying the information, he raised his eyes at what was stated before him. It looked like Vargon was in for a rough time, this time when caught, as the penalty for what she'd done was a slow death. He patted Lance on the shoulder, congratulating him on the quick find. Dairan turned to Mac at communications, ordering him to contact the Osmarea Headquarters Base and inform them of what had occurred on Entronet. Mac nodded, immediately beginning to carry out the communications request. Dairan turned, heading on into the DC. He walked over to Tayce's desk and walked around to sit on her chair and wait until it was time to return to the surface. After a few minons, the Telelinkphone sounded. He reached over, picking up the handset. Mac informed him that the head of Planetary Representation on Osmarea was waiting to speak to him.

"Put them through, Mac… I'm Acting Commander Loring of the exploration cruiser Amalthea Two. Who am I addressing?" asked Dairan after Mac connected the call.

"I am Chief Panasoe Corvayoss. You can start, Acting Commander Loring, by telling me who this female is I'm getting reports about, who has attacked the base on Entronet—which, I might add, is one of our top planets in the headquarters group, in your sector. It did have a population of over 4,500 inhabitants. What this female law breaker has done is a serious violation of our laws, to our people, and is classed as breaking the law in a third degree. She will be severely punished for what she's done," began the female chief in a well-educated authoritative tone at the end of the Telelinkphone.

"Believe me, we share your views on this woman in question. Her name is Countess Vargon—we all call her Vargon. My captain has had first-hand dealings with this woman. She's a true criminal of the worst kind. Your base on Entronet isn't the first to suffer at her treacherous hands. She's famous for her criminal acts throughout the Universe. Whatever she likes the look of she sets out to claim against any odds. She, in fact, destroyed my captain's home world," informed Dairan—he wasn't holding back.

"Have there been any survivors of this woman's acts on Entronet? If so, where are they now?" asked the Chief, calming down in her tone.

"Yes, we have them here on board the cruiser. Our physician, Dr Tysonne, is at present attending to their injuries and shock," assured Dairan politely.

The Chief surprised Dairan by announcing that as soon as the survivors had been treated they were to be returned to the surface of Entronet, where a rescue cruiser from Osmarea would be on its way to pick them up. Dairan thought the Chief was being unwise, placing her people back on the surface, because if Vargon showed up again she would pick the rescue cruiser off and it could be right when the survivors were being rescued from the surface.

"Pardon me for saying this, Chief, but I think you would be unwise to attempt such an act. Your people could be in a dangerous position. If you leave your people on the surface after we return them there, they might not be there for you to rescue," said Dairan seriously.

There was a deadly silence that filled the communications line for a moment. Dairan figured the female chief had taken to heart what he'd said. She knew that he was right. Dairan suggested he should have a discussion with his captain, namely Tayce, and perhaps they could all find a solution all round and get back to her, but he said he would fully understand if she felt she wanted to carry out her proposal. Chief Corvayoss, after a further few minons of silence, agreed, informing Dairan she would permit him to talk to his captain, and she would wait to hear what was decided. Dairan signed off, ceasing communications. He placed the handset back and sat silently for a moment in thought.

*　*　*

Down on Entronet, Craig had done what he could to repair the communications system and transmission circuitry, but most of the whole facility had been unrepairable. Tayce, meantime, had decided to wander about, despite the threat of the onslaught of the Entrodroids. As luck would have it, she walked from one room and into another and came face to face with something that was along the lines of the Securidroids that once patrolled the corridors of Greymaren. It was sat in the middle of the room, stationary but operative. She slowly drew her Slazer. She could tell by the way in which the silver barrel-shaped Entrodroid hovered that it was scanning her presence. Craig, who was looking for her, called out, but Tayce wished he hadn't. Just as he rounded the doorway of the room she was standing in, he realised she was in a prime position for the Entrodroid to attack. He looked alarmed towards her, then at the Entrodroid. Tayce gave Craig a far from impressed look—he'd probably just made her its enemy. She was right. It began slowly towards them, lights blinking on either side of its small protruding head. She had to take it out, and she would only get one shot and make it count. Before she had time to open fire, Twedor came into view. Upon seeing his mistress and Craig in the line of fire of the metlon security Entrodroid, he activated his Slazer finger; and as Tayce backed up, Twedor came forth, both fired on the advancing menace, hitting it right in the centre of its body. Direct hit! The Entrodroid sent sparks flying and caught fire, sending out thick black smoke erupting all around its mainframe, and it shut down in the middle of the room, still smoking. Craig sighed a great sigh of relief that he hadn't got Tayce killed by his thoughtless act.

"Tayce, I'm so sorry—I had no idea you were pinned down by one of those things," he said, pointing back at the Entrodroid as they began away.

"Don't worry, it's OK," said Tayce, forgetting the incident. She could see Craig felt guilty.

"I was nearly spare parts. If I hadn't had my scanner in scan mode, you two would have been killed," said Twedor as they walked.

"If you've finished repairing the communications system, I suggest we all get together, get out of here and return to Amalthea," announced Tayce, wondering if the Countess might push her luck and return.

Soon everyone, including Paracrose and some uninjured Entronians, gathered together in the open air. Tayce raised her Wristlink, activating it, contacting Amalthea and requesting immediate Transpot. Within a few cencrons the Amalthea Two Transpot engulfed the Amaltheans and the remaining Entronians, dematerialising them from the Entronet surface.

* * *

On board Amalthea Dairan was informed that Tayce and the others were returning to the cruiser. He decided to go and visit the ones brought aboard for medical treatment earlier and to also see Governor Cinva. As he entered the MLC she crossed to him in a slow but elegant way. Dairan thought for an oriental lady she was very exquisitely attractive. Her make-up made her look like a porcelain doll of oriental origin. The Governor began by thanking him for the generosity he'd shown to her remaining people. Dairan immediately explained that Dr Tysonne and Medic Nurse Tysonne should take all the credit as far as care went. He had merely come to her aid with his captain upon receiving the distress call. As the Governor and Dairan stood talking over the overhead Revelation Announcement System, Amal's voice requested him to report to the DC and to bring the Governor with him. Both immediately began towards the entrance doors. As the doors opened, so Dairan allowed the Governor to go first. She paused, turning back for a few minons to thank Treketa for the replacement clothes. Treketa smiled. Dairan glanced at the uniform the Governor was wearing and thought it looked familiar. It had been a medical one.

After passing through the open doors, Dairan guided the Governor in the direction of Level 1, leaving the MLC doors to close behind him.

* * *

Tayce, having arrived back on board, let Sallen take Paracrose to meet the rest of his people in the MLC. She then entered the DC with Twedor not far behind. She crossed to her desk. Walking round it she sat down relaxingly in her seat, waiting for the arrival of Governor Cinva. Twedor came to a pause beside her. He could see she had something on her mind. The words the Countess had said about one dayon both fighting on the same side kept repeating over and over again in her head. She sighed. The idea was something that would never happen—not while she was alive anyway. Twedor reached out, lightly tapping her on the arm as Dairan and the Governor were walking into the DC. She turned her chair to face them, rising to her feet. Twedor quickly stepped back, allowing her to walk out.

"Captain, I would like to thank you for your assistance in coming to our aid and the kind hospitality you've shown my people and myself," said Cinva in a gentle, appreciative way.

"You're welcome, though as far as the Countess goes I don't think this is over yet. I would advise you to be extremely careful of her. She's the kind of space criminal that doesn't give up easily," said Tayce, speaking as someone in the know.

"Your advice is taken seriously, thank you, Captain," said Cinva in softly spoken appreciation.

"If I may, Governor, your headquarters base is sending out a rescue cruiser to pick you and your remaining people up from the surface; but I said I would talk to you, Tayce. I think it would be too dangerous; I don't know what you think. I said this to Chief Corvayoss," said Dairan, greatly concerned.

"Totally unwise! Vargon could return and it would be a case of losing everything you have, Governor?" said Tayce, totally surprised and in agreement with what Dairan had said.

"I see," said the Governor, surprised her chief would be prepared to put them back in danger.

"I can't force you to remain here, where you'll be safe. You obviously have rules which you have to abide by. Anyway, your communications is back—my tech team managed to repair the system for short-term use so you will be able to contact the rescue cruiser, or us, should trouble arise," said Tayce, feeling awkward. She wanted the Governor and her people to remain where she would be safe, but she couldn't interfere with the headquarters ruling. It might be taken as an act of wrong-doing, by the Governor's people. If they wanted her to be picked up from the surface, there was nothing she could do.

"Thank you for your concern, Captain. My concern is that all our protection weaponry has been used," expressed Cinva.

"If you would allow us, and it's permissible, as you can't stay here, by orders of your chief, we could give you some of our weaponry to tide you over until your rescue people arrive—just in case the Countess should return," offered Tayce casually.

"It is permissible, Captain. Thank you. I will feel a lot safer knowing we have something. I shall be reporting your excellent conduct towards us to my headquarters base, stating what you have all done," said Cinva in a kind way with a slight appreciative smile.

"There really is no need. It's our duty out here in the Universe. Before you go, your defective Entrodroid—I'm afraid myself and my tech officer came face-to-face with it. It's very much out of permanent operation and will need to be replaced. It tried to kill me and my officer, and we had to stop it by weaponry means," said Tayce, expecting to hear she would have to pay for a replacement via her mother.

"Believe me, it's a relief to know it's not operable any more. We have been trying to bring it under control for the best part of four weekons," replied Cinva with a reassuring smile.

Tayce felt glad she hadn't done wrong in what she had done to the Entrodroid. Just as Cinva was about to say her farewells, her slim silver wrist-bangle-type communication device sounded. She gave a look as much to say duty called. Paracrose announced, on her answering, that everyone was waiting for her orders.

"Goodbye, Captain. I'm glad we had the chance to meet, even if it was through such an evil woman as the Countess," said Cinva politely.

"Take care. She'll never be far away until she's apprehended. We will let your chief know what has been decided and we'll keep watch until the rescue cruiser arrives, before we leave orbit," suggested Tayce.

Cinva nodded understandingly. Tayce suggested to Dairan he go with Cinva to make sure she had enough supplies of weaponry for the duration she would be on Entronet, until the rescue cruiser arrived. Dairan nodded understandingly. Cinva walked on out, back through Organisation, in the company of Dairan. Tayce watched for a while, then went on out of the DC, watching the team, all back at their duty positions, talking. She crossed to Mac, asking him to inform Chief Corvayoss what had been decided. Mac nodded and immediately carried out the communication in urgency. She paused by Kelly, ordering her to operate Transpot when the Governor was ready to leave. Kelly nodded. Mac, after finishing the request, turned, announcing she had a call coming in from Marc on Enlopedia. Tayce headed towards the Organisation entrance, ordering him to put it through to her quarters. He agreed. Tayce called Twedor, then continued on out. Breaking into a light sprint, she wondered what the call was about. Twedor was running to keep up with her, not far behind. As they went Tayce thought to herself that she had wanted to go against the rules set by Chief Corvayoss, but it wouldn't have been right—it could have caused trouble. Whatever happened to her people, it was now in her hands, but she had to remain, like she had said, in orbit until the rescue cruiser arrived.

* * *

Lance would in her absence take temporary command in Organisation until Dairan returned from helping the Governor with the dispatch of weaponry and helping her people to return to the Entronet surface. Mac, while Tayce was en route to her quarters, kept Marc in pleasant conversation on what had been happening until he could connect him to Tayce. Lance, as he began to compile the Quest report, hoped the Entronians would be safe until the arrival of the rescue cruiser. He knew what Vargon was like, and he too knew how Tayce was feeling. She probably would have liked to let them pick up the survivors from Amalthea somewhere other than on the planet surface of Entronet, but that was the rule and rules are made to be obeyed, not broken.

10. The Sexton Berenices

A weekon had passed since the unexpected emergency Quest to Entronet. Marc Dayatso had returned to the cruiser very glad to be back, though he had told Tayce before he boarded that he didn't want any unnecessary fuss; he just wanted to return to duty and carry on as normal. Tayce understood and briefed the team about Marc's wishes.

* * *

The team were all gathered in a meeting discussing the Quests that had been achieved to date. Everyone was seated around the meeting table, putting over their points, back and forth. It was vastly becoming a loud debate, but a happy one. Nothing hostile. The doors to the DC opened. Everything fell silent around the table and all eyes were looking in the direction of the entrance. Marc sauntered in wearing the temporary tinted eye-protection shields he'd been given at the Medical Dome to protect his eyes for a further period, to aid the healing process. The team all stood and simply welcomed him back aboard. Donaldo announced they'd talk later, as he sat down in his seat. Tayce explained that they were discussing various Quests they'd done since he'd left. Marc gestured for her to continue. He'd heard the latest about Tremanexor being shot by marksmen on Enlopedia for his murderous acts. He began realising, as he looked around him at the others in the discussion going on, that he had to put what happened on the Astrona Star to the back of his mind and move forward. He continued to listen to the many points of interest as they came up, but said nothing as he felt his absence from the team didn't give him the right to jump in on a point he hadn't been there for.

At the end of the meeting the team once more said to him, on the way out, it was good to have him back. Donaldo suggested he attend the MLC to discuss the final stage of his treatment. He'd received the information on what had to be done to get him back to normal from the Medical Dome and Dr Sellecson in his aftercare. Donaldo nodded to Tayce, then followed Treketa on out, leaving

Marc to talk to her. Dairan stood to one side silently. He knew his time as acting commander was over. After a few cencrons of Tayce and Marc talking, he informed her he'd see her later—he'd be down in the Astrono Centre. He had some work to do that was long overdue. He patted Marc on the arm, telling him it was good to see him back and he'd catch him later. Tayce nodded. She knew it wasn't easy for him to step down and hand things back to Marc. He'd been used to being her right-hand man in Marc's absence and had enjoyed it. He briskly walked from the DC, the doors closing behind him. Marc could see he was doing a good job at hiding his disappointment that he had to step down and hand things back to him.

"Is it my imagination, or is he peeved about standing down?" asked Marc casually.

"He's probably feeling down because of the fact he enjoyed his time as acting commander in your absence and finds it hard to take a step back, but he also understood it was only temporary," explained Tayce, feeling Dairan's disappointment, but she'd talk to him later off duty.

"Did a good job, then?" asked Marc, curious, giving her his full attention.

"Let's put it this way: you would have been proud of the way in which he filled your duty shoes. I think he did an excellent job. If I could have two commanders on this team, I would," replied Tayce with true praise.

Marc nodded understandingly. He could understand Dairan not wanting to give up something that made him feel important. He guessed he wouldn't want to step down either if it were him. He sauntered over to the DC sight port and paused, looking out into the ebbing Universe in thought. Tayce sat at her desk and turned to face him, studying him for a moment.

"So! Truthfully, how are you feeling? I thought those protective eye shields were only on for a short while. I hope you haven't returned to us before you should have—I don't want Dr Sellecson contacting me to inform me that you felt better, so discharged yourself," began Tayce in a firm tone.

"No, he won't contact you. These shields are only on for a couple of weekons more and Donaldo has to check my eyes on a dayon basis. It's only because of the glare from bright light, as my eyes are still sensitive," he replied, turning to face her.

"Take them off. I want to try something, and if it works, you can take them off for good."

"But the brightness," he protested, a little unnerved by what she was requesting.

"Twedor, lower the lighting and lock the DC doors," ordered Tayce.

"Right!" replied Twedor, doing as requested.

He left his stationary position and sauntered over to the doors. Placing his right hand on the mechanism panel to close the doors, he waited until a click and hum tone sounded, to signify they were locked; at the same time he sent a signal request for the DC lighting to dim, so it was safe for Marc to remove his tinted eye-protection shields. Tayce looked up at Marc as he removed the shields from his sensitive eyes. He smiled down at her, a bit nervous, but trusting. He knew she would never hurt him intentionally—they were too close as friends. Some had said they acted almost like a loving brother and sister, not captain and commander. Marc wondered what she was going to do to him. Tayce sat him down on her chair and ordered him to relax, exclaiming that if what she was about to do worked, then he could tell Donaldo he was through with the aftercare before it had started. She proceeded to put both her hands either side of Marc's head, in the temple region.

"Close your eyes and relax. Think of nothing," ordered Tayce softly.

She concentrated, using her powers of healing, and within a few cencrons a powerful orange aura materialised around the upper part of Marc's face, where his eyes were. Firstly Tayce concentrated on healing the inner eye and damage that had nearly healed, then restored his eyes to what they were originally. The whole time Tayce was working she made sure Marc was relaxed. He had nothing to fear as she went about the healing process. Slowly the tissue that had been damaged by the Tremanexan Bore-radds reverted back to normal. After a while she decreased her power and ceased the healing, opening her eyes she'd closed to concentrate earlier.

"Open your eyes and look at me," she ordered softly.

He opened his eyes cautiously, half afraid that what she'd done hadn't worked; but to his surprise his eyes were back to normal—no sensitivity. They were just as they'd been before the attack. He looked up at her and stood up, taking her into a strong thankful hug, thanking her over and over. She was glad she'd achieved what she'd hoped. Now he could truly put the Tremanexan Bore-radd attack behind him. After a few minons, they broke apart as the Telelinkphone sounded on the desktop. Tayce turned, picking up the handset and placing it to her right ear. Mac Danford's voice came through, requesting her out in Organisation. She acknowledged. Upon replacing the handset, she headed across the DC, pausing briefly to put her hand on the doors' mechanism panel, unlocking the doors to walk on out into Organisation. The lights in the DC rose to normal on Twedor's signal, then he and Marc followed on. Marc was glad that for the first time his eyes were no longer sensitive to the overhead lights. Tayce was greeted by a large hexagonal vessel as she exited the DC. It was at least the size of Amalthea, if not bigger, seen through the sight port. It was omitting a colour that seemed to bathe the whole vessel in a wave movement from bow to stern. Tayce wondered if this was its defence shield and it was classing Amalthea as an enemy. She ordered Kelly to stand by in case the crew or being in control of the vessel decided to open fire on them. Kelly agreed, poised ready to up the shields and return fire if necessary. Marc came to a pause beside Tayce. He could see she was unsure of the best move to make. He immediately took back his command as commander, suggesting he handle the problem. She glanced at him, studying him for a few minons, then decided he was not quite ready. She ignored him and headed over to Lance, leaving Marc in silent displeasure at her actions.

"Anything coming through on our hovering vessel?" she asked, coming to a pause beside him.

"Research scan information coming through now. Let's see what we can get," replied Lance, keying away in front of her, checking and sifting the final points to know.

"Mac, are they trying to make any form of communication with us?" asked Tayce, turning.

"Nothing so far and we're open for link-up," he assured her.

"Kelly, keep scanning that vessel. I want some answers. I want to know why it's here in our orbit. It's all yours, Marc. You can contact me on Wristlink should you need me urgently," said Tayce, heading towards the Organisation entrance, leaving Marc surprised once again by her actions and that she suddenly felt he could take over.

"Finally I get command back. She thinks I'm up to it!" said Marc under his breath, now beside Kelly.

She smiled, amused at Marc's words. Tayce walked from Organisation, leaving the strange alien sight through the sight port in Marc's hands. When they were ready to visit the stationary vessel, and it was proved safe to a certain degree, he would contact her, she thought. In letting him take back his duty, she realised she was taking a chance on him really being fit and able to command, but she also realised he had done what he had wanted to do all along, and that was get back on duty and continue on as normal. As Tayce walked along she wristlinked back to Lance in Organisation and discreetly ordered him to keep an eye on Marc in his first duty hourons. Any sudden sign of fatigue, then he was to call her. Lance agreed in a near whisper. She ceased communications, continuing on with Twedor by her side. Twedor could see she was concerned over Marc's eagerness to throw himself back into his duty upon his return. Tayce found herself worried he'd bottled up his feelings over the Tremanexan Bore-radds' attack back on the Astrona Star and he was doing a good job at hiding the fact, throwing himself into his duty to hide the pent-up nightmare obviously simmering beneath, and she didn't like it at all. There was no telling where and when it could suddenly erupt and what the outcome would be. Would he suddenly flip? She even wondered whether he had in fact discharged himself from the Medical Dome and had lied when he said he hadn't. Only time would tell, and no doubt she would receive a call from Dr Sellecson if he had, and a call from Lance telling her to return to Organisation in a hurry.

* * *

Kelly suddenly in Organisation picked up an unauthorised source boarding the cruiser. Her screen before her lit up, with the words in the centre saying

'UNAUTHORISED INTRUDER BOARDING'. She immediately drew Marc's attention to it. He quickly ordered her to try and obtain the identification, wondering if the crew on the stationary vessel before them were playing games, trying to take them totally by surprise. Kelly immediately began keying away on her keypad to find an identification through a scan of the onboard image pickup system. Marc paused, greatly interested, by her side, waiting and watching in seriousness.

* * *

Down in the Lab Garden Dome a shaft of pure invigorating purple light began to form without warning. It moved towards Sallen, coming up behind her as she finished with the blooms she'd been tending. She turned and, before she had the chance to scream, she was engulfed and disappeared. The shaft of light moved on, going through the Lab Garden Dome wall like it didn't exist. It moved in the direction of the Weaponry Design Centre. Aldonica, like Sallen, was hard at work and didn't feel or see anything out of the ordinary. Again it moved up behind her and engulfed her quickly, and she vanished. The shaft pulsated on, going up through the ceiling on Level 5, emerging on the next level, Level 4. Jaul Naven, who had been contacted by Marc in Organisation to inform him of the fact whatever had boarded the cruiser was heading his way, had dived out into the corridor, Pollomoss in hand, just in time to see the pulsating purple shaft ascend again, up to the next level, through the ceiling. He quickly wristlinked Mac, informing him that the phenomenon was heading his way. Jaul ceased communication and broke into a sprint to go and try to stop it in its tracks as Kelly informed him en route, via Wristlink, it had already claimed Sallen and Aldonica. He ran as fast as his legs could take him, up the Level Steps, hoping to catch the shaft on Level 3, to fire off a warning shot. On Level 3 it rose up from the previous level at just the same time as Jaul rounded the corner of the Level Steps, hoping to open fire on the shaft, which was heading along the corridor. The shot bounced off, much to his annoyance.

Tayce was walking with Twedor, totally unaware what was coming towards her. Both she and Twedor paused at the quarters entrance as it came through the corridor wall and moved towards her. She studied the shaft, trying to figure out what it wanted. Then her gift gave her the feeling it was aboard for no good reason but to cause trouble.

"Twedor, get out of here—go for help," ordered Tayce.

The little Romid squealed, then ran for help as ordered. The shaft moved towards Tayce. She stood her ground, not feeling the least intimidated by it. It paused for a moment, as if studying her. Tayce tried to concentrate and read what it wanted again, but she found it blocked her searching to find its identity and came forth to engulf her. As Twedor paused at the Level Steps, he turned to see his mistress become the next victim of the bright purple shaft phenomenon. He watched powerless as his mistress lashed out, trying to break free, and fail as the shaft increased its energy further, making her pass out and vanish to wherever the Amalthean women were being abducted to. Twedor turned back to meet Jaul brandishing his Pollomoss.

"Tayce has just been abducted by that thing," said Twedor angrily.

"She's not the first. It's taken Sallen and Aldonica," replied Jaul in his Canardan soft tone.

"It's going on up again," said Twedor, watching the phenomenon rise up to the next level.

Both broke into a sprint up the Level Steps, but would they get to where it would next strike in time, or would another of the female members of the team fall victim to being abducted again? they wondered.

* * *

In the MLC on Level 2, Donaldo Tysonne spun around on the alert when Treketa screamed behind him. The phenomenon had arrived in the centre. It began moving towards Treketa and she kept backing way until she was pinned up against the wall, unable to move. Donaldo quickly hurried over and put his arms around her to try and protect her. The shaft merely engulfed the pair of them, but after a few cencrons Donaldo was ejected and thrown through the air across the centre, with force. He hit the floor and rolled up against the far wall, and before he had a chance to sound the alarm Treketa became victim number four. The MLC doors opened and Twedor and Jaul hurried in, just in time to see Treketa disappear, as the others had. Jaul raced over to help Donaldo to his feet. Donaldo was angry and shaken as he hurried to his desk to inform Mac what had just occurred. As Mac came online, he angrily informed him that Treketa was the latest victim; also the shaft was on its way and it would be wise to let it take what it wanted, as he had tried to stop it and got knocked back for trying.

"All right, I'll tell Marc," replied Mac.

Communications ceased and both Jaul and Donaldo stood discussing why all the women of the team had been abducted so far. Had it something to do with the vessel that was right in their flight path?

* * *

Up in Organisation, Kelly had just identified the point of origin of the shaft-type phenomenon when, without warning once more, the shaft came out of the deck floor right under Kelly's position and engulfed her. The team present had to shield their eyes from the blinding purple brightness.

"What do you want with our team? Leave her alone," said Lance, coming forward to stop Kelly going as he was nearest to her.

"No! Lance, leave it. You know what happened to Donaldo when he tried the same thing," snapped Marc, grabbing Lance back by the upper arm.

"What are we going to do—stand here and do nothing?" replied Lance, turning on Marc, eyes like fire.

"That's exactly what we're going to do," said Marc in a sharp commanding tone.

Within minons Kelly was engulfed like the other women of the team. She screamed and vanished, leaving only the male members of the Amalthean Quests team on the whole cruiser, looking helplessly on. Just as the shaft-type phenomenon vanished for the last time, Donaldo, Twedor and Jaul ran into Organisation, but it was too late. Mac and Lance seated themselves back at their consoles, wondering where Tayce and the other female members had vanished to. Lance tracked the phenomenon. Upon finding the information he wanted, he explained to Marc where it had emitted from, and that was the vessel right in their path, confirming Donaldo's suspicions. Marc gave a look that said it all. There were no words to describe the anger he was feeling. He sighed, extremely concerned at what was unfolding. What next would this non-communicative vessel before them throw at them, besides abducting the women of the team?

* * *

The female members of the Amalthean Quests team found themselves in what could only be described as a glassene enclosed cell. The glassene panes were from the floor almost to the ceiling, frosted over so they couldn't see out. There were elaborate furnishings and red silkene drapes that hung on alternate glassene walls. The lighting was small lights strung on silver-toned thread here and there. Treketa glanced around, wondering just what they had been brought to. It was certainly first class. Were they on a vessel, or far away on a remote planet or colony, undetected and invisible from other vessels? Would Donaldo and the others of the team find them before it was too late to be rescued? Aldonica, who was also awake, sat beside an unconscious Tayce. She wished she would wake up.

"Isn't she awake yet? Let me take a look," said Treketa, crossing to check Tayce's pulse.

After checking Tayce's pulse and finding she was all right, she lightly patted her face to rouse her and bring her back to them, calling her name softly. Tayce slowly woke with the mother of all headaches. Treketa helped her to carefully sit up, guessing she'd tried to use her powers to resist being abducted earlier.

"Where are we? Where is this place? Don't tell me whoever was using that shaft of light succeeded in doing what they wanted to do," said Tayce, far from pleased, rubbing her head.

"Afraid so. Whoever they are, they have first-class taste. It seems it's only us women they've taken," replied Aldonica.

"Not Dion!" said Tayce, remembering he had women caught for his entertainment and pleasure, and it seemed like the sort of cheap trick he'd try.

"No! I don't think this is his taste," said Kelly out of the blue, remembering back.

"You know something about that barbarian we don't—care to share?" asked Treketa, giving Kelly a taken-aback look of surprise.

"She's right. When I come to think of it, I don't know why I thought of him. This isn't his taste. But why us and what for?" asked Tayce concerned.

"I've heard of vessels like this before. This one might be along those lines. It's classed as a pleasure slave vessel," spoke up Sallen.

"So you think whoever has this vessel took us for that reason?" asked Tayce, looking at Sallen questioningly.

"The decor certainly confirms it; and if this is so, I was once told that pleasure vessels travel to many sectors of the Universe, and every time they find a vessel or colony that has women, they abduct them, like we have been, and keep them detained until they can sell them on as pleasure slaves at the next market, to the bidder that pays the highest sum of currency," explained Sallen.

"When did you hear of this?" asked Tayce, somewhat surprised and curious as she had only been cleared of her memory programme about eight months previously.

"You'd be surprise what you hear after hourons in the bar back on Enlopedia," she replied.

"I've no intention of becoming a pleasure slave for anyone. We've got to get out of here, and the sooner the better," said Kelly, disgusted at the fact, rising to her feet.

"Kelly, calm down. None of us do, and I have no intention of letting it happen either," said Tayce in her tone of authority.

Everyone got to their feet. Aldonica wished Twedor had been abducted too, even though he wasn't a woman. He would have come in handy. He could have helped, by thinking of ideas of what to do next, of where they were and of how to escape. Upon mentioning the idea to Tayce, she said it was a good idea, but was quick to explain that he would no doubt have been sold on the unlawful market for his circuitry and anything else that could be considered currency-making. Aldonica nodded, agreeing. She could see where Tayce was coming from.

"Listen—we don't have our Slazers, or any other form of hi-tech equipment to help us make our escape, but we have all in some way been trained for this type of situation we find ourselves currently in, so we have to rely on our past training in combat to make our escape. If and when the chance arises, we have to work as what we are—a team," pointed out Tayce.

"Agreed," replied Treketa eagerly.

At that moment, behind them a door that formed part of the wall slid open. In marched ten giant stomping Robotoids in bronze. Aldonica, Tayce and Sallen immediately gathered around Kelly and Treketa, to protect them. The Robotoids, approximately 1.90 metres in height, built for combat, came to a halt encircling the women with silver powerful-looking weapons primed ready to use. Kelly swallowed hard. Her whole body began to shake with fright. It was known she wasn't the strongest of the females in the team—that's why she was glad of the protection of the others. A short, stout humanoid male walked in, rubbing his hands with glee at his latest batch of beauties he'd managed to abduct. He was in his late forties early fifties. Aldonica tried not to stare, but found him quite appealing to the eye. She'd never met a slave merchant before, if this was what he was. Sallen raised her eyes. He was everything the group of males back on Enlopedia after hourons had said he was—the typical slave merchant, slimy, mischievous, artful and handsome. It could be seen in his devious expression and his twinkling green eyes that he couldn't be trusted. To finish off his unlawful appearance, and all he stood for, he had short, dark curly hair and something that resembled a moustache on his upper lip. His attire was a colourful patterned expensive-looking suit in a silk material, obviously purchased with money from his last sale. He came to a pause, admiring Tayce for a few minons, impressed, then turned to the team with a thoughtful smile, thinking how much he would possibly make from this latest group.

"I demand to know why you've abducted me and my team. You've violated the space laws of Enlopedia by taking us from our vessel by force, and once they find you they'll show you no mercy. I suggest you return us at once before you pay for your actions," ordered Tayce sternly.

"Spirit! That's good in a pleasure slave. I should get a fair price for you. I'll make sure, my beauty, you go to the highest bidder. Yes, you could make me very rich," he said, studying Tayce, rubbing his hands with glee once more, delighted that he just might have found the best catch to date.

"It's a pity you won't be around to enjoy it," replied Tayce sharply, finding him disgusting.

"Enough of your talk, female. I am Lord Baldhere. You will silence that beautiful tongue of yours until I order you to speak—understand?" ordered Baldhere, pointing at Tayce with his right hand; but instead of a finger, he had a powerful pencil-shaped weapon that emitted a thin purple beam.

It was about to strike Tayce, but she was too quick for his actions and retaliated using her own powers. She put up her hand to block the laser, sending it back. It struck his hand, burning it severely. Baldhere glared at her in anger. Tayce continued. She silently used her gift to close his hand, almost crushing it—a trick she'd learnt from Dion on the first voyage—bringing the slave merchant to his knees, destroying the powerful laser finger into the bargain. He'd just picked the wrong woman to meddle with, thought Tayce. The others of the Amalthean team looked on in stunned silence and surprise at what Tayce had just done, but didn't blame her.

"Seize her!" ordered Baldhere, holding his injured hand in agony.

"Hold it right there, unless you want to destroy your surroundings," said Aldonica, stepping forward. She'd found a PolloAld bomb in her all-in-one-suit pocket. She was about to start modifying her latest weaponry design, back on the cruiser, when Baldhere grabbed her during her work.

The Robotoids stepped forward until Aldonica began to set the timer for destruction, then they stomped one pace back. One didn't—the one that was nearest to her grabbed her around her slim waist and lifted her and the visible PolloAld bomb off the floor into the air. The Robotoid's grip pinched Aldonica in her middle, but she withstood the pain. There was no way she was prepared to let go of the PolloAld bomb in her possession. She wriggled, jerked and shook the Robotoid, but it merely tightened its grip. Baldhere did nothing but look coldly at her in mid-air. His Robotoids were his protection against such acts as Aldonica was threatening to carry out. That's why the one that held her suspended in mid-air was doing its duty, serving its master.

* * *

Back on Amalthea, Lance had found a breakthrough, in that he now knew the vessel in front of them was where Tayce and the other female members of the team were being held. He had also found a small entrance on the underside of the vessel through its strange-looking force field. Dairan was making progress also. He'd searched through a blueprint screen map of the vessel retrieved from the criminal records on Enlopedia. After Lance found that Tayce and the others were on the vessel before them, he set about finding a possible section where they could possibly be. He was in the process of narrowing it down. Marc leant on the back of Lance's swivel chair, exclaiming that he didn't like the situation at all. He just wished there was some way they could pinpoint the exact location where Tayce and the others were. To make things worse, since Lance discovered the entrance earlier on the underside of the hull, an impenetrable shield had been put up around the vessel and the vessel was moving off to wherever it was destined to go. Amalthea followed on behind, protected by its Invis Shield.

"One of my capabilities, Commander, is to search through the shields when we are in Invis Shield mode and obtain information on who is aboard a vessel," announced Amal helpfully.

Marc turned upon hearing what Amal said, immediately ordering her to do it without a further word. Amal didn't need telling again. She began the operation, and after a few minons announced she had managed to penetrate the opposing vessel and pick up what appeared to be a Wristlink signal. She transferred the signal to Lance's computer screen and any other subsequent interesting information. Marc turned back to lean on Lance's chair to see the information materialise before them on-screen, to read, and to follow where the small on-screen cursor would head on the blueprint map of the vessel. Dairan quickly crossed. All three studied the screen as the cursor dashed to the Wristlink's pinpointed signal.

"Amal, transfer this to the main Sight Screen," ordered Marc, standing and turning to the wall screen.

"Transferring now, Commander," replied Amal in her soft, clear tone.

"At present it looks like they're in the near centre of the vessel," said Marc, studying.

"You're not going to like this one bit," said Lance, reading from the information Amal had managed to obtain when doing the penetrating search.

"What now?" asked Marc, turning towards Lance, giving a look that said, "Let's hear it."

"According to the information just in with the bearings from a Wristlink on board the vessel, it's the Sexton Berenices; and what's more, it's a pleasure slave vessel, owned and commanded by a pleasure slave lord and merchant named Baldhere. He apparently abducts female members from crews around the Universe and takes them to be sold to the highest bidder at planetary pleasure slave markets. Their memories are wiped of where they used to be as crew," explained Lance, who then turned to face the more than angry-looking faces of Marc and Dairan, increased at what might happen to the women of the team.

"Oh, he does, does he? That's what he thinks. We've got to get Tayce and the others out of there before it's too late," said Marc, realising this unexpected mess had just become dangerous beyond belief.

"He's increasing speed," said Lance in outburst.

"Amal, prepare to match their speed. Keep up with that vessel at any cost," ordered Marc in the true tones of commander.

"Our power is an equal match for them, Commander. We can keep up with them comfortably," assured Amal.

"Good! Stay with them. Also take control of navigations and operations for the time being, please. Craig, do you think you could find something to enable us to interfere with the Sexton Berenices' protection shield long enough for us to get aboard and get the rest of our team back?" asked Marc, turning to Craig.

"Yeah, sure. I'll give it a go. Lance, download from your console information on the protection shield to mine, so I know what frequency I'm working with," suggested Craig, taking to the tech console, which hardly ever got used—only when called for.

Craig soon slid into his duty-position chair and began to study the information feeding down to his position from Lance's computer. He was soon beginning to come up with ideas to compile a device to do what Marc requested—to rescue Tayce and the others. Twedor crossed and stood by the side of him as he sifted and keyed away at the information needed for the design in mind. After a few minons of studying and keying away, he rose to his feet, pressing a blue transfer key, transferring the end result to the Weaponry Design

Centre. He then informed Marc he was heading off down to the centre to see what he could come up with. Marc nodded understandingly, suggesting Dairan help. Dairan nodded, leaving his seat and following Craig and Twedor on out of Organisation. Halfway down the corridor Dairan turned to Craig, confiding in him his concern about Tayce. He didn't like things the way they were one bit. As they walked he asked him as a friend what he thought of the situation for the women of the team. Once they had boarded the Deck Travel with Twedor, Craig explained that it made him feel somewhat uneasy, as Aldonica had become a good friend and he didn't like to think she'd end up as a pleasure slave. Dairan nodded understandingly, seeing where he was coming from. Quite out of the blue—and it took Dairan by surprise—Craig put it to him that there was a lot more than friendship growing between him and Tayce, wasn't there? Dairan was surprised and quickly sidestepped the question, remembering what Tayce said about keeping the closeness they shared discreet in duty times. He simply replied that he was just greatly concerned for her safety and the fact that if this Lord Baldhere discovered she was gifted it might make things worse for her.

Craig gave Dairan a look that said, "Come on, mate, I can see it's a lot more than ordinary concern here.

Dairan laughed slightly, seeing Craig was not convinced, and decided to come clean about him and Tayce, in that, yes, their friendship was growing a lot deeper than just captain and lieutenant commander. He knew Craig wouldn't say anything to anyone—he wasn't the kind. He clapped him on the shoulder, wishing him luck, and added that he wouldn't say a thing, he promised.

The Deck Travel came to a stop on the required Level 5. As the doors drew apart, both men and Twedor walked on out along to the Weaponry Design Centre. Upon reaching the doors, they drew apart. All three entered. Craig ordered Amal, through the overhead Revelation Channel pickup, to activate the design systems. A few cencrons elapsed, then all the design equipment came from standby to functional, ready to use. He further requested the design worked out earlier be downloaded to the design-and-specification computer. The information soon appeared on the designated screen. Craig crossed and sat down. Dairan and Twedor soon joined him. They all began working on the special jamming device to temporarily halt the magnetic protection shield surrounding the Sexton Berenices, so they could board and rescue the women of Amalthea before they arrived at the destined slave market to be sold to the highest bidder as pleasure slaves.

* * *

Over on the Sexton Berenices it was stalemate. Aldonica was not prepared to let go of the PolloAld bomb—it was her key to freedom. Baldhere didn't want his merchandise damaged, so calmed himself, ordering his Robotoid to release her. Aldonica was dropped back on to her feet and released. In a split-cencron movement, the Robotoid whipped the PolloAld from Aldonica's hand, pushing her back with the others. Treketa steadied her as she rubbed her waist after the Robotoid's tight grip. Baldhere ordered Tayce and the others to be escorted to the Transfer Room. They were marched out of where they'd been held and down the corridor towards maroon-coloured floor-to-ceiling arch-shaped doors. As the doors drew open on their approach, inside it could be seen was as first class as the previous surroundings, only in maroons and reds. Tayce and the others were pushed inside, the doors closing behind them.

"Tayce, why don't you tell him who you are and who we are?" asked Treketa.

"Because I believe in the element of surprise, and for Lord Baldhere that will happen later, you'll see," replied Tayce, sensing the team aboard Amalthea were already in the throes of planning a rescue.

"Do you think the men on Amalthea know we're on this vessel?" asked Kelly, hoping so.

"If I know Marc like I do, and the men of our team, they're already in the swing at this moment of getting a way to get us out of here before we reach our destination," assured Tayce.

"Tayce is right, Kelly, Marc is not the type to leave us out here to be sold as pleasure slaves—not if he and the others of our team can help it. We'll be rescued, you'll see," said Aldonica, trying to cheer Kelly up.

"Marc has pulled me out of quite a few situations in my time, and successfully too," assured Tayce, seeing Kelly was feeling worried.

"All I can say is let's hope it's soon," said Sallen, glancing around.

Treketa crossed to the triangular sight port and looked out into the stars. They were moving forward in a travelling motion, definitely en route to somewhere. She called to the others, announcing they were heading to wherever Baldhere wanted them to be taken to. Tayce and the other female members of the team crossed and joined Treketa at the sight port, wondering where they were all heading. Tayce figured it had to be the next pleasure slave market. Aldonica, as she looked back at the entrance and the wall by it, found her sight was drawn to a tile set in the wall. It didn't quite sit properly, like the rest. Studying it, she figured it had to be concealing something beneath. It intrigued her. She left the others and walked across. Upon coming to a stop before it, she began to tug at it with her slender fingers. Tayce turned, seeing what she was up to, and crossed, wondering what she was hoping to do.

"What are you doing—we could be being watched?" asked Tayce, interested.

"I think the door's mechanism controls could be beneath this," began Aldonica, concentrating on what she was trying to achieve.

"What do you have in mind?" asked Tayce curious. "You just tried to help in a possible escape."

"If you fail the first time, keep trying until you succeed, that's what I say. We'll be better prepared this time. I don't know about you, but I certainly don't want to spend another cencron on a vessel bound for the pleasure slave market," said Aldonica, determined to get out of where they were at any cost.

"All right, I'm with you, but how are you going to know which cables are which, to activate and open the doors? Also, have you thought that the Robotoids could be on the other side, keeping us under lock and key, so to speak, until we reach the designated destination?" put Tayce seriously.

"This will work, I promise," assured Aldonica, determined.

She successfully and slowly removed the top tile-type cover, to be confronted by a mass of different-coloured wires. Tayce, watching, could see it was not going to easy, discovering which ones would open the doors to the corridor. To save time, she offered to help, using her ability to determine which wires were the right ones. Aldonica eagerly agreed. Tayce concentrated and soon her gift was telling Aldonica where the right wire was. She passed it on to her to pull. She reached in and pulled the wire from its connector. There came an array of white sparks, signifying success had been achieved. Both women smiled at the fact. The doors to their surroundings slowly opened.

Tayce had been right earlier when she said there would be Robotoids guarding the other side. There were two. They turned to walk in. Tayce ordered Kelly to stay back—they could handle it. Treketa, Tayce, Sallen and Aldonica quickly began making the Robotoids topple to the ground. The giants rocked back and forth, swaying their arms to try and grab one of the female members of the Amalthean Quests team in the process. Kelly watched on as the others dodged the shiny bronze arms trying to grab hold of them. The Robotoids soon began to malfunction. Tayce, not realising it, found herself in the wrong place at the wrong time, as a Robotoid reached down with its strong mechanical hand and knocked her aside with force, like she was nothing. Tayce sailed across the room with force and hammered into the wall on the far side, sliding to the floor and into unconsciousness. But, just before she did, she gave one brave final try to bring down the Robotoids by throwing a powerful energy ball, scoring a direct hit. The huge Robotoids shut down and fell backwards to the ground with a resounding thud. Aldonica quickly reached down for the Robotoids' weapons just in case others turned up.

* * *

Over on Amalthea, Craig and Dairan had successfully designed a palm-sized hand-held device for interaction between themselves and the protection field around the Sexton Berenices, enabling them to board the vessel to rescue Tayce and the others. Craig and Dairan, with Twedor not far behind, hurried from the Weaponry Design Centre and sprinted on their way back up to Organisation. Later, upon entering, Marc turned in eager anticipation to hear what both had come up with. He explained, as they came to a pause, that the team had already been picked to go. It would be both of them, himself, Lance, Mac and Jaul.

Donaldo would be remaining behind on standby, ready for any casualties. Both Dairan and Craig nodded in total understanding.

"Who's going to be in overall command while we're over there?" enquired Dairan.

"Amal! She's been in control since Kelly left," replied Marc.

"The key to the Sexton Berenices!" said Craig light-heartedly, handing over the small hand-held device.

It was a metallic round shape that would fit in the palm of the hand. Marc studied it, impressed. Turning it about, he suggested he hand round what he'd made. Craig took the other five he'd processed and handed them around to the others. Craig announced, as he noticed them studying them, that they were called Interacrai, because they were made to interfere with non-penetrable force fields. It would be like cutting through the shield with a Slazer knife. Donaldo entered Organisation. He'd been told he was to remain on board, but he wanted to know what was required of him. Marc quickly explained that he wanted him to be ready in case of an emergency. Donaldo agreed with a firm understanding nod.

"Right, everyone, let's get going. The sooner we rescue the others, the sooner this unfortunate mess can be cleared up," said Marc, heading for the entrance eagerly.

All six of the Amalthean Quests men walked from Organisation, each wearing the new Interacrai on their sleeve, ready to activate on Marc's command. Donaldo seated himself at Mac Danford's duty position; Twedor came to a pause beside him, waiting for any orders he needed to carry out in the others' absence. Amal began, the moment the Quest team left Organisation, to take overall control. The moment the Quest team was ready to transport, she would place them over on the Sexton Berenices. Donaldo sat and waited for his emergency request, hoping he wouldn't get one and that the women of the team would return safely, uninjured.

* * *

Marc, a while later, once they'd all arrived on the Sexton Berenices ordered Craig to scan the area with the portable handheld scanner to find Tayce and the others. Craig did as requested, protected by the Interacrai, aiming the scanner in different directions to get a possible reading on the handheld device. After a few cencrons he struck lucky. Turning, he showed Marc. The men of the Amalthean Quests team set off in the direction of the strongest reading, keeping alert and ready to draw their weapons if they needed to.

* * *

Further along on the same vessel, Aldonica and Tayce, who had regained consciousness with the mother of all headaches after the encounter with the Robotoid earlier, were trying to work out where they were on the vessel in relation to where the exit or escape pods were. Aldonica glanced through one of the sight ports and couldn't believe what she was seeing. Suddenly, just for a few cencrons, she saw Amalthea materialise then dematerialise. Was it wishful thinking? she wondered.

"Tayce, I swear I've just seen our cruiser materialise outside, then disappear," began Aldonica.

"I thought I was the one with a bump on the head. Are you sure?" asked Tayce in surprise.

"Yes—well, it was there a minon ago," replied Aldonica, looking back to see normal dark space.

All the women hurried to the nearest sight port, and as if by magic Amalthea Two materialised again out of Invis Shield. Tayce realised Amal must have picked up their presence on board and was letting them know. Marc was obviously attempting a rescue. She felt a whole lot better knowing, just when they thought they might never see Amalthea or the others again. She advised, despite the occasional bleariness she was experiencing from her impact earlier, that they keep moving and stay alert for the first sign of Lord Baldhere, who would be searching for them the moment he knew they'd escaped. Also she suggested they head for the centre of their current surroundings as they might find something there to help them leave and return to Amalthea if a rescue attempt by the others wasn't successful. Aldonica, after they'd all been walking for quite a while without the familiar sight of a Robotoid, suddenly and alarmingly whispered to them to take cover. She could hear the familiar stomping sound of a Robotoid approaching. Tayce listened, and sure enough the sound of a stomping Robotoid could be heard approaching just around the next bend in the corridor. They all raced to hide in a corridor alcove, out of sight of the advancing Robotoid. Treketa and Tayce peeped around the alcove wall back into the corridor cautiously. Tayce was cursing silently about her bleariness, which kept coming on, then clearing. They watched to see all the Robotoids escorting their leader, Lord Baldhere, to the Transfer Room, where they'd all been placed before their escape. Tayce, thinking for a moment, decided to take this no good pleasure-slave merchant on. Putting the way she was feeling to the back of her mind, she ran out into the corridor telling Treketa and Aldonica to get ready for action. The two Amalthean women took the Robotoid's weapons, retrieved earlier, and followed Tayce discreetly. Treketa caught sight of a weaponry wall store. She paused, reaching up for more weapons. Turning, she handed them to Sallen.

"Sallen—here, catch! Tayce, catch!" said Treketa in a near whisper as she threw the two small silver metallic handguns, one in the direction of Sallen, the other in the direction of Tayce.

"Thanks, Kelly. Stick with me," ordered Sallen, making Kelly get behind her.

"Thanks!" replied Tayce, glad that at last she had something to fight with.

She and the others very stealthily followed behind Lord Baldhere at a distance waiting for the right moment to go into action. Tayce ran round the corner into the corridor they'd just been in, before they reached the Transfer Room, close behind Lord Baldhere and his Robotoids. She paused in the middle of the brightly lit white corridor and took aim as they got a bit further away from her and were about to turn into the Transfer Room.

"Stop where you are, Baldhere, and turn around. It's over," commanded Tayce, fighting to focus and keep her mind on possibly shooting Baldhere.

'Damn it,' she thought. Her vision was suddenly becoming blurry again. It would have to get worse now, of all times! Without a further word the silver Robotoids turned to face Tayce and the others, who ran out to join her, aiming their weapons.

"Command your Robotoids to stop, Baldhere, or I'll make them a pile of flickering junk," backed up Aldonica, beside Tayce, as she could see she was finding it hard to keep her mind on what was happening, because of the coming and going of her blurry vision.

"If I were you, Lord Baldhere, I would take note of what this young woman's saying. She's an ace shot—never misses," announced Marc suddenly, walking up the corridor behind the team, much to their surprise, with the other male members of the Amalthean Quests team following on, weapons primed. Lance, Dairan and Craig all came on behind, pointing their weapons at Lord Baldhere's Robotoids. Jaul came in just behind Treketa and Aldonica. The Robotoids ceased moving on Lord Baldhere's command to do so. He figured he had just been outnumbered. Kelly didn't realise it, but she was nearest to Lord Baldhere and was quickly grabbed by him. He pulled her roughly in front of him, holding her in a restraining grip with his arm across her upper body. Tayce, on this latest move, found anger growing inside her and figured it was about time this situation was brought to an end. After all, none of them wanted to be in their current surroundings in the first place.

"Who is this army of fools? Lower your weapons or I'll take her life," demanded Baldhere, his hand forming an open grip, ready to strangle Kelly if Tayce and the others didn't do what he wanted.

"The fools, as you ask, are the men of my team, which you abducted us from. I'm Captain Traun of the Amalthean Quests team. If you harm that member of my team you have in your grip, you and your precious Robotoids won't be leaving this Universe in one piece, and I have the authority to make sure you don't," warned Tayce sternly. She was angered to think Kelly was being used as a protective pawn.

"You forget, Captain, I have as much power as you and your merry band here; and in places aboard this vessel you wouldn't imagine, I can cause you to be rendered helpless and at my mercy with one command," he replied, turning cold in his attitude, his face taking on a plain look.

Tayce gave Baldhere a look as much as to say, "Let's see it!" She was calling his bluff—as she figured he was doing the same to her—and she thought he didn't have anything. Also anything he tried would be no match for her and the team. All at some time during their training had been trained to handle situations such as the one they were currently in. He did just as she expected: he brought out a stun weapon from his jacket pocket and placed it against Kelly's delicate neck, pressing the small release key. The stun weapon rendered Kelly unconscious and he let her drop to the ground. Without warning, his eyes took on a bright burning whiteness, in pure energy. He sent it straight at Tayce. She wanted to match him with her ability, but there was no time. The power lifted her up off her feet and threw her further up the corridor. Dairan ran after her and she landed at his feet, cursing angrily. Now she was really mad. She pushed Dairan's offer of helping her to her feet away, climbing to her feet ready to finish it once and for all despite the fact she felt really unwell.

"You're such a pathetic child. To try anything would be unwise. You thought I was bluffing," warned Baldhere confronting an angry Tayce.

This did it for her. Even though she wanted to use her own ability, she was feeling too weak to attempt it, as she would no doubt end up dead in the attempt. She turned to the team and ordered them to give Baldhere a demonstration of the fact they didn't tolerate his actions towards Kelly, or his conduct in the Universe. Tayce nodded to Kelly, who had regained consciousness and was back on her feet. She struck out with her heeled boot, kicking Baldhere in the midriff. He pushed Kelly with force and anger across to impact with the wall beside Lance, who quickly grabbed her and checked she was all right. Marc, as soon as she was out of the way in the protection of Lance, turned his gun on the Robotoids and opened fire, filling them full of Slazer fire. He was quickly joined by Jaul, Mac and Craig. The Robotoids fell to the ground, sending out sparks and vocally dying until no more.

"Stop!" shouted Lord Baldhere in outrage, knowing he'd been beaten.

Dairan aimed at the ceiling just above Baldhere's head, firing one shot. This brought it down on and around the pleasure-slave merchant, until he was cut, battered and covered in dust.

"You fool, you've ruined my vessel," he bellowed, beyond control and furious.

"Take it as a warning not to stray across our path again," announced Marc.

Dairan glancing at Tayce. He could see she'd taken enough. He quickly contacted Amal on his Wristlink, ordering immediate Transpot. A few cencrons later, the Amalthean Quests team departed in the usual swirling way, leaving an angry Lord Baldhere behind, defeated until the next encounter he tried on another unsuspecting crew and vessel.

* * *

Upon arrival on Amalthea, Donaldo was standing by. Marc quickly took command, ordering Dairan to escort both Tayce and Kelly under Donaldo's care to the MLC Treketa put a gentle supporting arm around Kelly, guiding her on out of the Transpot Centre. Dairan supportingly guided Tayce. He was concerned that she looked suddenly pale. Just as they all reached the MLC and the doors parted Tayce passed out. Dairan steadied her, quickly scooping her up in his arms and carrying her over to the nearest bunk. Treketa explained that Tayce had been injured twice during their ordeal on the Sexton Berenices. Donaldo quickly paid full attention to her. Kelly glanced at Tayce, hoping she'd be all right, as she was escorted by Treketa to another bunk. As Dairan gently placed Tayce down on the nearest bunk, Donaldo picked up the Examscan and began to guide it around Tayce's head. He then pressed a code, which sent the diagnosis readings to the overhead monitor for considering the best course of action to take in treating her. Upon making sure Kelly was comfortable, Treketa crossed to discuss the matter with Donaldo, upon seeing the diagnostic readings on the overhead screen, whilst Dairan stood by, looking down at Tayce, concerned and wondering what they should do.

"Amal, full scan of internal damage, please?" ordered Donaldo via the overhead pickup.

"Internal scan under way. This will take forty-five cencrons. Scanning for internal skull and brain damage," confirmed Amal.

The small ceiling-suspended imager above Tayce's head descended on a long arm and stopped just above her, then slowly adjusted into position to take the deep-scan images from every available angle and covering the whole of her head and skull section in deep-scanning imagery, until finished.

"Diagnostic scan and imaging complete, Dr Tysonne. Scan confirms cranial bruising and severe concussion. No skull fracture, internal bleeding or formed clots. Brain damage is nil," confirmed Amal.

"Thank God," said Dairan with a sigh of relief.

"Thanks, Amal. Treketa, get me a Tryclane injection, level A2," ordered Donaldo.

The imager retracted back up to its resting station in the MLC ceiling and shut down until needed again. Treketa soon returned with what Donaldo requested, handing it to him. He took the small inject pen and placed it against Tayce's upper arm, pressing a small silver inset button. The injection hit home, releasing the required healing compound into Tayce's bloodstream, making its way to the point of concussion to begin healing. Donaldo stepped back, draping a heat-sealing blanket over Tayce, up as far as her chest, so she could sleep and heal with the aide of her own ability, plus the treatment he'd just given her. He looked at the overhead monitor and was satisfied the treatment was beginning to work, judging by the readings he was getting. Dairan crossed closer to Tayce and looked down at her beautiful face as she slowly began on the way back to full recovery. Treketa placed a reassuring hand on his shoulder, assuring him that Tayce would be fine in a couple of hourons, then went on to assist Donaldo with Kelly.

* * *

Up in the Organisation Centre, Marc ordered the defence shields to be activated. Aldonica, who had volunteered to stand in for Kelly, was seated at Kelly's console, busy. Marc paused beside her, patting her on the shoulder in an appreciative way, glad she'd volunteered at such short notice to assist. She looked up and smiled, then looked back at what she was doing. He requested she open the main sight-port shutters. Immediately, she did as requested with ease. The main sight-port shutters opened with a quiet hum. The sight that greeted them was Lord Baldhere's Sexton Berenices, still in orbit. Marc didn't like the way in which it was still present when he'd given Lord Baldhere his marching orders earlier. At that cencron, as they were looking, the Sexton Berenices opened fire on Amalthea. The cruiser shook from the impact, as the projectile rebounded off the ordinary defence shields. The team present nearly lost their seats. Marc gave a look that said they'd taken enough from this Lord Baldhere. He turned to face Mac.

"Give me an open communication with that vessel—now!" said Marc, trying to keep his cool. "This is Commander Dayatso. You have been ordered to leave this area. Firing on this cruiser won't help. If you don't want us to show you the kind of weapon power this cruiser can use in retaliation, I advise you to respond to the order and go at once. I'm giving you ten minons. After that you won't be here," said Marc, to the point, to everyone's surprise.

Lance smiled to himself on Marc's warning, but he understood him and didn't blame him. Lord Baldhere had been a pain in the rear since his vessel had shown up before them. Lord Baldhere appeared on the main Sight Screen. He grunted something unmentionable to Marc, then ceased communication. Marc raised his eyes at the sudden uncouth communication, not surprised. After a few cencrons elapsed, the Sexton Berenices turned around, suddenly departing from their current orbit, heading off like a shot from a gun. Everyone in Organisation cheered at the departure.

"Good riddance," said Aldonica sarcastically, glad to see the back of Baldhere.

At last Lord Baldhere was gone. Marc sighed, glad the whole situation was over. He turned, congratulating the team present and on open communication around the cruiser, he praised their good work as a team. He then turned to Aldonica, ordering her to get them back on voyage course. She nodded, continuing to do so. Marc glanced at his Wristlink time display, then turned, walking on into the DC, thinking it was nearly the end of yet another perilous duty stint. Not bad for the first duty back on the team, he thought. Everything had turned out well in the end. As he entered the DC, so the desktop Telelinkphone gave the sound that indicated someone was calling. Mac, back out in Organisation, called out to him that it was Commodore Traun, on Enlopedia. Marc, upon reaching the desk, lifted the handset, placing it to his right ear, beginning to listen as Darius Traun began on the other end.

"Marc, where's Tayce? I wanted to talk with her," began Darius, surprised Marc had answered the call.

"She's busy at the moment and away from her desk. That's why I'm answering. Is there a message I can give her?" asked Marc, trying to be helpful.

Darius, to Marc's way of thinking, had sensed something was wrong, even though he had tried to pretend everything was just the opposite. But he hadn't realised Darius had known him a long time, so he knew when he was trying to do a good cover-up.

"Is Tayce all right?" asked Darius suddenly, to Marc's surprise.

"Yes, sir, she's fine. It's just she's on a project on board and doesn't want to be disturbed. She's searching for information—and those were her exact words before she left the DC," assured Marc, hoping Darius would buy it.

"All right, I know how engrossed she can get. Tell her to contact me when she's free, or pass on this: I'd like her, you and the rest of the team to come to Enlopedia for a council ceremony," commanded Darius.

"Yes, sir, will do. Any special arrival time we have to be there?" enquired Marc.

"Mid dayon tomorrow," replied Darius.

"We'll be there," assured Marc meaningfully.

Marc signed off then replaced the handset on its supporting base, relaxing back into Tayce's seat, thinking that was tomorrow sorted, and he hadn't even gone off duty yet for a good night's sleep.

* * *

Tayce meantime in the MLC began to slowly regain consciousness. She opened her eyes slowly focusing. As her vision cleared, she found herself looking up into Dairan's warm, concerned eyes. He looked at her for a few minons before saying anything.

"Welcome back. How are you feeling? Better?" he asked gently, looking down at her.

Tayce nodded slowly, then began to sit up. Treketa crossed to assist her. Donaldo crossed, studying her. He began as Tayce swung her legs over the edge of the bunk, saying he wanted her to take things easy for a while and to stay off duty until mornet to give the treatment he'd administered time to repair the internal bruising. As Tayce slid to a standing position on the floor, Dairan assured Donaldo he'd make sure she did. Tayce turned, telling Kelly, who was receiving heat treatment to her neck for her injuries, she was to do the same and not report for duty until mornet. Kelly nodded, glad to have the time off, the way she felt. Dairan slipped a gentle arm around Tayce's shoulders and she leant against him. He escorted her on out of the MLC, off to her quarters. They both turned at the entrance as the doors drew apart, thanking Donaldo and Treketa, then walked on out. Donaldo and Treketa turned their attention back to Kelly and getting her back on her feet.

Marc walked from the DC out into Organisation. He ordered Amal to take night control. Aldonica, at Kelly's console, waited until the switchover, then rose to her feet, feeling tired. It had been an exhausting duty stint, and now all she wanted was to head for her Repose Centre. She waited for Craig, and they both walked on out together talking about Lord Baldhere.

Lance stood up; he crossed and walked out with Marc. Marc informed him as they left that he'd better have his ceremonial uniform ready. Lance looked at him questioningly. Marc continued, saying they were needed tomorrow at a special ceremony on Enlopedia. Commodore Traun had requested they all be there. Lance nodded, wondering what the ceremony was about.

Amalthea had resumed course, bound for Enlopedia, to arrive next dayon for the ceremony. Lord Baldhere had escaped this time, but in his crooked merchant attempts to steal the Amalthean women he had paid the price in his vessel being damaged and now he was heading to the nearest port for repairs.

11. A Traun Elected

Before turning in for the night, Marc called at Tayce's quarters to check how she was. As he'd heard from Donaldo en route, when he wristlinked for an update on Tayce, Dairan had escorted her to her quarters with strict instructions that she should take it easy until first light. Twedor was the first to enter, as the quarters doors opened. Marc followed in and found the lighting on a dim setting. He wondered if he was calling in too late and she'd already turned in for the night. Twedor ran a silent scan for his mistress and picked up her life signs quite close. He followed the reading and walked around the mouldable soffette before him. He found her stretched out, resting on the cushions with her eyes closed. Over at the sight port, Dairan turned, not hearing Twedor or Marc enter. Marc was surprised to see him present. Dairan crossed.

"How is she?" whispered Marc, interested.

"Fine! Only concussion, thank goodness," replied Dairan in almost a whisper, so as not to wake Tayce.

"I can hear you two whispering—I'm only resting my eyes. Amal, lights to normal mode," ordered Tayce.

Upon request, the lights in their immediate surroundings rose to the equivalent of artificial daylight. Marc apologised for the late visit, but he figured she'd want to know he'd just received a call from her father. Upon this, Dairan suggested he see them both at first light and walked from the quarters.

"Thanks, Dairan. See you in the mornet," said Tayce after him.

"Yeah, sure—night, Marc," replied Dairan casually on the way to the entrance.

"Night, Dairan," replied Marc, thinking about what he had to say to Tayce.

Dairan continued on out through the opening quarters doors, back into the corridor to head along to his own quarters. Marc carried on explaining: her father was somewhat displeased he hadn't been able to talk to her, but he'd made the perfect excuse for her absence, saying she was doing some research and couldn't be disturbed. Tayce smiled, thinking he had always managed to cover for her pretty well over the yearons.

"Thanks! What did he want?"

"He wants us all at Enlopedia at first light for a council ceremony. What's more, we all have to be in ceremonial attire," replied Marc calmly.

Tayce was somewhat intrigued to know why. She was about to think about the next dayon, and meeting up with her father, when Amal's voice came over the quarters Revelation Channel, announcing there was an urgent call coming in on Satlelink relay link. Tayce, via the overhead pickup, ordered her to put it through to the wall Sight Screen in the quarters. After a few minons the wall Sight Screen flashed into life and Jan Barnford appeared. Both Tayce and Marc gave him their full attention. He began, saying that if she'd been asked to attend the re-election ceremony tomorrow, then she'd better bring the team and put them on alert with Pollomoss weapons. On this, Tayce and Marc exchanged alarmed surprised looks, wondering what was coming next.

"What's up? Is trouble being expected?" demanded Tayce.

Jan leant in close to the screen, so nobody passing could hear, and almost whispered that there had been a threat against the proceedings. As yet, though, they hadn't been able to locate the source of the threat—only a message was sent to her father with the following words: *'Don't expect to rule for long as the elected one.'* Tayce rose to her feet quickly and realised she'd done it too quickly as her dizziness washed over her. She took a few minons to let it fade.

"I think we should meet on arrival in the mornet," replied Tayce, realising her father's life could be in great danger.

Marc stood in thought, shaking his head, wondering, like Tayce, who would cast such a life-threatening threat against Darius. He hadn't been back in normal duty-orientated circulation for long. He turned, seeing her in deep wondering thought, concerned for her father, and understood.

"When is the ceremony exactly tomorrow?" she put to him.

"Mid dayon. Why?" asked Marc, curious, recalling what Darius had told him earlier.

Tayce raised her Wristlink, keying in the code that would put her in contact with Amal. Within a few cencrons, Amal answered her call. Tayce began, saying that if it had not already been done, she wanted the course to Enlopedia started so they would arrive before first light and the speed to be increased to hyper-thrust turbo. Amal came back, informing Tayce that course was already ongoing—they'd be at Enlopedia under hyper-thrust turbo in the time requested. Tayce, hearing Amal had everything in hand, signed off, turning back to Marc. He suggested she get some sleep. He'd see her in five hourons, at first light. Tayce nodded. She could feel the drug Donaldo had given her making her sleepy once more. Marc walked from the quarters. Twedor set the quarters alarm for his mistress to wake on time, next dayon. He then dimmed the lights and followed his mistress into the Repose Centre. Once inside, he crossed to stand by the side of her bunk, then went to standby mode as Tayce changed attire for her much needed sleep.

* * *

In the early hourons, just outside Enlopedia's orbit, Amalthea Two arrived. On board Amal brought the cruiser in to commence a smooth docking. Dropping the speed from hyper-thrust turbo to a slow docking speed. Handling the whole procedure whilst her crew slept on unaware they were arriving at their destination. She conversed with the arrival chief and announced she was docking and what the nature of the visit was. Not that the Chief didn't already know, considering he knew the cruiser and captain and her link with Enlopedia.

* * *

Tayce, a couple of hourons later, was admiring herself in the imager, dressed in her ceremonial dress. She studied the way she looked from sideways, over her shoulder and frontally, to make sure there wasn't anything out of place. She quite liked the way she looked, in her body-hugging cream full-length wrap-over gown. Her hair was clasped up in a cream clasp, her footwear matching cream calf-length high-heeled boots, just showing under the split of her gown that ran from her knee to her ankle. The quarters doors opened. Marc sauntered in looking exceedingly handsome in his new cream high-rank official dress uniform. His dark, slightly curly hair shone in the reflection from the overhead lighting, finishing off his immaculate look of commander. Tayce turned, somewhat taken aback at how good he looked. He was truly inviting to the eye, she thought. He smiled and admired the way she looked. Studying her up and down, thinking that for a commodore's daughter she was one breathtaking beauty. Dairan was a lucky man. Glancing down, Tayce saw his Pollomoss handgun in his hip holster. This brought back the fact that the ceremony they were attending wasn't going to be one they could all relax at. Marc could see she was having trouble with the clasp on the necklace she wanted to wear. He crossed to come to a stand just behind her and take both sides of the gold chain.

"Allow me," he said softly.

"Thanks! I could be trying for hourons," she replied thankfully.

"You're a little unnerved by the threat against your father at this ceremony, aren't you? Listen—nothing will go wrong, I assure you. Remember Jan's men are going to be a strong security presence and I have no doubt he'll have every available man and weapons secretly primed to ensure it doesn't. We'll be carrying our handguns too, so there's no need for concern," he said, coming round to the front of her once he'd secured the clasp, looking down at her softly.

"I know Jan will do his best to protect Father; it's just the fact I've just found him and I don't want to lose him or Mother again," replied Tayce, remembering the last time she'd lost touch with both her parents, back on Traun, and how long it had taken to be reunited with them again.

But somehow this latest threat from the being who cast it, whoever they were—she knew it could be goodbye to her father again if they carried it out. Probably forever this time! It didn't bear thinking about. Marc understood where she was coming from. It had been tough on her the first time around, when she thought she'd lost both Darius and Lydia, until she discovered her mother was alive on Micacer. Tayce glanced at herself in the reflection imager one last time, then checked her Pollomoss was fully loaded. Marc wondered where she was intending to keep it, until once she checked it she slipped it under her gown and into an upper-thigh holster.

'That's a new place,' thought Marc, amused. He hoped it didn't go off by accident—she'd end up shooting her leg off! He smiled to himself about what she'd just done, then suggested they all get going.

All three of them—himself, Twedor and Tayce—walked from the Living Area out through the opening doors, on up to meet with the others in Organisation that would be ready to leave, to support her at the special ceremony in honour of the election of a new person in charge of Enlopedia. Her mother had decided to step back from being in charge of the base, to being just chief of the council for reasons which she'd decided not to divulge to Enlopedian and ex-Questonian inhabitants, though Tayce had wondered why, when her mother had seemed so happy in her position, she had decided to return to being just chief councillor of the council.

* * *

Docking had been completed. In the Organisation Centre the team stood ready, watching through the main sight port as the lights from the headquarters base shone from within and many vessels were arriving of all shapes and sizes to drop off delegates, then depart. Lance found every time he dressed in his ceremonial uniform he'd always see his father, the late Jonathan Largon, flash into his mind with a proud nod, pleased at the way he looked, and somehow he figured he would probably see this until the dayon he joined him in eternity. Marc and Tayce walked into the centre with Twedor not far behind, looking like he'd been through a polishing session, to look his best. Everyone present turned their attention away from watching what was happening at Enlopedia towards Tayce as she came to a pause before them.

"This ceremony is of great importance. You've probably been wondering why we are taking hand weapons. We've been asked to keep on alert, as there has been a threat to the ceremony and my father. Who has made this threat at this time, we don't know, but you can bet whoever cast it is likely to carry it out in public at the ceremony. All I want to say is you know there could be trouble where we're going, so stay on your guard at all times. If we need to act, we'll do it fast," explained Tayce in a true leadership tone.

"We'll be ready when you need us, right?" said Lance, glancing around the others.

"Definitely," replied Craig as the others nodded in agreement.

"Shall we go?" suggested Tayce, heading on back to the entrance.

She paused at the entrance; then turning, she ordered Amal to lock the Docking-Bay doors once they were off the cruiser. Amal acknowledged. Everyone continued on out of Organisation on the walk down to the Docking-Bay doors. They'd all come a long way from the first dayon of the new voyage and were one special team. Everyone felt proud in their ceremonial uniforms. Dairan walked beside Tayce. He discreetly whispered close to her that she looked truly breathtaking. She looked at him, meeting his warm, handsome smile. Even though Dairan had whispered what he had, Treketa and the others caught the gist of it. Treketa smiled. She could see, and had had a feeling for a long time, there was a certain deep closeness growing between Tayce and Dairan. Lance and Craig checked their Pollomoss handguns, pretending not to notice the exchange between Tayce and Dairan. Aldonica checked she'd brought her new invention, which she knew would come in handy if the person who had made the threat carried it out. It was a small finger-sized capsule, silver in colour, and when fired from a handgun, such as the Pollomoss, upon hitting the enemy it would release a liquid that would render the target immobile. Both Kelly and Sallen watched what she was doing in wonderment.

"What's this—another Aldonica invention?" asked Sallen, curious.

"Yes, it may come in handy at the ceremony, especially if whoever cast the threat on the Commodore's life tries to carry it out, though Jaul should take half the credit for what's in the capsule," said Aldonica, glancing towards Jaul.

Sallen turned towards him. He shook his head, exclaiming in a soft Canardan tone that Aldonica was the one who designed the capsule to carry the liquid in the first place. The team and Twedor on reaching Level 2 walked along to the Docking-Bay doors. The doors opened in front of Tayce on approach. The sound of gentle hydraulic compressed air accompanied the doors' opening. The team followed Tayce on out, walking on up the boarding tube. As they neared the end, so Tayce could see Adam and Jan dressed in their ceremonial attire, keeping an eye out for anything suspicious. Upon seeing her walking towards them, they stood waiting to meet with her. Everyone in the Amalthean Quests team paused upon coming to meet Jan.

"Welcome back," said Adam, smiling, glad to see Tayce and the team again.

"It's nice to be here, but I'm not happy with the aspect of a threat hanging in the air over my father," began Tayce as guests passed her.

"I need to talk to you before the ceremony," said Jan, taking hold of Tayce's arm lightly and guiding her to a discreet area where they could talk freely.

"I agree. I'd like some answers—let's hear it," agreed Tayce, eager to know what was happening.

"While Adam here takes the team down to the Celebrational Hall, I have orders to personally escort you, Twedor and Marc up to the Chief Councillor's Chambers—well, until the election ceremony todayon. We'll talk en route if that's OK?" expressed Jan, looking at her questioningly.

"Right! Marc, you're with me; the rest of you, stay alert and go with Adam. I'll see you later," ordered Tayce, taking her attention away from Jan for a moment.

The team all nodded in agreement, then walked away in the company of Adam. Marc crossed to join Tayce with Twedor and they all walked away with Jan on the walk towards the newly installed lift. It was only used for high-ranked officers and dignitaries who needed privacy where they needed to go. It had been constructed in the last monthons since Tayce's last visit to the base. They soon reached the clear-vision doors to the Slazer-proof oval lift. Jan slid an ID card in the slot, waited as it read the card, then gave permission to enter. The doors slid back. Tayce ushered Twedor in ahead of her, behind Jan. Marc followed. Jan, once inside, slid the card again through the ID reader. The doors closed and the lift began to ascend to the required level. As they went, Jan began explaining the reason for the new high-rank Level Travel, as it was called. It was because so many high-ranked dignitaries had expressed concern about travelling with unknown travellers in the ordinary Vacuum Lift to various departments in the Assignments Building, for confidentiality reasons. It had proved a great success so far. Her mother used it all the time, and her father.

"Tell me: any idea of who cast this threat to be carried out during todayon's proceedings?" demanded Tayce casually.

"No. We're still keeping every available officer on alert for the time being and during the ceremony," replied Jan.

"That's good, though whoever has cast this threat—I'd like to know why Father? He hasn't been back long."

"I agree. Who would want to hurt the Commodore? He's never crossed anyone intentionally in his life—not that I can recall, unless you take into consideration the Vargons," said Marc, also surprised.

"You're right, Marc. He's always been for the good side of the law," said Tayce, agreeing.

"We think it coincides with your mother deciding to step down and your father finding out about the ceremonial change of who is to be in charge of the base. We think someone has a grudge," expressed Jan, thinking about it.

"Did they receive the threat directly?" asked Marc, looking at Jan questioningly as they ascended in the lift.

"Luckily it came via Adam Carford in the form of a computerised threat, but was delivered by a female messenger. She hasn't been identified or seen since. Unfortunately she was disguised like one of our messengers—all ours have been through an emergency identification check and have come out clean," confirmed Jan.

"I can see the heavy presence of security," said Tayce, glancing around through the clear glassene walls of the Level Travel at the different levels as they rose.

"We're out to stop this assassination attempt, if we can, before it's too late," said Jan seriously.

"How are my parents bearing up through this?" asked Tayce, concerned, "It couldn't have come at a worse time."

"Fine, considering no one knows who's intending to carry out the threat. I think your mother is more concerned than your father. His words were he'd like to take on whoever is casting the threat in the first place, single-handedly," explained Jan, amused by her father's outlook on the situation.

"It doesn't surprise me. He never could tolerate threats of any kind. He used to say anyone casting a threat of this kind is a coward that doesn't have the guts to face the person they are threatening," announced Tayce.

"She's right. I used to be his aide on Traun—I heard it many times," backed up Marc.

"I appreciate the way he feels, but this time around I wish he would leave this particular matter to me and my men," replied Jan in near exasperation, wishing the Commodore would take a back seat in getting to the bottom of the situation. He wasn't on Traun any more.

"Gets to you, doesn't it?" asked Marc, understanding Jan's plight in handling the situation safely, as he had been in Jan's situation many times on Traun in the past.

"Yeah, I just wish he would realise my men are there for his safety and protection—to watch his back, so to speak," replied Jan.

"Leave it with me. I'll have a word with him, tell him things are a lot different todayon than what they were when we were on Traun. He may listen, considering I'm not that naïve little girl I was on Traun of old, though I can't promise anything," suggested Tayce, understanding Jan was only trying to protect her father.

"Thanks!" said Jan in appreciation.

The Level Travel came to a gentle stop. Jan, as the doors opened, stepped aside, allowing Tayce and Twedor out first, then followed on with Marc. Once out, he informed them he would see them later. Both nodded, beginning along the corridor to her mother's chambers with Twedor. Tayce realised that as her mother said she was stepping down from being in overall charge of Enlopedia, then the chambers might soon belong to the new leader of Enlopedia. Adam Carford entered the corridor from behind a glassene wall, out of breath. He'd run up all the steps to get to meet them. He came up behind Marc and Tayce, glad he'd made it before they entered the chambers' outer anteroom. Both turned upon hearing someone out of breath behind them.

"Are you all right?" asked Tayce in surprise to see him looking so shattered. "You look all in."

"I've a feeling it's going to be one of those dayons. I've just run all the way up. I need more exercise," he said light-heartedly, trying to get his breath back.

All three, with Twedor, walked the rest of the distance to the outer anteroom, to Tayce's mother's chambers, otherwise known as the Chief Councillor's Chambers, or, as they had come to be briefly known, the Chief's Chambers. They all discussed what the dayon would entail. Soon they entered into the anteroom, walking on in. The doors automatically opened on approach. Inside Lydia turned, dressed in her councillor's ceremonial gown, with high collar in oyster-pink satinex. She smiled upon seeing Tayce and Marc. Tayce studied her mother, thinking how beautiful and official she looked in her satinex gown with her shoulder-length blonde hair resting on her shoulders. She looked the true leader she had come to be.

"It's good to see you both. Thank you for coming back for the ceremony," said Lydia, gently hugging Tayce as she came to a pause before her.

"Mother, we had to come. I'm concerned for yours and Father's safety," expressed Tayce, hugging her mother affectionately.

"You needn't be. Chief Barnford has men posted all over this base, as you've no doubt noticed on the way up here. Everything is in hand. Where are the others?" asked Lydia, wondering if Tayce had come with just Marc and Twedor and left the team back on the cruiser.

"They're down in the Celebrational Hall, waiting," assured Tayce.

"Hello, young lady, Marc, it's good to see you again," said Darius with a nod, walking into the chambers dressed for the celebration ahead, in his navy suit with a stand-up collar which had the 'QE' insignia on in gold.

Tayce thought to herself that her father looked every inch the handsome leader he once was again. It made her cast her mind back to when he was in charge of Traun. She remembered how authoritative he looked back then. He had always been someone she had been proud to look up to and call her father. He hadn't changed a bit, she thought.

"Father, Jan is extremely concerned about the fact you'd like to take on this threat merchant single-handedly. Promise me you won't. Let Jan take charge—he knows how to handle criminals like this," said Tayce, almost pleading.

"I'm the one the threat's aimed at. Relax. What I said about taking on the threat merchant single-handedly was said in a moment of anger, on hearing what had unfolded. You know what it's like—something said without thought—and you're right, Chief Barnford is a good man. If anyone can pull in this threat merchant he can," said Darius, trying to put Tayce's mind at ease. He could see she was worrying.

"We're ready to act at a cencron's notice too. The team have been briefed," assured Tayce, making her father see he had double the protection, should it be needed.

"You can count on it," backed up Marc, listening.

"It's good to know so many people are looking out for me, as I will be totally vulnerable upon that platform later. I don't mind telling you, it makes me feel uneasy not knowing who's issued this threat, even though I have to seem brave," confided Darius.

The doors opened to the back stairs that would take everyone down to the Celebrational Hall. Four armour-clad security officers entered in through the chambers' open doorway, coming to a halt. They saluted to their soon-to-be new chief. Marc stepped back and gently pulled Tayce back beside him, by the upper arm. Adam Carford quickly but discreetly explained that the officers were there to escort her parents to the Celebrational Hall and to the platform for swearing-in. Two aides walked in from the anteroom carrying ceremonial cream robes. The male uniformed aides quickly went about draping the robes, one around Darius's shoulders, then the other one around Lydia, fastening them before stepping back with a salute to the forehead, then left. Both Darius and Lydia walked over to be in the centre of the four weapon-wielding armoured officers and walked off within the foursome, out down the back stairs to the Celebrational Hall. Tayce waited until her parents were out of sight, then raised her Wristlink, contacting Dairan down where her parents were heading. She warned him, as he answered, that her parents were on their way and to tell the others to stand by for watching for the threat merchant. Dairan could be heard agreeing. Tayce signed off. Herself, Twedor, Marc and Adam crossed the chambers and began walking on down the back stairs, to follow on behind her closely guarded parents. Marc reached out, seeing she was worried, and squeezed her arm reassuringly. He silently told her everything would be fine—she'd see.

* * *

In the Celebrational Hall, Aldonica sat between Jaul and Sallen. She was silently checking her new weapon, called a Vicdayne. The rest of the team were spread out in different places throughout the divided seating areas on both sides of the aisle, amongst the guests already arrived and seated. Dairan, Lance and Craig were on the front row. To the right of Dairan were two empty seats, which were for Tayce and Marc when they arrived. Twedor would stand before Tayce. Kelly, Mac, Donaldo and Treketa were further back, keeping an eye out for anyone suspicious that might wander in during the final moments. In amongst the seating area also were Jan's patrol-squad officers in plain clothes, looking like standard guests. All were discreetly scrutinising everyone entering the hall, wondering if any particular person, or being, needed to be kept under close watch. The hall soon became packed with high-ranked dignitaries, who were friends and duty-related colleagues of both Lydia and Darius. Some were seated at the rear left side of the seating area, talking amongst themselves. The topic was the uncalled-for threat hanging over Darius Trauns' head.

Tayce and Marc soon appeared through the main entrance doors and walked along to take their seats with Twedor.

Up on the stage area at the front Darius and Lydia came into view. A thunderous applause erupted from the seated audience. Waynard Bayden, who had been deputy to Lydia and had always been there, as requested by the late Jonathan Largon on his deathbed, to assist Lydia when she needed, stepped up on to the platform and walked to the central shiny woodex podium, where a micro-announcer had been placed for addressing the entire audience. He came to a pause, asking for everyone's attention. Tayce, as she seated herself next to Dairan, glanced around suspiciously. Suddenly her telepathic senses were giving her terrible vibes of looming trouble. But what? she wondered. So far nothing had surfaced, and she hoped her senses were just owing to her concern getting the better of her. She looked forward. Waynard, seeing everyone was now giving him their full attention, began by announcing good points about how Lydia Traun's leadership to date had been a good one; people from all walks of life and duty on the base every dayon had spoken very highly of her.

Tayce found herself half listening as she was finding it hard to concentrate. Her senses were suddenly working strongly overtime. There was something materialising outside the great Celebrational Hall. The vibes were growing extremely strong. Every moment she sat where she was she looked up and around, hoping to find Empress Tricara somewhere in the hall. Using her powers, she telepathically communicated, using her mind, asking Tricara if she was present and where? Tricara soon came back, asking what was wrong? Tayce silently asked, couldn't she feel something was about to unfold which could have disastrous consequences? There was a long pause on Tricara's side. She advised Tayce through a mind link-up to do what she thought was right to protect whoever the materialising feeling was aimed at. Tayce nodded. She knew her father's life had already been threatened and what she was feeling could be the beginning of that threat being carried out. The being, or whoever had cast it, was in the near vicinity. She came back to the present just as her father was being sworn in as the new admiral and overall chief of Enlopedia.

Just as the last words were spoken, the entrance doors to the hall burst open and a woman burst in brandishing a mini Slazer cannon. Adam immediately recognised her as the messenger that had delivered the printout threat earlier. She was dressed in an all-in-one grey combat jumpsuit, and her face was partially covered by a masquerade-type mask in dark crimson, so her features weren't so easily recognisable—or so she thought.

"You have control, Admiral Traun, but not for long. I've been sent here to stop your reign as admiral taking place. Don't anybody move. I'll shoot the first guest that stands," she commanded, striding forward down the aisle with meaningful intent, her gun aimed solely at Darius.

"God, no! Somebody stop her," called out Lydia, coming forward to Darius in panic.

The young female took aim with a cold look in her piercing dark eyes, her partially covered features directed at Darius. They were eyes full of evil intent.

Before the young obvious assassin could carry out her threat, Aldonica waited till she was nearly opposite and brought out the Vicdayne weapon, getting ready to fire. She stood up, shouting for everyone to get down, then fired it directly without thought of what she was doing. The Vicdayne went off, hitting the ginger-haired female assassin straight in the neck. Within cencrons the paralysing drug entered her bloodstream, rendering her unable to concentrate, sending her mind into an uncontrollable panic. She dropped her weapon and went into outright panic, shouting that she would kill the person who fired the weapon at her, in between decaying like a whimpering child. The audience were looking at the assassin, not moving. Some watched as her attitude went from being in control to that of a helpless uncontrollable child, feeling sorry for her threatening actions. Two of Jan's men came from the audience and apprehended the young female, hauling her away in spite of her uncooperative manner.

Silence filled the hall as calmness reigned once more. As the doors closed, the audience came back to paying attention to what was returning to near normality. Darius Traun gestured for Aldonica to receive thanks for what she'd done. Various members of the audience turned and gave Aldonica praise. Darius, out front, beckoned for her, asking her to go up on to the platform. Tayce turned to Dairan, feeling a lot more like her normal self and proud of what Aldonica had done. As Aldonica walked past, Tayce quickly and whisperingly congratulated her.

"Nice work, though why do I have the feeling this isn't over yet and that it was too easy?" confided Tayce discreetly, then turned to Dairan, informing him the same—it had been too easy.

"Do you think so? All we can do is wait for anything else suspicious to occur," advised Dairan in a whisper.

"As that girl said, she was acting for somebody else. I'm still a little concerned just who, but I guess all we can do is, like you say, wait for something to happen," replied Tayce, feeling there was still something more to come.

"Don't you think you'd better let your father or Chief Barnford know there's more to possibly come?" asked Dairan, thinking she should inform her father at least.

"But if it's just my mind playing tricks, I'm going to look stupid when It doesn't happen," replied Tayce in a near whisper looking about.

"I get your point," he replied, seeing where she was coming from—that without any evidence she would look just as she said, stupid. It worried him, though, that there could be further trouble and they didn't know when.

Darius, up on the platform asked for everyone's attention. The audience fell silent, giving their new leader their full attention. He began by firstly thanking Aldonica for her quick-thinking actions in saving the new leader of Enlopedia. Her actions would be noted for a commendation. With this, Aldonica smiled, thanking Darius politely, then stepped back out of the way. He announced further that he was honoured to be leader of such an up-and-coming base and, above all else, to be made Admiral of Enlopedia. He would serve the base and its people in the same way the late Jonathan Largon served Questa: with pride. He would serve with the best he could possibly give. He would listen and advise where necessary. The audience gave a thunderous applause at Darius's promise. He finally went on to declare he was going to make Enlopedia as good if not better than Questa, to be a base to be proud of and one that would be remembered long into history for being number one in everything.

Upon these words, the doors to the hall burst open once more. Everyone turned on the alert. In walked a man in the same attire as the young female assassin was dressed in earlier, only he was in black. Tayce turned her head. She knew her hunch had been right. Darius looked at the male as he walked forth, silently waiting for some explanation of who he was and what his purpose was in their surroundings. The audience began whispering, wondering who it might be. Tayce watched the male as he walked forth, thinking his arrival had something to do with the female's earlier. He brandished a powerful-looking weapon that looked like it could blow the roof off the hall. Jan and his men were watching as the male assassin made his way towards Darius, down the aisle, with scrutinising interest, getting ready to act and do what was necessary to bring him down before their new leader and admiral.

Tayce was contacted via a mind link with Tricara. She informed Tayce she had to do something as she was feeling feelings of extreme hostility to the extent that it was criminal to read what he wanted to do to her father since being elected as the new leader of Enlopedia. He paused and drew the weapon, ready to take aim. Aldonica felt helpless beside Lydia. She had left the Vicdayne weapon with Jaul Naven, back at her seat. She looked across to him, trying discreetly to get his attention. Sallen caught on to what Aldonica was trying to do. She grabbed the Vicdayne weapon from Jaul's hold and, before Jan's men had a chance to move in, loaded the weapon with the spare cartridge, discreetly, ready to fire.

"So you've made admiral. Let's hope you last longer in charge than I did," began the male coldly.

"What do you mean by that statement? Who are you?" demanded Darius.

"I, Admiral, am someone Chief Traun was hoping had disappeared forever. You see, she was in charge of casting me out to some remote deserted colony, deep in the depths of forgotten space, but I found a way to freedom. I'm back to stop some fool who was once part of the planetary council, and owned his own world, claiming my position. So you see, Admiral, your reign will be somewhat short. But for those of you who don't know who I am, let me show you," he announced, peeling away his mask slowly.

Lydia and Darius watched on in uneasy anticipation. Jan's men were itching to pounce. Slowly, to everyone's surprise, the mask revealed someone Lydia had hoped had gone forever. She shook her head in total disbelief as it became clear who was under the mask.

"Barkin! You're not welcome here. Leave this base at once, before you're arrested," said Lydia with cold hatred in her normally gentle voice.

"The beautiful Lydia Traun! I'm unable to fulfil your request. You see, I came here with one intention, and that is to finish off what my assistant didn't achieve. Say goodbye to your new admiral and partner," he said, beginning to move the weapon into a position where he could kill Darius with one single shot.

As Barkin took aim, so did Jan Barnford, his men and Sallen with Aldonica's Vicdayne weapon from different parts of the hall. The audience were subjected to another panic and lowered themselves to avoid being shot. Commodore Travern took out his Pollomoss and rose to a standing position beside his wife, aiming ready to shoot. Barkin was under gun watch from a lot of people around the hall, ready for his sudden move. The hall was filled with a deathly silence. Darius looked at Barkin, cold and unemotional. At the back of the hall Jan was discreetly ordering his men to help the guests leave discreetly. But before they had a chance to leave their seats, Barkin heard a movement and fired a powerful warning shot into the air. Lydia flinched. Bits of the Celebrational Hall ceiling fell to the ground. Barkin stepped aside, not bothered by his actions.

"Stop, or I'll take out Chief Traun first. After all, she did do me out of my position," bellowed Barkin.

Jan was getting really twitchy with his finger on the firing button. He was staring coldly with a look of sharp intent in his eyes. He wished Barkin would either make a move or back down. His patience to control the immense anger he was feeling inside was making him fired up to the point of explosion. Craig studied the weapon Barkin was holding. As a point of technological interest, it was silver in colour, like a mini cannon—the same kind the female assassin had been brandishing earlier when she'd burst in. Tayce glanced at Jan at the back at the hall, wondering what he was waiting for, though she could see by his composure and fixed sight on Barkin he was ready to wipe him out if he made the slightest move to shoot her father. Tricara looked over to her, telepathically mind-communicating with her, suggesting she should join forces and force Barkin to his knees. Tayce heard her friend, but glanced around the hall to see Commodore Martin Travern still poised with his gun directly aimed at Barkin, then she looked at Sallen with Aldonica's Vicdayne weapon. She could see her father had enough people to protect him. She looked back at Tricara and slowly nodded. Together they focused their minds on sending Barkin's mind out of control, so much so that it would reach the point of rendering him a blithering idiot and sending him in an unconscious state to his knees. As they were doing what they were doing, Jan and a couple of his officers, Sallen and Commodore Martin Travern, opened fire on Barkin. He dropped to his knees, the gun in his hold dropping to the floor as he fought unsuccessfully to gain his composure. He hit the ground, staying there. Barkin died like a whimpering child before Darius, Lydia and Aldonica on stage. Waynard shook his head in disgust at what Barkin had become. He remembered how he'd showed promising potential and vision for the future of Enlopedia and how things had turned out so wrong because the power of command had gone to his head.

Aldonica walked down the steps from the stage and picked up the weapon Barkin had dropped, making it safe. Two of Jan's officers came forth, dragging Barkin's dead body away. The audience once more gained their composure after what had occurred. Dairan glanced at Tayce as she opened her eyes from calming down after joining forces with Tricara. He had a feeling she'd assisted in bringing Barkin to his death in order to save her father, but said nothing. Tayce looked up at the platform and her mother in the comforting hold of her father. Lydia smiled back upon seeing her looking. As soon as peace had been restored, the proceedings were once more taken over by Darius, now as the new leader of Enlopedia, in the new rank of admiral. He looked down at the audience and was glad to find they were giving him their undivided attention once more.

"This is what you could say is somewhat of an eventful ceremony. Shall we continue, honoured guests?" asked Darius light-heartedly, making everyone laugh in the hall.

This broke the tense atmosphere. Commodore Martin Travern spoke up from the audience, exclaiming that it could only get better from then on, carrying on the situation to make the moment light. It worked. Everyone in the hall continued, laughed and relaxed. Darius looked down at Martin, thanking him silently, then went on, exclaiming that as the new leader and Admiral of Enlopedia he hoped the various colonies and other races that had worked well with Chief Traun would now consider working with him. Darius gave a nod, then stepped back to allow Waynard back to talk.

"Thank you for your address as admiral. I'm sure you will make us proud. It's good to have you as our new replacement for Chief Traun—not that she hasn't done a wonderful job in power, whilst being in the position of leader of this base at such short notice. I for one consider she has done an excellent job. As from todayon I will be changing my duty position also—I will be Chief Councillor Traun's new council deputy. And as for Adam Carford, he will be working with the admiral as his personal assistant in every-dayon matters relating to sorting any problems that arise and need sorting on this base," announced Waynard, gesturing with his hand for Adam to walk out and say a few words.

Adam stepped up on to the platform to applause as Waynard stepped back, allowing him to speak. He simply began by saying it was an honour to remain as part of the important side of every-dayon life on the base he called his home and enjoyed serving on. He would serve and uphold the law to the best of his ability and would continue to do so no matter how small or troublesome the problem would turn out to be. He would always be ready to help in any way he could—the Admiral could be sure of this. With that he nodded in thanks to the audience listening to him and stepped back down to his seat.

Darius stepped back to the micro-announcer and began explaining about how lucky he was. How in 2414, when things began to change dramatically for his Traunian world and family, he never thought something like being elected in as the new head of such a wonderful base as their current surroundings would turn out the way it had. Traun's destruction would live on in many minds. It was also hard to imagine Tayce, who was cast out on the dreadful night of terror with a guidance computer as her only companion, would now be on her second voyage with the Amalthean Quests team. It just went to show that not every change was considered a bad one in life. Darius gestured for Tayce and the team to head up onstage—something Tayce was not expecting. She rose to her feet, much to the astonishment of those that knew Darius by sight, but didn't know he had a daughter and that she was the successful captain of the Amalthean Quests team. Everyone in the team began on their way to the platform, including Twedor, accompanied by thunderous applause in their honour. Once up on the platform, Darius hugged her proudly, then let her speak. Twedor came in front of her as the rest of the team gathered round.

"Firstly, I would like to say you'll never find a better man than my father, as leader, and I'm not just saying this as his daughter. Secondly, let me introduce you to my team. This is Twedor, followed by Dairan, Marc, Craig, Aldonica, Sallen, Mac, Jaul, Dr Donaldo Tysonne and his wife Treketa, Kelly Travern and, finally, Jonathan Largon's son Lance," introduced Tayce proudly.

Everyone took a bow before the gathered honoured guests. Darius watched his daughter proudly. He was glad to see what she'd become and how she'd grown into an exceptional young woman, taking things in her stride. He broke the moment by asking for another round of applause for the legendary Amalthean Quests team. Once more the applause erupted, only this time around it sounded louder than ever. Some of the gathered guests that knew of Tayce and the team rose to their feet, clapping as a thank you for what the team had done for them in the past. many had had dealings with them, either in the course of solving crimes or rescuing them, or their crew, or people like the Travern family, whose daughter Kelly had become part of the Amalthean Quests team. When everything had died down and the various members of the audience had regained their seats from the standing ovation of appreciation of Tayce, Darius asked for everyone's attention for the final time.

"My honoured guests, thank you for sharing this special, eventful time with us todayon. Please enjoy the after reception and hospitality laid on, before heading back to your place of duty and life. Thank you for coming," said Darius, feeling proud and pleased that the whole occasion, even though eventful, had gone well. The gathered audience slowly rose to their feet, talking amongst themselves with others they hadn't seen for some time and began to ferry on out into the adjoining centre, where refreshments had been laid out in a buffet style.

Tayce turned to her team. "Feel free to join the others for refreshments, or whatever you want to do, but be back on board the cruiser ready for departure in three houroнs," commanded Tayce.

They all nodded understandingly, then dispersed, going their separate ways. Some stayed for the refreshments and to talk with other guests, whilst others headed off around Enlopedia. Dairan stayed for a few minons to talk with Tayce. She turned towards him with a warm smile.

"Do you want me to remain, because I would like to go to the Astro Supply Centre, in the city square—I need some supplies?" he enquired casually.

"No, you go ahead and get what you need. I'll see you later," assured Tayce positively.

"Thanks. Catch you later," replied Dairan, heading off.

Marc remained, watching the various male and female guests head into the adjoining centre for refreshments and to mingle. Darius turned to Lance, as he'd asked him to remain for a few minons. He began, as Tayce neared and listened, by saying that when the transfer of personnel archive material occurred from Questa to Enlopedia, the archives building found a sealed capsule that was left to him by his father. They wondered if he would like to go and collect it? Lance turned to Tayce, asking if he could do so and take it aboard Amalthea to his quarters. Tayce nodded, suggesting Twedor go along for support. She knew how hard it would be for him to collect the capsule full of old mementoes belonging to his father. He patted Twedor on his metlon head and suggested they get going.

"At last, something exciting to do," said Twedor, glad to be getting out of their surroundings.

"See you two later. Have fun and stay out of trouble, both of you," said Tayce.

Lance guided Twedor on across the floor to the entrance of the centre, where the refreshments had been laid out. They passed through guests talking and laughing with each other on matters of mutual interest. Adam Carford, upon seeing him approach, used his Wristlink to contact the archives building, to let them know Lance was on his way with one Romid to pick up his father's capsule. He also arranged for the capsule, on identification, to be transferred to Amalthea. Adam informed Lance what he'd done and let him go on. Tayce heard the name Jonathan Largon in Adam's conversation with the archives building and her thoughts drifted back to the first dayons when Lance joined the team as a naïve young officer—and an innocent one at that. She realised his father would be proud if he could see him todayon and what he had managed to become. As she came back to the present and glanced around the many gathered talking guests, she caught the watchful eye of her father, who was studying her, watching Lance. He sauntered over to her, leaving Lydia talking with a group of dignitaries.

"Jonathan would be proud of him, I'm sure. He'd be as proud of him as I am of you," said Darius, like the true proud supporting father he was.

"Thank you. Would you like me to stay, only you said when I spoke to you, before arriving here, you had some disk documents for future possible Quests? I'd like to study them before we depart," she said, glancing around at the many gathered guests.

"Yes, that's right. No, you go right ahead and do what you have to. I'll have them brought down for you. You do what you want with them afterwards—I don't need them back," replied Darius, not minding that she couldn't stay. He fully understood she had a voyage to return to.

"Thanks," replied Tayce, glad her father understood she had to get ready to resume duty.

Darius walked away across to Adam, asking him to do one last duty as assistant to Lydia. Adam soon agreed obligingly and hurried off to do what Darius asked of him. Darius continued on back to his guests as Tayce sauntered on over to the nearest sight port. She stood watching the arrival and departure of different types of space transportation, with interest. Marc sauntered over through the mingling guests to her, studying her concerned expression. Something was wrong, he thought. She didn't hear him approaching her and slightly jumped when he put his hand on her shoulder.

"Sorry!" he said quietly by her side, not meaning to startle her.

"No, I was far away," she said, turning to face him.

"Is anything the matter, only you're not mingling with the guests? There's some interesting people here."

"No, I'm fine. I'm waiting for Adam to bring down some disk documents Father has left me, then I'm going to head back to Amalthea. I want to study them before we leave, in case there's anything we need to take on immediately," said Tayce, glancing at the talking guests again after hearing a loud sound of laughter.

"I'll come with you if you don't mind. There's nothing I need to remain here for. It's mainly business talk between the powers that be," replied Marc, glancing around the centre, thinking the scene was one filled with high-ranked dignitaries and not really his scene.

"No, you stay. Father would welcome questions asked about Amalthean Quests answered by you, and I know he would love to share this celebration reception with you present," she replied.

"All right, but couldn't you stay for a little while too? We could go through the information on disk documents later together?" he asked, hoping she would change her mind.

"No, because as soon as everyone's back aboard, and the three hourons are up, we'll be departing. I want to be ready for the first possible Quest ahead," Tayce insisted.

Marc nodded understandingly, though he thought she was just trying to get out of mixing with dignitaries, which was understandable. Adam crossed the Reception Centre with the documentation case containing the requested disk chips and information for Tayce. He was slightly out of breath as he came to a pause before her. He handed her the case, exclaiming that he'd just done his last job as assistant purely to her mother. As from that moment on, he would be working for both her parents indirectly. Tayce congratulated him and jokingly informed him he would have to get a lot fitter, because working for her father was a lot more hard work than working for her mother. He thanked her for the warning, laughing, then noticed he was wanted on the other side of the centre. He quickly excused himself. Tayce informed him she'd see him next time she was in port. Adam nodded, then continued off across the centre. Marc followed Adam, leaving Tayce to head on back to the cruiser. She pushed her way through the mingling crowd, heading to the entrance. Upon reaching the entrance, she turned briefly, looking for her mother and father. They saw her and nodded a goodbye. She continued on out into E City Square.

She was about to head back to Amalthea Two, leaving Marc behind to represent her and the team, when she saw Chief Jan Barnford heading in her direction with a relaxed smile. She sighed. She was hoping she wouldn't get stopped any more. Time was passing and, the way things looked, she wasn't going to get much studying done of the information enclosed on the disk chips. They both met in the middle of E City Square.

"Getting too boring for you then?" he asked light-heartedly in his usual gruff tone.

"No! I have to look through these disk chips before departure; so I figured as the cruiser would be quiet for a while, I'd start," she replied casually.

"Oh, it's a case of duty calls, then, and there was me thinking if I get Barkin and his female accomplice taken care of, I could get off duty and head back to the centre and catch up on what's been happening since I last saw you, over a drink," he said, disappointed she was leaving so soon.

"Sorry—not this time. Maybe next time," she said in an apologetic way.

"I'll hold you to it. Old friends should catch up now and again. Take some advice from someone of high rank: all work and duty can soon tell on you; you should learn to relax once in a while. It doesn't do any harm and your team aren't going to think any less of you," he said discreetly close to her.

"I'll keep that in mind when this Universe runs out of Quests to solve," she replied lightly.

"Oh well, I might as well find someone else to treat to a drink in the reception I'll see you later," he said, pretending his feelings had been hurt, heading away.

She continued on, also feeling, in a way, she'd been unfair to Jan. He had been a real buddy since the demise of Tom, Still, he knew how busy she was and the kind of responsibility she had as captain on Amalthea. She rounded the building corner and came upon Dairan, departing from the Astro Supply Centre, loaded down with items for the onboard Astrono Centre. An assistant from the supply centre, walked behind him carrying more supplies. He was around seventeen and blushed upon seeing the legendary Captain Traun herself, in the flesh. Tayce asked Dairan, surprised, what was he intending to do with all the supplies? He gave her a straightforward reply: the onboard Astrono Centre stores were running low, but she needn't worry now he'd get everything in. She raised her eyes, hoping he was right. There seemed to be quite a few.

Upon arrival back at the cruiser, the young assistant who had been struggling with the supplies gave a look that said he was glad they'd reached where they had to take the supplies. They were getting rather heavy. He had been a student in first-grade astronomy and even though he had found his job somewhat heavy at times, he was chuffed he'd helped the legendary Amalthea team in some way. Tayce glanced at him and thought to herself, after he headed back to the supply centre, he wouldn't be able to contain himself in telling his friends who he'd assisted earlier. He smiled shyly, then placed the supplies nervously inside the Docking-Bay doors, finding it truly out of this world to serve the captain of Amalthea.

"Thanks for your help," said Tayce as the slender young lad with mousy-coloured hair stepped back out of Amalthea.

"You're welcome, ma'am," he replied in nervousness and bolted before Dairan had a chance to reward him with a tip of currency for his help.

Tayce smiled and shook her head, then remembered she too had been like the young man once—impressed by people in high-up places—and was so nervous when her father had introduced her to someone of high rank. She felt sorry for the young lad. He'd probably felt awkward being in the presence of two members of the Amalthean Quests team. But he needn't have been—she and every other member of the team always had time for the young people of Enlopedia and would talk to them about their travels, and tell them whatever they wished to find out.

Tayce helped Dairan with the supplies as far as quarters level. They both worked out who would carry what and walked on, arms full, talking as they went.

* * *

Later Tayce entered her quarters carrying just the document case. She set it down on the mouldable soffette, then walked on across the Living Area to the drinks dispenser to retrieve a fresh cup of Coffeen. The lights from Enlopedia reflected on the quarters wall. She ordered Amal to have the occasional lighting beside the soffette on the cream square tables activated to full illumination. Amal did as requested. The lighting rose to full illumination. Tayce sat down on the soffette and sank back into the cushions relaxingly, removing her calf-length boots. She grabbed the case and opened it. Behind her the quarters doors opened. In walked Twedor, making a sound that indicated he was totally displeased about something. Tayce leant around the end of the soffette, surprised by his under-breath mutterings of intolerance at what had just happened.

"Twedor, is there a problem—you seem angry over something?" asked Tayce, wondering what was wrong.

He walked around the soffette, his head down, looking totally bored. He paused before Tayce, who was ready to listen to his problem before commencing the disk work.

"For the past couple of hourons, I've been totally bored out of my plasmatronic brain by all the officialdom at the ceremony, then helping in the search for the capsule in the archives with Lance," he expressed, sounding gloomy.

"That's a first for you. You generally like official visits and looking for something. Will you fetch me my Porto Compute, over there, then if you like you can help me go through these disks Father has sent over," said Tayce casually.

"Sure. Can I say something?" began Twedor as he fetched the Porto Compute.

"Of course—what is it? You know we've always been able to talk freely," said Tayce, giving Twedor her full attention as he came back with what she wanted.

"You would think Lance led a boring life as a child, considering what we found in the capsule. It was filled with study books on disc and things you wouldn't have thought Jonathan Largon's son would be interested in," confided Twedor.

"Perhaps they belonged to Jonathan and they were his past treasures, instead of Lance's. Perhaps they were belongings Jonathan wanted to hand down from father to son, but it's not for you to pass judgement on. People live their lives in different ways, Twedor. Some aren't as privileged as I was. Perhaps Jonathan left the contents for Lance as a reminder of his life on Questa, as he lost everything when it was destroyed, remember?" pointed out Tayce seriously.

"Yes, maybe you're right. Who am I to judge? It's got nothing to do with me," replied Twedor seeing her point.

Tayce loaded the first disk into the Porto Compute, then pushed the activation key, bringing on screen the contents for a possible Quest ahead. Twedor watched for a while, but Tayce could tell he was still agitated, suggesting perhaps he could go and help Dairan. Twedor nodded, then turned, heading for the quarters doors. Tayce glanced up as they opened, watching the little Romid leave. She smiled and shook her head, then went back to what she was studying.

***

Amal, two hourons later, informed Tayce that everyone was back on board and Dairan Loring was on his way to see her.

"Prepare to pull out of the High Rank Private Port, Amal, and inform Officer Largon I want to see him at first light, duty hourons," ordered Tayce in reply.

Behind Tayce, as she closed down the Porto Compute, the quarters doors opened. Dairan and Twedor entered, Dairan carried a ten-by-eight image frame in gift wrap. He reached over the back of the soffette, handing it to her.

"Present for you," he announced softly.

"What is it?" she asked, curious.

"Open it. It's something you probably never knew there was an image of," he suggested calmly.

As Tayce opened the soft gift wrap that was wrapped around an average-sized square she was amazed to see the image was of her old home world, Traun. The sight almost made her catch her breath. All the memories of the fateful night came flooding back. She could hear the horrendous sounds of distress as her people suffered at the hands of the Vargon Warriors and smell the horrendous smell of burning as her whole home planet fell apart all over again. A sad tear came to her eyes. On this, Dairan suddenly felt he'd made the wrong move.

"Sorry! I didn't mean to upset you. I should have known. I'm such an idiot," he said softly.

"No, it's all right. It's just memories. They will always be with me, no matter what. It's a nice image—how did you get it?" asked Tayce softly.

"I had a buddy of mine at the Astro Supply Centre print it. He owed me a favour, so I asked him if he could find any images of Traun. He came up with what you're holding—even put it in a frame when I said it was for you."

Tayce turned her head, smiling thankfully at him. She rose to her feet, exclaiming that she would treasure it forever. She crossed the Living Area of the quarters and hung it on the spare wall attachment, so it was noticeable every time she walked into the quarters. As she turned to cross back, so Amalthea slightly jolted as she departed from the tractor-beam hold at Enlopedia. Tayce fell towards Dairan—he was there to steady her. Reaching out, he quickly brought her gently into his arms.

"We've got to stop meeting like this," he said softly to her, almost laughing.

Tayce smiled, but stayed where she was, in his loving hold. He gave her a long lingering kiss. A few minons later, he let go of her, said nothing and headed for the entrance, leaving her speechless, wondering why he'd cut dead their intimate moment.

"I'll see you in the mornet on duty," he announced briskly, walking from her quarters, leaving the doors to close behind him and leaving Tayce wondering why he'd left her so quickly.

Twedor looked up at his mistress, seeing she was wondering why Dairan had made such a swift exit. Had she done something wrong? Tayce shrugged her shoulders, thinking, 'Oh well, maybe he was tired.' She felt a bit disappointed, though, that he hadn't wanted to stay for a while. Twedor could see as much. Thinking back over the visit to Enlopedia, all in all it had been a good time, thought Tayce, even with the untimely intervention of Barkin and his female ginger-haired accomplice. Her father was back in a position of great power, as leader of Enlopedia instead of Traun this time, in the new rank of admiral. Now the base would really pick up, she thought. In a way, she hoped it would be as good if not better than her old home world, Traun.

12. Virus and Apprehension

Amalthea Two, two weekons later, was on what the team termed a trip to anywhere, As the cruiser wasn't logged in to any particular course. The reason was that the team had mysteriously contracted a form of influenza. The only two members who hadn't been affected were Tayce and Jaul Naven. Jaul, being science and medical botany officer on the team, had been given orders by Tayce to come up with a cure—and sooner rather than later. He set to work with Donaldo, working as a mini team. The symptoms were growing weirder by the cencron. Donaldo took a sample of Tayce's blood because she hadn't been affected, for some strange reason. Donaldo figured Tayce might hold the key to a certain immune gene that stopped her from contracting the current strain. Hence taking a sample of her blood. Where the strain had originated from Tayce had no idea, only it could have come from someone on Enlopedia at her father's swearing-in ceremony. So far, though, her father and mother hadn't been victims of the virus—or Adam, or any of the Enlopedians—but the headquarters base was on alert. As Tayce didn't like being without her team, she willingly volunteered to be the hoped-for cure blood donor. Jaul's reason for not contracting the mysterious strain was that he had been given a special antiviral life booster when he was a child, which protected him against space viruses for the whole of his life on Canardan 5, a colony that originated from Earth 1 Canada many centuries ago. A cure had become difficult to find for influenza because the virus turned into a super-strain, which was very difficult to treat as it resisted treatment. People that caught the super-strain were monitored and their systems boosted to eventually get them through. Jaul was glad he wasn't being affected, looking around at his team colleagues, sneezing, coughing, having hallucinations and high temperatures, some faring worse than others.

Two hourons into the onslaught of the mysterious virus, Tayce was standing in Organisation surrounded by her sneezing worse-for-the-virus team members. They were struggling, yet determined to keep their minds on their current duties.

Without warning, Kelly keeled over at her duty position, falling off her chair, slumping to the Organisation floor in a heap. Tayce quickly went about trying to get her back on to her chair, whilst ordering Amal to take over navigations. Tayce, once Kelly was seated, ordered Mac, who was looking like death warmed up, to forget his duty and take Kelly and himself to the MLC. They were relieved of duty. Mac eagerly obliged, taking hold of Kelly in a supporting hold and guiding her as she regained consciousness on out of Organisation. Marc let another sneeze go. He could hardly see out of his eyes for congestion. It was bad luck for Twedor. He was in the line of fire from Marc's unscheduled sneeze and got the full force of the germs all over him at tremendous speed. It made him glad he was a Romid and not human, otherwise he would have become the next victim.

"Thanks! Like I needed a shower of germ microbes," said Twedor sarcastically, looking up at Marc.

"Sorry, buddy," replied Marc, feeling awful.

"You're spreading infectious microbes and I think I just got a third of them," continued Twedor. He was far from impressed to know he had just been coated in influenza microbes.

After a few minons Marc patted Twedor, apologising, but explained that there was nothing he could do as a human sneeze comes without warning. He'd be wise to step aside next time. With this, Twedor decided he would be better getting out of Marc's line of fire. Slowly, one by one, the whole team in Organisation were falling too ill to continue with their duty and staggered off in the direction of the MLC Amal ended up taking control of each team member's console, until she was taking overall charge of the main operations of the cruiser. Finally Tayce, Twedor and Amal were the only ones left in charge. For Tayce it was like going back to the old dayons with Twedor in his former form as Midge, guidance computer. She hoped they didn't get called upon for a sudden emergency, otherwise God knows what she'd do. As if some external force was hearing her, Amal suddenly announced she had an urgent call coming in from Admiral Traun on Enlopedia. Twedor followed Tayce as she ordered Amal to put it through to the DC. They both entered the DC, pretending it was like the old dayons and that there was nothing wrong, so her father would not be suspicious. As Tayce reached her desk, she turned and sat on the edge, waiting for Amal to transfer the call to the Sight Screen. Twedor came to a pause by her side, also looking at the Sight Screen that was activating. Admiral Darius Traun appeared. Tayce was silently hoping he wasn't going to ask her to take on a sudden emergency. He was unaware the Organisation team were not on duty. Tayce braced herself as her father began explaining about what the next Quest would entail, thinking the team were all right. Twedor glanced at Tayce, thinking she was doing a good job in convincing her father all was OK. As Darius continued, Tayce found as she listened she was thinking less about the team's current predicament and becoming interested in the forthcoming Quest.

* * *

Meantime down in the MLC lab, Donaldo and Jaul, in between Donaldo letting the odd untimely sneeze go and feeling like death warmed up, had by sheer luck come across a cure using a sample of Tayce's blood. It had taken seven hourons trying this method and pinpointing the very tiny resistant antibodies in her blood that could knock out the influenza. Many antibodies had been tried on a computer simulation to no avail, but now one had proved successful. Both shook hands and clapped each other on the back, excited about their achievement. Donaldo suggested that as they'd made the successful cure he would volunteer to try it out. Jaul, without a further word, picked up the newly loaded Comprai Inject Pen, a new injection device brought from Enlopedia after the last visit, filled with the right amount of dosage for a first dose, then reluctantly pressed it against Donaldo's upper arm, waiting for the unforeseen worst to occur.

"Tell Treketa I loved her," said Donaldo, making light of the fact that Jaul looked somewhat nervous, worried that if the cure didn't work, against all odds, he could have just killed Amalthea's medical man.

"Very funny," said Jaul, seeing Donaldo was winding him up.

Jaul was a gentle-natured young man in his late twenties. He'd been picked for the team because of his expertise in both human and plant ailments. He was top of his class back on Canardan 5. He had warm friendly features, soft brown eyes and short sandy hair. His build was somewhat stocky, but he was very fit in appearance. Treketa smiled at Donaldo waiting for the unpredictable to occur, against all odds, as she entered the lab wondering if they'd had any luck. A few minons elapsed. Donaldo took the Examscan and began guiding it over himself, checking the readings. He gave a smile of relief as the injection seemed to be working. His vital signs were showing the influenza was leaving his system. Jaul handed the rest of the vials to Treketa, after injecting her with a dose, suggesting she load the Comprai Inject Pens and administer it to the rest of the team around the cruiser whilst they took care of the team present. Donaldo followed on out into the MLC and began across to the members present to give them the cure. Whilst Treketa took loaded inject pens and went in search of the others around the cruiser, Donaldo began to administer the cure, to Kelly first, then Mac. Treketa briskly headed for the entrance doors and as they parted she continued on out on the walk around the cruiser in search of the other members of team, all suffering from the mysterious strain of the influenza.

* * *

Marc and Dairan sat in the Leisure Centre feeling cold and like their bodies were being invaded by every ache imaginable. Finding it nearly impossible to relax, both had managed to get Amal to sift through the drinks archives for some warm, soothing citrus beverages to help stop their throats feeling like sandpaper.

Each one was trying to find topics to discuss, keeping their minds off the near-to-death experience they were enduring. Occasionally they'd glance out at the stars through the sight port beside them. Treketa, feeling a lot more like her old self, entered the centre carrying the cure.

"At last! I had to have Amal find you two. Here is the cure for your unwanted virus, though it would have been a lot quicker if you'd come to the MLC with your symptoms earlier," said Treketa, checking the Comprai Inject Pen before giving the cure to Marc.

"We figured you already had enough germs down there without us adding to them," joked Marc.

"I still say you would have had this a lot quicker. We have Tayce to thank for this cure—she gave us a sample of her blood as she's immune to this virus for some strange reason. Jaul and Donaldo spent seven hourons coming up with this and—before you ask is it safe?—Donaldo has checked it. It's fine," assured Treketa.

"Can we head back to duty?" asked Marc.

"Give it one houron, then you should be back to normal. I would suggest that en route you stop off at the MLC for a Vitboost injection, to boost your system back to full health," replied Treketa, putting the main part of the Comprai Inject Pen back in the small, slim grey case and the cartridges back in the case for disposing.

She turned and left both Marc and Dairan coming back to their normal selves. Marc rose to his feet. He wanted to cleanse and change before returning to duty, as he'd been sweating from the sudden temperature surges. He discarded his cup in the waste incinerator chute, then began on out, pausing in the doorway to suggest the same to Dairan. He'd see him up in Organisation.

* * *

Up in Organisation a while later Tayce sighed upon walking from the DC. She was glad she would soon be getting the team back on duty and that she'd been successful in helping to find a cure to the mysterious influenza. Lance was the first to return to duty, feeling a lot more like his old self. He'd cleansed and changed his uniform and was about to take up his duty position when he glanced over at Tayce, seeing her in thought.

"Problem?" he asked casually.

"We've got an urgent Quest come in. It's on Solarseano. It's to apprehend an Enlopedian female criminal who has broken security hold and escaped to the planet to hide out there and avoid being recaptured. Before fleeing she vowed she was en route to kidnap the Commodore's son and heir of Solarseano."

Lance gave her a surprised look, but carried on listening as Tayce continued to explain that this was obviously not a run-of-the-mill female criminal, as Chief Barnford was on his way out with two officers of the SSWAT team to assist in the recapture of the female. Lance thought about the whole situation for a minon, then suggested he get on with the research to see what he could find out about Solarseano and what was so special about this female criminal. If he turned up anything interesting, he would let her know.

"Keep it to one side and we'll study it later," ordered Tayce.

He nodded understandingly, then turned to his console and began keying in the request for information on Solarseano. Kelly walked in, feeling almost back to her normal self. She crossed to navigations. Tayce smiled gently down at her as she took up her duty position and took back the controls from Amal.

"I speak for the whole of the team when I say thank you for your help to find a cure for what we've been through. It's nice to be back to normal," said Kelly, glancing at Lance and back again at Tayce.

"I'm only too glad it was that easy, as we've a Quest to take on. I had to pretend earlier when I was talking with Father that everything was fine and you were all here on duty. Believe me, it wasn't easy," confided Tayce quietly.

Kelly began taking on the journey to Solarseano now that Amal had released the controls back to her. She and Lance exchanged glances, asking each other was the other one all right now? Before getting back to their duty. Craig entered Organisation and headed straight to his console, saying thanks to Tayce for her help with the cure. He was still carrying a disposable wipe as he had the sniffles. Mac was last to walk back in. He nodded to Tayce in a grateful way for what she'd done, as he headed over to take up communications again. Once seated, he placed the small, slim communication device on his head, where he could hear through his left ear and speak through the small, slim mouthpiece which was connected, via a slim arm, to the earpiece. This was known as Microceive. Once Tayce had found everyone was back in their duty positions, she asked for everyone's attention.

"Solarseano is our next Quest. Our aim is to track down a female criminal that's escaped from holding on Enlopedia. Her name is Orell Anitra. She's the gang leader of an underground group, if you know what I mean?" asked Tayce, glancing around the team, who were looking back at her, listening.

"Orell Anitra, did you say? You're joking, Tayce," spoke up Lance, giving her an alarmed look.

"No, I'm not. Enlighten me and the rest of us with what you know," demanded Tayce giving him her full attention.

"Father had quite a few dealings with her. She's a deceptive bitch; and from what Father use to tell me, she's real trouble. She'll vanish in the blink of an eye and reappear when you least expect it. She'll kill you in the same way too. As she appears, she strikes and you're dead. That's probably how she escaped her holding on Enlopedia. I'm surprised they didn't encase her in some kind of protection field, considering the ease with which she can escape," expressed Lance.

"Thanks for the insight. At least we know what we're up against," replied Tayce, still thinking about what Lance said. She knew they'd have to be extremely careful.

"Chief Barnford has just informed me that he and his two officers will be boarding in roughly one houron," said Mac, turning at communications.

"Amal, activate heating and operation facilities in the guest quarters for the duration of their stay," ordered Tayce, turning to face Amal.

"Activating as requested now, Captain," replied Amal in confirmation of her orders.

Marc, who had been standing just inside the centre listening, glanced at Tayce as she handed over command to him and headed into the DC. Dairan was the final member to enter Organisation. He caught sight of Tayce heading into the DC and decided to follow on. Twedor was already heading in the same direction, so he followed him in and made it through the doors just as they were closing. Tayce turned, apologising as she took up her seat relaxingly at her desk. Dairan began across, thanking her for her help in curing him. It had been the worst kind of flu he could ever remember, and he'd had various types in the past.

"There's no need to thank me. Kelly already did. I was just glad to get everyone back on their feet so quickly, especially as Father has handed me a somewhat emergency Quest."

"I've already done some research on my pocket-sized link to the Astrono Computer, and in order to travel to Polar Solarseano, known as just Solarseano, we have to travel down what is termed the polar corridor, which is made up of dense ice," he explained, perching on the end of the nearest soffette arm.

"Here I go again, freezing my systems. It took ages to settle back down last time," spoke up Twedor.

"You'll be fine, Twedor. Continue on, Dairan," said Tayce, ignoring Twedor's whinge.

"It's almost half a milon in thickness, and if we don't keep on the exact navigational course, and slightly touch the sides, we will end up like other vessels that have travelled the corridor before, being blown into a trillion partecs."

"What are those?" asked Twedor interested.

"Bits!" replied Dairan without a further word

Tayce, upon hearing this, suggested he start working with Lance to find out how long the journey would take. Secondly, what safety factors needed to be taken into account for the safety of the team during transit? Dairan nodded, standing. He turned and headed for the doors. They opened on his approach. Tayce followed as the cruiser suddenly started to experience slight turbulence, and she wanted to know what was going on. She soon stepped out into Organisation behind Dairan and found Marc requesting an immediate orbital view of their current position. The sight port's main shutters drew apart, revealing a sight

252

none of them was expecting to see so soon. It was the entrance to the polar corridor to Polar Solarseano.

"Someone care to explain why we're here so soon?" asked Tayce, coming to a pause beside Marc.

"Sorry—can't explain it. We shouldn't be here for at least another houron. Maybe something is pulling us inside, hence us being here sooner," said Kelly over Tayce's shoulder.

"At this rate we'll be inside that corridor before we've had a chance to plot a safe journey, and Chief Barnford will be left behind, wondering where we are," said Marc with concern.

"Is there anyway in which we can decrease power and put Amalthea in a reverse pull, to hold back from entering the corridor before Chief Barnford gets here, Kelly?" asked Tayce, turning and giving her her full attention, waiting.

"I can decrease the engine power right down to a minimum and do as you've suggested, putting the engines in reverse power for roughly one houron. Any longer and we'd be risking trouble, including possible instability of the cruiser's outer hull and damage to the engines," suggested Kelly, working with Tayce.

Both Marc and Dairan looked towards Tayce questioningly, wondering what she would do, considering the possibilities of what could go wrong. Tayce sighed. She knew Jan had to be on the current Quest to take Orell Anitra back, once apprehended. She thought for a few minons about the best course of action to take.

"Do it, Kelly. Amal, the minon Chief Barnford comes into our orbit, place a high-frequency tractor beam, mark 4, on his vessel and bring it into the Hanger Bay," ordered Tayce in a true tone of command.

"Yes, Captain. Preparing request," replied Amal.

"Dairan, find the exact location of the Polar Solarseano orbit on the other side of this polar corridor, then give the coordinates to Kelly, ready for when we depart from the corridor on the other side," ordered Tayce.

"I'll get right on to it," assured Dairan.

Craig gave up his duty console so Dairan could commence Tayce's request. He seated himself and began keying in the details for the orbit of the Polar Solarseano home world. Craig watched over Dairan's shoulder, interested in what was materialising on screen and the way in which he quickly picked the information he wanted and discarded what he didn't want. In his estimation, Dairan was certainly expert at his job. He noticed how he calculated the exact navigational bearings from the simulated journey and the safety factor of Amalthea's transition through the ice-encased interior of the corridor. The moment the answer surfaced, saying what was required, Dairan sent it to Kelly's console and she turned, acknowledging it had successfully arrived. Craig watched, then listened as Dairan announced what he'd done to make sure when the cruiser exited on the other side of the ice corridor it would head straight for the home world and take on the Quest in hand. Tayce nodded.

"Any sign of Chief Barnford yet, Kelly?" asked Tayce, hoping there was.

"Yes! His Quest 3 shuttle is approaching scanner range now," said Kelly, rather relieved.

"The moment he comes within tractor-beam range, lock on and pull him in using that mark-4-high-density force and bring his shuttle into the Flight Hangar Bay as I suggested," ordered Tayce, noticing the entrance to the ice corridor was growing closer by the cencron, and she could feel the engines straining to hold back from the gravitational force from within.

"Of course!" assured Kelly, nodding and turning back to her console, watching the nearing Quest 3 on-screen just waiting for the exact moment to put into operation Tayce's request.

"Marc, you're in charge. Dairan, you can come with me," said Tayce, heading towards the entrance with Twedor in tow.

"Right with you. All yours, Craig," said Dairan, handing back his console, standing to head on out.

He quickly hurried after Tayce and Twedor. They both walked on together, talking about Polar Solarseano and the concerns she had about their transition through the polar corridor. Dairan nodded, but assured her he'd taken every consideration into account during the journey, in his calculations, and they should have a smooth journey. This made Tayce feel a lot more at ease. They discussed Orell Anitra on the way to meet Jan coming aboard. Tayce, as she neared the Level Steps, wristlinked Donaldo in the MLC to find out if Jan and his officers needed to be vaccinated against the influenza virus. Donaldo quickly confirmed that it would be a safe precaution and he'd meet them in the Flight Hangar Bay. Tayce ceased communications, beginning the walk down the Level Steps with Twedor and Dairan.

* * *

Outside, Amalthea was in the process of bringing the Quest 3 aboard under high-frequency tractor beam at a fourth-degree level, the highest strength able to be gained under the current conditions. It drew near slowly and under great strength towards the opening hanger-bay doors. In the final stage of the Quest 3 boarding the cruiser, Amalthea Two began to enter the below-freezing average conditions of the interior of the corridor to Polar Solarseano, unable to hold back any longer from entering. The force of the gravitational pull had increased to such a degree that it was risking all onboard operational functions and the outer hull, straining it to the extent it might rip apart at any cencron. The journey was on for Polar Solarseano. The hanger-bay doors closed just in time, sealing the Quest 3 shuttle safely inside with cencrons to spare.

***

Inside Amalthea, the Quest went through the usual decontamination procedure—electronically cleansing the whole Quest 3 against dangerous space-orientated microbes. Once through and the shuttle was safe, Tayce and Dairan began across the bay followed by Twedor and Donaldo. Donaldo carried a small silver case with the Comprai Inject Pen inside, with the Javen cure, as it was now termed, ready to inject Jan and his officers the moment they stepped off the shuttle. He came to a pause beside Tayce, waiting as the Quest was cleared from decontamination by Amal. As the entrance slowly opened, Jan Barnford soon appeared in the doorway, coming out down the three retractable steps to the bay floor. He carried a small short-stay holdall. His two strong and fit-looking officers, one of oriental origin, followed. They stood patiently back while their chief came forth towards Tayce. It could be seen that Jan had obviously briefed them on being on their best behaviour whilst on Amalthea. They were men from the SSWAT and they were dressed in their dark navy all-in-one combat suits, with their guns in their side holsters. Jan looked at Donaldo, wondering why he was present and withdrawing a Comprai Inject Pen from the case he had in his hand.

He looked at Tayce in a questioning way, as much as to ask, "Care to explain what the Doc's doing with a Comprai Inject Pen in his hand?"

Tayce glanced at Donaldo. She knew how Jan hated injections.

"You going to use that thing, Doc?" asked Jan, uneasily eyeing up the Comprai Inject Pen in Donaldo's grasp, which he hated at the best of times.

"I need to give you, and your two officers here, a precautionary dose of flu vaccine. It's for your own protection. We had an outbreak of a mysterious strain of influenza on board. This will protect you against any chance of catching it," assured Donaldo.

"He's right—it's just a precaution so that when you return to Enlopedia it won't be contracted by anyone there. It could spread around the base fast if we don't do this. It would be like an epidemic and the Admiral certainly wouldn't thank me for not having you treated against it," said Tayce, knowing her father would be furious, to say the least.

"I understand what you've got to do, Doc, but I'm not to keen on inject pens. I don't really care for injections of any kind—you never know what the side-effects will be," began Jan, trying to talk Donaldo out of it.

"I can understand how you feel, Chief. The Comprai Inject Pens of Enlopedia are not the best, but with ours you won't feel a thing. They are the latest models and inject without the least pain. It will be over in a couple of minons," assured Donaldo. He, like Jan's two officers, were finding the fact the chief of a security force, such as Enlopedia's, was scared of injections somewhat amusing, even though he shouldn't.

"Fire away. I hope you're right, Doc," said Jan, much to the stifled amusement of his officers.

Jan gave Tayce a look that said he was waiting for the worst when the injection hit home and entered his bloodstream. But nothing. All he could hear was a click and it was all over. Donaldo smiled to himself as he moved away on to Jan's two officers, giving the injection without a problem. Once finished, he picked up the small case he'd brought with him, slipping the Comprai Inject Pen back inside and headed away to the MLC Tayce turned, asking Dairan to show Jan's officers to their guest quarters. She then looked at Jan, wondering what his orders to his men would be. Jan dismissed them with an abrupt command.

"At ease. Dismissed. Be on Wristlink alert," said Jan without a further word.

On their chief's words, they walked away, leaving Jan and Tayce with Twedor to talk. Tayce gestured for them to leave the Flight Hangar Bay, suggesting a liquid refreshment in her quarters, where they could discuss the forthcoming Quest at ease. Jan nodded, beginning to move away with Tayce with Twedor following behind. As both his mistress and Jan walked along, Twedor discreetly listened to what Jan knew about Orell Anitra. As Tayce listened, the first part was pretty much what she already knew. He further informed her that Orell had resided on Questa before the base was destroyed, then she moved to Enlopedia until she escaped from holding after being captured. She'd shot through to reside on Polar Solarseano, where once again she'd been briefly apprehended until she slipped through the hands of the crime police and was somewhere on the surface, as yet not found. No doubt she was in hiding. He further asked whether she was aware of the fact that Orell could take on any form of appearance she so wished—even someone like Tayce herself—to evade being recaptured. This made Tayce resolve to be even more cautious in handling Orell if she came face-to-face with her. They all soon entered Tayce's quarters on Level 3. She crossed to the drinks dispenser and key-selected two cups of fresh Coffeen. Jan crossed to the sight port to look out at the white solid walls of ice within the tunnel as they passed through. Twedor stood at ease by the nearest soffette.

"Your Coffeen. Not the most attractive sight, is it?" she said, coming towards him with the cup.

"Thanks! No, it's strange the many phenomenal things there are out here in this Universe, such as this corridor of ice. It amazes me. It certainly is a rare sight, but has its dangers, no doubt," he said, continuing to look out at the scene, sipping his Coffeen.

"We've certainly found some different phenomena on this voyage," replied Tayce, studying the icy scene whilst drinking her Coffeen.

"You seem to be gaining what you hoped with this voyage, considering the trouble you had getting it off the launch pad, so to speak," he said, glancing at her casually.

"Yes, it's working out fine, considering, like you say, the trouble I went through to get this cruiser back out here. As you recall, I nearly got arrested at one point, but it was worth it," she reminded him, laughing.

"Tell me about it," he said, laughing with her at the thought, recalling when she nearly had a confrontation in the Council chambers with Barkin, telling him he was an idiot in so many words, and he was sent for.

"This Quest—any special requirements needed?" asked Tayce casually.

"Your weaponry specialist will need her skills to come up with something to halt Orell escaping again. You know, I've never met a woman like her. She's good in her field, especially how she can just make something out of nothing in weaponry. It truly astounds me. She's an asset to you and this team. You were extremely lucky to get her," praised Jan, meaning Aldonica.

"Believe me, she astounds me sometimes too. I read her personal report when I was recruiting for this team and that's what made me pick her as the weaponry specialist—her ability to design. She comes from Clavern 2 and was top of her group in her field," explained Tayce.

"She's certainly impressive. On this Quest, we'll not only need her, but we'll need members of your team that are good at combat—especially those who are good a capturing someone such as Orell Anitra. It won't be easy, there is no good saying otherwise," said Jan, thinking of past experiences he'd had with the female criminal.

"Don't worry—most of this team have good capabilities at taking on someone like her. Most have had dealings with Vargon, remember. But if you'd like to address them, I can have a meeting called so you can fill in any blanks I may have missed out. If there's one thing I don't like doing, that's leaving this team in the dark when it comes to information they may need for the task ahead," pointed out Tayce seriously.

"Point taken. I'd feel the same if it were my team. I like to have every available piece of information going."

"Then that settles it—I'll get everyone together for a meeting."

She left Jan finishing his Coffeen and went about arranging the meeting in the DC for later. She crossed and lifted the Telelinkphone handset, pressing the connect code to connect her to Amal. Amal soon answered, requesting her orders. Tayce immediately requested a combat Quest team to be sorted for the Quest ahead then to announce to those members there was to be a meeting in the DC in roughly fifteen minons. Amal confirmed her orders, ceasing communication. Tayce put the handset back and turned her attention to Jan, now seated on the mouldable chair opposite. She noticed he was looking up at the image print of her father, herself and Lydia all being reunited when her father recently was sworn in as the new Admiral of Enlopedia.

"Your father has already made some improvements since taking up his new position on Enlopedia."

"That's good, isn't it?" asked Tayce casually. "It did need some improvements."

"Very! Since his election many people have already begun praising his good work—not that your mother hasn't done a good job in her time in power, but many have expressed, and I've heard say it's nice to deal with someone along the lines of the late General Largon," explained Jan,

This pleased Tayce. She felt good to hear of the way Enlopedia had taken well to her father being in charge. Twedor stepped up beside her, reminding her she'd arranged a meeting in ten minons. Tayce suggested they get going. Jan rose to his feet and together they both discarded their empty Coffeen beakers in the usual disposable way, then carried on out through the opening doors as they parted before them, on the way to Level 1, Organisation. Twedor hurried to keep up with his mistress and Jan as they walked at a brisk pace to get there in time for the meeting ahead. On the way up the corridor Tayce turned to Jan, asking why had she and the team been picked for this particular Quest? Jan began, in return, saying it was because she'd had dealings with the likes of Countess Vargon—and how slippery she'd been when they were trying to apprehend her. The powers that be figured she'd be more than capable of handling Orell Anitra and her unpredictable powers, particularly her power to be in one place one minon and another the next or her power to take on many different disguises, or to appear with a sudden flash of blinding light right in front of a person. They figured Tayce herself, with her powers, would be able to handle the situation a lot easier and apprehend Orell with a lot more ease than anyone else had been able to at other times. Tayce smiled, slightly amused. It had been the first time she'd been considered for a Quest just because she was gifted, but it felt good just the same. On approaching the Level Steps, they began discussing the many new things that were coming in on Enlopedia since her father had taken over. Jan also confided to her that it looked like Orell Anitra was turning out to be another Countess Vargon all over again.

* * *

Up in Organisation, the small Quest team who had been selected to go on the Quest assembled in the DC awaiting the arrival of Tayce and Jan. Marc, before going in to join them, leant on the back of Mac's seat, ordering him to keep him informed of any changes during the journey through the polar corridor interior and when they were in range of Polar Solarseano. Mac nodded in agreement. Marc continued on into the DC to be with the others waiting, leaving Mac, Kelly and Craig working away in Organisation, as they hadn't been picked for the forthcoming Quest. Tayce soon entered with Jan, Twedor and Dairan, and Jan's two officers were not far behind. All went through to the DC and to the waiting gathered members of the team. Tayce stood back as Jan commenced the meeting, at her gesture to do so. He began explaining how the Quest team would be working in amongst the inhabitants of Solarseano with his officers. Tayce, as

Jan answered any questions in between briefing, suddenly found herself feeling like she wanted to pass out. She tried hard to ignore it. Without warning her whole body went from underneath her and she dropped to the floor, where she had been standing. Both Jan and Marc went to her side as she lay on the floor before her desk, out cold.

"Get Donaldo up here—that's an order," commanded Marc, crouching beside her as she lay unconscious.

Jan took a scatter cushion from the nearby mouldable soffette and went about placing it under Tayce's head, wondering what had made her suddenly collapse. Dairan stood looking on with true concern as to what might be wrong. Lance announced that Donaldo was on his way up. Everyone present couldn't understand either why Tayce should suddenly drop like she did, with no warning. They all hoped it wasn't anything serious, because she was a good leader and captain, also a good friend who had always put them first. Donaldo came rushing into the DC, Emergency Medical Kit in hand and the white and chrome Hover Trolley. Treketa followed on, wondering what the emergency was. Donaldo pressed a key on the slim control pad and the Hover Trolley lowered. Marc and Dairan lifted Tayce gently on to it. Donaldo pressed another key on the slim control pad and the trolley rose back to its normal level, which was almost waist height. Treketa covered Tayce with a heat-sealant blanket. Donaldo pushed another key and the Hover Trolley moved off slowly in front of him. He quickly assured Marc he'd call him the moment he found what was wrong. Marc nodded and Donaldo began on out with the Hover Trolley and Treketa.

Marc didn't like the way it looked and wondered if it had something to do with the influenza virus after all. He knew it was down to him now to lead the Quest in Tayce's absence. Jan sighed. What had just happened had just made the Quest a lot trickier unless Tayce made a miraculous recovery, as they were relying on her powers to succeed. Marc began by suggesting Jan continue on with the briefing in hand. He then turned to Dairan, expressing that he was in charge when they were on the Quest. Dairan nodded in total understanding. Marc turned away to contact Treketa via Wristlink, discreetly telling her that should he be on the forthcoming Quest before what was found to be wrong with Tayce surfaced, she was to let himself or Dairan know the moment they found out what was wrong. Treketa agreed, ceasing communication.

"What do you reckon is wrong?" Dairan asked Marc discreetly. "She just dropped."

"Not sure. I hope it's nothing serious. She's one special lady to all of us," replied Marc, just as discreet.

Marc turned to face the team, listening to the final points of the brief. Jan was warning them about Orell Anitra and saying to be totally aware at all times as she could change her appearance so quickly.

Mac stepped just inside the DC, exclaiming that Amalthea had just left the polar corridor and the cruiser had made it through unscathed. All that remained was to head into the orbit above Solarseano and the Quest could commence. He walked on across the DC and out into Organisation to head over to Mac's position, leaving Jan to wind up the briefing. After checking where they were, Marc turned his attention to the sight out through the main sight port, of Polar Solarseano. It was a strange egg-shaped world in a shade of green with blue and white markings that covered some areas in patches. It was approximately 93,000 kilometres in diameter and the fact that some areas of the surface were populated was shown by a grey shading. Marc turned towards the DC as Dairan walked out. He informed him he would resume command until they were ready to go on the Quest. Dairan nodded understandingly, exclaiming that he'd just hang around and help where he could until it was time to step into temporary command when the Quest got under way.

* * *

Down in the MLC Donaldo had placed Tayce on a medical bunk, with help from Treketa. He then took the Examscan and guided it up and down Tayce, still unconscious. He pressed a key, which relayed her current condition to the monitor overhead. He picked up the slim diagnostic handheld computer and requested the information to study for a hoped-for easy diagnostic analysis. But what he was getting were somewhat puzzling readings. Treketa looked at his concerned, puzzled expression, but stayed quiet as he decided what he was going to do for the best. He suddenly paused upon trying various means to diagnose what was wrong. He sighed and shook his head, wondering why was it every time Tayce was ill it was always difficult to pinpoint what was ailing her? Perhaps it was because of her powers getting in the way of the electronic frequency of relay from both the Examscan and the diagnostic computer. Treketa could see Donaldo's frustration and could understand it. He always liked to get to the heart of a problem and find a hoped-for solution. He'd, over the last couple of yearons, grown truly professional in his attitude and had on several occasions become annoyed when he couldn't find a solution, which was understandable, being who'd he become.

"I take it it's not an easy analysis. Can I do anything?" asked Treketa softly, glancing down at Tayce and then back at the above-normal readings that were being displayed.

"I've got it. Hold on—one of the readings here is telling me Tayce has the same symptoms as Kelly and Lance had during the influenza virus. What she's in is termed the unconscious phase, but she shouldn't be getting it. It was her blood that successfully brought about the cure for the virus. Get Jaul up here now. Let's hope he can help—tell him it's urgent," ordered Donaldo, not taking his eyes off what he was trying to decipher.

"Right! What are we going to do? Do you think somehow the virus has invaded her immune system after all and caused her to become the way she is?" asked Treketa, interested, as she headed across the MLC to contact Jaul via the Telelinkphone on the wall.

"I'm not sure, but it looks that way. I'll start by taking a blood sample and keep her under constant watch. She should be resistant to the full-blown virus; but because of the way her immune system is, if it's been invaded in some way, there's no telling what side-effects she's going to undergo," said Donaldo, concerned, as he took the blood sample with the Comprai Inject Pen.

Treketa, when Jaul answered the call, asked him to report to the MLC as he was needed. Jaul agreed. She put down the cordless handset and began back to Donaldo. As she did, she began informing him Jaul was on his way.

Donaldo thought to himself, 'Whatever they attempt to do in finding a cure for Tayce, we have to consider the possibilities of a reaction occurring, and they have to avoid that at any cost. The cure would most definitely have to be exact, without problems. He took the blood sample across to the side counter that ran around the whole of the MLC and transferred it to a container for Jaul. The doors to the centre opened and Jaul walked in with a small kit, exclaiming that he'd been told they needed his help? His sight was immediately drawn to Tayce lying on the medical bunk unconscious. He looked at Donaldo in a questioning manner.

"What's happened? Why is Tayce like this?" asked Jaul, concerned.

"She passed out in a briefing about twenty minons ago. I've taken a blood sample. I've a feeling she has a strain of the virus, which has managed to bypass her immune system somehow. I've a feeling, also, it could have happened when we took the last sample of her blood to help find the first cure. As you're aware, the virus has side-effects, one of which is a sudden onslaught of long unconsciousness. I'd like you to find a cure, like yesteron. She was due to go on an important Quest. But we have to take the utmost care; also you can have up to twenty-five hourons maximum. That's the longest I can keep her on life support, or it could damage her internally and her whole system could collapse," explained Donaldo as Jaul listened.

"I'll get right on to it. Where's the sample? I'll see you with a cure hopefully in half that time," replied Jaul, taking the blood sample from Treketa as she crossed with it in the vial.

Jaul turned and in urgency heading back to the entrance doors, wondering already as he went how he was going to get the exact match and cure for Tayce. He headed out through the opening entrance doors and off down the corridor, leaving the doors to close behind him.

"Continue with the constant checks. If anything should decline or worsen, which we hope it doesn't, then an alarm will sound," said Donaldo quietly to Treketa, who was looking at Tayce, worried.

She looked at him, nodding understandingly, continuing on with the other duties she was attending to around the MLC. As she passed one of the three sight ports looking out on the Universe, she caught sight of the distant world Polar Solarseano and paused for a moment, studying the somewhat interesting egg shape.

* * *

Marc Dayatso up in Organisation was in mid communication with the Commodore of Polar Solarseano about apprehending Orell Anitra. Jan was nearby listening. The Commodore expressed how glad he was to have the help of the Amalthean Quests team to assist in the trickiest of tasks. He granted Marc permission to land on Polar Solarseano or go to a stationary orbit above the planet. Marc immediately announced he would be going to a stationary orbit and would use transportation to the surface. The Commodore nodded in understanding. Marc ceased communications with the words "Meet soon." Then he signed off. Marc turned, suggesting the selected Quest team head to the Flight Hangar Bay. They were leaving soon. Marc turned back to Dairan.

"Command is all yours. I'll see you after the crime catch of the century—namely, Orell Anitra," said Marc light-heartedly, heading to the entrance.

"Good luck," said Dairan in reply, knowing that as Orell was one slippery female he was going to need it.

"You know me—I love a good challenge," replied Marc, knowing the apprehension of Anitra was going to be just that without Tayce: a challenge.

"We've got that already, haven't we, in Tayce?" joked Dairan.

"Don't let her hear you say that," replied Marc, laughing.

Dairan took over full temporary command as Marc followed Jan with his two officers. They were getting closer to a stationary orbit. Dairan watched as Polar Solarseano drew slowly closer as they came into a stationary orbit where they would remain until departure—or until the Quest had been accomplished. He turned, ordering Kelly to follow any special planetary requests Mac passed to her in obtaining their designated orbit above Polar Solarseano as requested by Commodore Havelious on the surface. Kelly agreed. Dairan then turned to Mac, ordering him to stay in contact with Marc at all times during the Quest. Mac nodding in agreement. Twedor followed him as he next headed into the DC. He wanted to find out from Donaldo why Tayce had suddenly collapsed. Twedor stood patiently waiting as Dairan sat in Tayce's command seat behind her desk and went about contacting Donaldo down in the MLC. He listened as Dairan mentioned about Tayce collapsing earlier, hoping he too could find out why she had suddenly dropped like a stone during the briefing. It concerned him greatly. Considering all they'd gone through to date, he didn't like to think he was losing his mistress. Dairan smiled to himself, thinking Tayce had joked and teased them all when they'd gone down with the virus. Now it wasn't so funny when she herself was unwell, probably with the same thing. He'd always told Tayce never to laugh at someone else's misfortune—it could come back on her. It looked like it had. Donaldo immediately answered. Dairan began enquiring what was happening with Tayce to get her back on her feet. The current Quest had been made slightly harder with her not being able to go. Donaldo began explaining what had happened to make Tayce pass out and said he needn't worry as Jaul was at that cencron working on a cure. He told Dairan he would let him know the moment success had been achieved. Both continued to discuss Tayce and the virus in general, particularly how it had affected all the team in different ways.

* * *

Down on lower levels of the cruiser, Jan walked beside Marc as they made their way to the Flight Hangar Bay. Jan enquired whether Tayce had been overdoing duty hourons again and gone down with exhaustion. Marc shook his head, explaining that it wasn't that. Since he'd been on the team in the current voyage he'd been keeping an eye on her for that very reason. This was something more. What, he had no idea, but Dr Tysonne would no doubt find out. Jan nodded understandingly. Once down on Level 3, they both headed along to the entrance to the Flight Hangar Bay, where the Quest team would be waiting inside. Jan, as they all neared, exclaimed that it was a shame Tayce hadn't been able to go on the Quest and whatever had befallen her had lousy timing. The Quest had been given to them for the reason Tayce would be able to use her powers and halve the problem in dealing with Orell Anitra. Marc nodded in understanding and could see Tayce being present would have given the task ahead an added bonus. Everyone grouped in the hangar bay as Marc asked for a final word in general.

"Be on your guard at all times. Orell Anitra is one treacherous female and Tayce is not able to be here to detect her presence, so we have to do the best we can. And at all costs stay alive," said Marc seriously.

With this, the team and Jan's officers began walking over to the awaiting Quest shuttles/fighters and climbed aboard. Marc headed straight through to the pilot section and took up his seat at the controls. In no time the vast-sized hangar-bay doors drew apart and both Quests lifted off, one behind the other, swiftly leaving the bay to head into space and the orbit of Polar Solarseano.

* * *

Meantime Jaul Naven was busy working on a successful cure for Tayce, without side-effects, and one that would also replenish her immune system after it had been invaded by the rare strain of influenza. No one could put a finger on how it had come aboard. He sat at his desk in Medical Lab B, currently separating Tayce's blood samples into different small slim glassene test tubes and adding various possible mixtures to try to find a cure in the time allocated. He put one after another in under the computer analytic reading tray, watching the readings, hoping what he had done would bring the cure a step nearer. He was so engrossed, that he didn't hear Treketa enter the lab behind him. She crossed quietly towards him so as not to distract him from his work.

"How's it coming along? Any progress? Tayce is somewhat complex to treat at the best of times. Do you notice how sometimes this cruiser seems quiet? It's like that now," began Treketa, making conversation, but she had a feeling Jaul was too engrossed in what he was doing to hear her.

"What? Did you say something? Sorry—I think I'm getting near to a cure," replied Jaul, trying something more with one of the samples he'd added to previously.

"No, it's fine. You mean it's nearly there?" she asked, coming to his side, interested.

"Damn! Just when I thought I'd nearly got it! I think I'm going to need all that allocated time after all. I've a feeling I'm going to need it at this rate. Why does Tayce have to be so complex in her immune system and blood make-up?" he said, continuing on, trying to work with other samples he'd separated.

"Maybe because, unlike us, she comes from the planet Traun. Relax Jaul—you'll get there. I'll tell Donaldo you're working flat out," promised Treketa, heading back to the entrance.

"Yeah, all right. Thanks," he replied, continuing to work on.

"Tayce is going to be angry knowing she contracted the virus strain in a different way to everyone else and had to miss this current Quest, when she awakes," announced Treketa.

"I would be too. I hear she was going to be a key factor in helping in the apprehension of this escapee from Enlopedia. It's certainly going to be a tough Quest without her. I wouldn't want to be Donaldo and have to break the news when she wakes up. Let's hope the Quest will be successful, and over, when the cure is found," said Jaul over his shoulder.

"Let's hope so. I'll leave you to it."

"I'll be there just as soon as this cure materialises," promised Jaul, working on.

As the doors opened Jaul glanced over his shoulder to watch Treketa leave. He then went back to finding the cure before him. And he hoped it was found soon. He began thinking about Treketa—how she had helped make his arrival on the team less stressful, considering his type of duty was mostly alone. She had become a good friend.

* * *

On Polar Solarseano the Quest 3s set down under the expert guidance of both shuttle/fighter pilots on the landing area allocated by Ground Control. The Commodore could be seen in the distance waiting to meet the Quest team. The area in which they landed was very much along the lines of Questa: tall buildings, surface one level domes and visable Vacuum Lifts of a cylindrical shape were ascending and descending in the obviously busy throng of alien and human every-dayon life. People were heading to places of duty or pleasure, or just heading back to their place of dwelling.

'Not bad,' thought Marc as he activated the entrance hatch to open it, as did Jan on his shuttle/fighter.

Marc left the Quest and was first to exit and step down on to the concretex-type surface, followed by the rest of the small Quest team, who glanced around, glad the atmosphere was a normal, living, breathable one. Marc walked from the Quest shuttle/fighter over to meet the approaching commodore. Jan and his two officers followed on with the Quest team members, Lance, Sallen and Aldonica.

"Welcome to Polar Solarseano, ladies and gentlemen. I'm Commodore Havelious. I wish your visit was under better circumstances and not concerning the tricky matter we have in hand," announced the Commodore in a pleasant voice of authority.

He held out his hand for Marc to shake in greeting. Marc grasped it in the true manner of commander of the Amalthean Quests team, shaking hands.

"Commodore, I'm Commander Dayatso. Captain Traun sends her extreme apologies. She is, much against her wishes, unable to be here to help and has asked me to lead the Quest team. This is Lance Largon, Aldonica Darstayne and Sallen Vargon—all combat-trained and able to stop the likes of this Orell Anitra. We have the official backup of Chief Barnford here and two of his top skilled officers from Enlopedia," introduced Marc.

"Chief Barnford, let's hope you can catch this female and her band. They have been causing untold misery and damage to our people, including enrolling my son in her actions just because we won't comply with what she wants," expressed the Commodore seriously.

The Commodore was a tall, broad man, around forty-seven yearons old. His hair was a coppery brown in a short, neat style. His features were warm and friendly, yet they were the kind that could turn serious and commanding should the need for it arise. His eyes were bluey-grey and showed great intelligence. His attire was a green tunic-type suit with a gold-and-white trim running down the front. He looked truly the man in command. Jan stepped forth after Marc shook hands with the Commodore.

"Sir! Don't worry—we'll bring this young woman to justice and see the safe return of your son. I and my men are aware of how elusive she can be, and is, through past dealings with her," assured Jan.

"Pan Yan Tore, at your service, sir," introduced Jan's oriental officer politely.

"Greg Bergetson. It's an honour to meet you, sir," introduced Jan's second officer.

"Let me introduce you to the head of Crime Section, Laytra Palton," said the Commodore, stepping aside for a young woman in her late twenties to walk forth. Jan felt a strike of cold ice go right through him suddenly at the mention of the young woman's name. She was just as he remembered her—slim, blonde and stunning in looks, but above all else she was trouble to him. She had tried to compete for the gold trophy in combat trials and lost. She was disqualified for cheating and Jan had been the one to rumble what she was doing and inform the authorities, who had disqualified her for misconduct. As he recalled, she had been caught blackmailing a judge in the tournament, using unconventional after-hourons means. It turned out the Judge was the head assessor, and she threatened to disclose that he had seduced her. In reality it was other way round—she had been the one doing all the seducing. But Jan, being suspicious that she wasn't playing by the rules, had her investigated and, when it came to the announcement of the winner, all she'd done surfaced. Hence her disqualification. She now stared at Jan with an uncomfortable look in her piercing blue eyes, then turned that look to try to unnerve Jan, but without much success, much to his amusement. Jan could see his presence was making her feel very uncomfortable and she looked away after a brief introduction and exchange of forced pleasantries. Lance caught the cold exchange between Jan and Laytra and figured something wasn't right—they'd obviously had bad dealings with each other in the past. He found her to be a stunning woman, also the kind he would be interested in. Jan leant close, when Laytra wasn't looking and discreetly advised him to forget any interest in her. She was both treacherous and downright poison. Lance took note of what Jan had advised and returned to thinking about the task ahead: helping to apprehend Orell Anitra. The Commodore asked for everyone's attention.

"I am hereby handing over the whole situation of apprehending Orell Anitra to Laytra here," he said, proudly gesturing for Laytra to take over immediately.

"I hope she's changed; otherwise it will be something he'll regret as well as the rest of us," said Jan discreetly to Lance beside him.

"Would you like to say something, Chief Barnford?" asked the Commodore, noticing he was whispering about something to Lance.

"Yes, Chief, if you have something you'd like to add, I'd like to hear it," said Laytra with a hint of sarcasm in her voice.

"No, nothing. I was just thinking out loud," said Jan without a further word, giving Laytra a mistrustful look.

The Commodore didn't know what to make of the icy exchange between Jan and Laytra. He looked at Jan, wondering what it was that made him so abrupt with his head of Crime Section. He suggested to Laytra she continue, then walked away, leaving the Amalthean Quests team, Jan Barnford and his officers with Laytra to commence the operation. Laytra immediately began by asking for everyone to accompany her. She would take them to the point where Orell Anitra was known to recruit her young recruits, including the Commodore's son, for her criminal acts.

"It's a shame your captain couldn't be here to help us, Commander. Perhaps she could join us later?" began Laytra trying to make pleasant conversation with Marc as they went.

"Yes, perhaps she could," replied Marc.

Everybody walked off towards a vacant glassene Vacuum Lift. Laytra explained that the point where the youngsters were recruited was the crew recreational bar. There, under one of her many disguises, Orell misled many of the young cadets astray, including the Commodore's son. After boarding the lift and arriving at the requested level, the Quest team and Laytra headed to what was known as the Seano Bar, where loud synthesised music seemed to come from. All entered an atmosphere of neon lighting, flashing to the rhythm of the beat of the music. A mixed array of off-duty personnel were chatting, laughing and downing alcoholic drinks in a somewhat loud fashion at times. Up front, in what could be described as a stage area, in the near darkness a group sang in high-pitched harmonic voices. Marc paused, as did Laytra. He looked about suspiciously. Laytra began explaining over the rowdy noise that Orell Anitra was known to entice young cadets away from their duties, making them think they were heading off to better things in life—promises that were so enticing they'd jump at the chance to join her, though nothing came of the promises. Many of Anitras young victims were never heard of again.

"What do you think happens to them, and particularly the Commodore's son?" asked Marc above the noise.

"Not known, but myself and my officers reckon she takes them below the city level. We once went down there to investigate, but found nothing except some young dead cadets. The Commodore's son wasn't amongst them, thank goodness. They were not a pretty sight to see. We put it down to the fact the young cadets, male and female, realised the promises were false and she tortured them for letting her down," explained Laytra casually.

"Aldonica, Lance, Sallen and Pan, you remain here in case Orell shows up. If she does, call us immediately on Wristlink. Do not take her on by yourselves—is that understood?" ordered Marc with Jan in agreement.

"Leisure hourons will be in twenty minecs. That's when she generally comes in," said Laytra, informing Aldonica discreetly.

"Keep watch and look after the Amaltheans. Contact me," ordered Jan to Pan in true authoritative tone.

With this, whilst the others went about mingling with the the Seano Bar visitors, Jan, Greg, Marc and Laytra all walked from the Seano Bar to head on across to the glassene Vacuum Lift. Laytra warned everyone they'd better stay on alert, especially if they were going below the city level. It could be extremely dangerous with rough travellers of the worst galactic kind hanging around.

* * *

Back on Amalthea Jaul Naven had found the perfect cure with help from Amal. He placed the end result into a Comprai Inject Pen, then left Medical Lab B in a tearing hurry, with Twedor in hot pursuit as he had come down from Organisation to assist him in the final preparation to complete his mistress's cure. Twedor found it near impossible to keep up with Jaul as he raced along Level 2 towards the MLC. Upon reaching the entrance doors, they parted in front of him and he rushed in, heading towards Donaldo, who had just walked from his Officette. Jaul came to a pause, out of breath.

"One successful cure to rid Tayce of the virus, side-effect free," said Jaul, holding the Comprai Inject Pen out to Donaldo to take, trying to get his breath back.

"Nice going, and just in the nick of time," expressed Donaldo.

"Glad I could come up with a cure. This cruiser wouldn't be the same without Tayce," said Jaul, glancing at her still unconscious.

"Quite!" agreed Donaldo and Treketa.

Donaldo turned to Tayce and prepared to administer the cure. Treketa and Twedor stood by watching as he placed the Comprai Inject Pen against Tayce's delicate neck and pressed the small release button. The cure entered her in cencrons and began to do its work. Donaldo stood back, watching with the others, waiting, then glanced to the overhead monitor, as did Jaul and Treketa, waiting for the first signs of improvement. Jaul smiled as the cure began to take effect. After a few minons Tayce slowly opened her eyes. Once she'd fully focused on her surroundings, she began sitting up. Treketa gently, in a caring way, assisted her. Tayce was surprised to find she was in the MLC instead of where she'd passed out, in the DC.

"What happened? Why am I here?" asked Tayce, somewhat puzzled.

"You passed out in the DC during a Quest briefing. You had symptoms of the influenza virus after all. It depleted your immune system, but Jaul here came up with a cure. You're now fine," explained Donaldo softly.

"Thanks, Jaul. Good work. How did the Quest go? Did I miss much?" asked Tayce, thinking the Quest was over.

"It's still under way at the present time. Everyone left less than an houron ago," spoke up Twedor.

"Marc took command in your absence, leaving Dairan in charge here," explained Donaldo.

"Just as long as the Quest still went ahead," replied Tayce, glad.

She began climbing down off the bunk and was about to stand up when Donaldo caught her doing so.

He sighed and began by saying in a concerned tone, "Where are you going? I want you to take it easy for a while." He was worried she was going to do too much too soon.

"You said yourself I'm fine. I need to be on Polar Solarseano, on that Quest, and that's exactly where I'm heading. Come on, Twedor," said Tayce, beginning to walk over to the MLC entrance, ignoring Donaldo's words.

Donaldo briskly began forth. He grabbed Tayce's arm, wanting her to think twice about her actions. She pulled her arm free, throwing him a look to tell him not to stop her. Donaldo gave a look of total impatience that she wasn't going to take his advice—but she was captain; he could only advise. Jaul and Treketa could see the look of slight concerned anger in Donaldo's eyes, at Tayce. The doors to the MLC soon parted and closed behind her and Twedor as they left. Donaldo stood shaking his head. He hoped she didn't get a sudden unexpected side-effect, despite what Jaul had said.

Tayce, as she began up the corridor with Twedor by her side, wristlinked to Amal, ordering her to pinpoint where Marc was on Polar Solarseano then, when she reached Transpot, put her down in the vicinity. Amal could be heard agreeing. Tayce and Twedor soon entered the Transpot 2 Centre and crossed to the Transpot dematerialising area. She didn't trust her own ability to travel to the surface. As she was still recovering from the virus symptoms, she could end up God knows where. Upon taking up her position, she ordered Amal to commence immediate Transpot. Both she and Twedor dematerialised to the Polar Solarseano surface.

* * *

Down on Polar Solarseano, Marc Dayatso had been parted from the others. He'd received a Wristlink call from Aldonica and chased Orell Anitra with another unsuspecting group of cadets to below the surface. Laytra had hurried to the surface, leaving Marc to look around, gun poised. Jan and Greg had gone into uncharted underground territory, armed with Pollomoss handguns, ready also to cut Orell off and save the cadets, possibly including the Commodore's son. Marc heard approaching boot steps coming towards him. He took aim with his gun, ready, looking in a searching way into the near darkness for the first signs of the evil female gang leader. Anitra walked into view, coming towards him alone, without her gang or the cadets she'd enticed. It was as if she'd walked out of nowhere. Marc realised she could have been invisible, but must be thinking it was safe to be visible. But where were the cadets and the gang she was running with? wondered Marc. Orell looked in Marc's direction and homed on his essence of being present. She used her ability to read minds and found Marc's was on a female named Tayce and how she was doing back on a vessel named Amalthea. This intrigued her, wondering if she could turn herself into this female and lure Marc in like an unsuspecting fool. Little did Orell know that Tayce was on her way. She decided to do it anyway. Marc gave a total look of surprise. He shook his head. Was he seeing things? he wondered.

"Tayce! What are you doing here? You're not well—let me handle this. Come on," said Marc, not suspecting it was Orell in fact playing him for a total fool in the guise of Tayce.

"I've come to help you," replied Tayce/Orell.

Orell, having thought she'd managed to fool this idiot, namely Marc, was wrong. For down the corridor came the real Tayce with Twedor by her side. Twedor activated his Slazer finger and stepped out of Tayce's way. Tayce sensed Orell's powers had worked on Marc and she knew she had to do something fast before he became another victim of the gang leader. Orell was making up to Marc in a big way. She was all over him like a rash—something she'd never do. Tayce shook her head, wondering why Marc couldn't see she wouldn't ever act this way.

"Enjoying yourself, Orell? Really, Marc, you of all people should know I wouldn't act like this. Game's over, Orell. Nice try," said Tayce, coming to a pause just a short way from what she didn't want to see.

"What! Get away from me, you evil bitch," said Marc, pushing Orell away from him angrily.

He was horrified to think he'd been suckered into thinking it was Tayce, but he came to his senses, realising she wouldn't act like Orell was behaving. Orell spun with a powerful evil look in her dark-brown eyes. Tayce stood her ground. She was an equal match for this trashy replica of herself. Instead of sapphire-blue eyes like Tayce, she had dark evil ones. As with many intergalactic criminals, she was far from perfect. Once she'd reverted back to her true appearance, she was as attractive as Tayce, but in a trashy kind of way. Her outfit was purple in colour and hugged her body like a second skin. She was of average build and around 1.63 metres in height. Her hair was short, cut close to the head in an urchin style, and rusty brown. She looked from Marc to Tayce, then, just as she thought she could pull her vanishing trick, Tayce picked up on the fact with the aid of her own powers, stopping her before she left.

"Who are you? What are you doing? Let me go," demanded Orell, outraged at being caught by Tayce's sudden power force holding her in her current time and position.

"Your worst nightmare, and one you won't want to repeat again," said Tayce, enjoying using her ability to stop Orell from vanishing.

An invisible force field detained Orell. She'd tried to escape for the last time. She protested to no avail in the grip of the force field. The rest of the Quest members came into view. Jan was somewhat amazed to see Orell struggling against an invisible field and Tayce present.

"Greg, Pan, set up an immediate force field, maximum strength, now!" ordered Jan.

He could see Tayce was finding it difficult to keep Orell in her powerful hold. Both Pan and Greg managed to set up the force-field prison just as Tayce dropped her hold on Orell, who had tried to match Tayce in power ability. Tayce sighed, glad Jan had made such a request. Blue force-field handcuffs were in total control of Orell with a force-field prison set at an extremely high degree. It was sparking as Orell tried to escape, without much success.

"Captain, we haven't met. I'm head of Crime Section here on Polar Solarseano. Pleased to meet you," began Laytra, casually stepping forward, pleased Tayce had caught Orell Anitra once and for all.

"How do you do?" replied Tayce, grasping the young woman's hand, shaking it.

"Shall we head on out?" said Jan, beginning to walk away with his two officers and Orell struggling and cursing in the hold of both forms of high-density field.

Everyone fell in and began on the walk back to the surface of Polar Solarseano. Laytra talked with Tayce, expressing how glad she was that Tayce had managed to step in at the last minon and detain Orell for the last time. To Jan's surprise, Laytra even thanked him for his assistance in stopping Orell in her escapades. Tayce sensed a frosty atmosphere between Laytra and Jan and wondered why, but didn't say anything.

Once on the surface, Commodore Havelious had left his current duties and had come to rendezvous with Laytra on the city level. As the teams and Orell Anitra came to a pause, the Commodore looked at her with utter disgust for what she'd done to the many innocent cadets, his son included, corrupting their young minds. Not having met Tayce and Twedor, the Commodore looked at them questioningly. Laytra quickly introduced Tayce and Twedor to him, explaining that sadly there was no sign of his son, but Tayce had managed to join the Quest after all and stop Orell in her tracks. The Commodore thanked her. Tayce stepped forth, shaking hands with him, introducing Twedor as her escort, who the Commodore was delighted to meet. He then turned his attention for the final time to Orell, angered by the thought that his son was gone forever at her hands.

"You, young woman, are going to get the kind of punishment you deserve, and not before time. As for your gang, they are no more. They were apprehended an houron ago and met an untimely fate, of no return," he plainly stated to the silence of all gathered in both Quest teams.

Orell spat at him in enraged disgust at her failure to continue her endeavours of corruption, then looked away. Jan abruptly ordered his men to move out. His two officers roughly hauled Orel Anitra away under close watch and powerful restraint. The Commodore was glad he wouldn't have to encounter the likes of her again. Jan shook hands with him, exclaiming that he had to get her back to Enlopedia, where she would endure fitting punishment for her crimes, including the death of the Commodore's son. The Commodore nodded, letting him leave with a thank you.

As Jan walked away, he glanced back over his shoulder at Laytra. She was looking right back at him, managing a slight smile. He shook his head, smiling to himself, thinking back to what she had pulled on him the last time they'd met. If she thought one action on working together would put right what had happened and make him forgive and forget, she could think again. He walked on, letting Tayce and the team shake hands with the Commodore and Laytra before following on.

The two Quests finally departed with all aboard and Orell Anitra under continued watch. They headed away from Polar Solarseano, heading back to Amalthea, leaving the world to return to normal and the young cadets to return to a normal future, without the threat of being enticed to their deaths by Orell Anitra and her gang. It had been a shame that they hadn't managed to find the Commodore's son alive. The people of Polar Solarseano could live in peace once more, but for the Commodore it was a time of grief over the loss of his son.

Tayce, even though she still felt in somewhat less than full health, felt pleased with what she'd pulled off and sat back relaxingly on the journey back to the cruiser. Marc glanced at her, seeing she wasn't quite back to normal after her illness. He was proud of what she'd done. As she glanced at him, he gave her a warm smile that said it all—it had been another successful Quest.

13. Deluca

Upon returning to Amalthea, Jan Barnford ordered his men to collect their overnight holdalls and his from the guest quarters. He didn't want Orell Anitra left unattended. Both his officers nodded understandingly. Jan headed over to meet up with Tayce and Marc, to explain that he was going on ahead down the polar corridor. He didn't want Orell breaking free and causing trouble aboard Amalthea. Upon explaining this to Tayce, she in turn wristlinked to Kelly back in Organisation, ordering her to have the return journey coordinates sent to Jan's navigational computer and be prepared to lock tractor beam on for a safe return journey. Kelly could be heard acknowledging. Tayce didn't like the fact Jan was travelling the treacherous return journey alone. Anything could go wrong. He could see she was uneasy about the fact and reached out his right hand, putting it on her left shoulder in a reassuring way.

"Don't worry—we'll both make it. I don't want Orell breaking free here and causing untold trouble for you." he assured with a slight reassuring smile.

"She is quite a remarkable woman, even though it was in the field of criminal recruitment," replied Tayce thinking about Orell in general.

"Yes! It's a shame she wasn't on the good side at Enlopedia. She would have made a first-class recruitment officer for my division," he agreed.

"Before you leave—Laytra. What is it between you two?" asked Tayce, wanting to know. "I sensed a frosty atmosphere when we left?"

Jan looked at Tayce, then away and back again, raising his eyes. He could tell she wasn't going to let him leave without some kind of explanation. Not that he minded. He began by saying that Laytra, in her past, had literally tried to cheat him out of a gold award. Tayce raised her eyes in surprise, then prompted him to continue. Jan explained that Laytra had slept with the head assessor of a tournament they were both in. Then, in order to get what she wanted, namely the gold award, she blackmailed the head assessor, saying that if he didn't award her the award over Jan she would tell all. He got wind of what she was up to and, before the assessor landed up to his neck in trouble, he blew the scheme up in her face. Hence the award stood in pride of place in his Officette back at Enlopedia. Marc shook his head in disbelief, laughing. Tayce laughed. She would never have guessed Laytra was anything like Jan had just said, when she met her earlier. Twedor just tutted at the explanation. Almost everyone thought Laytra was a first-class officer. Marc wished Jan a safe journey and assured him that he would keep an eye on his Quest at all times. If Orell was in any way found to be putting his life or his men's lives in danger, then he'd have them transpoted aboard and ditch the Quest with her in it. Jan nodded in total agreement. He would rather lose Orell than two of his finest officers. Marc turned and began moving away, leaving Jan and Tayce to finish up. Jan put a friendly hand on her upper left arm and suggested she take things easy for a while. It was nice to see she was all right after her brief illness. He glanced at his Wristlink time display, then exclaimed that he'd better go.

"Thank the Doc for the precautionary influenza jab. At least I won't have to do it again for another yearon," said Jan.

"I'll see you next time, either at Enlopedia or on another Quest—or sooner if Orell tries to escape."

She stood watching as Jan walked over to the entrance hatch of the Quest and boarded as its pilot. One of the two officers that had come on the Quest was going through final procedures for take-off. The entrance hatch soon closed. Tayce stepped back and turned with Twedor to head on across the Flight Hangar Bay floor. At the entrance, before walking back into the corridor, Tayce paused and turned to watch Jan's Quest heading on out through the open doors, back into space for the journey back down the polar corridor to Enlopedia.

"Come on, Twedor, let's go and see what's going on in Organisation, shall we?" suggested Tayce, beginning on up the corridor.

"Right with you," replied Twedor, catching her up.

Together they headed for Level 1. Tayce realised she hadn't thanked Marc for stepping in and taking charge of the Quest at such short notice. She caught up with him on the Level Steps. He turned surprised to see her so soon. He thought she and Jan would be talking for quite a while.

"I thought you'd be on Level 1 by now," she said, catching him up.

"I would have been, but I was just talking with Donaldo about the Quest. He was on his way back from a duty break and asked how it went," he replied.

"I've been meaning to thank you for taking over the Quest during my untimely illness. Thanks!" she said with a smile.

"Don't think anything of it. I enjoy being in charge in your absence. I know you wanted to do this Quest and what this Quest meant to you, but, considering the outcome, it worked out well," he replied as they continued on up the Level Steps together, with Twedor in tow.

Once on Level 1, they both headed along into Organisation, wondering what was next on the voyage when they exited back to normal space from the polar corridor they were about to travel back down. Upon entering Organisation, Tayce looked across to Kelly, to see she was in communication with Jan's pilot and giving him the procedure to be placed under tractor-beam hold. Dairan was watching her with interest, listening to how it was unfolding in case she needed any assistance.

"Good Quest, I hear?" asked Dairan, turning as Tayce approached.

"Yes! Orell Anitra is on her way back to Enlopedia under high-frequency lock and key, so to speak," replied Tayce.

"Donaldo is far from pleased at the way in which you ignored his advice and headed on down to Polar Solarseano so shortly after you recovered from the unconsciousness caused by the virus," informed Dairan, keeping one eye on Kelly in case he was called to assist at any moment.

"He'll get over it," replied Tayce, not bothered.

Without a further word she walked away from him in the direction of the DC. Marc smiled and shook his head in amusement. She never changed. She was in charge and Donaldo could think what he liked. He followed Tayce in. Dairan turned his attention to the Universe out through the main sight port and the approaching polar corridor back to home space. He knew the next three hourons was going to be tricky, considering Chief Barnford was on tractor beam for the duration of the journey.

* * *

Three hourons later Amalthea Two emerged from the polar corridor, back into home space. The journey, much to everyone's relief, had been a calm, trouble-free one, considering Orell Anitra's last couple of escapes. Jan Barnford's Quest had successfully stayed on tractor beam through the entire journey under the watchful eye of Kelly, following his course, informing him of any sudden changes in direction. Jan commended her on getting him through unscathed. In the blink of an eye he was free of the tractor beam and had left at great speed to get Orell back to Enlopedia, where she would have a punishment fitting her crimes.

* * *

Tayce stood watching the familiar Universe through her quarters sight port, glad they were back in familiar territory once again. She was taking time out from duty. It was what was termed 'leisure time'. She'd gone to her quarters to relax after she and Marc had discussed the Quest and filed a report with Enlopedia.

As she stood in thought, without warning the whole of the cruiser shook and the lights and power shut down. The lights in her immediate surroundings dropped into total darkness and operations went offline.

"Brilliant! Now what?" said Tayce, stood in the dark.

The emergency power soon came online and a soft shade of emergency lighting illuminated her immediate surroundings where she stood. Her Wristlink bleeped. She raised it, pressing the Comceive button. Craig's face lit the small screen on her wrist. He began by saying they'd a big problem. Tayce raised her eyes to the ceiling in jest, then prepared to listen as Craig explained that the whole of the cruiser was rendered totally powerless. They were flying blind, in a manner of speaking, and were target practice for anyone who wanted to attack.

"Don't panic—I'm on my way just as soon as I get out of here," she replied reassuringly.

"Hurry. Something doesn't feel right around here," said Craig in a tone Tayce found most unusual for him—like he was fearful of something.

"Stay calm," ordered Tayce softly, wondering why he seemed nervous. He generally wasn't the kind to be nervous.

She ceased communication and quickly realised as she depressed the Comceive button that even though she said she was on her way, she wasn't able to get out of her quarters with the power down. The doors wouldn't open without power. Then she remembered that the quarters doors had a manual release control, with enough backup energy to release the doors to open in an emergency. But she couldn't remember where Jamie Balthansar had installed it. She remembered it was behind a concealed panel by the entrance. She crossed to the entrance and called Twedor to run a scan of the wall by the doors, in search of the panel.

"A little to the left, down, right there," said Twedor, picking up something that scanned as the mechanism for the entrance.

"Here?" asked Tayce, placing her hand on the exact area Twedor was suggesting, then pressing lightly.

"Yes, you've got it. I hope we get out of here soon. For some strange reason my power source is draining," said Twedor, sounding like his volume was being decreased as the battery was wearing down.

"Twedor, stay with me. I need you. Just remain calm, otherwise you'll blow a circuit on low power," ordered Tayce, wondering just what was going on on board.

"I'm trying, Tayce. I don't like this. It's as if someone else is controlling me. I wish they'd pack in trying to access my systems," protested Twedor.

"At last! Got it! I must remember to get Craig to put some kind of indication label on this panel so if there's a next time I'll know where to find it. Thanks, Twedor," praised Tayce.

She pressed an orange square panel on the standby controls and pushed a silver lever down flat. After a few minons the doors drew apart slowly, much to her relief. She turned to see Twedor looking somewhat near to standby power and decided to leave him where he was. Upon telling him, he didn't much like the idea. But he knew he wouldn't get far if he went with her. Tayce squeezed through the opening and out into the emergency-lit corridor on Level 3. She activated her Wristlink and shone the light down the corridor. She headed in the direction of Organisation. As she went, she realised whatever was affecting the cruiser was obviously affecting Twedor. But what, or who, was it? Further up the corridor on the same level she found Dairan standing by his quarters doors. Her Wristlink illumination caught him in the beam.

"At least you've found some kind of light. My light pencil torch is back in there, so I figured as I couldn't see too well in this emergency light I'd remain here until help arrived. What's going on? Why the sudden power drain?" asked Dairan, wondering.

"I don't know. Craig called me on Wristlink just after the power failed. He informed me we're powerless and flying blind, but he can't find out why," replied Tayce, coming to a pause.

"I could try and help. Let me do what you're doing with your Wristlink. It will give us double the light to light the way ahead," he said, pressing for the illumination on his Wristlink, on Tayce's instruction.

"Let's go," said Tayce, beginning on down the corridor

She knew Dairan had a qualification in electronics and figured he might be able to assist Craig when they reached Organisation. She'd remembered this from the beginning of the voyage, when she'd rescued him on Naninda and he'd tried to repair her smashed Wristlink. They both broke into a sprint in the light towards the Level Steps. As they began on up, so Tayce explained that even Twedor had been affected by the power drain. Dairan raised his eyes in surprise, wondering what the influence over the whole cruiser was. It was certainly weird, to say the least.

As both he and Tayce reached the top and stepped on to Level 1, Tayce looked and saw the doors to Organisation hadn't closed during the power drain. This was a relief, she thought, going on into Organisation. The sight of Craig Bream half sticking out from under the main access port to Amal's main circuitry panel greeted her as she walked in. He slid out upon seeing her enter.

"Everything checks out. I can't understand it. I've even done a portable deep scan of all the cruiser-wide functions. I've done every test I can think of. As far as I can figure, this is an outside influence beyond our control," explained Craig.

"Right! Twedor is affected too. I had to leave him behind in my quarters," explained Tayce looking down at him.

Organisation was team-less. All the team were on leisure time, not expecting what had occurred to happen. Tayce suddenly felt like someone was watching them as they stood talking about the power loss and the fact it could be due to an outside influence.

Glancing around discreetly to check no one was on board in the dark areas of the DC up ahead, she continued.

"Are you OK?" asked Craig, seeing her shudder uneasily and look again into the darkness.

"I don't know. There's a strange feeling here, like we're being watched," said Tayce.

"Maybe we are. Maybe that feeling you're getting is someone seeing everything we're doing from afar. Perhaps he has the power to watch us without us knowing it," said Dairan.

"Craig, I know everyone's on leisure time, but do you know exactly where they are at present?" asked Tayce.

"Marc is stuck in the Combat and Training Practice Centre. Sallen and Kelly are stuck in the Recreation Room, playing a strategy game. Treketa and Donaldo are stuck in the Supplies Store, doing a stock-take. In fact everyone is stuck just about everywhere throughout the cruiser, doing something," replied Craig.

"Without the chance to bring power back up online it's going to be difficult to free everyone. Can't we restore power by rerouting other functions, maybe using the current emergency power to gain full power? I'm not happy knowing we're currently target practice for every criminal in the Universe and half this team are trapped unless they use manual control to leave where they are, if they can find it," expressed Tayce seriously.

"I'd need to gain entry to the Total Shutdown Centre for the whole cruiser, outside on this level. With power down, there's no way I can get in. I've been down to try," said Craig sadly.

"You two, go and try again. If you have to use Slazer force to disengage the lock, do it. I don't like us being in the current situation we're in as possible selvage for anyone who fancies taking us on," said Tayce in a worried tone.

"Don't worry—we'll sort it," assured Dairan, seeing her worried.

He and Craig left Organisation in the light of Craig's light pencil torch. They headed down the corridor in the direction of the Total Shutdown Centre for the whole cruiser, further along on Level 1. Tayce found herself completely alone in the near-darkness, unable to do anything. Everything was silent around her. All lights were in semi-darkness on the consoles around the centre and Amal was on emergency power only. Her screen was blank. It reminded Tayce of the first night she'd arrived on Amalthea One at the beginning of her life amongst the stars. She was older now. She had to get a grip, she thought. But it still didn't stop her from hating the fact she was in deadly silence and semi-darkness. She crossed to the light pencil-torch emergency-supplies drawer and retrieved a newly charged torch, activating it. It came on full beam, which made her feel a lot more at ease. She ventured on into the DC and set it down on her desk in such a way as to give her maximum light. No sooner had she done so than quite suddenly Amalthea went into a violent shake. Her light pencil torch rolled off her desk and under the soffette.

"Damn it!" she said, grabbing hold of something solid, watching the torch roll under the soffette.

Now she knew something or someone was in charge of her cruiser from afar. Looking around, she wondered if whoever or whatever was doing what they were doing was putting her and the team through some kind of intergalactic test. She wished they had the decency to at least return the cruiser to full power whilst doing it.

* * *

Further along on Level 1, Dairan decided Tayce's order to disengage the lock on the access door to the Total Shutdown Centre using Slazer force was the only way to get in. Both himself and Craig stood back and took aim, pointing their Pollomoss handguns in a direct line with the lock region, then opened fire on full power. Suddenly there was a brilliant red flash, but not one that had come from the Pollomoss handguns. It occurred for a few cencrons, filling the whole of Level 1, engulfing the area where Dairan and Craig were standing. When it had gone, all that remained was an empty corridor, with a pair of discarded Slazers on the floor where both Dairan and Craig had been. The entrance to the centre was still firmly shut. Whoever or whatever had done it, they now had two of the Amalthean Quests team. But where? In Organisation, back along the corridor, Tayce jumped in surprise as the power started up and everything became fully operational once more. She sighed, thinking Craig and Dairan had succeeded, and raced out of the centre to go along and congratulate them. As she neared the spot where they had been, she found the two discarded Pollomoss handguns on the floor.

'What the hell is going on?' she wondered. Where were they? Now two of her officers had been abducted. She didn't like this at all. Marc came running up the Level Steps as she bent down to pick up the handguns and make them safe. He paused, dressed in combat practice attire, looking exhausted and damp from his practice. He looked at her, seeing something was wrong.

"What's going on?" he demanded, his eyes wide and alert with extreme concern.

"You tell me. Whoever or whatever is behind this now has Dairan and Craig," replied Tayce sharply.

"Really? How?" he replied, calming down.

"I'm not sure. Craig and Dairan came to see if they could gain entry into this centre, and the next thing power was restored. I rushed out to tell them well done, only to find nothing more than these two guns and Dairan and Craig gone," explained Tayce, uneasy.

"Don't worry—we'll sort this out," reassured Marc in thought.

Just as Marc said what he did, over the Revelation Channel came a deep, male, commanding abrupt voice. He simply informed Tayce that if she wanted to reclaim her two officers she was to travel to a planet by the name of Marrack under his guidance. Upon this, Tayce and Marc exchanged looks of outrage at what had just been cast. Mac, who had come up the steps as the words had been spoken, looked at Tayce, seeing her far from pleased with whoever was behind what was happening. All hurried on back along Level 1 into the Organisation

Centre. Upon entering Organisation, all three were greeted by a sight through the main sight port of a white pulsating cloud that filled the whole of the sight port. Amal began announcing, much to Tayce's relief, that the cloud was harmless. But it was surrounding the whole of the outer hull and she was coming under the guiding influence of it. The abrupt voice that was heard earlier began again, informing Tayce she was permitted to communicate with the computer known as Amal, but every other function aboard the cruiser was under the control of Marrack. This infuriated Tayce. She sighed in anger.

"Who does this being think he is, putting Amalthea under his control?" began Tayce furiously.

"Someone who thinks he pulls all the strings in controlling this cruiser," said Marc in reply.

"Mac, get me communication to the source that keeps on dictating orders," ordered Tayce angrily.

"Trying now," replied Mac, beginning to key in commands to gain some kind of communication link.

After a few minons Mac had traced the source of the orders. He turned to Tayce, informing her that he had a link and to go ahead.

"This is Captain Traun of the cruiser you have forcibly taken command of. I demand to know why you have done so. Why have you also abducted two of my crew?" demanded Tayce, straight to the point.

"Captain Traun, all your questions will be answered on arrival at Marrack," spoke up the male commanding voice once more overhead, without much feeling and to the point.

That was as good as nothing, thought Tayce, but at least she'd let him hear her displeasure at this so called Marrack taking over her cruiser. She didn't like Amalthea being under someone else's control without good reason. The rest of the Organisation team arrived, having been able to get out of where they'd been trapped during the power failure. Lance, upon walking in, looked at the white cloud through the main sight port. He looked back at Tayce with a questioning look as he took up his duty position. Kelly glanced at what was before them, then continued on to hers.

"We're caught under the control of someone on the planet Marrack. They've kidnapped Dairan and Craig, though for what purpose I can't find out at the moment. We just have to do what they want," said Tayce, addressing everyone present.

"Why us in particular? And why take Dairan and Craig?" asked Lance, curious.

"If I knew that, don't you think everyone here would be the first to know, Lance?" retorted Tayce without thought.

"Sorry!" replied Lance. He could see Tayce was angry about the current situation.

Marc paused by Lance, discreetly telling him to ignore Tayce's attitude—she was under great pressure. He then turned, informing Tayce he was off to get cleansed and changed, as at present he was far from dressed for duty. Tayce nodded, but her mind was on what was happening before them. Marc could see she was feeling uneasy about the controlled trip to Marrack and she had every reason to be. This was a classic case of the Arkarans all over again. In the first voyage, they'd taken over some of the crew and made them take them home to Arkanoss. It made him shudder when he thought back to the incident. It was one he'd rather forget. Yes, this current situation was similar, he thought. He exited Organisation with it still on his mind. Tayce, not wanting to continually see the white cloud right before her vision through the sight port, turned and headed on into the DC. Lance watched her go. He nudged Kelly, asking her to watch his console for any sign of the research screen unfreezing itself from the controlling force and telling her he'd be in the DC. Kelly quietly agreed. Leaving his seat, Lance figured Tayce could do with a friend to talk with about the current forced trip. He headed on into the DC, waiting for her to tell him to get back to duty. Both had, most of their lives, been like almost brother and sister. Their relationship had the same closeness as the real thing. Even the late Jonathan Largon, Lance's father, had noticed how both of them acted like the real thing without realising it. Jonathan had thought the world of Tayce like the Trauns had thought, and still did think, the world of Lance. He paused mid floor in the DC.

"Need someone to talk this over with, other than Marc?" he cautiously asked.

"Sure! Why not? Sorry about earlier. This just feels like the Arkarans all over again. I keep expecting Dairan and Craig to come through that doorway, like you have, with those same strange eyes you had when under the influence of the Arkarans," began Tayce confidingly.

"It's not easy, I know, and I would probably be thinking the same way you are right now," he said, dismissing the incident earlier when she'd snapped at him.

"You're right. It's the fact I don't know what they could be putting Dairan or Craig through right now," replied Tayce, thinking about all the worst possible things that could be occurring.

"Don't worry—I think Dairan will put up one hell of a fight, whatever they try," assured Lance.

"Yes, you're right," replied Tayce, smiling, then she glanced at Twedor walking in.

But his presence wasn't right. She'd left him power-drained in her quarters. 'What is going on?' she wondered. 'He should still be there.'

He came to a pause almost before her, by Lance, and began to speak to her. But not in his usual voice—in the tone of the male who had spoken to her earlier and had taken over the cruiser.

"Twedor is temporarily out of communicative function. He is purely under my operational guidance for the duration of this journey to Marrack," said the commanding voice without feeling.

"No! You said only the operational functions of this cruiser—you didn't say anything about taking control of my Romid. Release him at once!" demanded Tayce, beginning forward, forgetting it was Twedor for a moment.

"Tayce, don't! Remember it's Twedor. They'll damage him if you try anything," reminded Lance, quickly pulling her back gently.

He wondered what she was going to do, she was so angry. He was concerned about the fact she could get hurt by whoever was controlling Twedor. She looked at him, realising he'd been right to do what he did, pulling her arm free. They'd no choice but to obey who was controlling Twedor and do what was asked until the journey ended. Lance shook his head in disgust over what the latest takeover was. Tayce sighed impatiently. How much longer were they going to be helpless victims of the Marrackans? She crossed to look out through the sight port to try and calm herself. After a few minons, she turned back to the controlled form of Twedor.

"I would like to inform you, if you're listening, you can tell your superiors I'm far from pleased at the way in which you want us to travel to your home world; and what's more, I'm holding you responsible for any damage done to this Romid here whilst under your control. Is that understood?" said Tayce sternly.

"This Romid form is purely for communications—for you and I to be able to talk at all times. You have our total assurance he will be unharmed and will be returned to you in operational function, as he was before we acquired him for communication purposes only," replied the voice from Twedor.

Lance tried not to laugh as he imagined for a cencron what Twedor would say to some being taking over his entire form—something like "Find your own vessel, pal!" Tayce looked at him, not seeing what was so funny. She didn't like seeing Twedor in this current state. They'd been through too much together, and she considered him a friend.

"Captain, if it helps, I apologise," said the voice coming from Twedor.

"I don't know who you are, other than you're in control of this unscheduled journey to your home world. And you're probably not going to tell me, but I don't like being kept in the dark—especially when it comes to what's happened to my two male team members and the taking-over of Twedor. I feel you're making this journey one-sided. You want us to come to Marrack, so why don't you come clean and tell us why this has to be the way we travel to your world, and tell me what's currently happening to my two crew members," demanded Tayce, straight.

"All will be revealed when you arrive at Marrack. I am not permitted to explain any more at this moment," replied the voice from Twedor, to the point.

Tayce shook her head, thinking he didn't want to. She walked back to the sight port, angry enough to explode. Lance could see the fact and sauntered over to be with her, coming up close beside her.

"We—that's the team and I—don't like this any more than you. It will be OK," he assured whisperingly.

"Thanks for your support. Someone on Marrack is going to answer for this when we get there, believe me," replied Tayce in a whisper, trying to keep her anger in check.

"I'll leave you with it. Call me if you need me," he said, walking away towards the entrance.

Tayce nodded. But her mind had moved on to thinking about what Craig and Dairan might be enduring at the hands of the Marrackans. She hoped Dairan kept his cool. Marc entered the DC as Lance exited. He didn't realise Twedor was under the control of the Marrackans and asked was there any news on their current situation? As he came to a pause beside Tayce she discreetly announced that Twedor was the latest victim to come under the control of their unwanted guests. Marc glanced over at Twedor, feeling just as angry as Tayce. He discreetly began explaining that whilst in his quarters he had done some research on his Porto Compute and discovered the Marrackans were a race with a knack to achieve anything they so wished—even taking control of Twedor, in spite of the Romid's high-density security system. They had gone to great lengths to penetrate it. It would have to be upgraded when he came back to normal. Twedor couldn't have stood a chance against them taking him over. They were a force who obviously didn't take no for an answer. He continued, saying if she wanted him to try and stop Twedor being used, he was quite happy to pull the main circuit cut-off in the base of his skull. Even though Tayce was unsure of what would happen on the part of the Marrackans, she didn't like the idea of Twedor being used and nodded in agreement. Marc, so that Twedor, under the control of the Marrackans, didn't suspect what he was about to attempt, slowly crept up behind Twedor's form and bent down to release the small concealed cover quietly. Behind it was the main circuitry and system-cut-off inset key. Just as he went to press the small blue metlon key, he received a severe electrical shock which sent him through the air across the room and up against the far wall, where he landed on his backside with a thud. It winded him for a few cencrons. He was far from impressed at the rebuff, and decided not to try it again. Tayce rushed to his side and helped him back on to his feet as Twedor turned.

"Marc, are you all right? Are you hurt? They really aren't having any of our meddling in their plans, are they?" she began, outstretching her hand to help him back on to his feet.

"I'm fine. I agree—there's only one set of rules in this game, and that's the ones they want us to follow. Make no mistake on that one," he replied, coming to a standing position with Tayce's help.

"Are you sure you're going to be OK? That was some jolt," she said, letting go of Marc's right hand.

"Yes, absolutely. I was just winded, that's all. It will take a lot more of a surge than the one I just felt. Luckily for me, they don't know of the various degrees Twedor can go to in electronic surges," he confided.

Both he and Tayce decided to leave Twedor and went out into Organisation to see what was happening under the control of the Marrackans in the guidance and general main operations of the cruiser. The Organisation team looked totally at a loss for something to do as their duties were currently under Marrackan control. Mac sat on his chair in a state of total relaxation, his Microceive still on his ear, hoping he might get something coming through any cencron. Tayce crossed over to him.

"Any chance you're picking anything up, or anything's coming through?" asked Tayce casually.

"Nothing! Sorry—just a load of old static atmospherics," replied Mac, feeling bored.

"I know you're bored, and it's understandable, but keep listening. We may have something materialise when we reach this planet Marrack, or when they decide to restore our communications system. Take a break in forty-five minons if you still haven't got anything, OK?" she ordered, understanding his frustration at not being able to do his normal duty.

Turning away from checking with Mac if they were picking up any kind of conversation of the Marrackans, she turned to see through the main sight port that the white cloud that had surrounded the cruiser was gone. Now it didn't feel so claustrophobic any more. Clear space was restored again. In the distance and drawing near was a muddy-coloured planet. This, presumed Tayce, had to be their destined port of call, Marrack. Marc came to her side, seeing the view also.

"What do you reckon?" he asked quietly.

"Not the most attractive planet, is it?" replied Tayce, just as discrete.

Kelly gained navigations and announced in surprise that Amalthea's speed was decreasing, like they were getting ready to come into land or dock. Tayce glanced at Twedor, who was now standing in the doorway to the DC. She wondered if he had been returned to them in a full operating capacity, free of the Marrackan influence. Marc and she exchanged wondering glances, considering the matter.

"Twedor, are you back with us yet?" asked Tayce, hoping he was.

"No, Captain, he's not. I am guiding you in for final approach to our home world," came the voice from Twedor. Much to Tayce's disappointment, the Marrakans still had him.

"There go my hopes," said Tayce under her breath.

"You may take a small team with you to Marrack, Captain, if you so wish," announced the voice coming from Twedor.

Tayce, upon these words, immediately chose Lance and Mac and ordered Mac to contact Donaldo, if he could, via Wristlink and have him ready for a Quest and to inform him to bring his Emergency Medical Kit and Treketa. Mac agreed, raising his Wristlink. He found communications had been enabled, so he proceeded to make contact with Donaldo down in the MLC. He was glad at least the Marrackan controller was letting him do it via Wristlink. Before him suddenly, at the same time, his communications console sprang to life, lighting up as the keypad should do when in normal operation. He quickly ceased his Wristlink call and proceeded in the normal way. Tayce smiled in the direction of Twedor—at least communications were back. The controller made Twedor nod his head. Tayce began thinking about the journey they'd been forced to make to Marrack. Why had they been requested in such a non-negotiable way? Why hadn't herself and the team been requested in a more normal way such as using communications to make an urgent request? It would have prevented all this power failure and taking-over of controls. It was still on her mind to speak severely with the leader of Marrack, as what he or she had done, whether they realised it or not, was classed as a possible act of war. It was one of Enlopedia's rules. No one shall take over any vessels, etc., in the Enlopedian realm without consent unless authorised by the headquarters base with purposeful legal authority. If he or she was not aware, then she would make sure they were. So the next time they wouldn't be engaged in a possible war they didn't want. Marc glanced at her. He could see she was in deep thought. He had a feeling she couldn't wait to meet whoever had caused all the unnecessary trouble, to give them a piece of her mind. It made him smile at the thought.

* * *

A while later Donaldo and Treketa entered Organisation. Once the Quest team were ready to leave, Twedor, in the control of the being from Marrack, ordered everyone to accompany him down to the Transpot Centre. It felt weird, to say the least, following Twedor, as it was usually the other way round. Tayce realised the Marrackans must have given Amalthea a severe information search, as they knew where the Transpot was. But did they get it through Twedor? she wondered.

"How did you know this cruiser has such a facility?" asked Tayce as she walked along.

"Your Romid, Captain, is a very interesting source of information. There is very little left to study about your cruiser and team. We Marrackans have found the information interesting. There is little more we can discover from you—or need," replied the Marrackan/Twedor.

"Damn cheek!" said Tayce under her breath.

"Did you say something, Captain?" said the voice coming from Twedor, as they went.

"Just that, as you may recall I informed you earlier, I hold you responsible for any damage caused to the form you're currently occupying. The fact is he is not just my property; he belongs to Enlopedia Headquarters Base, so it won't be just me you'll be answering to for any damage that's caused by you. It will be them as well," began Tayce, but she was cut off by the voice coming through Twedor.

"Enough, Captain! I am not prepared to discuss this matter any further," came the male voice, as if he didn't like what Tayce had said.

Twedor, under the guidance of the Marrackan, proceeded forth with the small team towards the Transpot Centre and Marrack. Before leaving Organisation, Tayce had decided to leave Marc in command for the simple reason that she didn't trust the Marrackans and what they'd done so far. Marc had wholeheartedly agreed. He didn't trust them either. Mac Danford had been picked to take care of Tayce, at any cost, if her life was suddenly in danger and to fight to get away.

* * *

Marrack was a planet in entire darkness—no daylight, ever! It was far from ideal for a living environment. The atmosphere was damp. Poor visibility was the main factor, which was the result of dense fog. You couldn't see further than right before you if you were stood on the surface. The air was far from breathable, filled with noxious gases. The planetary every-dayon lives of the inhabitants was under threat because of the severe weather conditions that were in a continuous repeating loop in the planet's daily cycle. It was a far cry from the paradise world of Entronet. In the middle of the surface was a vast dome-shaped construction. Attached to it were various one- and two-storey square buildings in grey stonex. Purple lighting emitted from inside what could only be described as a complex, where the Marrackans tried to live an every-dayon normal existence. Inside one of the large square two-storey buildings, visable through one of the floor-to-almost-ceiling clear Look Views on ground-floor level, sat a slim young girl with startling brown eyes and a slightly tanned complexion. She tossed back her long, straight chestnut hair, which cascaded around her shoulders. She seemed to be in deep thought as she stared out into the near-impossible visibility and darkness. It was as if she was longing for something to happen or wanted to be somewhere else—anywhere but where she was.

She stretched and continued to finish doing up her body-hugging suit in purple silkene. She rose to her feet and began, in a fed-up way, walking from the room, not looking back at the contents she had left scattered around the room upon deciding what to wear. This was obviously her dwelling place. She was average in height, which matched her slim physique. The oval doors opened automatically on her approach and closed behind her as she passed through. She briskly made her way to the leisure area. As she went, you could tell she'd been brought up to hold herself in high esteem. There was a certain pure upper-class breeding about her. You could tell this by the way she walked. As she walked past some young male techs of the area, going about their duty, she playfully maintained teasing eye contact with them—something, if her father caught her doing it, she would be severely reprimanded for. One had even called out her name to make her turn her head in his direction. Deluca was her name. She gave the young working tech a look as if he was beneath her in breeding, which he was. She quickly reminded him verbally that he was addressing the Admiral's daughter and to show some respect. The group of young mischievous working techs laughed. They knew they could get away with teasing her. One hit the other doing the teasing and told him he was in trouble now. She would tell her father. They all laughed, knowing they'd done what they wanted to achieve, and that was to wind up Deluca playfully. She walked on to where she was heading in disgust.

* * *

In a holding room elsewhere in the vast complex Dairan sat looking out of the Look View, wondering if he or Craig would ever see the Amalthean Quests team or Tayce again any time soon. Suddenly the oval cream entrance doors drew back into the wall on either side. Deluca walked in cautiously and paused, studying both Dairan and Craig nervously. She had been contacted by her father, as she was en route to the leisure area, and ordered to forget her plans and go and fetch the two officers from Amalthea.

"Gentlemen, I'm Deluca, daughter of Admiral Marrack. My father wishes to meet with you," she announced in a soft yet polite tone.

"When are you going to be returning us to our cruiser?" asked Craig plainly, his patience wearing thin, annoyed that he and Dairan had just been left where they were for what seemed ages. He reached out and grabbed Deluca, wanting answers.

"Craig, mate, she's just a kid—leave it," said Dairan, stepping in to stop him.

"Actually, I'm sixteen," replied Deluca, pulling herself free of Craig's grip, unimpressed by Craig's behaviour.

Craig walked away from Deluca, trying to calm down. He knew he wouldn't generally act the way he did, but after being abducted from the corridor on Amalthea, then bundled into their current surroundings without a word, he was entitled to feel irate. Deluca smiled nervously at Dairan, who smiled back gently in return. He advised her to lead the way—they'd follow. On this, Deluca turned and began walking on out. Dairan called Craig to follow on and, as he approached, he suggested discreetly that he try and calm down—remember who they were representing. Craig nodded understandingly. No sooner had Deluca exited the room with Craig and Dairan than they all walked along the corridor of created natural lighting towards a walkway. Walking to the end, Dairan glanced around at the marblex yellow walls and beige shiny floor underfoot and the sculptured patterned archway they passed through into a purple soft-lit chamber. Upon Deluca seeing her father, she smiled and crossed to him, announcing that she'd brought the two officers from Amalthea. Admiral Marrack crossed with an outstretched hand for Dairan to shake, apologising.

"Gentlemen I'm Admiral Marrack. My sincere apologies for the unconventional way you were brought here by my staff. But please do not concern yourself—there is nothing to fear. No harm will come to you. The reason for you being brought here will be revealed when your captain arrives," he assured most sincerely, shaking Dairan's hand.

"It did make us a little unnerved, sir," said Dairan as Craig stood silent.

Dairan studied the Admiral, who decided to begin explaining partly why he had to bring them to Marrack so unconventionally. It was so he could make sure their captain would come to rescue them, and he could meet her to ask something important of her. Dairan nodded. But he had a feeling Tayce wouldn't be happy when she arrived, and he wondered if the problems they were having on the cruiser had something to do with this male being before him. The Admiral was a tall man of average build and had an air of great supremacy about him. He had warm features, but the kind that showed he was in charge. His eyes were, like his daughter's, brown, but showed a certain great intelligence about them. Even Dairan could see he was a man who would not suffer fools easily. He could also see he was a man who could be trusted, despite the way in which they'd come to his world. Admiral Marrack suggested he and Craig make themselves comfortable until the arrival of their captain—take some refreshment. He then turned and sauntered back to his operations console to check on the progress of Tayce's arrival. Dairan noticed his command attire—the colour of his robe. In fact it was the same as Deluca's all-in-one purple body-hugging satinex suit, which was decorated with a thin outline of black piping to the collar and cuffs. His robe opened down to the floor to reveal a black high-collared undershirt, matching black close-fitting trousers and grey calf-length boots. Dairan thought to himself that these were obviously the Marrackan colours and it was smart. He figured the race obviously took great pride in their appearance, to create a good impression. The Admiral broke his train of thought as he spoke some words to a person who appeared on-screen. Then the V-shaped screen went blank, deactivating.

"Your captain and small team are on their way. I hope she's not too cross with us," announced the Admiral.

"Can I ask how you brought us here?" asked Craig casually, but interested.

"We Marrackans have a great power to reach far across the Universe and bring to this world anyone and anything we so wish. I have brought not only you here, but your captain, by that means, even though I hear she is far from pleased at the way in which we have done so. I fear I shall probably feel the wrath of her tongue because of our unconventional means of invitation to bring her here. The Universe your cruiser had to travel through is classed as somewhat dangerous, known only to the worst form of traveller, so my people taking overall charge of the course and your cruiser were able to protect your cruiser from danger and destruction. I have considered most stations and other cruisers in the Universe, but none of them came up with what I wanted. Your cruiser the Amalthea Two, had my exact requirements for the proposal I have to put to your captain. It is said it is the best exploration vessel in your headquarters base fleet, and you and your team are something of galactic legends. I feel you're right for what I have in mind to put to your captain. I hope she understands," explained the Admiral, sauntering about, his hands clasped behind him as he thought about his proposal and how angry Tayce might be when they met.

"If you explain your reason for controlling her journey here, I'm quite sure she'll understand," assured Dairan, but he wondered if she'd be mad as hell first.

"Father, do you need me any further at present?" cut in Deluca politely.

"No, but stay within contact distance. I will need you when the Captain arrives," he said, waving her away with his right hand.

"Of course, Father. Nice to meet you, Dairan," she said, not giving Craig a second look. She turned and ran on out like a child let out to play.

"Bang goes my chance of a friendship," said Craig under his breath.

"Don't concern yourself, Officer Bream. She's a high-spirited girl, but she's considerate and she never holds a grudge for long. I and her mother are extremely proud of her, but alas we realise she needs to find a world outside Marrack— 'spread her wings' I believe is the term you use. She needs to gain experience of life other than here," said the Admiral, running a broad hand through his short chestnut-coloured hair.

Both Dairan and Craig walked with the Admiral over to the largest of three Look Views, discussing Marrack in general. After a while the Admiral turned to Craig, exclaiming that he understood from his people he was something of a genius in sorting out computer problems. He said he wondered if Craig wouldn't mind taking a look at the Marrack weather-computer system, which was responsible for the awful weather the planet was currently experiencing. It had proved impossible to track where the problem lay, but the computer controlled the atmosphere and temperature of the environment they occupied every dayon. The Admiral explained that the weather had changed drastically just on three monthons ago—hence the dark and near-impossible visibility they saw before them. Craig looked at Dairan, consulting him on whether he should help. Dairan nodded in total agreement. Craig, on this, asked if there were any tools he could use as his full kit was back on Amalthea. With a wave of his hand the Admiral magically materialised Craig's tech kit on the floor in front of him. As Craig picked up his kit, amazed, the Admiral in a sharp authoritative tone summoned an aide to take Craig to the Weather System Computer Centre and make sure he had help, should he need it, as he was going to repair the computer. Craig headed off in the company of the aide, dressed in a white-and-purple body-hugging suit-type uniform. At the same time, out of the shadows of the chambers came another young male aide with dark hair, roughly the same age as Deluca. Behind him came Tayce, and to either side of her were Lance and Mac. Behind them came Donaldo and Treketa with Emergency Medical Kits in case they were needed. Admiral Marrack walked forth to the far-from-pleased expression of Tayce.

"Welcome to Marrack, Captain, all of you. Firstly I must apologise for the way you were so determinedly brought here by my staff. They do get a bit carried away sometimes," began the Admiral in a true apologetic tone.

"Admiral, I trust Twedor here will be returned unharmed to his normal state," said Tayce straightforwardly.

"He's back under his own operation. He's quite an amazing piece of technology. We found him fascinating during our time in his form. Apologies again for my staff and their overambitious behaviour."

"I accept your apology, but would like to add that there was no need for a forced trip to your world. If you had contacted us in the normal way, we would have been quite willing to come here," Tayce pointed out in her true tone of unamused captain, feeling slightly peeved the journey had been out of her control.

"Captain, let me explain the reason I brought you here in the way I did. My people did it to protect you and your cruiser, because there is an area of space known as Avarus space—nobody without our protection has lived to tell the tale of passage through it," explained the Admiral.

Twedor who had been standing silently wondering what they were all doing in their present surroundings, after the Marrakan control had vacated his form, looked up at Tayce, suddenly asking, "What are we doing here?"

Tayce looked at the Admiral, as much to say, "Would you care to enlighten both of us?"

The Admiral asked for a quiet word. Tayce ordered Twedor to stay with Lance. Lance, on this, looked concerned as she walked away in the company of the Admiral over to the Look View. After a while, out through the Look View the weather began to change. The darkness gave way to brilliant daylight and the poor visibility cleared to reveal warm sunshine. Both the Admiral and Tayce stopped talking for a moment, to witness the rapid change for the better. A warm smile crossed the Admiral's features. He was glad to see the beautiful sight of his planet coming back to normal. It was a breathtaking scene—just as it used to be. The Marrackan hills in the distance and the panoramic views were returning to their former glory. Blooms and bushes were coming back to what they should look like, instead of poor, dying replicas. Tayce was taken aback by the beauty of what was forming before her. It reminded her of her home world, Traun. Deluca walked back into the chamber with Craig and his tech kit.

"Sir, your weather computer is now fixed. I've left instructions with one of your techs and explained what needs to be checked regularly," exclaimed Craig.

"Thank you, young man. You've done a wonderful job. You've given the people of this world the chance to venture outside again. You've made this world a beautiful place once more. Captain, this young man is quite something—hang on to him," said the Admiral, pleased beyond words.

Deluca paused, seeing Twedor. For a moment she didn't quite know what to make of him. She looked at Lance, Mac, Donaldo and Treketa, all standing patiently, wondering who they were. She looked at her father who was now back in discreet discussion about something of great importance with Tayce. She knew better than to break into the conversation when her father was talking with someone important, like the captain of Amalthea. Admiral Marrack glanced at Deluca and smiled. He was discussing the idea of having her join the Amalthean Quests team, and telling Tayce the reason he wanted her to join such a good team and why he had picked the team in the first place. Treketa crossed to Deluca, seeing she felt awkward waiting to be introduced to the team present. Treketa began by introducing herself to Deluca.

"Hello. I'm Treketa. I like your outfit," began Treketa, trying to make friendly conversation with Deluca.

"Thanks! What's your captain discussing with my father? It looks serious," said Deluca, keeping her sight on her father, seeing him nod and glance at her occasionally as he spoke with Tayce.

"I don't know, but I think we're about to find out," replied Treketa kindly.

Tayce and Admiral Marrack turned on the shiny floor in the direction of Deluca and the others. The Admiral began to point out to Deluca that the time had come, discussed a couple of dayons previously, when she was to join the Amalthean Quests team on Amalthea Two for her outside-Marrack experience. On this, Deluca, to everyone's surprise, turned on her father and yelled at him in an outspoken tone of voice. She wasn't leaving Marrack, not then, or ever, she didn't care what he'd decided for her. With this she turned and ran from the chamber, leaving her father somewhat embarrassed by his daughter's behaviour. Tayce looked at Lance, giving him a look to suggest he go after Deluca. He nodded and excused himself. Lance recalled the fact that he'd felt the same way when his father started him in his now settled career. Admiral Marrack looked ashamed at his daughter's behaviour, not quite knowing what to say next.

"What purpose will your officer serve, Captain?" asked the Admiral disappointed. "It looks like my stubborn daughter has decided what she wants and there will no changing her mind."

"He's gone to talk with her, Admiral. Officer Largon has been in the same position as your daughter—he didn't want to leave his home world, but now he's more than glad he did, and I think he'll change her mind. But if you have done your research on us, as you claim, you will know this about Lance," said Tayce casually.

"Yes, we do—let's hope he can change her mind. Change is what she needs. Thank you, Captain," he said with an appreciative smile.

"You're welcome," replied Tayce, quickly forgetting what had occurred with Deluca.

The Admiral glanced towards the entrance, hoping Lance could turn Deluca's decision around. He went over to meet some of the team. Tayce turned, meeting Dairan's warm brown eyes looking at her gently. She silently enquired was he all right? He nodded and gave her a warm, handsome reassuring smile, then walked over to be with her. The Admiral, upon meeting everyone from the cruiser, turned, informing Tayce the Amalthea Two was now back under normal guidance and her cruiser's guidance computer was back in full control, as it should be. He had just been informed of as much in his ear communications device. Tayce nodded, feeling a lot more relaxed knowing the fact. The doors opened on the left side of the chamber and serving aides entered with a tray of refreshments. The Admiral gestured to the only piece of furniture in the chamber: a large ornate mahoganex table with matching chairs, set in an alcove. The chairs were swivel ones and decorated in a soft fabric in navy blue.

"Please, come and take some refreshment," gestured the Admiral politely.

The team and Twedor crossed over and sat down at what was the equivalent of a dining table. Dairan sat next to Tayce, Treketa next to Donaldo and Mac finally at the end of the table. The Admiral began by telling everyone about Marrack and the way of life on the planet in general.

*　*　*

Lance, meantime, after an aide had shown him to Deluca's chambers, stood outside. The aide assured him she was inside, then left Lance to it. He braced himself for what Deluca might do when he entered her chambers if she didn't want to cooperate with her father's wishes. This was not going to be easy, he thought. He reached out and pressed the green-lit diamond announcer to signify he was outside waiting to enter. Within a few minons the doors drew back. Inside Deluca turned, giving Lance a 'What do you want?' look.

"Do you mind if I come in?" enquired Lance politely.

"If you feel you have to. Don't go trying to change my mind. I said what I want," snapped Deluca like a spoilt child.

She turned away, looking back into the now sunny daylight the computer had created, in a careless way. She wasn't really bothered whether he stayed or walked out. Lance remembered, of all the times to remember it, that Tayce had been like Deluca once—a real stuck-up miss. So he now knew how to handle Deluca.

"Can I call you Deluca?" he asked, entering the chambers and coming to a pause as the doors closed behind him

"Only if I can call you Lance?" she replied, turning her head to look at him, seeing how surprised he was she knew his name.

"If you don't mind me saying so, you remind me of myself a couple of yearons ago, not wanting to leave the place I loved so much," he began, trying to break the icet with her.

"So what do you want me to do about it?" she retorted, giving an uninterested look, shrugging her shoulders.

"You could try listening to me for a moment and I'll explain why I think you should try what your father wants you do," he replied, thinking that even Tayce hadn't been this bad when she threw a paddy yearons ago about what her father wanted of her.

"If you think I need to, though, like I said, I've made up my mind I'm staying," replied Deluca.

She really wasn't interested in this male Questonian and member of a team. She also wasn't really interested in what he had to say. She didn't see the point. There was no way she was leaving Marrack todayon—or any other dayon for that matter.

"Right! Well, my father some yearons ago was like yours—he forced me into becoming part of the Amalthea One team. At the time, like you, it was the last thing I wanted to do, but I did it and after being with the team for four monthons I wouldn't have returned to my old way of life for anything. Still wouldn't todayon. So what I'm saying here is give it a chance—do what your father is suggesting. If it doesn't work out after the same amount of time, I'll personally fly you back here myself," said Lance. He could see she was thinking about what he was saying, with more interest.

"You will?" she said, calming down.

"Sure! All I'm saying is give it a try," he replied, crossing and sitting opposite her on a nearby seat in a relaxed way.

"I'm sorry, Lance—it's just that what you said about yourself is how I'm feeling. I feel I don't want to lose my friends and Father should have asked me first whether I wanted to go to Amalthea Two. He just said it was best for me—it would broaden my horizons. I'll miss everyone and it scares me. Marrack is all I've known. Once I leave here I won't be able to talk to my friends," expressed Deluca, looking down sorrowfully.

"Firstly, our team are all easy to get on with—OK, we all have our moments, but we're always there for each other—and, believe me, you'll soon fit in. Secondly, you can still talk to your friends here. We have a type of communication system that will still allow you to talk to your friends back here, just at the touch of a button. Our weaponry specialist uses it to call her home and keep in touch. You won't be shut off just because you join our team; and if you can't get through here, you can talk to any of us on the team, including the Captain. We'll always be there to talk and help," pointed out Lance, having the feeling he was convincing Deluca that being a part of the Amalthean Quests team wasn't quite so bad after all.

Deluca thought for a moment about what Lance had said and gradually realised that maybe life on Amalthea might not be so bad after all. She rose to her feet, ordering Lance to hand her her travel holdall and garment bag from the closet near him. He eagerly did, having the feeling she'd changed her mind. He asked her as much. Deluca just gave him a look and smiled, confirming that she was convinced life on Amalthea wouldn't leave her isolated from her home and friends after all. She was going with him. As she began to pack, a smile of slight amusement crossed Lance's warm, tanned, handsome features, because he had managed to convince her to join the Amalthean Quests team. He knew Tayce would be proud of what he'd achieved. He helped Deluca pack what personal items she wanted to take with her, knowing what her new quarters would hold.

* * *

A while later Lance and Deluca walked back into the chambers. Deluca brought her holdall and garment bag with her. Admiral Marrack turned upon hearing her enter with Lance, surprised to see them laughing. Upon seeing her packed ready to leave home, he walked towards her. She put down her holdall and garment bag. She hugged her father as he stopped before her. He then held her just away from him, exclaiming that he should have informed her of what was happening when they'd had their discussion, and he said he'd seriously meant what he wanted her to do. He and Parella, her mother, who was now in the chamber, wanted her to gain off-world experience and get the best she could in life, in the field of exploration. He had no idea she had not taken him seriously. Hence he had found the best team he could for her—namely the present Amalthean Quests team. He released her completely. Tayce stepped forth and after reassuring Parella that Deluca would be watched over whilst being part of the team, said she had nothing to worry about.

"Deluca, at any time during your time with us on Amalthea, if you become totally unhappy, we will contact your father here and have you flown back; but I hope you will enjoy your time with us and find it rewarding enough not to want to," announced Tayce gently, but in the tone of leader.

"Thank you, Captain—I'll give it a try," replied Deluca softly with a nervous smile.

Tayce turned to the Admiral and suggested she and the team with Deluca get going back to the cruiser—there was a voyage to continue. The Admiral agreed wholeheartedly, exclaiming that he'd taken her and the team off course long enough. Tayce turned, ordering Dairan to contact Amalthea and have them transpoted back. Dairan agreed. Tayce took off her Transpot bracelet and handed it to Deluca, ordering her to put it on. Lance turned, helping her, showing her how to do it in future. Tayce shook hands with the Admiral and his beautiful wife, Parella Marrack, who was like her daughter in beautiful looks. In fact she could even have been mistaken for an older sister. The same beautiful big brown eyes and clear peach-like complexion, only with a soft application of make-up to emphasise her true Marrackan beauty. Her long chestnut hair was swept up in a bun at the back of her head with a few strands hanging loosely. She was slender like Deluca, but had a certain regal air about her. Parella at a rough guess was in her late forties, but in the Universe it was never easy to judge anyone's correct age, as had been proven before in the first voyage. Just because someone looked a certain age, didn't mean they were that age.

Once everyone was ready, Tayce gave Dairan the nod to order immediate Transpot. It commenced and Deluca, with her holdall and garment bag, dematerialised with the Amalthean Quests team back to the cruiser. The Admiral put a loving arm around Parella and watched their loving daughter dematerialise for the last time, hoping she would like her new life as part of the Amalthean Quests team and it would go well. Admiral Marrack discreetly assured his wife that Deluca would be all right, she'd see.

* * *

On board Amalthea the team and the new recruit, Deluca, arrived in the Transpot Centre. The team, all except Lance, quickly left Deluca behind with Tayce, heading off back to their duty. Tayce ordered Twedor to look after Deluca—take her to the guest quarters to unpack. Twedor willingly agreed and began on out of the Transpot Centre with Deluca in tow. Tayce smiled to herself, exclaiming to Lance that although Deluca knew nothing about the cruiser, by the time Twedor was through with her she would be well versed on everything. He laughed and shook his head in amused agreement at the thought. Both he and Tayce continued on out of Transpot back up to Organisation. En route Tayce turned, thanking him for encouraging Deluca to take the chance to be part of the team, then she enquired as to what he had said to convince her. He quickly explained that he had told of his reluctance to join the Amalthea One team, but he was glad he did join. Tayce patted him on the shoulder thankfully, informing him that he'd done a great job and she was proud of him. A warm smile crossed Lance's features. He was glad she was pleased.

* * *

In the guest quarters, a while later, Deluca was standing looking at her home world, Marrack, through the sight port. It was now ebbing away into the distance. In a way she felt sad, knowing it would be a long time before she saw her home world again, if ever. But in another way, she felt she was starting a new beginning, a new chapter in her life, and from what Twedor had told her so far it was going to be an exiting journey from that moment on. But something made her wonder what it would entail.

14. The Aemiliyana Threat

One weekon later, Mac Danford out of the blue informed Tayce he was leaving the team. She wasn't pleased at the short notice, but was aware of the fact it might happen sometime. She understood he wanted to move on. He was heading back to Enlopedia to take up a new position in charge of the communications section at the Planetary and Personnel Search and Rescue building. A job he'd put in for before accepting the position on Amalthea as communications officer. Lydia Traun had talked the fact through with Tayce and, even though she had been somewhat surprised and disappointed, she knew she had no right to stand in his way as he had put in for the position before joining the cruiser.

* * *

Dairan was in charge of flying him back to Enlopedia. He called in at Mac's quarters to find out if he was ready to leave the cruiser. Mac, upon Dairan entering the quarters, picked up his holdall and garment bag, took one last look at the spacious surroundings he'd made like a second home for the duration of his duty, then followed Dairan on out, back into the corridor, allowing the quarters doors to automatically close behind him. Dairan, on walking down to the Flight Hangar Bay, asked Mac how he felt about leaving. Also had he enjoyed his time on board with the team? Mac nodded, exclaiming that he couldn't think of a better start on the Universal career ladder than serving on the Amalthean Quests team. On this, Dairan was somewhat mystified as to why he was leaving in the first place. If it had been him, he would have declined the offer at Enlopedia and continued his life on Amalthea. He put the question to Mac: why leave when he was so settled on board? Mac exclaimed that it was unavoidable as he'd put in for the other position as a change of duty and responsibility; then he was asked by Chief Traun to temporarily take the duty he had done on board until the position he'd been after was ready to take up. Dairan raised his eyes and silently felt Mac was making an unwise step. He'd be on Enlopedia all the time, not, like he was on Amalthea, travelling to the stars. They soon reached the Flight Hangar

Bay. Walking in, they walked along the small walkway and down the steps to the bay floor. Tayce and Twedor were waiting to fly to Enlopedia with Mac, to meet his new replacement. Tayce held a small blue cube-shaped gift box. She turned as they began walking over to her.

"Ready to go? I'm not going to say I'm disappointed you're leaving so soon, because I am. You've been a good communications officer here and I will never forget what you did in the Empire of Honitonia with me over the Telepathian test. I have a small reminder of that time—it's a replica of the blue power crystal and it's not just from me—it's from Emperor Honitonia, would you believe?" announced Tayce, handing the small box to Mac.

"I'm sorry for the short notice, believe me. I wouldn't have left if this position hadn't come up, but, as you know, it's a once-in-a-lifetime chance and I just have to take it. Thank you for making me feel so welcome and part of this team," he said, taking the box.

"When we're on Enlopedia look us up, if you have time," said Tayce. She felt sad to see him go, as they'd become good friends.

"Marc's in command," spoke up Dairan informatively.

Tayce nodded, then suggested they all get going. She had been requested to meet her father to meet with Mac's new replacement, and suddenly found herself wondering what he would be like. As they began moving away, Mac announced he would put the crystal on his new shelving if he had any in his new quarters. Tayce nodded.

Upon the Quest shuttle/fighter entrance opening, Mac climbed aboard first and placed his holdall and garment bag in the luggage section. Tayce lifted Twedor on board, then with Mac's help climbed aboard also. Dairan was last on board, and whilst Tayce was securing herself and Twedor he went through to the pilot seat. Mac, once strapped in, glanced out through the sight port at the magnificent Flight Hangar Bay for the last time. Tayce looked at him and could read his mixed emotions about what he was doing.

Under Dairan's expert guidance the Quest shuttle/fighter lifted up off the hangar-bay floor, heading out through the opening bay doors into space. Once free of Amalthea the Quest 3 went to turbo speed, leaving Amalthea behind like a fast-disappearing object, growing smaller by the cencron. Mac watched the sight until the cruiser was no more. He thought to himself that he'd been proud to serve on the Amalthean Quests team and cruiser. He'd been glad to call the cruiser home and the team his friends for the past eight monthons. Now he had to look forward to his next step on the career ladder. He looked at Tayce; she smiled softly at him. He silently wondered if she was reading his thoughts, but said nothing. Without warning, a wave of uneasy anticipation washed over him at what lay waiting for him in his new position as communications chief at the Planetary and Personnel Search and Rescue building. After flying for almost two hourons continuously, the Quest 3 came under the docking procedure of the

Enlopedia Headquarters Base. As the procedure progressed, the Docking-Bay doors of the docking area drew closer. Dairan decreased his speed almost to a crawl, manoeuvring in, waiting to feel the docking port lock on and secure the small Quest. When docking was complete, Dairan pressed for the entrance to open. Tayce was first out of her seat, She unsecured Twedor, then stepped down outside, allowing Mac to lift Twedor down on to Enlopedia for the last time. Mac grabbed his luggage and followed Dairan on out. Once everyone was off, Dairan turned, locking the Quest securely with the sonic key, which he pushed into a slim slot by the entrance. A young male brown-haired flight attendant walked across in a determined way to meet them. He looked like he was fresh out of training. His uniform looked new and he had a certain eager-to-please way about him. He came to a pause gently, as not to appear threatening in any way. Tayce looked at him, meeting his unusual green eyes—they were almost reptilian in appearance. Tayce wondered what he was going to say and, judging by his appearance and tall stature, she wondered if it was going to be in English or a language they couldn't understand.

"Captain Traun, it's an honour to meet you. I'm Hames. I'm here to ask if there is anything I can assist you with during your visit. Your Quest 3 is perfectly safe where it's situated," he began in perfectly understandable English, much to everyone's surprise.

"Thank you, Hames. No, everything is fine this time. We don't require your assistance, but we'll let you know if we do," said Tayce, trying to let the lad down gently.

"In that case have a good visit with us," he replied, then turned, heading away, not the least bit offended.

Dairan looked at Tayce, thinking to himself, 'That was subtle.'

Tayce read his thoughts and nudged him, giving him a look as much as to say, "What else was I going to say?"

Tayce, Dairan and Mac walked on across the Flight Arrival and Departure Dome to the entrance. Mac paused, turning to Dairan and Tayce. He glanced at his Wristlink time display. It was time to say his final farewells for the time being. Tayce hugged him, wishing him luck in his new position and ordered him to stay in touch. Dairan shook hands, suggesting he see him around, also wishing him luck.

Twedor raised his metlon hand and, as Mac grasped it, said, "It's been nice knowing you. I hope your new job goes well."

Mac nodded, then turned, walking away to take up his new position. Tayce watched him go, hoping his replacement was going to be as good and easy to get along with. Her mind drifted for a moment to when she and Mac were on Honitonia for the Telepathian test. He'd been a good friend, even if it was for a short space of time. Dairan softly, behind her, suggested they move on as they were blocking the entrance.

They walked off out of the Arrival and Departure Dome into E City Square shopping mall, which seemed to be extremely busy. Many end-of-year celebrations were in full swing, with personnel in the spirit of full festive jovial mood. Tayce ordered Dairan to take the list of supplies needed for Amalthea to the stores and see about having them sorted for delivery to the Quest 3. He agreed with a nod, suggesting he meet her later. With this he took the list of printed requirements, heading off in the opposite direction to Tayce and Twedor, to the Space Wares Complex. Twedor followed Tayce on across the square, past the central cascading water fountain, with water coming out of the giant silver metal 'E' in a pouring motion, down into the pond surrounding it. Twedor glanced at it and continued on behind Tayce towards the Vacuum Lift. Celebrating off-duty personnel in festive spirit passed Twedor. Some expressed how cute he was. Some dropped their thin festive silver celebration streamers over him with a merry laugh, much to Twedor's annoyance. He turned, reminding them he wasn't a festive tree for decoration! He was a very highly sophisticated Romid. Tayce paused, guiding him towards her so she could remove the streamers, seeing the funny side of his predicament.

"Lighten up, Twedor—it's the season to be happy," said Tayce, laughing as she removed the streamers.

"If you ask me, they're way beyond happy," replied Twedor, glancing after the merry group.

They walked into the newly arrived Vacuum Lift. A young dark-haired attendant, recruited especially for the festive season to attend to the needs of passengers, asked Tayce her destination.

"Top level, please," replied Tayce.

"Captain, if I may, if you're visiting the Admiral, he now has new chambers known as the Admiral's Chambers on that level, but if you're visiting Chief Councillor Traun, hers are where they were before," explained the middle-aged uniformed attendant politely.

"Thanks for telling me," said Tayce, appreciative of the information.

She placed her hands on Twedor's shoulders, in front of her, to steady him during ascending to the top level. The Vacuum Lift rose above the city square and stopped at the requested level. Once the lift stopped, the doors drew back, and Tayce, with Twedor, walked on out along the shiny-floored corridor, around the first corner and up to the entrance to the Admiral's Chambers. Outside the entrance was the new sight of two blue platex-armoured guards, one on either side of the entrance. This, thought Tayce, was obviously a sight that would be a permanent fixture. They greeted her with a nod, then stood at ease until she'd entered the outer anteroom with Twedor. Then, as the doors closed, they returned to a guarding stance, in an official way. Inside Tayce found Aidan Lord present. He was once her mother's aide for a while; he was now relief assistant for Adam Carford and together they now shared her parents' workload. He smiled a relaxed smile and rose to his feet, walking around the desk to meet both herself and Twedor.

"It's good to see you again, Captain, I'm afraid your father's in with someone at the moment, but please wait—he shouldn't be long," announced Aidan in a soft-spoken educated tone.

"Thanks! Tell me, why is there another set of doors beside the entrance to Mother's chambers?" asked Tayce curious. "I've never noticed them before?"

"They're new. There's been some changes since you last visited. Your mother still has her chambers, known as the Chief's Chambers, where she conducts her council business, whilst your father has his own chambers, known as the Admiral's Chambers, and now the third set of doors leads to a Meeting Centre," explained Aidan.

"That could be confusing if you're not careful. Where's Adam?" asked Tayce concerned. "I expected to see him here—no offence."

"It's his off-duty time at the moment. When he needs a break, he hands the area out here over to me; then when I want a break he does the same for me," replied Aidan.

"Is Father very busy at the moment in general?" enquired Tayce, interested.

"Yes! He hasn't stopped being that way since he took over from your mother. Everyone has said he's like the late Jonathan Largon—willing to work with the people of this base, just like Jonathan did. In fact he's thought very highly of!" exclaimed Aidan, recalling what he'd heard.

"Twedor, how are you?" asked Aidan, bending slightly and patting him on the head.

"I'm fine, though I just wish people would stop trying to turn me into a festive tree," replied Twedor, looking at Aidan.

"What's he referring to?" asked Aidan, puzzled as to what Twedor was talking about.

"Oh, some revellers tried to decorate him in glitzy festive streamers a while ago," explained Tayce, amused.

"Oh, I see," replied Aidan, raising his eyes and laughing.

The doors to the Admiral's Chambers suddenly opened and Darius walked out, concluding a meeting with a male who Tayce recognised as being the head of one of the complexes on Enlopedia. He didn't look too pleased the last time she'd seen him, on a previous visit. He looked a lot happier this time. He shook hands with her father, smiling, exclaiming that they'd meet again soon. He was roughly the same height and age as her father, she thought. As she studied him, without being rude, she found he was neither handsome nor plain-looking. She guessed he was termed average in looks. He left looking a lot happier and nodded in acknowledgement of her, seeing her present, waiting.

Darius welcomed Tayce with a warm fatherly smile, holding out his left hand, gesturing for her to go into his chambers first. She rose to her feet and ushered

Twedor off in front of her, going on behind. Once all three were inside, the doors closed behind them with a quiet hum. Darius crossed, and turned upon reaching the front of his desk. He perched just on the edge.

"Nice room, and done out in the same colours as Mother's. You two haven't fallen out, have you? Is that why you're working in separate rooms? I thought you'd want to work together—that you'd change the way it's set out," said Tayce, giving her father a look as much to say, "Is there a problem I should know about?"

"No, young lady, we've not. I need more space than your mother, and there isn't enough room for both of us to conduct different kinds of business in the same vicinity," replied Darius, amused at Tayce's cheekiness.

"OK, just as long as you're both all right—no cross words. I'm here to meet Amalthea's new recruit, Nick Berenger, the communications chief and replacement for Mac Danford, who as you know was communications officer. I stipulated the next recruit would be totally in charge of communications aboard, so he should have the rank of chief. I expected him to be here. Where is he?" asked Tayce, far from impressed that he was late.

"He preferred to meet you down in the Twone Bar, in the city square," replied Darius, seeing a far-from-impressed look suddenly creep over Tayce's beautiful features.

"Oh, he did, did he? Well, before I go and meet this Mr Berenger, do you have any new assignments for us?" asked Tayce in a tone which told her father she was far from pleased at Nick Berenger's choice of place to meet his new head of cruiser and his employer.

Darius turned on his desk and picked up a small black box that held disk-chip assignments the Amalthean Quests team might be interested in taking on. He handed the box to her. She accepted it. The doors opened behind her and Lydia entered, pleased to see her again, even if it was for another of her fleeting visits. Tayce turned.

"Hello, Mother. I can't stay long—I just came to pick up our new replacement for Mac and to say a quick hello before heading back to Amalthea. Father has just informed me Mr Berenger is waiting for me in the Twone Bar, would you believe? I can't take Twedor in there. Why couldn't he have met me here? He's off to a great start as part of a successful team like mine!" began Tayce angrily.

"He did come up to see me and stayed for a while. As I had other business to attend to, I suggested he meet you down there. But you're right—the moment you arrived in port he should have come back here to meet you," replied Lydia.

"Dairan's with me. He's currently picking up supplies we need. I'll wristlink him and request he meets us outside the Twone Bar," said Tayce, sighing.

"I hate to cut and run, but the council is convening in ten minons to consider a decision I must be there for. See you next time. Have a good festive time on Amalthea. Say hello to Dairan for me," said Lydia, turning and hurrying back to the chambers entrance, walking briskly on out as the doors parted, leaving

Darius and her daughter, as the doors closed behind her, talking. Darius shook his head, smiling at the way in which Lydia seemed to never be around long enough before heading away somewhere else in a hurry. Tayce looked at her father, wondering what was so funny, and asked as much. Darius explained that he'd never imagined for one cencron, back on the dayons on Traun, that some yearons later Lydia would become head of a council and even take charge of vast bases such as Questa and Enlopedia had both been. Tayce smiled. She could see how happy her father was for her mother and glad he still thought of her in a warm, loving, affectionate way, as he had always done.

Suddenly her Wristlink bleeped on her wrist. She raised it, pressing 'Comceive'. Dairan's voice came through. He informed her the supplies were being ferried out to the Quest as he spoke and he would meet her there. Tayce stopped him, explaining that there had been a change of plans in the meeting place. She wanted him to meet her outside the Twone Bar, as she had to leave Twedor with him while she went to meet their new replacement for Mac inside. Dairan made a sound that said it all. He was thinking along the same lines as she was—this new replacement was making a great start to becoming a fully fledged member of the Amalthean Quests team, meeting in such a place as a bar! But he agreed. Darius watched his daughter proudly as she handled the situation with such calmness and independence—something he thought, all the past yearons ago, he would never see. Tayce ceased communications with Dairan.

"That's settled. Dairan will meet us at the Twone Bar. I must go, Father, before this Nick Berenger thinks I've changed my mind about recruiting him. Believe me, the way I'm feeling right now, I'm wondering," said Tayce, laughing.

"Of course—you go. You look after yourself. I hope this Nick Berenger turns out to be a good team member, despite what you're going through to meet him," he said, walking over and giving her a warm, fatherly hug.

"Enjoy your festive dayons off; and as for looking after myself, with Dairan and Marc around I think they've got it covered," she replied, amused, knowing how watchful Marc and Dairan both were over her.

Father and daughter broke apart. Tayce began walking over to the entrance with Twedor. As the doors drew apart she and Twedor left her father's new chambers, heading on out through the anteroom and saying goodbye to Aidan on the way through. Twedor began to complain about how he wasn't allowed to go into the Twone Bar. He informed her he could more than handle himself. Tayce quickly and in a no-nonsense tone informed him she didn't want him falling into unscrupulous hands. At such a celebrating time of the year, he would be lost in cencrons without a trace. It wasn't the personnel of Enlopedia she was worried about—she knew they all respected him—it was the travellers passing through. They wouldn't hesitate to grab him and make a lavish amount of currency by selling him on, and not necessarily in his original form. Twedor saw her point and said no more on the matter. He intended to stick to her like glue.

They approached the waiting Vacuum Lift and met the same male attendant who had brought them up earlier. They both boarded and Tayce requested the city level. The attendant put the request into operation, then began talking with Tayce, as the Vacuum Lift descended back down to the city square, about the impressiveness of the new command level. Once down, Tayce walked out, off across to the Twone Bar, with a tight hold of Twedor's left hand.

When the doors opened Dairan came into view, waiting at the entrance. A young woman for pleasure was trying strongly to entice Dairan into celebrating a night of festive spirit with her he wouldn't forget in a hurry. But he wasn't having any of it. He'd heard the kind of reputation this somewhat breathtaking beauty had. He walked away from the eye-catching brunette and over to meet Tayce, raising his eyes in jest regarding the unwanted attention he'd been getting. The leatherex-clad voluptuous beauty, upon seeing Tayce, gave a spiteful look of disgust then stormed off.

"I think she liked you. I give her points for persistence to entice at least," said Tayce, laughing.

"Stop it, please—you're making the situation worse. She's not my type," said Dairan, laughing, amused.

"She'd be mine," said Twedor out of the blue, much to Tayce's surprise.

"Twedor, that's enough! The reason I wanted to meet you here is that I have to go in there and meet our replacement for Mac. Nick Berenger is his name and he's our communications chief," said Tayce, gesturing towards the loud festivities of the interior of the Twone Bar.

"I'll take Twedor back to the Quest. Are you sure you're going to be all right, going in there alone?" Dairan asked concerned.

"Yes, I'll be fine. You take care of Twedor. I'll meet you back at the Quest just as soon as I've met this Nick Berenger," assured Tayce casually.

She braced herself and headed across to the entrance to the Twone Bar. Dairan watched her with concern as she went, though he could see, by the way she walked, she could take care of herself if any situation arose once inside. Considering the criminals she'd been up against to date. He continued on with Twedor by his side. Tayce hated entering crew and personnel after-hourons bars, as you never knew what you'd encounter. She entered into the smoky, noisy festive atmosphere, which nearly made her ears burst. She felt the unwanted looks of various people and beings, eyeing her up in a curious manner, wondering who she was and what she was doing in their vicinity. The feeling of great uneasiness grabbed at her senses and burnt right through her from the various cold and wondering stares of men of all calibres as she made her way to the long counter at the front of the bar. She gained the somewhat surprised attention of the serving tech because he recognised she was the Admiral's daughter. She had to talk loud enough to be heard above the female singers, for the tech to hear.

"I'm looking for a man by the name of Berenger. Do you know who he is and if he's here?" asked Tayce, almost shouting the question.

The scruffy-looking serving tech pointed to a booth in the near darkness, in the far right-hand corner. Tayce turned to see where he was pointing and saw a man with dark short hair and of medium build sipping a drink. She began across. She couldn't make out his features in the poor lighting as the bar progressed into a very bad light the nearer she came to the table. She came to a pause, fed up with this Mr Berenger, and began in a far-from-pleased commanding tone.

"Are you Nick Berenger, communications replacement for Amalthea Two?" asked Tayce, to the point, far from pleased at being messed about on meeting this new member of her team in a less than desirable place. She didn't like the atmosphere and interest growing in her direction.

"Who wants to know?" he asked, not caring, unaware of who he was addressing.

"Your new chief. I'm Captain Traun of Amalthea Two, the vessel you've been assigned to as part of my team," replied Tayce, not the least impressed by this Nick Berenger's attitude.

"Pardon! You're Captain Traun? I'm sorry, ma'am—I had no idea I was waiting to meet a woman," Nick replied, then realised, if he wasn't already in trouble, he'd just insulted his new captain by saying he wasn't expecting to meet a female.

"If I being a female, am someone you'd rather not work for, as part of my team, then I'll let Chief Traun know you've changed your mind and you can report back to her," began Tayce, being just as abrupt to him as he had been to her.

"No, Captain, it's fine. I'm quite happy to work for a woman, believe me," replied Nick, trying to smooth over what he'd said. He felt he'd just got off to a bad start.

"Then let's go. I don't want to be here a minon longer," said Tayce, heading away towards the entrance, not waiting for Nick to catch up.

He grabbed his holdall and other personal luggage, hurrying after Tayce, moving through the mingling noisy crowd celebrating the end of duty, heading on towards the entrance. At one point he lost sight of her altogether.

Once outside, Tayce turned to see if he was following on. He exited, apologising in the most sincere way, once more, for having insulted her. His recruitment officer had made him think he was waiting to meet a man because all he'd said, and also Chief Traun, was that he was meeting a Captain Traun, not whether it was a man or a woman. Tayce raised her eyes in surprise, then looked ahead as they began on across E City. Nick figured he wouldn't say any more. He figured he'd done all he could to make her look at him differently—to make her see that he hadn't meant to be rude to her. Tayce figured she was probably being mean, but she was his superior and he'd got off to a great start in his new duty on her team! She could tell by the tone of his voice that he was trying really hard to put the offence he'd caused right. She glanced at him as they walked together. He had a rugged face, but one that was quite pleasant. She could see there was more to this Nick Berenger than met the eye. Studying his casual dress, it could be seen he took great pride in his general appearance, judging by his smart clothes and short neatly styled hair. Despite their first meeting, Tayce could see he was going to make a first-class communications chief. There was a certain intelligence in his blue eyes that showed he was clever.

"Captain, I'd like to say it's going to be a great honour to serve as part of the Amalthean Quests team. I've heard so much about what you do," said Nick, trying to make conversation, still trying to smooth over what he'd done.

"In that case, welcome to the team. I guess I can understand you were waiting to meet a male captain if you were told you were meeting a Captain Traun. I guess I would assume the same as you—that I was meeting a man. Call me Tayce. We call each other by our Christian names on the team and work as just that—a team. We only address each other by rank when we visit planets of great importance, or on ceremonial occasions," explained Tayce.

"In that case, call me Nick," said Nick, relieved the icet had thawed between the two of them.

They both soon entered the Flight Arrival and Departure Dome after crossing the busy, bustling city square. Another happy group of off-duty personnel passed them, wishing them a happy festive season. Both Nick and Tayce laughed as they seemed to be somewhat worse for wear. Dairan and Twedor soon came into view. She could see Dairan supervising the supply loading on board the Quest. Both Nick and herself walked over. Dairan turned upon her approach.

"How's it coming along?" Tayce asked as she paused.

"Fine! They're loading the last of it now," he replied, watching.

"This is our new communications chief, Nick Berenger. Nick, this is Dairan Loring, lieutenant commander and astronomer on Amalthea Two," introduced Tayce.

"Welcome to the team, mate," said Dairan, extending his right hand for Nick to shake, in friendly greeting and welcome to the team.

"Thanks!" replied Nick, grasping Dairan's hand and shaking it.

"What about me? Don't I get an introduction?" spoke up Twedor, down beside Dairan.

"This is Twedor. He's my escort, a Romid and high-frequency link-up to our onboard guidance computer. Twedor, this is Nick," said Tayce.

"Hello, Twedor," said Nick, like he was addressing a small child.

Twedor put up his metlon hand, grasping Nick's with just the right amount of pressure, shaking it in greeting.

Nick, not knowing what Amalthea Two looked like, looked at the Quest 3 through the glassene sight port, wondering if it was the legendary Amalthea cruiser. He was greatly disappointed if it was.

Loading was soon completed. The head supervisor handed Dairan a document of contents, then walked away. Tayce placed the box her father gave her earlier aboard. Nick climbed aboard and stored his holdall and other luggage away ready for departure. Tayce took the loading documentation from Dairan, studying it whilst he shut the rear compartment using a sonic key.

Tayce was about to board when she heard the familiar voice of Empress Tricara calling out to her, trying to get her attention. She turned, looking about, seeing Tricara coming towards her through the arriving crowds that had just come off a shuttle. Tayce walked to meet her halfway. Both paused mid floor. Tricara put to Tayce, was there a chance they could talk before she left for Amalthea Two? Tayce nodded. She knew whenever Tricara asked for a discreet word and a moment of her time there was something wrong. Without warning, and out of nowhere, as Tayce went to walk to one side to talk with Tricara, a Slazer shot rang out. Tayce suddenly dropped to the ground where she'd stood. She'd been hit. Pandemonium broke out in the moments that followed. Screams came forth from female travellers in the arriving crowd and panic quickly set in. Within minons the Enlopedia Security Patrol was quickly arriving, taking action to find out who had fired the shot, sealing down the scene in gun-brandishing manner, officers going here and there to catch the would-be assassin who had brandished the offending weapon. Jan Barnford ran across to Tayce alarmed, issuing orders to his men to track the assassin and shoot on sight. He watched on in alarm as Empress Tricara crouched beside Tayce. Dairan, who had run to Tayce's side also, was now supporting her in his arms, worried. She'd taken a direct hit in the upper arm, near the shoulder.

"My officers are searching now. How is she?" asked Jan in alarmed concern, looking down.

"She'll be fine in a moment," assured Tricara as she placed her slender right hand just off the site of the wound, palm face down, and began to heal Tayce's wound.

Within minons a pink glow appeared from Tricara's palm and began to heal Tayce's wound. Tayce had passed out from the impact, but now she began to come back to consciousness. She looked up at the new recruit, Nick, who like the others around her was looking worried. He had hold of Twedor. Empress Tricara rose to her feet when the healing was done, exclaiming that Tayce would be fine.

"I don't think you'll catch this assassin, Chief," announced Tricara, knowing who it possibly was.

"Really! What makes you think my officers won't? You know they are very highly trained," said Jan, finding it suspiciously strange that Tricara should feel his men wouldn't apprehend the assassin.

"I second that. Why, Tricara? Who is this assassin?" backed up Dairan, helping Tayce back on to her feet.

"I'm sorry, Tayce—I wish I could have found you earlier. Your assassin is someone connected with Witch Queen Aemiliyana and she's out to wreak revenge on you," said Tricara, sorry her close young friend had to be the unfortunate victim of such an evil and very powerful witch.

"That does it, I'm assigning two security officers to your cruiser until this Witch Queen is stopped," said Jan in a no-nonsense tone. He didn't like the fact that Tayce was in extreme danger.

Tayce knew the name well. She'd read it many yearons ago and everything she could about the powerful witch. She was ten times worse than Vargon. She remembered reading something about the witch's involvement with her great-grandfather—but what, she couldn't remember off hand. But for some strange reason the woman made Tayce shudder at the thought of her and the mention of her name.

"I'll be fine. I can protect myself if this Aemiliyana makes an appearance," insisted Tayce.

Jan knew Tayce was gifted and was more than capable of protecting herself. But he didn't like the idea something should happen to her at the vengeful powerful hands of some Witch Queen from some unknown realm. Tayce read his thoughts of great concern. She placed a reassuring hand on his right arm, informing him if things got out of hand she would summon the help of Tricara. On this, Tricara backed her up, assuring her she would be watching from afar, via her own gift of powers and would assist should a confrontation occur, joining forces with Tayce. Jan, hearing about powers, shook his head. It was way beyond him. Tricara gently advised Tayce to be on her guard. With this Tricara handed Tayce a disk chip.

"Here, this will help. Study it. It's all about your great-grandfather, Grandmaster Alexentron Traun and the confrontation he had with Witch Queen Aemiliyana. It will give you an insight into how to handle her," announced Tricara.

"Good. I need all the help I can get, by the sound of it. I remember something about Grandfather having dealings with her, but it's such a long time ago now," said Tayce, thinking hard and trying to remember back to when she'd heard it.

"Yes, he was known to many on your world and mine as the Grandmaster of the Empire of Past Traun and he had his reasons for putting Aemiliyana where she's resided for centuries, until now—where she's obviously escaped from," announced Tricara seriously.

"Thanks! I'll certainly give this a study. It might give me the reason she's picked me," replied Tayce, thinking about what might lie ahead.

"Ready to go?" asked Dairan, glancing at his Wristlink time display.

"You take care," said Jan in a sincere concerned way. She wasn't just a friend; she was the Admiral's daughter and someone they all cared about.

"I always do. Believe me, it will take a lot more than some Witch Queen to get rid of me. I'm a galactic legend, remember?" said Tayce light-heartedly.

"Dairan, watch her and tell the rest of the team to be on their guard too. Tayce is one special lady," said Jan discreetly to Dairan, by his side.

"I know, believe me. She'll be perfectly safe," replied Dairan reassuringly.

Nick walked on and climbed aboard the Quest 3 followed by Tayce, Twedor and Dairan. Twedor was already thinking that when Tayce studied the information on the disk Tricara had given her he'd be there making computer notes to protect her, if he could. Dairan went straight through to the pilot compartment and seated himself ready for departure. After everyone was seated safely on board, and he was ready in the pilot seat, he activated the control to close the entrance hatch. It sealed with the gentle sound of compressed air. Outside the Quest, at the Docking Port, Jan gently pulled Tricara back for her safety as departure began. The Quest 3 withdrew slowly from the docking hold and turned to head out, away from the Docking-Port Area. Once in position, under the expert guidance of Dairan it shot away in the direction that would take them back to Amalthea.

Jan and Tricara meanwhile walked back to their duties, with Jan wondering if they'd turned up anything on the assassin who fired on Tayce earlier. For Tricara it was concern for Tayce that filled her mind, and she was off to see Darius Traun to inform him of what had happened.

* * *

Halfway back across the Universe, Nick Berenger on board the Quest 3 found himself wondering what the sudden incident was involving Tayce being wounded by a strange assassin earlier. He turned, studying her without blatantly being rude, wondering why someone would want to take a shot at her. She sensed he was looking at her and looked back, smiling reassuringly.

"We'll soon be arriving at Amalthea. It's not long now," assured Tayce, breaking the silence.

"I hope you don't think I'm being nosey, but that incident back on Enlopedia—any idea why?" he asked gently, somewhat curious.

"There's something you have to know about me, which all the team already knows: I'm a gifted member of the Telepathian Empire of Honitonia and I'm able to use mind-controlled powers, but they are used for good, never bad. I may have to use them to defend myself against the likes of this threatening Witch Queen Aemiliyana. I would never misuse my gift. Most of the time it's used when I'm seeing justice done," explained Tayce.

"Empress Tricara talked about this Witch Queen in such a way that she sounds vicious, and as I am now part of your team I'd like you to count me in on helping against her when the time comes to face her—that's if you should need me," replied Nick in a true friendly tone, with an added smile.

"Thanks! It's much appreciated," replied Tayce, glad he was turning out a lot better than he was when she met him in the bar, for attitude.

Dairan suddenly announced Amalthea was coming into orbital view. Tayce, on this, turned to look out through the nearest sight port at the approaching sight of Amalthea. Nick whistled in sheer utter disbelief at the vast and graceful-looking sight that was Amalthea Two. He couldn't believe what he was seeing. It was certainly impressive for an exploration cruiser, he thought. Tayce smiled to herself, amused by Nick's amazement. Even though she was glad to be going back on board, it was tinged with uneasiness because of the threat of Witch Queen Aemiliyana and wondering how she would make her first strike.

* * *

On board Amalthea, in Organisation, Marc was watching the approaching sight of the Quest 3 returning from Enlopedia, through the sight port. He wondered how things had gone. Turning, he ordered Kelly to stand by ready for arrival procedures for the Quest 3; then he turned back, ordering Amal to activate electronics in Quarters 8, Level 3. Amal acknowledged. Kelly started procedures for bringing the Quest 3 safely into land in the Flight Hangar Bay. Marc stood in a commanding stance, watching the safe arrival of the Quest 3 as it came in for its final approach to land in the Flight Hangar Bay.

"Final procedure under way," announced Kelly, working at her keypad as she said it.

She continued to track and make sure the final moments before the Quest set down on the bay floor went smoothly, whilst Amal stayed in contact with Dairan. Once through the final stage of landing the Quest 3, she went back to normal duties. Marc turned, placing Lance in overall charge, informing him he would be in the Flight Hangar Bay. If needed, he could get him on Wristlink. Lance nodded. Deluca suddenly turned on her chair in the temporary position at communications, informing Marc a call was coming in from Enlopedia from Empress Tricara. Marc sighed, pausing midway towards the entrance to Organisation, turning back.

"Put it through to the DC. I'll take it there," he said, heading towards the DC.

Deluca did as requested with a little help from Lance, who was overseeing her, in training.

Marc soon entered the DC, crossing to Tayce's desk. He gave an impatient sigh as he sat in Tayce's chair and waited for the call to come through. He understood Deluca was learning, so he waited patiently.

* * *

Down in the Flight Hangar Bay, the entrance hatch opened on the Quest 3. Tayce stepped down followed by Nick with his holdall and other personal luggage. Dairan then lifted Twedor down on to the bay floor and jumped down after him. The team waiting to collect their supplies were Aldonica, Donaldo and Craig. Tayce turned, introducing Nick to the present members. Nick saw someone he couldn't believe he was seeing: Sallen Vargon. He gave an unimpressed look that said it all as she entered the Flight Hangar Bay to collect her supplies for the Lab Garden Dome. Nick, upon being introduced to her, found he had to cover up what he truly felt for her, from past dealings with her and her mother. Tayce saw what was going on and wondered once more whether, after all this time, they were going to have trouble regarding Sallen's past. She could see Nick was relieved when he moved to shake hands with Aldonica. Sallen quickly dismissed the awkward moments and went on to get her supplies. Dairan exchanged raised-eye glances with Tayce over the incident, but said nothing.

"See you later," said Tayce to Dairan.

"Yeah, sure," replied Dairan, waiting for the others to get their supplies.

Tayce and Twedor with Nick walked from the Flight Hangar Bay, leaving Dairan to distribute the allocated supplies. Once out in the corridor, and out of earshot of Sallen, on the way down the corridor Tayce brought up the subject of his apparent shock at seeing Sallen. She could tell the atmosphere between them had become difficult once more, like back on Enlopedia in the Twone Bar. As she began talking about Sallen and the way he'd looked at her on greeting her, she quickly assured him anything he thought about Sallen was now in the past and that's where it must remain. He quickly exclaimed that he'd had dealings with her mother in the past and they'd not been pleasant ones. He was in continued thought about whether he'd done the right thing in joining the Amalthean Quests team, now he'd seen Sallen all over again.

"Nick, before we continue any further, there's something you should know about Sallen which the rest of us already know," said Tayce, stopping in the corridor and turning.

"What? I had no idea she was serving on your team. I'm sorry, Tayce—I don't know if I'll be able to stay," he said forthrightly before Tayce had a chance to say what she wanted to say.

"Hear me out. The Sallen of old with the evil countess for a mother is no more. She underwent what is termed memory reprogramming treatment. Anything that happened in her past was wiped. She has no recollection of who she once was. She has a completely new life—the past does not exist for her, as the old Sallen Vargon, once evil sidekick and daughter to the Countess. She's now a science tech on this team and takes great pride in the Lab Garden Dome and runs the botanical side of things around here," pointed out Tayce.

"Really... I'm sorry," he said in a soft, almost speechless apologetic tone.

"It's not me you need to apologise to; it's Sallen. If it's any consolation, whatever Sallen did to you in the past, or her mother did, you're not the only one of this team to feel the way you do. Lance Largon felt the same way the moment he saw her at the beginning of this voyage, until, like yourself, he found out she'd changed. Of course if you feel you still can't be on this team with Sallen, then I will arrange for the next Enlopedian Launch to pick you up and take you back to headquarters," said Tayce, disappointed.

"No! No, there's no need. I guess I could bury the past and accept the fact that what she did was in a previous life. I'll go and see her and apologise properly. I'll introduce myself. There won't be any trouble after what you've said. What's in the past will remain there, I assure you," he announced in a sincere way.

They continued on along the present level. Twedor figured Tayce had tackled the issue very well. She was somewhat curious though to know what involvement Sallen had in Nick's past, but she didn't like to pry. They all had their past occurrences with the Countess, and past Sallen, they'd rather forget. Upon reaching his new quarters, she left him to unpack and ordered Twedor to remain to escort him to Sallen, then up to duty when he was ready. She then walked away in the direction of the Level Steps, glad she'd left Twedor to escort Nick to see Sallen as he had told her he was prepared to forgive Sallen and make a fresh start. Sending Twedor was her way of keeping an eye on him, making sure everything went well. Twedor informed Nick, after Tayce had walked away, that her bark was worse than her bite regarding the protection of the new Sallen. Nick smiled and they both entered through the opening doors of his new quarters—Mac Danford's old quarters. Nick, as he set his holdall and other personal luggage down, realised that if he was going to get on on this team, then what Tayce said about what had happened in his past where Sallen was concerned should be left in the past. She was right. The doors behind them closed and he began to unpack, with Twedor telling him how things went in their current surroundings.

*   *   *

Marc meantime in the DC put down the handset of the Telelinkphone and sighed an exasperated sigh, giving a look of pure concern for Tayce over what he'd heard from Tricara about Aemiliyana. He rose to his feet and turned to look out of the full-length sight port in deep worrying concern about the danger Tayce was going to face according to Tricara, wondering what more evilness would emerge for Tayce because she was gifted. It seemed this Witch Queen was even more evil and treacherous than Vargon. She was out to wreak revenge for being locked away in another realm by Tayce's grandfather—another gifted being. How he wished it was him instead of Tayce this vengeful Witch Queen was after. He'd certainly know how to handle her. He figured Tayce had suffered enough at the mercy of vengeful beings like this Witch Queen. Tayce soon entered the DC, much to his surprise. He turned, looking at her silently for a moment. She used her telepathic thought-probing technique and read his thoughts. She found all she wanted to find in a matter of minons—that Tricara had told Marc about Aemiliyana. He smiled a warm, handsome smile, beginning to think back to the first time he'd met her yearons after Traun's destruction on Questa. He wondered why criminals or vengeful powerful beings couldn't find another target in the

Universe other than Tayce. She was a wonderful person. It just wasn't fair—especially the latest threatening force. Tayce walked towards him. He opened his arms to her, seeing her worried about what was coming, namely Aemiliyana. He closed his arms around her and gave her a warm, affectionate hug, assuring her she would be fine—she'd see.

"I heard what happened on Enlopedia. Empress Tricara just called. Are you all right?" he asked softly as he held her.

"I'm fine, thanks. You needn't worry as far as Aemiliyana is concerned. I have something in mind for her, which she knows nothing about yet," assured Tayce, letting Marc go.

"The crystal—do you think it will be enough to fend her off? I don't like the sound of this woman. She could kill you, Tayce. I heard this from Tricara just now," said Marc, finding the whole situation somewhat uneasy.

"Listen, I know you care about me, but she doesn't scare me. I've encountered beings like her before, when it was just me and Midge, now Twedor. They didn't defeat me or kill me then; nor will she now," assured Tayce, meeting the concerned look in his eyes.

"Tricara said something about a disk chip she's given you with everything about Aemiliyana on?" asked Marc, interested.

"Yes, it was compiled by my great-grandfather. His name was Grandmaster Alexentron Traun. He came from the Empire of Past Traun, where he sent Aemiliyana to trap her for eternity. But she's escaped and, because he is no longer around and I'm a Traun descendant, and the one that's gifted, I'm the one she's decided to wreak revenge on because of what happened to her in the past," explained Tayce.

"Interesting, yet worrying at the same time," replied Marc seriously.

"The disk chip records what happened to my great-grandfather when he and this Witch Queen came face-to-face. Let's see what he's got to say and what we're up against," said Tayce.

Marc crossed and perched on the front of Tayce's desk whilst she crossed to the large DC wall Sight Screen. In the area just below the screen was a disk slot. She slid the disk in so far and it was taken inside to start spinning and loading to play. After a few minons, the screen flashed into life. A man with a slight similarity to Tayce's father, in his mid fifties with a white beard and Telepathian blue eyes, flashed up on-screen wearing the strangest of colourful robes Tayce had ever seen. He was along the lines of her father for build, tall with the same broad shoulders. There was an air of supreme power about him, thought Tayce as she studied him. Dairan entered the DC, coming to a silent pause, looking at who was on-screen, wondering who the being was.

He quietly asked Marc as he turned. "Who's this?" asked Dairan, whispering.

"Someone who's going to help Tayce. His name is Alexentron Traun. He's Tayce's great-grandfather and goes by the title of Grandmaster Alexentron

Traun, from the Empire of Past Traun," explained Marc in discreet whisper as Dairan came to stand beside him.

Dairan nodded understandingly. He perched on the desk next to Marc, watching the man resembling Darius Traun talking on-screen like he was actually lecturing Tayce.

"You have no doubt received this disk chip because either you're a member of the Traun family, somewhere in my future, or the worst has occurred: Witch Queen Aemiliyana has escaped from where I sealed her for what I hoped would be eternity. My sincere apologies. You're about to be the target of the revenge of this vile, evil woman. I pray you're on the powerful side of our Traun ancestral line, with the great ability of power to take on this witch. Let me introduce myself. I'm Alexentron Traun and what you are about to hear is first-hand knowledge of one of the most vile, evil and powerful women in the entire group of wrong-doing beings on our Telepathian worlds. Whether you're a man or a woman, in encountering such a female this information will stand you in good stead for what you are about to take on. Let me explain the various tactics that can be used to survive such an encounter," began Alexentron as the others watched and listened with great interest.

Tayce backed up and sat on the edge of the soffette, continuing to watch what her great-grandfather was explaining, with interest. Alexentron continued on about the many ways in which Witch Queen Aemiliyana might strike. All three sat engrossed in what was being said, watching the screen. Tayce ordered Amal, over the Revelation Channel pickup, to search and store for Twedor and further study reference the ways to tackle Aemiliyana, for retrieval at a later date. Amal confirmed Tayce's request, immediately beginning to pick up certain points, like the way in which the Witch Queen might arrive and how best to use any force to protect Tayce. Both Marc and Dairan decided to leave Tayce to watch the remainder of the disk chip and headed on out into Organisation. After a while, Alexentron Traun finished his briefing, wishing the viewer the best of luck and offering some further advice, in that he or she should not let their guard down when the time came to face Aemiliyana and, above all else, to show no fear as she would use this to her advantage.

With this, the screen went blank and deactivated. The disk chip slid back out. Tayce decided to sit at her desk and start to sift through and study the finer points Amal had collected and transferred to her Porto Compute. She wanted to be prepared for this Aemiliyana when the time came.

After a while the DC doors opened and Dairan sauntered back in. She looked up and was surprised to see the guest he was showing in.

"Emperor Honitonia! This is an honour and somewhat unexpected," said Tayce, surprised, rising to her feet, amazed that he was on board and in her presence as he hardly ever left the empire.

"Relax! No need to stand on ceremony. I had to come and see you and bring you a gift that will protect you against Witch Queen Aemiliyana in your forthcoming encounter with her," began the Emperor.

Tayce walked from the back of her desk and towards the Emperor like an obedient child coming towards its master. He gave her a slight smile to relax her. He could tell she was feeling nervous in his sudden presence, but there was no need for it. He could tell by reading her thoughts, she was feeling great apprehension about the forthcoming encounter she faced. He understood her feelings. Dairan decided to leave the Emperor and Tayce to talk and headed on back out. The doors closed behind him as he went.

The Emperor walked up to Tayce as she came to a halt at a respectable distance from him. He raised his right hand just off her forehead, ordering her to close her eyes. Tayce did as he ordered. A crimson glow appeared in the centre of her forehead, increasing from the size of a small marble to that of a small ball. It pulsated as it increased to the desired size. Tayce tried to stop herself from feeling like she wanted to collapse, as the progress of what the Emperor was doing with his left hand was very powerful in her mind. He took hold of her arm and guided her gently to the soffette, sitting her down. After a few minons, he took his hand away and the crimson glow continued increasing in speed. The doors to the DC opened. Marc entered and was immediately surprised by what greeted him—the Emperor working with Tayce, implanting a power in her mind. Emperor Honitonia turned his head and gestured to Marc to remain silent, which he did, fascinated by what he was witnessing. When it was safe to leave Tayce to endure the latest gift of power as it melted into her mind, the Emperor walked to meet Marc.

"Hello, Commander. I'm Emperor Honitonia. I expect Tayce has told you about the test and the empire and who I am?" said the Emperor, introducing himself politely and in a friendly, educated way.

"It's an honour to meet you, sir. Call me Marc. I've heard quite a bit about what happened at the test and of your Empire. Yes, welcome aboard Amalthea," said Marc in true awe of greeting.

"It's good to be here. Through Tayce's mind I have seen many things and learned quite a bit about this cruiser and team, also what a good friend you are to this young woman. It's something I sense she needs right now with what's approaching her," replied the Emperor gently.

He was dressed all in white satinex—a white three-quarter-length jacket with stand-up collar, close-fitting trousers—and low-heeled boots of grey leatherex. Marc thought to himself that for a powerful ruling emperor he wasn't quite what he expected. There was nothing regal about him, and his attire was just like that of a high-ranked officer. He expected him to be in white robes. Also, as he studied him, he noticed he wasn't a strong-looking man—quite the reverse—and he was pale. He was not like any emperor he'd encountered before in his career so far. They always seemed to be elaborately dressed and rotund in build. But he guessed he could put Emperor Honitonia on a different list. The Emperor smiled slightly to himself at Marc's thoughts about him, as he read Marc's mind. Both stood talking about Tayce and the forthcoming threat from Aemiliyana. Behind them the ability the Emperor had bestowed on Tayce completed in joining her abilities. She began to come back to consciousness from the completed task. She opened her eyes.

"Am I finished with what you had to do?" asked Tayce, wondering if there was more, as she found herself feeling slightly drained.

"Yes, the task is complete. You now have the ability to match the likes of Aemiliyana. You won't feel intimidated when she strikes, but it will only last until you have placed her back where she belongs. I will be watching over you during the encounter. Take care, Tayce," he advised.

With this, the Emperor nodded in a goodbye gesture to Marc, then vanished in a blinding blue light from the DC. Marc shook his head in amazement, then crossed to where Tayce stood. He began announcing that for the time being she would be guarded by Twedor at all times and during the night hourons her quarters would be protected by the onboard alarm system until the Aemiliyana incident was over. Tayce, on this, assured him she could more than handle Aemiliyana now. There was no need for extra security procedures. Marc put his hands on her slim shoulders, looking concernedly at her like any true friend would.

"I don't want you to be caught off guard by that evil witch and for you to be hurt by her powers. Remember I'm the one your father's going to blame if she takes you by surprise and you end up dead," said Marc with meaning in his voice.

"Will you stop worrying! No matter where I am, I'll be ready for the likes of her and whatever powerful tricks she might pull," promised Tayce in a stern reply.

Even though she was now more than capable of taking on Aemiliyana, she was still a little uneasy deep down as to what the Witch Queen might do to commence her strike of revenge against her, when she showed up. She broke from Marc's hold and began walking over to the entrance, pushing all thoughts of Aemiliyana to the back of her mind for the time being—or at least until the encounter occurred between the two of them. The moment she walked out into Organisation, she began ordering Kelly to resume their voyage course, if she hadn't already done so. Dairan leant close to her as she came to a pause in the middle of Organisation.

"Course is already taken care of," he assured discreetly.

Tayce looked over to the empty communications position, wondering why Nick Berenger wasn't at his new duty post. Twedor entered Organisation alone. Tayce looked at him questioningly, wondering if when Nick had gone to apologise to Sallen it had all gone wrong. Twedor looked up at Tayce, seeing she was looking at him in a questioning way.

"Where's Nick, Twedor?" asked Tayce concerned. "I left him in your care."

"It's all right—he's making peace with Sallen, as you suggested. He'll be here soon," promised Twedor.

This annoyed Tayce. She didn't mean for Nick to spend any length of time he liked talking with Sallen. She meant for him to apologise and be on duty as soon as possible. Communications needed manning. What did he think he was doing? Did he think duty aboard Amalthea was to be taken lightly? That he could just show up when he felt like it? She crossed to Craig.

"Tell Nick his communications duty is waiting—it started a while ago," ordered Tayce.

"Right!" replied Craig. He could see Tayce was far from pleased, but she had a right to be—she was chief.

He carried out her request. He could see she was not impressed by Nick's failing to turn up for duty. Dairan crossed to Deluca to see how she was getting on in working hard on trying to sort out the information Lance had left her to sort out whilst he went for a break. Upon approach, he could see she was struggling, so offered to help, much to her relief. She listened as he explained. Dairan, whilst Deluca did what he told her, glanced at Tayce and could see she didn't need the lack of urgency to report for duty from Nick Berenger on top of the threat of Aemiliyana arriving at any moment. He wondered how long it would be before this Witch Queen would make her appearance. He guessed none of them knew for sure. All he hoped was that Tayce would win through against the evil female.

Quite suddenly, as Tayce stood looking through the sight port into the Universe, she heard the following words: *"I'm coming, Traun. Revenge will be mine."*

15. Influential Forces on Maldigri

It had been almost seven dayons since Tayce first learnt of Witch Queen Aemiliyana and her wish for revenge for being locked by Grandmaster Alexentron Traun in the Empire of Past Traun. The thought of what might occur was constantly surfacing during her quiet moments of thought. That the Witch Queen could strike at any cencron. Nick Berenger, the new replacement communications chief, was becoming a good team member, mixing in both on- and off-duty tasks and pursuits on board. He'd buried the past with Sallen and was slowly becoming friends with her. It was leisure time aboard. Tayce was sat in the Leisure Centre, a room off the Refreshment Centre, watching *Trial Houron*, a programme on criminal trials on the centre's vast-sized screen, transmitted from the Enlopedian News and Vision Complex. Present was Lance, Dairan, Treketa, Twedor and Craig, each following the current trial with great interest. Without warning in big bold white letters across the centre of the screen flashed the words 'URGENT NEWS BULLETIN'. Everyone looked at each other, wondering what was wrong. A young pretty dark-haired announcer began reporting.

"Latest news just in: teacher of gifted children and other students on Enlopedia, Empress Tricara has gone missing during a solo flight by Transpo Launch, en route to the planet Trinot for a seminar. There's a report of an explosion occurring in the vicinity of the last known coordinates of the Empress's Launch. The news I'm receiving states it's disappeared from the tracking scanner. It's believed the Empress has perished. That's all the news I'm receiving at the current time," said the young announcer, holding her hand on her communications earpiece, fighting back the tears as she knew of Tricara.

The screen returned to the *Trial Houron* programme. Tayce rose to her feet, horrified and upset. Someone or something had done away with her friend. But something didn't feel right, she thought. She couldn't stay in the centre. Her mind began telling her there had to be more. This was just too cut and dry. Tricara was very tight regarding her security, especially after the incident on voyage one, regarding Trinot. Her thoughts became conflicting. One minon her mind was saying yes, it was possible Tricara had perished, then the next she found herself disagreeing with that thought altogether. She briskly hurried on out of the centre. Dairan could see she wasn't thinking straight and hurried after her. He knew what Empress Tricara meant to her. Treketa followed on as well, in urgency, not just as Tayce's friend, but as her medic/nurse, worried how the shock would come out in her as she was already showing signs of stress, judging by the way she'd rushed from the centre. Dairan soon found Tayce outside, staring at the millions of stars through the full-length sight port. She lowered her head into her hands, crying over the thought that her friend had perished, as she couldn't reach her with her thought transference. He gently approached her and turned her to face him. She looked at him with tears in her eyes and a tear-stained face. He pulled her towards him into a comforting hug as she broke down on his shoulder.

In between the sobs, she said, "I refuse to believe it's true. Tricara can't be gone—I'd feel it if she was—but I can't reach her. There's a blank where I should hear her answer me, see her face. Oh, Dairan," said Tayce, trying to make some sense of what was happening and why she wasn't receiving a reply from her gifted friend.

"Tayce, are you all right? They say there will be more news later," said Treketa in a gentle, caring tone.

"Something is telling me Tricara didn't perish in that mysterious explosion. A strange feeling washed over me as the announcer made her announcement. I can't explain it," she replied, turning in Dairan's gentle hold, confused by her conflicting thoughts.

"You mean you feel the Empress was trying to contact you in some way?" asked Treketa, interested.

"Do you think it is possible Tricara could have been telling you all was not what it seemed just before the explosion, that it was a cover-up for something else?" asked Dairan, trying to help Tayce make some sense of what she felt.

"I don't know. Maybe. I can't work it out. There's something—what, I just don't know," replied Tayce, breaking away from him.

"What do you want to do?" he replied, studying her.

"I want to find out if, as you say, it's an elaborate cover-up, if her Launch didn't explode and she's on a planet nearby injured somewhere. Whatever has happened, I want to know," replied Tayce firmly. She didn't want to think of the worst.

She began away, heading back to the Leisure Centre. Upon entering, she announced all leisure time had been temporarily suspended. She then ordered Lance to find the route from Enlopedia Tricara could have taken to Trinot. He nodded understandingly and ran on out, heading briskly towards Level 1, Organisation. Treketa began, saying that if they eventually found the Empress she might need medical treatment, So she'd go and inform Donaldo. He'd need to be prepared for a possible emergency. Tayce agreed. She suggested to Dairan and Craig they all head back to Organisation. Tayce, Craig and Dairan began on out of the leisure part of the Refreshments Centre, back to Organisation with the notion of finding out if Empress Tricara was alive somewhere. Twedor followed, doing his own thought processing on the idea of whether Tricara was alive or dead.

* * *

Later in the DC the Telelinkphone sounded on the desktop. Tayce picked it up and placed it to her right ear. Nick informed her the call to her father was online and he was ready to talk to her from his chambers on Enlopedia. Her father's voice soon came through and she noticed he too was upset from what had unfolded. She decided to tell him of her plan.

"Father, I don't believe Tricara is dead. I don't know how, but something tells me she's alive somewhere, that the explosion was a cover-up to make us think she's no longer alive. I didn't sense any sudden break between us, as i would have if she'd died. We've always had a certain communicating bond between us. We've decided to try and trace her journey to find out if she crashed on some planet near to where the explosion occurred. Sometimes a tracking signal can fail at the most inopportune moment. Maybe that's what happened with Tricara," confided Tayce.

Darius thought for a few minons. He also wanted to think what had happened to Empress Tricara had all been some elaborate set-up, but he also wondered if Tayce was just refusing to believe their family friend and her teacher of abilities had perished.

"All right, go ahead, but keep me informed of what you find," expressed Darius. He couldn't see what harm it would do—they'd be sure one way or another of whether Empress Tricara was alive or dead, and he felt Tayce had to do it to clear the uncertainty she was feeling once and for all.

"Let's hope it's Tricara and she's alive," replied Tayce optimistically.

"Good luck with the search," replied Darius with a fatherly smile, wondering if she was setting herself up for a fall.

Tayce smiled back, glad her father was looking at what had happened to Tricara with the same idea as she was. Communication ceased. Tayce sat in thought for a few minons, thinking about Tricara. Marc entered the DC as Dairan suggested he go and tell Kelly the Admiral had given his go-ahead for the search. Tayce nodded in agreement. Marc came to a pause, ready to listen.

"What's happening?" asked Marc, concerned and greatly interested. "Kelly said something about a news report stating Empress Tricara is missing presumed dead, and that there was some kind of explosion to confirm it."

"It appears she was heading to another of her regular seminars on Trinot, and en route she disappeared from tracking under the Enlopedia tracking security trace and there was an explosion at the same time she disappeared off the signal. It appears both Tricara and the Transpo Launch have vanished, but, in spite of my link with her, I can't feel she's alive or dead. I don't know why, but something wants me to find out for sure whether she is alive or not," explained Tayce seriously.

"Count me in. What are your plans?" he asked, interested. The Empress had always been fair with him.

"I've put into motion the tracing of her journey. Maybe we can find the planet near to the area she vanished. There's got to be some kind of answer to what really unfolded at the time of that explosion—if it's a cover-up of some kind and why and who's done it?" said Tayce confidingly.

Marc hit the doors' mechanism panel and the doors drew closed, sealing them off from the busy Organisation team. He walked around the desk and came to a stand beside Tayce, who was now stood looking out of the full-length sight port, still trying silently to contact Empress Tricara through thought transference. He studied her—he knew how she felt. Empress Tricara was an exceptional woman and dear friend to both of them. He took hold of Tayce by the shoulders and turned her to face him.

"I know you don't want to believe the inevitable, but you have to accept that what has been broadcast may be true. Don't get me wrong, I want to believe she's alive somewhere too. I and the team will do our utmost to find her, I promise you," he said, softly looking at her.

"I couldn't ask for anything else. Thank you," she said in soft reply.

He pulled her into a warm reassuring hug, holding her for a few minons. Tayce was glad to feel his warmth and gentleness at a time when she needed it most. Marc realised the situation with the Empress was the last thing she wanted with the threat of Aemiliyana hanging over her. He released her gently, looking down at her in a caring way, with a reassuring smile, just like a brother would a sister. She looked back, her beautiful Telepathian blue eyes sparkling.

"Why is it you're always here when I need you most?" she began casually.

"That's what friends are for, and you've been there for me when I needed help most. I'll always be here when you need me. Your father would probably kill me if I wasn't," he assured, joking.

Both laughed.

The intercom on Tayce's desktop sounded—three electronic sounds. She turned, reaching over and pressing the answer button. Lance's voice came through, suggesting she go out into Organisation. He might have found something which seemed to resemble a crashed Transpo Launch, on a scan of the planet nearest to where the Empress was supposed to have disappeared. Also, he'd picked up a signal that was something like a distress homing beacon. On this, both Marc and Tayce exchanged hopeful glances then hurried over to the entrance. Marc hit the doors' mechanism panel and the doors began to open. As soon as they opened enough he hurried out followed by Tayce, across to Lance at his position. Lance pointed to the planet on his research screen as they paused and gave their full interest.

"The planet is Maldigri. It's about two milons from where the Transpo Launch is supposed to have exploded and disappeared off the tracking screen. The signal started strong and suddenly. It happened the moment I long-range-scanned the planet nearest the orbit the launch disappeared in, but it's fading as we speak," explained Lance, looking from Marc to Tayce then back to the screen.

"You don't think there's a chance it could be coming from anything other than a Transpo Launch?" asked Tayce, wondering.

On this, Lance double-checked, then confirmed it was emitting from a Transpo Launch, which seemed to be the only kind of signal on the planet surface that could be easily read. For some strange reason Tayce found she was feeling a sudden strong connection with Maldigri, other than that they crashed there on their first voyage.

"Didn't we crash-land there last voyage?" spoke up Marc, thinking.

"Yes!" replied Lance, thinking back.

"Check the orbit around Maldigri. Make sure there's no unwanted activity waiting for us, then place a quick route with Amal for travelling there, to the surface. We're going in at first light. I want to find out one way or the other if Tricara is alive or dead down on the surface," said Tayce commandingly.

She placed Marc in command, then advised him to keep in Wristlink contact. If anything was found waiting in orbit, she wanted to know. Marc agreed with a nod. Tayce continued to walk on out of Organisation, heading off down the corridor in thought. She was quickly joined by Dairan and Twedor. Dairan came to a pause beside her, asking about Maldigri. He was interested to know what happened in the last voyage. Tayce began, saying that Amalthea One had crash-landed on the surface due to a strange phenomenon forcing them out of space. She continued more fully about what happened, as they progressed down the corridor. Dairan found himself becoming more interested by the minon as they went. But, for Tayce, Tom flashed in her mind in a memory of when they were on Maldigri and he'd kissed her in the old ruins. 'It was a nice memory,' she thought.

* * *

Treketa walked into the MLC as the doors parted in front of her. Donaldo looked up from studying his notes. He could see by the look on his beautiful partner's face that something was on her mind. He studied her in a questioning way as she walked over.

"What's wrong—you look concerned about something?" he asked gently.

"It's the Empress—she's gone missing en route to a seminar on Trinot. They say there was an explosion, so everyone assumes she's dead, except Tayce. She feels otherwise," she explained, sitting down on the nearby chrome and black leatherex stool.

"Tricara! Missing? Are you sure?" asked Donaldo, almost speechless in disbelief.

"Yes, that's what the news said, and Tayce, because she has a special link with the Empress, feels she isn't dead and wants us ready for a possible emergency in case the Empress is found alive but injured. All I can say is let's hope the hunch Tayce has is true, for her sake," said Treketa, worried for Tayce.

"I agree. Well, Tayce has asked us to be ready when the time comes and that's what we'll be. We've changed course," said Donaldo, glancing out through one of the sight ports, noticing as much.

"Perhaps the course is to bring us in line to find the location of the Empress," replied Treketa, looking out, noticing also.

"Poor Tayce, as if she doesn't have enough to worry about right now with the threat of this Aemiliyana showing up without warning. This isn't good for her health," said Donaldo, concerned.

"You're right. I was worried when she got the announcement about the Empress. She kind of reacted to the news badly, until Dairan went after her to comfort her," replied Treketa, thinking back.

As the cruiser's main medical man and friend to Tayce, Donaldo was worried for her and what the two situations might do to her health, through stress. Treketa was as concerned as Donaldo, considering Tayce was prone to exhaustion and this could drain her. She knew how much the Empress meant to Tayce and could understand her concern as, despite what happened at the end of the first voyage, when she was mistaken for the Empress, she herself liked her. She realised that when the incident had occurred she had been very hard on her, but it was a situation she wouldn't want to find herself in ever again. Tom flashed into Treketa's mind. There were dayons when she still missed him, after his demise on the first voyage. She found herself wishing he hadn't been killed. Donaldo brought her back to the present with a quick kiss on the cheek, when passing. He suggested they get the Emergency Medical Kits ready, so when they were called they'd be ready to go. With this, she did just as he suggested. But her thoughts were on Tom. It made her wonder whether by some strange phenomenal way he would return in the future.

* * *

On the paradise world of Maldigri it was daylight hourons. Deep in a massive area of trees and bushes was the badly damaged Transpo Launch belonging to Empress Tricara. The front glassene shield was cracked in a pattern resembling a spider's web. Inside was a male pilot, slumped forward in the pilot seat, even though it was thought Empress Tricara had flown solo on this trip as she was qualified to do so. It didn't seem like it after all. The Empress was lying slumped back with her head on one side in the passenger seat. She too was unconscious. Her generally neat swept-up brown hair was dishevelled, with strands rested over her beautiful face. Blood slowly trickled from her temple down her left cheek, where she'd been struck by falling bits of the interior upon crashing. At the corner of her delicate perfectly shaped lips was a drop of blood, which was setting. Her perfect make-up was slightly smudged, but this was the least of her worries should she regain consciousness. Something wasn't right. Tricara had the inner ability to heal herself and she should have been showing signs of regaining consciousness within an houron of crashing on the surface. A cool breeze blew in through one of the front glassene cracks in the shield and lightly blew her hair.

Outside, on a high-up distant part of the landscape, a white satinex-robed female in her mid forties stood bathed in great illuminating brilliance, smiling in an evil, pleased way. She was exceptionally beautiful in every way, showing she was a powerful witch of the highest galactic order. Without warning she suddenly burst out laughing in a triumphant, callous way, pleased she'd accomplished her perfect trap to bring Tayce Traun, great-granddaughter of Alexentron Traun, to the present surroundings. This white-satinex-attired beauty was none other than Witch Queen Aemiliyana. She had just made her second strike towards achieving her confrontation with Tayce.

* * *

Night hourons. Amalthea was less than a couple of hourons from the once remembered planetary world of Maldigri. Remembered for all the wrong reasons, it was where the first Amalthean cruiser had been forced out of space by a somewhat controlling space phenomenon, which sent fireballs towards the cruiser.

In Tayce's quarters, sleep was the last thing on her mind. She checked the clasp on the neckline of her all-in-one Quests suit. Twedor was nearby in the Living Area, tapping his metlon foot in silent disapproval of what his mistress was thinking of doing. He also didn't like the orders she'd given him—to cover her tracks on what she was about to do. It was against all he stood for, in protecting her. He should be with her in this dangerous and downright stupid feat she was about to attempt. Not remaining on the cruiser, whilst she was putting her life at risk in going on ahead of the team to Maldigri. It infuriated him to the point where he could blow something vital because he couldn't do the job he was suppose to do, and that was protect her. Tayce had given him the order to be silent about her leaving the cruiser without assistance. But he figured he'd wait till she'd gone then disobey that order by telling someone as soon as possible about what she was doing, as it was too dangerous not to.

Tayce glanced at her Wristlink time display, thinking to herself she had to go. In an houron or so it would be first light and duty would commence for another dayon. She hadn't realised it, but it had taken the best part of four hourons to prepare for the journey to Maldigri. Tom suddenly flashed into her mind and she could hear him saying didn't she think it would be safer to wait until first light, when the Quest would start properly? She sighed and wished he wouldn't remind her that what she was attempting was downright stupid, but she wanted to be the first person on the planet surface, to discover whether her friend was alive or dead. It was only an houron—what harm could it do? she wondered. The rest would be along later for the Quest. If she could speed up the process of getting help to the crashed Transpo Launch and Empress Tricara, then so be it. She was unaware that her friend was not alone where she had crash-landed. Plans had been put in place to return the Transpo Launch via the tractor beam to the Flight Hangar Bay for transporting back to Enlopedia, so if she could cut down the time, all well and good. Tayce couldn't shake her uneasy feeling of uncertainty about whether Tricara was alive or dead. It had crossed her thoughts whether Aemiliyana had had something to do with what had happened, and the more she began to think of the possibility, the more it plagued her thoughts that the evil bitch could possibly be lying in wait for her on Maldigri. Well, if she was, she was in for a hell of a fight, she thought.

"It's time to go. Remember what I asked you, Twedor," she said commandingly.

"I wish you would take me with you. I don't like you attempting this alone—it's too dangerous," said Twedor, sounding far from pleased at what his mistress was going to do.

"I'll be fine," she replied, heading towards the entrance.

The doors drew apart. She slipped out into a dimly lit night-hourons corridor, leaving behind a disappointed Twedor standing in the centre of the Living Area as the doors closed behind her. As she made her way up the corridor, all that could be heard was the sound of the cruiser's engines turning over smoothly at cruise warp 5—744,000 milons a cencron. She was beginning to relax, as she figured she had successfully sneaked away from the team's quarters, where they were all in night-hourons sleep, and she was going to make it off the cruiser without being detected. Without warning a hand came out of nowhere in the darkness on the way, grabbing hold of her arm. She nearly flipped, thinking an intruder had boarded. She sailed across the corridor and into the hold of the person who had grabbed her. As she impacted, she looked up hesitantly and found herself looking into Dairan's warm, brown questioning eyes. He looked down at her, then eyed her up and down, looking especially at her state of dress.

"Going somewhere?" he plainly asked in a near whisper.

"Why aren't you in your quarters like everyone else?" she demanded, far from pleased that he was standing in the way of her plan.

"Where do you think you're off to dressed like that at this houron? Tell me, Tayce." He returned the demand, ignoring her question. He was suspicious that she was going to do something rash.

"I knew we would be making a start at first light on going down to Maldigri, so I thought I would make an early start with the final preparations," replied Tayce, hoping she'd fooled him into thinking differently to what she really had in mind.

"So you're thinking of hanging around in this get-up for the next houron—interesting you've never done it before," he said giving her a look as much to say he was far from believing what she was telling him.

Tayce had no idea Twedor had ignored the request she'd given him and informed Dairan of what she was attempting. He was enjoying hearing her good effort at making up a story to cover up what she was truly going to do, but he wasn't buying it. He didn't take his eyes from hers, almost waiting for her to tell him the real reason—her true plans—and he knew she wouldn't be able to hold out on telling him the truth. Tayce found it downright uncomfortable the way he was making her feel. Why was it, one look in those brown eyes of his and there was no way she could resist caving in and telling the truth?

"All right, you win. If you must know, I'm going down to Maldigri," she announced without a further word, much to his raised-eyed surprise.

"I'm coming with you. There's no way you're going alone with the threat of that Witch Queen hanging above your head," he said firmly.

"Well, considering you're already dressed in your Quest suit too, I can't say no, can I? How come you're dressed like you are anyway?" asked Tayce, finding it somewhat suspicious.

"Twedor told me what you had planned when you'd left your quarters," replied Dairan casually, seeing a taken-aback look cross Tayce's beautiful features, which said it all.

"I asked him not to say anything, that little snitch!" said Tayce, far from pleased.

"Talking about me, Tayce? I'm not letting you go alone—this goes against my principles to let you walk into danger," said Twedor, coming up behind her, hearing what she'd just called him.

"I gave you an order, Twedor, and you disobeyed it…" began Tayce, looking down at him and speaking in an angry whisper.

"Before you're too hard on him, it was my turn to watch your quarters, remember, in case Aemiliyana showed up? But now I'm here, I'm volunteering to go with you. After all, I'm already dressed and, what's more, I'm not going to let you attempt this alone," he pointed out to make her see sense.

"Oh, very well, you can come too, Twedor. Let's go before we wake up the rest of the team. I've got to pick up an Emergency Medical Kit en route," said Tayce as they began moving on.

"You go on and collect the kit; I'll take Twedor and meet you in the Flight Hangar Bay," replied Dairan.

Tayce agreed. They went their separate ways at the Level Steps. Tayce headed for the MLC on Level 2, leaving Dairan to continue on to the Flight Hangar Bay, talking with Twedor as he went. Tayce smiled to herself. She could hear Dairan and Twedor talking as they walked away about how she thought she was going to get away with going on ahead to Maldigri. At the top of the Level Steps, a while later, on Level 2 Tayce lightly ran along to the MLC. Upon reaching the entrance, she paused as the overhead sensor picked up her presence and the doors automatically opened before her. They'd hardly parted when she slid inside and hurried around, looking for Treketa's Emergency Medical Kit. On finding it prepared for going down to Maldigri, she reached for it, closing the white-and-blue lid, and headed back out to the entrance with it in her hand. As the doors opened before her, she quickly ran through and back along Level 2 to the Level Steps. Once back on Level 3, she quietly walked up the corridor, so the kit in her hand wouldn't make any noise, and entered into the Flight Hangar Bay.

Dairan was on board the Quest 3 with Twedor. He'd placed two Slazers into the onboard charger, ready in case they were needed on the Maldigrian surface. He'd also packed a pack of PolloAld bombs in case they were also needed. There was no telling what was lying in wait when they arrived on the surface—especially the threat of Aemiliyana arriving at any moment. He turned upon hearing footsteps approaching, glad it was Tayce. He'd wondered if any of the others had been contacted by Amal and informed of what they were attempting. He looked and saw the Emergency Medical Kit. As Tayce came to a pause, he took the kit from her and stored it safely as she climbed aboard. Without thought, Dairan started to laugh.

"What's so funny?" asked Tayce, giving him a puzzled look, wondering why he was laughing.

"I was just thinking of Donaldo's face in roughly an houron's time, when he discovers Treketa's Emergency Medical Kit has mysteriously vanished during the night hourons," he replied.

"Ha ha! Let's go," said Tayce, seeing the picture of Donaldo's face in her mind, puzzled.

Soon the entrance closed on the Quest 3. Before Dairan and Tayce, the large Flight Hangar Bay doors drew apart in front of them. Tayce contacted Amal, requesting immediate clearance for departure and ordering her not to inform Commander Dayatso where they'd gone until they'd landed on Maldigri. Dairan waited until the hangar-bay doors had drawn back on either side of the bay, into the wall, then expertly put the actions in place to leave Amalthea. The engines soon roared into life and the Quest 3 shuttle/fighter lifted off the bay landing area and headed straight out into the Universe at great speed under Dairan's control towards Maldigri.

* * *

It was around 0900 hourons the same dayon. The Quest team that were going to Maldigri were waiting in the DC for Tayce and Dairan, totally unaware that Tayce had left the cruiser in the company of Dairan and taken a Quest to Maldigri already. Marc walked into the DC, wondering why everyone was standing around looking lost. Glancing around the members present, he noticed not only was Tayce not present, but neither was Dairan or Twedor. He had a hunch and didn't like it. He hoped he was wrong.

"Amal, where are Tayce, Twedor and Dairan?" demanded Marc with a sigh.

There was a long pause before Amal came back. This only fuelled Marc's suspicions that something wasn't right. He remembered the night hourons before: when he left Tayce at her quarters doors she had something on her mind. He hoped she hadn't done anything stupid, like gone on ahead of them to Maldigri.

Amal came back: "I can inform you, Commander, a Quest 3 left the Flight Hangar Bay earlier this mornet. Aboard were Captain Traun, Lieutenant Commander Loring and Twedor. They were bound for Maldigri," informed Amal.

"Damn it! I had a feeling she'd try something like this…" began Marc angrily.

"That explains where my missing Emergency Medical Kit disappeared to," spoke up Donaldo, glad to know at least it hadn't mysteriously disappeared during the night hourons. But he didn't like the fact Tayce had taken it without leaving so much as a note.

Marc sighed. He was far from pleased at Tayce's irresponsible and downright stupid behaviour. He suggested they all get going. The Quest to Maldigri was under his lead. Briefing was cancelled and they needed to be on the surface—like then. The Quest team rose to their feet and hurried on after Marc. He informed Lance he was in charge of Organisation until he returned, as he walked out through Organisation.

"Good luck," he called after Marc as he walked from the centre.

Outside in the corridor Marc walked along with Donaldo. Both felt angry at Tayce, Marc because she'd deliberately gone ahead and put herself in what could be a dangerous situation, and Donaldo for the fact she'd removed one of the Emergency Medical Kits without permission. Marc glanced at him, seeing he was angry. He confided that it was a good thing Dairan and Twedor had gone with Tayce to Maldigri as at least she had some kind of protection should anything dangerous unfold. Donaldo nodded in total agreement. The Quest team were almost running to get to the Quest 3, to leave for the Maldigrian surface, considering what had unfolded in the last hourons.

* * *

Down on Maldigri, the Quest 3 had found a place to set down. The entrance had opened and Dairan was the first out with a Pollomoss handgun, fully charged.

Checking their immediate surroundings, he glanced about in the early mornet sunshine for anything that might be considered suspicious. Everything looked reasonably natural, nothing out of place that could be considered a threat. But he wasn't going to let his guard drop, he thought. He headed back to the entrance and took out the Emergency Medical Kit from the passenger section and waited as Tayce and Twedor exited the interior. Already the atmospheric temperature was growing increasingly warm. But Tayce remembered what the weather was like on Maldigri and how it could change so quickly. There were the familiar sounds of the Maldigrian paradise. Birds of different species and sizes, from the smallest to the size of an earth eagle, soaring high above and swooping in to land on trees and bushes, making their singing sounds. Dairan found the sun was too brilliant to look normally about in, so reached into the left pocket of his jacket and pulled out his own personal pair of sunlight-sensitive self-polarising protection eye shields, made specially for blocking out the harmful glare of the strong sunlight. He turned, advising Tayce to do the same. Twedor adjusted his sight-circuit light receivers to cancel out the harmful glare. He began to run a scan of the area in search of the crashed Transpo Launch, which the Quest 3 had picked up on scan as it was coming into land. Tayce's thoughts turned to Tom for a few minons, as Maldigri was where they'd shared a Quest together when he was alive. She stood looking around at the trees and the straw-coloured grass, in thought. Suddenly she felt a cold, evil feeling, as if something or someone was watching them. A sudden unnerving shiver rushed through her. The feeling was one that could be classed as extremely threatening and very powerful. One name fell into Tayce's thoughts: Aemiliyana! Was she somehow in their current surroundings, watching her, waiting for the right moment to strike for the first time? Tayce's face took on a somewhat uneasy look. Dairan turned, noticing as much.

"What is it? What are you sensing?" he asked softly.

"Something extremely powerful—it's watching us. I can feel it—it's giving me the creeps," whispered Tayce in case they were being watched.

"Found the Transpo Launch—it's about half a milon in that direction," said Twedor, pointing to the left.

"Let's go. I don't want to be on this planet any longer than we need to. It doesn't feel right—it feels different to when I and the team were here last time. There's a threatening uneasiness hanging in the air and it seems to be getting stronger by the minon," said Tayce, glancing around once more to see if she could see anything suspicious.

Dairan securely locked the Quest 3 and they set off on in the direction Twedor had pointed to. The surface underfoot was stony with the odd patch of uneven grass that nearly made Tayce and Dairan trip if they weren't careful. They both passed bushes with beautiful blooms in various shades of pastel and deep colours. Some were scented. Dairan began, saying that it was like walking through the equivalent of a botanical garden with the various species. He also added it was like earth before the pollution time occurred. Tayce agreed. She remembered studying earth during her schooling yearons on Traun. Twedor was finding the surface hard on his underfoot sensors and didn't much care for the fact. But he said nothing, as he'd insisted he go along on the Quest to protect Tayce.

* * *

Tayce had every reason to feel uneasy about the atmosphere on Maldigri. As she, Dairan and Twedor were searching for the Transpo Launch, Witch Queen Aemiliyana was watching them from her powerful space fortress in orbit above the planet, undetectable to scanning devices, even from Amalthea. She powerfully laughed at her successful actions over enticing the great-granddaughter of Alexentron Traun into a trap for the revenge she sought. She elegantly crossed to her obedient slave, in her white satinex gown that had a long train and slid on the white marblex floor behind her as she walked. She soon paused beside him. He was in his mid twenties and dressed in a white hard-wearing baggy uniform. He paid immediate attention to her powerful presence. 'Adarrent' was the name printed on his lapel badge. He looked like he had been kept down at heel most of his life and dared not speak unless spoken to.

"Adarrent!" she exclaimed with her commanding powerful voice.

"Yes, Your Highness," he replied obediently in a soft voice, as if he was somehow afraid of her.

"Fetch me the Traun girl. I want her here before me. Now!" she snapped in arrogant tone of order.

With her order cast, she tossed back her shoulder-length ginger curly hair and gave a look that conveyed she was looking forward to coming face-to-face with the great-granddaughter of the being who had locked her in the Empire of Past Traun before her powers fully matured. A smug, wicked smile crossed her beautiful yet treacherous features and a glint of dark evilness shone in her dark eyes.

"Adarrent, before you go, use your ability to change form if you have to. If you fail to bring me the Traun girl, you know what the punishment will be," she said after him.

He nodded, then continued on out through the large cream arch, off to do as his queen ordered. He knew if he didn't return with what Aemiliyana wanted, it would be the worst form of torture for him and she would do it by draining every vessel of his body, slowly until death. Aemiliyana was a thin but tall, shapely woman with flawless beauty. She was everything a Witch Queen should be, from the dark, evil side of the Empire of Honitonia. She turned at the conjured image of Tayce, Dairan and Twedor, progressing towards finding Empress Tricara. She knew time was on her side in meeting Alexentron Traun's great-granddaughter. She thought of the fact that the long-awaited revenge would soon be hers.

* * *

Tayce and Dairan reached the crash site of the Transpo Launch. Twedor came to a halt, glad the stones were not making his walking hazardous any longer. The whole Transpo Launch was securely embedded in a large group of pink-bloom-type bushes. Dairan tried to look for a way in, though he felt it was impossible. Behind Tayce and Twedor, the Quest 3 from Amalthea suddenly came out of the presently clear sky and in to land. Tayce turned, wondering what kind of reception she was going to get, considering her act of leaving ahead of time to come to the planet surface—especially from Marc. No sooner had the Quest 3 landed and the entrance had opened than Marc was out and striding towards her with a far from pleased look on his face. Upon coming to a near pause, he gave her a look that showed his total disapproval of her heroic act of stupidity. He then, after a few minons, at Dairan's request helped him find a way to reach the Transpo Launch. Twedor helped too as he was able to bend through small openings. Donaldo looked at Tayce, also far from pleased, but she ignored him. She knew what he was getting at—the taking of the Emergency Medical Kit without a message to reveal the fact she'd taken it. There had been little time to leave such a message, but he wasn't going to let her get away with what she'd done.

"Next time you feel like borrowing one of my kits, please leave a message on my Porto Compute."

Tayce ignored him. Her interest was solely on the men of her team and watching them try and find a way in. Just as Marc ventured in, Empress Tricara came towards him, covered in the small pink petals that had come from the blooms on the nearby bushes. Her normally neat hair was dishevelled, out of place. As Marc backed up and helped her out into the open, he called to the others outside to say he'd found her. She looked tired and shaken and far from the normal calm, serene empress she generally was, as she came out into the open.

"Oh, Tricara, thank God you're safe. I knew you didn't perish in that explosion," said Tayce as she rushed forth to give her friend a hug.

"What explosion? I'm fine. It's a good job you're gifted. I could have been here for eternity. Donaldo Jaran, my pilot—he's been badly hurt. I can't understand what happened—one moment we were both en route to the seminar, the next we were nosediving towards this planet. It was as if something or someone plucked us right out of space and flung us here. It baffles me," said Tricara in disbelief at what had happened.

"The news service reported there was an explosion and you had disappeared off the tracking system, and everyone presumed you were dead," expressed Treketa.

"Really?" replied Tricara, surprised.

"Come and sit over here and let Treketa check your injuries," said Tayce, guiding Tricara over to some nearby rocks that were high enough to sit on. Tricara, with the guidance of Tayce, walked over and sat down. Treketa took her Emergency Medical Kit, which Tayce had already brought down earlier, and proceeded in checking the cuts Tricara still hadn't healed with her inner healing power.

"I still can't believe how the accident happened. It wasn't Jaran's fault. He's one of Chief Barnford's elite pilots. He's an expert in avoiding space dangers. Chief Barnford assigned him to me for that very reason," expressed Tricara as Treketa listened.

"I'm quite sure all will be revealed," said Treketa softly as she attended to the wounds.

"Jaran is not to blame—I want to make that quite clear. It was as if some kind of force took the controls away from him. He fought to hold on," persisted Tricara, this aspect of the crash bothering her.

Tayce and Treketa exchanged surprised looks, but said nothing. They were wondering if it was Witch Queen Aemiliyana after all. Donaldo, a few minons later, emerged from the Transpo Launch with Jaran on a Hover Trolley. Treketa, once she'd finished treating Tricara, crossed and immediately draped a medical heat-sealant blanket over the pilot to keep any body heat in. Tayce glanced at Jaran. She remembered him as one of Jan's best pilots. He was in his mid forties and considered very experienced in his flight capabilities. Donaldo operated the Hover Trolley, taking it off towards the Quest 3 to place Jaran on board and prepare him for returning to Amalthea. Treketa crossed back to the Empress and draped a heat-sealant blanket about her shoulders whilst Aldonica and Nick stood by, their Pollomoss handguns primed in case any trouble materialised. Marc began, saying that maybe they should leave their current surroundings and head back to the cruiser, considering Jaran's injuries and Tricara's condition. Tayce agreed, but suggested to his surprise he go on without her. Marc looked at her questioningly, wondering why she wasn't going with everyone else. He began ordering the other team members to head back to the Quest. Empress Tricara with Treketa's kind support walked over to the Quest followed by Aldonica and Nick. Marc looked at Tayce again, waiting for her explanation of why she wasn't going with everyone else.

"You're not coming with us—why?" he asked, curious and to the point.

"No, I'll head back with Dairan and Twedor," she replied.

Marc sighed, then walked on and, upon reaching the entrance to the Quest he'd travelled down in, called out to Dairan to take care of Tayce and stay alert.

Dairan gave a wave of acknowledgement. Marc boarded and the entrance soon closed. Soon the Quest was lifting off and heading for Amalthea. As the Quest was becoming well and truly airborne, Dairan, Twedor and Tayce began on the walk back to their Quest 3. They'd only been walking for about twenty minons when the Transpo Launch behind them, which was going to be placed on tractor beam by Tayce's Quest 3, suddenly exploded with a terrific boom, throwing Tayce, Twedor and Dairan off their feet through the air and on to the grassland ahead, a few yards. A shower of debris and dirt rained down on them and around them. After a few cencrons, when he figured all had settled, Dairan lifted his head and looked around to see Tayce had landed just a short distance from him and Twedor was face down almost beside her. Dairan reached out and tried to touch her, calling her name. Tayce, much to his relief looked up and towards him, shaking the dirt from her hair.

"It looks like we won't be taking the Transpo Launch back to Amalthea," said Dairan, rising to his feet, brushing himself off, removing all the dirt.

"Why did it explode like that?" asked Tayce in sheer amazement as she got back on her feet.

"No idea. All I know is it's a good thing it wasn't earlier, or It could have been a catastrophe," he replied, watching the burning wreckage.

"Help! It's all gone dark—is someone trying to snuff me out?" came a cry from Twedor in panic, still face down.

Dairan hurried to the little Romid's side and stood him on his feet. As Twedor did a quick systems check to see he hadn't damaged anything operational, Tayce looked about. Something had to cause the explosion, she thought. Transpo Launches, once the engine power ceased, were not prone to suddenly exploding after a crash.

"I hate to say this, but I have a feeling we're not alone down here. That explosion just confirmed it. You know as well as I do Transpo Launches don't just explode," said Tayce, suspicious.

"No serious damage sustained," announced Twedor, relieved.

Just as he said it, gunfire came from out of nowhere. Dairan dropped to the ground and took out his handgun, rolling towards a group of nearby trees for shelter and for quickly hoped-for retaliation. Tayce crouched and ran in the same direction, telling Twedor to move it and keep his head down. Twedor found it near impossible to avoid the weapon fire heading in his direction as he hurried to keep up with Tayce, with one good sight circuit working in one eye and the other damaged from when he'd hit the ground earlier. He was beginning to think maybe his mistress was right: he should have remained back on Amalthea. Upon reaching the shelter of the group of trees, with oncoming weapon fire still whizzing past them, Tayce took out her Pollomoss handgun and began joining Dairan in returning fire. Whilst Dairan took on the sudden firepower coming from one direction, she took on the firepower coming from another. Both were back to back, firing in opposite directions. After a while of exchanging weapon fire on both sides of the vast open area, the enemy abruptly ceased fire. Birdsong could be heard once more. Both Dairan and Tayce looked at each other, wondering what was next.

"Did we win, do you think?" asked Dairan in a near whisper, glancing in the direction the weapon fire had come from.

"There's only one way to find out," replied Tayce.

"Count me out on this one," said Twedor, staying where he was until it could be proved the coast was clear. Cautiously, Dairan and Tayce stepped from their retaliation spot. Nothing materialised in the way of a commencement of gunfire. Dairan suggested that whilst it was quiet they should forget about sightseeing and head quickly back to the Quest 3. Tayce nodded in total agreement. Together they grabbed Twedor by his metlon arms, lifted him up and ran in the direction of the Quest 3 shuttle/fighter.

* * *

Aemiliyana, on her space fortress, was finding the amusement of pinning Tayce and Dairan down by one of her elaborate conjuring spells with Adarrant—creating the illusion of a shooting band of guards—almost too much to bear. She was splitting her sides with out-of-control evil laughter. Everything was progressing nicely, she thought. She continued to watch Tayce and Dairan through the image of what was occurring on the Maldigrian surface, as they ran like scared micets towards the Quest 3. She was eager to put the next part of her revenge in place when they boarded the Quest. Her eyes showed she wanted them to move faster as she waited.

As the Quest 3 lifted off the Maldigrian surface, she concentrated with a great power force, raising her hands as she conjured the next move with extreme force. She brought the Quest 3 towards her domain, for bringing aboard, as Dairan fought without much luck to control the shuttle/fighter. Adarrent walked in and over, pleased for his mistress. He was back from the surface, via trans beam.

"You've done well, Adarrent," praised Aemiliyana, continuing her actions.

"The actions are all yours, Your Highness. I merely assisted. Our combined forces on the Maldigrian surface were quite convincing, I believe," he announced in obedient praise.

"For once, Adarrent, you're correct. The explosion was lovely to see," she said, looking down at him proudly, though she was merely letting him think they were partners, kidding him they'd joined forces. There was only room for one powerful being in her world—that was her. But she'd praised him nonetheless, thinking if it made him feel good, so be it. It meant nothing to her. They both stood in the vast white chamber of elaborate architectural design, which was filled with every possible powerful electronic gadget ever invented, and an operating team to keep the space travelling fortress flying. Both watched as the Quest 3, drew nearer and nearer by the cencron. After a while, Aemiliyana looked over to a semicircular area of white desks, to the operatives before them, in their heavy-duty white uniforms, like Adarrent's, and gave the command.

"Prepare the Power-Draining Holding Chamber. We have a much awaited guest."

"Yes, Your Highness" came the obedient reply from one of the nearest operatives.

* * *

On board Amalthea in the MLC, Empress Tricara and Marc stood in discussion about their concerns for Tayce where Aemiliyana was concerned. Tricara suddenly stopped talking, as if she was sensing something was about to happen and it wasn't good. Marc looked at her in questioning concern.

"What's wrong?" he asked, seeing the look.

"It's Tayce and Dairan—they're in the throes of being taken aboard Aemiliyana's fortress," she said, greatly worried.

"What! No!" said Marc in alarmed disbelief, thinking that if only Tayce had returned with them, what was about to happen wouldn't be happening.

After calming down at the anxious thought of what Aemiliyana could possibly do to Tayce, he raised his Wristlink and contacted Nick Berenger in Organisation. Nick soon answered, out of breath. He'd been helping Deluca and had rushed back to his duty position. Marc ordered him to check where the Quest 3 was at that cencron. Nick checked, then confirmed Marc's worst fears. The Quest 3 had been placed under a powerful force and taken aboard the fortress. Marc signed off. Donaldo and Treketa, who heard what Nick said, were now looking at Marc, worried.

"There's something you all ought to know," began Tricara suddenly.

"What? Let's hear it?" said Marc, snapping, bracing himself for the worst.

"Aemiliyana's fortress isn't in our normal Universe," explained Tricara, sensing Marc was far from pleased at the idea as she said it.

"So, where is it?" asked Marc, sighing, his patience wearing thin.

"It's tricky to explain. It's here, but not here, so to speak," replied Tricara.

"I'm listening," said Marc, giving her his full attention, standing at ease and folding his arms.

"It's located in an area of space known as the Mid Dimensional Zone. It's space that's undetected to any vessel, etc., not clearly visible to the naked eye. Oh, she's out there, but we can't detect her and can't see her, and it allows her to retrieve what she wants—namely Tayce," explained Tricara.

"She's using a kind of doorway, then, to come and go from this Universe to others, so at the moment she's hanging halfway in this one, just long enough to set a trap for Tayce, which she has, and cause trouble—am I not right?" asked

Treketa, much to everyone's surprise. She knew what Tricara was trying to explain.

"Yes, Treketa, that's right," replied Tricara softly, glad that at least Treketa had an idea of what she was trying to say.

"That confirms how you crashed on Maldigri. She set you up, knowing it would be a way to get her hands on Tayce," said Marc, trying to contain his anger at the act Aemiliyana had pulled.

"But surely it could be dangerous. It might work for Tayce to travel back and forth the way the fortress works, because she's gifted; as for Dairan it could be fatal. His body might not take the immense force of power, especially if that doorway collapses. They'd all be trapped in the mid realms of space forever. What's more, Dairan would probably die," said Donaldo seriously.

"Believe me, Emperor Honitonia and myself wouldn't allow it to happen. We're watching Aemiliyana very closely. If she shows any sign of what you say will happen, we'll deal with it," said Tricara seriously.

"What are our chances of going in with a small team and getting them out?" Marc asked Tricara.

Tricara thought for a minon, beginning to pace the floor of the MLC, then paused and turned, exclaiming that it was possible, though she would have to consult Emperor Honitonia. In case anything went wrong, he would be able to return everyone safely to the present orbit and cruiser. Marc agreed. As Tricara saw it, Aemiliyana was breaking the rules of the Telepathian Realm of Honitonia by being where she was, in the area that was occupied by the Empire of Honitonia. In normal circumstances, no human that wasn't gifted would be aloud in the vicinity of the empire without an invitation from the powers that be. She was unsure whether a small team would be granted permission to rescue Tayce and the others. The Emperor was already having to make exceptions for Dairan being present, because of what had occurred at the hands of Aemiliyana. He might, though, because of the circumstances, allow a small rescue team just once. She would have to tread carefully in gaining permission. Marc knew he had to allow her to discuss the matter with the Emperor and nodded in total understanding as she explained as much. Right there and then, she excused herself and vanished in a blinding yellow flash.

"Let's hope she can get the Emperor to listen," said Donaldo, worried for Tayce and Dairan.

"Poor Dairan—he only went on this unexpected Quest to look after Tayce," backed up Treketa, feeling sorry about the fact of where he had ended up.

"It's going to be the other way around on the fortress. Tayce will be watching out for him," replied Marc casually.

All three stood in silent thought for a moment. Marc turned, suggesting that when Tricara returned they should tell her he'd be in Organisation. Both nodded. With this, he walked casually, not with his normal commanding stride, over towards the entrance. The doors parted on his approach, allowing him to walk out, on up the corridor. Donaldo went back to checking on the progress of the young Transpo Launch Patrol pilot and how he was coming along in recovery, whilst Treketa made sure he was comfortable.

* * *

The Quest 3, containing Tayce, Dairan and Twedor, arrived on board the fortress. It descended on to the white marblex landing area. Four cream armour-clad armed officers of Aemiliyana's guard ran forth across towards them in unison. They came to a pause with guns pointed at the entrance to the Quest 3, ready to shoot if need be. Dairan looked at Tayce. She nodded in a way that suggested they should proceed with caution. He pressed the command to activate the opening of the entrance. It opened slowly to reveal officers aiming their weapons directly at whoever would emerge. Their purple eyes homed in on who might appear first. Dairan, before emerging from inside, discreetly checked his Pollomoss, in his side holster, in case it was needed. He was glad to see it was still fully charged.

Tayce was first to exit the Quest 3, taking hold of Twedor's metlon hand as they both stepped out together. Dairan slowly followed Tayce and stepped down on to the landing area beside her. Tayce found the guns aimed at her and Dairan somewhat threatening. Twedor stuck close to her, almost hiding behind her. Dairan looked at the officers, realising one false move and they'd be dead. He didn't like the look of the threatening situation. Tayce flinched as the officers suddenly gestured for them to move on, with their weapons. Tayce, as they did, found that a feeling of extreme pure hatred washed over her. It was like the feeling she'd felt earlier, back on Maldigri, only ten times stronger. After being escorted for some time through the cream marblex corridors, Tayce, as they turned a corner, saw the elaborate-style entrance to what she assumed to be their destined point for meeting the leader. She had no idea at this moment that it was Aemiliyana she was about to face, but something was telling her there was evil ahead and of the most extremely powerful kind.

The first thing that greeted her when she walked into the vast white chamber was not the leader, but someone she knew shouldn't be present in the first place. Tom Stavard, her late husband. Now she knew who was behind their current situation, and it came to her exactly where she was and how Tom was present: Aemiliyana. The being like Tom stood at ease, looking at her softly. Tayce looked at him, then away at Dairan, who was looking at her in a questioning way, wondering who it was. But, as she looked back to where Tom had stood, he was gone. Vanished into thin air. Up ahead, after summing Tayce up, comparing her with her great-grandfather, Grandmaster Alexentron Traun, Aemiliyana walked forth. As Tayce saw her come towards her, she showed no fear, as she had everything in her grasp to fight the likes of this powerful witch. Aemiliyana came to a pause and looked at Tayce as if she was below her in status. Tayce read her evil thoughts and there was only one thing on her mind: revenge for being held in the suspended Empire of Past Traun for the past yearons by her great-grandfather.

Dairan stepped up protectively beside her, so she felt his reassuring presence. Twedor summed Aemiliyana up. He could see she was an equal match in beauty to his mistress, but what beauty she held was hiding the evilness she conveyed. He glanced at the officers that had escorted them into their current surroundings. He was just waiting for them to start taking action. If they did, he'd activate his heat shield and Slazer finger—they weren't getting their hands on him.

"Welcome, granddaughter of Alexentron Traun. Welcome to my fortress," began Aemiliyana slowly, eyeing Tayce up and down in an evil-summoning way. She continued to compare Tayce to her late great-grandfather in power ability.

"I'm not going to say it's an honour to meet you—it's not," replied Tayce coldly, to the point.

Dairan watched the frosty reception between the two women, and in Aemiliyana's case he thought to himself there was real strong and powerful hatred present—the kind that scared even him. The friction between both Tayce and Aemiliyana could be cut with a Slazer knife as they stared at each other for a moment. Once she had summoned Tayce up enough to gain all she wanted to know, she moved on to him. He looked right back at her with just as much coldness as Tayce and as if just as uninterested.

"He's quite handsome—you have good choice in male attention, Tayce Amanda. He'll make an excellent slave—after his training, of course," she said, walking over to Dairan and around him, interested.

Dairan found himself growing impatiently more angry by the minon. He found the witch's attentions somewhat intimidating and unwanted. It was hard for him to try and keep his cool as she stood before him, looking at him in a provoking way, waiting for him to lash out. She studied his warm, handsome features, his brown eyes. She reached out to stroke his right cheek. Dairan quickly, in a split-cencron action, did as she expected. He grabbed her wrist midway and held it sternly, looking at her with a cold, dark look of pure anger.

"I'm not interested. There's only one woman I serve, and she's not you," retorted Dairan, continuing to look at her with angered darkness in his eyes.

Aemiliyana pulled her slim wrist from Dairan's grasp, unimpressed, changing her look to cold evilness once more. Now, knowing she couldn't turn him to her advantage against Tayce so easily, she turned and walked back to her white high-backed marblexan throne. She seated herself in thought. Tayce waited, looking at Aemiliyana without any emotion in her normally beautiful features. Dairan lowered his right hand discreetly towards his holster, where his Pollomoss was loaded. Twedor saw what he was doing. He silently readied himself so the moment Dairan decided to go for it he would be ready to assist. Both were ready for any action that would materialise if Tayce decided she wasn't going to play to Aemiliyana's antics. If Tayce decided to make a run for it, he didn't blame her.

* * *

On board Amalthea Marc stood in the DC, discussing what had happened so far, with Lance and Nick, who were both good at combat, including evasive action. They were also considering what could possibly be done to get Tayce, Dairan and Twedor out of their present surroundings. Marc exclaimed that he had an idea: if in some way they could gain entry into the witch's fortress, they might be able to take Aemiliyana by surprise. Both Lance and Nick found the idea a good one.

"Can I ask what the hold-up is? If you believe in this idea, why aren't we leaving now?" asked Nick.

"Empress Tricara has to return with permission from the Realm of Honitonia, which occupies what's termed as the Mid Dimensional Zone. This is where Aemiliyana's fortress currently resides, and as humans that aren't gifted we're forbidden to enter without permission—it has to be requested. Just as soon as the Emperor gives the go-ahead, then we'll leave," promised Marc.

"Just give the word—we'll be ready," assured Lance.

Just as Lance and Nick were about to head on back to duty, Empress Tricara came through the entrance doorway, entering the DC, coming to a pause. Marc, Lance and Nick all gave her their immediate attention.

"I've spoken with Emperor Honitonia and, in this instance, he has granted his permission for you to go ahead and attempt a rescue. He's furious beyond all recognition with Aemiliyana. He's already stated that she's breaking and violating Honitonia space by taking Dairan and Twedor, who are non-gifted members of the realm, into the Mid Dimensional Zone. I've never seen him so furious before. He and the committee are at this moment trying to find a way to handle her withouther violating any more rules," explained Tricara.

"She certainly is something! Thanks for what you've done, Tricara," said Marc in an appreciative tone.

"You're welcome. I just want Tayce out of Aemiliyana's clutches," replied Tricara in a concerned tone.

"Lance, you lead the Quest. Nick, tell Aldonica we need her on this one. Tell her what it involves and tell her to bring what she thinks would be ideal in weaponry," ordered Marc.

"I think you should know, when I spoke to the Emperor he informed me Aemiliyana has already gained the upper hand in revenge over Tayce. She's taken Twedor and placed him in some kind of freezing liquid that freezes solid. Also Dairan has been considered as a prospective slave. As for Tayce, for some strange reason I can't get through to her using my mind link," informed Tricara.

Lance, Nick, Tricara and Marc all walked back out into Organisation. Marc walked straight across to Craig. As he approached the computer-analysing technical officer, so he explained what had happened to Twedor and that he would need him to stand by in the Robot and Technical Service Section ready to start work on reverting Twedor back to normal functioning capabilities, just as soon as they returned. Craig agreed, then headed away to get things ready down on Level 5. Marc crossed back to Tricara, waiting to find out from Nick if Aldonica had got the request.

"Aldonica will meet us in the Flight Hangar Bay," informed Nick, standing, removing his Microceive.

"Come on, let's go. Ready, Lance? Amal, you're on standby command," ordered Marc, heading for the Organisation entrance.

"I will be ready to act as requested, Commander," assured Amal in her clear eloquent tone.

Tricara called after the small team, wishing them luck with the rescue. She knew they were going to need it. She turned to look out through the main sight port at the Universe in thought. After a few minons, she turned to Kelly.

"Has Marc informed Donaldo he may be needed?" she asked casually.

"Yes, everything is in place for the return. I informed Donaldo in case Marc forgot to," assured Kelly.

Tricara returned to looking back out into the Universe. She felt a strange feeling that conveyed Tayce was in extreme danger at the hands of Witch Queen Aemiliyana. She felt terrible that there was nothing she could do to help her young gifted friend.

* * *

Twedor, in Aemiliyana's fortress, was lifted motionless out of the freezing purple solution he'd been lowered into earlier. He looked like a stiff stonex statue, glazed and void of all life. Tayce had been placed much against her will on a marblex cream bunk, large enough to hold one person, in a lying position under Aemiliyana's force. She had been placed in force-field restraints to stop her from escaping, even though she had fought hard against the action to get her there. Above her a silver metallic machine was suspended from the ceiling of the vast chamber. Inches from her forehead was a needle point on the end of a long arm that was primed with a bright orange light, aimed at the centre of her forehead. She didn't like this. She struggled in the force-field restraints as the arm began to lower at Aemiliyana's command to commence the befitting demise. As it lowered towards Tayce, millitron by millitron, every sense in her very existence was on alert. She didn't want what was about to happen, but she found herself powerless to stop it. Aemiliyana watched with a look of great glee in an evil way, thinking soon revenge would be all hers. Dairan was unable to do anything to stop what was happening. He'd been rendered helpless as Aemiliyana had ordered one of her men to stun him and place him in suspended time in a force field. She had made sure he was induced into a time-suspended deep sleep before moving on to Tayce. Guards were close at hand should they be needed for any reason by their queen. Aemiliyana walked to the side of Tayce and looked down at her.

"You're feeling how I felt when your great-grandfather committed me to the Empire of Past Traun, Tayce Amanda. Soon you will have paid that debt in full—you'll be useless to anyone," she said, watching Tayce struggling with tears in her eyes.

"You bitch! It is my great-grandfather your revenge is concerned with. I had nothing to do with what happened to you. You'll pay for this. You think you'll be able to roam this Universe a free person; you won't," retorted Tayce, continuing to struggle as the orange illuminated point on the extending arm came within cencrons of piercing her forehead.

"You have little chance of escaping, so why don't you accept the punishment for your great-grandfather's actions? Look around, if you can. Your little robot is helpless to help you and the handsome Dairan is in a deep suspended sleep, locked in time until I free him," she replied, then burst out laughing evilly, knowing her torment would soon be through and she would be plagued no more by what happened to her.

Tayce felt the situation was helpless as Aemiliyana had blocked her powers to contact Empress Tricara. She was totally in this witch's hands. Aemiliyana looked across to Adarrent, ordering him to activate the power drain of Tayce's abilities. He didn't move. He just stood where he was, with his fingers poised above the activation keys. Something was making him disobey his orders. But what, he didn't know.

"I gave you an order, Adarrent. You know what the penalty will be if you defy my orders," she began coldly, slamming her hand down on the nearest surface in frustration that her devoted servant for the first time in his life refused to do as she was ordering.

"Tom!" said Tayce in a whisper, catching the sight of her dead husband out of the corner of her eye to the right of her, in the far part of the chamber.

"He won't listen to you. I brought him back to life. He makes an excellent slave, as will your Dairan when the process of transformation is complete. What's more, he will serve by my side in a personal way, so you've lost both the men in your life, Tayce Amanda. Now, Adarrent!" shouted Aemiliyana, getting impatient because he wouldn't cooperate.

Tayce had a feeling Aemiliyana's ordering Adarrent around had just come to an end. Maybe her situation wasn't so hopeless after all. Maybe her crime-fighting dayons weren't over after all. Without warning, overhead and all around the vast chamber bellowed the familiar voice of Emperor Honitonia, which filled the air.

"Cease this action at once, Aemiliyana, over this young woman. Stop where you are, Witch. This has gone on long enough," commanded the voice of the Emperor.

"Honitonia!" said Aemiliyana in shock and surprise that he'd been witnessing what she was doing. But she soon regained her determination not to let him interfere. She was an equal match for him—or so she thought—with powers to countermand anything he cared to throw at her.

"I've witnessed enough of this rule-breaking behaviour. Release these beings at once. I need not remind you you are in gross violation of the Realm of Honitonia rules," he continued, and appeared in the chamber looking far from pleased, but unimpressed and unmoved by Aemiliyana's outraged look.

"She has to pay for what her great-grandfather, Alexentron Traun, did to me—locking me in time. For yearons I remained in torment, unable to gain back my powers," blurted Aemiliyana, not prepared to back down.

"Tayce Amanda has nothing to do with this, other than she is linked to Alexentron Traun by her family line. Now do as I command or I'll put a halt to what you crave, myself," announced the Emperor, becoming impatient with Aemiliyana's defiance.

"I have no time for your idle threats, Honitonia. Leave!" she ordered and took the stance to continue her wanted revenge.

"Do not order me, Witch. I can put you right back where you escaped from with great ease. I have more power over you than you will ever have. Now release these beings, or I will carry out the necessary action to deter you from completing your revenge," shouted the Emperor with a strong tone of command in his voice.

Tayce could see the Emperor was furious beyond words, out of the corner of her eye. She'd never known him to sound so angry. It showed in his eyes. He stood silently waiting for Aemiliyana to make the next move. Tayce thought to herself that he was waiting for Aemiliyana to continue her plan of punishment and then he would carry out what he'd stated: send her back to the Empire of Past Traun and crush the fortress forever. After the brief silence, Emperor Honitonia used the first degree of his power on Aemiliyana and she found herself chocking. She grabbed at her neck. The Emperor asked Aemiliyana was she going to do as he commanded, or was she going to draw her last breath with her continued act of total defiance? Aemiliyana ignored him and put up her own power against him. He laughed off the attempt. Tayce felt Aemiliyana was losing badly against the immense power hold Emperor Honitonia had over her. Minon by minon Honitonia gained control of what Aemiliyana had done to Dairan, Tayce and Twedor. The power that had held Dairan where he was slowly drained and he began to come back to a normal conscious state. The blue sparking force field that had held him where he was suddenly collapsed. He fell out and was quickly steadied by Adarrent. Both men watched as Emperor Honitonia drained the very life force that held Aemiliyana together, in all her evilness. Slowly she began to disintegrate into nothing. The fortress began to come apart at the seams as the Emperor increased his powers. Aemiliyana's workforce began to lose their grip and collapsed to the fortress floor, disintegrating where they dropped.

"Release Tayce, Commander Loring," ordered Honitonia whilst he continued his actions.

Dairan, now fully coherent and aware of his surroundings once more, didn't need telling twice. He raced over and quickly released Tayce from the restraints, whilst Adarrent, who had been under the influential forces of Aemiliyana, found he could once more think for himself and immediately deactivated the power-draining machine. Dairan helped Tayce up on to her feet, checking she was all right. She nodded and looked around the fast-deteriorating state of their surroundings for Twedor. Her eyes fell on the solid sight of the little Romid. Dairan suggested they get him and leave. Tayce turned to see the Emperor continuing to torture Aemiliyana, not feeling sorry for her, whilst Dairan lifted Twedor down, with help from Adarrent. Tayce then glanced towards where Tom had been standing earlier, only to see he was no more. All she heard in her head were Tom's words, telling her she would be all right now.

"Once you have your Romid, Tayce, go!" ordered the Emperor.

"Won't you come with us, Adarrent?" asked Tayce.

"I cannot, Captain. Please go. Save yourselves," he softly replied.

Dairan reached out and grabbed Tayce's arm and pulled her to go on with him. He suggested they head for the shuttle/fighter before it was too late. Tayce glanced back over her shoulder as she ran on out of the chamber. The sight she saw was Aemiliyana on the floor, drained, and the whole of the vast chamber where they'd been taken to for the torture was falling apart from the powerful force of the Emperor's destruction. Inside Tayce's mind she heard the Emperor tell her he would see her back on board Amalthea. Upon reaching the white-floored landing area, much to their relief they were met by the small Quest rescue party. Marc was watching, as well as Aldonica, Nick and Lance, the work servants freeze solid in their duty actions, then implode.

"What the hell's going on around here? It looks like the next best thing to an all-out self-destruction taking place," began Marc, finding what was happening unbelievably amazing, to say the least.

"Emperor Honitonia has taken over. He's making Aemiliyana pay for her actions towards me and breaking the rules of the realm," replied Tayce.

"Are you all right?" asked Aldonica.

"We are, but Twedor suffered at the hands of Aemiliyana. He'll need a little work when we get back," said Tayce, then showed her Twedor's current state.

"Craig's standing by to take him to the Robot and Technical Service Section upon our arrival," assured Marc.

He turned, heading back to the Quest that was waiting beside the one Tayce and Dairan had arrived in. He paused halfway, calling back to Dairan, asking what of the Witch Queen? Would she show up again in the near future? Dairan replied that all would be revealed when they were back in safe space on Amalthea. The Amalthean Quests members, with a somewhat solid Twedor, boarded the

Quest 3 shuttles/fighters. As soon as everyone was safely on board, the entrance hatches were sealed for take-off. Marc was first to lift off in his Quest, followed by Dairan and Tayce in theirs. Both shuttles/fighters broke through the fortress's falling-apart roof and headed back out into the Mid Dimensional Zone, back along the corridor to normal space, under the sudden guidance of Emperor Honitonia. After about an houron, both Quests found the entrance to emerge back into normal space.

Tayce, in the Quest 3 she arrived in on her way to the fortress, heard an ear-piercing scream, as did the others. Then she was suddenly plunged into a unconscious state, slumping back in the seat, her head falling to one side. Dairan glanced at her in alarm. Whatever had happened? It was serious and connected with the hold Aemiliyana had over the empire and the Mid Dimensional Zone. He continued flying, knowing they'd be back aboard the cruiser in a matter of minons.

* * *

Tayce was not the only one to suddenly become unconscious. Back on Amalthea the Empress had suddenly collapsed in Organisation. Jaul Naven, who was present in the centre and had been talking to Kelly, turned, catching Tricara smoothly and quickly and placing her down on Lance's vacant seat. But just as he went to call Donaldo she began to regain consciousness, helped by the caring support of Kelly. Deluca crossed with a drink of plicetar, handing it to the Empress.

"Are you all right?" enquired Jaul with great concern in his Canardan (Canadian) polite accent.

"Yes, I'm fine. I can't understand why it happened—I'm not one for fainting," she replied in a soft tone.

"Don't think anything of it—we are all prone to it sometime in our lives and it can be something so trivial that causes us to do so," assured Jaul.

"They're on their way back," announced Kelly, having returned to her duty position, looking at the scanner in front of her.

Deluca crossed to Kelly's side to watch the two Quest 3s heading back to the cruiser and Flight Hangar Bay. Jaul and a recovered Tricara crossed to see them also. Tricara went suddenly silent for a minon. Jaul glanced at her, worried, until she announced everyone on the team was all right—that was except for Twedor. He was damaged. She excused herself and hurried from Organisation. As she passed the first sight port she came to, so she saw the arriving Quests approaching and hurried on much more quickly in order to meet everyone.

* * *

In the Flight Hangar Bay, Donaldo and Treketa stood waiting in case there were any medical emergencies. Craig Bream also waited, wondering what kind of condition Twedor would be in, considering what he'd heard. He'd brought with him a special Robot and Technical Service Section container, big enough to transport Twedor back to the service section. The Quest 3s came in to land one behind the other, setting down on the bay floor.

No sooner had they landed than the action commenced. Both entrances on the shuttles/fighters opened. Marc stepped down from his and headed across to help Tayce from hers as she had not long regained consciousness, like the Empress. Tayce looked at Marc with tired eyes. She felt drained from her ordeal at the hands of Aemiliyana. She had tried to use the powers the Emperor had bestowed on her, but the Witch Queen had been too strong for her in ability. Marc looked back at her, giving her an understanding look. Dairan called out to Craig and beckoned for him to come forth. Once Craig had boarded the Quest, he and Dairan lifted a still and silent frozen Twedor together out into the clear Perspexon container in an upright position. Craig thanked Dairan, then quickly began away to begin work on getting Twedor back to a fully operational state.

"Poor Twedor—I hope Craig can get him back to normal," said Tayce, watching her friend and Romid being taken away in a sorry solid non-working state.

"Don't worry—if anyone can bring him back to normal, it's Craig. After all, he designed him," Marc assured her in a kind way. He knew what the little Romid meant to her.

Tayce found herself wishing she'd stood her ground at the beginning of the Quest, in not letting Twedor go with her to Maldigri, but what was done was done.

"I suggest we head for some refreshment. The Quest report can wait," suggested Marc, putting a comforting arm around Tayce's shoulders and guiding her on out like a brother would a sister.

"Tayce, how did it go?" asked Tricara, walking into the Flight Hangar Bay to meet Tayce.

"Let's just say this: I think Emperor Honitonia has put Aemiliyana back where she belongs," replied Tayce, assuming as much.

"Did he say anything to you?" asked Tricara

"Only at the end. He said he would see me back here," replied Tayce casually.

"I'm glad you're safe, considering what you were up against. She was a very difficult opponent to try your gift against so early in your abilities," praised Tricara softly.

Marc suggested Tricara join them for refreshment in the Leisure Centre. Tayce agreed. Dairan suggested he head back to Organisation and see her later, maybe. Tayce nodded. With this, Nick, himself and Lance all walked back to duty in Organisation, whilst Aldonica went in search of Craig to see if there was anything she could do in getting Twedor back to normal. As for Donaldo and

Treketa, not having a medical emergency to attend to, they sauntered back to their duty in the MLC.

* * *

As Tayce walked in the company of Marc and Tricara, to her surprise she heard Aemiliyana's voice in her mind once more, saying the following words: *"It's not over. We'll meet again, Tayce Amanda. I will return."*

16. Lance

Roughly one houron later, Tayce entered her quarters to find, to her surprise, Dairan and the emperor waiting for her. The emperor turned from watching the Universe through the almost-floor-to-ceiling sight port and Amalthea leaving the planetary world of Maldigri behind. As Dairan stood at ease, Tayce walked to the middle of the Living Area floor, coming to a gentle pause, looking questioningly at the Emperor as he turned to face her. Firstly he looked past Tayce to Dairan, congratulating him on keeping his calm throughout the ordeal with the Witch Queen and her treacherous enticing ways. Tayce smiled, glad the Emperor was pleased. She felt Dairan had done his best too to protect her in such difficult circumstances.

"Please sit!" the emperor gestured to the nearest soffette.

Tayce did as requested, ready to listen to what the Emperor had to say. He began, saying he'd managed to put a temporary restraint on Aemiliyana, but was unsure how long she would remain where he'd placed her before she escaped again. This bothered Tayce—knowing where the Emperor had placed Aemiliyana wasn't 100 per cent secure. She thought about the words she'd heard in her head earlier about Aemiliyana returning. It was now a distinct possibility that she would, despite what the Emperor had done to her. Tayce rose to her feet, sighing, annoyed at the fact, and began to pace her Living Area floor. She turned to face the Emperor, who had picked up on her thoughts and was looking at her calmly.

"So does this mean she could come back for me all over again any time soon?" asked Tayce, hoping not.

"This, I'm sorry, I cannot say. I'm hoping the force field the Honitonian powers that be and myself have placed her in will hold her where she is for a very long time in her drained state," he replied, seeing Tayce's thoughtful face.

He could also see Tayce was feeling great irritation at the fact that she and Aemiliyana might have to come face-to-face again sometime in the near future. Tayce slapped the back of the chair nearest to her in frustration. The Emperor was obviously present to take back the force he'd given her to take on the Witch

Queen. What good would it be if she didn't have the same power next time around? Did this mean she would lose?

The Emperor was one step ahead of her in reading her thoughts and began, saying, "The empire's Higher Minds Committee and myself have realised you would be at a disadvantage when and if Aemiliyana returns if we were to take back your extra ability at this time. As you're one of our most promising students, we value what you do with your gift; so we feel the power we've bestowed on you should remain with you until after the next confrontation," he announced, much to Tayce's relief.

Tayce knew she shouldn't, but wanted to hug the Emperor for making this decision. She felt the next time Aemiliyana showed up it wasn't going to be going all the Witch's way. The Emperor was still reading Tayce's thoughts and a slight smile of amusement crossed his chiselled features, owing to her thoughts on the next possible encounter with Aemiliyana. He assured her that both he and the Empress would be watching over her in the future. With this, he rose to his feet and wished her luck. Tayce walked around from the back of the chair to the centre of the floor to face him. He walked towards her. Taking hold of her by the upper arms, which surprised her, she wondered what he was going to do.

"You will succeed the next time, if it arises, and I have no doubt it will be the last time, but don't let her think she has an advantage over you. Well the empire minds are calling—until next time," said the Emperor.

"Before you leave, what happened to Adarrent?" asked Tayce, curious.

The Emperor paused before getting ready to vanish back to the Empire of Honitonia and turned, exclaiming that Aemiliyana had played some very powerful cruel tricks in her attempt to get her hands on Alexentron Traun's great-granddaughter, namely herself. One was to make Tom Stavard appear. The Emperor promised Tom was at peace in the Empire of Peace, after his untimely demise and having once been joined with a gifted member of the empire, as Tayce was. The Emperor also informed, her to her surprise, one dayon Tom might find a way to return in some form—what he couldn't say but she'd know. As for Adarrent, Aemiliyana had taken him from the same place as Tom, only he'd been a new arrival at the empire and within easy manipulating reach for Aemiliyana's powerful greed. But he was also back where he belonged; that's why he couldn't return to Amalthea with everyone else. Aemiliyana had brought him back to life for her purposes only. Tayce was glad to hear that Adarrant was OK. The Emperor stood silent for a few minons, then vanished in his blinding blue aura of transportation back to the Honitonian realm.

Tayce crossed over to the Living Area sight port with Tom on her mind and where he'd been sent since he was killed. She paused upon reaching the sight port, looking out into the darkness of space. Hatred for Aemiliyana rose in her mind. She knew the next time they met she would have something to throw at her.

Behind her the quarters doors opened. Lance entered, wondering if he'd called at a wrong time. Tayce turned, seeing him looking troubled.

"Come in—what's wrong?" she asked, seeing something was seriously bothering him.

"Is it possible I can have a brief word with you—it's of great importance?" he asked awkwardly hoping that she would help.

"Yes, of course. What's on your mind?" asked Tayce, studying her long-time friend.

"I'll catch you later. I'll head back to Organisation. I merely came to wait with the Emperor, as he'd asked for me to be present when you arrived," said Dairan, standing and heading towards the entrance.

"Yes, fine. Thanks, Dairan, for being here," said Tayce after him.

"I don't know how to say this…" Lance began apprehensively, waiting for Dairan to leave.

"Come and sit down. Tell me," asked Tayce, walking over to the soffette and sitting down, giving Lance her full attention.

He sat across from her on one of the two mouldable chairs. As Lance began to explain to Tayce what was on his mind, she gave him her undivided attention, because she could see he was greatly troubled and it worried her.

"You remember Father left me a capsule which I now have in my possession? Well, I've been through all the disk chips in a set of forty and there's one missing. I've double-checked, but it's missing all right. What's more, it has a record of the events leading up to his death on it," explained Lance seriously. He then removed the disk prior to the one that was missing from his jacket pocket and set it down.

"So what do you think the one missing could possibly contain?" asked Tayce, interested.

"I know I shouldn't jump to conclusions here, but I think the one that's missing contains the evidence my father was murdered and didn't die of just his heart problem. They—whoever they are that took the disk—are making a good effort to cover their tracks to conceal what they've done," expressed Lance.

"That's a serious accusation, Lance," said Tayce, hoping he was certain in his assumption.

"Maybe so, but let me show you this and I'll let you form your own opinion on what you think," replied Lance.

Before Tayce could say another word, Lance had jumped to his feet and put the disk chip prior to the one that was missing into the slot for activation on the wall Sight Screen. He pressed the activation button then suggested they watch. The large wall Sight Screen flashed into life and the universal date of the recording flashed up across the middle in bold white lettering, plus the disk-chip number. Lance crossed back and sat down. Jonathan Largon materialised on screen with an arch-enemy of Tayce—namely, Layforn Barkin. The scene was

Jonathan's Officette Chambers, and he was discussing assignments and other business matters.

"Watch what happens in the next few minons," spoke up Lance.

Without warning the debate between Jonathan Largon and Layforn Barkin became heated. Barkin seemed to be enjoying with little effort making Jonathan's voice go from one of normal stern opinion, to an enraged violent one. He could be seen reminding Barkin of his position, his rank, and where he was. Barkin verbally retaliated at Jonathan with full fierceness, saying he was a downright idiot and couldn't see further than tomorrow. With this Jonathan ordered Barkin in outright enraged anger to leave his Officette Chambers immediately. As Barkin headed to the entrance of the chambers he paused, turning, retaliating, saying he would see there was a stop put in place to the present matter regarding designated assignments, one way or another. The wall Sight Screen in the Living Area went blank, signifying the end of disk 39. Tayce for a moment was left speechless in shock. She'd never seen Jonathan so angry.

"What assignments will he put a stop to? I don't think I've ever seen your father so angry. I know Barkin could be an absolute bastard—I had a few awkward heated moments with the man myself over this second voyage and the rebuilding of this cruiser," said Tayce, disgusted.

"I can't believe Father reacted like he did—and come to think about it, whenever Barkin's name came up it just seemed to wind Father up in a way I would consider was not like him at all."

"Your father had every right to be angry at Barkin. He was the kind of man who rubbed everyone up the wrong way he came into contact with," assured Tayce.

"Where the missing disk chip has ended up is unknown, but it's my guess it contains evidence needed to prove a point once and for all. I think Father was murdered. In fact I think his last moments weren't caused by what we all thought—induced severe heart trouble. And if so, did Barkin have anything to do with it in some way at the time?" replied Lance seriously, far from pleased.

"I don't know what to say, but as far as the disk chip goes, I have to agree. Someone has it somewhere and they could have a purpose for holding on to it to cover their tracks. Like you say, this calls for a meeting, I think, where we can discuss the points more thoroughly," said Tayce, turning over in her mind what was unfolding.

"Who with?" asked Lance, curious.

"Marc and Dairan. I want to hear what their thoughts are on this," replied Tayce.

"Sorry if you think I'm keeping this between you and me, but the fewer people who know about this matter at the moment, the better it will be. If the murderer is still at large and gets to find out they are about to have their cover blown because of what I've discovered, it would allow them to make a run for it before we catch them, but I don't mind Marc and Dairan finding out," explained Lance.

"That's understandable. Give me the disk chip and return to duty. I'll meet you up in the DC. I think I'd better keep this evidence for the moment, don't you?" said Tayce, taking the disk chip from him.

Lance thanked her for believing in his theory as he headed to the entrance. As the doors parted he continued on out, feeling a little easier having shared what he thought with Tayce. As the doors closed Tayce continued on to the Cleanse Unit for her cleanse and to change into a clean uniform. The assumption Lance had shared with her occupied her immediate thoughts as it was certainly something to think about.

* * *

Four hourons later, Tayce, Dairan and Marc were in the DC with Lance. They were all seated around the meeting table in discussion about Lance's thoughts on the missing disk chip and the possibility it might contain evidence of Jonathan's untimely demise. Marc asked him why he'd waited so long before coming forward with his thoughts on what had occurred and why he had a feeling his father's untimely death was possibly murder. Lance explained that he'd viewed all the other disk chips and found one was missing. In his own mind, what he'd viewed up to the missing disk chip seemed to point to his suspicions that his father's death was not solely due to an exhausting work schedule.

Nick Berenger stepped into the DC, apologising for the intrusion, but Chief Barnford and two officers of SSWAT were about to dock with them. What's more, they were carrying orders to arrest a member of the team. Tayce, on this announcement, rose to her feet in urgency, alarmed at the fact.

"Dairan, come with me. We'll meet Jan as he walks aboard," said Tayce, beginning to move over to the entrance.

Dairan stood and hurried over to go with her, wondering just who was going be arrested. Both himself and Tayce briskly walked passed Nick, heading out, going on through Organisation on the way to head down to meet Chief Jan Barnford in urgency. Tayce didn't like the fact that one of her team was about to be arrested and wanted to get to the bottom of it. Meanwhile Lance continued to talk with Marc and explained what he'd told Tayce earlier. Marc listened intently, forming his own conclusion, and found himself believing the possibility someone could have done foul play towards Jonathan Largon and covered their tracks for Barkin at the same time.

* * *

Tayce and Dairan soon walked from the Deck Travel on Level 2. They briskly headed in the direction of the Docking-Bay doors. As they approached, so the doors slid open. Jan Barnford stepped aboard accompanied by two of his SSWAT uniformed officers. He came to a halt on meeting Tayce, feeling pretty awkward about what he was about to do. He greeted her with an acknowledging nod.

"This is unexpected. What's this all about, Jan?" asked Tayce in a straightforward way.

"Quite. I'm afraid I'm here on official business for Enlopedia. I have documentation stating Lance Largon is to be taken into close arrest," announced Jan, producing the confirming documents from his uniform pocket.

"What! What for?" asked Tayce in utter disbelief at what Jan had just delivered.

"I'm sorry, Tayce—this is out of my hands. He's wanted in connection with the murder of the late Jonathan Largon," announced Jan awkwardly. He could see Tayce was far from amused.

"You've got to be joking! Lance is no murderer. Sure enough Jonathan might have been murdered, but not by his own son, whoever sent out this order is way off the mark," said Tayce angrily, exchanging alarmed looks with Dairan, who looked just as shocked.

"Believe me, personally I feel like you. I believe he wouldn't, but the powers that be say otherwise and I have to carry out my orders or be held responsible for disobeying them," expressed Jan in all sincereness.

"When you say powers that be, I can't believe for a cencron this came from Mother or Father," began Tayce. She knew her parents wouldn't even consider such a thing.

"Council gave the orders. They say they want to see Lance face-to-face. That's why I'm here to escort him back," replied Jan, gesturing to his two accompanying officers, standing behind him at ease.

"Is there any chance there could be a severe mix-up—maybe a name sounding like Lance Largon?" asked Dairan over Tayce's shoulder, somewhat surprised.

"I'm afraid not. I double-checked that fact myself before I came out here. Believe me, I don't want to be here and arresting a member of this team unnecessarily," replied Jan, not happy.

"Before you take Lance away, gentlemen, I want to discuss this further with you in the DC, Jan," said Tayce, angry with the council's act towards Lance.

"Men at ease, take a break," ordered Jan, allowing his men to stand down and go for a Coffeen.

"Sir!" came the reply from the two smart-looking officers.

The two officers, who had been on Amalthea before and knew where the Refreshment Centre was, headed away to do just as suggested. Tayce, Dairan and Jan began on the walk up to the DC. Jan, as they went, began explaining that the accusation regarding Lance had surprised him a bit—that was why he had double-checked right back to the council. But, even then, something somewhere just didn't add up, to his way of thinking. Something somewhere was being elaborately covered up, because Lance was close to Jonathan, the council or someone on the council passed it through to make Lance the scapegoat for reasons he just didn't understand. It seemed to him there was an elaborate cover-up going on, and the real culprits were hiding their tracks. The council had been known in the past to make some bad decisions—why should this one be any different? He felt they were being threatened by an undisclosed source. As they entered the Deck Travel and the doors closed, Dairan requested Level 1, whilst Jan and Tayce continued to talk about the far-fetched accusation.

* * *

Marc, in the DC, retrieved the disk chip from the Sight Screen Disc Reader, as Lance decided to show him just what happened. Lance could see Marc was somewhat concerned by what he'd witnessed between his father and Layforn Barkin in the Officette Chambers.

"What do you think?" asked Lance.

"I don't know what to think, to be honest. I must admit what you're thinking is a distinct possibility," replied Marc, thinking back to what he'd just seen.

Tayce soon walked into the DC followed by Jan and Dairan. Marc turned, surprised to see Jan looking so official. He looked at Tayce questioningly, only to see something wasn't right. Jan began in an official way and to Lance's utter amazement.

"Officer Largon, I'm here on behalf of the Enlopedian Council, to arrest you in connection with the murder of your father, the late Jonathan Largon, in the year 2417. It is advised you accompany me without fuss or I will be forced to summon my two officers to escort you back to the Patrol Cruiser under close restraint," said Jan, to the point, even though he hated doing what he was doing.

"Arrested for murder? This has to be some mistake," protested Lance in outburst, finding the whole accusation somewhat absurd, to say the least.

Marc was speechless at the sudden announcement. Like Lance, he found it hard to believe. His features took on a far from pleased expression. There had to be something drastically wrong, he thought.

"You have nothing to fear, Lance. I'll back you up should you need help. We will get this sorted," said Tayce assuringly.

"Lance, do this and tell the council what you've just told us—take the disk chip you've just shown me, leading up to the one that's missing. It might give you something to throw at the council as possible evidence," suggested Marc in an advising tone.

"I'm going to accompany you, Marc. Tell Treketa to prepare Tricara's young injured pilot, ready for returning to Enlopedia. Also tell her she's going along as well. Tell Tricara she can join us also," ordered Tayce.

"Sure! But are you going to be all right on Enlopedia alone?" he asked, referring to the fact there was still the threat of the Witch Queen hanging over her. There was no telling when the witch might break out of the empire the Emperor had placed her in, or what she might do.

"Yes, fine, but if it makes you feel more at ease, I'll take Dairan with me. He's had first-hand experience of Aemiliyana, but I feel it's going to be a while before we see her again. You'll be in charge until I return. Hopefully, it might only be a couple of dayons," replied Tayce casually.

"While you're waiting, Chief, I'll get on with your requests and have Craig get Twedor ready. Hopefully he can pull it off in time for you to take him with you when you go," suggested Marc.

"I can hold out for a couple of hourons if it will help, then I have to get Lance here back to base," said Jan, glancing at his Wristlink time display.

On this, Marc left Tayce, Jan, Dairan and Lance, heading back out into Organisation to put in place the orders Tayce had requested. Firstly, he informed Tricara her flight to Enlopedia was leaving in two hourons. He then crossed to Nick Berenger, ordering him to call Treketa and tell her she was to prepare young Jaran for transfer to Enlopedia and that she was to accompany him during the transfer. Nick agreed, commencing the requested orders. Marc turned and headed on out of Organisation, heading down to go and see Craig personally on Level 5, to explain that Twedor was needed in two hourons and to assist if he had to in getting Twedor up and back to an operational standard by then.

Back in the DC Tayce ordered Lance to go and change his uniform, ready to face the council at Enlopedia, also to pack an overnight holdall. He nodded, then began towards the DC entrance. Jan, before he'd got too far, reached out and gently detained him. Lance looked at him, wondering what he was going to say.

"If it's any consolation, I'm on your side. What's more what I have to do makes my duty very difficult because I know you," assured Jan, to Lance's surprise.

"It's fine—I totally understand you're just following orders," replied Lance, glad Jan could see he wouldn't do what he was accused of—murdering his late father.

He continued on out. Tayce watched him go and felt sorry for him—to think he had to relive the demise of his father all over again, who he loved so much, like any proud son would. How could someone convince the powers that be behind the scenes or the Enlopedian Council that Lance had done the unthinkable—murdered his own father? It was awful, she thought, and downright spiteful. She wished she knew who could have pulled such an act. Nevertheless, she was going to do her utmost to convince the council otherwise, even though she didn't have to prove something that deep in their own minds they knew was a set-up by the real culprit covering their tracks. But she also knew that if the council, being the narrow-minded bunch they were, had been got at by some unknown source—the real culprit—and did not listen to her evidence of where Lance was on the dayon Jonathan died, then they might simply dismiss her evidence altogether to suit their assumptions of what they'd been forced to believe and Lance would take the blame for something he was innocent of. She certainly had her own thoughts on how the council handled situations to make sure they appeared to be in the right, no matter what the outcome and they didn't seem to care what anyone else wanted. Hence Tayce calling them, under her breath, a narrow-minded bunch of no-good decision-makers. In this instance, the idea of Lance murdering his father was totally wrong and unrealistic—he was innocent.

"Personally, I don't like this, Tayce. I feel Lance is taking the blame for some other idiot who did the dirty deed and convinced council they're innocent, using Lance as a scapegoat," confided Jan.

"Maybe there's someone somewhere who knows Lance, besides me and you, and knows Lance couldn't have murdered Jonathan and will come forth with the evidence, as Lance faces the council," said Tayce hopefully.

Jan studied Tayce. He could see she wanted what was best for Lance and understood it. He would feel the same if one of his men had been wrongly accused in the same way. He also knew if she didn't do what she thought was right, then she wasn't the leader and exceptional woman he'd come to respect and admire as a good close friend, since the demise of Tom Stavard. Tayce turned and caught him studying her casually. She suggested she'd better go and pack for leaving.

"Would you mind if I tag along?" he asked casually.

"Of course not—it won't take me long," she assured.

Both walked from the DC on out through Organisation, discussing the kind of questions council might put to Lance, heading into the Level 1 corridor, to walk on down to Level 3.

* * *

Two hourons passed. Tayce walked from her quarters with Jan Barnford. They'd arranged to meet Treketa, Jaran and Empress Tricara with Lance and Dairan at the Docking-Bay doors on Level 2. Tayce had changed uniforms, to one that met with the dress code required to meet with the council. It was an all-in-one wrap-over cream gown, gathered in at the waist, with a belt and calf-length cream low-heeled boots. Her hair was swept up and secured at the back of her head neatly. She truly looked every inch the galactic successful captain of a crime-fighting team she was, and one that could take on the likes of the council, like she'd done so many times before this current voyage. Jan smiled to himself. He knew from past hearings that the council was a bunch Tayce had no fear of taking on and, dressed like she was, he knew they were in for a hard time. What's more, as her father was now Admiral to the whole base, they didn't want to push their attitude too much when dealing with her because there might be repercussions. On the way to the rendezvous with the others, Jan discussed Marc with Tayce and how he'd made a good recovery after the attack on the Astrona Star, in resuming his duty to the team. Tayce agreed.

On Level 2, Empress Tricara and Dairan stood waiting. She'd explained how she had been talking with Marc about the safety of Tayce, over Aemiliyana, and how he'd come to the decision to let Tayce do what she thought was right and to just be there if she needed him. Dairan nodded understandingly, expressing that he too was worried about Tayce as far as Aemiliyana went. As Tayce approached with Jan, Tricara discreetly assured Dairan he needn't worry—everything had been sorted.

Jan looked from Dairan to Tricara, wondering what they'd been discussing. He then continued on aboard the Patrol Cruiser. His two officers, who had taken a break, came forth and, under their chiefs orders (namely Jan), immediately helped take their team buddy Jaran on board on the Hover Trolley. As Jaran left her side, Treketa turned her attention to Lance, who was stood waiting to board, reassuring him that things would work out—he'd see. He smiled, thanking her silently. He was glad she was on his side, realising that there was one thing they'd always been and that was there for each other in times of trouble. Each was willing to support the other in any way they could, as good friends should. They both walked aboard the Patrol Cruiser. Jan was about to order Lance to be placed into confinement, unaware that Tayce had read what he was thinking of attempting.

She gave him a no-nonsense look and simply demanded, "Why?" in a point-blank tone.

"Because it's a formality—it's a rule that's standard in a case such as Lance is facing," replied Jan without thought, noticing her far from impressed look.

"Just this once you can drop the formalities. Lance, firstly, is innocent and, secondly, not a stranger. He travels freely with us. If I thought he was guilty, do you think I would be travelling to Enlopedia to clear his name?" replied Tayce in a discreet whisper, surprised at Jan, considering what he'd said earlier about not believing Lance did what the council accused him of.

"This won't look good when he turns up on Enlopedia walking free without some kind of restraint," persisted Jan, becoming impatient because Tayce would not comply with the Enlopedian ruling.

"Who is going to know? You can put him in restraints when we arrive, not before," replied Tayce, giving Jan a plain look, conveying that she was not prepared to back down.

She ordered Lance up front with Treketa. As she saw it, rules in this instance didn't apply, no matter what the council wanted. If they caught wind of the fact Lance wasn't under criminal restraint during transit, then they could take it up directly with her or her father. Jan shook his head, wondering why it was she had to force her hand of authority with him at times. But he guessed he would just have to take it in his stride as usual. Tayce followed Lance and Treketa, not looking back. Dairan ushered a restored and fully operational Twedor on board and passed Jan. He could see he had a look of exasperation on his face and it was in the direction of Tayce. Jan pushed past him and discreetly asked Tayce, even though she wouldn't hold with the transit in confinement, would she allow him, once they reached Enlopedia, just for the sake of his duty, to allow his two officers to lead Lance off the Patrol Cruiser, as a pure formality, in restraints. She thought about it for a moment, then agreed. Jan further continued, saying if the real culprit was waiting to see Lance arrive under escort out of sight, it would make him or her think they'd won and got away with their convincing the council that Lance was guilty. They'd feel a kind of evil satisfaction in what they'd achieved—that's when they'd be apprehended for suspicious behaviour on the base and questioned, because they'd be looking somewhat dubious. Tayce could see the idea was a good one and suggested Lance should be informed of what Jan wanted to carry out. Jan nodded, exclaiming he'd have one of his officers do it. He was pleased—at least she wasn't going to cost him his duty position and was willing to give in a bit. He went back to his pilot at the front and took his seat. Tayce sat in hers, thinking about what she had to do when they arrived at Enlopedia. The vastly sized bluey-grey Patrol Cruiser, slightly smaller than Amalthea, departed smoothly from the Docking-Bay and began on its way, turning out and heading back to Enlopedia. Within the blink of an eye, it shot off into the distance leaving Amalthea behind.

* * *

Tayce a while later on the Patrol Cruiser was relaxing in transit with Dairan in the onboard Refreshments Lounge. It was time she was enjoying before the audience with the council. It had been an houron since leaving Amalthea behind. One more and they'd be arriving. Jan had suggested earlier to everyone that it would be a good idea if sometime during the two-houron journey they grab some refreshment. Dairan sat opposite Tayce, studying her in a soft, understanding way. He was glad he wasn't in her shoes, considering what the Emperor said earlier—that there was no knowing how long the Witch Queen would remain where she'd been placed before she showed up again. He knew one thing: he would do what Tayce asked of him to help her fight against the witch, when she did appear again. He guessed they all would.

"Not the ideal situation, is it?" he asked, reaching his hand across the table and touching her arm gently.

"What do you mean?" she replied, taking her gaze from looking out at the stars, meeting his warm, handsome features.

"This unnecessary accusation against Lance, with Aemiliyana in temporary hold, not knowing when she's going to make her return appearance." he said softly.

"I'm fine. I've come up against worse than Aemiliyana. The first time she had the upper hand, but next time I'll be ready for her. But thanks for your understanding," she replied with a soft smile.

"You know I'll always be there for you should you need me," he assured her, grasping her delicate hand and squeezing it gently.

"Tayce! Dairan!" said Jan, entering the area and walking towards them.

Both Dairan and Tayce returned to normal team behaviour as Jan paused with a fresh cup of Coffeen by their table, which was one of four in the small Refreshments Lounge. He began explaining, in between sips, that he himself had told Lance what was to happen when they reached base. He figured it was best coming from him—he knew Lance well enough to make him understand that the procedure was purely formality and it was solely for the council's benefit. Lance in turn to avoid any unnecessary problems, expressed that he was quite happy to go along with what had been proposed, in being brought before the council. Tayce raised her eyes in surprise, but could see his point in the fact he didn't want to cause any trouble and it just might flush out the real culprit. Jan suddenly smiled in thought, beginning by saying that Lance had to be the most cooperative accused man he'd had to date! But then again, he was Jonathan Largon's son and had probably been taught to keep good conduct in whatever current particular situation he found himself in. Dairan smiled at the thought that Lance didn't want to put a foot wrong, but could understand his reason for doing so too. Jan finished his Coffeen, suggesting he get back to duty as they'd be arriving at Enlopedia soon. With this, he discarded the empty disposable cup in the nearby waste incinerator slot and carried on out, leaving Tayce and Dairan to continue what they were discussing before he had intruded.

*　*　*

Enlopedia Headquarters Base, 14:20 hourons, the SSWAT Patrol Cruiser docked home. A medic team from the Medical Dome was present and standing by, waiting to take Jaran, Empress Tricara's young injured pilot, away for continued medical treatment. Jan, the moment the entrance doors drew open, ordered Treketa to leave the portable Hover Trolley when Jaran had been transferred on board the cruiser, as he would be flying everyone back to Amalthea later. Treketa nodded and did as ordered, leaving the two officers to take the Hover Trolley and store it safely once Jaran was in the safe medical hands of the other medical team waiting. She walked on quickly, catching up with Tayce and Dairan. All three watched whilst Lance was led away by the two patrol officers. Silently Treketa wished him luck. Before Jan left the team, he wished Tayce luck in trying to clear Lance of the suspected murder of his father. She nodded, half listening, with thoughts of what she was going to say and do in doing just that. She began off in the direction of her father's Officette Chambers with Dairan, Treketa and Twedor walking beside her. Empress Tricara waved to Tayce and headed off to her apart-house for some much needed rest after her ordeal on Maldigri. Dairan paused halfway with Tayce, suggesting he take Treketa and they head off towards their short-stay accommodation. Tayce agreed. Twedor stayed with her, watching both Treketa and Dairan walk away in the direction of the apart-house accommodation area with his and her overnight holdalls. Tayce continued on. As she neared her father's building, where his Officette Chambers were, she felt glad to be on solid ground for a while. It wasn't that she was complaining about her life in space. She loved it, but at times it was nice to be on Enlopedia. It felt like the dayons when she used to reside on her home world. The environment was a daylight/night-time rota, rather like the artificial environment created for Enlopedia. She and Twedor approached the vacant and waiting Vacuum Lift. A young male attendant welcomed them with a warm, pleasant smile and a nod as she walked aboard with Twedor.

"It's nice to see you again on Enlopedia, Captain; you too, Twedor," announced the young brown-haired attendant. Everyone knew Twedor on the base—he was one of a kind.

"Thanks. It's nice to be here, sometimes, it's a break from duty," replied Tayce casually.

"The Admirals Level?" enquired the young, slender male attendant.

"Yes, please," replied Tayce, wondering what her father was going to say about the situation with Lance.

The doors drew closed and the Vacuum Lift began to ascend, after the attendant had keyed in the requested level. The lift whisked Tayce up smoothly and stopped on the required level. The doors drew open. Tayce ushered Twedor out, then followed on behind, saying farewell to the young attendant who had been chatting to her on the way up about how the new second voyage was coming along. He smiled, then began putting into procedure for the lift to be taken back down. As Tayce began along the corridor towards her fathers outer anteroom, she almost collided with Aidan Lord, who was hoping to catch the Vacuum Lift.

"Sorry, Captain, Twedor! I was thinking of something else. Are we expecting a visit from you todayon—we haven't received word from Amalthea to say you were coming?" asked Aidan, surprised to see them both.

"It's fine—don't worry. Is my father in his Officette Chambers?" asked Tayce in a casual way.

"Yes! Go on in," suggested Aidan, continuing on to where he was heading in a hurry.

Tayce continued on along the corridor, entering through the opening doors on approach, into her father's outer anteroom and on into his Officette Chambers. As the doors drew apart, inside the Officette Chambers Darius looked up from keying in at his desk on the computerised touch keypad. He rose to his feet upon seeing it was Tayce and smiled. Crossing, he asked why hadn't she let him know she was coming?

"What brings you here so unexpectedly—not that I'm not glad to see you? I am. Did you fly here alone?" asked Darius, somewhat concerned that something was wrong.

"It's good to see you too. This isn't a social visit—please continue with what you were doing. I don't want to disturb you and keep you from your work," said Tayce as she and her father hugged mid floor.

"What's the reason for being here, then?" asked Darius, seeing something was bothering her as he pulled away.

"Jonathan Largon's death. Someone is trying to frame Lance for it," began Tayce.

"What!" replied Darius, wondering if he'd heard right.

Tayce sauntered over to the large sight pane, pausing for a few minons in thought, looking down on E City, then turned. She met her father's questioning look. He was waiting for an explanation.

"The council, or someone who has great influence over them, are claiming Lance murdered Jonathan. They even went as far as to send Jan Barnford and two of his officers out to Amalthea to place Lance under arrest and bring him back here for an audience with them," began Tayce, disgusted, but she was cut off by her father, interrupting furiously.

"I've never heard of anything so preposterous in all my galactic life. Believe me, Tayce, this is the first I've heard of this. You did well to come and tell me," said Darius in thought, trying to digest what Tayce had just said, though finding it totally absurd.

He just couldn't believe such a wild and untrue accusation had been cast. He'd known the Largon family for many yearons, right back since the dayons when Traun was a living, thriving world—especially Lance and his father. They were as close as any father and son could be. He knew that Lance had the greatest respect and love for his father, and Jonathan was extremely proud of Lance's achievements. He knew also, from Lydia, that Jonathan was proud of the fact Lance had become a member of the Amalthean Quests team.

"Preposterous or not, I'm here to clear Lance of this accusation. I need Amalthea One's log entry 14. This is for the date Jonathan passed away. It will state where Lance was at the time of Jonathan's demise," continued Tayce.

"Leave it with me. The moment Aidan returns I'll have him retrieve it from the archives. Are you sure the council ordered Chief Barnford to do what he did?" asked Darius, somewhat curious as to why the council had left him out of what had been cast and hadn't run the accusation by him first. Who was behind this? he wondered.

"Positive! As you have no idea of what's been cast, it goes to show someone somewhere is placing great influence over them and covering their own tracks and avoiding you at all costs," said Tayce, angry.

The whole idea that someone somewhere outside the council was causing trouble bothered Darius greatly and why hadn't Lydia told him she had some idea something underhand was going on behind the scenes in the council? But perhaps she didn't know either, he thought. Was it the council that was at fault, or someone pretending to be a councillor causing trouble, like before with Layforn Barkin. Twedor stayed silent. He'd been like it since he and Tayce walked in earlier. He could see the Admiral was far from pleased. Tayce said no more either on the matter. The incident involving Layforn Barkin was rising in her thoughts too, as she'd read her father's mind.

After a few minons Darius turned.

"How soon do you want this log entry and where do you want it?" he asked calmly.

"Aidan can drop it off at the apart-house where Dairan and I are staying," she replied.

Darius nodded and didn't pick up on the fact she'd said she and Dairan were staying together in the apart-house. He figured she was a grown woman, and once legally joined, she knew what she was doing being intimate with Dairan. Without a further word Tayce called Twedor and headed over to the entrance of the Officette Chambers, exclaiming that she would see him later at the council hearing, no doubt. He nodded as the doors parted and Tayce continued on through with Twedor by her side. Behind her, Darius took steps to find out why the idea of arresting Lance hadn't been brought before him before action had been taken to do so? Out in the anteroom, one of Jan Barnford's officers had been sent to find Tayce. He stood waiting with Aidan Lord. The young oriental officer informed Tayce the hearing with the council was set for 1100 hourons next mornet, the following dayon. Tayce nodded in understanding, then continued on out through the open anteroom doors with Twedor, back into the marblex corridor.

As she began towards the Vacuum Lift, Dairan, to her surprise, stepped from the lift and began walking to meet her. He smiled a warm, loving smile.

"I thought I would come and meet you. Is everything all right?" he asked, noticing she was in thought as she came towards him.

"Fine! Father had no idea Lance was here to go before the council tomorron to answer the accusation that he'd murdered Jonathan," replied Tayce casually as they began to head to the waiting Vacuum Lift.

"Really? Did you say anything about the missing disk chip to him?" enquired Dairan.

"No, but Father is going to retrieve the log entry from Amalthea One's voyage that states where Lance was at the time of Jonathan's death. He's having the report sent over later," said Tayce.

Tayce ushered Twedor into the lift and followed with Dairan. All three stood waiting for the doors to close. They slid shut with the gentle sound of compressed air. The Vacuum Lift began to descend back to E City Level. Once down, the lift doors opened and they all walked forth. Tayce's thoughts were on what was going to possibly happen next mornet with Lance. What he might go through. They both began on across E City Square towards the corridor that would take them along the path to the apart-house. Twedor, once clear of the city square, explained that he was already probing into Enlopedia's computer system, trying to see if he could help find the missing disk chips location.

"Be careful, Twedor," warned Tayce.

"I will. If there's any sign I'm being detected, I'll cover my tracks," promised Twedor.

They all soon entered the apart-house after meeting various people they knew on Enlopedia on the way. Twedor crossed and stood out of the way, silently seeing what he could retrieve from the Enlopedian computer system without being rebuffed. Tayce began, saying she was off to get cleansed and changed before refreshment time. Dairan watched her walk away admiringly, then turned back to Twedor, hoping he didn't blow vital circuits in his probing process.

* * *

Later on that same dayon in the apart-house Twedor, during evening refreshment without warning shrieked and shut down. Both Tayce and Dairan looked at him alarmed, as did Treketa. Dairan jumped to his feet and ran over to the little Romid, kneeling down as Tayce wondered if he would reboot himself. Dairan began to check the little Romid out to see what had happened. After a few cencrons of examination, he came to the conclusion that Twedor had sustained overload. Tayce figured it had to be serious, otherwise he would have rebooted. Dairan reached the reboot/reset button under Twedor's circuitry panel and pressed it. A few cencrons passed and suddenly Twedor came back on full operational power, his systems coming back up one by one.

"Oh boy, that had a kick in it! I guess I pushed my luck in probing for information," he announced in his childlike male voice.

"What happened?" asked Tayce, truly relieved that he was going to be all right.

"I guess I was a little too nosey. I hit an electronic frequency block and it rebuffed me with a bolt of pure energy for my nosiness. Take my advice: never want to be a Romid. When something like that happens it knocks you powerless," explained Twedor.

"Are you all right now?" asked Dairan before rising to his feet.

"Fine! I'll just have to be careful when I probe around the main system next time," replied Twedor, patting Dairan's hand reassuringly.

Treketa decided once the meal was through to return to her short-stay accommodation as she wanted to contact Donaldo back on the cruiser before turning in for the night. With this, Twedor volunteered to escort her back. He figured he'd done enough searching around in the Enlopedian main computer system for one dayon. Tayce warned him to be careful, but let him go.

When the apart-house doors closed behind Treketa and Twedor, Dairan crossed to Tayce. He took hold of her hands and pulled her in close, swiftly. Their eyes met. She felt the warmth and strong passion and mysteriousness he conveyed enticing her softly. Soon they were locked in a tender kissing embrace, neither one interested in where they were. They let their feelings soar for each other. Tayce draped her arms around his neck, lost in what they were sharing. As they became engulfed in each other's wants and needs, they completely lost all recognition of time.

He whispered close to her ear. "You're the most sensual woman I've ever encountered. I love you."

"I truly love you too," she replied in a melted whisper.

As they both were so lost in each other, they didn't hear the entrance doors opening behind them. Lydia and Darius walked in and stood waiting, looking at one another in amused surprise at what they were witnessing in both their daughter and Dairan Loring. Darius raised his eyes in jest. Lydia was taken back, but glad the friendship had blossomed. As neither Tayce nor Dairan noticed they were there, after a few cencrons Darius coughed to let Tayce know he and Lydia were present. Tayce, hearing the cough, broke from Dairan, feeling somewhat awkward, even though she had no need to. Dairan was stuck for words and wondered if the Admiral would look down on him for his behaviour with his daughter.

"Mother! Father! This is a surprise," said Tayce, breaking the icet.

"Yes, it was for us too. We thought we would deliver the report you wanted for Lance ourselves and stay for a while. We had no idea you had plans," said Darius, teasing his daughter, with a cheeky grin. Lydia studied Dairan, a little surprised that Tayce should go for him, for attraction. Not that he wasn't handsome—he was—but she always thought it would have been Marc Dayatso that would be her daughter's type as she knew he felt a lot for Tayce and they'd always been close. But if Dairan was what Tayce wanted, she was a grown woman and it was fine by her. After all, the last relationship Tayce had, had a somewhat tragic ending.

"Thank you," said Tayce, taking the report and setting it down on the table.

"Everything all right, Dairan?" asked Darius, trying to keep a straight face. He could see Dairan was slightly unnerved by him being caught with Tayce in his arms.

"Yes, sir," replied Dairan somewhat awkwardly, having no idea Darius was winding him up.

Darius could identify the way Dairan was feeling as he'd once been like it with Lydia in the early dayons when he wanted her to be his for long term. He could see Dairan becoming a possible member of the Traun family, in a manner of speaking, by the way he seemed to be looking to Tayce for help in their awkward moments.

"We've also brought some bad news, I'm afraid. The council have stated not only must there be evidence from the last Amalthean voyage, which you have here, but they are also calling for the missing disk chip information to be presented," explained Lydia.

"That's ridiculous—we don't have it. We have the one prior to it," said Tayce, worried.

"Oh, but you will have. I think that's where I come in," said Twedor, hearing what was said and pushing past Darius.

"What do you mean, Twedor—where you come in?" asked Tayce, surprised, looking at Dairan questioningly, wondering if he might know what Twedor was on about.

"You know the temporary shutdown I had? Well, I was probing for the whereabouts of the missing disk chip information"explained Twedor.

"Did you have any luck?" asked Darius, interested.

"No, but I'm willing to have a go again," he volunteered.

"All right, but be careful this time," advised Tayce.

Lydia and Darius watched as Twedor ventured once more into the high-frequency link-up and gained access under Darius Traun's nose to the main Enlopedian computer system, in search of the missing disk chip. Tayce looked on, concerned that he might get another rebuff from the security defences set in place against hacking and probing. Dairan was ready to act and save the little Romid when it occurred. All stood around watching and waiting as Twedor silently worked away in search, this time with hoped-for success in finding the missing disk chip for evidence that Lance did not murder his own father. Without warning, Twedor once again began to shake violently, just like he had the first time. Tayce didn't like the fact he was not shutting down, like he did. Then, just as the inevitable seemed about to happen, Twedor calmed down, coming back to normal operation.

"Did you find anything this time?" Dairan asked Twedor.

"Yes! The missing disk chip—wait for this—in Layforn Barkin's sealed capsule in the Archives building," said Twedor, to everyone's utter amazement.

"Good work, Twedor," praised Tayce, hugging the little Romid.

Darius and Tayce began walking over to the entrance of the apart-house, to go on out. Dairan suggested he go instead to the Archives building. Darius looked at Tayce, waiting for her to decide who she wanted to take. He didn't mind either way. She gestured to Dairan. With this, Darius suggested to Dairan that he take the master key for the Archives building as it would be out of Officette hourons to gain entry. Dairan accepted it. Darius continued, saying he would contact Chief Jan Barnford and have him meet them at the entrance to the building. Both continued on out of the apart-house. Outside they both ran down the shiny marblex path towards the area where the Archives building was. Soon they were in the corridor that would take them to the Archives building. They ran along, passing off-duty after-hourons revellers and young cadets on the way to some relaxation leisure club where music and merriment took place. Dairan, upon arriving at the Archives building, noticed the lights were on half-power and the staff had gone off duty. He took the sonic master pass key out of his pocket and slid it into the de-locking reader by the entrance doors. Just as he did, Jan Barnford came across to them.

Jan winked at Tayce then began speaking. "Burglars will be severely dealt with," he light-heartedly announced.

Dairan laughed, knowing it was Jan by the sound of his voice. The glassene-and-steelex doors before them began opening once the pass key had been read.

"Don't worry about the intruder alarm—I'll take care of that once we're inside," said Jan helpfully.

He entered first and headed away briskly to deactivate the intruder alarm. Tayce followed Dairan into the anteroom of the vast-sized building. They stood waiting for Jan's return before venturing any further, waiting until it was safe to do so. After Jan depressed a sequence of keys to deactivate the alarm system, he briskly walked back to join them.

"Your father tells me you're looking for the missing disk chip to clear Lance (besides the one you've got already) and it's in Layforn Barkin's capsule. I was quite surprised to hear this," he said seriously.

"It was Twedor that found it. We are just as surprised as you are, but that's what we're here for," replied Tayce.

"Right, once we've found the capsule, it must be taken back to my Officette in the Security, Crime and Patrol Division building, where it can be opened in a safe, secure environment," ordered Jan.

All three of them walked across the anteroom to almost floor-to-ceiling wide gold-coloured vault-type doors, which lead to the Capsule Containment Room. Jan unlocked the door with another master key. After a few minons the thick and heavy doors drew back along the equally thickly constructed walls on either side. Tayce slipped inside with Jan, with Dairan following on. Inside was vast and filled with capsules on shelves from floor to ceiling and from one end of the room to the other, as far as the eye could see. It looked like the end of the room went into infinity. There were centre aisles for walking down to find what was required and special lifts to travel to the high-up shelves, which would move along at keypad command. The interior of the whole room was in the same shiny gold colour as the entrance doors. It was believed to have been constructed of the same metal, but ten times thicker. Dairan paused, amazed by the great vastness of their surroundings.

"We'll never find it—there's too many," said Dairan, looking up and all about at the shelves of gold-coloured capsules.

"Don't worry—the high-ranked officers' capsules are along here, in alphabetical order, so it shouldn't be too far along," said Jan, taking the situation in hand and beginning to walk down a row, looking.

All three walked along for a few minons, looking in different directions, high and low. Dairan spotted the capsule.

"Found it—Barkin!" announced Dairan triumphantly, glad they didn't have to spend hourons searching the whole vastness of the room.

"I wonder what the P stands for?" asked Tayce, curious.

"Probably pain in the ass," replied Jan, much to everyone's amusement.

"Jan!" replied Tayce, laughing at his sudden outburst.

"He's got a point, though," said Dairan, trying to stop laughing.

"Right, what do we do now?" asked Tayce as Jan took down the gold square-shaped capsule with help from Dairan.

"Follow me back to my Officette," replied Jan.

All three began on out of the capsule-orientated storage vault and out through the anteroom, where Jan activated the building alarm before joining Tayce and Dairan, then leaving the building and heading across the city square to his Officette in the Security, Crime and Patrol Division building. Dairan left Tayce halfway across the square, exclaiming that he'd head on back to the apart-house and inform her parents that the capsule had been retrieved. Tayce agreed. With this Dairan walked away leaving Jan and Tayce to continue on.

Upon entering the Security, Crime and Patrol Division building ,Tayce was somewhat surprised to see the main Arresting Area was not busy. Jan caught her surprised look.

"Problem?" he asked.

"It's just I don't think I've ever seen this area so calm and empty," she replied.

"Don't worry—it will be busy later and tomorron, especially at the time of the trial," he replied, knowing so.

"Don't remind me—tomorron will come soon enough. I guess it will be people looking for a scoop on the story that they can fabricate to hide the truth of what happened," she said.

She knew she was in for a tough time with the council next dayon. They never saw eye to eye on matters relating to the Amalthean Quests, or her team and voyages.

"Well, it's not every dayon Lance Largon comes before the Criminal Council for the death of his father; and before you react, I'm on your side, remember? Now, let's see what's inside this thing," he said, walking on through to the doors of his Officette.

They soon entered into Jan's Officette and the doors closed behind them. Inside he crossed to his light-brown desk and sat the capsule down. Tayce watched with great anticipation as Jan went about breaking the security seal with a sharp thin opening laser device. Once open, he undid the lid and there, much to their surprise, right before their eyes, was the evidence that would clear Lance in the form of the missing disk chip. Jan glanced at Tayce, then lifted the small, thin, clear, 87.5-mm-in-diameter disk chip container containing the missing disk chip out and handed it to her.

"I think this is what we've been looking for, don't you?" he announced, pleased.

"Yes definitely. I'd like to see Lance while I'm here—give him the good news," replied Tayce, glad about what they'd found.

"Of course. I'll take you down to the holding cell," he replied casually.

"What will happen to Barkin's belongings now?" asked Tayce, curious, as Jan closed the capsule ready to be resealed.

"His son will have them," replied Jan without compassion in his usual gruff tone.

"His what! He hasn't got one, has he?" asked Tayce, somewhat surprised to learn Barkin had a son.

"Yes. Would you believe he adopted one of the orphan children many yearons ago. His name is Nayarn. He's probably about eighteen yearons old now and top of his class in the Science College Colony. That's what I was told last time I heard," explained Jan, thinking about it.

"Does he know about what his father did regarding the loss of all the innocent cadets?" asked Tayce, curious.

"I'm not sure. The last I heard about him was that he'd put in for a transfer to some far-off colony, when he leaves the Science College Colony," replied Jan.

Both began walking on out of the Officette to visit Lance. They were soon walking through the main Arresting Area on their way to visit Lance in the holding cell. Two young criminals were discussing Lance, and not in the most flattering way. Tayce was about to put the two of them straight when Jan reached out and squeezed her shoulder discreetly, advising her to let it pass. They knew no better. Tayce glanced back over her shoulder and Jan shook his head. She continued on, but somehow wished she could meet the person or being who had framed Lance face-to-face. This whole situation with Lance reminded her of what had happened to Tom, her late intimate joining partner, who was accused of the murder of Alenea, his first wife, on the first voyage.

After walking for a while through various corridors, both Tayce and Jan came to a force-field grid type entrance to a holding cell. Inside Lance sat on the far bunk, under the clear vision sight pane, staring out in thought into the bleakness of the immediate Universe. He didn't even notice Tayce enter his surroundings until she touched him on the shoulder. He turned, glad to see her standing beside him, holding his key to freedom: the missing disk chip container, containing the much needed disk chip information to clear his name.

"You've found it! Does this mean tomorron I'm off the hook, so to speak?" asked Lance, greatly relieved he was going to be a free man, considering what had come to light, plus the evidence leading up to it on the other disk chip.

"You are in one way, but you still have to come before the Criminal Council. I wish it was a case of just handing this in and the other disk chip and returning to Amalthea—end of story. Sorry, Lance," replied Tayce.

"Can I ask is there any chance of retaining the disk chip, after the audience with the Criminal Council for my personal collection?" Lance asked Jan.

"After the evidence has been heard and stored, I don't see why not. It belongs to you anyway. Tayce tells me you have Twedor to thank for finding this. Apparently, he nearly blew his circuits," explained Jan.

"Tell him, Tayce, he's the best little Romid in the Universe," said Lance, praising Twedor.

"No, you can tell him yourself in the mornet. Now get some sleep—you've a date in the mornet neither one of us wants to face, but must," ordered Tayce in the tone of friend and captain.

She turned and began on the way out, pausing as Lance thanked her, feeling a lot easier in his mind even though he wasn't guilty. Tayce looked back at him and smiled, then followed Jan on back out into the corridor. The security guard on duty activated the force-field grid-type door for the last night Lance would have to be where he was. Tayce walked with Jan back out of the holding-cell area to the sound of various confined criminals' innuendos regarding what they would like to do to her, as she passed. She ignored it—it was nothing she hadn't heard before, in her dayons before voyage two.

They soon came out into E City Square, where Jan said goodnight and they parted.

* * *

Back at the apart-house, Dairan had given Lydia and Darius the news that the disk chip had been found. Lydia, on hearing it, gave a great sigh of relief to think Lance had been proven innocent after all. After the death of his father, Lance had always thought of Lydia and Tayce, and now Darius, as his new adopted family, and Lydia looked upon him as the son she could never have. Darius put his arm around her, noticing she looked tired. It had been a long and busy duty time. He informed her of as much as she glanced at him, glad everything would work out well for Lance in the mornet—especially now the disk chip had been recovered safely. She smiled a relaxed smile. Darius suggested they head back to the residence and catch Tayce in the mornet. Lydia, even though tired, refused. She wanted to stay a bit longer. Dairan, on, this offered another refreshing drink. Both thought about it for a few minons, then accepted. Dairan, as he crossed to the drinks area, began explaining about the confrontation with Aemiliyana, what had happened and how he had managed to keep Tayce safe through it all.

"You went on the Quest; why not Marc?" asked Darius, somewhat surprised Marc hadn't been included.

"Believe me, sir, it's a long story. Tayce will have to tell you that, I'm afraid," replied Dairan. He figured it was between father and daughter.

At that moment, the apart-house doors opened. Tayce entered. Lydia looked up from sitting with Darius on the soffette.

"How's Lance holding up?" she enquired.

"Fine! He's glad to know the missing disk chip has been found for the audience with the Criminal Council in the mornet. He already knows that with the evidence the disk chip may contain, plus the one we've got leading up to it, he's walking free," explained Tayce, crossing to Dairan.

"Thanks for the drinks, Dairan. Now we'll leave you two alone. Come on Lydia, it's going to be another busy dayon tomorrow," said Darius, rising to his feet and helping Lydia to hers.

"I want to see you before you leave tomorrow, if everything goes all right," requested Lydia to Tayce.

"Yes, of course. Will you be in the audience in the chambers or part of the council tomorrow, Father?" put Tayce. She figured, with her father being Admiral of Enlopedia, if he was present then he would have some clout behind the decision on Lance's freedom and innocence.

"I don't know, but your mother may be there. I know you've requested to be present haven't you, but whether they'll allow me is another thing. It's a criminal matter and they don't try to get me in there too often, if you know what I mean.

"They can try and push your father aside, but me—that's another matter. Night, you two," announced Lydia.

Tayce smiled at her mother's determination, but whether or not she would be present, they'd have to wait and see. Darius shook his head at his wife's attitude—her determination to be present the next dayon. Dairan caught on and smiled to himself. As he saw the Admiral give Lydia a raised-eye look, thinking of what she had become since being in charge. He realised Tayce was like Lydia in her impulsive and stubborn way. It was a case of like mother, like daughter.

Darius said goodnight to them both, then walked over to the entrance to leave. The entrance doors drew back on approach. Darius paused, waiting for Lydia, then together they walked on out. When the doors closed, Tayce turned to see Dairan standing holding two glassenes filled with a coloured liquid. She walked towards him.

"Did Mother or Father ask anything about us?" asked Tayce, studying him, wondering if they'd given him an approving lecture regarding the fact they were now an item.

"No, they didn't say much at all—just general conversation about Amalthea and the Quests we'd done to date," replied Dairan tiredly.

"Well, I'm turning in for the night. How about you? We've a busy dayon tomorron" replied Tayce, just as tired.

"In a while. Where are you going to keep the disk chips for safekeeping tonight?" asked Dairan, interested, knowing how important it was for them to be safely guarded until the next dayon.

"Twedor, would you mind looking after the disk chips for me until mornet?" asked Tayce, looking down at the little Romid.

"Of course not—they will be quite safe with me," assured Twedor, taking the disk chips.

He pressed a panel in the mid section of his torso. It slid back and he placed the disk chips inside then closed the panel with the push of his first metlon finger.

Tayce, as she walked away in the direction of the Sleep Centre, called back to Twedor, "Goodnight."

Dairan was about to enter his Sleep Centre when Tayce reached out and grabbed him into hers. Dairan didn't protest. There was the sound of soft laughter as the doors closed. Twedor did a synthesized whistle, then went to standby for the night hourons.

* * *

Next dayon came round soon enough. It had been decided that everyone would meet outside what was termed the Grand Dome, which housed the council building. But upon walking into the area, they found it surrounded by a chanting mob, slagging Lance off in the most unflattering of ways. Security officers that were watching the crowd saw Tayce and her team members and immediately went to assist in getting them safely inside the building. Tayce grabbed Twedor close to her as they went. Dairan and two security officers made sure both Treketa and Tayce entered the building in their protection. The mob, as both Amalthean Quests members and the security officers made it inside, turned very rowdy—so much so that the rowdiness was climbing to an almost out-of-control pitch, which made the officers wonder if they'd have to call for drastic backup measures. Tayce caught sight of where the violent shouts and yells of abuse were focused on. It was Lance, approaching the council building with six armour-clad SSWAT officers. Jan Barnford walked out into the square from his building, looking like thunder ready to erupt. The crowd were beginning to disrupt the every-dayon peaceful existence of Enlopedia city and base. It had to stop. He raised a loud announcement handheld device to his mouth.

"Enlopedia has heard enough of this rowdy disruption. I am hereby ordering immediate silence and dispersal of this crowd. I understand your anger and you've had your say—now, as Chief of Security of this base I would suggest you head off to your every-dayon duties, or there will be significant arrests. Is that clear?" Jan shouted loud enough to be heard above the angry crowd of men and women in their mid twenties to fortie's.

The crowd fell silent and looked in Jan's direction. Officers placed their hands on their Pollomoss weapons ready for any trouble, ready to restore order to the city square if need be. As the crowd failed to move, Jan fired a blank warning shot from his Pollomoss into the air. After a few cencrons, the crowd began to slowly disperse, mumbling to themselves as they did as ordered and headed away. Jan ordered his men via Wristlink to keep the crowd moving and watch for any troublemakers. He continued on into the council building to check that Tayce and others were all right. Just as he was about to walk to Tayce, a young blonde male clerk in a turquoise uniform walked from the Council Chambers for criminal hearings and approached.

"Captain Traun and Officer Largon," he called out in a precise no-nonsense tone.

"Here!" replied Tayce.

"Would you accompany me?" he prompted, turning and walking away back to the chambers entrance.

Tayce and Lance followed the young clerk in the direction of the chambers. Jan paused with Dairan and Treketa with Twedor and followed on in to see how the hearing was going to go. Once inside, they were escorted to the private viewing balcony, where they could watch the hearing through a glassene partition. Dairan and Treketa, as they caught Lance looking in their direction, wished him luck. Tayce walked into the centre of the Council Chamber under the watchful eye of the seated selected delegates present. Lance walked to come beside her. He came to a pause. Before them sat the thirteen selected delegates, experts in criminal law, in their red-and-blue robes. It was an all-male council. All had serious expressions. They were ready to hear and pass decisive judgement on Lance, if it had to be passed. Tayce was somewhat surprised to see her mother was not on the council of thirteen present, or her father. This gave her the idea something wasn't right in the set-up. Lance being present, when the council felt everyone was ready they began.

"Officer Lance Jonathan Largon, you stand here todayon in the presence of this criminal investigation council, accountable for the death of the late General Jonathan Largon of Questa Headquarters Base. How do you plead in this instance?" asked the central delegate of thirteen, a man with short brown hair and of thin build.

"Not guilty, sir. Somebody else killed my father," replied Lance with a mixture of anger and hurt on his features, to think he was where he was.

"Captain Traun, you are here to present evidence to substantiate that Officer Largon was on board Amalthea One during the time of his father's death, are you not?"continued the central delegate as the others muttered around him.

"Yes. I have here the missing disk chip, plus the one prior to the missing one, of a collection of disk chips left to Officer Largon by his father. Both contain what we believe is evidence—as you will all discover upon viewing these disk chips—that Officer Largon was not responsible. He's innocent. Where's Layforn Barkin, who was the one to provoke the late Jonathan Largon into a severe heart attack, causing his death, and not my officer beside me, as you claim," pointed out Tayce seriously, trying to keep her cool.

"That's quite an accusation, Captain. How did you come by this missing evidence that suggests Layforn Barkin is somehow connected?" asked another delegate on the panel of thirteen, giving Tayce a scrutinizing look with his somewhat plain, cold features.

"It was discovered in Layforn Barkin's capsule of belongings, which was kept in the Archives building. Chief Barnford assisted in retrieving and opening the capsule," replied Tayce.

"Nice speech, Tayce—thank you," said Lance discreetly by her.

"Let's hope they see the connection with your father's death when they study the disk chips," replied Tayce, just as discreetly.

Suddenly there was a lot of whispering amongst the thirteen-strong Criminal Council before them. The audience on the private viewing balcony were also discussing amongst themselves Layforn Barkin's possible connection. Tayce glanced up and caught Dairan looking down. He smiled and winked at her affectionately. She turned her attention back to the panel of delegates as they'd stopped whispering. The head delegate began, saying that he had discussed the possible evidence and would like to view the disk chips. A young clerk of average looks walked forth and took the disk chips from Tayce. He then crossed to the head delegate, who put one in the disk chip reader, which was built into the desktop. A few cencrons elapsed. The large circular wall screen in the far end central wall of the chambers flashed into life.

In the moments that followed, the screen showed the heated debate between Jonathan Largon and Layforn Barkin in Jonathan's Officette on Questa. The second disc was played right behind the first. Lance felt he didn't want to see the incident all over again, but he had no choice. Both he and Tayce stood watching the scene unfold once more—the threatening actions of Barkin. The audience and seated delegates watched in interested wonder and judgement of what was going to happen. Then came a scene Tayce hadn't seen before as it was on the second disc played. It shocked her, as it did Lance. Just as Jonathan had turned his back on Barkin in anger, Barkin slipped something like a blue powder into Jonathan's Coffeen on the desktop. Tayce gasped in shock. She looked at Lance, seeing that he too was in shock at what had just unfolded. His eyes were wide with alarm. She could sense the hatred and furiousness rising in him and could understand it. The second disk chip soon ceased.

There was talking amongst the delegates once more. Then the lead delegate announced that they, the Criminal Council, had seen sufficient evidence to know they were wrong in their assumption about the death of the late Jonathan Largon. The other delegates, all ranging between the ages of forties to mid sixties and distinguished in appearance, all looked at Lance, a lot more at ease.

"Officer Largon, the members of this council and myself have considered the visual evidence, and it is plain to see it's sufficient to clear you of any involvement in the death of the late Jonathan Largon. A further investigation will ensue examining Layforn Barkin's background to find out what truly happened. I hereby announce that you are a free man," announced the head delegate.

"Thank you, sir. I am just glad Captain Traun here was able to prove I am innocent and she could help in providing the evidence you needed to prove I wasn't connected with my father's death, I loved and respected my father, sir," spoke up Lance beside Tayce, with tears of great relief forming in his eyes.

As the Criminal Council stepped down from their position and began on out, the audience began leaving the private viewing balcony, looking at Lance with a lot more respectful looks on their faces. Paclan Sellecson, who was on the Criminal Council, on behalf of the Medical Dome, crossed to Lance. He came to a pause and began, saying that Jonathan's death was due to the drug Layforn Barkin had dropped into his Coffeen, but it wasn't detected until after his death. It had been a heart-stopping drug, very lethal, especially when mixed with Coffeen, and it had been the sole cause of Jonathan's death. Then he discreetly informed Lance he couldn't understand why the powers that be ever considered him responsible. Lance shook his head, knowing that if he could get his hands on Barkin and he wasn't dead, he soon would be.

"Well, duty calls, you two. Take care of yourselves," said Paclan politely as his paging bleeper had sounded on his Wristlink—he was wanted back at the Medical Dome urgently.

"You too," replied Tayce as Paclan headed briskly away back to duty.

"Tayce, would you mind if I meet you back at the Patrol Cruiser?" asked Lance.

"Why? We have to get back to Amalthea," said Tayce, curious to know, though it had crossed her mind that Lance, seeing his father had been murdered, might take it to heart and head off to the Twone Bar and down a few drinks, like he did when his father had died and he couldn't cope.

"I want to collect the disk chips for the completion of my collection," he replied, much to Tayce's relief.

"All right, an houron, then we depart for Amalthea," replied Tayce warningly, thankful it hadn't been what she suspected.

"OK, I'll be there, don't worry," he assured.

Once outside the Council Chambers, in the large anteroom area, Dairan, Treketa, Twedor and Jan met up with Tayce. Once Lance had received the many congratulations for proving his innocence, he excused himself and headed off to collect the disk chips containing the evidence. Jan asked where he was off to, wondering, like Tayce had, with Lance seeing his father again on-screen earlier, was he off to the Twone Bar? Tayce explained that he wanted the disk chips used as evidence, for his collection. Jan nodded in understanding.

Everyone continued on out of the Grand Dome. The crowd that had gathered to see Lance's downfall earlier had dispersed and the square was back to normal. Adam Carford was passing the building as Tayce and the others exited into the square. Tayce called out to him, asking him as he crossed towards her to tell her mother she wouldn't be able to keep their meeting after all and she'd see her next time they were in port and had time to visit. Adam nodded understandingly, going on. Jan glanced at his Wristlink time display, announcing it was time for refreshment. He would treat. With this, Tayce, Dairan, Treketa, Twedor and himself headed off to get something to eat and drink. It had been a long mornet. They crossed the city square towards the new 'Enlo' Refreshment Dome.

* * *

An houron later Lance walked from E City on across to the Arrival and Departure Dome and on towards the walkway that would take him to the Patrol Cruiser. He carried the disk chip container that contained the disk chips he wanted back from the trial, plus the purchases he'd made from the E City shopping mall. He smiled to himself, thinking how two hourons ago there had been sceptics waiting outside the council building ready to see him fall for something he hadn't done. Now they were nowhere to be seen and anyone that did pass him wasn't interested in him in particular. 'Yesteron's news!' he thought. He passed through the automatic sensor, which scanned his body for offensive weapons. This was standard on the base, whether leaving or arriving. He could see Treketa waiting at the top of the walkway, just on board the Patrol Cruiser. She waved and he broke into a sprint. As he reached the end of the walkway, he ran up on board thinking he had arrived at the base an accused man; now he was leaving with a clean record. He stepped aboard behind Treketa, heading to find his seat.

Slowly the entrance closed and the Patrol Cruiser began to reverse out of the Docking Port, ready for turning to head off out into deep space. Amalthea was its destined port of call.

17. Final Confrontation

A couple of weekons later, after the unexpected trip to Enlopedia, Amalthea was travelling at a comfortable speed and many of the team aboard were taking time to catch up on duties and workloads that had been put on hold for various reasons, unaware of what was about to unfold. Out in space, without warning, massive explosion occurred and the whole cruiser shook violently. Kelly Travern, on duty in Organisation, was startled by the sudden brilliance of the glare that filled the whole of Organisation. She gasped at the suddenness as she was taken totally by surprise, as were the rest of the team on duty. Marc, who was present, quickly crossed over to her console. He paused beside her, looking down at her softly.

"Are you all right?" he asked in a caring way.

"Yes, I'm fine. It was just so sudden," replied Kelly, her eyes coming back to normal from the glare.

"It was a surprise for all of us. What was it—any information?" asked Marc.

Kelly quickly gathered herself together after the suddenness of the shock and began finding out what it could have been. Marc suggested she run an immediate scan of the near vicinity to find out what they were heading towards, or through. Kelly began the scan procedure without a further request. Marc watched as she did so, interested as to what they'd find. Tayce, who had been working in the DC, came into the doorway area and to everyone's surprise called out to Marc and dropped to the floor where she stood. Marc left Kelly and rushed to Tayce's side, ordering Nick on the way to call Donaldo and tell him they'd an emergency—it was Tayce. As Nick carried out the request, Marc knelt down beside Tayce, lifting her gently up into a sitting position, supporting her in his arms. She opened her eyes, slightly meeting his concerned look.

"The Empress—she's dead. The Honitonian realm is gone—destroyed," she said softly in a heartbroken way.

As she continued to look up into Marc's concerned eyes, he noticed her Telepathian blue illumination of force rise in her sapphire-blue eyes for a few cencrons, then fade away. She slipped back into unconsciousness, slowly closing her eyes and becoming lifeless in Marc's arms. He felt for her pulse, concerned. It was faint. He wished Donaldo would get a move on—something wasn't right. The team members around them watched on in extreme concern. Donaldo could be heard approaching and soon rushed into Organisation with his Emergency Medical Kit, accompanied by Treketa, who was ready to assist him. He went straight to Tayce's side and set down his kit.

"What happened?" he asked, looking at Marc as he opened his kit.

"She just appeared in the doorway, called to me, then collapsed. She said something about Empress Tricara was dead—yes, dead!—and the Honitonian realm was destroyed—all gone," replied Marc.

Donaldo didn't know what to make of it. He took his Examscan from his kit and began to guide it all over Tayce as she lay still lifeless, eyes closed. After a few minons, he finished the examination and looked at the display on the Examscan, waiting for the diagnostic readings to appear. He studied them the moment they materialised, then shook his head in disbelief as the reading was normal. Nothing seemed wrong. But there had to be something it didn't add up. He guided the Examscan around Tayce's head, and as he did so it became unbearably hot and he had to drop it. He quickly crossed to pick it up and quickly threw it into the waste recess compartment before it exploded, just behind Craig. Craig quickly helped in pushing the button to close the seal for immediate and safe disintegration. Everyone present wondered what was going to happen next. Donaldo suggested Tayce be moved to her quarters and Twedor be present to watch over her. Marc nodded. He suggested that as he hadn't brought the Hover Trolley he carry Tayce down there. Donaldo agreed. Marc scooped Tayce up in a supporting hold and began on the way to the Organisation entrance, the team watching on as he went, telling Dairan as he had entered the centre that he was in command until he got back. As Marc went with Tayce, Twedor, Donaldo and Treketa all walked from the centre.

Kelly looked back at her navigational screen just in time to see a sight she wasn't expecting to see. Right in their flight path was the menacing sight of Aemiliyana's massive space fortress in all it's threatening glory. She was back! It was a sight no one on board Amalthea wanted to see again. Lance ordered immediate Invis Shield; but before Kelly had a chance to do anything, Amal had taken the threatening situation in hand, which was showing itself, and already taken precautions to protect the cruiser and team. Dairan came to the entrance of the DC and, upon seeing the return of Aemiliyana, gave an alarmed and furious look.

"What the hell is she doing back here—I thought that fortress was destroyed?" demanded Dairan without thought.

"It just materialised. I guess she's conjured up a new version and it looks more powerful than the last, judging by the readings I'm receiving," replied Lance at his research console.

"She's picked a good time to appear—maybe she's the reason for Tayce's current state," said Dairan, wondering if the Witch Queen had cast another of her vicious spells and rendered Tayce helpless, so she could gain the upper hand in a confrontation once again.

Behind Dairan in the entrance to Organisation, in shimmering holographic projection, Aemiliyana appeared in all her evil prowess. Deluca, upon seeing her, called Dairan. He spun round to see the sight of Aemiliyana giving him a commanding and powerful yet interested look.

"We meet again, Loring. Where is she—the threat to my existence and one that must be destroyed? Isn't she here to witness the display of my new power force?" she asked in her commanding sarcastic tone.

"You rendered her unconscious, you bitch! Now I would suggest you back off," retorted Dairan furiously.

"Really! That's such a shame. Inform her what has been cast is just a start in the increase of my power ability. There will be more shows of power forthcoming if she doesn't surrender within three hourons," stated Aemiliyana.

"Didn't you hear what I just said?" replied Dairan. His eyes were dark and angry-looking.

"We have unfinished business over her great-grandfather, Grandmaster Alexentron Traun. If she does not do as I demand, I will crush your cruiser and kill everyone on board," she announced with real meaning in her voice, then faded out of existence.

Dairan gave an exasperated sigh. His features were still filled with anger. He punched the air in madness. Lance raised his eyes, but understood Dairan's fury. Both exchanged unimpressed looks over Aemiliyana's delivered speech. Dairan wished what Emperor Honitonia had done to her had worked, for Tayce's and all their sakes.

"Has Invis Shield been activated?" asked Dairan as he crossed to Kelly.

"Yes, it's now been increased to the maximum level," replied Kelly, checking.

"Keep it that way—it will keep Aemiliyana guessing where we are and buy us some time," replied Dairan, knowing with the whole cruiser under Invis Shield it would stop Aemiliyana finding out when Tayce was back on her feet so she could be prepared for the final meeting with the witch.

*　*　*

On Aemiliyanas fortress, which had been re-established through her powers. She was immediately alarmed when one of her operatives informed her, that Amalthea had disappeared from the universal path before them. Another expressed that Amalthea had also vanished off the Detection Scanner. She glared angrily at the young blonde operative and her breathing quickened in fury. He ignored her increasing anger and simply explained that he couldn't explain what had happened—all his systems were fully operational; there should be no reason why they could not detect or see the Amalthean cruiser.

"I don't care how you do it—find that cruiser. I've come too far to let Tayce Traun slip through my grasp this time around. I'm not prepared to lose her at any cost," shouted Aemiliyana, her eyes wide in enraged anger at the thought that she might miss the chance to carry out her final confrontation once and for all.

The operative that had delivered the news Aemiliyana didn't want to hear tried keying in every sequence he could figure to find the possible whereabouts of Amalthea. But nothing he tried would work to his advantage. He looked at Aemiliyana and shook his head, almost afraid of what she might to do him.

"Apologies, Your Highness—there's nothing to uncover. The whereabouts of Amalthea are not available," he announced obediently.

"Curse and damnation! They're out there—keep trying I want that cruiser found!" she ordered impatiently with simmering fierceness.

"Your Highness, it is possible Amalthea is hiding behind some kind of undetectable shield that is hard to break through," came back the first young operative, in his white uniform.

"Find a way to detect it—now! Is that clear?" she demanded, almost about to explode, pacing about the floor in agitated exasperation.

Her eyes were enraged and dark-looking, conveying her powerful anger from within. She could see Tayce Traun getting away all over again and she wasn't prepared to let her, even if she had to take on getting through whatever Amalthea was hiding behind, or wherever it had gone.

* * *

On board Amalthea, Marc placed Tayce gently down on her bunk in her quarters. Donaldo, who had decided to accompany them, attached a diagnostic counter alert disc, or DCAD for short, on Tayce's right wrist so she could be monitored from the MLC in case her condition changed. It was a small, silver, round, almost flat disc, roughly 2.3 mm in diameter. He then activated it. Amal overhead confirmed activation had taken place. Marc removed Tayce's boots so she was more comfortable, whilst Donaldo picked up his Emergency Medical Kit and briskly walked from the Repose Centre, heading on out through the Living Area of the quarters, on through the opening entrance doors, back to the MLC Marc's Wristlink bleeped on his wrist. He raised it and pressed the Comceive button. Dairan's voice came through in urgency. He warned Marc that Aemiliyana was back and she'd created a new fortress similar to her old design, but more powerful than the last. Marc gave a look of anger, then glanced down at Tayce. Dairan continued, he had Invis Shield raised to the highest setting, so it was now in full operation to buy them some time.

"Nice work. Just make sure she can't penetrate this cruiser. With Tayce in her current state, she'd be right where Aemiliyana wants her—easy for the taking," said Marc, concerned.

"Don't worry—we'll do everything we can up here until Tayce is able to confront Aemiliyana on her own terms," assured Dairan meaningfully.

"I'll remain here until she regains consciousness. Keep me informed," said Marc, signing off and deactivating his Wristlink.

Marc shook his head, watching Tayce, hoping she would wake up soon for her own sake. He thought to himself, why couldn't Aemiliyana have stayed where the Emperor had put her? What was it with her and this revenge thing? What had Tayce's grandfather really done to this woman that made her seek revenge on Tayce so badly especially as Tayce had nothing to do with what happened in the past? He sat on the bunk. There was no way he was going to leave Tayce alone in her current state. Fair enough, Twedor was present; but after what had happened to the little Romid the last time Aemiliyana got her hands on him, he wasn't taking any chances. He was staying put until Tayce regained full consciousness. He reached down and checked his Pollomoss handgun, in his side holster just in case the almost inevitable happened and the Witch Queen showed up. Without warning, Tayce moaned but stayed asleep. Marc reached out, taking hold of her delicate slim hand, reassuring her that she was safe. But, as he said it, deep down he hoped the Invis Shield surrounding the cruiser didn't fail until she was awake again.

Kelly, up in Organisation, announced that the fortress was beginning to head towards them. Dairan turned quickly on her words, to see as much through the main sight port. He immediately ordered an orbital shift in position. Once again, before Kelly had a chance to carry out Dairan's request, Amalthea under Amals guidance was already moving out of the vicinity of the fast-approaching massive fortress. Amal was the kind of computer to protect her outer hull, as well as the crew, and was programmed to avoid life-threatening situations to the crew if need be. Hyper-thrust turbo was activated and the cruiser put some distance between them and the fortress. Dairan gave a look that said it all. He had an idea the Witch Queen remembered that before they'd gone under Invis Shield they were in front of her and figured she'd try ramming them. There came a huge shout and a triumphant cheer at the action being taken, from the team present, as Amal shifted the cruiser further away in orbit relative to the fortress, leaving behind Aemiliyana, none the wiser that Amalthea and Tayce were anywhere near. Dairan's face changed to an amused smile as he thought about the fact they'd fooled the evil witch.

"Do we still need to remain in Invis Shield now we've put some distance between the witch and us?" asked Kelly, curious.

"Give it two hourons, then if Aemiliyana doesn't suspect we've jumped to another orbit and followed, return us to normal Invis Shield," replied Dairan, thinking about it and playing it safe.

"There's a call coming through. It's Enlopedia—Admiral Traun. He wants to find out if Tayce is OK, only Empress Tricara has collapsed in her duties and has been rushed to the Medical Dome," explained Nick at his communications position.

"Could he have more perfect timing? Make a good excuse—and make sure it's good enough to convince him she's busy but all right," suggested Dairan.

"Leave it with me," assured Nick, beginning to wonder how he could tell the Admiral enough to convince him Tayce was busy but fine, even though they all knew otherwise.

Marc, much to Dairan's surprise, walked into Organisation. He put to him that he'd thought he was remaining with Tayce while she was in the condition she was in. Marc exclaimed that Twedor had assured him they'd left the orbit of the fortress, so Tayce was safe for a while in his care. So he had decided to return to duty and leave Twedor on watch. He had promised that if there were any suspected visits from Aemiliyana he would be alerted. Dairan explained what was happening in that the Admiral had called from Enlopedia to check whether Tayce was all right, as Tricara had collapsed suddenly on duty at Enlopedia and been rushed to the Medical Dome. Marc, on this, gave a raised-eye look of surprise. It seemed to him Aemiliyana was making quite a spectacular return. She'd now rendered both Tayce and the Empress unconscious and probably thrown the Honitonian realms into utter chaos, just to get what she wanted—and it looked like she wasn't going to be defeated. Dairan continued, saying they'd hopefully managed to put some distance between Aemiliyana and themselves, buying some recovery time for Tayce. Marc nodded in total understanding. Dairan further announced that Invis Shield had been downgraded to normal undetectability; it would remain like it unless the fortress entered their new Universe. Then Amal would raise it at a minon's notice to protect Tayce again, if need be. Marc could see Dairan was doing his utmost in his absence. All he hoped was that Aemiliyana stayed patrolling the old Universe, where they'd left her. They both turned their attention to the present time and duty, keeping on alert, in case the inevitable should happen: Aemiliyana suddenly appearing without warning.

* * *

Down in Tayce's Repose Centre, she began to wake slowly from the induced unconsciousness, created by Aemiliyana's power force. Twedor was standing by her bunk, looking down at her, running a silent test on her well-being, making sure she was fully back to normal. He reached out his little metlon hand and lightly prodded her on the arm.

"Are you all right, Tayce?" he asked, waiting.

Tayce opened her eyes, looking up at him, quickly realising something within herself wasn't right. She felt strange. Then it came back to her, how back in the DC she had suddenly lost all her inner power ability and collapsed. As she adjusted to her familiar surroundings, so she realised she couldn't sense things like she normally would. Sitting up, she tried to conjure a small power ball with her hands, using her mind, as Twedor watched. Nothing was happening, as hard as she tried, she was powerless. This, she thought, wasn't good. If Aemiliyana showed up, she would be totally vulnerable and totally at the Witch Queen's mercy once more. She turned to Twedor.

"I'm powerless. I can't communicate using my powers. I can't reach Tricara, the Emperor or sense Honitonia is still in existence. Oh, Twedor, what's happened?" asked Tayce, looking at him, hoping he would answer her questions.

"Let me explain, but you're not going to like this: Aemiliyana is back. She tried catching us in the last sector until we went to hyper-thrust turbo, putting some space between her and us," explained Twedor, seeing the look of upset on his mistress's beautiful face.

"Aemiliyana! She can't be back so soon. Emperor Honitonia placed her locked away in the realms of the empire. I have no powers to fight her. What am I going to do?" confided Tayce, panicking.

"You know I'll help protect you. She may have got her hands on me last time, but this time I'm ready for her. Oh and one other thing: she's managed to resurrect her space fortress. It's even more powerful than the last time around," replied Twedor.

"God, her fortress! Then she's back for the final confrontation and I'm powerless. Brilliant, I'm a sitting target," replied Tayce, far from pleased at the thought just when she wanted to be at her best, power-wise.

"If it's any consolation, both Marc and Dairan are doing everything they can to buy you some time in case your powers return in time for coming to face-to-face with the witch. Dairan's furious at the fact she's back and what she's currently done to you. She's already come aboard in the form of a holographic message to demand a showdown with you," continued Twedor.

"Bitch!" replied Tayce, angered, without thought.

Tayce swung her feet around to the edge of the bunk from under the coverlet, sliding down to stand beside the bunk. She stood for a few minons, then walked on out into the Living Area of the quarters. But what she didn't realise was what was waiting for her as she exited the Repose Centre. Aemiliyana was a lot closer than any of them on board, including herself, had visualised. Twedor, who was just ahead of her as they walked out, saw what was waiting for his mistress and came to an abrupt stop, making Tayce almost run into the back of him. She looked to where he was pointing and, right in the centre of the Living Area stood the witch, in all her powerful glory. Somehow she'd found them and broken through the protecting shield that surrounded the cruiser. Tayce felt her heart sink. Without her powers, she was no match for Aemiliyana and was not quite sure of just how she was going to escape with her life—if she was lucky. Aemiliyana looked at Tayce almost smiling, evilly.

"Powerless—interesting," announced the Witch Queen, knowing she had an advantage.

"You bitch! As if you didn't know what you've done!" said Tayce spitefully.

"Given me a little advantage, I'd say," replied Aemiliyana, standing at ease in a powerful kind of way.

"That's debatable. I may not have my powers, but there are other ways to strike back at you—ways you won't even anticipate," retorted Tayce.

"You thought you'd outrun me, evade my final triumph; you thought, with leaving the orbit I first found you in and vanishing so neatly, I wouldn't find a way to track you. You underestimate the new power of my new improved space fortress, Tayce Amanda," said Aemiliyana coldly.

"You can count that as one of the moves you didn't know I could make. I had no idea you were back so soon. What's the matter—did you grow tired of where the Emperor placed you? What have you done with the empire realms of Honitonia anyway?" demanded Tayce, coming to halt a few feet away from the witch, in such a way that it was clear Tayce was facing Aemiliyana in a no-nonsense stance.

"It's merely placed in a time freeze. I want you to be at my mercy. It took me a while to realise that in order to do it I had to freeze everything, including your powers," replied Aemiliyana as she paced back and forth.

"It shows you how shallow you are, doing what you've done, eliminating everything power-wise just to gain a hoped-for advantage. Nice try, but I won't fight you here on board this cruiser. Is that understood? This crew and cruiser are not part of what you want—your revenge is with me," said Tayce, sounding suddenly not the least bit scared, though she didn't know why.

Twedor figured she was being crazy, considering the amount of power this witch now possessed. He stood silently watching, ready to activate his Slazer finger to try and protect Tayce if he had to.

"Let's see if you can handle this without your powers."

Aemiliyana used her powerful eye energy force, in a thin beam emitting from her eyes, which lifted Tayce up off the floor, spun her around, then threw her over the mouldable chair nearest to her with force. Tayce crashed up against the wall behind the chair, winding herself. She sighed in anger, quickly gaining her composure, knowing it was not going to be easy fighting for her life. She reached for a heavy marblex ornament nearest to her, in the shape of a small ball. It was an ornament she never much cared for, but it would make a good missile. She hurtled it at Aemiliyana with force. She laughed, amused in her evil way and struck it aside with another powerful strike, as if it meant nothing. Twedor realised he had to do something to try and help his mistress—she was losing badly. He activated his Slazer finger and began to move around to come behind the Witch Queen. Tayce caught sight of her Pollomoss handgun. She reached for it and saw what Twedor was attempting.

"Twedor, stay out of this—it's too dangerous," ordered Tayce in an abrupt tone and one Twedor knew that she didn't use too often.

Aemiliyana caught sight of the fact Tayce had grabbed her gun and was poised ready to use it. This enraged her even more. She decided to wreak revenge on her current surroundings. It didn't matter that it was Tayce's quarters. She began with random strikes around the Living Area. With powerful energy emitting from her hands, she struck at various places, causing fires to erupt, ornaments to smash on Shelving, etc., image frames and mementoes to smash to the ground, glassene to shatter and soft furnishings to burst apart on impact. Tayce was beginning to seethe with anger at what her surroundings were turning into—a wrecked and burning mess. She'd had enough. Seeing her chance, she went for it. She rose to her feet and fired directly at Aemiliyana. Both Slazer power and Aemiliyanas powerful energy locked across the room in joint firepower midway—a long continuous beam of two powerful forces, joined as one.

"Give it up, Tayce. You're no match for me without your ability," warned Aemiliyana in full power force.

"Never! I told you I won't fight you here," retorted Tayce above the noise and chaos going on around her.

Neither Tayce nor Aemiliyana would give in to the others means of power. Tayce found it hard to hold on to the Pollomoss and keep her finger on the activation key in continuous firing against Aemiliyana's continued energy force. But the Witch Queen picked up on the fact and increased her power with very little effort. Tayce put all her ordinary strength into holding off the power getting nearer, for as long as she could. Outside the quarters, Marc, Lance and Dairan could be heard trying to gain entry as Amal had announced there was trouble. Donaldo had rushed down to try and help save Tayce when it was all through, knowing she was in danger without her powerful ability.

"Give it up. Give me what I want, you can't hold that weapon forever, girl," advised Aemiliyana.

"So the likes of you can win? You underestimate me, witch," retorted Tayce with a look of pure cold hatred on her normally beautiful features.

"Then you make my job easier," said Aemiliyana coldly.

Slowly Tayce felt herself moving back against the wall. In no time she was pinned there, but still keeping her finger on the activation key of the Pollomoss. Without warning, as Tayce felt she was about to kiss her life goodbye and become the victim Aemiliyana so craved, a warm powerful surge shot straight through her, signifying her ability was returning. But it ceased just as quickly as it began. She wondered whether she had enough strength to finally take control of the situation and gain the upper hand. But before she had the chance to find out, Twedor had disobeyed her order and fired his Slazer finger at the Witch Queen, hitting her between the shoulder blades. She wasn't expecting his action and cried out in agony as the shot burnt into her body like a hot poker. Her strength diminished and her grip holding Tayce up against the wall with her immense energy beam dropped to nothing. Within a few cencrons Aemiliyana dematerialised from what was left of the quarters. But before she went, she warned Tayce that she needn't think she'd won—she would return again.

Tayce let out a sigh of relief and fell back against the wall she'd been pinned up against from the force of Aemiliyana's powers, sliding to the ground. At least she'd managed to hold her own, even though she didn't have her powers and had help from Twedor. The doors to the quarters finally opened. Dairan rushed in first, surveying the damaged interior, thinking the worst from what he saw. He looked around for Tayce. He was followed by Marc and Lance, brandishing Pollomoss handguns, ready to use, and Donaldo followed with an Emergency Medical Kit in hand. No one was expecting to see the sight that greeted them—almost total destruction. Upon seeing Tayce, Dairan hurried, stepping over an upturned smashed glassene occasional table, the glassene crunching underfoot as he went. Upon reaching Tayce, he reached out and pulled her up into a reassuring and comforting hug.

"It's all right—it's all over." We're here now, this won't happen again," said Dairan reassuringly.

"I'm all right. I had no powers to stop her—she's taken them—but Twedor saved me. He shot her right between the shoulders," she assured.

Dairan held her comfortingly. Her hair was dishevelled and her normally beautiful features dusty. She had a slight wound on her left cheek from flying glassene in the onslaught. She was shaking slightly from her ordeal, even though she was trying to convey she was fine.

"Are you sure you're OK. We hurried here just as soon as Amal informed us of what was happening—that Aemiliyana had broken through the protection shield," said Dairan in a caring tone.

"Thanks! But I feel we haven't seen the last of her. Once she's recovered, she'll be back. Let's hope I have my powers back by then. Then I'll make her pay for this—that she can count on," assured Tayce, watching Lance put out the small fires with a small extinguisher, in the mess that was once her beautiful Living Area.

"It seems like our Invis Shield around Amalthea isn't substantial enough," spoke up Marc, considering the fact Aemiliyana had just penetrated the highest level.

"I don't think any degree will keep her off this cruiser. She's a powerful Witch Queen and you can see just how powerful by what she's done here," replied Tayce.

"I take it that when you passed out earlier in the DC, and I saw the powerful ability glow rise and fall in your eyes, that was when you lost your powers?" enquired Marc, interested.

"Afraid so. I woke up and found everything seemed blank—everything had gone. I tried to use my ability to it's furthest degree and concentrated really hard—but nothing. Then Twedor told me she was back, so I put two and two together," explained Tayce as Donaldo attended to the cut on her cheek.

"So you're no longer a member of the Telepathian Empire unless she releases it from what she's done with it?" asked Lance curious.

"No! Ouch! Don, be careful—that smarts," snapped Tayce as the spray he used on her cheek stung.

"Sorry—I'm being as gentle as I can. This won't take long," he promised in a true reassuring doctor's manner.

"I have to think of some way to protect myself for the next time she visits if my ability isn't restored—but what?" asked Tayce, thinking about what she could use that would have enough power.

"Leave this with me—I've got an idea, see you later," said Marc, heading away in thought, on out through the entrance.

His destination was Level 5. As he went, so he began wondering how Tayce would cope if her powers never returned, thanks to Aemiliyana. As he reached the Level Steps, he began down two at a time until he reached Level 5. Upon setting foot on the destined level, he briskly walked along until he came to the Robot and Technical Service Section. He rounded the corridor corner and heard the voices of Aldonica Darstayne and Craig Bream in the Weaponry Design Centre. He continued along the corridor towards the doors to where the voices were coming from inside. As he walked in, Aldonica and Craig were in the process of working on something new together, on the weaponry design bench. Aldonica looked up, putting down the cordless pencil-shaped sealant gun. Marc crossed.

"I'm glad I've found the two of you here together. I need your design and tech skills. Tayce has just endured the first of what could be more confrontations with Witch Queen Aemiliyana and it would appear she's ceased every way of Tayce using her abilities to fight back. In a nutshell, Tayce is vulnerable," explained Marc, far from pleased.

"My god, poor Tayce! What can we do to help?" asked Aldonica, giving Marc her full attention.

"We need some kind of invisible shield that Aemiliyana can't detect, to protect Tayce," said Marc seriously.

On this, Aldonica began keying in the requirements on the design computer keypad. She then brought up the human silhouette form, and with another few keystrokes the silhouette began to turn and show ways to protect Tayce with a possible shield.

"For how long does this have to work, and how long do we have to work on it?" Aldonica asked, looking at Craig, who was watching and listening.

"Long enough for Tayce to win, and long enough for you to come up with something—three hourons maximum. Any longer and I think we'll be taking a risk, to Tayce, as Aemiliyana will be making another return," warned Marc, thinking about the fact.

"Leave it with us. Tayce will have something to protect her from Aemiliyana. What's more, we'll make it low in detectability, so she can't see Tayce is protected," promised Craig.

"Good! Go to it. Three hourons," reminded Marc.

He turned and, without a further word, headed back on out of the Weaponry Design Centre. He paused in the doorway before walking back out into the corridor, suggesting they bring the completed device to Guest Quarters 1 as this was where Tayce would reside until her own quarters could be restored on the next visit to Enlopedia, as her own had been trashed by Aemiliyana. Aldonica gave a look of surprise. Craig shook his head in disgust—Aemiliyana, in his eyes, was a real venomous bitch. Marc continued on out, leaving Aldonica and Craig to put their skills to the test, to come up with a protection shield.

* * *

Tayce, feeling more like herself, on Level 3 was beginning to take her belongings, or what was left of them that hadn't been trashed in the attack, to Guest Quarters 1. Twedor and Deluca were helping. Deluca had volunteered her off-duty time to help. Donaldo had left Tayce, knowing she was going to be OK considering what she had endured, and was heading back to the MLC Lance had walked with him so far as he headed on back to duty in Organisation. Marc soon was walking back along Level 3. He paused just outside the guest quarters. Dairan informed him he'd head on back to Organisation and take command in his absence; he'd also keep him and Tayce up to date on what was happening with Aemiliyana. Marc agreed with an understanding nod. Dairan, with this, walked away on the walk back to Level 1. Tayce walked from the guest quarters just in time to see him walk away. She studied him, wondering why he'd just walked off, until Marc explained why he had.

"How are you bearing up?" he asked, putting a friendly arm around her.

"I told you I'm fine—a bit shattered. But you know me.—I'm gearing up ready for the next strike. Where did you go when you said I should leave it to you earlier?" asked Tayce, curious.

"To hopefully find a solution to your power ability, or lack of it, and the threat of that witch turning up again. I have some good news for you: Aldonica and Craig are going to work on creating a special low-detectability Invis Shield for you to wear. Aemiliyana won't know what's hit her," assured Marc, hugging Tayce to him, trying to cheer her up, walking together to her old fire-damaged and almost destroyed quarters.

"Thanks—it means a lot. If I could have an advantage over her, it would be a bonus," she replied.

"Believe me when I tell you that I and the team don't want to lose you to that evil crone. We all want to help in any way we can—even Twedor," assured Marc, hugging her again in a warm sincere way.

* * *

Upon letting Marc go, she reached for the last box of undamaged possessions, walking on out. Once outside, Twedor put a command in place to seal the quarters doors until they could get to Enlopedia for a design-and-refurbish team to put the quarters back to the way they should be. Deluca came out of the guest quarters and paused, watching what Twedor was doing, interested. She then walked on to her own quarters.

"Thanks for your assistance, Deluca," said Tayce with a gentle smile.

"You're welcome, Captain. I hope you get your old quarters back soon," replied Deluca softly.

When the old quarters had been secured, Tayce figured how lucky she'd been. If it hadn't been for Twedor disobeying another order, she would be dead. Sometimes he was a real little lifesaver. Other thoughts went through her mind, like what move Aemiliyana might attempt to continue her revenge and would Aldonica and Craig come up with something in time to protect her? Would Aemiliyana involve the team, or try to destroy the cruiser? Somehow this unwanted situation was not over by a long shot, she thought.

* * *

Aldonica, two hourons later, was trying out the new protection Aura Bracelet, which was incorporated in a Wristlink, disguised in appearance. Craig stood in the Test Chamber wearing the Wristlink, ready to activate it on Aldonica's command. He wondered what was going to happen this time around, as he was always Aldonica's willing guinea pig. He'd been fine so far. Aldonica laughed at the apprehensive look on Craig's face. He looked at her and suggested she get on with it.—Tayce was waiting. She gave him the order to activate the Wristlink / Aura Bracelet key. Craig did as asked, touching a small blue sensor key on the device. It bleeped to signify activation. Aldonica checked the reading on the computer screen, showing that the whole of Craig was protected by the invisible shield to withstand a tremendous force. Then she activated the test attack simulation, increasing the power to the bracelet as the simulation of attack energy strikes hit home on the protection shield surrounding Craig. Sparks bounced off as the shield held perfectly. Next Aldonica tried a weapon simulation of power arrows hitting the shield. They, much to Craig's relief, bounced off again in spectacular fashion. Aldonica felt elated to know success had been achieved. She quickly deactivated the test, leaving the bracelet set at the frequency to protect Tayce when she wore it against the force of power Aemiliyana might unleash. Craig stepped from the Test Chamber, taking off the Wristlink / Aura Bracelet.

"I do declare it's another fine marvel of yours, Officer Darstayne," said Craig cheekily, removing the bracelet and handing it to her, putting his own Wristlink back on.

"Yep! It certainly looks that way," she replied, pleased with her achievement.

She and Craig always got on and worked well as a small team, collaborating in joint creations on board. They'd formed a good friendship and had hit it off from the moment they first met and worked together, when joining the team. Craig occasionally teased her, but she gave as good as she got.

"Shall we go? Tayce will be waiting and the three-houron deadline is nearly up for completing this latest marvel of yours," said Craig, checking his Wristlink time display.

"Yes! Thanks for your input. I definitely think Tayce stands a good chance at defeating Aemiliyana with this, don't you? She won't know what's hit her, especially as she won't be able to detect Tayce will be wearing it."

"Yeah, too right," replied Craig casually, thinking about the fact.

They exited the Weaponry Design Centre with the Wristlink / Aura Bracelet and headed on through the Robot and Technical Service Section towards Level 3. As they went, so Craig informed her he'd enjoyed once again helping to create another gadget for the greater good. It made a change from making sure Amalthea ran smoothly. On this, Aldonica suggested that, from that moment on, should anything else come up in design and she needed his input she would give him a shout.

＊＊＊

Tayce was on her own in the guest quarters, trying to make them feel like her own, putting her personal touches here and there. She was on alert, knowing Aemiliyana's fortress was somewhere in close proximity to Amalthea, where the witch was no doubt licking her wounds and planning the next strike. Behind her, the quarters doors opened, making her turn in alarm. Dairan walked in and she sighed, glad it was him. He smiled at her reassuringly, seeing her so freaked, and explained that he'd been relieved from duty by Marc, who suggested he head down and stay with her while he resumed command. He studied her as he neared her. He could see she was under great strain and her mind was elsewhere. He could guess where—Aemiliyana's next strike. He walked around the soffette and sat down relaxingly. Tayce joined him.

"Oh, what can I say?" asked Dairan, studying her troubled beautiful features, then he kissed her on the forehead.

"I'm all right, considering what's going on," replied Tayce softly, glad he was there for her.

"That witch has got a lot to answer for. Why couldn't she find a way to go through time and head back and have this out with your grandfather, instead of taking her revenge out on you?" asked Dairan, feeling angry at the pain and torture Aemiliyana was putting Tayce through.

"I wish she had," confided Tayce.

Tayce felt fidgety, knowing that at any moment Aemiliyana could return. She couldn't relax in Dairan's company like she normally did, and he understood it. She rose to her feet and crossed the guest quarters to the sight port to look out at the uninterrupted space-scape. But it was quickly marred by the sudden appearance of the fortress materialising. Tayce glared in anger at the sudden sight. It hung in orbit, looking somewhat menacing once more. The quarters doors opened behind Tayce. Dairan rose to his feet, turning. Craig and Aldonica walked in carrying the new modified Wristlink / Aura Bracelet. Tayce crossed the room, waiting to hear what they'd come up with. Aldonica held out the Wristlink / Aura Bracelet to her.

"This should give you a very good chance against Aemiliyana. It withstands the highest degree of firepower and energy strikes, plus power arrow strikes, which I checked, and she could use any of these against you. It has a low-emitting energy field and is well below pickup range," began Aldonica.

"It emits an invisible protection shield around the whole of your body, anything she throws at you, will repel back at her," backed up Craig.

"It can be used as a normal Wristlink as well, so when you defeat her, contact us and we'll pull you out," said Aldonica.

Tayce removed her Wristlink and slipped on the Wristlink / Aura Bracelet instead, doing it up. Aldonica explained that Craig had been the one to suggest the light weight of the Wristlink and to disguise it's appearance so that it wouldn't raise suspicion in front of Aemiliyana. She further explained that Craig had been the tester and it was a success.

"You're still standing, then mate?" quipped Dairan, finding it funny that Aldonica had used him as test subject again.

"Yeah, until next time. I should get a reward for my extra danger duties," laughed Craig.

Tayce was glad about what her two team members had achieved in the short time. It certainly looked like she had no fear of Aemiliyana winning their next encounter. She hugged Aldonica, grateful for what she'd done, then Craig.

"We just want you to be safe and to win," said Aldonica, hugging Tayce.

"We'll leave you to it—good luck," said Craig, looking at Tayce with a friendly smile as he let her go.

"Thank you again, both of you. You don't know what this means. Considering I'm without my ability, this will give me a fair advantage," said Tayce, tears welling in her eyes.

"We hope you stop this Witch Queen once and for all. Give her hell from us," said Craig.

"I will," replied Tayce as Aldonica and Craig headed back to the entrance.

Dairan studied the Wristlink / Aura Bracelet as the entrance doors opened and Craig and Aldonica walked on out, both hoping that this time around Tayce would finally put an end to Aemiliyana.

The doors closed to the outside corridor and Tayce turned to look back out to the fortress, silently saying. "Come and get me—let's get this over with, I'm ready."

Dairan saw a smile cross Tayce's features and wondered what she was thinking. With the new Wristlink / Aura Bracelet, he had a hunch it was something to do with Aemiliyana and what Tayce was going to do to her. An idea crossed Tayce's mind as she turned back to face Dairan. He gave her a questioning look. She gave him a 'trust me' look in return, informing him he'd find out what she was thinking in time. Dairan, even though he didn't like the sound of it, figured she knew what she was doing. Tayce felt that at this moment she wasn't going to tell him for fear Marc would try and get the idea out of him and stop her, as he would consider it impulsive and stupid. Both crossed back and sat down, discussing, amongst other things in general, Aemiliyana.

* * *

On Aemiliyana's fortress all the operatives serving her, as her commanding and operations team, had returned to their not so pleasant quarters on the lower levels—Level 4, to be exact—below the main deck. Here they were permitted to rest for the duration of three hourons before their Queen wanted them back at the controls. Meantime Aemiliyana was resting, ready for her final powerful confrontation with Tayce in her personal chambers, having taken an elixir of power from the secret store of energy she had taken from the empire she'd been locked in by Emperor Honitonia, on her return. The impact of Twedor's weapon still smarted. Her chambers were known as the Grand Central Chambers and were elaborate in design, colour and furnishings. She was in a reclining position, thinking up her strategic moves, working out how to take Tayce on and gain overall control of the whole of the empire realms of Honitonia and do away with the one being who had stopped her the last time she tried to destroy Tayce—Emperor Honitonia. Little did she know that her plan wasn't going to succeed. The Empire of Honitonia, even though severely depleted because of her powerful actions, would not easily succumb to losing their chief—namely Emperor Honitonia—as she so wished.

* * *

Tayce on Amalthea, in the guest quarters, glanced at the time on the wall digital time display. It read 0100 hourons. She was alone. Dairan had gone back to his quarters for the night hourons—or she presumed he had as he had left her some while ago, saying he'd see her later. Before Dairan had left, he ordered Twedor to guard her and any sign of trouble he was to raise the alarm immediately. She too, like Aemiliyana, was putting into action the idea she had had earlier that dayon to take her on, finishing the situation once and for all. Twedor stood watching her. He had recorded a transmission to be played back in the mornet, when she'd left, much to his annoyance. He felt he should immediately inform Dairan or Marc of what had happened, but once more Tayce had forbidden him to do so. But once she'd gone, he would decide what was best for her, even if it meant disobeying orders once more. The transmission stated that if anything happened to her where she was going, then it was to be relayed to the team and Marc was to take overall command of Amalthea and the Amalthean Quests, as new leader, with Dairan being second in command. Twedor wanted to go with her, but she had refused and had ordered Amal, under no account was she to permit Twedor to follow her. Amal had confirmed her request and would shut Twedor down, should the need arise, via high-frequency link.

Tayce checked the extreme power arrows in the grey pouch she'd collected earlier, making sure she had set each one to maximum of diminishing energy drain, which would rid the Universe of Aemiliyana once and for all once she was struck by one. She double-checked the the Power Arrow Launcher. This she'd discovered in the weaponry hold, after Aldonica had told her earlier that power arrows were something Aemiliyana might use, only Aemiliyana's would be self-made with pure energy of the highest degree. This was something Tayce couldn't do, so she had Amal produce high-grade arrows in hard form to equal what Aemiliyana would dish out. The Power Arrow Launcher was a weapon to shoot faster than a human eye could blink and was shaped like a small crossbow made of silver. Finally, when she was all set to leave, she took one more look at her appearance in the reflection imager. She felt pleased at the way she was dressed for action in her all-in-one cream body hugging suit. She patted Twedor, then headed over to the entrance. Once the doors drew apart, she crept out.

The doors closed behind her with the usual sound of compressed air. She began on the way quickly and quietly to the Transpot Centre, cautiously making no sound, passing her team's quarters doors. She eventually and successfully made it up to Level 2 and sighed a sigh of relief. Amal was the only one to know she was moving about the cruiser and was watching her progress as she headed through the levels, aware of what she was doing. Upon entering the Transpot Centre, she crossed to the podium and activated the Transpot setting that would deliver her to where she wanted to go. She added a few cencrons delay, so she could cross and take up the standing position ready to transpot. After standing for a few minons, the Transpot activated with its swirling motion of dematerialisation, starting underfoot and working its way up her body, sending her on her way to the fortress. Before she departed from Amalthea, she had activated the Wristlink / Aura Bracelet to protect her on arrival.

* * *

Upon arriving at the fortress, Tayce glanced around, then at her Wristlink to make sure it was protecting her as it should. It was near darkness. There were voices coming from somewhere in the distance—male voices. Tayce realised she had to find a layout section map so she could find out where she needed to head. Just by sheer luck, opposite her across the corridor in the dim light she could make out a map of levels, it showed all the levels of the fortress in detail—just what she wanted to know. Where Aemiliyana would be at that moment in time. As she studied the layout, she kept her ears open for anyone advancing in her direction. An amused smile crossed her features at the thought of what Aemiliyana would do if she knew she was on the fortress and protected from revenge. After discovering the obvious place Aemiliyana would be, she began to think of her next move in the task she had ahead: putting an end to Aemiliyana and returning her to where she had originally escaped from and bringing the empire back to its full standing. When this was done, she would regain her power ability and everything in the empire realms of Honitonia would be back to normal.

Suddenly there was the sound of movement just ahead, then the sound of two sets of heavy boots marching towards her. She had to find somewhere to hide—and fast, before she was detected. Just as she was about to head for a small alcove, hoping it would shield her from detection, a hand reached out around her mouth and she was grabbed back out of sight, with swift but soft force. She fought to gain her footing—she was not going to give in without a fight against her assailant. She felt his warmth against her as she backed into his strong restraining hold. She turned her head around to face whoever had restrained her, after the two sets of boots had passed in the form of obvious night guards, and was shocked and amazed to find, as she looked up, she was staring right into the warm brown eyes of none other than someone she didn't want present: Dairan Loring.

"What the hell are you doing here? Go back—you're going to get us both killed. That's an order," said Tayce in an angry whisper. She didn't want him there.

"Thanks for saving me, Dairan. Glad you're here," replied Dairan in a sarcastic tone.

"Not funny! I don't want you here. I don't want you in danger as a result of being in the way when I take on Aemiliyana. Now return to Amalthea this instant. That's a direct order, as your captain," ordered Tayce with strong meaning in her tone.

"Not before you hear me out. Amal contacted me and told me she'd picked up an intruder in Sallen's quarters. Who? She had no idea as they were only present for a short space of time then disappeared just as quickly as they'd materialised."

"What are you saying?" asked Tayce in an interested whisper.

"The intruder was traced to this fortress, so you're stuck with me in case Aemiliyana has called up someone else she can use to help kill you," said Dairan, straight.

"You're putting yourself in danger without the kind of protection I have, in fact you've probably already been detected by the night guards. I can handle this myself—now leave," said Tayce in a casual whisper.

He studied her for a few minons, then hugged her, telling her to take care—they wanted her back in one piece. With that he pressed his Wristlink, but nothing happened. Tayce looked at him in alarm, concerned as to why he hadn't dematerialised. He shrugged his shoulders, unsure of why he hadn't begun to return to Amalthea. Dairan had no intention in returning and had made it look like his Wristlink/Transpot was malfunctioning. He had no intention of leaving her at the hands of Aemiliyana and he'd just activated his anti-scanning-detection device. Aldonica had made a second one for possible passing on to Enlopedia for commissioning to be made for wide usage. Tayce could say no more—it looked like she was stuck with him whether she wanted him along or not.

At that cencron, weapon fire could be heard in the form of shots in their direction. Tayce cursed as she wanted to take care of this Quest by herself. But now it looked like both she and Dairan were in it together and somehow they'd been detected, neither knew how. Dairan took out his Pollomoss handgun, setting it to 'disintegrate'. Tayce shook her head, explaining that the operatives and night guards could belong to the Honitonian realm, but were under some kind of spell cast by Aemiliyana to serve her in her treacherous deed. She told him to stun them only. Dairan looked at her, puzzled as to what good stunning would achieve in an onslaught. Tayce continued, saying if they stunned instead of disintegrat the night guards and the operatives, then they could hold them in an unconscious state until the empire was out of Aemiliyana's hold: then they could return to their rightful place. Dairan thought about it for a few minons and could see her point. Agreeing, he changed the setting to 'stun' on his Pollomoss.

She let Dairan go first. He raised his gun and cautiously stepped out of the alcove and around the corridor corner. He immediately saw the advancing night guards, and they weren't a small party. He began firing, taking them out, and the following operatives in their white uniforms as they came. Slowly they dropped to the corridor floor, one by one, as both he and Tayce continued on to the point of great importance—Aemiliyana. As they went, so the corridors of the vast fortress became littered with stunned night guards and operatives in different positions, falling where they'd been struck down. Once outside Aemiliyana's Chambers, which Aemiliyana termed the Grand Central Chambers, Tayce quickly put into action for Amal to retrieve Dairan. Before he had time to protest, he vanished, leaving Tayce to continue on. She took the Power Arrow Launcher and loaded it with the first of many power arrows she expected to use.

She pressed the cream-coloured doors' mechanism panel. The arch-shaped doors slid back to reveal the elegant interior of Aemiliyana's domain. Tayce walked in with the protection shield in place and took aim, searching for the Witch Queen. She fired the first shot above Aemiliyana's head when she found her lying on the lavish red silkene sheets. Aemiliyana screamed and sat bolt upright, looking startled and wide-eyed at the sight of Tayce standing, showing no mercy, with a face of angered intent, with the Power Arrow Launcher loaded and aimed, ready to fire off another shot.

"Afraid? You will be," said Tayce, getting ready to fire again, a cold look in her sapphire-blue eyes.

"Stop! Enough! You've made your intentions clear—I know why you're here, Tayce Amanda—but you're forgetting where you are. I only have to summon my guards and you'll soon be rendered free of that weapon you're holding, young woman," said Aemiliyana, getting up off the double-sized bunk into a standing position.

"What's the matter? Don't you like surprise visits? After all, that's what you did to me when you showed up on Amalthea. Let me see—as I recall you destroyed my quarters. Maybe I'll start with your possessions," said Tayce, ignoring Aemiliyana and glancing around. She was in no mood to be the loser this time around.

"Guards! Guards!" summoned Aemiliyana through the open doorway behind Tayce.

"You're wasting your time. They are, you could say, taking a nap, care of me."

"You think you hold all the aces, young woman—wrong. You haven't met my new accomplice in finally helping me get the revenge I seek—you!" announced Aemiliyana, looking past Tayce.

Tayce turned to see a sight she thought was gone from her life forever, after what Chief Corvayoss said when she'd invaded Entronet. Countess Vargon in all her evilness. Tayce summed up the situation. This seemed to be nothing more than one of Aemiliyana's latest conjuring spells, making her believe the biggest bitch next to the witch herself was present. But a hint of wonder entered Tayce's thoughts on seeing Vargon. Had she evaded being caught by the Entronians and escaped again? Then she remembered what Dairan said earlier about Sallen having a sudden visitor to her quarters on Amalthea and Amal not knowing who it was for some strange reason they were undetectable to detect. It was puzzling. She decided to play along with Aemiliyana. There was only one way to find out—play along.

"Vargon! I didn't know you had joined forces with Aemiliyana. The last I saw of you was leaving Entronet. I presumed you'd finally met your demise, considering the Chief of the Entronians declared that you would be dealt with for your actions on Entronet. But then again, this could be one of your elaborate tricks to fool me, Aemiliyana," said Tayce, giving Aemiliyana a look that showed she was suspicious.

"Oh, I can assure you, Traun, I'm no illusion. Aemiliyana here you could say sprung me from the colony the Entronians sent me to for the rest of my life. Sorry to disappoint," began the Countess convincingly.

Tayce gave a sheer look of alarm. She wished she had the use of her powers—then she could work out what the Countess was, real or fake. It was really frustrating trying to decide. Tayce began wondering how Aemiliyana had pulled off this latest treacherous act. She figured she had to get some distance between the two evil women. She wasn't taking any chances. She glanced at her Wristlink display, glad the protection shield around her was still activated. At least from anything Aemiliyana, or the conjured-up or real Countess, threw at her she was protected. She still kept her Power Arrow Launcher primed ready to fire another arrow. But who would be first to make their move against her? she wondered. The real or conjured version of Vargon, or Aemiliyana?

* * *

On board Amalthea it was first light—duty time. The team were slowly going on duty. Marc Dayatso in his quarters walked from the Cleanse Unit, fastening up the Velcro collar of his uniform. He was somewhat startled to find Twedor standing in the Living Area, waiting for him.

"This is an honour, Twedor. What's up? Has Tayce sent you in here to tell me something that can't wait?" he asked, looking down at the little Romid, wondering why he wasn't with Tayce.

"She's gone. Dairan went after her last night, but she sent him back," began Twedor.

"Gone where? Explain. Don't tell me she's done what I think she's done?" demanded Marc, alarmed.

"She's recorded this to play to you," replied Twedor, ignoring the alarmed look Marc was showing.

Twedor, as Marc watched, crossed the Living Area of the quarters to the wall Sight Screen and put the disk chip in the reader, just below the screen, pressing the activation button. The wall Sight Screen flashed into life and Tayce's recorded transmission began. Just as Tayce appeared on screen, Marc's quarters doors opened behind him. Dairan sauntered in, not knowing quite how he was going to tell Marc what he had to. Before he could say anything, as he came to a halt, Twedor prodded him in the leg and pointed to the screen. Marc glanced unimpressed at Dairan, then looked at the screen as Tayce began.

"I've asked Twedor to give you this recording because what I have to do I have to do alone. By now you'll know I'm not on board, via Twedor or Amal, but what

I am doing has to be done without any help from the team. Don't blame Dairan, Marc—this is totally my decision. Don't think of coming to the fortress to assist me in this task ahead. If for any reason I fail, I want you to command Amalthea, Marc. You know her better than anyone. If I succeed, I'll see you when I have accomplished what I left the cruiser for. Get ready to pull me out when I call. Tayce out," said Tayce, deactivating the recording.

"God dammit! I knew she'd do this. She's downright crazy. She knows what Aemiliyana could do to her. God, why does she do these impulsive acts?" said Marc, extremely angry that Tayce had deliberately placed herself in extreme danger.

"She's wearing the protection device and has taken a Power Arrow Launcher!" exclaimed Twedor.

"I did try and stop her. I even went as far as to follow her to the fortress wearing another one of Aldonica's devices. I managed to help her on board—put the night guards under, stunned, along with the operatives—but then she sent me back, ordering Amal to pull me out," said Dairan.

"Don't worry—when Tayce wants something badly enough and she doesn't want anyone else involved, she'll do what she feels is right to her advantage. It's not the first time she's done it," said Marc, knowing so.

Marc did one more check of his appearance for duty in the reflection imager, then gestured for Dairan and Twedor to walk on towards the entrance of the quarters. The doors parted and they began on out on the walk up to the Leisure Centre for the first meal of the dayon. On the way Dairan began saying how he had insisted to Tayce that he remain to help her on the fortress, but she didn't want him putting his life in dire danger. Hence he was returned to Amalthea by Amal. Marc nodded in understanding and once more pointed out that he'd done his best. All they could do was hope Tayce's act of foolish pride would end with her safely returned to them and alive. Both approached the Level Steps and lightly sprinted up to Level 2, with Twedor following on at his own pace.

* * *

Tayce meanwhile, on the space fortress, was still standing primed ready to open fire on any false moves from either Aemiliyana or the Countess, whether real or otherwise. She had decided to continue to play along with Aemiliyana's tricks. The idea of using a convincing yet false Countess was very old and far from convincing. If it was meant to scare her, it didn't. Tayce wondered what else the revengeful witch was going to use and began thinking. She guessed it was the way she got her spiteful kicks in any situation, trying to win by casting spells and seeming to retrieve people the victim, in her eyes, would be afraid of. But Tayce had rumbled her on this occasion, she thought.

"There's one thing you fail to see: I hold the Empire of Honitonia in my grasp and if you want it back, then you'll have to take it from me," said Aemiliyana coldly.

"Ready when you are. So be it," replied Tayce sharply without thought.

Aemiliyana unleashed an energy ball directly at Tayce, for her taunting words of defiance. As she did, Tayce sidestepped it with quick preciseness in avoidance. The Countess took the full force of the throw. Tayce couldn't help laughing as Vargon diminished to nothing. She wished she knew for sure if it was the real one.

"Getting sloppy in your strikes, witch," said Tayce spitefully, amused by Aemiliyana's anger.

Aemiliyana was furious beyond words as her creation exploded, vanishing in spectacular fashion.

Glancing down for a minon Tayce checked that she was still protected and, much to her relief, she was. She opened fire with the Power Arrow Launcher, unleashing a power arrow which sailed straight across the chamber and, before Aemiliyana had chance to react, impacted in her left side. She suddenly found herself fading. She glared at Tayce, wondering what power force had struck her, as it seemed to be stronger than her own. She found much to her madness, she was unable to retaliate with an energy strike.

"What's the matter, Your Highness—can't fight back? Pity!" announced Tayce, pleased her shot had done what she wanted it to do. She had made sure this was a force greater than Aemiliyana's power, to take her out once and for all.

"What the blazes have you done? You'll pay for this, Tayce Amanda," replied Aemiliyana, trying with all her might to gain enough power to strike back.

"What I had to do. The empire is my first thought—I'll do anything to get it back, even if it means destroying you once and for all," replied Tayce as Aemiliyana's force before her depleted.

Quite unexpectedly Tayce felt the sudden return of the inner Telepathian power, strength rushing back through her very existence with force. She knew from this that the Empire of Honitonia and everything connected to it was slowly returning to normal.

"Damn you, Tayce Amanda! You can't win, you just can't," protested Aemiliyana, failing miserably.

Tayce stood with a look of cold joyous achievement at the slow depletion of Aemiliyana and everything she stood for. She could sense the anger in the Witch Queen and wondered why she didn't explode.

"Face it—you've lost what you thought you had," said Tayce, trying to annoy Aemiliyana before her.

Just as Tayce was getting the feeling of becoming the outright winner, Aemiliyana found an inner strength source for one last attempt to finish Tayce. This time it emitted from her eyes. They turned an illuminated white with powerful burning brilliance and a thin line of pure energy shot towards Tayce. The strike hit home before Tayce had a chance to retaliate. It quickly broke the protection shield, making Tayce something she didn't want to be—vulnerable. She was thrown into the air and against the chamber wall and, as she hit it on the far side, her Wristlink smashed on impact. She realised she had to think, and think fast, if she was to stay alive. The Power Arrow Launcher was gone. It had been jolted from her grasp during her hurtling across the chamber. It was now on the floor, a distance from her. Aemiliyana came forth in full powerful fury with one aim in mind: the final attack of revenge to pay back Tayce's great-grandfather, Grandmaster Alexentron Traun and all would be hers. She felt elated to know she had gained the upper hand against this mere girl.

"You thought you could defeat someone as powerful as me, child. No one ever defeats me, least of all the great-granddaughter of Grandmaster Alexentron Traun. I have enough force in me to finish you once and for all, girl," said Aemiliyana in a cold, evil tone.

"I'll never give in to the likes of you. Good prevails over evil," retaliated Tayce as Aemiliyana towered above her whilst she lay pinned to the floor by the witch's powerful hold.

Tayce, much to Aemiliyana's surprise, used her own powers to break free and roll in the direction of the Power Arrow Launcher. As Aemiliyana went to go after her, she grabbed the Power Arrow Launcher and rolled over, coming face-to-face with the witch, and took aim right at Aemiliyana's heart, firing repeatedly until all the arrows were firmly embedded in the Witch Queen, burning and diminishing her very existence. Aemiliyana stumbled backwards in a blaze of a pure brilliant energy glow, panicking for probably the first time in her powerful life. Tayce climbed to her feet, watching as the Witch Queen slowly dropped to the fortress floor and screamed in tortured agony whilst glaring at Tayce. Tayce was shaking from her ordeal, glad she'd survived. In a way she knew she shouldn't, but she felt sorry for Aemiliyana. Revenge had consumed her beyond all recognition and had been her downfall. Right before her, Aemiliyana withered away to nothing. It was over.

Tayce felt her full Telepathian power and communication with the Honitonian realm slowly returning. But all around her the fortress was beginning to fall apart. With Aemiliyana gone, so her creations were going too. Tayce knew she had to get off her surroundings and fast. She picked up the Power Arrow Launcher and, as the floor shook beneath her feet and the walls began to fall, she made a run for it. The fortress was coming apart around her. She quickly realised she would have to try and use her powers to send herself back to Amalthea. She concentrated, hoping they wouldn't fail her.

The voice of Emperor Honitonia could suddenly be heard. "Relax, Tayce. You've done well. Let us place you where you need to be," he said calmly.

Within a few minons Tayce was removed from the falling-apart fortress, where Aemiliyana was no more, by the Empire of Honitonia, and sent back to Amalthea, under powerful protection.

No more would Aemiliyana be heard of. Tayce had won. She could relax, knowing she would never return.

One thing Tayce still didn't know, even though she had her powers back: was the Countess an elaborate and convincing version of the real thing? Had Aemiliyana done her a favour? Only time would tell.

18. Thealysis HB 2

Two weekons later Amalthea was back on voyage course after the rendezvous with Aemiliyana a couple of weekons later and travelling at a comfortable warp speed. It was heading off into a new sector, on the journey to rendezvous with Tayce's father, Admiral Darius Traun, on a planet proposed to be the new possible second headquarters base to Enlopedia, Thealysis.

* * *

Tayce was standing in the newly refurbished quarters that had been restored a weekon ago after Jamie Balthansar and his reconstruction-and-design team had rendezvoused during transit, putting the quarters back to first-class condition, working around the clock to finish them. She was thinking about the woman who had caused the destruction in the first place. Aemiliyana. Glad she would never have to come face-to-face with her ever again. It felt good to be back in her own quarters. She sauntered over to the sight port. Here she paused to look out into the calm passing Universe, sighing, glad it was peaceful, just for a while. It was hard to imagine that a couple of weekons previously, Aemiliyana's menacing space fortress was the main focal point.

Without warning, behind her, in the middle of the Living Area, Emperor Honitonia materialised. He stood waiting. He could read Tayce's thoughts and could see the trouble with the Witch Queen was still very much on her mind. He walked to come to a pause beside her, breaking her silence, beginning to explain that he'd personally come to thank her for restoring the empire to what it should be, freeing it from the clutches of the most powerful and evil woman in the Universe.

"I did what had to be done. I couldn't let the likes of some witch, seeking revenge against one of my ancestors, think she could make me pay for past dealings she had with my great-grandfather," replied Tayce.

"You showed great endurance during your difficult time with her, considering you took her on without your ability, but you managed to free the Honitonian realm from the 'time set' that she placed us all in. I commend you and this will be noted in the empire's recordings of the part you played," expressed the Emperor kindly.

"Thank you, but I would do it all again if I had to," replied Tayce sincerely.

"There is another reason I am here—the extra power ability I bestowed on you no longer needs to serve you and needs to be handed back. I guess we could say that because of the loss of your ability at a time you needed it most it really wasn't helpful when it should have been. I guess you could say it was beyond our control," said the Emperor with a smile.

Tayce agreed, understanding what the Emperor was saying. Without a further word, he suggested she take care and have a continued safe voyage and said that she wouldn't even notice the removal of the extra ability given to her for the endurance with Aemiliyana. With this, he stepped back and vanished just as quickly as he had arrived.

Just as the Emperor vanished, Amalthea was attacked by some kind of incoming force of energy. It made the cruiser shake violently. Tayce had to struggle to stay on her feet during the unsteady moments. She quickly gathered her thoughts together, heading across the Living Area of the quarters towards the entrance. The doors soon opened on her approach. She quickly passed through, beginning on the urgent walk towards Organisation, trying to contact Amal via her Wristlink en route.

* * *

Down on Level 4 in the Astrono Centre, as another strike of energy force hit home on the outer hull shaking the cruiser, Dairan Loring was flung across the centre with force. He crashed into the computer-filled wall and slid down it into a heap on the floor in an unconscious state, his head coming to a tilt on one side.

* * *

Twedor was on the Level Steps on his way to meet Tayce. In the bombardment of strikes he lost his footing and balance, tumbling head over metlon heels back down the steps. As he rolled in a tumbling way, so he began wondering where he was going to stop. After rolling for what seemed like eternity, he came to a halt on Level 4, going into a shutdown hibernation state in a lying position until someone could rescue him.

* * *

In Organisation 'red alert' sounded, signifying an emergency situation was under way. Sparks were flying from various operational points around the centre, such as research and communications. Panels suddenly exploded. Marc was helping Kelly back on to her feet, from being thrown off her seat at his feet. He quickly glanced around, asking everyone present if they were all right. There came replies from various members saying they were.

Marc demanded from Amal in an impatient tone, "What the hell's going on, Amal? What just happened?"

Amal began running an investigation, ignoring Marc shouting at her, whilst the Organisation team began trying to find out what damage had been done to the cruiser, if any, around the various other sections as they gained their seating once again.

* * *

Down in the MLC Treketa was sat on a medical bunk, looking at Donaldo as he attended to a wound she'd sustained during the attack. Something had slid off the shelf and caught her where she had been standing. As Donaldo cleaned the wound, Treketa draped her arms around her husband's neck and studied him in a true affectionate way. He glanced down at her and smiled softly, warning her that the spray he was about to use was going to sting, but it was unavoidable. Treketa braced herself as he proceeded to seal the wound. The whole of the MLC around them was littered with upturned equipment and smashed jars that had contained liquid. They had fallen in the onslaught of attack.

* * *

Nick Berenger heard the sound of Tayce calling somewhere in the distance through the open Organisation entrance doors. He left the centre and ran down towards where she was calling from. He soon caught sight of her on the Level Steps, struggling to get back on to her feet. He quickly went about helping her in a supporting way. He helped her up on to her feet, checking to see if she was hurt anywhere. She soon found her ankle hurt, explaining that she must have twisted it in falling back down the steps during the recent strike.

"Let's head on to Organisation" she suggested, then grimaced as she put weight on her aching foot as she went.

Nick reached out and took hold of her in support, helping her up the rest of the steps on to Level 1. As they slowly went, so Tayce demanded to know what was going on. Who was making them target practice of the yearon? She also asked had the defence shields been activated? Nick nodded in a confirming way, explaining the team were all working on finding out what the source of attack was and why. As they neared Organisation, Marc turned, hearing them talking. As they entered, he noticed Tayce limping.

"What happened? You're limping—are you OK?" he asked in true concern.

"I'll be fine. It's just a sprain. Any identification as to who's attacking us?" replied Tayce, ignoring her injury.

"Amal just ran a long-distance wide scan. Nothing as yet," replied Marc.

"Keep trying. I want to know who they are, and I want to know what their reason is for attack. I'm damned if this cruiser is going to be used for target practice for no reason at all," said Tayce, straight.

"Sure! We did return fire a while ago; so if they are hiding behind something like our Invis Shield, then I guess we might have hit home, as we haven't heard anything. I just wish they'd make themselves known—become visible even. Then we would know why they seem to have picked us as target practice" he put to her, glancing out through the sight port into the stars.

"Quite!" she replied.

Tayce left him discovering what was going on and borrowed the steady arm of Nick to get into the DC, where she could use her powers to heal her ankle. Marc crossed to stand beside Kelly's console to wait for any further updates of the identity of their attacker. Nick soon was heading back to communications to see if he could pick up any distant conversations. Tayce had told him that if any update was available she wanted to know.

* * *

Down in the Astrono Centre, meanwhile, Dairan had regained consciousness, but as he opened his eyes he found everything was blurry. It threw him completely for a few moments, not knowing what to do next. He decided to raise his Wristlink and really try and focus enough to see the outline of the Wristlink's controls. He found the display was jagged—it had been smashed.

"Come on, what next!" he said angrily.

He recalled the way in which he'd put out his hand to minimise the impact of hitting the wall, realising this was how he must have smashed the face. How was he going to raise the alarm for help? he wondered. After a few minons, he began groggily to climb back to his feet. Once up, the centre swayed slightly and an extreme dizziness came over him. Staggering with an immense feeling of nausea, he made his way over to the operations console. Upon reaching it, he again tried to focus intently on what he had to try and do. It was hopeless, he thought—he couldn't make out any numbers on the keypad in front of him, no matter how hard he tried. He decided to press the Comceive button—he remembered it was red in colour. Upon hitting it, Nick Berenger within a few cencrons answered on the other end, much to his relief.

"Nick, it's Dairan. Help! I need Donaldo—I'm hurt," said Dairan. All life seemed to be draining from him as he supported himself on the console top with great effort.

Before Nick could answer, a wave of immense nausea washed over Dairan and he collapsed back on to the floor, staying put, silent. Nick could be heard calling him. After a few minons of Nick asking him to repeat what he was saying, nothing could be heard. His voice of request went unanswered.

* * *

Back in Organisation Nick turned to Tayce in urgency as she exited the DC, walking normally after healing her own ankle with her powers. He informed her he'd just received a very distorted message from Dairan in the Astrono Centre. He couldn't make out what Dairan was trying to say, only it sounded like a cry for help. He had asked him to repeat the request, to make sure—but nothing. Tayce didn't like the sound of it. Placing Marc in overall charge, she was about to head on out to go and find out what was going on with Dairan, when she turned to see that out through the main sight port the attacking vessel had become visible. It was sleek in design and white in colour. It was also fully armed for any possible target it fancied using as target practice.

"I'm leaving you with it, Marc. Keep me informed of any hostile further activity. I think Dairan's in trouble in the Astrono Centre. Come on, Lance," said Tayce, heading on out.

"Sure!" he replied, his mind on studying the sight through the main sight port.

Marc turned to Kelly, ordering her to keep an eye on the vessel before them and make sure they we're protected from any further strikes. He also decided to fire a warning shot across their bow, just to let them know Amalthea was not a sitting target solely for their practice time. Kelly questioned the decision, wondering if the vessel would think it was a hostile act to start a fight. Marc listened, considered what she was saying, then simply announced they would dematerialise under Invis Shield so they couldn't be brought into the game of attack.

"Warning shot released. Preparing to go under full Invis Shield," confirmed Kelly.

Amal, behind Marc, began announcing the latest information on the enemy attackers, including the fact they'd upgraded their defence shields too.

Marc laughed. "I guess they didn't like a taste of what they've been dishing out," he announced, amused.

The whole of Organisation erupted in laughter, agreeing. Marc suggested to Deluca that she take over watching research in Lance's absence, whilst he was helping Tayce. She nodded.

* * *

As Lance and Tayce hurried down the Level Steps, he noticed she wasn't limping like earlier. He guessed she'd used her powers to heal the problem, but said nothing. He was just glad she had the ability to do it. To Tayce's surprise she saw Twedor lying on his side on Level 2. They both went to him, wondering what damage he'd sustained. It was soon discovered he'd gone into standby mode.

Together they lifted him up into a standing position and Tayce went about resetting his systems, hoping he would come back online with a quick key press. Both stood back, hoping Twedor would come to life. But nothing happened. Lance raised his Wristlink and depressed the connection to connect him to Craig Bream. Craig soon answered.

"Craig! Twedor's been damaged in the attack. He's on Level 2, at the bottom of the Level Steps," informed Lance.

"I'll grab my tech kit and be right there," replied Craig, ceasing communications.

"He's on his way down," announced Lance, seeing Tayce looking at Twedor, concerned over what could have happened.

"Right, there's nothing we can do here. Let's go and see what's happened to Dairan," suggested Tayce, walking over to the Level Steps to continue on down to Level 4.

Lance agreed, walking away from Twedor to follow on behind her. Soon they were stepping on to Level 4. Both hurried along to the Astrono Centre, being joined by Donaldo with an Emergency Medical Kit in his hand, stepping from the Deck Travel. They soon paused outside the Astrono Centre. Donaldo enquired who had attacked Amalthea? Tayce was quick to point out that as yet it couldn't be identified, only the vessel was white and armed with every available weapon for a good all-round space fight. Donaldo gave a look of surprise, then continued to ask what kind of emergency were they dealing with inside the Astrono Centre, to get an idea of what he could expect?

"It's Dairan. Nick received a somewhat strange cry for help a while ago," said Tayce, concerned.

"Let's see what's waiting for us, shall we?" suggested Lance, hitting the doors' mechanism panel.

The doors to the Astrono Centre opened. Inside was a sight of scattered star charts and debris all over the place. It was one big mess. It looked like the centre had taken most of the last strike. Tayce was amazed to see the sight ports were still intact; otherwise they would have lost the whole interior and more through the vacuum out into space. She walked around the central large work desk Dairan usually was seated at and found him face down on the floor, out cold.

"Donaldo, quickly! Over here! I've found him," she called in alarm.

Donaldo hurried to Dairan's side and upon reaching him immediately set down the Emergency Medical Kit, opening it. Tayce knelt by Dairan's side and felt for a pulse as Donaldo reached into his kit and retrieved his Examscan.

"It's weak—we have to hurry," said Tayce, looking worriedly at Donaldo.

"Don't worry—he'll be all right," he assured, getting to work to save him.

He began to guide the Examscan all over Dairan to determine what injuries he'd sustained, paying particular attention to scanning Dairan's head in case he'd hit it and had a brain injury—hence his unconscious state. He then pressed the 'Diagnosis' command and waited for the diagnosis reading. Tayce looked up at

Lance, worried. He smiled reassuringly back at her, knowing what Dairan meant to her, besides being a team colleague and friend.

"No serious head injuries, except slight concussion maybe, though he has sustained damage to his left shoulder, ripping muscle tissue. The reason for his unconsciousness is that his head took one hell of a blow, and it's letting him know. It probably would have interfered with his vision, and explains Nick not quite hearing his cry for help. He probably would have had trouble concentrating and blacked out in mid communication, but he's made of the tough stuff—he'll pull through," assured Donaldo in his true medical manner, giving Tayce a slight smile of reassurance.

Behind the three of them, the Astrono Centre doors opened. Treketa entered, bringing with her a Hover Trolley. Upon seeing Dairan, she looked at him, concerned, then to Tayce, giving her a reassuring smile that everything would be OK.

Tayce thought to herself that whoever the attackers were, they'd caused a lot of unnecessary trouble for both the cruiser and her team, and she didn't like it. Treketa immediately assisted Donaldo in activating the Hover Trolley, ready for him to use. She pressed a small key on the handheld slim keypad, and the Hover Trolley slowly manoeuvred to a convenient level to place Dairan on it. Both Lance and Donaldo carefully lifted Dairan up on to the trolley, with Lance supporting his shoulders, Donaldo at his feet. Once Dairan was settled, Treketa covered him with a heat-sealant blanket. Donaldo, as he pressed the activation key on the slim handheld keypad, began off out behind the trolley as it slowly began forward, exclaiming that he would compile a medical report. Tayce nodded understandingly. Treketa smiled and touched Tayce's upper arm in a reassuring way again—Dairan would be all right—then followed Donaldo on out.

Tayce's Wristlink sounded. She raised it, activating it.

"Go ahead," she announced.

Marc's voice came through, sounding pleased. He happily informed her that Amal had successfully found a way to disarm the opposing vessel in their flight path and she'd brought their engines to a total standstill. At present the vessel was under tractor beam and being drawn to a distance from which they could transpot it's occupants on board. Tayce looked at Lance, wondering if it was the right thing to do, considering they'd been using Amalthea as target practice. Marc continued, saying that notification had just come in informing them that he vessel—or should he say first-class small warship?—that had been attacking them was stolen from the high-rank security section of their destined port of call, Thealysis. It appeared the two cadets aboard—one named Nickrotrae, a young male in his teens, the other named Traytanna, a female of the same rank and age, had apparently decided to take the expensive vessel for a joyride and have some space fun at Amalthea's expense. Tayce noticed Marc's tone changed to one of anger as he was talking about the young cadets.

"Don't do anything when they arrive, until I meet you in the Transpot Centre. These two joyriders are going to answer for their acts of stupidity," announced Tayce, just as angry as Marc.

Marc agreed, signing off. Tayce walked with Lance on out of the Astrono Centre, back into the corridor, asking had he heard what Marc just said? He nodded, suggesting the reckless youngsters be placed in confinement until they reached Thealysis, where they would be handed over to answer for their irresponsible behaviour. His father would have done it—made them accountable to the head of their colony or planet for their actions. Tayce nodded. She knew Jonathan would have too. But she had to keep in mind that the situation was delicate, considering Thealysis was in line to become the proposed second base to Enlopedia. But she would have to think of some form of reprimand for their foolish and irresponsible behaviour, considering that Dairan had been injured because of it. Lance could see she was in a difficult position when it came to dealing with the cadets. She had to be careful not to risk jeopardising the joining of the two bases because of her actions to two of the inhabitants of Thealysis. Both discussed it, and the best course of action to take, as they both began on up the Level Steps, heading for Level 2. Upon reaching the destined level, Lance wished her luck, then continued on back to Level 1 and his duty in Organisation, leaving Tayce to head off along Level 2 to meet Marc in the Transpot Centre. She began getting into the attitude to deal with the young joyriders, even though she didn't want to take the stern hand towards these two youngsters. She knew what it was like to be young and want to have fun, but Amalthea was her cruiser and they had to be brought to task for attacking it just for the fun of it.

Marc was waiting in the Transpot Centre, thinking over how he was going to assist Tayce, having heard in the last half an houron that Dairan had been injured because of these youngsters' reckless behaviour. The doors opened. He turned to see Tayce walk in looking far from pleased. Suddenly the Transpot activated and two uniformed cadets began to materialise in the swirling aura of arrival. When Transpot was completed, two young cadets, no older than sixteen or seventeen, stood looking somewhat apprehensive about what was going to happen to them. Their uniforms were all-in-one suits in a dull khaki and mustard colour with matching bottle-green knee-length boots. The female, named Traytanna, was a slim, pretty dark-haired girl with big brown eyes with a yellow centre to them. Nickrotrae, on the other hand, was tall and athletic-looking, with a certain cockiness about him. He had fair hair, but the same eye-colouring as Traytanna. They stood in silence, seeing Tayce was not prepared to tolerate their actions.

"You're on board Amalthea Two, the cruiser you've no doubt found it fun to use as a kind of game to attack. Well, this is not a game and not a simulation and the damage you've caused in one of my crew being injured is very real. At the moment he's in the medical facility here, unconscious," said Tayce with no nonsense in her tone.

"You were lucky you weren't picked up by pirates," said Marc, to the point, just to the side of her.

"You mean there are pirates out here?" asked Nickrotrae.

"Yes, pirates of the worst kind. They are always looking for unsuspecting victims and easy targets. You would do well to remember that for future reference," snapped Marc.

"Are you going to punish us? We're sorry—really we are," spoke up Traytanna sheepishly.

"No! You'll be placed in confinement, where you will remain until we reach your home world. There you will be handed over to answer for your irresponsible actions, to your superiors," said Tayce in the true tone of commanding captain.

"There's no way I'm going back there," blurted Nickrotrae, producing a small handgun from his uniform jacket and aiming it at Tayce with intent, not truly realising what he was doing, panicking.

"Drop that at once!"commanded Marc abruptly and angrily at Nickrotrae, taking his Pollomoss out of its side holster, ready to stun the youngster.

Marc grabbed the handgun as Nickrotrae lowered it. Grabbing him without thought, he angrily hurtled him up against the wall for his actions, his face full of fury.

"You do not threaten the captain of the cruiser who just rescued you. Your superiors are going to hear of this," said Marc angrily, keeping a tight grip on Nickrotrae as the youngster struggled in his hold.

"Please, sir, he doesn't know what he's doing," pleaded Traytanna, near to tears.

"Commander Dayatso, that's enough," commanded Tayce, halting Marc in his angry actions.

"Come on, move! There's only one place you're going until we reach your home world—that's confinement on Level 5," announced Marc, impatiently hauling the young Thealysian without compassion across the centre, out through the entrance that opened before them.

Traytanna looked at Tayce nervously, apologizing for her friend's behaviour. Tayce quickly realised Traytanna hadn't been the instigator of the whole space joyriding idea. She had a feeling it was all down to Nickrotrae, not realising his idea was wrong and they would end up in trouble for it. Tayce listened as Traytanna began to explain—she'd been an idiot to go along with Nickrotrae and what he'd proposed as a bit of fun, in the first place. But he was the kind to make any idea seem exciting and wouldn't take no for an answer. Both Tayce and Traytanna walked from the Transpot Centre. Tayce was intrigued to know why Nickrotrae had acted like he had in pulling a weapon on her earlier. Could it have something to do with Enlopedia joining forces with Thealysis? Perhaps Nickotrae didn't like the idea. Would this incident and what he'd done jeopardise the signing of the treaty? Something suddenly didn't feel right, thought Tayce.

Was her father in danger in some way? If the people of Thealysis were undecided and, like Nickrotrae, didn't want the treaty, was this the reason she and the team had been asked to go to Thealysis in the first place? Trouble was expected. Maybe she was letting her imagination run away with her. But was she? She'd keep it in mind in case she needed to pull her father off Thealysis at a moment's notice, because of her suspicions. Maybe the treaty wasn't wanted by the people—only their leader.

Once on Level 5, Tayce handed Traytanna over to Marc, discreetly warning him to go easy on the youngsters. He agreed. Tayce turned and headed on the walk back to Organisation in thought about Nickrotrae and his behaviour earlier. It still bothered her why he felt he had to act the way he did.

* * *

Outside in the Universe the first-class small warship belonging to Thealysis followed on behind Amalthea, via tractor beam, on its unscheduled return to the planet under Amal's guidance. Lights shone from on board Amalthea as it cruised at a comfortable warp for towing such a vessel. The Thealysian vessel wasn't what was termed large. It was what could be considered average size, as small warships went. It measured three-quarters of a milon in diameter compared to some that were bigger than Amalthea. It certainly wasn't a type of vessel to be taken for a joyride by two inexperienced cadets. It wasn't attractive to look at, it was quite dull-looking. Its colour was dark maroon. It didn't have the attractiveness that Amalthea had. No sleek lines to its shape. It may have been considered first class, but it wasn't in its design. It was totally built for battle.

* * *

Tayce soon reached Level 1 on Amalthea. She sauntered along the corridor and entered into Organisation. Upon entering, she called over to Lance, asking him and Deluca to join her in the DC. As she continued on in the direction of the entrance, both Lance and Deluca exchanged glances, wondering what she wanted them for, and followed on. As soon as she entered the DC, she crossed to her desk, going round to the back to sit down on her swivel chair relaxingly.

"How did it go with our couple of galactic joyriders?" enquired Lance, entering the DC and coming to a pause at ease mid floor.

"Marc has placed them both in confinement until we arrive at Thealysis. I feel the idea to take the vessel they did was down to the male of the two; the young girl was just obviously enticed by his fancy persuasion. He thought he was playing an impressive game to such a degree that he pulled a handgun on me," announced Tayce.

"No! What happened?" asked Lance, almost speechless.

"Marc disarmed him, and not in the most gentle of ways," replied Tayce casually.

"I know I was probably a little tearaway in my early cadet yearons, but nothing on a grand scale such as what these two pulled off. You could say they got what they deserved," replied Lance.

"What I want you to do is sift through anything on our onboard guests. See what you can find. See if you can uncover anything about why they don't want to return to Thealysis. Nickrotrae the male of the two, said what he did in a way that's concerning me. I want you to delve deep—see if there's another reason for those two being out here in such a powerful vessel as they were in, other than what we think—joyriding. It unnerves me this whole situation we're heading into," said Tayce, concerned.

"Sure! What's making you feel uneasy?" asked Lance, prompting.

"I'm wondering about the real reason Nickrotrae pulled the weapon on me like he did, other than being impressive to Traytanna. Was it something to do with a small protest by his people about joining forces with Enlopedia? Perhaps he was conveying their feelings about being joined with outsiders—that they didn't want to be part of a treaty. It makes me wonder if Father is safe on Thealysis. I want to know if there is anything hostile we're heading into, because of this joining treaty, that could surface once it's all signed and sealed and we are there," explained Tayce.

"Don't worry—if there is anything unlawful, we'll find it—right, Del," assured Lance.

"Right! The Admiral's safety is of the utmost importance," backed up Deluca, knowing how Tayce was feeling. She would have felt the same about her own father if he was in the same situation.

"I'll leave it with you; but if there is something, I want to know before we arrive on Thealysis, just in case we need to act to pull Father out quickly," pointed out Tayce.

"Right! Come on, Del, we've got work to do," announced Lance, turning and briskly walking on out of the DC.

Deluca followed on. Tayce watched them both go, thinking to herself how well Lance had taken Deluca under his wing and was working with her, training her in research, which she seemed to enjoy. But Tayce knew he always did have endless patience to guide and teach someone and he was the right man to teach Deluca patiently, considering she hadn't known anything other than her life on Marrack. Tayce turned her swivel chair to look out of the full-length sight port. Twedor entered the DC and crossed the floor. He walked around the desk to come and stand beside her. He lightly prodded her in the arm. She looked down and smiled, glad to see him operational once again, considering the fall he taken earlier. It had been the kind of tumble that could have put him out of action for a couple of weekons at least. She realised she'd picked the right man in Craig Bream for performing miracles in keeping both the cruiser and Twedor functioning well.

"Back to normal and ready for action," announced Twedor obligingly.

"Glad to hear it—we'd be lost without you. I would be lost without you, my little friend," said Tayce, glad he was back.

"You didn't think a slight bump could finish me off, did you?" asked Twedor.

"Of course not. Look, we're approaching Thealysis. We're meeting Father there. It will be good to see him again," confided Tayce, thinking about it.

"It certainly is a strange shape for a hoped-for new headquarters second base. It seems to have appeared ahead of schedule, according to my calculations," said Twedor, surprised.

"Maybe we made good flying time. I have to agree, it's a strange shape for a proposed sister colony to Enlopedia—an elongated white hexagon is somewhat different from other planets we've encountered to date," said Tayce, thinking on the fact, studying the strange planetary shape, which almost covered ten milons in overall diameter.

"Strange shape or not, it's Thealysis," proclaimed Marc, entering the DC behind them.

"How are Nickrotrae and Traytanna?" enquired Tayce, turning her chair to face him across the desk.

"She was having a go at him when I left. I think he's learning the error of his ways," replied Marc casually, smiling at the thought.

"I bet it didn't turn out the way he expected it to. I feel they've been used as innocent pawns. Go easy on them. I'm having Lance delve into the background of our joyriders. I feel someone else is behind Nickrotrae's action earlier with the gun and them being out here in such a vessel. You were a little rough on Nickrotrae earlier. Fair enough, he did draw that gun on me, but I doubt he would have had the courage to use it. He was scared and it was his way of lashing out. I picked up conflicting thoughts, as if someone had given him orders to do what he was attempting to do," began Tayce.

"But if I hadn't taken action to stop him, he may well have been trained to kill you—you just don't know," protested Marc sincerely.

"But he didn't and, like I said, I don't think he would have," replied Tayce.

"It didn't look like that from where I was, and now you're having him investigated. Better safe than sorry—that's what I say," protested Marc. He figured what he'd done in protecting her had been right.

"I appreciate your actions, but you were a cadet Once, you know, as was I in a roundabout way. Didn't you do anything that was irresponsible or reckless—break the rules maybe?" she threw at him.

"Not so much as to draw a gun on someone of great importance. He's going to have to curb that temper, otherwise I can't see him turning into a first-class officer," replied Marc in thought.

"Maybe so, but, like I said, I feel he acted on orders from someone else. They were just using him because he was young and impressionable, with little thought of what the repercussions were," replied Tayce, persisting.

"Are you mad at me? I was just doing my protective duty, that's all?" he said, giving her a wondering look.

"No, I'm just saying you could have shown a little restraint, where Nickrotrae was concerned, regarding your rough treatment, that's all. Remember, Father is in the middle of a treaty. What you did, if Nickrotrae reports it to his superiors or whoever, could have a knock-on effect, especially if they are trying to cause trouble where this joint treaty is concerned," said Tayce in a forthright manner.

"All right, point taken—sorry!" he replied, realising what she was saying could be right.

"You're in command. I'm off to get changed into my ceremonial attire, ready to meet with Father and the hoped-for leader of the second base to Enlopedia," she announced, rising to her feet.

"While you're gone, I'll see how Lance and Deluca are getting on research wise. I want to find out if there's anything that should be known about the Thealysians, considering Nickrotrae's behaviour. You're not the only one that's unnerved by his actions. To be honest, Lance told me earlier what you suspected and I have to agree with you—there may be a problem regarding the inhabitants of Thealysis not wanting any treaty. We have to be prepared. I'll let you know later in the Docking-Bay area, before we leave, if we need to be on our guard," suggested Marc.

"Good idea. See you later?" she replied, beginning to walk over to the entrance to the DC.

Twedor followed on like an obedient servant. Marc smiled to himself at the way in which he had become a real pal to the team, especially Tayce, and was ready for any action that might come his way. Marc headed back out of the DC into Organisation. He soon paused at Nick Berenger's side, asking if there was any reply from Thealysis regarding the small vessel they were towing there. Nick looked up, removing his Microceive, and began explaining that Thealysis was extremely grateful that Nickrotrae and Traytanna had been apprehended safely. They were sending out a tow vessel to relieve Amalthea of the unnecessary transportation of the confirmed small warship. Marc raised his eyes in jest. Also there was a message to say Ambassador Wiljan, his daughter Nadinea and Admiral Traun were awaiting their arrival. Marc nodded in understanding.

Amal suddenly announced the Quest team for visiting the proposed second headquarters base. Marc turned, listening.

"The following members are selected for the Thealysian Quest: Captain Traun, Marc Dayatso, Lance Largon, Nick Berenger, Dr Tysonne and, lastly, Aldonica Darstayne," announced Amal.

Marc was glad he was going. He was quite looking forward to it. He also would be on hand should Tayce quickly need his assistance. It was also his duty to accompany Tayce on important Quests, such as this was. He glanced out into the Universe through the sight port, then suggested that all named Quest members head off and get changed into their ceremonial attire for the arrival at Thealysis.

"Nick, before you head off, inform Aldonica and Donaldo they're going on the Quest, will you?" asked Marc as Nick stood up and was about to head off.

"Sure!" replied Nick, seating himself again, carrying out the order.

"Before you go, Lance, anything on the terrible twosome down in confinement? Anything we should know about in their background before we head down to their home world?" asked Marc, pausing beside Deluca's chair.

"No, nothing out of the ordinary. The two down in confinement have as clean records as any other cadet of their age. They've only done the normal acts young cadets get up to. The latest feat has to be their most daring one so far, according to their records," replied Lance in a definite tone.

"Thanks for checking anyway," replied Marc in an appreciative tone.

As he turned back to look out through the main sight port, so his eyes caught the arrival of two sleek-looking pointed Transpo Cruisers from Thealysis. Kelly at her duty position turned, informing him the two vessels were there to take over the tractor beam hold and return the Thealysian warship back to Thealysis. Marc, on this walked across Organisation to come and stand by Kelly. He reached for Nick Berenger's Microceive, which Nick had left on the communications console, before heading on out and slipping it on.

"Hand communications over to me for a minon," ordered Marc.

Kelly, on his words, depressed a few keys that activated communications. Marc stood listening to the leading pilot explain to him that he'd come to take back the small warship currently under tractor beam. Marc agreed. He then ordered Kelly to release the vessel into the hands of the tow cruisers. The Pilots were in position to take over. Kelly nodded and did as requested, watching the screen. Marc stood watching for a few minons to make sure the switchover went smoothly. He then placed the Microceive down at Kelly's side as she would be in charge of communications in Nick's absence. After the switchover, Marc informed her he was off to get changed for the Quest ahead. Any problems, Amal would take full control. With this he headed on out, leaving Kelly in Amal's capable guidance.

* * *

Thealysis, the proposed new second headquarters base to Enlopedia, could only be described as having an environment of a blizzard-blown snowy surface, with below-freezing temperatures. The snow blew in sheets of whiteness. It was hard to see in the extreme weather conditions the concretex columns that rose from below the surface of the planet with one-, two- and three-storey round buildings on top, of a blue-and-white mottled design. There were quite a few of the protruding structures rising from the white snowy landscape and they seemed to be linked by a travelling tunnel system, for personnel to travel back and forth from one construction to the other. This was the Thealysian base. The whole base was constructed approximately twenty yearons ago, and the first building to be constructed was the Flight and Service Dome. It was a three-storey glassene-and-steelex domed design. It enabled workers to bring in teams to work and bring in the materials to build the entire complex-type base in a yearon and a half.

Inside the centre dome of the complex, which was considered the centrepiece of the base, was Admiral Darius Traun, along with Chief Jan Barnford and Ambassador Janard Wiljan. They all stood on the top floor in the Ambassador's Centre, looking out at the ill-tempered winds and the blizzard conditions. The Ambassador had commented that the winds whipping the snow around their present surroundings were an estimated 140 milons a houron. It was considered far from ideal, as it had lowered the temperatures to below zero. But he had added that of late the conditions had been somewhat of a common occurrence. Darius Traun thought to himself that he was glad the weather on Enlopedia was computer-generated. There was no fear of extreme conditions, like the ones he was witnessing then. The Ambassador was an authoritative yet kind-looking man, around 1.83 metres in height and of strong build. He had short whitish-grey hair and warm brown eyes. A real fatherly type, thought Jan as he glanced at him for a brief moment. But he could also see the true leadership he held, by the way in which he stood. The Ambassador began to pace around the large simply furnished centre. He began in a pleasant forthright and sincere way, voicing his concerns over the treaty where his people were concerned and the big change it would bring. He wanted them to feel the benefits and advantages for Thealysis. Darius listened and nodded in an understanding way. He then assured Janard that he had his word there would be no one left out or not beneficially affected where the benefits of a joint treaty were concerned. This was not his or Enlopedia's way of doing things. Upon these words, Janard Wiljan gave a relieved smile at the thought. He began, saying that his people had always shown great loyalty to him as a leader, and he felt it only right he consider them as well as himself in the joint treaty. Darius fully understood and confirmed as much. Janard further explained that there would be a ceremonial celebration evening for the meeting of some of the people from both Thealysis and Enlopedia, where there could be the chance of exchange and possible recruitment on both sides. There would also be the discussion of duty and position changes to be considered. Darius knew this treaty with Thealysis was a difficult one. He was glad he'd been in the rank he was in, with the experience to simply play along with what the Thealysians were requesting. He nodded once more, agreeing to what Janard Wiljan had asked and proposed. Jan Barnford, as he stood listening, figured there was going to be quite a transformation under way in this significant change. He just hoped there wasn't any trouble and it all went smoothly. He watched the snowy landscape through the large sight pane, listening as both Darius Traun and Ambassador Wiljan continued in discussion.

* * *

Tayce, back on Amalthea was in her quarters. She checked her appearance in the reflection imager. The entrance doors opened behind her. Dairan stepped in from the corridor, his sight falling immediately on her breathtaking beauty. She caught him studying her, interested, as she looked in the imager to see who had just entered. He smiled a warm, loving smile, winking at her. She turned to face him. God, he thought, why was she so damn gorgeous? He wanted to take her there and then in his arms. Tayce smiled. She was reading his thoughts and played along with them in a playful, flaunting way. She could see he liked what he was seeing.

"Need I ask what you think of the gown?" she asked in a playful way.

"From where I'm standing, you take my breath away just looking at you like that," he replied, trying his hardest not to think of what she was making him feel.

He walked forth, not able to contain his feelings any longer. Reaching out, he grabbed her gently around her waist, drawing her in in a soft, determined way, knowing what he wanted to do.

She sailed towards him and announced as she looked up at him, "We don't have the time," she laughed, reading his somewhat interesting thoughts.

He felt the softness of her cream silkene wrap-over gown as she stayed in his gentle hold, both looking into each other's eyes for a minon. He lowered his head slowly to kiss her on the lips fully, in a strong wanting way. Tayce once more gave into his warm seductiveness and draped her cream-sleeved arms around his neck. She could spare five minons, she thought. They stayed in a lost nothingness for each other for a few moments, then Tayce was jerked back to reality by the thoughts of Thealysis flashing into her mind. She broke away. He let her go gently, looking at her, concerned because she'd cut short their intimate moment.

"Was it something I did?" he asked softly, wondering.

"No. I wanted it too, but we've got the Quest to Thealysis. We'll reschedule," she promised softly.

"Well, I hope you've put your thermals on under that gown. I've been told it's freezing down there," he said, changing the subject swiftly.

"You bet, and this gown is made from a thermally insulated material, even though it's soft and luxurious to the touch. It's a new technology—the material doesn't have to be thick any more to be insulating."

"Really? I know I won't be booking a break to Thealysis any time soon with temperatures like they've got, freezing cold snow and high blizzard-type winds.

It won't be top of my vacation list. It might be ideal for a second headquarters base, but that's all," said Dairan, thinking about it.

"I'm keeping an open mind on that second headquarters base," replied Tayce, reserving her judgement. Something was still making her feel uneasy about the joint treaty with both bases.

"Oh, why?" asked Dairan, interested.

"Because of what happened with Nickrotrae. It still unnerves me. We don't know if something could go wrong regarding this treaty and the people of Thealysis."

"I guess I don't blame you," replied Dairan, seeing her point of view.

"I want you to take care of Organisation whilst I'm down on Thealysis—that's if you feel up to it after your ordeal earlier. I'll understand if you don't feel you can do it. How do you feel in yourself really?" she asked in a caring way.

"Like I've been ten rounds without protection on a combat simulator and lost badly, but the sight of you and the way you're looking makes me feel ten times better," he replied, giving her a mischievous look.

"So are you up to taking charge in my absence?" she persisted, finding his reply amusing.

"Sure! Don't worry about a thing—you go. I'll be ready to act if there's any trouble. You give the word and I'll have you out of there at a cencron's notice," he promised.

Tayce glanced at her Wristlink time display. It was time to leave. Twedor came on normal operational mode and stood ready to accompany his mistress. Tayce began walking over to the quarters entrance, followed by Twedor. Dairan, as the quarters doors drew back, informed her he'd catch her later and told her to have a good Quest but to keep in touch. Tayce agreed, letting him walk on out, up to Level 1. She then followed on out to go on to the Docking-Bay doors with Twedor, letting the quarters doors close behind them.

* * *

Marc, Lance and Craig were dressed in their ceremonial thermal Quest uniforms and were heading up towards the Docking-Bay doors on Level 2. The topic for discussion was Countess Vargon and how they felt glad for Sallen that the evil woman hadn't proven to be the real one when Tayce had her final confrontation with the Witch Queen. It would have been very tricky, considering Sallen's memory reprogramme and not remembering what the evil woman meant to her before—that they were related. They approached the Level Steps and began up to Level 2 from 3. As they stepped on to Level 2, so Tayce, Aldonica and Nick all came down the corridor from the Deck Travel. Nick had a restraining hold on Nickrotrae, and Aldonica lightly restrained Traytanna. They would be handed over to their section superiors to be made accountable for their actions, when they all arrived on Thealysis.

Tayce paused upon reaching the Docking-Bay doors. She turned, addressing the two young Thealysians.

"Whatever your reasons for doing what you thought was fun, as from this moment on you're answerable to your superiors. I will not be lodging an official complaint with my headquarters base. Consider this as a warning. Owing to the fact your world is to join with Enlopedia, I'm prepared to take no further action. I would urge you, though, the next time you try such a foolish act, to think. The vessel you try it on may see it as an act of war, and you want live to tell the tale," said Tayce plainly, speaking like a true captain.

"You two will learn that the Universe is not a playground," backed up Marc seriously.

"Captain, I never wanted this to happen. It was him. Please help us," pleaded Traytanna.

"You two can think yourselves lucky. At around your age I was cast out into this perilous Universe alone. I had to fight to just stay alive for the next three yearons of my life. I faced pirates and beings that can only be described as ones you'd never want to meet. And there's one still at large that would have found you both easy victims, for different reasons, if we hadn't discovered you. Value what you have—think before you act," pointed out Tayce, noticing Traytanna was seriously listening.

"Docking complete," announced Amal overhead.

As the Docking-Bay doors opened, the Amalthean Quest members, with the two cadets, walked off the cruiser on the walk down the boarding tube on to Thealysis. At the end of the walkway, a khaki-uniformed male officer could be seen awaiting their arrival, looking like thunder ready to erupt as his sight caught Nickrotrae and Traytanna. He was present to escort the Quest team into the clear-view lift that would take them to the high-ranked Ceremonial Dome. Two strong-looking officers dressed in dark turquoise, with security labels on their uniforms, stepped into view, looking somewhat unnerving as Nickrotrae and Traytanna reached them. Both youngsters were quickly and swiftly apprehended and led away in a no-nonsense way in total silence. Traytanna glanced back at Tayce and gave a small apologetic smile, then looked forward. Tayce glanced at Marc. He looked back, raising his eyes in surprise at the swift way the two youngsters were apprehended. He began wondering what was going to happen to them. The official-looking officer, there to meet the Quest team and Tayce, caught Tayce's surprised look at the way Nickrotrae and Traytanna had been led away so roughly. He quickly began saying that both would be all right—they would be reprimanded for their actions—but their punishment would be no more than any other cadet breaking the law would endure. Everyone walked aboard the clear-all-round lift, ready to head to where they needed to be taken. Tayce, in the clear-vision lift, rested her hands on Twedor's shoulders to steady him as the lift began forth. It travelled through clear glassene tunnels on the journey towards the Ceremonial Dome. The sight was of the blizzard-type landscape and the vastness of the whole of Thealysis as they travelled from one destination to another.

"This is our home, Captain—Thealysis in all her glory. Though not very impressive because of the weather conditions, which I must apologise for, our base here covers four milons wide by five milons in length," explained the young uniformed officer, who had met them earlier and who was also a courier.

"Why so much snow?" asked Marc, curious, leaning close to Tayce.

"Unfortunately, at present we are in what is termed Arctic Inclemency. It lasts for up to five monthons of our yearet. At the end of that time, our season changes to summer conditions, with very strange heat and storms and is known as daystaran. Temperatures can reach up to 100 degrees," explained the young officer/courier.

"One extreme to another, then?" asked Tayce without thought.

"How do you cope with such conditions, as they are at the present time?" cut in Marc before Tayce had a chance to have her question answered.

"Certain rules have to be obeyed during this time, as for daystaren. We have to take care then—especially our senior inhabitants regarding heat-related incidents—until the season passes," replied the officer/courier in a clear informative tone.

Tayce glanced at the young officer's lapel badge and his name. It was Jaranel. He was roughly in his his mid twenties and looked like he was relatively new to the position, judging by his behaviour—doing his best to please them as new guests important to Thealysis. He had sandy blonde short hair and was of slim to medium build. There was a certain military look to his features. They showed he was disciplined. His eyes were green, and showed the same kind of yellow pupil as Traytannas. Tayce tried reading the kind of man he was inside and found he was totally different to what he was showing. There was a warm, sincere inner peace, which she found somewhat strange because, on duty, he was showing none of what she was reading. She turned her attention to steadying Twedor, who looked up at her in his special close-fitting thermal suit, glad she was holding on to him. Donaldo was next to ask questions as they all travelled along.

"If you don't mind me asking, how do you manage in coping with ailments and emergencies of the medical kind, especially with the climate change you have here?"

"Fine! Doctor, we have top medical and science personnel. The moment a virus or other disease arises in any of our people, they are removed from what they're doing and put into total isolation. Then the teams work around the time dial to find a cure. They have never been beaten yet in restoring any member of the Thealysian race to normal health. As for medical emergencies, they are taken care of quickly and swiftly," explained Jaranel.

Donaldo found himself impressed by what Jaranel had said. He had no idea the medical and science teams were so advanced. But he also realised that if Enlopedia and Thealysis were going to be joined, then the medical and science teams would have to be advanced too, considering Enlopedia's medical and science teams were considered elite in their field. As the clear-vision lift began to decline to a slow speed before it began descending down a deep slope towards the High-Ranked Ceremonial Dome, Marc put to Jaranel what were the clear-vision tunnels used for? They looked like they ran round the whole base and he could see that not only were people travelling like themselves, but walking to and fro and riding in hover vehicles. Jaranel explained that the tunnels system was a means of travel for everyone, to get from A to B. The capsule-shaped hover vehicles were the means to carry people and needed equipment and supplies to other areas of the vast complex-orientated base. Some personnel walked to their destinations, but it all depended on how much time one had. Marc nodded in understanding, looking out and watching the throng of Thealysian personnel toing and froing.

The clear-vision lift finally slowed to a gentle stop. Tayce looked out and could see her father and was glad to see he was all right, considering what she'd been thinking. She was glad he was part of her life again. Beside her father, she could see who she thought was Ambassador Wiljan and a young, pretty girl of shapely figure that had to be the Ambassador's daughter, Nadinea. The most striking thing about Nadinea was her long, dark hair, which hung loose about her shoulders and down to the mid section of her back. Beside her were two guards from the Cadet Training Dome. Marc glanced at Tayce in wonderment, curious to know what they were present for. Tayce, sensing Marc was looking at her, looked back, wondering why the need for security? Had it to do with the fact Twedor was with them and they were uneasy? Tayce bent down and discreetly ordered Twedor to be on his best behaviour. He nodded in a understanding. The doors to the lift drew open with a humming sound. Jaranel stepped to one side, allowing Tayce to take Twedor and walk forth, over to meet with his ambassador and her father.

"Welcome to Thealysis, the new second headquarters base to Enlopedia. Captain Traun, who's this?" asked Ambassador Wiljan, looking down at Twedor, amazed and impressed by him.

"This is my escort, Twedor. He will cause no threat to Thealysis," announced Tayce, sensing the guards were summoning up Twedor suspiciously.

"At ease, men. In that case, Twedor, welcome to Thealysis," said the Ambassador, taking hold of Twedor's hand as he held it out to shake.

The Ambassador was truly impressed by Twedor, finding him fascinating. Twedor grasped the Ambassador's hand in gentle slow motion, applying the right amount of pressure.

"Thank you, sir. It's an honour to be here," announced Twedor politely, in his little way.

"Ambassador, this is Commander Marc Dayatso and here are some of my Amalthean Quests team," introduced Tayce, gesturing to the various members that had come with her.

Tayce introduced each of the team she'd taken with her, from Lance down to Aldonica, and in such a way that conveyed she was proud of each member. Darius Traun stood back, impressed by the way in which Tayce introduced the members of her team. Nick Berenger and Lance Largon seemed to impress the Ambassador's daughter, Nadinea. Tayce noticed how she returned their smiles of interest as they individually met her. She realised she'd have to keep an eye on both team members where protocol was concerned. The Ambassador turned, suggesting to Tayce that she and the team accompany him. With this, he began away through to the Great Ceremonial Hall, where there was a gathering of high-ranked delegates and important planetary people, who represented each section on Thealysis.

Tayce, Twedor, Marc and the rest of the team followed the Ambassador and headed in through the entrance towards a white stage with a podium at the far end of the Great Ceremonial Hall, under the studying watch of the people present, who represented Thealysis and everything it stood for, wondering what the Amalthean team would be like to meet? The group gathered were men and women, all ranging from the ages of twenty to fifty yearons, in differently designed uniforms. Some wore robes; some dressed in all-in-one suits. The colours ranged from royal blue to different shades of cream, brown, orange and white. The people ranged in height and build. Some were tall, some short, but most smiled and nodded in a welcoming gesture at Tayce. She studied them discreetly as she passed. Tayce figured there had to be around fifty or so people present. The Ambassador, as he stepped up on to the stage, began to address his mixed group of very authoritative-looking delegates as the Amaltheans stood silent.

"My people of Thealysis, todayon daylight houron I signed our base to become the second sister base with Enlopedia, to give us continued good life, I therefore give to you Admiral Traun of that base, to firstly say a few words," announced the Ambassador, gesturing for Darius to step forth.

"So glad to see so many new faces. This is a great honour for our base in this first of, it is hoped, many meetings, as it is no doubt an honour for you to meet myself and some of my people from a base that we hope you will enjoy becoming a big part of. Our aim is to bring peace, restore justice throughout the Universe and slow the crime rate that has been growing in the last yearons. I would like to introduce you to, if I may, some people I feel proud to introduce you to—a crime-fighting team that is somewhat becoming legendary, I give you the Amalthean

Quests team, headed by my daughter," announced Darius, proudly turning to Tayce, indicating for her to step forth.

"Welcome to you all in becoming part of Enlopedia. I'm Captain Traun and these are some members of my crime-fighting team. Every one of them is dedicated in their line of duty. I hope that we will all come to work together in the near future. It's an honour to be here todayon on Thealysis to share in the joining of both bases. I hope that our venture is a successful one, for all of us. If there are any questions you'd like to ask myself or any of my team, please do. We will be glad to answer them," announced Tayce casually.

She then stepped back, allowing Ambassador Wiljan to speak to his people. Darius gestured for Tayce to go first down into the gathered crowd, then followed on behind with the Amalthean Quests team members. Nadinea crossed to Lance and began to ask him about his duties as a member of a crime-fighting team. Also about Enlopedia. Tayce watched from a distance and smiled to herself in an amused way at the way in which Nadinea had taken a shine to Lance. Darius interrupted her amused watch by congratulating her on a good yet simple speech. He then enquired how the team were in general. Tayce felt she would have liked to tell him about Aemiliyana, but realised it wasn't the time or place. She also noticed Ambassador Wiljan approaching from the stage through the crowd. She simply gave him a simple answer—they were fine.

As Ambassador Wiljan paused, Tayce's attention was caught by some young members of the delegation taking an interest in Twedor. She excused herself and crossed to be with them and answer any questions they might have about him.

"You've a daughter to be proud of, Darius. I wish—and this is between you and I—Nadinea would take an interest in the aspects of leadership. I wish she would see that one dayon this will all be hers, but she doesn't, I'm afraid," said the Ambassador, looking at Tayce admiringly.

"Leadership for my daughter was not through choice; it was thrown at her. Our home world was destroyed and Twedor, beside her, was her only companion back in those dayons. He was her first cruiser's guidance and operations computer, but she doesn't regret what happened. Yes, I am proud of what she is todayon. Nadinea will find her way, you'll see," assured Darius in friendly tone.

"I certainly hope so," replied Janard.

"Excuse me, gentlemen—have you seen Tayce around?" asked Marc politely to Darius and the Ambassador.

"Over there talking, I presume about Twedor," replied Darius.

"Thanks!" replied Marc, walking away.

He headed on across the Great Ceremonial Hall towards Tayce. He soon paused and took her lightly by the upper arm, guiding her to one side of the hall. She looked at him as he began speaking discreetly, saying that one of the couriers had just informed him there was a call for her from Dairan, on the cruiser. It sounded urgent. On this, Tayce nodded, then guided Twedor away from the small group of young people and walked on, with Marc in pursuit, to find out what was so urgent. Once outside the Great Ceremonial Hall, Marc paused, waiting.

"Where is the courier? Where do I take this call?" asked Tayce, becoming alarmed, thinking something was wrong.

"Relax! There isn't a call—I just needed to talk to you discreetly out of the earshot of the others," put Marc, glancing around the outside area, making sure no one was listening to what he was about to say.

"You dragged me away from a discussion with young people who will be part of Enlopedia's future on a false pretext. This had better be good, Marc," said Tayce, growing angry at the fact.

"Take a look around—don't you feel something isn't right here?" he began discreetly.

"Oh, at last you feel uneasy, like I do! Everything does seem just a bit too perfect, like it's staged. It's like at any cencron something could go wrong. I've been feeling this right back since when Nickrotrae drew that gun on me and said what he did about not coming back here," replied Tayce.

"You want to know the truth—the feeling's mutual. It's like we're only seeing what they want us to see. It's just too cut and dry in the 'good impressions' way. I didn't like the way both Nickrotrae and Traytanna were hauled away in the manner they were and the way Jaranel swiftly covered up the way the youngsters were taken. It didn't seem right. All right, they did wrong, but the way that young girl looked at you made me wonder about things around here, punishment-wise. There's also an uneasy feeling of pretending—a kind of cover-up of some sorts is being played out, so that your father and us will believe everything is OK," confided Marc.

Quite suddenly, just as both Tayce and himself were thinking suspiciously that their new surroundings were just a bit too perfect, Thealysis became the target of an unexpected attack, shaking the entire base to its foundations. Tayce grabbed Marc to steady herself and pulled Twedor under her arm to shield him. The doors to the Great Ceremonial Hall drew back and all the people that had been gathered inside began to pour out in screaming panic. Tayce grabbed Twedor even closer to herself, ordering him to hold on tight. She then pushed on through the rushing crowd to a scene that suddenly took her back to many yearons previously. For a minon it was as if she had shot back in time to the night of Traun's destruction. Before her was a sight of fallen masonry and scorched and torn celebrational banners and dead bodies scattered here and there from the strike of attack. Nadinea was kneeling over Ambassador Wiljan's lifeless body, sobbing her heart out, pleading with him not to die. Darius Traun looked at Tayce as he tried to get Nadinea to rise to her feet and leave her father. Chaos was raining all round as the base had taken a direct hit. Snow was blowing in where the walls had fallen.

"Marc, find out if the Ambassador is alive?" asked Darius in a discreet way.

"Of course," replied Marc, crossing and crouching down by the Ambassador's dusty and bloodstained body, which had taken a direct hit from the falling masonry.

Marc placed his right hand to the pulse region on the Ambassador and, after cencrons of waiting, looked up at Darius and Tayce, shaking his head. Donaldo came rushing in to see what he could do to assist in any way he could. He soon was with them and took his medical Examscan out of his top left-hand pocket, ready to see if anything could be done to save the Ambassador. Tayce looked around and saw other members of her team helping Jan Barnford to try and get the crowd to safety and calm them, but to no avail. She glanced back to Donaldo, who was at the side of the Ambassador, guiding the Examscan over and around the Ambassador's body.

"We'd better get him back to the MLC on Amalthea. I can try more there—it may not be to late," announced Donaldo in a true medical tone.

Nadinea looked around at what was her beautiful and peaceful home, which was now quickly becoming a wreck around her, worsening by the cencron. Her eyes were brimming with distraught tears. Was this the end? she wondered. She looked down at her father, hearing words he'd spoken to her so many times before, saying she would have to grow up one dayon; Thealysis would be hers to be in charge of. She suddenly wondered if his words were going to come true and she was going to lose him, just like she had her mother all those past yearons ago during the attack on their cruiser, out in space, on the way to their new surroundings to settle.

"First my mother, now my father," she said softly, tearfully clinging to Darius.

Tayce read her thoughts on her mother and shook her head. Nadinea was going through what she had yearons ago. She knew the pain she was feeling.

Jan Barnford left the base security chief in charge when he arrived with a team from the far side of the base. He thanked Jan for his assistance. Just as he did, another incoming missile hit home on the base. In the moments that followed, more attack strikes, both missile and Slazer fire, hit home over the different parts of Thealysis. It was helpless, thought Tayce. If they stayed where they were any longer, it would be too late to leave for all of them—not least the Thealysians. Marc suggested they leave before they became targets themselves. The Quest team soon gathered, along with Darius Traun, Nadinea and Jan Barnford. Tayce gave order via Wristlink to transpot and get them off the surface. With that, after a few minons, as the base security tried to get people to vessels, to escape, Tayce grabbed Nadinea and Darius so that they could be included in the Transpot, whilst Donaldo and Lance held the Ambassador. Then the whole team dematerialised off the surface to the safety of Amalthea.

* * *

What was left behind was a burning and bloodied sight, with screams and sheer panic as the Thealysian Security Force fought to rescue some of the inhabitants, taking them to awaiting rescue ships. They were putting up a good fight in returning fire on the attacking enemy. Some were being destroyed with people aboard, which meant the loss of more lives. As it looked at the present time, Thealysis was not to be the second headquarters base to Enlopedia after all. What had seemed the ideal first treaty between Enlopedia and a distant world had failed.

19. The Boglayons' Final Return

Upon arrival on Amalthea, Treketa was waiting with the Hover Trolley prepared for Donaldo to quickly take the Ambassador to the MLC to see if there was anyway in which he could to save him. Just as soon as the Ambassador was placed on the Hover Trolley, Nadinea went with Treketa on behind. As Donaldo began off in the direction of the MLC Tayce raised her Wristlink and contacted Amal, ordering her to scan the attack force annihilating Thealysis and find out who was responsible. She wanted to know the moment she reached Organisation. Amal acknowledged Tayce's request. Tayce broke into a sprint, heading for the Organisation Centre, passing the small group heading to the MLC Darius looked at Tayce as she passed, with Twedor not far behind in hot pursuit, knowing that if anyone could find out the identity of the attackers, she would—and find out the reason for the unprovoked attack on the proposed, but not to be, second headquarters base. He continued to comfort the upset Nadinea and for the first time realised that in a way Tayce must have felt the same as this young woman in his care. She too was alone, those many yearons ago, when she had been cast out in the Universe that fateful night of Traun's demise. His thoughts went to the treaty, that had been signed between the two bases. He guessed the document was now void and, what's more, Nadinea could be without her father if Donaldo was unable to revive him. The more he looked at it, the more Nadinea seemed like Tayce back in 2414: homeless, without a family or friends she knew and loved. The whole situation was becoming an unfortunate mess.

On Level 1 the team members who had been on the Quest with Tayce and worked in Organisation ran into the centre, over to their duty positions. Upon seating themselves, they immediately began to find out why Thealysis was under unprovoked attack. Why had it occurred in the first place? Tayce paused by Dairan upon entering Organisation. He began to explain that Amal had just announced the attack force had just shown up in orbit and began firing on the surface and base just an houron after herself and the others landed there. They had come out of nowhere, which would confirm that they must have been hiding behind some kind of Invis Shield. Amal had received a warning to stay out of the plan of attack or they would become the next target. Tayce pulled a face that conveyed she didn't like being told what to do by total strangers, let alone some attack fleet. Quite suddenly, behind her, at his position, Lance cursed. Tayce turned, as did Dairan, wondering why. Lance looked across to Tayce, knowing she wasn't going to like what he was about to relay to her—the information he had on-screen before him.

"You're not going to like this. You'd better brace yourself. Information has just come through revealing the identity of the attack force," warned Lance.

"Who?" prompted Tayce, giving him her full attention.

"The Boglayons, would you believe?" announced Lance, to the point.

"Lord Dion," said Tayce, then felt a surge of a feeling that unnerved her, like her encounter with him was yesteron. It rushed through her very existence and she saw the Pirate Lord's face appear in her mind.

It was quickly replaced by a look on her beautiful face which showed her anger at the thought about Lord Dion and the last time they had met—how he had nearly crushed her hand and made her fight against being seduced by his powerful powers of the mind. 'God!' she thought. 'Why did it have to be him?' She looked at Marc in frustrated anger at the Pirate Lord's return, wondering what he wanted this time, besides annihilating Thealysis. Marc raised his eyes in jest. He shared her feelings of anger, particularly because of the fact the Pirate Lord had escaped being brought to justice the first time. Kelly, at her duty position, shivered at the thought of the Boglayons' return also. They were the bunch of pirates that had kidnapped her parents and taken them prisoner to be held at the old Boglayon hideout. She'd hoped she'd seen the last of Lord Dion and wouldn't have to come face-to-face with the barbarian ever again.

"Captain, Dr Tysonne requests your presence in the MLC immediately," announced Amal suddenly.

Dairan returned command back to Marc, now that he was back from Thealysis, and accompanied Tayce to go and see what was happening in the MLC Both he and Tayce walked from Organisation into the first level corridor. Darius Traun was coming up the corridor as they began walking down. He smiled, seeing Tayce. All three came to a pause in the middle of corridor.

"Donaldo has just asked for me in the MLC. He said it was urgent."

"In that case, I better return with you," replied Darius, turning round ready to walk back.

All three continued walking on down to Level 2. Tayce, as she went, had a feeling the news Donaldo was going to deliver wasn't going to be good. Her senses confirmed her thoughts. As they stepped on to Level 2, Darius informed Tayce whatever the outcome where the Ambassador was concerned, he would take Nadinea back to Enlopedia and get help for her there.

"What will happen if her father can't be revived and returned to normal health? Considering she has no family, isn't it going to be difficult on Enlopedia for her, not having anyone she knows?" asked Tayce, feeling sorry for Nadinea, having been in the same situation once herself.

"Chief Barnford is currently sorting out a search party to find out if there is the slimmest chance some of her people escaped in those vessels that were departing Thealysis. If there isn't any hope, then your mother and I will make sure she gets the best support to start a new life on Enlopedia, or wherever she wants to go," assured Darius in a sincere way.

The doors to the MLC were soon before them. They parted and the sight that greeted Tayce confirmed her worst thoughts. Nadinea was being comforted by Treketa in the Officette, as the young girl sobbed her heart out. Tayce turned her attention to Donaldo as he approached, solemn-faced. He gestured to Janard Wiljan, who lay in a still, silent condition on the first bunk. Tayce studied the battered and bruised appearance of the Ambassador, then looked at Donaldo questioningly. He shook his head, announcing that he'd died just over twenty minons ago. He'd done all he could possibly do to save him. It had been a hopeless situation. His injuries were too intense and life-threatening.

"Don't worry—you did all you could do. You couldn't do any more," assured Tayce.

"I second that," backed up Darius.

Nadinea walked from the Officette, her delicate elfin features tear-stained from the crying she'd done over the demise of the only family she'd had, now gone forever. She slowly walked on over to the sight port, where she paused and stood looking out, hoping she'd be able to see her home world. She backed away in emotional hurt and horror at the sight she saw, the planet fast becoming a wreck of what was Thealysis, her beautiful snowy home. She began to shake with the hurt and emotional turmoil she'd been plunged into. Donaldo realised as he looked over Dairan's shoulder that she was going into severe traumatic shock. Without warning she passed out. Dairan quickly turned, catching her in a quick supporting hold. Donaldo quickly retrieved an anti-shock relieving injection (ASR), designed by Jaul Naven, and administered it, pressing the Comprai Inject Pen against Nadinea's arm. The shock relaxant entered her system with the sound of compressed air. Within minons Dairan, on a nod from Donaldo, lifted her up and carried her over to the nearest vacant bunk, setting her down gently. Treketa covered her with a heat-sealant blanket up as far as her shoulders, then moved to cover the Ambassador so Nadinea wouldn't have any more problems when she came back to consciousness, in seeing her dead father.

"Donaldo, I would like you to prepare the Ambassador for transference, ready to be given a proper burial when we reach Enlopedia," requested Darius.

"I'll get right on to it. Leave it with us," assured Donaldo quite calmly as he checked Nadinea's vital signs.

"Much appreciated," replied Darius casually.

"Treketa as soon as Nadinea is up to facing things, I want her brought to the DC," requested Tayce, glancing at the still unconscious form of the young Thealysian.

"Of course. I'll do it just as soon as she's ready," assured Treketa.

"I'll leave you to it. You know where I'll be if you need me," said Tayce, heading back to the entrance with Dairan in tow. As the doors parted, upon Tayce's approach, she and her father were first through, followed by Dairan, beginning the return walk back to Organisation.

* * *

Jan Barnford who was on board Amalthea, having returned with the Quest team, was in the process of arranging for the next Patrol Cruiser that was in the area to take him back to Enlopedia. As luck would have it there was one nearby. He arranged for them to call in and pick him up. He was glad he'd managed to find one on patrol. He headed on down to the Docking-Bay doors, leaving a message with Nick Berenger, on the way out of Organisation, to inform Tayce he'd see her later. He was in the final moments of walking in the direction of the Docking-Bay doors when Nick, overhead announced to his surprise that the Patrol Cruiser was in the process of docking alongside. Jan broke into a brisk sprint the rest of the way. Just as he reached the doors they opened, and he walked off Amalthea on to the Patrol Cruiser, leaving the Docking-Bay doors to close behind him. Within minons the Patrol Cruiser was departing from Amalthea, heading for Enlopedia, where Jan had urgent security business waiting, unaware of just who the attack fleet was that had attacked Thealysis.

* * *

A while later Tayce, Darius and Dairan walked into Organisation. They weren't prepared for the sight that grabbed them through main sight port and had appeared just after Jan's Patrol Cruiser had left the vicinity. Tayce, before Lance announced who it was, sensed he was back and heard his seductive pirate's voice in her head.

A shiver—and one she didn't want to feel—ran up her spine as she heard him say, "Hello, Fairness. I said we'd meet again," he said in his enticing sexy voice.

Tayce gave a look that showed her total disgust that he was back. The last thing she wanted was to come face-to-face with him again. He unnerved her for all the wrong reasons. He was one powerful being and one that tried to undermine her own powers for his amusement and advantage in the sensual stakes. The vessel was the same in colour as the Boglayon hideout in the first voyage: muddy brown. But it was armed with every available weapon imaginable, ready for battle at a cencron's notice, as it had proven against Thealysis. In size it was roughly four milons in diameter. What were they back for besides annihilating

Thealysis? wondered Tayce. Dairan had no knowledge of this leader and was getting information from Lance. He turned, announcing that in the last houron it had been uncovered on research that the leader—namely, Lord Dion—had escaped to regroup with a new band of men over two yearons ago.

Not meaning to, Tayce snapped. "I know who he is, but what's he doing here? What does he want besides destroying Thealysis?that's What I want to know?" said Tayce sharply without realising it.

"Tell me, Dairan, wasn't this the attack fleet that attacked Greymaren?" asked Darius, watching the sight on-screen, interested.

"Yes, sir, it was," cut in Kelly before Dairan had a chance to say a word, confirming it with a tinge of hatred in her voice.

Marc put a reassuring hand on Kelly's shoulder and squeezed it to calm her. He knew how she felt about Lord Dion. Tayce crossed to Nick, asking if any communication had been made since Dion's arrival in orbit above Thealysis. Just as Tayce asked him, he received a communication at that cencron from the man himself. He was demanding open-screen communication with the Colonel of Amalthea, not knowing Tayce had changed rank since they last met.

"Transfer that barbarian to the main sight screen. Lets hear what he has to say," said Tayce in a couldn't-care-less tone, walking to stand in the centre of Organisation, hands on hips, waiting for Lord Dion—or Dion, as she liked to address him—to appear.

"Transferring now. He's all yours," announced Nick, pressing a few buttons to activate the screen for face-to-face communications.

"I'd rather he wasn't," replied Tayce under her breath.

The main sight screen flashed into life and the leader of the Boglayons, Lord Dion, appeared. He silently studied Tayce and she felt it, trying to resist, to his amusement, using her own powers to try and block him. He was a little older, but conveyed just as much power in his dark, smouldering brown eyes. His features were just as she remembered them—amazingly handsome, dark and bearded. His almost jet-black hair was a little shorter, yet styled in a short layered wavy look to the nape of the neck. Tayce thought to herself that a pleasure slave would think he was the best thing in an overpowering encounter of the intimate kind to grace the Universe. She'd sampled what he'd like to do to her, on their last encounter in the first voyage. She'd felt his power. Poor unsuspecting victims of the female kind, she thought. But despite this fact, he was as bad as they came and he had just proven this by attacking the peaceful snowy world of Thealysis. He studied Tayce further, trying to entice her with intense interest, playing with her feelings much against her resistance to him doing so, trying to unnerve her to no avail. He remembered their last encounter at his hideout. It had been one that had somehow fascinated him. No female had ever challenged him and stood up to him in quite the way she had. He found her appealing, to say the least.

"This is an unexpected pleasure, Colonel," began Dion, playing with her with his mind powers.

"It's not a pleasure for me, Lord Dion. And it's Captain," said Tayce in a tone of coldness, fighting what he was trying to make her feel.

"You wandered in last time, hell-bent on taking me to hand, you failed and as you can see, I'm back, so state the nature of why you're interested in my current movements, or get the hell out of my way and don't interfere, woman. I warned you some yearons ago to stay out of my business," he said, suddenly turning cold in his tone.

"Pretty hostile words! You warn *me?* The planet you have just annihilated, Thealysis, was joined in a treaty with Enlopedia todayon, so that makes your business my business. Why are you interested in Thealysis? I'm waiting, Dion," said Tayce, not prepared to put up with Dion's brash response.

"All right, my business is with the Thealysian woman Nadinea Wiljan, and my scan just confirmed that you have her on board; so hand her over, Fairness, or I'll be forced to take her through unconventional means," he said, growing impatient.

"Try taking her, Dion, and I guarantee you will not be leaving this Universe with her. This is not the original Amalthean cruiser and it's an equal match for you in fire power any time," replied Tayce in a warning tone. She was not prepared to just hand over Nadinea Wiljan easily.

Lord Dion just gave her an impatient furious look, sighed and abruptly ceased communication. The screen went blank. At this moment in the Organisation Centre doorway Treketa stood with Nadinea. Dairan drew Tayce's attention to the fact by touching her on the arm and gesturing towards the entrance with his eyes. Tayce turned. Nadinea walked across to her. Darius looked questioningly at the young female Thealysian as she did so. He wondered just why a man so evil as Lord Dion wanted her. He noticed he wasn't the only one that was looking at Nadinea in a curious way, wondering what the connection with Lord Dion was. Kelly swallowed a lump in her throat as it brought back old memories. She realised that maybe Nadinea could be like she'd been—one of Lord Dion's proposed conquests-cum-pleasure slaves. The air could have been sliced with a Slazer knife it was so silent as everyone waited. Upon Nadinea pausing before Tayce, she suggested they have a private talk in the DC. Nadinea agreed with a slow nod. The team silently watched on as Tayce guided Nadinea on into the DC with Twedor and Marc in pursuit. Tayce paused as her father approached.

"Go easy on her, but find out just what's going on?" he advised discreetly.

"Don't worry—I will. I want to find out what we're up against, and if there's a way to stop that barbarian getting his hands on Nadinea," she assured her father in a returned whisper.

Tayce continued into the DC. She had to find out, if she was to protect Nadinea by using the Amalthean Quests team and her cruiser. Darius knew it would be a while before they learnt the truth of what was going on between the Thealysians, Nadinea and Lord Dion, so he decided to head off to his guest quarters for a bit of rest and call Lydia privately. He informed Dairan of as much. Dairan nodded, but continued to keep his sight on the view of Lord Dion's vessel through the main sight port. Now he'd learnt just what Lord Dion stood for, he didn't like him or trust him any more than Tayce did. Darius walked from the Organisation Centre. It had been a long dayon and a demanding one at that, with more to follow, he thought.

In the DC, Tayce walked around to the back of her desk and sat down in a relaxed way in her chair, ready to listen to what Nadinea had to say regarding her involvement with Lord Dion.

"I want to hear what your planet's involvement is with Lord Dion?" demanded Tayce, finding it worrying but not surprising as she had had her suspicions the moment they'd arrived at Thealysis that something wasn't quite right over the treaty. Dion had just proven her suspicions were justified.

"It's a debt that's owed to him. My parents owed him a great sum of currency for past protective favours in order to keep our world alive and safe. The understanding was that I would be handed over to him on my father's death. My father dismissed the fact that the debt was in place when he signed the treaty with Enlopedia, pretending it didn't exist, I told him it was wrong—hence Lord Dion destroyed our world and now he's after me because my Father shut Lord Dion out and pretended the debt wasn't in place," began Nadinea in a sorrowful way.

"Your father signed the treaty with Enlopedia with this in place?" asked Tayce in total shock and disbelief.

"Yes, Captain," replied Nadinea softly and ashamed. She could see Tayce wasn't pleased.

"Is this all, or is there more?" asked Marc, just as surprised as Tayce at what he'd just heard.

"It all started when I was a small childling," began Nadinea, but she was interrupted by the doors to the DC opening behind her.

Darius Traun entered. He wanted to hear what Nadinea had to say in regard to her involvement with Lord Dion. He headed across to the nearest soffette and sat down in a relaxed way, gesturing for Tayce to continue.

Nadinea, on a nod from Tayce, continued. "It all started like I said, when I was a childling, five yearons old, my mother was killed by one of Lord Dion's men in the battle for our new home. Lord Dion to cover up what had been done offered to protect our world. Father paid the money for a while, then there was a row over the fact Father owed him a large sum of currency for behind payments building up. Another agreed time for the next payment time came around and there was a further heated discussion between my father and Lord Dion. Father couldn't repay him and it was decided, in order to keep our world alive and safe,

I was to be handed over to Lord Dion at the age I am now—eighteen, or on my fathers death, to be taken as a pleasure slave for his personal selection. That time, Captain, is now," finished Nadinea, lowering her head in shame.

"I can't believe I'm hearing this," said Tayce in utter disbelief and disgust.

Marc cursed, using the strongest swear words Tayce had ever known him to use. He shook his head in utter disgust at the fact. Nadinea began to break down and cry. She didn't want to be handed over to Lord Dion—he was a barbarian of the worst kind and she had never liked him. Tayce rose to her feet and crossed the room, sighing.

"Nadinea, why did your father go ahead with the signing of the treaty with Enlopedia if he knew of this connection with Lord Dion? Tell me, was it to pay the debt off and set you free with the sum of currency that was to come from the joining?" asked Darius, feeling he'd been foolish to connect an upstanding base such as Enlopedia to a planet that was working with the likes of the leader of the Boglayons. He gave a look that conveyed that he was far from amused at what had been uncovered.

"Yes, sir, I'm afraid so," replied Nadinea awkwardly, meeting Darius's angry eyes.

Tayce understood one thing: Nadinea was an innocent pawn in an evil game Dion was playing. She draped an understanding arm around the young Thealysian's shoulders. The way she felt right then made her wish Dion was within shooting distance of their current orbital bearings. If he was, she'd unleash enough firepower on him to finish him off once and for all, for putting Nadinea through the equivalent of a fearful hell.

"Captain, please help me. I don't want to be serving that creep for all the wrong reasons for the rest of my life," said Nadinea, looking up at Tayce in a pleading way.

"Then you won't. Leave this with us. In the meantime, I'll have you shown to quarters where you can rest until we reach Enlopedia," said Tayce, much to Marc's surprise.

Both Darius and Marc wondered if Tayce was playing with fire, getting involved in the situation with Lord Dion concerning Nadinea. Darius realised Enlopedia had had a narrow escape, considering the leader of the Boglayons was in the picture secretly before the treaty had been signed. Next time there would have to be more vetting done when Enlopedia joined with another planet, etc., for a treaty.

A few minons elapsed. Nick Berenger walked through the opening doors of the DC.

"Sorry for interrupting, but I thought you'd like to know the Boglayon vessel is in a stationary orbit nearby and Dion is growing restless, wanting to know when you will be handing over Nadinea, who he claims is rightfully his," explained Nick.

"Ignore him. Have Kelly come in here. Make sure our defence shields are at maximum. If need be, go to Invis Shield—that should provide something to anger him for a while," ordered Tayce. She didn't care what Dion wanted—he could wait. His threat wasn't going to get him anywhere.

"Right!" replied Nick, trying not to smile as he headed back to his duty position.

Darius looked at Marc, who looked back, sharing his look of concern. He wondered how much longer the Boglayons and Dion would remain patient before they began to open fire on Amalthea. Kelly acknowledged Darius as she entered the DC with a nod and smile. Tayce turned, requesting she escort Nadinea to the guest quarters. Kelly nodded, then gestured for Nadinea to follow her. Both were soon walking from the DC. Darius looked over his shoulder to make sure Nadinea was out of earshot.

"Do you think that move was wise, sending Kelly down with Nadinea, considering Kelly was once a victim of Lord Dion? What happens if he arrives on board during their transit to Nadinea's temporary quarters?" put Darius.

"Relax, Father. The way Kelly feels about Lord Dion, he'd be wise not to try such a thing," replied Tayce.

"What do you think about this whole situation?" Darius put to Tayce, confidingly.

"I believe she's an innocent pawn in Dion's evil game. I want to help her," said Tayce.

"But what are you going to do? Surely you're not going to just head back to Enlopedia under Invis Shield and leave Lord Dion sitting out there waiting for you to hand Nadinea over! I can't see it happening. I can see the moment he has the slightest inkling you're manoeuvring off towards headquarters, he'll begin his attack on this cruiser," said Darius, concerned. He thought Tayce was showing tendencies of irresponsibility.

"Don't worry—that's what I'm banking on. And before you say another word, I know how to handle Dion and if he's as clever as he makes out, in his powers of the mind, he'll read my thoughts and think twice."

Darius could see the thoughtful look on his daughter's face as she said what she had, and he realised she was going to make Lord Dion pay, once and for all, when the time came. He said no more. Amalthea was her cruiser and she obviously knew what she was doing. He decided ages ago she was now an independent young woman who was used to making dangerous decisions in the past yearons, during his absence in the Universe. If she made mistakes, she had to live with them. He was not treating her like the privileged daughter any more. What she said went.

Tayce glanced at her father. She could see he was in deep thought.

"Like I said, don't worry. I have no intention of making a decision over Dion that would put this team at risk. Any decision I do make will be one that I think this team and cruiser can handle," promised Tayce.

"I know—it's just me being the old protective father. Lord Dion's not what you call a gentleman, is he?" said Darius, smiling gently.

"No, he's certainly not. I know how to handle him, though," replied Tayce with a smile.

In her estimation, Dion was nothing more than an uncouth powerful Pirate Lord of the worst kind. He thought he could take any female in the known Universe, including her if he could get away with it, for his personal pleasure if he so wished. Using his powerful influence to do it too. Not if she had anything to do with it, she thought. She headed back on out into Organisation. Darius followed her, and as they walked out into the centre of Organisation Nick turned at his communications console, exclaiming that the Boglayon leader, Lord Dion, was still plaguing him for the handover of Nadinea and was getting just a bit more heated with every cencron he was kept waiting. In the last call he had informed Nick that he wanted Nadinea Wiljan and soon. Otherwise he would be taking steps to put his actions into place to get what he wanted.

As Nick finished what he was saying, so the onboard intruder alarm sounded. Craig Bream, who had taken over Kelly's console in her absence, turned.

"Quarters Level—intruder nearing guest quarters," announced Craig urgently.

"He's trying that move, is he? He couldn't wait. Nadineas in danger," said Tayce, knowing Kelly had just taken the young Thealysian to the lower levels to her temporary quarters. Maybe what her father had said about it being unwise to let Kelly take Nadinea to guest quarters was coming true.

"Hold on—you're not going alone. You'll need backup. There's no telling what you'll encounter down there," said Dairan, checking his handheld Pollomoss and hurrying after Tayce as she ran on out in urgency.

"Craig, any chance of finding out who it is?" asked Marc, crossing the room.

Both Craig and Nick worked hard in trying to find out the identity of the intruder, or intruders. He keyed in the code that would show the corridor where the intruder, or intruders, had boarded, and picked up one voice—Lord Dion himself, speaking with curses about wanting to find Nadinea. Craig confirmed Nick's findings. Marc gave an angered look, knowing Lord Dion was on board. Darius saw his expression and shared his thoughts on the idea. He could see Marc was far from amused, realising that Nadinea Wiljan and the attack on Thealysis by this leader and his band had led to a situation that was getting out of hand. His own daughter, namely Tayce, was beginning to put Nadinea's welfare above her own and it concerned him. But there was nothing he could do. Tayce was leader of the team around him and if she decided to take matters into her own hands, then he had to abide by what she decided, even if it went against what he thought. He clapped his hand on Marc's shoulder assuring him everything would be OK—Tayce wouldn't let the likes of Lord Dion beat her or prevent her from saving Nadinea. Marc nodded in understanding of where Darius was coming from, and he realised he was right. All they could do was wait to see what materialised and be ready to act if need be.

* * *

Dairan and Tayce, with their Pollomoss handguns primed, ran down the Level Steps with Twedor, who had activated his Slazer finger to assist if he had to. Without warning, Tayce's Wristlink sounded—much to her annoyance, as she was hoping to surprise Lord Dion. She sighed and pressed the Comceive button, raising her wrist. Marc's voice came through, informing her she needed to hurry. It was Lord Dion and he was on board searching for Nadinea. Tayce acknowledged and signed off, ceasing communications. She went on down the last steps, wanting to deal with the likes of Dion once and for all. Dairan glanced at her as they went. He could see she was not in the mood to stand for any nonsense from Lord Dion. He shared her thoughts on what she was thinking. There was the threat to Kelly as well as Nadinea, considering how Kelly felt about Lord Dion and what he did to the Greymarenians, her people, back on Greymaren during the last voyage. There was no telling what she would try and do to get him back.

On the next level, the Quarters Level, Kelly Travern was in the process of shielding a frightened Nadinea from the vicious threatening likes of Lord Dion, and she was finding for the first time since he'd ambushed her home, Greymaren, that she was no longer afraid of him. In fact she felt nothing but hatred towards him. She stood her ground with a look of pure hatred in her beautiful brown eyes. Dion stood in the middle of the corridor, growing tired of this female refusing to hand over Nadinea. Kelly couldn't believe the feeling of braveness she was feeling, considering Dion's large, muscular, threatening attitude towards Nadinea and herself at that moment. In the past she would have been frightened, but she wasn't. He glared at Kelly, trying to intimidate her. His breathing conveyed he was approaching the end of his patience. He moved towards Kelly—so much so that he seemed to tower over her. Kelly didn't budge. She pushed Nadinea behind her. Dion stared at her with a malicious look in his dark eyes, which conveyed that if she didn't move in the next ten cencrons he would do what he should have done to her all those yearons ago on Greymaren and kill her.

"Move, Travern—otherwise you know what I'm capable of. And the way I'm feeling right now, nothing would give me greater pleasure than to take you out with one blow," he said, looking down at her and speaking in a cold tone.

"If you think I'm scared of you, think again. Those dayons are gone. Nadinea stays with me," replied Kelly, not feeling the least intimidated—and she liked it.

"Please, Kelly, don't risk your life for me. What must be, must be," said Nadinea, almost petrified by Dion's powerfulness.

"No, Nadinea, you have a choice—stay where you are. I'm not giving into this barbaric murderer," said Kelly, refusing to let the young Thealysian go past.

"So be it, woman. You leave me no choice but to take what is mine. Move aside," commanded Lord Dion in the true tone of a pirate leader focused on getting what he wanted.

Dion raised his Slazer weapon and pushed it in Kelly's face. Nadinea fought to slide out from behind Kelly's protective shielding. Kelly, in the tussle with keeping Nadinea in place, moved out of position for being shot in the face by the Boglayon leader's weapon. Instead it went off and she was shot in the left shoulder. She glared at Lord Dion and tried to stifle the pain, but without success. Then she dropped to the Quarters Level floor, out cold. Lord Dion looked down at her unconscious form, sighing impatiently, thinking that if she had complied with what he wanted, she would still be all right. He reached out his black leatherex-clad strong muscular arm and grabbed Nadinea towards him roughly, ignoring her protests not to be hurt.

"You've given me enough trouble, miss—silence!" commanded Dion in a near whisper by her right ear.

With that he stood with a tight grip on Nadinea ready to transpot back to his vessel. Upon giving word to his officer back on board, he vanished just as Dairan, Tayce and Twedor came running down the last steps, seeing him disappear with Nadinea in his grip. Dairan saw the unconscious Kelly lying on the floor.

Tayce quickly contacted Donaldo via Wristlink and ordered him to come to the Quarters Level as Kelly was injured—she'd been shot by Dion. Donaldo confirmed he was on his way. Tayce, as soon as she had ceased communications with Donaldo, contacted Amal, requesting that herself and Dairan be immediately Transpoted to Dion's returning coordinates. Dairan gave a look of surprise. He had no idea they could be sent via Transpot to another destination from where they were. He didn't relish the idea of boarding the Boglayon vessel, but in order to protect Tayce he had to. Amal scanned both Tayce and himself, bathing them in a orange glow, then they vanished in the swirling aura of the Transpot to the Boglayon vessel, leaving Donaldo and Treketa watching on as they came down the corridor towards Twedor, watching over Kelly, left behind. Twedor was far from pleased. First he was going to miss all the fun, and secondly he wasn't doing his job in protecting Tayce again. But a pirate vessel was no place for the likes of a Romid, such as he was. There was no telling what they would do to him.

Donaldo slowly crouched down and turned Kelly over carefully. Taking his medical Examscan from his kit, he began to find out just what had been done to her as Treketa prepared the Hover Trolley to take Kelly back to the MLC Treketa knelt by her wounded friend, concerned she was going to be all right.

"Don't worry—it looks worse than it really is. She's suffered a weapon burn in the muscular tissue region of her shoulder. It's enough to knock someone unconscious, but nothing else, thank God," whispered Donaldo to Treketa, glad it wasn't worse, considering the powerful weapons he'd heard the Boglayons used.

"She's coming round," replied Treketa quietly, looking down at Kelly coming back to consciousness.

"Nadinea—he can't take her. I've got to help her," began Kelly, sitting up determinedly, forgetting the pain that was burning in her shoulder.

"Take it easy. You can't do any more for her, but Tayce is on to it," said Donaldo in the true doctor's tone of reassurance.

"I couldn't stop Lord Dion, though I tried," protested Kelly. She felt she'd failed.

"You did your best, Kelly. Lord Dion is a formidable force," assured Treketa.

"We need to get that shoulder wound sorted. Come on, let's get you to the MLC," ordered Donaldo.

Both Treketa and Donaldo helped Kelly up on to the Hover Trolley. Once she'd lain down, Donaldo took a pain relieving filled Comprai Inject Pen from the Emergency Medical Kit he'd brought with him. He pressed the pen into the side of Kelly's arm. The liquid entered into Kelly's system and she immediately began to feel relaxed, then drifted into a soft sleepiness. Treketa draped a heat-sealant blanket over her, up to her shoulders. Donaldo, when ready, operated the handheld pad and the Hover Trolley began to move off slowly before him, heading towards the MLC on Level 2 with Treketa and Twedor following on behind.

* * *

Over on the Boglayon battle-type vessel Tayce and Dairan materialised in an area that could only be classed as some kind of storage area. It was near-darkness, so it was hard to make out what the containers were that was stored all around them. Dairan took his light pencil torch out of his top left pocket and activated it. He crossed in the light of the beam to one of the large white storage containers, interested to see just what was inside. The light beam hit a label, picking out black letters forming some kind of code. He studied it, trying to make out what it was.

"What are you doing? This is hardly the time to be reading labels. I'm not interested in Dion's cargo—I'm here to rescue Nadinea from that barbaric creep, so let's go," ordered Tayce in an urgent and impatient whisper."

"That's interesting," said Dairan, ignoring her.

"Now, Dairan! I don't want to stick around here any longer than I have to. Let's just find Nadinea and get off this rust bucket and get her back where she truly belongs," said Tayce, getting fed up with his lack of seeing just how dangerous it was to remain in their present surroundings.

"Just a minon—hold on. This supply merchandise doesn't belong here," said Dairan, continuing on.

"I don't care. Now move it! Are you coming or am I going to leave you here for the Boglayon Pirates that have begun on their way here, having detected we're on board," began Tayce angrily.

Tayce, after he still wasn't budging, didn't take any more of his disobeying her orders. She reached out upon coming out from behind the container they had arrived behind, and activating her light pencil torch she pulled Dairan away in a rough manner, pushing him forth, ordering him to get going.

"I'm going. Knock it off," he whisperingly protested, walking on.

"Don't make me pull rank on you, because I will. You're here as a team member to assist, so do it," said Tayce. He was in the process of jeopardising the urgent rescue—they could be caught.

He said no more, checking his Pollomoss handgun, making sure it was still fully charged, and much to his relief it was. He decided to change the setting to 'Disintegrate'. He followed Tayce and they slowly walked out into a dimly lit grey corridor, both checking there weren't any oncoming Boglayon Pirates in sight first. Tayce found the atmosphere was filled with the strong smell of the usual alcohol of the vardox kind, which the Boglayons consumed in large quantities when they were celebrating something pleasing to them—namely the spoils of a raid on some unsuspecting vessel, or the capture of female unwilling victims from that raid for their pleasure. As they progressed along the corridor on full alert, without warning Lord Dion's smiling features entered Tayce's mind. She found him too strong to almost resist, but tried. Dairan broke her thoughts and she was glad of it.

"Where do you think he's holding Nadinea?" asked Dairan quietly.

"Knowing him, as close as he can get. He knows I wouldn't give up that easily in my determination to get her back," replied Tayce, once again seeing Dion's face in her mind, this time with a look that said, "Come on, I'm waiting."

Suddenly, much to the surprise of them both, they were joined by Aldonica. She crept up along the corridor behind them, carrying with her a case containing the latest in weaponry to get rid of the likes of the Boglayons once and for all, called Pollocrai.

"Need some help?" asked Aldonica in a near whisper.

"What are you doing here?" asked Tayce, turning to face her approaching weaponry specialist.

"Marc sent me. I've brought the ideal thing to get rid of Lord Dion—Pollocrai," said Aldonica, holding up the slim silver case containing the Pollocrai—small marble-sized bombs that packed a mighty explosion when set.

"Nice going. He's not going to know what hit him," said Dairan, impressed he'd heard what they could do.

"I want you to set them in sequence to go off every ten to fifteen cencrons, one behind the other. Start when we find we're near to finding Nadinea," ordered Tayce.

"Sure! Where do you think Nadinea is, poor girl?" asked Aldonica, wondering what torture she could be enduring at the hands of Dion's men. It made her cringe just thinking about it.

"Like I said to Dairan, he's probably got her close because he knows I'll be coming after her," replied Tayce.

"Poor Nadinea! Hasn't she suffered enough?" said Aldonica, thinking about what had happened so far for the young Thealysian.

"Oh, I agree, but this is out of her hands. Apparently her father agreed with Dion that she would be his as a pleasure slave for not paying a debt he owed him. Father knew nothing of this when he joined with Thealysis in the treaty," explained Tayce, recalling what Nadinea had told her earlier in the DC.

"Rather her than me! That's awful. I've heard he's quite a powerful being in the ways of intimate mind persuasion and the other, if you know what I mean," replied Aldonica, shivering coldly at the thought.

Dairan interrupted the whispered exchanges of conversation between Tayce and Aldonica by suggesting they start looking for their point of emergency—Nadinea. All three began moving along what must be considered the main corridor of the vessel, listening out for the first signs of oncoming Boglayons. Aldonica looked up across the corridor they were in and caught sight of a maroon and white lettered sign on the grey wall. She drew Tayce's attentions to it. It read 'Operations Central', followed by an arrow heading in the direction they were walking. Tayce thought to herself they seemed to be heading in the right direction.

A sudden scream filled the air and it was female and sounded like she was being tortured in some way on the next level. All three Amaltheans looked at one another with only one concluding thought: it had come from Nadinea.

Aldonica began to set the timing on the Pollocrai marble-sized bombs, then began to place them one at a time in succession as they walked on. She crouched and pushed them out of sight, ready to explode when the timer hit zero. She smiled as she thought about the small size of the bomb to bring down Lord Dion and the Boglayons once and for all. After laying the fourth of the Pollocrai she followed on up the steelex steps.

As they neared the top there came another piercing female scream. This time Tayce knew it was Nadinea for sure. She felt anger rising within her at what Dion could be doing to her. Dairan sighed, displeased. He hated the idea of what Nadinea was going through. Tayce looked ahead, down the long winding corridor to the far end, which was the front of the vessel. She could see in through a large opening, there was something untoward going on. On her word, and with Pollomoss at the ready, they walked on ready to shoot should a pirate emerge from the opening ahead. Dairan glanced around, noticing the interior of the vessel had seen better dayons. Tayce was surprised Dion was travelling the Universe in such a rust bucket, considering the various connections he had in the Universe. She expected something a little more to his taste—at least something that looked like it could hold together to enable him to do the deeds he wanted to do. They all neared the entrance and, within a few cencrons, chaos erupted. Boglayon Pirates were coming from everywhere. Aldonica pulled the last Pollocrai marble-sized bomb from the case and activated it as a smokescreen, dropping it to the ground. A gawky gun-toting pirate looked down at the bomb just as the smoke bellowed up. It started to make him cough and he dropped like a stone. The smoke slowly filled the corridor and entered into the open room before them. Looking into the Pollocrai case, Aldonica found Craig had loaded one more Pollocrai in the reserve compartment, which she was glad of.

"Tayce, I'll set this one for in there," she announced, setting the marble-sized bomb and throwing it into the room ahead of her.

The bomb rolled in and immediately began sending forth further blue smoke, which enabled Tayce, Dairan and herself to gain an advantage over the Boglayons, as they were only slightly affected by the blue smoke.

"Dairan, tell Amal to stand by," ordered Tayce, near to shouting, as she couldn't see him in the smoke and commotion, that was going on around her. She was wondering whether Aldonica's smokescreen was a good idea after all.

"I'm trying to do it now," he replied, lashing, out to take out another of the fifty or so advancing pirates.

Dairan finally brought the pirate to his death that had lunged at him through the smoke. He raised his Wristlink, contacting Amal back on Amalthea, ordering her to stand by. She acknowledged. Dairan quickly ceased communication upon seeing all the pirates were gone and Tayce was heading on into the room ahead in search of Nadinea. Tayce called out to Nadinea in the smoke. Now she too was beginning to find it difficult to breathe in. She noticed Dion was missing—Gone from the scene. But where was he? she wondered. Had he done to Nadinea what he wanted and moved on to the next unwilling victim in another part of the vessel or jumped vessel and escaped again? Nadinea called back, much to Tayce's relief. She and Dairan moved in the direction of Nadina's cry while Aldonica fought on with the odd stray pirate, coming up from other levels, making an unexpected appearance and taking them out one by one until there were no more.

Tayce, upon finding Nadinea after a few minons, found her dressed in a scanty 'glad suit', which revealed every best asset she had to offer. She was bruised and bleeding through her mistreatment at the hands of Dion's men; and if she had been innocent, that was gone. Dion's men had broken her from being the daughter of an Ambassador to being another pleasure slave. It made Tayce mad, seeing what had been done to her, but there was nothing she could do at present. Nadinea's face showed the turmoil she had endured. This young woman had been through the worse torture that could ever be imagined. If only she had listened to Kelly Travern's advice about staying protected back on Amalthea, she wouldn't have endured the torture in the first place. Nadinea began to shake through the shock of what she'd been through. Dairan, being the gentleman he was, took off his uniform jacket and carefully draped it around her bare shoulders. Aldonica walked over and quickly suggested they leave their present surroundings because the first of the set Pollocrai were due to go off in minons. Dairan raised his Wristlink, ordering Amal to commence Transpot. The smoke gave them enough cover to fight the odd straggler of Lord Dion's army, still coming forth. An exchange of gunfire took place. Tayce wondered where Dion was. He was generally at the heart of an attack and liked to rile her, but he was still nowhere to be seen.

As Transpot took on with it's usual swirling motion, and Nadinea was under the comforting arm of Dairan, and Aldonica was poised with her handgun to shoot anything that advanced in their direction, suddenly Tayce heard Dion speaking in her mind.

"We'll see each other again, Fairness, in the future," he announced seductively.

Tayce, upon this, dematerialised off the Boglayon battle-type vessel with the others, just as the Pollocrai began exploding below on the level Aldonica set them on. The vessel shook every time a bomb exploded. Eventually it would be destroyed forever.

* * *

On board Amalthea, Darius and Donaldo stood waiting for the hoped-for safe arrival of Tayce, Dairan, Aldonica and Nadinea. The swirling aura began signifying their safe return. Darius sighed, glad Tayce was safe, as she fully materialised. Donaldo crossed the floor and gently guided Nadinea off to the MLC for treatment. On the way across the floor Nadinea paused. She took off Dairan's jacket and passed it back to him, shaking still from her ordeal, giving him a weak slight smile of thanks. Tayce wristlinked Marc up in Organisation, ordering him to get them out of their current orbit and fast. Marc could be heard agreeing. Tayce ceased communications and turned her attention to her father.

"Are you all right, young lady? That was some daring decision you made, but I'm glad you pulled it off. Well done," praised Darius with a fatherly smile.

"Thanks! Let's put it this way: I went in with one thing in mind and that was to get Nadinea out of the clutches of Dion, and I won, thanks to Aldonica here and her latest invention, the Pollocrai. As for the man himself, he vanished— probably couldn't face me for his actions," confided Tayce, wondering just where the Boglayon leader had vanished off to.

"I have a feeling he's the kind of being that lives to fight another dayon and we'll no doubt see him again sometime. When he does make another appearance, I also have no doubt you'll be ready for him," said Darius.

Just as Darius had said what he did, through the Transpot sight port the Boglayon vessel exploded in the distance, signifying the end of the Boglayon

Pirates once and for all. Amalthea caught the aftershock of the explosion. The cruiser shook for a few cencrons. Darius lightly steadied Tayce until everything became calm again. A smug look crossed Aldonica's features, realising she'd placed the Pollocrai just right after all. Darius caught her look and smiled.

"Tell me, Aldonica; did you do something over on that vessel to make such a spectacular explosion?" asked Darius, giving her a light-hearted look.

"Yes, sir, I laid the Pollocrai and set them in succession, so they would go off one behind the other, and I even used a couple to help create a blue smokescreen to help us get Nadinea to safety," replied Aldonica, pleased.

"Very clever. Well done you," praised Darius in an impressed tone.

"Thank you, sir," said Aldonica, feeling pleased the Admiral was pleased.

As Aldonica headed away, Dairan, having stood listening, suggested he see Tayce later up in Organisation. Tayce agreed. With this, he turned and walked from the Transpot Centre, leaving Tayce and her father to talk. Darius began enquiring what were her plans from that moment on?

"Heading off to my quarters to get cleansed and changed, whilst Marc takes us to Enlopedia. Why?" asked Tayce, curious.

"Do you mind if I come along—I'd like to run something by you?" asked Darius.

"Of course not. Twedor, there you are," said Tayce, glad to see him coming to meet her.

"As always, your obedient servant. I've come to tell you we will be docking at Enlopedia in roughly two hourons, that's all," said Twedor. With that, before Tayce could say another word, he'd turned and walked out on her.

"What have you done to him—he seems to have had his computerised feelings hurt?" asked Darius, somewhat amused at Twedor's behaviour.

"It's probably because I didn't take him over to the Boglayon vessel. I expect he figures he missed out on the action and protecting me again. He seems to think lately he's indestructible, but he'll get over it," replied Tayce, forgetting the incident.

As father and daughter walked on out of the Transpot Centre, both talked about the whole fiasco that was supposed to have been a good treaty with Thealysis. Darius apologised for the fact she'd just been asked to Thealysis to represent Enlopedia and had been drawn into rescuing Nadinea and become caught up with Lord Dion once again. As they briskly headed towards the Level Steps, Tayce shrugged the apology off, informing her father to think nothing of it. What had happened was planned in a roundabout way before they got there; they were just kept in the dark about the whole situation with Dion. She'd thought there was something going on by the way the young students had seem reluctant to be handed back to their superiors over their actions in using Amalthea as target practice at the beginning.

As they began down, Darius brought up the intimate clinch he and Lydia had caught herself and Dairan in the last time they'd all met together. He began to tease her, like any father would. But he found that if there was one thing she hadn't changed in, it was the fact that she never liked being teased. She still didn't, as old as she was. He could see this in the way she behaved. She truly thought something of Dairan—more than just as a teammate—and in the yearons that would follow he could see them growing a lot closer than the clinch he and Lydia had caught them in. He was pleased for her. He'd heard how hard she'd taken Tom Stavard's death and he figured she deserved to be happy once more. He draped a fatherly arm around her slim shoulders and hugged her to him as they walked down the last steps on to Level 3. But there was one thing Darius couldn't tell his daughter, which was that there were to be cutbacks on spending on voyages like the one Tayce was currently on. He had decided he was going to fight the axe falling on the Amalthean Quests if he could, no matter what. But in the meantime he would keep it under wraps.

* * *

Marc Dayatso, up in Organisation, watched the view through the main sight port, glad the Boglayon vessel was gone from their immediate orbit. He was glad they were leaving behind what could only be described as one hell of a messy Quest, figuring the Quest report was going to take some filling in. They'd arrived at Thealysis to peacefully represent Enlopedia and ended up embroiled in rescuing a young woman from the clutches of Lord Dion. There would be questions asked over the whole treaty, that was for sure, at the next council meeting, he thought. He, however, was finding it hard to believe what Dairan had just told him upon returning to duty—that Lord Dion had just vanished from his vessel during the rescue of Nadinea. He figured the pirate leader was out in the Universe somewhere, escaped in a 'life craft' or even another battlecruiser that had been undetected by the scanning process. Kelly looked up at him, then back at her console, working even though she felt sore. She informed him that their orbital sector had been changed; they were now en route to Enlopedia. Marc nodded, but his thoughts were still on where Lord Dion—or Dion, as some people addressed him—had gone. Would he surface in the future and in what way?

Nick Berenger tore off a suddenly arriving printout from Enlopedia. He turned, handing it to Marc, exclaiming that it had just come in from Chief Lydia Traun. Marc reached out, accepting it, and began to read it. It concerned Chief Jan Barnford. Marc suggested Nick leave it with him—he'd make sure Tayce received it. Nick nodded, then went back to his duty.

* * *

Lord Dion had in fact escaped, unbeknown to the Amaltheans, in a battlecruiser and was well away into the next Universe to live another dayon. But as he left the current Universe, he sent a message back to Tayce, and it was one that sent a shiver through her suddenly, in the company of her father.

"Until the future, Fairness, I'll be waiting." Then he broke into a callous laugh.

20. Last Duties

A couple of dayons later, when everything had settled down on board the cruiser, a private Transpo Launch rendezvoused with Amalthea. Darius Traun had arranged for a high-ranked launch to come and collect him, as Tayce had been asked to assist Chief Jan Barnford, who had found himself stranded on Pellasun 1. Darius fully understood she had to head off to Pellasun, to rendezvous with the Chief, so went about arranging his transport home with Nadinea Wiljan and a little help from Nick Berenger. The destined port of urgency for Tayce and the cruiser was Pellasun 1. It was a planet with a dayon/night rota. A paradise environment with a perfect weather pattern and breathable atmosphere for a possible living and working base. It had been found during a planetary search for a second base to replace Questa and was found to be ideal for the construction of a new headquarters base. The reason for Chief Barnford's visit was to assess security whilst the new headquarters base was under construction, in case any law-breaking passers-by fancied helping themselves to materials during construction. He had to compile a report of how many security men were needed in order to protect the workers during construction, staying over until completion.

* * *

The high-ranked Transpo Launch couriers that had come from the Eternity Life Complex on Enlopedia boarded Amalthea quickly and smoothly, taking Ambassador Wiljan's body, with the dignity it deserved, from Donaldo's Hover Trolley and placing it into a special container for taking it back on the Transpo Launch under the respectful watch of Marc and Tayce. Nadinea watched sadly, fighting back the tears at seeing her father leave. Tayce felt the young woman's sorrow. It took her back to the night she thought she would never see her parents again. She'd been lucky—not like Nadinea. Eventually both Marc and Tayce wished her luck with her new life on Enlopedia, suggesting she stay in touch. Nadinea agreed, thanking Tayce for her understanding and help. She felt she'd caused a lot of unnecessary trouble all round. Marc took hold of Nadinea's hand and assured her that what the team and Tayce did was all in a dayon's duty—everyone just wanted her to be safe. Nadinea walked away in the company of a new life male counsellor, pausing in the doorway of the Transpo Launch to turn and lightly wave to Tayce and Marc, who were still watching. Darius hugged Tayce in a fatherly goodbye way, then suggested he'd better get going—they had a new life to sort out and a decent burial to undertake. Tayce nodded. Darius walked on aboard the Transpo Launch, the doors closing behind him, sealing off the Transpo Launch from Amalthea. Marc and Tayce watched it depart and head for Enlopedia, through the sight port. Marc put his right arm around Tayce's shoulders and suggested, as course to rescue Jan Barnford was already under way, it might be wise to take a refreshment break before they arrived at Pellasun. Tayce agreed. She'd missed her Coffeen break that dayon. Both turned and began on up the corridor towards the Refreshment Centre, in discussion about Pellasun and its similarities with Traun, their old home world.

* * *

They were an houron into the locked course to Pellasun 1, a planet that was to be placed under the Enlopedian colonisation programme in a joint venture with Canardan 5 as a recruitment-exchange world. Bringing together people from all walks of life, from the two joint worlds: Enlopedia and Canardan 5. It would be a planet upgraded in status to colonisation—a habitable world and the first one in centuries since Traun. It would also be the first dayon/night world that had been in normal occupancy for families, couples and single people for centuries—since the demise of Traun, which was not an artificial world, but a real, fresh, breathing, living one. Being the second headquarters base, it would uphold the priorities Questa and the late Jonathan Largon upheld: peace and justice. Enlopedia and Canardan 5 would work closely together to expand in its future to make it a first-class planetary inhabitable world. Dairan entered the Refreshment Centre to find Tayce and Marc. He crossed to retrieve a much needed fresh cup of Coffeen from the drinks selector in the far alcove.

"Who's watching our journey?" asked Marc, curious, seeing Dairan.

"Lance. He'll contact me on Wristlink if something comes up. Nick told me Jan let the team of scientists take his cruiser to return to Enlopedia, not realising, with all that was going on in the first steps towards planning for construction, that he didn't have a lift back himself. Hence he called us," explained Dairan, sipping his Coffeen, amused.

"What on earth is that?" said Tayce, looking out of the sight port at an illuminated blue cloud pulsating out in the near vicinity of Amalthea's flight path.

"It wasn't there a minon ago," replied Dairan, looking at the same sight through the wide sight port.

Marc immediately raised his Wristlink, contacting Amal, ordering her to raise shields to the highest level. Amal could be heard acknowledging. All three studied the strange phenomenon, wondering what it could be. It was as if it was just stationary, in orbit, in its pulsating state, watching the cruiser. Was it studying them? wondered Tayce, or was it scanning silently, waiting for them to unleash their firepower? She finished the Coffeen she'd been drinking and rose to her feet, watching the sight, trying to get some idea of what it was. Moving out from behind the table they'd been sitting at, apart from Dairan, she crossed to the waste incinerator recycler, pausing to deposit the empty beaker. Then she headed on out through the entrance, exclaiming that she'd head back to Organisation to see if she could shed some light on their mysterious visitor. With that, she left Marc and Dairan behind, elegantly walking on her way back to duty, pausing for a brief cencron to take a look back at the pulsating visitor through the nearest sight port en route to Organisation.

* * *

A while later Twedor came down the Level Steps that Tayce was walking up. He'd gone to find her, figuring she'd probably caught sight of the strange cloud that had suddenly appeared off Amalthea's starboard side in their current travelling orbit. He felt he had to be with her to protect her as her escort this time, considering he'd been left out when she'd gone aboard Lord Dion's vessel.

"Twedor, have there been any further calls from Chief Barnford?" asked Tayce, meeting him halfway up the steps.

"No, only to say that he's awaiting our arrival. The only thing that's occurred recently is that blue pulsating cloud. Have you seen it? It bothers me. It just appeared on Lance's research screen," announced Twedor.

"Oh, why? It could be harmless—not everything out here in the Universe, Twedor, is hostile. You should know that by now," replied Tayce.

"When I said there were no calls from Chief Barnford, it's because, whatever that thing is out there, it's blocking all communications—so much so that Nick had to remove his Microceive as it sent a piercing whistle down the earpiece, making him pull the Microceive from his ears and yell," continued Twedor.

"Is he all right?" asked Tayce, concerned.

"He's fine. It just left him deaf for a few minons. I scanned him," assured Twedor.

"So our last contact from Jan was before this strange pulsating phenomenon showed up?" asked Tayce, curious to know why, whatever the visitor out in space was, it should stop all communications getting through.

"Yes!" replied Twedor as they went up the steps to Level 1 together.

Just as Twedor and Tayce were about to step on to Level 1, a strange bright-blue 'lightning' entered the cruiser from the ceiling and began to strike out, here and there, moving slowly along the corridor towards them. Tayce quickly grabbed Twedor back down on to the Level Steps, out of harm's way. After a few minons, as they took a look around the steps' corner on to Level 1, the lightning passed their area, but nothing happened. It was as if the lightning was just scanning and wasn't interested in causing damage. Tayce and Twedor watched as it continued on up the corridor, on through the cruiser without damaging anything, just sending out the lightning flashes here and there. Tayce began to wonder if this was a way to scan Amals' many functions for some reason. She suggested to Twedor that they take it carefully and head on.

No sooner were they about to head on than Marc and Dairan came running up the Level Steps behind her. Marc reached out and grabbed Twedor, lifting him up the last step, setting him down on Level 1. All three ran with Twedor on into Organisation. Upon entering, Lance turned at his research console.

"Before you say anything, I've got everything you need to know about that thing out there," said Lance, pointing to the blue pulsating phenomenon through the sight port.

"We had a visit from it less than ten minons ago?" said Tayce.

"Right—the phenomenon is a defence shield. It came into operation in 2203 and was in operation from then up until 2267. It's used to protect weaponry stored aboard vessels behind the shield. There's obviously something behind it still that needs protecting, or for some strange reason it's activated itself. At this moment, I can't tell which—sorry," said Lance.

"It seems to me, whatever or whoever turned the shield off, that somehow, like you've said, it's managed to activate itself. 2267 is a long time ago. Why whoever owns what's behind it doesn't fly out and check it from time to time is beyond me," cut in Marc, glancing out through the main sight port.

"Is there any way we can find out what's hiding behind that shield in case there's anything we should be made aware of?" asked Tayce, curiously.

"Amal is in the process of doing a deep probe scan on high frequency. It shouldn't be long before we find out just what's behind it," confirmed Lance.

"While we're waiting, find out who owns whatever is behind our spectacular sight. Check the research on the shield—there may be a port or whatever to contact. Tell Nick when you find out," ordered Tayce.

"Right, I'll get on to it," said Lance, beginning to key away.

"Nick, I want you to tell the people responsible for the shield that it's activated itself. As we are in the vicinity on the way to the planet Pellasun, would they like us to find a way to deactivate it for them?" said Tayce as Nick listened.

"What if they refuse to acknowledge who we are and who we represent?" asked Nick, turning at his console.

"Then point out to them that under the Enlopedian headquarters ruling regarding galactic dangers to space travellers, if the shield is not shut down, either by us or by the owners, it falls into the category of breaking the law of hostile phenomena and will be treated as a danger, reported to Enlopedia and the owners made accountable for letting the shield activate itself without regular checks," explained Tayce, pacing in thought.

"Don't worry—I'll make sure they see it's in their best interest to deactivate it again permanently," assured Nick.

"Amal's findings are coming in. The defence shield is protecting a space station that was shut down back in 2214 because of lack of funds to keep it operational," explained Lance, reading from the screen before him.

"Well, at least we know what we're up against. Nick, let me know what happens—I'll be in the DC if you get a result," said Tayce, walking across the centre and up into the DC.

Upon entering the DC, Tayce crossed to her desk in thought, followed by Twedor. He asked Tayce why she hadn't said anything about the strange lightning that engulfed the whole of the Level 1 corridor earlier. Marc walked into the DC, hearing Twedor's question, and looked at Tayce, also wondering why she hadn't mentioned the lightning. Lance and Dairan entered, hearing the discussion going on.

"It didn't harm us or Amalthea, so I didn't think it was worth mentioning," announced Tayce, shrugging it off.

"You might not see it that way, but it certainly made my circuits act up," said Twedor.

"Maybe that would explain the sudden power surge we picked up earlier aboard," said Dairan.

"Yeah, my research console had it happen too, a while ago. Anyway, I and Nick have been working together, and in just a short time we've managed to come up with who owns the station behind the shield. It's owned by the Deltan Lorentz Corp, which is an earth-type planet roughly five sectors beyond this. They say they had completely forgotten all about the station way out here. Nick asked if they wanted us to shut it down, and they agreed—especially when he told them that if they didn't, they would be breaching Enlopedia's law of hostile phenomena. They then announced they were putting into operation the sending-out of a salvage team to tractor-beam the station back to their home world. They asked us if we could gain entry to the Scanner Centre on the station and shut down the activated shield, enabling them to take care of what they had to come out and do," explained Lance.

"Tell Nick to return the call to Deltan Lorentz and confirm that we'll take care of the shield for them. Tell Craig to get his tech kit together. Marc, you're in charge., Dairan, you're coming with me—you too, Twedor," said Tayce, rising to her feet and walking from behind her desk.

"Do you want me along?" asked Lance casually.

"No, not this time, but I want Nick, Craig, Deluca, Treketa and Aldonica along," replied Tayce.

"I'll tell them for you," replied Lance, heading on out.

Marc followed on, pausing in the doorway. He turned, suggesting it might be wise to take Pollomoss handguns. There was no telling what they'd find waiting for them on boarding the station, considering the fact the station had been vacant for 153 yearons. Tayce nodded in total agreement. She remembered there had been some really horrific stories of empty stations, etc., in the past, being left for many yearons, and what was in waiting when people went to investigate. Some people never came back to tell what was on the deserted stations. Strange and horrific space creatures had taken up occupancy and done untold things to explorers boarding such places. Marc then added that she surely remembered what Greymaren was like. Tayce laughed, recalling the fact of the Securidroids that patrolled there at the time of the Quest and how it was near impossible to outsmart them. Marc nodded, continuing on out back, into Organisation, to make sure the Quest emergency team knew they were going over to the station. Considering what Marc had said about taking a Pollomoss handgun, Tayce checked hers was fully charged in case she should need to use it. Dairan did the same, then slipped it back into his side holster.

"Ready, Twedor? Let's go," suggested Tayce, heading across the DC behind Dairan.

Twedor didn't need telling twice. He was right up beside Tayce. He had no intention of being left behind this time. Tayce headed on out of the DC and across to the Organisation entrance, quickly being joined by Craig with his tech kit to shut down the defence shield. Nick and Deluca followed on together. They all briskly headed on out and down to Level 2, to the Transpot Centre. But just as the team set foot on Level 2, the blue lightning returned, just like it had the first time. Tayce pushed Twedor behind her and everyone in the team stopped in their tracks for a minon, curious. Craig announced it was harmless, using his handheld scanner. He informed them it was merely scanning Amalthea like a routine scan. After everyone was bathed in the blue lightning and it had passed, Tayce checked Twedor was all right and they continued on towards the Transpot Centre. Tayce, upon walking into the centre, handed around portable breathing containers she'd retrieved from the corridor store on the way down for the Quest in hand. She wristlinked Marc, back in Organisation, to order him to activate Transpot in five minons. Aldonica ran into the Transpot Centre, apologising for being late and holding everyone up. Tayce assured her it was OK. She noticed Aldonica had her Quest bag draped over her slim shoulder and wondered what she was taking on the Quest to use this time, in the form of a creation to amaze them all. Finally, when everyone was ready, they took up their positions on the marked floor area of the Transpot, including Twedor, ready to dematerialise from the cruiser. Within a few minons the Transpot began and sent the small Quest team down to the Deltan Lorentz Space Station.

The Deltan Lorentz Space Station was dark, but the life support was still in recycling mode. As the team began to arrive and activated their portable breathing containers, holding the masks over their faces, they found the station in total abandonment. Everyone activated their torches to make out their surroundings. As illumination filled the immediate area, a dusty and dirty old-fashioned environment became visible in the beams of their torches. Signs of habitation long gone. Tayce considered the idea that where they had arrived had to be used for main operations and must have been considered as Operation Central. Instrumental panels that were old-fashioned qwerty keypads and dials seemed strange to see. Most of the instruments had frozen in time, stopping at the last houron they were finally operational in 2267. Silence filled the air with an eerie stillness, mixed with an icy feeling. Dairan felt that if something was dropped on to the concretex floor, it would probably be heard at the end of the station, in vibration. For a few cencrons, the team looked about in the glare of their torches. Craig announced that life support was on and working as well as the dayon it had been put into operation in the first place, which everyone found strange considering how long the station had lain dormant. Dairan had skipped lunch back on Amalthea and his stomach started to confirm as much. Tayce glanced at him, amused.

"Can I help it if I missed lunch?" he said, meeting her amused look.

Tayce tried to take her mind elsewhere, but everyone started to laugh, hearing the sound and finding the moment quite amusing. Craig assumed the life support must have been operational in case someone did board from the Deltan Lorentz Corp at any time during the 153 yearons. He suggested he try and look for the controls, to check it was set to be in constant operational power, whilst they were aboard. Tayce agreed, letting him head over to the long computerised consoles ahead of them. Twedor crossed also, ready to assist Craig in any way he could. Craig soon found what he wanted, and with Twedor's assistance activated the life support to maximum power, as it had been discovered that it was in fact on 'average' setting, as no one was on board prior to their arrival—or it was presumed so. As the readings before him began to rise on the old display, he checked to see how long they would be able to remain on board the station before the system became strained under the extra power. It had been running at minimum capacity. He linked the Porto Compute through a frequency link-up, waiting for a reading. After a few minons, he turned, informing Tayce they had five hourons at a maximum before the old system began to strain. Tayce nodded, deactivating her portable breathing container as Craig glanced at the system reading, declaring all was safe—they could breath normally. Five hourons was long enough for what they had to do unless unexpected complications arose. They had no idea what would happen.

"You two head off and find the Scanner Control Centre. The sooner we do what we came here to do, the sooner we can safely get out of here," suggested Tayce to Craig and Nick.

"Come on, Twedor, you may be needed," said Craig, heading off with his tech kit and activated light pencil torch with Nick following on.

"Where are you three going?" asked Tayce, looking in the direction of Aldonica, Treketa and Deluca, who were walking away.

"We'd like to check out this place. We'll be fine and won't be long," assured Treketa.

"In that case, stick together and look after Deluca. I don't want anything happening unnecessarily," warned Tayce.

"We will," promised Aldonica.

"Just be careful, all three of you. We don't know what secrets this station holds," replied Dairan, watching the three female members of the team walk on through a wide open archway and turn down a corridor out of sight.

Dairan realised he and Tayce were the only ones left behind. Tayce crossed to the computer console Craig had been working on, to see if she could gain entry into the station's frozen logs and find out anything about the station's past and the reason, other than financial cutbacks, for the crew up and leaving. Without warning—she hadn't realised it—Dairan had sauntered up behind her.

"Don't you think it would be wise to leave tampering with gaining entry? I don't know exactly what you're trying, but there's no telling what punishment you might receive for prying where you shouldn't," he said softly over her shoulder.

"Yes, you could be right. There's no good warning the others to take care, if I get injured through not being careful," she replied, feeling the warmth of his closeness.

"This could be a station worth salvaging—making good—don't you think?" he whisperingly asked, slipping his hands around her waist—pulling her back against him.

She fought the soft feelings of sensuousness he was trying to make her feel.

"Yes, I agree, but it would have to be a thorough overhaul. I don't fancy life on a space station. You'd be living in a stationary orbit all the time—I like to travel. I suppose the Deltan Lorentz team will tow this place back to some spare allocated port and leave it there until someone thinks of a new use for it and brings it back into service," replied Tayce, enjoying his warmth and closeness as she felt a little cold.

"Yes, I agree. I can't understand why they left this station vacant all these yearons. Surely they could have found a good use for it?" he replied, beginning to kiss her neck slowly, tentatively, whilst keeping an eye out for any of the team suddenly returning.

"The team could come back at any cencron. This isn't the time or place, Dairan, to fool around. Later," said Tayce in soft response, fighting the immense pleasurable feelings that were slowly overwhelming her.

She broke slightly away from him, turning to face him. She looked up into his warm, mysterious eyes. He looked back at her. God, she thought, why did she always feel like she could drown in those eyes? For a minon they just looked into each other's eyes, losing themselves in each other. Dairan glanced back over his shoulder to see if anyone was coming, then looked back at Tayce, pulling her into a warm full-on kissing embrace.

"Dairan, this isn't a good idea—we're on duty," said Tayce, protesting softly in between kisses.

"Relax! It's just the two of us—I've checked," he replied in a near whisper, lowering his head and bringing his lips back to hers in a full-on warm, meaningful kiss, ignoring what she'd said.

He kissed her gently at first, then slowly more meaningfully. Tayce couldn't fight the feelings he was making her feel. She succumbed to his persuasiveness, draping her arms around his slightly tanned neck, and became lost in the full-on moment, hoping the others didn't walk back in and catch them lost in each other.

Without warning, Tayce's Wristlink sounded on her wrist, making her come back to reality with a jolt. She and Dairan drew apart. He winked at her affectionately. She gathered her thoughts together—they were on their current surroundings—then answered the call. She walked away, leaving Dairan to cool down after their untimely interlude. The call was from Craig. He and Nick had found the Scanner Centre with the field unit to the blue pulsating phenomenon inside. He was just calling to inform her they were about to terminate the defence shield and would be returning in roughly one houron.

"Be careful, Craig. See you later?" said Tayce, sighing off.

Aldonica walked back into Operation Central without Treketa and Deluca. Tayce turned, giving a questioning concerned look, wondering what had happened.

"What's happened? Where's Deluca and Treketa? I strictly advised all three of you to stay together," said Tayce, sounding somewhat cross.

"It's all right. Treketa wanted to look at the hospital section here, and Deluca stayed with her. They are quite safe and won't be long," assured Aldonica, seeing Tayce was far from pleased.

Upon this, Tayce calmed down somewhat, but she didn't like the idea that the three team members she'd asked to stay together had disobeyed her orders. Dairan could see she was doing a good job in hiding her displeasure at the fact. He crossed to one of the round sight ports and looked out.

* * *

On board Amalthea Marc was glad to hear from Kelly that the space station's scanning defence shield had been deactivated. As soon as it ceased and dispersed, a call came through from Chief Barnford on Pellasun 1, demanding to know where his ride was back to headquarters. Marc crossed to Nick's console, taking the Microceive and slipping it on to communicate with Jan.

"Jan, this is Marc. We've run into some problems. As soon as were through, we'll be there, I assure you," said Marc in a sincere tone.

"Make it soon, please," replied Jan, signing off.

Lance and Kelly laughed over Marc's shoulder. They had a feeling Jan sounded somewhat desperate to get back to base and get out of his current surroundings. Marc glanced at them both in a reprimanding way, but he could also see the funny side of Jan's impatience at being kept waiting. Jan wasn't the kind of man to be kept waiting. But he wished the both of them had waited until communications had ceased between Amalthea and Pellasun 1 before laughing. He turned back to Amal, asking for a Quest update. There were a few minons of silence, then she came back and explained in her crisp, clear feminine educated tone of voice that Craig Bream, at the current moment, had shut down the scanner defence shield and the team were returning back to the cruiser.

"Has our course been readied to head off and pick up Jan?" Marc asked Kelly.

"Yes, I'm just waiting for the others to return safely, then I'll activate the course to Pellasun," confirmed Kelly at her position.

"Good. The sooner they're back, the sooner we can get under way," replied Marc.

He stood watching as Kelly keyed in the activation sequence to transpot the team back to the cruiser. He was glad the scanning defence shield was now permanently deactivated. Perhaps things could get back to normal on board. No more sudden power surges, no more strange scanning lightning aboard. He crossed back to Nick Berenger's vacant duty position, slipping the Microceive back on. He depressed the previously stored code for the Deltan Lorentz Rescue and Salvage Complex. The moment communications were linked up, he began explaining that the scanning defence shield had been successfully deactivated. The space station was safe and all theirs to do with as they saw fit. The Deltan Lorentz command thanked Marc for the assistance. He signed off and ceased communications. Marc placed the Microceive back on the console top and glanced out at the sight through the main sight port of the space station with its deactivated shield. He noticed the journey had cut in for Pellasun 1, they were under way and everyone was back on board. In the distance he could also see the tow vessels on their way to take the station back to Deltan Lorentz.

* * *

Down in the Transpot Centre, Tayce, Twedor and the other members of the Quest team had materialised back on board. Nick, Craig, Deluca and Dairan hurried on out back to Organisation to continue their duties, whilst Treketa, who had gathered some notes on her Quest Porto Compute about the Deltan Lorentz medical facility, walked on back to show Donaldo in the MLC what she'd found. Aldonica meanwhile, after having a few casual words with Tayce about the station in general, followed Treketa. Dairan noticed Tayce wasn't following on and paused in the doorway, turning. He waited for her and Twedor, noticing she looked like she had something on her mind, judging by the thoughtful look on her face.

"What's wrong?" he asked softly.

"Nothing! I'm OK," said Tayce, but she had the feeling something was about to happen, involving her and the team, and it wasn't good.

Dairan didn't pry any further. He figured she'd tell him when she was ready. They both walked from the Transpot with Twedor following on casually. As Tayce walked up the corridor, she couldn't help but return to the nagging feeling that something was about to happen that could possibly change all their lives forever. But she couldn't think what it could be. Dairan glanced at her. He could see something was occupying her mind, but again didn't like to ask her in case she didn't feel like sharing it. They walked along in silence.

* * *

Outside in orbit the Deltan Lorentz Space Station, which was oval in shape and in total darkness, was now heading further and further away as Amalthea Two headed in the opposite direction, off towards Pellasun 1. Tow vessels could be seen arriving at the space station to take it in tow back to the Deltan Lorentz colony—a journey that would take the best part of a weekon to undertake at slow speed, considering the age and wear and tear of the station.

* * *

Tayce soon entered Organisation followed by Dairan and Twedor. Marc turned, giving her a welcome-back smile, crossing to meet her mid floor. He also noticed she looked thoughtful about something, but, like Dairan, said nothing—she'd tell him when she was ready.

"The Quest was a success, then?" he asked lightly, bringing her back to the present.

"Sorry? What did you say? I was thinking," she said, not catching what he'd just said.

"I said the Quest to shut down the scanning defence shield was a success, then?" he asked again, wondering if she was all right. He could see something was strongly bothering her.

"Yes, Craig did a great job," praised Tayce, looking in Craig's direction.

"Thanks, but you know I love a challenge and enjoyed that one," replied Craig casually.

"How long until we arrive at Pellasun 1, Kelly?" asked Tayce, interested.

"Roughly one to two hourons and seventy-six minons," replied Kelly, turning at her keypad.

"Lance, research on Pellasun 1—let's hear it. You can bring it into the DC," said Tayce, turning and walking briskly on across Organisation, going on into the DC.

Lance without a further word, gathered the information printouts and rose to his feet, hurrying on across the centre to join Tayce in the DC. Dairan informed Marc that as he wasn't presently wanted he'd head on down to the Astrono Centre. With this, he walked on out, leaving Marc in command, watching the horizon through the main sight port. The Organisation team returned to normal duty in preparation for reaching Pellasun 1. Marc glanced around at all the team, busy, noticing they were discussing the Deltan Lorentz Space Station and how they wouldn't fancy working on something in a constant stationary orbit. He smiled to himself at the many comments that were surfacing, thinking they would have hated life on Traun. It had been a planetary world. But he noticed that Deluca wasn't saying anything. He guessed they all liked the lifestyle of travelling the stars, as they were, from one Quest to another.

* * *

On Pellasun 1 dawn had surfaced and the planetary sun was beginning to become a dominant object in the sky to form another beautiful paradise-like dayon. A light breeze blew, rustling the leaves and plants that were growing here and there. In one of the modern module units that were temporary quarters the flimsy netlon drapes blew out in a billowing fashion through the open sight pane into the room. Jan Barnford, fully dressed and ready to leave just as soon as the Amalthean team arrived in orbit, walked out through the open sliding doors on to a woodex balcony, drinking a fresh cup of Coffeen—the first of many in the dayon ahead. He paused, looking around at the vast and beautiful countryside and panoramic views as far as the eye could see, in thought. He wondered if the breathtaking scenery would be kept when the new headquarters base was constructed. He for one certainly hoped it would. He looked skywards. He could see the dayon's conditions weather-wise looked good. He hoped it stayed that way, considering how the weather so far had proven unpredictable— thunderstorms with lightning that filled the sky spectacularly, heavy rain that had caused flooding and winds that had done damage. It had been good weather for research in what could be expected when the new headquarters base was built for the science and design teams. He himself had been caught in no end of sudden heavy showers. They had come on without warning and stopped just as quick as they'd started, but they'd soaked him through a couple of times in the dayons he'd been there.

After finishing his Coffeen, he stretched and walked back inside the temporary residence. It was a one-storey unit with one part living area and one part for cleansing and sleeping. Big enough for two people. He crossed to his half-packed rusty-coloured holdall and carried on packing. His thoughts were on his Officette back at Enlopedia and how much work had piled up in his absence. How much paperwork he'd have to authorise regarding situations that had arisen in his time away. It was hard to imagine that in the age of computers he still had a certain amount of paperwork. It made him laugh at the fact. He remembered something the late Jonathan Largon said once, when they were talking casually: no matter what technology came into being, in handling every-dayon work there was nothing as solid and reliable as putting something down on paper, the old-fashioned way. It was never deleted, rubbed out or degraded by time. Upon packing the final items he'd take back as part of his security research, he remembered how right Jonathan had been. He did up his holdall, then checked his Wristlink time display. The call he'd received from Marc Dayatso yesteron, informing him he'd be picked up in Pellasun daylight hourons, was suddenly on his mind. He pulled on his off-duty brown leatherex flight jacket and fastened the Velcro clasp together, studying his smart appearance in the full-length imager on the wall before him. Glancing at his Wristlink again, he found there was a message from Amalthea, stating that the cruiser would be arriving in orbit shortly. Jan deleted the message, realising it was just a matter of killing time until arrival was accomplished. He wandered back out on to the balcony, wondering why the Enlopedian Council's new member and temporary deputy, Cartarn, had wanted him to be picked up by Tayce and the Amalthean Quests team. All he had been told, twenty-five hourons previously, was to wait for further instructions when he'd successfully arrived aboard Amalthea. He had found it strange that when he wanted to ask the reason why, he had been refused permission to ask any questions about the whole affair. He leant on the balcony once more in thought over the fact, looking at the panoramic views of green trees and grasses in different shades of colour and the many bushes and other plants in bloom. He changed his thoughts back to the fact it would be a shame if the views couldn't be preserved during construction.

In the unit behind him Transpot began and Tayce materialised from Amalthea. She was dressed in duty attire, as she'd resume duty just as soon as she returned to the cruiser. She glanced around for Jan, then looked out on to the balcony. As the netlon drapes blew out, she saw him standing looking out across the panoramic view. She sauntered on out through. As she did so, suddenly the feeling that had been bugging her since they had come back from the Deltan Lorentz Space Station, that something unexpected was going to happen to change the lives of herself and the team, hit her again. But why now? she wondered. Was Jan something to do with what she was feeling? As she approached him, so she tried to push what she was feeling to the back of her mind once again.

"Beautiful, isn't it?" she said, breaking the silence, stepping out to join him.

"Tayce! Yes, let's hope they keep it this way," he agreed.

"Are you ready to leave? Amalthea is waiting," she said, coming to a pause.

"You got here, then! I was beginning to wonder if I should take out a permanent residency on one of these units," he said jokingly, with a teasing look in his eye.

"I can't believe this view—it's like my old home world before it was destroyed by the likes of Vargon," said Tayce, turning to look out at the panoramic view with interest, thinking back for a moment.

"Take a good look. In about a monthon's time, they'll be building a new headquarters base and more than 150 new habitable dwellings. It's to be the new sister base to Enlopedia. It will be a shame if they destroy the views, but they'll probably call it progress," said Jan, leaning back on the rail beside her.

"So when did I turn out to be your taxi service, Jan? Why didn't you head back with the other teams?" asked Tayce, curious.

"Their research was done before mine," he replied without thought. He wanted to tell her about the council and how they had requested he have her pick him up, but he figured he couldn't—he'd probably lose his job. Despite the fact that she was a friend, he said nothing. He had been given his orders.

"I see. You bring me halfway around the Universe to pick you up and that's all the explanation I'm going to get. Why didn't you request one of your Patrol Cruisers patrolling—you've done it before?" asked Tayce. She was beginning to think there was more to her picking him up than she was hearing.

"You were nearest," he said, turning away, picking up on the fact she was becoming suspicious, and he wished she would stop it.

"Is there something wrong? You seem like something is bothering you. As friends, you generally hug me in greeting when we meet alone," she said, giving him a questioning look.

"Of course not—come here," he said, turning her around and pulling her into a friendly hug.

But as Jan broke away, she could see something was on his mind. Why couldn't he share it with her? she wondered. They'd never had secrets between them before, so why now? He noticed she was looking at him questioningly and looked away again, trying hard not to respond to the fact she was suspicious of the way he was behaving. She could see he wasn't going to share what he was hiding, so she headed back to the unit doorway, disappointed. He reached out and grabbed her, bringing her back before him.

"Is there a problem? Tell me, Jan. You and I have never had any secrets—why now?" ordered Tayce softly. She didn't like what she was feeling—like he was hiding something and had been told not to say anything. For the first time she found he was acting awkwardly towards her and it wasn't like him.

"I probably shouldn't be telling you this, and you haven't heard it from me, but the council at Enlopedia gave me orders I had to request you pick me up. That's all I know—they wouldn't tell me any more and when I tried asking questions I was told to do as requested and they wouldn't tell me any more," he said, far from pleased at being kept in the dark and keeping Tayce in the dark.

Tayce was now even more worried. Why should the council give the orders they had? She continued on into the residence-type unit, worried about what might unfold. Jan paused, glancing back at the panoramic view for the last time for a while. Then he followed on behind. Once inside he closed the doors and prepared the residence-type unit for shutdown after he had left. He then crossed the room and picked up his holdall and silver attaché case, which contained his Porto Compute and findings report. Tayce raised her Wristlink when he was ready and ordered immediate Transpot. A few cencrons later Transpot engulfed the both of them, removing them from Pellasun 1 for the time being, back to Amalthea.

* * *

On Amalthea Marc stood waiting in the Transpot for Tayce's arrival. The moment Tayce and Jan arrived, Marc welcomed Jan aboard, unaware of what was going to unfold in the next hourons, whilst he was with them. He glanced at Tayce, seeing she still had her worrying look. How he wished she'd just share her problem with him, as it was really bugging him wondering what was making her worried.

"Lydia just called. She says it's urgent. She needs to talk to you the moment you return. She was calling from her chambers on Enlopedia," announced Marc, unsure of what it was about.

"I'll take it in my quarters, where we can talk privately. I'll head back to duty just as soon as I've found out what it is," promised Tayce, heading away, leaving Jan in the company of Marc.

"Take your time. I can handle the command until you return," called Marc in reply.

Tayce continued on out through the opening doors, leaving Marc to escort Jan to the guest quarters. She ran down the Level 2 corridor, wondering what her mother wanted that was so urgent. As she neared the Level Steps she wristlinked Nick Berenger in Organisation and requested he contact Chief Lydia Traun in her chambers on Enlopedia and have it put through to her quarters, for her arrival. Nick agreed. She ran down the Level Steps and along Level 3 to her quarters, still wondering what her mother had to tell her that was so urgent. As she entered her quarters, she found Twedor already present, in standby mode. He quickly picked up her presence and came on full operational power. Tayce crossed to the soffette and sat down, ready to speak to her mother via the wall Sight Screen. Twedor walked to come and stand beside her. The Sight Screen flashed into life and Lydia Traun appeared. She was seated at her desk in her chambers. Tayce, as she studied her mother, could see something displeased her and she didn't know how to begin.

"Mother! Marc said you wanted an urgent word with me, is something wrong with Father?" asked Tayce, seeing and picking up from Lydia that something was seriously wrong.

"No, it's not him. You're not going to like what I'm about to say and there is no easy way to tell you," began Lydia, knowing Tayce would hit the roof when she heard the news she had been ordered to convey.

"Go on—I'm listening," replied Tayce slowly, growing increasingly alarmed that she was going to hear what her suspicions had been conveying—that something was about to change the lives of the team and cruiser forever.

"It involves your team, cruiser and current voyage contract," said Lydia, seriously but apprehensively.

"Why am I not surprised? What about it Mother? What's wrong with it?" replied Tayce, growing angry.

"Is Jan Barnford with you?" enquired Lydia, seeing Tayce suddenly becoming suspicious.

"Why? Hold on, Mother—does us picking up Jan have something to do with what you're trying to say?"

"All right, the council has appointed a new deputy councillor. His name is Carlyle Cartarn. As I seem to be assisting your father a lot more these dayons in the Council Chambers, we've become a mini team. This new deputy has been put in the position to cut back on voyages, missions and assignments. Unfortunately your voyage is where they decided to cut back again. They've decided your contract is hereby terminated and your cruiser is to return to Enlopedia," she announced, disregarding Tayce's question about Jan.

"What! You've got to be kidding me! I won't stand for this, Mother, not again," shouted Tayce in anger.

Twedor looked at his mistress. He'd never seen her so furious. He understood her anger—it wasn't right as she'd worked so hard this voyage. Tayce sighed and began to pace, agitated to think such a thing could happen again. She was furious beyond words at this Carlyle Cartarn's actions. How could he have done what he had and used Jan into the bargain to impound her cruiser.

"I won't allow them to do this. What does Father say? He is Admiral of the base, after all—surely he has some clout in all this?" argued Tayce, her face angry beyond all recognition.

"Your father tried to argue, pointing out the good things that you've done with this voyage on your behalf, but Cartarn insisted your voyage has not fulfilled certain criteria in the Quests set out by Enlopedia, as it anticipated in the first yearon of this new voyage. I'm afraid the axe falls in two weekons," said Lydia. She could see her daughter was so infuriated beyond words at what had unfolded and understood it.

"I'll come to Enlopedia and fight this decision. I will not allow this to happen again. I will not have this team disbanded and dispersed all over the Universe, do you hear me? And you can convey that to the powers that be, including this new deputy councillor," shouted Tayce.

"As much as you want to, you can't fight this decision. It's been made—it's out of your hands. They are already looking at new assignments for your team," replied Lydia, her tone sounding more like a stern councillor than a mother.

"Hold on, Mother—we helped during Questa's demise this voyage. Doesn't that count? Oh, I get it—when the axe falls let it drop on the Amalthean Quests voyage, just like the last time. No thought went into the decision at all," snapped Tayce.

"I understand where you're coming from. Your father argued until he could argue no more," assured Lydia.

"This is ridiculous. This Cartarn is dictating to you. You might not be in the full duty of chief of council at times, but you're still chief over him. There's more to this, Mother, than meets the eye, and I won't rest until I find out what," persisted Tayce. She was not going to give up; she was not going to lose her team and cruiser.

"Real stinkers the lot of them," spoke up Twedor, unimpressed.

"Be quiet, Twedor. Stay out of this," snapped Tayce, even though she didn't mean to snap at him.

"It appears that this new deputy councillor has been assigned overall control over the cutbacks of voyages, missions and assignments. It would appear he passed this new ruling in my absence whilst attending a seminar on Trinot and, what's more, he conveniently put in place that no family-related member can interfere with any decision made on another member of that family. They made an exception that your father may be heard because he is Admiral of the base. Believe me, he's already looking at ways to reverse such a stupid decision," assured Lydia. She was just as mad as Tayce.

"Well, Mother, you can tell that bunch of no-good decision-makers they've just brought themselves a fight in taking on this team and cruiser, that I can promise," replied Tayce, ceasing communications abruptly.

Twedor looked at his mistress as she began to pace the Living Area of the quarters, trying to calm herself and think of what her next move would be. The doors to the quarters opened. Tayce looked up. Marc stepped inside, noticing she looked like thunder about to erupt. He began to walk in, cautiously enquiring was everything all right with Lydia? Tayce said nothing; she just turned away and walked across to the sight port, where she paused to look out into the passing stars, trying to calm herself. Marc knew something had to be wrong by her silent composure. Thoughts of having to give up the team and cruiser after all they had been through during the current voyage went through her mind. Quite suddenly Tayce broke down.

"I can't do this, Marc. They want to cancel the Amalthean Quests again," she said sadly, trying to stop the tears.

"What! You've got to be kidding me! Why? Tell me," he said, crossing to her side.

He didn't like seeing her this way. They'd been friends for far too long and he didn't like it when something upset her, like something was right then. Upon reaching her, he reached out and turned her around, bringing her into his strong arms as she broke down. He began to comfort her with soothing words as she, between sobs, told him she wasn't going to lose everything again, not this time.

"Tell me—otherwise I can't help you. Tayce, please, tell me," he said, breaking away slightly from her and lifting her chin with his finger so she was looking at him with tear-stained eyes.

"It's Enlopedia and a newly appointed deputy of voyages, missions and assignments. After all we've done this voyage, including helping out during the demise of Questa, they've decided to terminate this voyage of Quests and our contract. Mother says there's no way I can fight this. What do I do?" said Tayce, upset.

"You're probably not the only one this idiot has cast this same decision on, but if you want to fight for the continuation of this voyage, you've got my backing and I'll help you in any way I can," he assured her.

Tayce broke away from him completely, feeling at least she had Marc on her side. But she wondered if the others would join him. She thanked him for his support. He hugged her to him again, assuring her she wouldn't get anything less. They had been through too much together for him not to be there for her. After he released her, Tayce felt there should be a gathering of the whole team in the DC to hear what their views were on what had arisen and suggested this to him.

"I totally agree, but I think you need to be careful. The council have ways of enforcing their laws and decisions against the person it's been served on," he advised her.

"What do you mean?" asked Tayce, curious.

"Jan Barnford's on board. He may be our friend, but he still has to be accountable to Enlopedia and has a job to uphold. If he had the orders from council to be picked up from Pellasun 1 by us and to await further orders, it means he has to act on them when they are given. I bet he feels pretty awkward as it is at the moment. His friendship with you, or his duty to carry out the orders from Enlopedia high up? He could lose his job if he doesn't obey. I wouldn't want to be where he is right now," explained Marc.

"This is still my cruiser and I'm not letting it go, but I see your point—he does have a difficult decision to make and one that has to suit both sides," she replied, seeing what a difficult decision Jan had.

"Let's go and play it by ear. Remember, whatever you decide, I'm right behind you" he assured her.

Both headed back to the quarters entrance with Twedor in tow. The doors opened and all three walked on out on the walk up to Organisation. En route Marc wristlinked Nick, requesting everyone on board attend an emergency meeting in the DC in twenty minons. Nick could be heard acknowledging the request. Marc ceased communications, slipping his arm around Tayce's shoulders, exclaiming that if they could stop the Enlopedian Council and this new deputy, then they would. This made Tayce feel a lot happier. Twedor offered his support too. He didn't want to work for anyone else—God knows what they'd have him do.

All over Amalthea the team left their duties and began making their way to the DC, wondering what the emergency meeting was all about. None of them had the slightest clue they were about to lose their duty positions, the life they had come to enjoy and take for granted and their home. Amal took overall command of the whole cruiser. Tayce had put orders in place that Jan Barnford was not allowed to override her authorisation code to take Amalthea over, for the council. She didn't care how many rules it broke. In the DC the team soon gathered, wondering what was going on. Donaldo and Treketa ran into Organisation and were quickly followed by Marc, Tayce, Jaul, Sallen and Aldonica from lower levels. Tayce walked to her desk and perched on the back edge. She waited till everyone was seated around the DC table, then began.

"What I'm about to say is going to come as a shock to all of you. It was for me. The council and a newly appointed deputy of voyages, missions and assignments has cast the order that this voyage is to end," announced Tayce to the sudden shocked faces of some of her team.

"What made them decide this—Father would never have allowed this, you know that Tayce?" asked Lance in outburst.

"That's disgusting. My father warned me about the Enlopedian Council. He said they were an underhand lot, if you don't mind me saying so, Captain?" spoke up Deluca.

"That's brilliant! Never mind what we've done for that base, just pack your bags and leave the job you have come to love. I'd like to come face-to-face with this decision-maker," said Nick, disgusted beyond words.

"I guess this will be the end of my career advancement," spoke up Aldonica.

"I share your points of view, all of you. I don't want this to end any more than any of you do. I'd like to think that we've built a good team spirit here; and if I can help it, I won't let it end," promised Tayce, glad she had the support of the team behind her for the continuation of the voyage.

The DC doors suddenly opened and Jan Barnford entered, looking like he was about to conduct official duty. But he hated what he was about to do. Everyone turned, looking at him, wondering what he was about to do and say. He sighed and looked down at the floor, then back up awkwardly, then began relaying the orders he had been forced to carry out.

"I have orders to hereby impound this cruiser until further notice. The orders are given by the Enlopedian Council. You are to take Amalthea Two back to Enlopedia as soon as our present course will allow. Any deviation from the current course will result in certain procedures being enforced to make sure this cruiser does reach base. I personally don't want to do this. I know you all, and I for one condemn this order from the top," said Jan, feeling somewhat displeased that he had to do the duty that was asked of him.

To make the order official, he placed his open ID wallet down on the meeting table, to mark his orders being cast. Dairan and Marc exchanged silent looks, wondering what would happen if Tayce decided she wasn't going to comply with what he'd cast. Lance could take no more. He sprang from his chair, looking at Jan angrily, not caring what the council or Jan did to him.

"If you do this, you're not the friend I thought you were to me or Tayce, or any of us," said Lance with a snarl. He knew what the Amalthean voyage meant to Tayce.

"No, Lance, leave it—don't," said Marc, dragging Lance away from Jan restrainingly.

Jan's look turned to one of hurt and surprise. He and Lance went back a long way together, having been friends on Questa, and it surprised him to see Lance's actions, but he put it down to loyalty to Tayce.

"You've said what you came to say. I now know what you were hiding back on Pellasun 1 and I can tell you I thought better of you. You of all people know how hard I fought for this voyage and yet you're prepared to help this Carlyle Cartarn stop it all over again," said Tayce, hurt beyond words that a friend she'd looked up to and had thought would always be there for her wasn't.

She pushed past Dairan and ran from the DC entrance, finding the sudden shock and hurt too much to bear. She felt she'd let her team down. She was disgusted with Jan at that moment.

"Nice work, Jan—she's not the only one who's surprised at you," retorted Dairan coldly, then ran after Tayce.

Jan felt like an enemy who should make a swift exit. The team were all looking at him plainly, some shaking their heads at what he'd just done. He himself hated the news he had to deliver, but his position on Enlopedia would have been at stake if he hadn't carried out the designated orders that had been given to him. Marc, even though he understood the team's anger, could also see where Jan was coming from, in that his hands were tied and he was carrying out orders given to him, like any officer would, by superiors.

"I suggest that as at present Amalthea is still ours to command, we all get back to duty," ordered Marc in the tone of commander.

No further words were spoken in Jan's earshot. Everyone stood and threw him a spiteful look as they walked from the DC silently. Marc watched each member leave, thinking to himself that this was one strained situation. He followed on with Jan behind him, discreetly suggesting he stay calm and out of the way of the team, in Organisation, if he had to oversee the journey back to base.

* * *

Tayce entered the Flight Hangar Bay a while later. Twedor was with her. He didn't like seeing his mistress as hurt and as furious as she was. He didn't know what to say to make her feel a little easier. Tayce wanted to be alone. She knew Marc would take over—he was good in the kind of situation they now found themselves in. She felt terrible. She felt she had just kicked the team back into the Recruitment Centre at Enlopedia.

Without a thought, Dairan ran into the bay out of breath, just behind her. Once she was within reaching distance, he grabbed her, pulling her to a sudden stop.

"I've failed again. What does it take to make this bunch of no-good decision-makers realise what I'm trying to do in restoring justice in this Universe," Tayce blurted through her tears, pulling herself free of him.

"Don't blame yourself—it's not your fault, we all know that," he told her firmly.

"Do you know something, I finally won through in facing the council at the beginning of this voyage and got what I wanted—this cruiser reinstated and this voyage. I thought this was a new beginning, a real chance to make this Amalthean Quests concept work. I never imagined something like this would happen, like the last time. I never thought for one moment it was going to happen all over again, but it has and I wish to God I'd known it was going to. I would never have done this voyage," said Tayce, pacing.

"You'll do it again, I'm sure of that, and we're right behind you. None of us want to lose all this. We've built up something strong here—a good team, and one that's not about to turn its back on you, I assure you of that. You saw the way they were with Jan when he cast what he did," he said, trying to calm her.

"Do you know something? When I was a child on Traun, I used to stand out in the night air at home and I would say to myself that one day on I'd be out here, travelling the stars, being the best leader I could possibly be. But now it seems every time I try to be what I wanted to be that bunch of no-good decision-makers on Enlopedia try and stop me from achieving my goal. I don't think I'll ever win," said Tayce, looking out through the Flight Hangar Bay sight port.

"Stop it, Tayce—you're beating yourself up. You're a damn good leader and one I know I would serve under any time, not just because I love you—and that goes for the team too," he said, studying her along with Twedor.

"But it's too late. I've lost it all again, just like before, and it doesn't matter what you say—nothing will change the fact. What's been done is done," she replied.

"No, it isn't. You might have been forced back to Enlopedia, but if you personally argue your defence over continuing this voyage, they have to grant you an audience—that's the law. Jonathan Largon put in place, when he was alive, that a leader of a voyage has the right to appeal against a decision they don't think is fair," said Twedor, recalling a rule set out when the late Jonathan Largon was in power.

"How do you know this?" asked Tayce, surprised that the little Romid knew what he did.

"You'll be surprised what I learn when nosing around the Enlopedian data systems."

"But if I march into Enlopedia's Council Chambers and tell them they can forget their idea to take this team and cruiser and terminate this voyage they'll probably arrest me and impound all this permanently, surely," she said, wiping her tear-stained face with her hand.

"You'll never know unless you try. You're a good captain and leader, though you need to prove you can be. This cruiser is still yours and this team needs you right now—that includes me. Now take your duty back and forget Jan's presence," said Dairan plainly.

"And me—I need you too," spoke up Twedor, backing Dairan up.

"Get back in command," said Dairan, walking up to her, taking her by the shoulders gently.

"You can't order me around. You forget I'm still the one that gives the orders around here at the moment," she replied, meeting his handsome brown eyes, realising he was right—she had to fight.

"That's what I wanted to hear. Your team awaits you," he said, kissing her on the cheek, knowing he'd made her realise who she was and the fact that she had to fight the current situation to keep the team and cruiser.

"Thanks, both of you!" she said, managing a smile, realising what she had to try and do.

With this, she briskly walked past Dairan and on out of the Flight Hangar Bay, knowing she had to get her act together if she wanted the continuation of her Amalthean Quests. She appreciated what Dairan had made her realise. Dairan smiled to himself, amused. His words had worked—he'd managed to convince her she needed to fight for the right to hang on to the Amalthean Quests cruiser and team. One dayon she would probably thank him for what he'd just made her do. He followed on with Twedor, back to duty in Organisation whilst there was still duty to do. Both he and Twedor discussed what had happened on the way out of the Flight Hangar Bay, on the way back up to Organisation.

* * *

The team were at their duty consoles in Organisation, under the watchful eye of Jan Barnford. It seemed like a case of Big Brother's watching you! The team guided Amalthea on what would probably be the last journey she would make towards Enlopedia. Marc ignored the fact that Jan was present and stood looking out of the sight port into the Universe in thought. He wondered if Enlopedia would be the final port of call for them all. Tayce briskly walked into the centre a while later and gave Jan a plain look and began speaking in a hostile tone.

"Chief Barnford, you may have orders to see this cruiser reach Enlopedia; but as captain of this cruiser until we arrive there, I would appreciate it if you stop treating my team like they were microbes under a microscope and stay out of my way. That way my team won't feel like they're under threat. I can tolerate all that you're doing as you have shown where your loyalties lie—just don't get in my way. Nick, get me a communications link to Chief Traun's chambers," demanded Tayce, crossing Organisation, leaving a taken-aback and surprised-looking Jan Barnford at her coldness towards him.

Jan sighed. He realised that being official with Tayce was not going to work. The council was a bunch of idiots, he thought. It had been a stupid idea to put him in a spot where he was the only one to fulfil orders where he would normally need a team to assist him. This team were more than capable of showing him the meaning of what an airlock was for, with just one order from Tayce to undertake the action if she decided to. He wished he could make her understand that he was really on her side and he was merely carrying out orders, which were out of his hands. Personally he didn't want to see the downfall of the Amalthean Quests happen. Nick turned at his console, exclaiming that communications had been obtained between Amalthea and Chief Lydia Traun.

"Put it through to the DC, please Nick," said Tayce, then began in that direction with Marc following on and Dairan, who had just entered the Operations Centre with Twedor. The doors soon closed behind them. Jan figured he'd stay out of it, because Tayce was not the kind of person who would disobey orders.

* * *

Inside the DC, Tayce crossed to her desk and walked around the back to sit down. The DC wall Sight Screen flashed into life. Lydia Traun appeared. She wondered what her daughter was going to say, considering what had happened the last time they'd spoken, a while ago.

"Mother, I decided I don't intend to give up on this voyage and lose this team and cruiser, so I want an audience with the council when I arrive. I want you to arrange it, please. I'll be bringing Marc and Dairan with me," said Tayce, to the point.

"I've told you, Tayce, it won't do any good. Deputy Councillor Carlyle Cartarn has firmly declined any further discussion on the continuation of the Amalthean Quests. Just todayon alone the head of an Enlopedian fleet was arrested for not complying with what had been cast for cutbacks," replied Lydia.

"Then they'll have to arrest me too, as under an old Questa ruling and Enlopedia's new ruling, I'm entitled to an audience with the council over this decision and I demand it," she said, getting angry.

"I'll see what I can do. I can't promise anything, but I'll try," said Lydia, sighing. She knew her daughter was determined to do what she wanted, lawfully or unlawfully.

"Can I ask something here, Chief? Why are they cancelling something that is doing a lot of good in the every-dayon task of justice being sought in the Universe here and around the universal system?" asked Dairan, curious to know.

"Deputy Councillor Cartarn feels funds should be spent on long-term projects, such as the constructing of stations and colonisation in space," replied Lydia.

"Hold on a minon. Amalthean Quests falls into that category of long-term projects, surely?" asked Marc.

"Long-term, yes, but it's not a project. No—you can argue that point when you meet with the council upon your arrival," replied Lydia.

Tayce gave a look that said it all. She had a feeling her mother was going to wash her hands of this idea altogether and she was beginning to feel suspicious. The whole situation was beginning to look like Layforn Barkin all over again. Her mother had been told to do as she was told and fall in with what this new deputy councillor wanted, just like the last time, or she would lose her position on the council. But this was a different councillor? The outcome couldn't be the same, could it? she wondered.

"Leave this with me—I'll call you back just as soon as I've tried something" said Lydia, thinking, then signed off.

"Maybe there's a light at the end of the tunnel yet, so to speak," said Marc.

The wall Sight Screen deactivated. Marc paced the DC in deep thought. Both Tayce and Dairan exchanged looks of wonderment at what he was thinking, then looked at Marc, waiting to hear what he was turning over in his mind. After a while, as he didn't say anything, Tayce began speaking.

"Care to share what your thinking?" she prompted.

"What if there's more to this Councillor Cartarn than meets the eye? It's happened before. Need I say more? I feel this time there's something more than just plain cuts here. The council know how hard we've worked and for your father, the Admiral of the base, to be pushed aside—it doesn't seem right somehow," said Marc seriously.

"You don't think you're being a bit too imaginative here? We have no proof yet, though there's one force that hasn't been heard of for yearons and suddenly, for some strange reason, he comes to mind. I can't think why, though he would go to great lengths to put a stop to this voyage, where his female partner failed. Count Vargon. He's been gone into exile for yearons. Some say he went there leaving the Countess to continue his work out in the open. Some say he was driven into hiding because of his evil acts," exclaimed Tayce as a shiver ran through her at the thought that the Count was back.

"You really think it's possible?" asked Marc, giving her a wide-eyed look.

"It's quite possible. He'd go to great lengths to cover up his actions to get back at me after all these yearons," said Tayce.

"If you're right and this man is as dangerous as you both suspect, shouldn't something be done before it's too late?" asked Dairan, having a feeling Count Vargon was just as bad as the Countess.

All three glanced at each other in thought about what they could do. Something had to be done to get to the bottom of why the axe had specifically fallen on the Amalthean Quests once again and especially by another elected deputy councillor. Varon Vargon was a dangerous and vicious man with more powers at his fingertips than his female partner in crime, the Countess. Tayce knew one thing: if Carlyle Cartarn thought she was a weak pushover when it came to her team and cruiser, he could think again. She would fight him any way she could. She was not going to give in easily, especially if she could somehow uncover that he was working for Count Vargon. There was a lot riding on the possibility of a further voyage, and, by God, if she could do it by the skin of her teeth, she would keep the team together.

* * *

Amalthea Two headed the last milons to an uncertain future. There was a lot at stake. But was there a further threat—one they hadn't anticipated—that would stop them from reaching Enlopedia, and it would unfold without warning. Was this the last of the Amalthean Quests and the last duty the team would ever do?

Was this the last duty for the team returning to Enlopedia?

Was there more to this new deputy councillor once more?

The Amalthean Quests Continue...

AMALTHEAN QUESTS
THREE

JERI DION

For My Readers

As author or *Amalthean Quests One* and now *Amalthean Quests Two*, which you've just read and enjoyed, I'd like to share how it all began with you.

I was at college in 1979 when, after an assignment to write a story, an English lecturer and professor told me I had a wonderful imagination and should seriously think about writing a book. I thought about it and decided to write a science-fiction book, but it was some years before I sat down to be serious as a writer, to write the first book about the Amalthean Quests. My first attempt by then was consigned to the bin. The first effort, you could say, of *Amalthean Quests One* was finished in the late '80s and no matter how it was written it just didn't seem right. Also at this time in my life I didn't have much time to pick up the first book, so left it.

In 2009 I was given a laptop. Well, I was always used to an electronic typewriter and never thought of using a computer of any kind to write. I wasn't keen.

When I hit fifty-four I suddenly found myself setting myself a goal, that if I didn't get published by the time I was fifty-five it was time to look for a new hobby. Quite suddenly I felt I had to take the first book in the Amalthean Quests series and pull it apart and throw a lot more into it and put it back together. I did this using the programme I love using today. As for the typewriter, well it was consigned to the loft to gather dust and has since gone to the charity people and found a new home.

After finding Amalthean Quests where I felt it should be with the extra ingredients I set about find a publisher once more. Whilst this was ongoing I went on to rewrite and do the same with book two. This was done against all odds with different situations creeping into my life that found me struggling to get the time I needed to get to my trusted laptop. But it happened. I was lucky to find the right publisher in the publishers I have today and they have been fantastic in being there every step of the process to get my series read for what it is: a first-class book.

It fills me with pride to know that you my readers have enjoyed reading *Amalthean Quests One* and *Amalthean Quests Two* and followed Tayce Traun and her team through the many Quests that unfold with each chapter. I would like to thank you.

If you feel when you've read books one and two, you'd like to leave a review when you've finished then please do.

Thanks again for following.

Jeri Dion